As Per Revised Syllabus

I0681457

CIDCO

ASSISTANT CIVIL ENGINEER EXAM

※ BY ※

Haribhau K. Gite
Assistant Engineer Grade – I
Water Resource Department
Government of Maharashtra

Sachin D. Gade
Assistant Engineer Grade – I
Water Resource Department
Government of Maharashtra

PRAGATI BOOKS

PP300

CIDO : ASSISTANT CIVIL ENGINEER

First Edition : January 2016

ISBN - 978-93-5164-647-1

© : Authors

Published By :

NIRALI PRAKASHAN

Abhyudaya Pragati, 1312, Shivaji Nagar,
Off J.M. Road, PUNE – 411005
Tel - (020) 25512336/37/39, Fax - (020) 25511379
Email : niralipune@pragationline.com

DISTRIBUTION CENTERS

PUNE

Nirali Prakashan
119, Budhwar Peth, Jogeshwari Mandir Lane,
Pune - 411002, Maharashtra.
Tel : (020) 24452044, 66022708; Fax : (020) 2445 1538
Email : niralilocal@pragationline.com

Nirali Prakashan
S. No. 28/27, Dhayari,
Near Pari Company, Pune - 411 041,
Tel - (020) 24690371
Email : dhayari@pragationline.com
bookorder@pragationline.com

MUMBAI
Nirali Prakashan
385, S.V.P. Road, Rasdhara Co-op. Hsg. Society, Girgaum, **Mumbai -** 400004, Maharashtra
Tel : (022) 2385 6339 / 2386 9976, Fax : (022) 2386 9976
Email : niralimumbai@pragationline.com

DISTRIBUTION BRANCHES

NAGPUR
Pratibha Book Distributors
Above Maratha Mandir, Shop No. 3, First Floor,
Rani Jhanshi Square, Sitabuldi, Nagpur 440012,
Maharashtra, Tel : (0712) 254 7129

HYDERABAD
Nirali Book House
22, Shyam Enclave, 4-5-947, Badi Chowdi
Hyderabad 500095, Andhra Pradesh
Tel : (040) 6554 5313, Mob : 94400 30608
Email: niralibooks@yahoo.com

CHENNAI
Pragati Books
9/1, Montieth Road, Behind Taas Mahal, Egmore,
Chennai 600008 Tamil Nadu, Tel : (044) 6518 3535,
Mob : 94440 01782 / 98450 21552 / 98805 82331
Email : bharatsavla@yahoo.com

JALGAON
Nirali Prakashan
34, V. V. Golani Market, Navi Peth, Jalgaon 425001,
Maharashtra, Tel : (0257) 222 0395
Mob : 94234 91860

KOLHAPUR
Nirali Prakashan
New Mahadvar Road,
Kedar Plaza, 1st Floor Opp. IDBI Bank
Kolhapur 416 012, Maharashtra. Mob : 9855046155

BENGALURU
Pragati Book House
House No. 1, Sanjeevappa Lane, Avenue Road Cross,
Opp. Rice Church, Bengaluru – 560002.
Tel : (080) 64513344, 64513355,
Mob : 9880582331, 9845021552
Email:bharatsavla@yahoo.com

RETAIL OUTLETS
PUNE

Pragati Book Centre
157, Budhwar Peth, Opp. Ratan Talkies,
Pune 411002, Maharashtra
Tel : (020) 2445 8887 / 6602 2707, Fax : (020) 2445 8887

Pragati Book Centre
Amber Chamber, 28/A, Budhwar Peth,
Appa Balwant Chowk, Pune : 411002, Maharashtra,
Tel : (020) 20240335 / 66281669
Email : pbcpune@pragationline.com

Pragati Book Centre
676/B, Budhwar Peth, Opp. Jogeshwari Mandir,
Pune 411002, Maharashtra
Tel : (020) 6601 7784 / 6602 0855

Pragati Book Centre
152, Budhwar Peth, Pune 411002, Maharashtra
Tel : (020) 2445 2254 / 6609 2463

MUMBAI
Pragati Book Corner
Indira Niwas, 111 - A, Bhavani Shankar Road, Dadar (W), Mumbai 400028, Maharashtra
Tel : (022) 2422 3526 / 6662 5254
Email : pbcmumbai@pragationline.com

www.pragationline.com   info@pragationline.com

Contents

1. Mechanics .... 1.1 – 1.28

2. Structural Analysis .... 2.1 – 2.26

3. Concrete Structure .... 3.1 – 3.32

4. Steel Structure .... 4.1 – 4.28

5. Soil Mechanics .... 5.1 – 5.40

6. Foundation Engineering .... 6.1 – 6.28

7. Fluid Mechanics & Hydraulics .... 7.1 – 7.42

8. Hydrology .... 8.1 – 8.32

9. Water Requirements .... 9.1 – 9.22

10. Air Pollution & Water Pollution .... 10.1 – 10.14

11. Municipal Solid Waste .... 11.1 – 11.24

12. Highway Planning .... 12.1 – 12.24

13. Surveying .... 13.1 – 13.28

❖ ❖ ❖

UNIT - 1 : MECHANICS

1. A shaft of diameter D is subjected to a twisting moment (T) and a bending moment (M). If the maximum bending stress is equal to maximum shear stress developed, then M is equal to
   - (1) T/2
   - (2) T
   - (3) 2T
   - (4) none of these

2. Shear stress is maximum at
   - (1) neutral axis
   - (2) top
   - (3) bottom
   - (4) none of these

3. Shear stress is minimum at
   - (1) neutral axis
   - (2) top
   - (3) bottom
   - (4) (1) and (2) both

4. A triangular section having base b, height h, is placed with its base horizontal. If the shear stress at a depth y from top is q, the maximum shear stress is
   - (1) $\dfrac{3S}{bh}$
   - (2) $\dfrac{4S}{bh}$
   - (3) $\dfrac{4b}{Sh}$
   - (4) none of these

5. The value of shear stress changes along depth
   - (1) linearly
   - (2) parabolically
   - (3) constant
   - (4) none of these

6. At a point in a strained material, the state of tensile stresses are σ along x and y axis. Radius of Mohr's circle is
   - (1) σ
   - (2) 0.5σ
   - (3) zero
   - (4) None of these

7. At a point in a strained material, the states of stresses are σ along x as tensile stress and along y as compressive stress. Radius of Mohr's circle is
   - (1) σ
   - (2) 0.5σ
   - (3) zero
   - (4) None of these

8. At a point in a strained material, the shear stress acting is τ. Radius of Mohr's circle is
   - (1) 0.5τ
   - (2) τ
   - (3) zero
   - (4) None of these

9. In a loaded beam, the point of contraflexure occurs at a section where bending moment is
   - (1) zero
   - (2) maximum
   - (3) minimum
   - (4) none of these

10. The shape of the bending moment diagram over the length of beam, having no external load, is always (B.M. due to self weight)
    - (1) parabolic
    - (2) linear
    - (3) horizontal
    - (4) none of these

11. At a point in a strained material, the states of tensile stresses are 75 MPa along x and 50 MPa along y-axis. Radius of Mohr's circle is
    - (1) 9 N/mm²
    - (2) 7.5 N/mm²
    - (3) 12.5 N/mm²
    - (4) 62.5 N/mm²

12. Principle plane is a plane on which the shear stress is
    - (1) zero
    - (2) minimum
    - (3) maximum
    - (4) none of these

13. The working stress in a material should be
    - (1) equal to its ultimate stress
    - (2) equal to its lower yield point stress
    - (3) more than its yield point stress
    - (4) less than its yield point stress

14. The ratio of the lateral strain to the linear strain is called
    - (1) modulus of elasticity
    - (2) modulus of rigidity
    - (3) bulk modulus
    - (4) Poisson's ratio

15. Which one of the following materials has the highest value of Poisson's ratio ?
    (1) wood   (2) rubber   (3) copper   (4) steel

16. Minimum bending stress which occurs in T section of beam is at
    (1) top   (2) bottom   (3) neutral axis   (4) none of these

17. The ratio of change in volume to the original volume is called
    (1) lateral strain   (2) linear strain
    (3) Poisson's ratio   (4) volumetric strain

18. Modular ratio of the two materials is the ratio of
    (1) linear stress to lateral strain   (2) linear stress to linear strain
    (3) shear stress to shear strain   (4) their moduli of elasticity

19. In Mohr's circle, the centre of circle from Y-axis is taken as
    (1) $\dfrac{\sigma_x - \sigma_y}{2}$ (2) $\dfrac{\sigma_x + \sigma_y}{2}$ (3) $\dfrac{\sigma_x - \sigma_y}{2} + \tau$ (4) none of these

20. The stress developed due to impact in the bar is
    (1) tensile   (2) compressive   (3) both (1) and (2)   (4) none of these

21. Unit of proof resilience is....
    (1) N/mm²   (2) N-mm   (3) N/mm   (4) None of these

22. The direct stress, across a principal plane, is known as
    (1) principal stress   (2) bending stress   (3) shear stress   (4) none of these

23. Mohr's circle is used to determine the stresses on an oblique section of a body subjected to
    (1) direct tensile stress in one plane accompanied by a shear stress
    (2) direct tensile stress in two mutually perpendicular directions
    (3) direct tensile stress in two mutually perpendicular directions accompanied by a simple shear stress
    (4) all of above

24. A beam of triangular section is with base 'b' and an altitude 'h'. It is placed with its base horizontal. Shear force in beam is 'S'. The maximum shear stress in the beam is
    (1) 3S/(bh)   (2) 3S/(2bh)   (3) 8S/(3bh)   (4) 8S/(6bh)

25. Stress of 400 MPa is applied on the same planes. The maximum normal stress will be
    (1) 400 MPa   (2) 500 MPa   (3) 100 MPa   (4) 1400 MPa

26. What will be the circumferential stress developed in case of thin cylindrical pipe with diameter 'd' and thickness 't', subjected to internal pressure 'p' ?
    (1) $\dfrac{pd}{4t}$ (2) $\dfrac{pd}{2t}$ (3) $\dfrac{p}{t}$ (4) $\dfrac{p}{2t}$

27. When a body is subjected to a direct tensile stress (σ) in one plane, then tangential or shear stress on an oblique section of the body inclined at an angle θ to the normal of the section is
    (1) $\sigma \sin 2\theta$ (2) $\sigma/3 \sin 2\theta$ (3) $\sigma/2 \sin 2\theta$ (4) none of these

28. When a body is subjected to bi-axial stresses 50 N/mm² (tensile) along x-direction and 50 N/mm² (tensile) along y-direction, the radius of Mohr's circle is
    (1) zero   (2) 50   (3) 100   (4) none of these

29. When a body is subjected to bi-axial stresses 50 N/mm² (tensile) along x-direction and 50 N/mm² (compressive) along y-direction, the radius of Mohr's circle is
    (1) zero   (2) 50   (3) 100   (4) none of these

30. A simply supported beam of span 'L' supports a concentrated load 'W' at mid-span, if the cross-section of beam is an I-Section, then the length of elastic-plastic zone of the plastic hinge will be :
    (1) L/3   (2) L/4   (3) L/2   (4) 3 L/4

31. Normal stress due to axial force in a bar of diameter D is
    (1) P/D   (2) P/(2πR)   (3) 4P/(πD²)   (4) none of these

32. The resultant stress on an inclined plane which is inclined at an angle θ to the normal cross-section of a body which is subjected to a direct tensile stress (σ) in one plane, is
    (1) σ sin θ   (2) σ cos θ   (3) σ sin 2θ   (4) none of these

33. When a body is subjected to a direct tensile stress (σ) in one plane, the maximum shear stress is ...... the maximum normal stress.
    (1) equal to   (2) one-half   (3) two-third   (4) zero

34. Strain energy is the
    (1) energy stored in a body when strained within elastic limits
    (2) energy stored in a body when strained upto the breaking of a specimen
    (3) maximum strain energy which can be stored in a body
    (4) proof resilience per unit volume of a material

35. Where does maximum shear stress occur in a rectangular shaft subjected to torsion ?
    (1) Centre   (2) Corners
    (3) Middle of smaller side   (4) Middle of longer side

36. A hollow circular shaft of 175 mm external diameter, thickness of metal 12.5 mm is rotating at 2 rps. The length of shaft is 2.75 m. The power transmitted is 229.8 kW. Modulus of rigidity is 80 GPa. The angle of twist is
    (1) 0.7°   (2) 0.75°   (3) 0.8°   (4) 0.85°

37. In the torsion equation the term J/R is called
    (1) shear modulus   (2) section modulus
    (3) polar modulus   (4) none of these

38. When two shafts of same length, one of which is hollow, transmit equal torques and have equal maximum stress, then they should have equal
    (1) polar moment of inertia   (2) polar modulus
    (3) diameter   (4) none of these

39. When a shaft is subjected to a twisting moment, every cross-section of the shaft will be under
    (1) tensile stress   (2) compressive stress
    (3) shear stress   (4) none of these

40. When a shaft is subjected to torsion, the shear stress induced in the shaft varies from
    (1) minimum at the centre to maximum at the circumference
    (2) maximum at the centre to minimum at the circumference
    (3) zero at the centre to maximum at the circumference
    (4) none of these

41. The torsional rigidity of a shaft is given by
    (1) T/J   (2) T/θ   (3) T/G   (4) none of these
42. Two shafts 'A' and 'B' are made of same material. The shaft 'A' is of diameter D and shaft 'B' is of diameter D/2. The torsional strength of shaft 'B' is ……….. as that of shaft 'A'.
    (1) one-eighth   (2) one-fourth   (3) two-third   (4) none of these
43. Resilience is the
    (1) energy stored in a body when strained within elastic limits
    (2) energy stored in a body when strained upto the breaking of the specimen
    (3) maximum strain energy which can be stored in a body
    (4) none of these
44. The stress developed due to suddenly applied load is …… of gradually applied load.
    (1) twice   (2) half   (3) equal to   (4) none of these
45. The stress developed in the bar due to gradually applied load is
    (1) force/area   (2) (2 × force)/area (3) force/(2 × area) (4) none of these
46. The stress developed in the bar due to suddenly applied load is
    (1) force/area   (2) (2 × force)/area (3) force/(2 × area) (4) none of these
47. Unit of modulus of resilience is
    (1) N/mm²   (2) N-mm   (3) N/mm   (4) none of these
48. The following assumption is not true in the theory of pure torsion :
    (1) The twist along the shaft is uniform.
    (2) The shaft is of uniform circular section throughout.
    (3) Cross-section of the shaft, which is plane before twist, remains plane after twist.
    (4) All radii get twisted due to torsion.
49. A shaft revolving at ω rad/s transmits torque (T) in N-m. The power developed is
    (1) T·ω watts   (2) 2π Tω watts
    (3) (2π Tω/75) watts   (4) none of these
50. The product of the tangential force acting on the shaft and its distance from the axis of shaft is known as
    (1) bending moment   (2) twisting moment
    (3) shear force   (4) none of these
51. The stress at which extension of a material takes place more quickly as compared to increase in load, is called
    (1) elastic point   (2) plastic point   (3) breaking point (4) yielding point
52. The ratio of strengths of solid to hollow shafts, both having outside diameter hollow and inside diameter D/2, in torsion, is
    (1) 1/4   (2) 1/2   (3) 1/16   (4) 15/16
53. A rectangular bar of width b and height h is being used as a cantilever. The loading plane is parallel to the side b. The section modulus is
    (1) $\dfrac{bh^2}{6}$ (2) $\dfrac{b^2h}{6}$ (3) $\dfrac{bh^2}{12}$ (4) none of these

54. Maximum bending stress, which occurs in a symmetrical I section of beam, is at
    (1) top   (2) bottom   (3) neutral axis   (4) (1) and (2)

55. Euler's formula states that the buckling load P for a column of length l, both ends hinged and whose least moment of inertia and modulus of elasticity of the material of the column are I and E respectively, is given by the relation
    (1) $P = \dfrac{\pi^2 EI}{l^2}$ (2) $P = \dfrac{nl^2}{EI}$ (3) $P = \dfrac{nEI}{l^3}$ (4) $P = \dfrac{n^2 EI}{l^3}$

56. The stiffness factor for a prismatic beam of length L and moment of inertia I, is
    (1) $\dfrac{EI}{L}$ (2) $\dfrac{2EI}{L}$ (3) $\dfrac{3EI}{L}$ (4) $\dfrac{4EI}{L}$

57. A hollow shaft, with internal diameter 76 mm and thickness 6 mm, is rotating at 2 rpm. Maximum permissible shear stress is 72 N/mm². Power transmitted by shaft is
    (1) 37 kW   (2) 35 kW   (3) 54 kW   (4) 45 kW

58. As compared to uniaxial tension or compression, the strain energy stored inside is only
    (1) $\dfrac{1}{8}$ (2) $\dfrac{1}{4}$ (3) $\dfrac{1}{3}$ (4) $\dfrac{1}{2}$

59. The law which states, "within elastic limits strain produced is proportional to the stress producing it", is known as
    (1) Bernoulli's law   (2) Stress law   (3) Hooke's law   (4) none of these

60. For a given material, if E, C, K and η are Young's modulus, shearing modulus, bulk modulus and Poison's ratio, the following relation does not hold good :
    (1) $E = \dfrac{9KC}{3K + C}$ (2) $E = 2K\left(1 - \dfrac{2}{\eta}\right)$
    (3) $E = 2C\left(1 + \dfrac{1}{\eta}\right)$ (4) $\dfrac{1}{\eta} = \dfrac{3K - 2C}{6K + 2C}$

61. A member which is subjected to reversible tensile or compressive stress may fail at a stress lower than the ultimate stress of the material. This property of metal, is called
    (1) plasticity of the metal   (2) elasticity of the metal
    (3) fatigue of the metal   (4) workability of the metal

62. If Z and I are the section modulus and moment of inertia of the section, the shear force F and bending moment M at a section are related by
    (1) $F = \dfrac{My}{I}$ (2) $F = \dfrac{M}{Z}$ (3) $F = \dfrac{dM}{dx}$ (4) $F = \int Mdx$

63. The section modulus of a rectangular section is proportional to
    (1) area of the section   (2) square of the area of the section
    (3) product of the area and depth   (4) product of the area and width

64. The property of a material by which it can be drawn to a smaller section, due to tension, is called
    (1) plasticity   (2) ductility   (3) elasticity   (4) malleability

65. Strain is defined as
    (1) deformation per unit area   (2) deformation per unit length
    (3) deformation per unit load   (4) deformation per unit volume

66. The unit of elastic modulus is the same as that of
    (1) strain, shear modulus and force   (2) stress, shear modulus and pressure
    (3) stress, strain and pressure   (4) none of these

67. Every material obeys the Hooke's law within its
    (1) elastic limit   (2) plastic point
    (3) limit of proportionality   (4) none of these

68. For a given material, Young's modulus is 200 GN/m² and modulus of rigidity is 80 GN/m². The value of Poisson's ratio is
    (1) 0.15   (2) 0.20   (3) 0.30   (4) 0.25

69. The resistance to deformation of a body per unit area is known as
    (1) strain   (2) stress   (3) elasticity (4) rigidity

70. The unit of stress in MKS system is
    (1) kg/cm²   (2) kg-cm   (3) kg/cm   (4) N/m²

71. The deformation of the bar per unit length in the direction of the force is known as
    (1) lateral strain   (2) linear strain   (3) shear strain   (4) none of these

72. Young's modulus of elasticity for a perfectly rigid body is
    (1) infinity   (2) unity   (3) zero   (4) none of these

73. Hooke's law holds good upto
    (1) yield point   (2) proportional point
    (3) elastic limit   (4) plastic limit

74. The diameter of a mild steel round bar, on which tensile test is performed at, fracture will
    (1) increase   (2) decrease   (3) be same   (4) none of these

75. True stress represents the ratio of
    (1) instantaneous load and instantaneous area
    (2) maximum load and maximum area
    (3) average load and maximum area
    (4) none of these

76. The value of modular ratio is always
    (1) less than one   (2) greater than one
    (3) equal to one   (4) zero

77. The effect of temperature on the value of elasticity for various substances in general
    (1) decreases with rise in temperature   (2) remains constant
    (3) increases with rise in temperature   (4) none of these

78. The maximum twisting moment a shaft can resist, is the product of the permissible shear stress and
    (1) moment of inertia   (2) polar moment of inertia
    (3) polar modulus   (4) modulus of rigidity

79. For a simply supported beam with a central load, the bending moment is
    (1) least at the centre   (2) least at the supports
    (3) maximum at the supports   (4) maximum at the centre

80. For a shaft, the shear stress at a point is …… the distance from the axis of the shaft.

    (1) equal to   (2) directly proportional to

    (3) inversely proportional to   (4) none of these

81. The shear stress at the centre of a circular shaft under torsion is

    (1) zero   (2) minimum   (3) maximum   (4) none of these

82. The ratio of the moment of inertia of a circular plate and that of a square plate for equal depth, is

    (1) less than one   (2) equal to one   (3) more than one   (4) equal to $3\pi/16$

83. If the width of a simply supported beam carrying an isolated load at its centre is doubled, the deflection of the beam at the centre is changed by

    (1) 1/2   (2) 1/8   (3) 2   (4) 8

84. For a simply supported beam of length L, the bending moment M is described as $M = a(x - x^3/L^2)$, $0 \leq x \leq L$; where a is constant. The shear force will be zero at

    (1) the supports   (2) $x = L/2$ (3) $x = L/3$ (4) $x = L/4$

85. The deflection of any rectangular beam simply supported, is

    (1) directly proportional to its weight

    (2) inversely proportional to its width

    (3) inversely proportional to the cube of its depth

    (4) directly proportional to the cube of its length

86. A beam is of triangular section with base 10 mm and height 12 mm. Its maximum section modulus is

    (1) 60 mm^3 (2) 90 mm^3 (3) 120 mm^3 (4) none of these

87. A beam of rectangular section is subjected to bending moment at 14.4 Nm. If b = 0.5 d, where b is breadth and d is depth and maximum stress developed is 100 MPa, the depth of the section is

    (1) 18 mm   (2) 12 mm   (3) 8 mm   (4) none of these

88. The value of bending stress changes along depth

    (1) linearly   (2) parabolically   (3) elliptically   (4) none of these

89. Due to hogging bending moment, the bending stress at bottom is

    (1) compression   (2) tension   (3) zero   (4) none of these

90. A bar is subjected to bending moment M and torsional moment T, then the principal planes can be located at

    (1) T/M   (2) M/T   (3) $T/(M^2 + T^2)^{1/2}$ (4) none of these

91. Unit of strain is

    (1) no units   (2) N/m   (3) N/m^2 (4) none of these

92. The shear stress at any section of a shaft is maximum

    (1) at the centre of the section   (2) at a distance r/2 from the centre

    (3) at the top of the surface   (4) at a distance 3/4r from the centre

93. What is the shape of influence line diagram for the maximum bending moment in a simply supported beam under uniform distributed load ?

    (1) Rectangular   (2) Triangular   (3) Parabolic   (4) Circular

94. The ratio of torsional resistance of a solid circular shaft of diameter D and a hollow shaft (external diameter D and internal diameter d), is
    (1) $\dfrac{D^4}{D^4 - d^4}$ (2) $\dfrac{D^3}{D^3 - d^3}$ (3) $\dfrac{D^4 - d^4}{D^4}$ (4) $\dfrac{D^3 - d^3}{D^3}$

95. Strain energy of any member may be defined as work done on it
    (1) to deform it   (2) to resist elongation
    (3) to resist shortening   (4) all of these

96. The angle of twist produced by unit torque applied is
    (1) torsional flexibility   (2) torsional stiffness
    (3) torsional rigidity   (4) none of these

97. Twist angle of a shaft of diameter 'd' is ...... to d⁴.
    (1) inversely proportional   (2) directly proportional
    (3) equal   (4) none of these

98. In a bar of large length when held vertically and subjected to a load at its load own-weight produces additional stress. The maximum stress will be
    (1) at the lower cross-section   (2) at the built-in upper cross-section
    (3) at the central cross-section   (4) at every point of the bar

99. In a square beam loaded longitudinally, shear develops
    (1) on middle fibre along horizontal plane
    (2) on lower fibre along horizontal plane
    (3) on top fibre along vertical plane
    (4) equally on each fibre along horizontal plane

100. Along the principal plane subjected to maximum principal stress
    (1) maximum shear stress acts   (2) minimum shear stress acts
    (3) no shear stress acts   (4) none of these

101. If a solid shaft is subjected to a torque T at its end such that maximum shear stress does not exceed f_s, then the diameter of the shaft will be
    (1) $\dfrac{16T}{\pi f_s}$ (2) $\sqrt{\dfrac{16T}{\pi f_s}}$ (3) $\sqrt[3]{\dfrac{16T}{\pi f_s}}$ (4) none of these

102. Shear deflection of a cantilever of length L, cross-sectional area A and shear stress under a connected load W at its free end, is
    (1) $\dfrac{2}{3}\dfrac{WL}{AG}$ (2) $\dfrac{1}{3}\dfrac{WL^2}{EIA}$ (3) $\dfrac{3}{2}\dfrac{WL}{AG}$ (4) $\dfrac{3}{2}\dfrac{WL^2}{AG}$

103. If a member carries a tensile force P on its area of cross-section A, the normal stress introduced on an inclined plane making an angle θ with its transverse plane, is
    (1) $\dfrac{P}{A}\sin^2\theta$ (2) $\dfrac{P}{A}\cos^2\theta$ (3) $\dfrac{P}{A}\tan^2\theta$ (4) $\dfrac{P}{2A}\sin^2\theta$

104. Ratio of the maximum bending stress in the flange to that in the web of an I section at any distance along the length of a beam is always :
    (1) less than one   (2) equal to one
    (3) more than one   (4) no relationship exists

105. Coulomb's theory of failure is also known as
     (1) maximum principal strain theory   (2) maximum principal stress theory
     (3) maximum shear stress theory   (4) maximum strain energy theory

106. Maximum principal strain theory is also known as
     (1) St. Venant's theory of failure   (2) Coulomb's theory of failure
     (3) Rankine's theory of failure   (4) none of these

107. As per the maximum shear stress theory, yield locus is
     (1) rectangle   (2) circle   (3) ellipse   (4) hexagon

108. A bar of certain material has bulk modulus 145 GPa and shear modulus is 100 GPa. The Poisson's ratio is
     (1) 0.2   (2) 0.22   (3) 0.26   (4) 0.28

109. A bar of certain material is 60 mm × 40 mm in cross-section and 2.8 m in length which is subjected to an axial pull of 120 kN. Modulus of elasticity is 200 GPa and Poisson's ratio is 0.3. Volumetric strain is
     (1) 0.0001   (2) 0.0002   (3) 0.00015   (4) 0.00025

110. A bar has base diameter 100 mm and length 3 m having density of material 78 kN/m³. Modulus of elasticity is 200 GPa. Elongation of bar is
     (1) 0.0001 mm   (2) 0.0009 mm   (3) 0.006 mm   (4) 0.001 mm

111. A solid shaft is rotating at 1 rpm. Maximum permissible shear stress is 55 N/mm². Power transmitted by shaft is 31 kW. Diameter of shaft is
     (1) 57 mm   (2) 67 mm   (3) 77 mm   (4) 87 mm

112. A solid circular shaft has to transmit 200 kW at 180 rpm. The maximum shear stress is 50 N/mm². The diameter of shaft is
     (1) 102 mm   (2) 92 mm   (3) 112 mm   (4) 82 mm

113. A solid shaft of 125 mm diameter is rotating at 95 rpm. Maximum permissible shear stress is 86 N/mm². Power transmitted by the shaft is
     (1) 228 kW   (2) 128 kW   (3) 328 kW   (4) 428 kW

114. A simply supported beam carrying a uniformly distributed load over its whole span, is propped at the centre of the span so that the beam is held to the level of the end supports. The reaction of the prop will be
     (1) half the distributed load   (2) 3/8th the distributed load
     (3) 5/8th the distributed load   (4) distributed load

115. The range within which a load can be applied on a rectangular column, to avoid any tensile stress, is
     (1) one-half of the base
     (2) one-fifth of the base
     (3) one-fourth of the base
     (4) one sixth of the base on either side of centroid

116. The torque transmitted by a solid shaft of diameter (D) is
     (1) $\pi \times \tau \times D^3/4$ (2) $\pi \times \tau \times D^3/16$ (3) $\pi \times \tau \times D^3/32$ (4) none of these

117. The polar moment of inertia of a hollow shaft of outer diameter (D) and linear diameter (d) is
   (1) $\pi \times (D^3 - d^3)/16$ (2) $\pi \times (D^4 - d^4)/16$
   (3) $\pi \times (D^4 - d^4)/64$ (4) $\pi \times (D^4 - d^4)/32$

118. A steel shaft, 150 mm diameter, is subjected to torque of 16 kN-m and bending moment of 12.7 kN-m. The maximum principal stress is
   (1) 65 N/mm²   (2) 70 N/mm²   (3) 50 N/mm²   (4) 60 N/mm²

119. A steel shaft, 150 mm diameter, is subjected to torque of 16 kN-m and bending moment of 12.7 kN-m. The maximum shear stress is
   (1) 29.3 N/mm²   (2) 48.3 N/mm²   (3) 41.3 N/mm²   (4) 30.8 N/mm²

120 A steel shaft, 85 mm in diameter, is subjected to torque 'T' and bending moment 6 kN-m. The maximum principal stress is 125 MPa. The value of 'T' is
   (1) 6.8 kN-m   (2) 7.5 kN-m   (3) 9.6 kN-m   (4) 8.5 kN-m

121. A member which does not regain its original shape after removal of load producing deformation is said to be
   (1) plastic   (2) elastic   (3) rigid   (4) none of these

122. Which of the under mentioned type is simple strain ?
   (1) Tensile strain   (2) Compressive strain
   (3) Shear strain   (4) All the these

123. A steel shaft, 75 mm in diameter, is subjected to torque of 4 kN-m and bending moment 'M'. The maximum principal stress is 87 MPa. The value of 'M' is
   (1) 2.5 kN-m   (2) 3.75 kN-m   (3) 2.9 kN-m   (4) 6.0 kN-m

124. Shear stress at the centre of shaft having 200 mm radius and subjected to twisting moment of 300 N.m. is :
   (1) 0.19 N/mm²   (2) Zero
   (3) 0.38 N/mm²   (4) 0.095 N/mm²

125. A rectangular plate is 300 mm long (x-axis), with cross-section 50 mm (y-axis) × 10 mm (z-axis). Axial tensile forces acting along y and z directions are 100 kN and 100 kN respectively. Young's modulus is 150 GPa and Poisson's ratio is 0.19. The compressive force acting along x direction, when volume remains same, is
   (1) 5 kN   (2) 10 kN   (3) 15 kN   (4) 20 kN

126. A compound bar ABCD is subjected to axial compressive load 30 kN. AB, BC and CD are 40 mm, 20 mm and 30 mm in diameter and 0.3 m, 0.6 m and 0.2 m long. Modulus of elasticity is 200 GPa. Contraction of bar is
   (1) 0.18 mm   (2) 0.36 mm   (3) 0.54 mm   (4) 0.72 mm

127. A copper bar, 36 mm in diameter, is enclosed in a steel tube of 50 mm external diameter and 5 mm thickness. Length of composite is 1500 mm, a compressive force of 140 kN is applied to the composite and E_s = 200 GPa and E_b = 110 GPa. Stress in copper is
   (1) 61 N/mm²   (2) 74 N/mm²   (3) 90 N/mm²   (4) 40 N/mm²

128. A conical bar has base diameter 100 mm and density of material is 85 kN/m³. Modulus of elasticity is 80 GPa. Elongation of bar is 0.01 mm. Length of bar is
     (1)   127 kN/m³   (2)   144 kN/m³   (3)   170 kN/m³   (4)   190 kN/m³

129. A compound bar ACDB, fixed at A and D, having 20 mm diameter, is subjected to axial forces. AB, BC and CD are 0.2 m, 0.2 m and 0.4 m long. Force 12 kN is applied downwards at C and 20 kN downwards at D. Modulus of elasticity is 200 GPa. Reaction at A is
     (1)   31.9 kN   (2)   13.1 kN   (3)   24.5 kN   (4)   18.9 kN

130. A steel shaft is subjected to torque 7.5 kN-m and bending moment 5.2 kN-m. The maximum principal stress is 95 MPa. The diameter of shaft is
     (1)   60 mm   (2)   70 mm   (3)   90 mm   (4)   80 mm

131. A hollow shaft is subjected to a torque 200 kN-m and bending moment 100 kN-m. Internal diameter of shaft is 0.5 times the external diameter. If maximum principal stress is 41 MPa, then the diameter of shaft is
     (1)   250 mm   (2)   200 mm   (3)   300 mm   (4)   350 mm

132. A hollow shaft having 200 mm external diameter, is subjected to a torque 125 kN-m and bending moment 75 kN-m. Internal diameter of shaft is 0.75 times the external diameter. Minimum principal stress developed is
     (1)   45.5 N/mm²   (2)   55.6 N/mm²   (3)   65.9 N/mm²   (4)   39.7 N/mm²

133. A hollow shaft having 300 mm external diameter, is subjected to a torque 250 kN-m and bending moment 135 kN-m. Internal diameter of shaft is 0.85 times the external diameter. Maximum principal stress developed is
     (1)   225 N/mm²   (2)   205 N/mm²   (3)   215 N/mm²   (4)   165 N/mm²

134. A solid shaft of 150 mm diameter is rotating at 125 rpm. Maximum permissible shear stress is 100 N/mm². Power transmitted by shaft is
     (1)   876 kW   (2)   867 kW   (3)   327 kW   (4)   723 kW

135. A hollow circular shaft of 150 mm diameter, thickness of metal 10 mm, is rotating at 2.5 rpm. The angle of twist is found to be 0.86°. The power transmitted is 120 kW. Modulus of rigidity is 85 GPa. The length of shaft is
     (1)   2 m   (2)   3 m   (3)   4 m   (4)   5 m

136. A hollow shaft of 280 mm external diameter and 220 mm internal diameter, has to transmit 1000 kW at 100 rpm. It is additionally subjected to bending moment 10 kN-m and an end thrust of 200 kN. Maximum shear stress developed is
     (1)   57 N/mm²   (2)   47 N/mm²   (3)   27 N/mm²   (4)   37 N/mm²

137. A hollow shaft of 250 mm external diameter and 200 mm internal diameter, is subjected to torque 'T'. It is additionally subjected to bending moment 35 kN-m and an end thrust 125 kN. Maximum principal stress developed is 61 N/mm². The value of 'T' is
     (1)   55 kN-m   (2)   65 kN-m   (3)   85 kN-m   (4)   75 kN-m

138. A solid shaft, 145 mm diameter, has to transmit power 'P' at 100 rpm. It is additionally subjected to bending moment 15.5 kN-m and an end thrust 53 kN. Maximum principal stress developed is 60 N/mm². The value of power 'P' is
     (1)   125 kW   (2)   105 kW   (3)   175 kW   (4)   95 kW

139. In a simply supported beam, hogging B.M. is 5 kN-m, N.A. from top is 250 mm, overall depth of section is 510 mm. M.I. of the section is 2×10^7 mm⁴. The maximum bending tensile stress is
   - (1) 62.5 N/mm²
   - (2) 60.5 N/mm²
   - (3) 65 N/mm²
   - (4) 67 N/mm²

140. In a simply supported beam, hogging B.M. is 5 kN-m, N.A. from top is 250 mm, overall depth of section is 510 mm. M.I. of the section is 2×10^7 mm⁴. The maximum bending compressive stress is
   - (1) 62.5 N/mm²
   - (2) 60.5 N/mm²
   - (3) 65 N/mm²
   - (4) 67 N/mm²

141. In a simply supported rectangular beam, width and depth is 200 mm and 500 mm respectively. The maximum stress is 103 N/mm². Maximum bending moment is
   - (1) 87.5 N-m
   - (2) 875 kN-m
   - (3) 87.5 kN-m
   - (4) 875 N-m

142. In a simply supported rectangular beam, width is 100 mm. The maximum stress is 80 N/mm². Maximum bending moment is 173 kN-m. Depth of beam is
   - (1) 320 mm
   - (2) 300 mm
   - (3) 340 mm
   - (4) 360 mm

143. In a cantilever rectangular beam, width of beam is 200 mm and overall depth of section is 570 mm. The bending stress is 150 N/mm². The concentrated load acting on 6 m span at cantilever end is
   - (1) 170 kN
   - (2) 270 kN
   - (3) 370 kN
   - (4) 470 kN

144. In a cantilever rectangular beam, width is 220 mm and overall depth of section is 450 mm. The concentrated load acting on 3 m span at 1 m from cantilever end is 100 kN. The maximum bending stress is
   - (1) 9 N/mm²
   - (2) 15 N/mm²
   - (3) 27 N/mm²
   - (4) 36 N/mm²

145. In a cantilever rectangular beam, width of beam is 100 mm and overall depth of section is 500 mm. The bending stress is 86.5 N/mm². Uniformly distributed load acting on 3 m throughout the span is
   - (1) 70 kN/m
   - (2) 60 kN/m
   - (3) 80 kN/m
   - (4) 67 kN/m

146. A bar of certain material has modulus of elasticity 110 GPa and Poisson's ratio is 0.2. Bulk modulus is
   - (1) 45.83 GPa
   - (2) 61.11 GPa
   - (3) 100 GPa
   - (4) None of these

147. A bar of certain material has modulus of elasticity 210 GPa and Poisson's ratio is 0.25. Shear modulus is
   - (1) 140 GPa
   - (2) 210 GPa
   - (3) 84 GPa
   - (4) None of these

148. A bar of 120 mm diameter and 300 mm in length is subjected to axial compressive load of 120 kN which increases diameter by 0.075 mm and decreases length by 1.1 mm. Poisson's ratio is
   - (1) 0.20
   - (2) 0.17
   - (3) 0.32
   - (4) 0.28

149. A bar of 75 mm diameter and 3.2 m long is subjected to gradually applied load 20 kN. The stress developed in the bar is
   - (1) 63.6 N/mm²
   - (2) 94.3 N/mm²
   - (3) 104.5 N/mm²
   - (4) 44.8 N/mm²

150. A bar is 15 mm in diameter. Elastic limit for the bar material is 300 MPa. Modulus of elasticity and the modulus of resilience of the bar is 300 GPa and 92.8 J respectively. Length of the bar is
   - (1) 3.5 m
   - (2) 4.5 m
   - (3) 2.5 mm
   - (4) 5.5 mm

151. A bar of 75 mm diameter and 3.2 m long is subjected to suddenly applied load 20 kN. The stress developed in the bar is
   - (1) 63.6 N/mm²
   - (2) 114.3 N/mm²
   - (3) 104.5 N/mm²
   - (4) 127.3 N/mm²

152. A weight of 2 kN is dropped onto a collar at lower end of the bar which is 20 mm in diameter and 3 m long, through a height of 35 mm. Modulus of elasticity is 210 GPa. Minimum instantaneous stress is
   - (1) 140 N/mm²
   - (2) 210 N/mm²
   - (3) 180 N/mm²
   - (4) 170 N/mm²

153. A vertical steel bar, 3.2 m long, is provided with a collar at lower end. A weight of 700 N is dropped through a height 120 mm. Maximum permissible tensile stress is 135 MPa. Modulus of elasticity is 210 GPa. The diameter of the bar is
   - (1) 24 mm
   - (2) 22 mm
   - (3) 26 mm
   - (4) 28 mm

154. A weight of 5 kN is dropped onto a collar at lower end of the bar which is 30 mm in diameter and 2 m long, through a height of 50 mm. Modulus of elasticity is 200 GPa. Minimum instantaneous stress is
   - (1) 239 N/mm²
   - (2) 259 N/mm²
   - (3) 189 N/mm²
   - (4) 169 N/mm²

155. A bar of 20 mm diameter and 1.5 m long has to transmit shock energy of 7.180 J. Instantaneous stress developed in the bar is
   - (1) 80 N/mm²
   - (2) 110 N/mm²
   - (3) 100 N/mm²
   - (4) 90 N/mm²

156. A vertical steel bar having 26 mm diameter is provided with a collar at lower end. A weight of 750 N is dropped through a height 68 mm. Maximum permissible tensile stress is 130 MPa. Modulus of elasticity is 200 GPa. Length of the bar is
   - (1) 2 m
   - (2) 2.3 m
   - (3) 2.8 m
   - (4) 3 m

157. A weight of 5 kN is dropped onto a collar at lower end of the bar which is 30 mm in diameter and 2 m long, through a height of 50 mm. Modulus of elasticity is 200 GPa. Maximum elongation of bar is
   - (1) 3.53 mm
   - (2) 4.56 mm
   - (3) 2.73 mm
   - (4) 5.20 mm

158. A bar of 18 mm diameter and 2.1 m long is subjected to gradually applied load 30 kN. The stress developed in the bar is
   - (1) 98 N/mm²
   - (2) 118 N/mm²
   - (3) 104 N/mm²
   - (4) 140 N/mm²

159. A bar, 3.5 m long, is subjected to suddenly applied load 100 kN. The stress developed in the bar is 160 MPa. Diameter of the bar is
   - (1) 25 mm
   - (2) 40 mm
   - (3) 55 mm
   - (4) 35 mm

160. A vertical steel bar of 18 mm diameter and 3.25 m long is provided with a collar at lower end. A weight of 1 kN is dropped through a height 'h'. Maximum permissible tensile stress is 218 MPa. Modulus of elasticity is 200 GPa. The value of height 'h' is
   - (1) 85 mm
   - (2) 80 mm
   - (3) 95 mm
   - (4) 75 mm

161. A steel beam of size 200 mm × d mm is simply supported over a span of 12 m. It carries UDL of 100 kN/m. The maximum shear stress is 6 N/mm². The value of 'd' is
    (1)   400 mm   (2)   450 mm   (3)   500 kN   (4)   550 mm

162. A hollow shaft having internal diameter 60 mm, is rotating at 80 rpm. Power transmitted by shaft is 18.3 kW. Maximum permissible shear stress is 90 N/mm². External diameter of shaft is
    (1)   77 mm   (2)   88 mm   (3)   68 mm   (4)   57 mm

163. A hollow circular shaft of 120 mm internal diameter and thickness of metal 20 mm, is rotating at 175 rpm. The power transmitted is 263.8 kW. Modulus of rigidity is
    (1)   75 GPa   (2)   80 GPa   (3)   85 GPa   (4)   90 GPa

164. The cross-section of beam is inverted 'T' section with flange 80 mm in width and 15 mm in depth and web with width 15 mm and depth 80 mm. The section is subjected to shear force of 35 kN. The maximum shear stress is
    (1)   14.1 N/mm²   (2)   2.65 N/mm²   (3)   15.1 N/mm²   (4)   17.2 N/mm²

165. A steel beam of size 225 mm × d mm is simply supported over a span of 20 m. It carries UDL of 180 kN/m. The maximum shear stress is 20 N/mm². The value of 'd' is
    (1)   500 mm   (2)   550 mm   (3)   600 mm   (4)   650 mm

166. A bar of certain material is 50 mm × 50 mm in cross-section and 100 mm in length. It is subjected to an axial pull of 200 kN. Modulus of elasticity is 200 GPa and the Poisson's ratio is 0.25. Width of section is
    (1)   increased by 0.007 mm   (2)   decreased by 0.007 mm
    (3)   increased by 0.009 mm   (4)   decreased by 0.009 mm

167. A bar of certain material is 80 mm × 30 mm in cross-section and 1.5 m long. It is subjected to an axial pull of 180 kN. Modulus of elasticity is 220 GPa and Poisson's ratio is 0.25. Width is decreased by
    (1)   0.0018 mm   (2)   0.0025 mm   (3)   0.0038 mm   (4)   0.0050 mm

168. At a point in a strained material, the states of stresses are σ_x tensile and 52 MPa tensile along x and along y-axis respectively and shear stress is 46 MPa making moment clockwise due to vertical shear stress. The maximum principal stress is 110 N/mm². The value of σ_x is
    (1)   63.5 N/mm²   (2)   65.5 N/mm²   (3)   55.5 N/mm²   (4)   73.5 N/mm²

169. At a point in a strained material, the states of stresses are 75 tensile and σ_y compressive along x and along y-axis respectively and shear stress 65 MPa making moment clockwise due to vertical shear stress. The maximum principal stress is 100 N/mm². The value of σ_y is
    (1)   60 N/mm²   (2)   75 N/mm²   (3)   55 N/mm²   (4)   65 N/mm²

170. A solid shaft, 125 mm in diameter, is subjected to shear stress 60 N/mm², bending stress 50 N/mm², and an axial stress σ. Due to these stresses maximum principal stress developed is 120 N/mm². The value of σ is
    (1)   43 N/mm²   (2)   35 N/mm²   (3)   23 N/mm²   (4)   33 N/mm²

171. If the Young's Modulus and Poisson's ratio of a material is 2×10^6 kg/cm² and 0.25 respectively, find the Bulk Modulus :

(1) $\frac{6}{5} \times 10^6$ kg/cm²   (2) $\frac{3}{4} \times 10^6$ kg/cm²

(3) $\frac{5}{6} \times 10^6$ kg/cm²   (4) $\frac{4}{3} \times 10^6$ kg/cm²

172. A solid shaft, 100 mm in diameter, is subjected to shear stress 'τ', bending stress 36 N/mm² and an axial stress 25 N/mm². Due to these stresses maximum principal stress developed is 95 N/mm². The value of τ is

(1) 43 N/mm²   (2) 35 N/mm²   (3) 63 N/mm²   (4) 57 N/mm²

173. A bar of 400 mm length and of uniform cross-section 20 mm diameter is subjected to tensile load of 50 kN, assuming E = 200 GPa, the elongation of bar is :

(1) 2.481 mm   (2) 3.203 mm   (3) 0.318 mm   (4) 0.187 mm

174. A beam of rectangular section is with width 'b' and depth 'd'. The shear force at a section of the beam is S. The ratio of maximum shear stress to average shear stress is

(1) 1.2   (2) 1.5   (3) 1.7   (4) None of these

175. A bar of certain material has modulus of rigidity 80 GPa and Poisson's ratio 0.28. Young's modulus is

(1) 205 GPa   (2) 220 GPa   (3) 284 GPa   (4) None of these

176. A bar of certain material has modulus of rigidity 120 GPa and Poisson's ratio 0.3. Bulk modulus is

(1) 225 GPa   (2) 312 GPa   (3) 260 GPa   (4) None of these

177. In a simply supported beam, section is 'I' section with vertical flanges 200 × 20 mm and horizontal web 20 mm × 500 mm respectively. The section is subjected to shear force of 250 kN. The maximum shear stress at the junction of flange and web is

(1) 45.8 N/mm²   (2) 39.7 N/mm²   (3) 35.2 N/mm²   (4) 41.2 N/mm²

178. The slenderness ratio of a vertical column of a square cross-section of 2.5 cm sides and 300 cm length, is

(1) 200   (2) 240   (3) 360   (4) 416

179. In a simply supported beam, span is 6 m and section is 'I' section with flanges and web 120 × 20 mm and 25 × 200 mm respectively. The maximum bending stress is 60 N/mm². Concentrated load at centre is

(1) 25 kN   (2) 35 kN   (3) 450 kN   (4) 55 kN

180. In a simply supported beam, span is 5 m and section is 'I' section with flanges and web 120 × 20 mm and 25 × 200 mm respectively. The maximum bending stress at bottom is 48 N/mm². UDL on beam is

(1) 7.6 kN/m   (2) 8.6 kN/m   (3) 9.6 kN/m   (4) 10.6 kN/m

181. A rectangular section having dimensions 100 mm × 325 mm which is simply supported on span 3.4 m, carries UDL of w kN/m. If the bending stress is not to exceed 115 MPa, value of UDL w is

(1) 100 kN/m   (2) 120 kN/m   (3) 170 kN/m   (4) 140 kN/m

182. At a point in a strained material, the states of tensile stresses are 72 MPa and 72 MPa along x and y axis respectively and shear stress is 38 MPa making moment anticlockwise due to vertical shear stress. The minimum principal tensile stress is
  (1) 29 N/mm²   (2) 39 N/mm²   (3) 24 N/mm²   (4) 34 N/mm²

183. At a point in a strained material, the states of tensile stresses are 72 MPa and 72 MPa along x and y axis respectively and shear stress is 38 MPa making moment anticlockwise due to vertical shear stress. The resultant stress on a plane making an angle 50° with the x-axis is
  (1) 92.6 N/mm²   (2) 129.6 N/mm²   (3) 99.6 N/mm²   (4) 112.6 N/mm²

184. At a point in a strained material, the states of stresses are 72 MPa tensile and 72 MPa compressive along x and along y axis respectively and shear stress is 38 MPa making moment anticlockwise due to vertical shear stress. The normal stress on a plane making an angle 50° with the x-axis is
  (1) 45 N/mm²   (2) 55 N/mm²   (3) 40 N/mm²   (4) 50 N/mm²

185. A bar of cross-section 15 mm × 15 mm is subjected to axial compressive load of 32 kN. The lateral dimension of bar is increased by 0.0035 mm. Modulus of rigidity is 85 GPa. Bulk modulus is
  (1) 346 GPa   (2) 129 GPa   (3) 237 GPa   (4) 185 GPa

186. A bar of 100 mm diameter and 500 mm in length is subjected to axial compressive load of 150 kN, which increases the diameter by 0.095 mm and decreases the length by 1.5 mm. Shear modulus is
  (1) 1.26 GPa   (2) 1.96 GPa   (3) 3.24 GPa   (4) 2.41 GPa

187. A rectangular plate is 500 mm long with cross-section 30 mm × 30 mm. Axial tensile stresses acting along x and z directions are 120 N/mm² and 75 N/mm² respectively. Young's modulus is 125 GPa and Poisson's ratio is 0.25. The volumetric strain is
  (1) 0.00027   (2) 0.00057   (3) 0.00078   (4) 0.00098

188. A rectangular plate is 200 mm long, with cross-section 10 mm × 10 mm. Axial stresses acting along y and z directions are 150 N/mm² compressive and 50 N/mm² compressive respectively. Young's modulus is 125 GPa and Poisson's ratio is 0.22. The tensile stress acting along x-direction when volume remains same, is
  (1) 200 N/mm²   (2) 180 N/mm²   (3) 160 N/mm²   (4) 140 N/mm²

189. A hollow circular shaft of 150 mm external diameter and thickness of metal 20 mm, is rotating at 200 rpm. The angle of twist on 3 m length was found to be 0.7°. Modulus of rigidity is 80 GPa. The maximum shear stress is
  (1) 42 N/mm²   (2) 36 N/mm²   (3) 24 N/mm²   (4) 50 N/mm²

190. A hollow circular shaft having internal diameter 50% of external diameter, transmits 800 kW at 150 rpm. The angle of twist on 4 m length was found to be 0.99°. Modulus of rigidity is 80 GPa. The external diameter is
  (1) 100 mm   (2) 150 mm   (3) 200 mm   (4) 250 mm

191. A hollow shaft having external diameter 110 mm and thickness 5 mm, is rotating at 90 rpm. Maximum permissible shear stress is 60 N/mm². Power transmitted by shaft is
  (1) 47 kW   (2) 27 kW   (3) 37 kW   (4) 42 kW

192. A hollow circular shaft having 130 mm external diameter and thickness of metal 15 mm, is rotating at 180 rpm. The angle of twist on 5 m length was found to be 0.75°. Modulus of rigidity is 85 GPa. The maximum shear stress is
   (1) 12.5 N/mm²   (2) 16.5 N/mm²   (3) 20.5 N/mm²   (4) 14.5 N/mm²

193. At a point in a strained material, the states of stress is 25 MPa compressive along x-axis and shear stress 45 MPa making moment clockwise due to vertical shear stress. The minimum principal compressive stress is
   (1) 64 N/mm²   (2) 56 N/mm²   (3) 45 N/mm²   (4) 34 N/mm²

194. At a point in a strained material, the states of tensile stresses are 72 MPa and 72 MPa along x and along y axis respectively and shear stress is 38 MPa making moment anticlockwise due to vertical shear stress. The maximum principal tensile stress is
   (1) 90 N/mm²   (2) 110 N/mm²   (3) 100 N/mm²   (4) 120 N/mm²

195. What is the greatest eccentricity which a load 'W' can have without producing tension on the cross-section of a short column of external diameter 'D' and internal diameter 'd' ?
   (1) $\dfrac{D + d}{8D}$ (2) $\dfrac{\pi\,(D^4 - d^4)}{32\,D^3}$ (3) $\dfrac{D^2 + d^2}{8\,D}$ (4) $\dfrac{D^2 - d^2}{8\,D}$

196. If a circular shaft is subjected to a torque 'T' and bending moment 'M', the ratio of maximum bending stress to maximum shear stress is ....
   (1) $\dfrac{2M}{T}$ (2) $\dfrac{M}{2T}$ (3) $\dfrac{M}{T}$ (4) $\dfrac{2T}{M}$

197. Where is the bending stress on a beam section zero ?
   (1) Depends on the shape of the beam   (2) Top fibre
   (3) Bottom fibre   (4) Centroid of the section

198. A timber beam, which is rectangular in section, is simply supported over 6 m span to carry brick masonry wall 150 mm thick and 3 m high. Density of brick masonry is 18 kN/m³, allowable bending stress is 10 N/mm² and b = 0.4d. The value of b is ....
   (1) 182 mm   (2) 152 mm   (3) 302 mm   (4) 352 mm

199. At a point in a strained material, the states of stresses are 72 MPa tensile and 72 MPa compressive along x and along y axis respectively and shear stress is 38 MPa making moment anticlockwise due to vertical shear stress. The maximum principal stress is
   (1) 81.4 N/mm² (T)   (2) 81.4 N/mm² (C)
   (3) 89.4 N/mm² (T)   (4) 89.4 N/mm² (C)

200. At a point in a strained material, the states of stresses are 72 MPa tensile and 72 MPa compressive along x and along y axis respectively and shear stress is 38 MPa making moment anticlockwise due to vertical shear stress. The minimum principal stress is
   (1) 81.4 N/mm² (T)   (2) 81.4 N/mm² (C)
   (3) 89.4 N/mm² (T)   (4) 89.4 N/mm² (C)

201. A circular bar is subjected to an axial pull of 70 kN. If the maximum shear intensity on any oblique plane is not to exceed 65 MPa, then the diameter of bar is
   (1) 23.1 mm   (2) 26.2 mm   (3) 27.4 mm   (4) 29.0 mm

202. A circular bar of 50 mm diameter is subjected to an axial pull of 120 kN. If the normal stress on an oblique plane is 45 MPa, then the shear stress on the plane is
     (1) 23.5 N/mm²   (2) 27.3 N/mm²   (3) 36.7 N/mm²   (4) 48 N/mm²

203 A circular bar of 25 mm diameter is subjected to an axial pull. If the normal stress on an oblique plane at an angle 65° with x-axis, is 65 MPa, then the axial pull is
     (1) 39 kN   (2) 25 kN   (3) 31 kN   (4) 45 kN

204. If a simply supported rectangular beam measuring $10 \times 18 \times 400$ cm carries a uniformly distributed load such that the bending stress developed is 100 N/mm². The intensity of the load per metre length, is
     (1) 54 N/mm   (2) 27 N/mm   (3) 60 N/mm   (4) none of these

205. A copper bar of 36 mm diameter is enclosed in a steel tube of 50 mm external diameter and 5 mm thickness. Length of composite is 1500 mm, a compressive force of 170 kN is applied to the composite and $E_s = 200$ GPa and $E_b = 110$ GPa. Contraction of bar is
     (1) 0.3 mm   (2) 1 mm   (3) 0.7 mm   (4) 2 mm

206. A bar of 20 mm diameter and 1 m length is kept between two rigid supports. The temperature is increased by 40°C. Coefficient of thermal expansion of material is 11×10^{-6} and modulus of elasticity is 200 GPa. Stress in bar is
     (1) 61 N/mm²   (2) 98 N/mm²   (3) 69 N/mm²   (4) 88 N/mm²

207. A circular bar, which is 1 m long, tapers uniformly from 45 mm. A pull of 50 kN is applied to the bar. Modulus of elasticity is 190 GPa. Elongation of bar is 0.5 mm. Diameter of bar at other end is
     (1) 10 mm   (2) 20 mm   (3) 15 mm   (4) 5 mm

208. A circular bar, which is 2 m long, tapers uniformly from 'd' mm to 40 mm. A compressive force of 19 kN is applied to the bar. Modulus of elasticity is 80 GPa. Contraction of bar is 0.25 mm. Diameter 'd' of bar is
     (1) 40 mm   (2) 50 mm   (3) 60 mm   (4) 70 mm

209. A circular bar of 25 mm diameter is subjected to an axial pull. If the normal stress on an oblique plane at an angle 65° with x-axis, is 55 MPa, then the resultant stress on the plane is
     (1) 70 N/mm²   (2) 50 N/mm²   (3) 80 N/mm²   (4) 60 N/mm²

210. A square bar with 25 mm side, is subjected to an axial pull. If the normal stress on an oblique plane, making an angle 27° with y-axis, is 120 MPa, then the resultant stress on the plane is
     (1) 46 N/mm²   (2) 37 N/mm²   (3) 56 N/mm²   (4) 41 N/mm²

211. A timber beam rectangular in section, is simply supported over 8 m span to carry brick masonry wall 230 mm thick and 4 m high, density of brick masonry is 20 kN/m³, allowable bending stress is 8 N/mm² and b = 0.5d. The value of d is
     (1) 305 mm   (2) 405 mm   (3) 505 mm   (4) 605 mm

212. A cantilever beam with 3.1 m span, rectangular in cross-section, carries brick masonry wall 150 mm thick and 3 m high, density of brick masonry is 18 kN/m³, allowable bending stress is 10 N/mm² and b = 0.4d. The value of b is
     (1) 200 mm   (2) 250 mm   (3) 150 mm   (4) 350 mm

213. A rectangular section of cantilever beam 200 mm × 275 mm carries UDL of 30 kN/m. If the bending stress is not to exceed 150 MPa, the span of beam is
   (1) 3 m   (2) 5 m   (3) 10 m   (4) 8 m

214. A rectangular cross-section of cantilever beam b × 500 mm of span 6 m carries UDL of 15 kN/m. If the bending stress is not to exceed 135 MPa, width of beam is
   (1) 48 mm   (2) 125 mm   (3) 150 mm   (4) 175 mm

215. At a point in a strained material, the states of stresses are 75 MPa tensile and σ_y compressive along x and along y-axis respectively and shear stress is 65 MPa making moment clockwise due to vertical shear stress. The maximum principal stress is 100 N/mm². The minimum principal stress is
   (1) 90 N/mm²   (2) 75 N/mm²   (3) 80 N/mm²   (4) 85 N/mm²

216. A steel shaft, with 100 mm diameter, is subjected to torque of 9 kN-m and bending moment of 3 kN-m. The maximum principal stress is
   (1) 63.6 N/mm²   (2) 76.5 N/mm²   (3) 56.6 N/mm²   (4) 69.5 N/mm²

217. A rectangular plate is 200 mm long with cross-section 10 mm × 10 mm. Axial stresses acting along x and y directions are 150 N/mm² compressive and 50 N/mm² compressive respectively. Young's modulus is 125 GPa and Poisson's ratio is 0.22. The tensile stress acting along z direction, when volume remains same, is
   (1) 120 N/mm²   (2) 180 N/mm²   (3) 160 N/mm²   (4) 200 N/mm²

218. A bar has diameter 100 mm and length 3 m having density of material as 78 kN/m³. Modulus of elasticity is 200 GPa. Elongation of bar is
   (1) 0.0011 mm   (2) 0.0015 mm   (3) 0.0025 mm   (4) 0.0018 mm

219. A steel shaft, 100 mm in diameter, is subjected to torque of 9 kN-m and bending moment of   3 kN-m. The minimum principal stress is
   (1) 31 N/mm²   (2) 41 N/mm²   (3) 46 N/mm²   (4) 33 N/mm²

220. A timber beam of size 150 mm × 300 mm is simply supported over a span of 8 m. It carries UDL of 10 kN/m. The maximum shear stress is
   (1) 2.33 N/mm²   (2) 1.33 N/mm²   (3) 3.33 N/mm²   (4) 1.67 N/mm²

221. A circular beam having diameter 'D' is subjected to shear force of V. The ratio of average shear stress to maximum shear stress is
   (1) 5/8   (2) 7/9   (3) 4/7   (4) 3/4

222. The cross-section of beam is inverted 'T' section with flange 100 mm in width and 20 mm in depth and web with width 25 mm and depth 120 mm. The minimum shear stress at the junction of flange and web is 11 N/mm². The shear force on the section is
   (1) 125 kN   (2) 100 kN   (3) 150 kN   (4) 75 kN

223. A rectangular section 100 mm × 325 mm, simply supported on span 6 m, carries UDL of w kN/m. If the bending stress is not to exceed 255 MPa, value of UDL w is
   (1) 60 kN/m   (2) 100 kN/m   (3) 170 kN/m   (4) 140 kN/m

224. A bar of certain material has bulk modulus 140 GPa and Poisson's ratio 0.24. Shear modulus is
   (1) 219 GPa   (2) 139 GPa   (3) 88 GPa   (4) None of these

225. Find the Euler's crippling load for a hollow cylinder column (E = 205 GPa) of 38 mm external diameter and 2.5 mm thick, with a length of 2.3 m and fixed at both of its ends.
   (1) 17.16 kN   (2) 14.29 kN   (3) 16.88 kN   (4) 21.49 kN

226. The cross-section of beam is 'T' section with flange 80 mm in width and 8 mm in depth and web with width 8 mm and depth 132 mm. The section is subjected to shear force of 50 kN. The maxium shear stress at the junction of flange and web is
   (1) 28 N/mm²   (2) 50 N/mm²   (3) 14 N/mm²   (4) 5 N/mm²

227. A propped cantilever of span 'L' is carrying a point load 'P' acting at midspan. The plastic moment of the section is Mp. The magnitude of collapse load is :
   (1) 6 Mp/L   (2) 8 Mp/L   (3) 2 Mp/L   (4) 4 Mp/L

228. A timber beam of size 125 mm × 250 mm is simply supported over a span of 10 m. The maximum shear stress is 4.8 N/mm². UDL on beam is
   (1) 15 kN/m   (2) 20 kN/m   (3) 25 kN/m   (4) 30 kN/m

229. The maximum shear stress is 6 N/mm². The value of concentrated load acting at mid span of beam is
   (1) 240 kN   (2) 200 kN   (3) 260 kN   (4) 280 kN

230. The cross-section of beam is inverted 'T' section with flange 80 mm in width and 15 mm in depth and web with width 15 mm and depth 80 mm. The section is subjected to shear force of 35 kN. The maximum shear stress at the junction of flange and web is
   (1) 14.1 N/mm²   (2) 2.65 N/mm²
   (3) 1.4 N/mm²   (4) 21.2 N/mm²

231. The cross-section of beam is 'T' section with flange 80 mm in width and 8 mm in depth and web with width 8 mm and depth 132 mm. The section is subjected to shear force of 50 kN. The maximum shear stress is
   (1) 61 N/mm²   (2) 52 N/mm²   (3) 48 N/mm²   (4) 57 N/mm²

232. A timber beam of size 160 mm × 300 mm is simply supported over a span of 8 m. The maximum shear stress is 2.5 N/mm². The value of concentrated load acting at mid span of beam is
   (1) 110 kN   (2) 130 kN   (3) 160 kN   (4) 180 kN

233. A timber box beam having hollow section with two horizontal plates 200 mm × 50 mm and two vertical plates 250 mm × 50 mm is connected by nails on both sides. The strength of each nail is 12 kN. The shear force acting on the section is 35 kN. The spacing of nail is
   (1) 220 mm   (2) 250 mm   (3) 270 mm   (4) 285 mm

234. A solid shaft is rotating at 85 rpm. Maximum permissible shear stress is 60 N/mm². Power transmitted by shaft is 44.2 kW. Diameter of shaft is
   (1) 55 mm   (2) 65 mm   (3) 75 mm   (4) 60 mm

235. A solid shaft of 60 mm diameter is rotating at 120 rpm. Maximum permissible shear stress is 50 N/mm². Power transmitted by shaft is
   (1) 46 kW   (2) 39 kW   (3) 27 kW   (4) 64 kW

236. A solid circular shaft of diameter 100 mm is subjected to a torque of 25 kNm. The angle of twist over a length of 3 m is observed to be 0.09 rad. The modulus of rigidity of material is
    (1) $7.64 \times 10^{-5} \text{ N/mm}^2$
    (2) $8.49 \times 10^4 \text{ N/mm}^2$
    (3) $2.1 \times 10^5 \text{ N/mm}^2$
    (4) $6.74 \times 10^4 \text{ N/mm}^2$

237. A bar of steel ($E = 2.1 \times 10^6 \text{ kg/cm}^2$) 70 cm long varies in its cross section with 2.5 cm diameter for the first 20 cm, 2 cm diameter for next 30 cm and 1.5 cm diameter for the rest of the length. Find the elongation if the bar is subjected to a tensile load of 15 tonnes.
    (1) 0.118 cms
    (2) 0.25 cms
    (3) 0.178 cms
    (4) 0.354 cms

238. A bar of certain material is 40 mm × 40 mm in cross-section and 90 mm in length. It is subjected to an axial pull of 120 kN. Length is increased by 0.05 mm and each side is decreased by 0.005 mm. The Poisson's ratio is
    (1) 0.21
    (2) 0.18
    (3) 0.26
    (4) 0.28

239. A bar of cross-section 10 mm × 10 mm is subjected to axial compressive load of 10 kN. The lateral dimension of bar is increased by 0.002 mm. Modulus of rigidity is 80 GPa. Modulus of elasticity is
    (1) 210 GPa
    (2) 120 GPa
    (3) 235 GPa
    (4) 185 GPa

240. A bar of certain material is 40 mm × 40 mm in cross-section and 90 mm in length. It is subjected to an axial pull of 120 kN. Length is increased by 0.05 mm and each side is decreased by 0.005 mm. Bulk modulus is
    (1) 109 GPa
    (2) 129 GPa
    (3) 57 GPa
    (4) 46 GPa

241. A timber box beam having hollow section with two horizontal plates 200 mm × 50 mm and two vertical plates 250 mm × 50 mm is connected by nails on both sides. The spacing of nail is 195 mm. The shear force acting on the section is 35 kN. The strength of each nail is
    (1) 25 kN
    (2) 20 kN
    (3) 15 kN
    (4) 30 kN

242. A circular beam 250 mm diameter is subjected to shear force of 100 kN. The maximum shear stress is
    (1) 1.7 N/mm^2
    (2) 1.3 N/mm^2
    (3) 2.3 N/mm^2
    (4) 2.7 N/mm^2

243. For the simply supported beam of length L, subjected to a uniformly distributed moment M kN-M per unit length as shown in the figure, the bending moment (in kN-m) at the mid-span of the beam is ....

    M kN-m per unit length

    |◄———— L ————►|

    (1) zero
    (2) M
    (3) ML
    (4) M/L

244. If bulk modulus and modulus of rigidity for a material are K and G respectively, then what will be Poisson's ratio ?
    (1) $\dfrac{3K + 4G}{6K - 4G}$
    (2) $\dfrac{3K - 4G}{6K + 4G}$
    (3) $\dfrac{3K - 2G}{6K + 2G}$
    (4) $\dfrac{3K + 2G}{6K - 2G}$

245. A hollow shaft with external diameter 70 mm and thickness 4 mm, is rotating at 80 rpm. Power transmitted by shaft is 19 kW. Maximum permissible shear stress is
   (1)　50 N/mm²　　　(2)　70 N/mm²　　　(3)　55 N/mm²　　　(4)　65 N/mm²

246. A solid circular shaft of diameter d and length L is fixed at one end and free at the other end. A torque T is applied at the free end. The shear modulus of the material is G. The angle of twist at the free end is ....
   (1)　$\dfrac{16TL}{\pi d^4 G}$　　　(2)　$\dfrac{32TL}{\pi d^4 G}$　　　(3)　$\dfrac{64TL}{\pi d^4 G}$　　　(4)　$\dfrac{128TL}{\pi d^4 G}$

247. A simply supported beam of span 4 m carries UDL of 6 kN/m throughout the span. The cross-section of beam is 'T' section with flange 100 mm in width and 10 mm in depth and web with width 10 mm and depth 100 mm. The maximum shear stress at the junction of flange and web is
   (1)　14 N/mm²　　　(2)　11 N/mm²　　　(3)　1.4 N/mm²　　　(4)　2 N/mm²

248. A simply supported beam of span 4 m carries UDL of 6 kN/m throughout the span. The cross-section of beam is 'T' section with flange 100 mm in width and 10 mm in depth and web with width 10 mm and depth 100 mm. The shear stress at neutral axis is
   (1)　14.4 N/mm²　　　(2)　15.3 N/mm²　　　(3)　1.4 N/mm²　　　(4)　21.2 N/mm²

249. The principal tensile stresses at a point across two perpendicular planes are 80 MPa and 50 MPa. The resultant stress on a plane at 20° with the major principal plane is
   (1)　70 N/mm²　　　(2)　96 N/mm²　　　(3)　77 N/mm²　　　(4)　87 N/mm²

250. At a point in a strained material, the state of stress is 25 MPa compressive along x-axis and shear stress 50 MPa making moment clockwise due to vertical shear stress. The maximum principal tensile stress is
   (1)　51 N/mm²　　　(2)　43 N/mm²　　　(3)　39 N/mm²　　　(4)　45 N/mm²

251. A body is subjected to two normal stresses 20 kN/m² (tensile) and 10 kN/m² (compressive) acting perpendicular to each other. The maximum shear stress is
   (1)　5 kN/m²　　　(2)　10 kN/m²　　　(3)　15 kN/m²　　　(4)　none of these

252. A bar of 120 mm diameter, and 300 mm in length is subjected to axial compressive load of 120 kN, which increases the diameter by 0.075 mm and decreases the length by 1.1 mm. Modulus of rigidity is
   (1)　3.68 GPa　　　(2)　2.56 GPa　　　(3)　1.24 GPa　　　(4)　4.44 GPa

253. A bar of certain material has bulk modulus 140 GPa and Poisson's ratio 0.24. Modulus of elasticity is
   (1)　219 GPa　　　(2)　239 GPa　　　(3)　88 GPa　　　(4)　None of these

254. A bar of cross-section 10 mm × 10 mm is subjected to an axial compressive load of 10 kN. The lateral dimension of bar is increased by 0.002 mm. Modulus of rigidity is 80 GPa. Poisson's ratio is
   (1)　0.27　　　(2)　0.32　　　(3)　0.54　　　(4)　0.47

255. The effective length of a column of length L fixed against rotation and translation at one end is ....
   (1)　0.5 L　　　(2)　0.7 L　　　(3)　1.414 L　　　(4)　2 L

256. A hollow shaft, with internal diameter 80 mm, is rotating at 75 rpm. Power transmitted by shaft is 35.9 kW. Maximum permissible shear stress is 85 N/mm². External diameter of shaft is
    (1) 90 mm   (2) 80 mm   (3) 100 mm   (4) 70 mm

257. A hollow shaft, with external diameter 90 mm, is rotating at 2.5 rps. Power transmitted by shaft is 45 kW. Maximum permissible shear stress is 98 N/mm². Thickness of metal is
    (1) 2 mm   (2) 2.5 mm   (3) 3 mm   (4) 3.5 mm

258. A short metallic column subjected to 500 mm² cross-sectional area, carries an axial tensile load of 100 kN. The shear stress on a plane inclined 70° with the load direction is
    (1) 32 N/mm² (T)   (2) 27 N/mm² (C)   (3) 36 N/mm² (T)   (4) 48 N/mm² (C)

259. A short metallic column subjected to 500 mm² cross-sectional area, carries an axial tensile load of 100 kN. The resultant stress on a plane inclined 70° with the load direction is
    (1) 75 N/mm² (T)   (2) 82 N/mm² (C)   (3) 94 N/mm² (T)   (4) 87 N/mm² (C)

260. The number of independent elastic constants for a linear elastic isotropic and homogeneous material is ....
    (1) 4   (2) 3   (3) 2   (4) 1

261. A solid circular shaft has to transmit 350 kW at 250 rpm. The maximum shear stress is 75 N/mm². The diameter of shaft is
    (1) 108 mm   (2) 9 mm   (3) 118 mm   (4) 88 mm

262. In a shaft subjected to bending moment and twisting moment, the greater principal stress is numerically four times the lesser one. Greater principal stress is tensile and lesser is compressive. The ratio of M and T is
    (1) 0.2   (2) 0.35   (3) 0.55   (4) 0.75

263. Two people weighing W each, are sitting on a planck of length L floating on water at L/4 from either end. Neglecting the weight of the plank, the bending moment at the centre of the plank is ....
    (1) $\dfrac{WL}{8}$ (2) $\dfrac{WL}{16}$ (3) $\dfrac{WL}{32}$ (4) zero

264. The major and minor principle stresses at a point are 3 MPa and – 3 MPa respectively. The maximum shear stress at the point is ....
    (1) zero   (2) 3 MPa   (3) 6 MPa   (4) 9 MPa

265. A simply supported beam of uniform rectangular cross-section of width b and depth h is subjected to linear temperature gradient, 0° at the top and T° at the bottom, as shown in the figure. The coefficient of linear expansion of the beam material is α. The resulting vertical deflection at the mid-span of the beam is ....

Temperature gradient

    (1) $\dfrac{\alpha \, T h^2}{8L}$ upward   (2) $\dfrac{\alpha \, T L^2}{8h}$ upward   (3) $\dfrac{\alpha \, T h^2}{8L}$ downward   (4) $\dfrac{\alpha \, T L^2}{8h}$ downward

266. A long structural column (length = L) with both ends hinged is acted upon by an axial compressive load, P. The differential equation governing the bending of column is given by : $EI \frac{d^2y}{dx^2} = - Py$, where y is the structural lateral deflection and EI is the flexural rigidity. The first critical load on column responsible for its buckling is given by :

    (1) $\frac{\pi^2 EI}{L^2}$ (2) $\frac{\sqrt{2}\,\pi^2 EI}{L^2}$ (3) $\frac{2\pi^2 EI}{L^2}$ (4) $\frac{4\pi^2 EI}{L^2}$

267. For linear elastic systems the type of displacement function for the strain energy is ....

    (1) linear   (2) quadratic   (3) cubic   (4) quartic

268. The symmetry of stress tensor at a point in the body under equilibrium is obtained from ....

    (1) conservation of mass   (2) force equilibrium equations
    (3) moment equilibrium equations   (4) conservation of energy

269. The components of strain tensor at a point in the plane strain case can be obtained by measuring longitudinal strain in following directions

    (1) along any two arbitrary directions
    (2) along any three arbitrary directions
    (3) along two mutually orthogonal directions
    (4) along any arbitrary direction

270. If principle stresses in a two-dimensional case are 10 MPa and 20 MPa respectively, then maximum shear stress at the point is ....

    (1) 10 MPa   (2) 15 MPa   (3) 20 MPa   (4) 30 MPa

271. The bending moment diagram for a beam is given below :

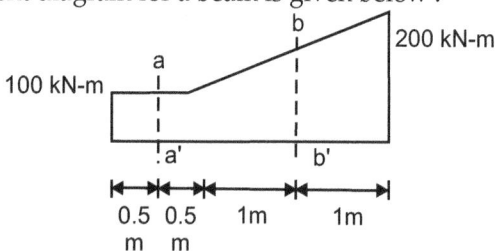

The shear forces at sections aa′ and bb′ respectively are of the magnitude
    (1) 100 kN, 150 kN   (2) zero, 100 kN
    (3) zero, 50 kN   (4) 100 kN, 100 kN

272. A circular shaft shown in the figure is subjected to torsion T at two points A and B. The torsional rigidity of portions CA and BD is GJ_1 and that of portion AB is GJ_2. The rotations of shaft at points A and B are θ_1 and θ_2. The rotation θ_1 is ....

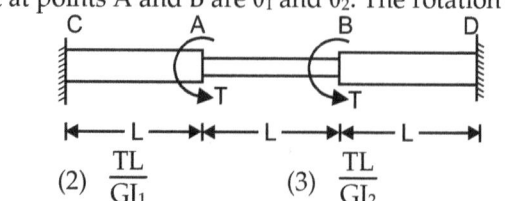

    (1) $\frac{TL}{GJ_1 + GJ_2}$ (2) $\frac{TL}{GJ_1}$ (3) $\frac{TL}{GJ_2}$ (4) $\frac{TL}{GJ_1 - GJ_2}$

273. Mohr's circle for the state of stress defined by $\begin{bmatrix} 30 & 0 \\ 0 & 30 \end{bmatrix}$ MPa is a circle with

    (1) center at (0, 0) and radius 30 MPa   (2) center at (0, 0) and radius 60 MPa

    (3) center at (30, 0) and radius 30 MPa   (4) center at (30, 0) and zero radius

274. A long shaft of diameter d is subjected to twisting moment T at its ends. The maximum normal stress acting at its cross-section is equal to ....

    (1) zero   (2) $\dfrac{16T}{\pi d^3}$ (3) $\dfrac{32T}{\pi d^3}$ (4) $\dfrac{64T}{\pi d^3}$

275. Consider the beam AB shown in the figure below. Part AC of the beam is rigid while Part CB has the flexural rigidity EI. Identify the correct combination of deflection at end B and bending moment at end A, respectively

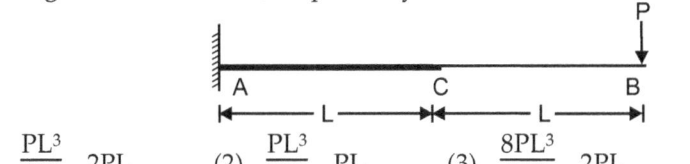

    (1) $\dfrac{PL^3}{3EI}$, 2PL   (2) $\dfrac{PL^3}{3EI}$, PL   (3) $\dfrac{8PL^3}{3EI}$, 2PL   (4) $\dfrac{8PL^3}{3EI}$, PL

276. For the section shown below, second moment of the area about an axis d/4 distance above the bottom of the area is ....

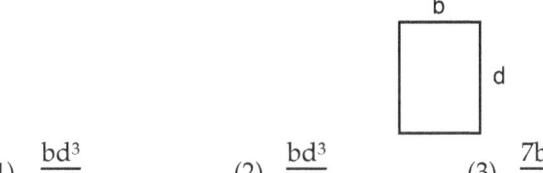

    (1) $\dfrac{bd^3}{48}$ (2) $\dfrac{bd^3}{12}$ (3) $\dfrac{7bd^3}{48}$ (4) $\dfrac{bd^3}{3}$

277. An axially loaded bar is subjected to a normal stress of 173 MPa. The shear stress in the bar is ....

    (1) 75 MPa   (2) 86.5 MPa   (3) 100 MPa   (4) 122.3 MPa

278. A steel column, pinned at both ends, has a buckling load of 200 kN. If the column is restrained against lateral movement at its mid-height, its buckling load will be ....

    (1) 200 kN   (2) 283 kN   (3) 400 kN   (4) 800 kN

279. For an isotropic material, the relationship between the Young's modulus (E), shear modulus (G) and Poisson's ratio (μ) is given by ....

    (1) $G = \dfrac{E}{2(1 + \mu)}$ (2) $E = \dfrac{E}{2(1 + \mu)}$ (3) $G = \dfrac{E}{(1 + 2\mu)}$ (4) $G = \dfrac{E}{2(1 - 2\mu)}$

280. A metal bar of length 100 mm is inserted between two rigid supports and its temperature is increased by 10° C. If the coefficient of thermal expansion is 12 x 10⁻⁶ per °C and the Young's modulus is 2 × 10⁵ MPa, the stress in the bar is ....

    (1) zero   (2) 12 MPa   (3) 24 MPa   (4) 2400 MPa

281. The shear stress at the neutral axis in a beam of triangular section with a base of 40 mm and height 20 mm, subjected to a shear force of 3 kN is ....

    (1) 3 MPa   (2) 6 MPa   (3) 10 MPa   (4) 20 MPa

282. A mild steel specimen is under uniaxial tensile stress. Young's modulus and yield stress for mild steel are 2×10^5 MPa and 250 MPa respectively. The maximum amount of strain energy per unit volume that can be stored in this specimen without permanent set is ....

    (1) 156 Nmm/mm³   (2) 15.6 Nmm/mm³

    (3) 1.56 Nmm/mm³   (4) 0.156 Nmm/mm³

283. Cross-section of a column consisting of two steel strips, each of thickness t and width b is shown in the figure below. The critical loads of the column with perfect bond and without bond between the strips are P and P_0 respectively. The ratio P/P_0 is ....

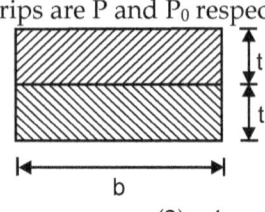

    (1) 2   (2) 4

    (3) 6   (4) 8

284. The maximum shear stress in a solid shaft of circular cross-section having diameter d subjected to a torque T is τ. If the torque is increased by four times and the diameter of the shaft is increased by two times, the maximum shear stress in the shaft will be ....

    (1) 2τ   (2) τ

    (3) τ/2   (4) τ/4

285. The stepped cantilever is subjected to moments, M as shown in the figure below. The vertical deflection at the free end (neglecting the self weight) is ....

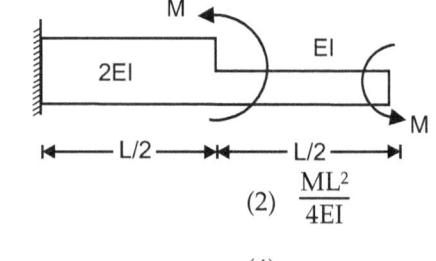

    (1) $\dfrac{ML^2}{8EI}$ (2) $\dfrac{ML^2}{4EI}$

    (3) $\dfrac{ML^2}{2EI}$ (4) zero

286. The point within the cross-sectional plane of a beam through which the resultant of the external loading on the beam has to pass through to ensure pure bending without twisting of the cross-section of the beam is called ....

    (1) moment centre   (2) centroid

    (3) shear centre   (4) elastic centre

287. A hollow circular shaft has an outer diameter of 100 mm and a wall thickness of 25 mm. The allowable shear stress in the shaft is 125 MPa. The maximum torque the shaft can transmit is ....

    (1) 46 kN-m   (2) 24.5 kN-m

    (3) 23 kN-m   (4) 11.5 kN-m

288. Match List-I (Shear Force Diagrams) beams with List-II (Diagram of beams with supports and loading) and select the correct answer using the codes given below the lists :

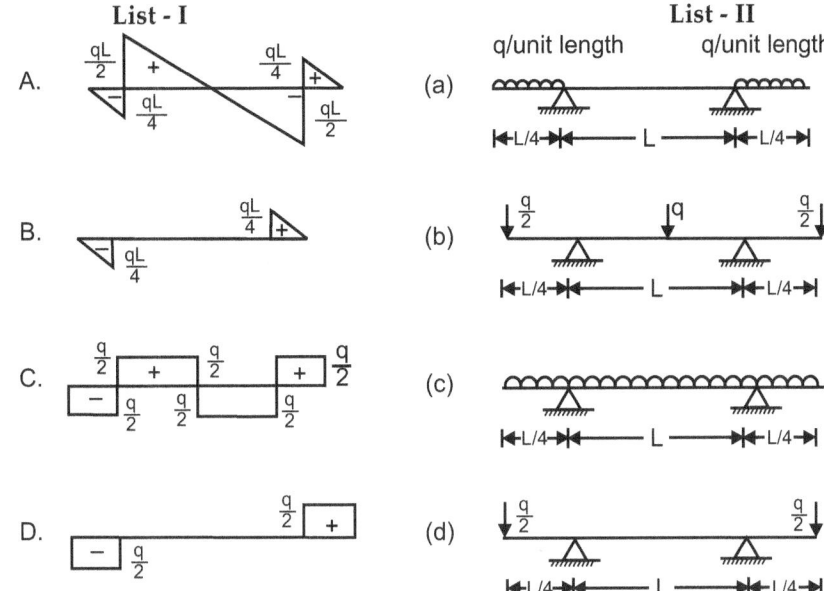

Codes :

	A	B	C	D
(1)	(c)	(a)	(b)	(d)
(2)	(c)	(d)	(b)	(a)
(3)	(b)	(a)	(d)	(c)
(4)	(b)	(d)	(c)	(a)

ANSWER KEY

1.	(3)	2.	(1)	3.	(4)	4.	(1)	5.	(2)	6.	(3)	7.	(1)	8.	(2)
9.	(1)	10.	(1)	11.	(3)	12.	(1)	13.	(4)	14.	(4)	15.	(2)	16.	(3)
17.	(4)	18.	(4)	19.	(2)	20.	(3)	21.	(2)	22.	(1)	23.	(4)	24.	(1)
25.	(4)	26.	(3)	27.	(3)	28.	(1)	29.	(2)	30.	(1)	31.	(3)	32.	(1)
33.	(2)	34.	(1)	35.	(4)	36.	(3)	37.	(3)	38.	(1)	39.	(3)	40.	(3)
41.	(2)	42.	(1)	43.	(4)	44.	(1)	45.	(1)	46.	(2)	47.	(1)	48.	(4)
49.	(1)	50.	(2)	51.	(4)	52.	(4)	53.	(2)	54.	(4)	55.	(1)	56.	(1)
57.	(3)	58.	(3)	59.	(3)	60.	(3)	61.	(3)	62.	(4)	63.	(3)	64.	(2)
65.	(2)	66.	(2)	67.	(3)	68.	(4)	69.	(2)	70.	(1)	71.	(2)	72.	(1)
73.	(2)	74.	(2)	75.	(1)	76.	(2)	77.	(1)	78.	(3)	79.	(4)	80.	(2)
81.	(1)	82.	(4)	83.	(1)	84.	(3)	85.	(3)	86.	(3)	87.	(2)	88.	(1)

89. (1)	90. (1)	91. (1)	92. (3)	93. (2)	94. (1)	95. (4)	96. (1)
97. (1)	98. (2)	99. (4)	100. (3)	101. (3)	102. (3)	103. (2)	104. (3)
105. (3)	106. (1)	107. (4)	108. (2)	109. (1)	110. (3)	111. (3)	112. (1)
113. (2)	114. (3)	115. (2)	116. (3)	117. (2)	118. (3)	119. (4)	120. (1)
121. (1)	122. (4)	123. (1)	124. (2)	125. (4)	126. (2)	127. (1)	128. (2)
129. (4)	130. (3)	131. (4)	132. (3)	133. (4)	134. (4)	135. (1)	136. (4)
137. (1)	138. (2)	139. (4)	140. (3)	141. (2)	142. (4)	143. (2)	144. (3)
145. (3)	146. (2)	147. (3)	148. (2)	149. (1)	150. (1)	151. (4)	152. (4)
153. (4)	154. (2)	155. ( )	156. (2)	157. (3)	158. (2)	159. (2)	160. (3)
161. (2)	162. (3)	163. (1)	164. (3)	165. (3)	166. (4)	167. (2)	168. (4)
169. (4)	170. (2)	171. (4)	172. (4)	173. (3)	174. (2)	175. (1)	176. (3)
177. (1)	178. (4)	179. (1)	180. (2)	181. (4)	182. (4)	183. (2)	184. (4)
185. (1)	186. (4)	187. (3)	188. (1)	189. (3)	190. (3)	191. (1)	192. (4)
193. (1)	194. (2)	195. (3)	196. (1)	197. (4)	198. (2)	199. (1)	200. (2)
201. (2)	202. (1)	203. (1)	204. (2)	205. (2)	206. (4)	207. (3)	208. (3)
209. (4)	210. (3)	211. (4)	212. (3)	213. (2)	214. (1)	215. (1)	216. (1)
217. (4)	218. (4)	219. (4)	220. (2)	221. (4)	222. (1)	223. (2)	224. (3)
225. (2)	226. (2)	227. (1)	228. (2)	229. (1)	230. (1)	231. (1)	232. (3)
233. (3)	234. (3)	235. (1)	236. (2)	237. (3)	238. (2)	239. (3)	240. (3)
241. (1)	242. (4)	243. (1)	244. (3)	245. (2)	246. (2)	247. (1)	248. (2)
249. (3)	250. (3)	251. (3)	252. (3)	253. (1)	254. (4)	255. (1)	256. (1)
257. (2)	258. (1)	259. (3)	260 (3)	261 (4)	262 (4)	263. (4)	264. (2)
265. (4)	266. (1)	267. (2)	268. (3)	269. (2)	270. (2)	271. (3)	272. (2)
273. (4)	274. (1)	275. (1)	276. (3)	277. (2)	278. (4)	279. (1)	280. (3)
281. (3)	282. (4)	283. (2)	284. (3)	285. (3)	286. (3)	287. (3)	288. (1)

❖ ❖ ❖

UNIT - 2 : STRUCTURAL ANALYSIS

1. The maximum bending moment due to a train of wheel loads on a simply supported girder
   - (1) always occurs at centre of span
   - (2) always occurs under a wheel load
   - (3) never occurs under a wheel load
   - (4) none of the above

2. Effects of shear force and axial force on plastic moment capacity of a structure are respectively to
   - (1) increase and decrease
   - (2) increase and increase
   - (3) decrease and increase
   - (4) decrease and decrease

3. A beam is as shown in Fig. 1. The ordinate at E for reaction at B is

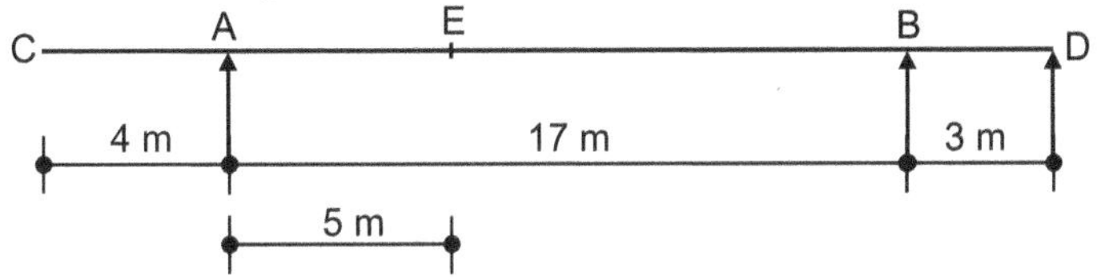

   Fig. 1

   - (1) 0.5
   - (2) 1.29
   - (3) 0.71
   - (4) one

4. A beam is as shown in Fig. 1. The ordinate at C for reaction at B is
   - (1) zero
   - (2) 0.24
   - (3) 1
   - (4) 1.24

5. A beam is as shown in Fig. 1. The ordinate at D for reaction at B is
   - (1) 0.3
   - (2) 0.18
   - (3) 0.25
   - (4) 1.18

6. A beam is as shown in Fig. 1. The ordinate at C for reaction at A is
   - (1) one
   - (2) 0.5
   - (3) 1.24
   - (4) 0.24

7. A beam is as shown in Fig. 1. Bending moment ordinate at E is
   - (1) 3.53
   - (2) 4.23
   - (3) one
   - (4) 4.25

8. For a two-hinged arch, if one of the supports settles down vertically, then the horizontal thrust
   - (1) is increased
   - (2) is decreased
   - (3) remains unchanged
   - (4) becomes zero

9. For a symmetrical two hinged parabolic arch, if one of the supports settles horizontally, then the horizontal thrust
   - (1) is increased
   - (2) is decreased
   - (3) remains unchanged
   - (4) becomes zero

10. A single rolling load of 8 kN rolls along a girder of 15 m span. The absolute maximum bending moment will be
    - (1) 8 kN.m
    - (2) 15 kN.m
    - (3) 30 kN.m
    - (4) 60 kN.m

(2.1)

11. A beam is as shown in Fig. 2. Reaction at C is

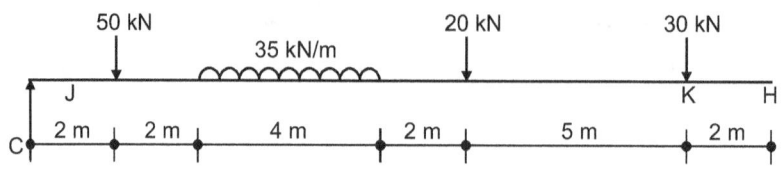

Fig. 2

(1) 137.69 kN   (2) 147.9 kN   (3) 152.85 kN   (4) 117.69 Kn

12. A beam is as shown in Fig. 2. Reaction at B is

(1) 145.56 kN   (2) 122.31 kN   (3) 195.56 kN   (4) 171.33 kN

13. Which of the following is not the displacement method ?

(1) Equilibrium method   (2) Column analogy method

(3) Moment distribution method   (4) Kani's method

14. Study the following statements.

(i) The displacement method is more useful when degree of kinematic indeterminacy is greater than the degree of static indeterminacy.

(ii) The displacement method is more useful when degree of kinematic indeterminacy is less than the degree of static indeterminacy.

(iii) The force method is more useful when degree of static indeterminacy is greater than the degree of kinematic indeterminacy.

(iv) The force method is more useful when degree of static indeterminacy is less than the degree of kinematic indeterminacy.

The correct answer is

(1) (i) and (iii)   (2) (ii) and (iii)   (3) (i) and (iv)   (4) (ii) and (iv)

15. Select the correct statement :

(1) Flexibility matrix is a square symmetrical matrix.

(2) Stiffness matrix is a square symmetrical matrix.

(3) both (1) and (2)   (4) none of the above

16 A continuous beam ABCDE is as shown in Fig. 3. If the support moment at C is 8.5 kN-m then the support moment at B is

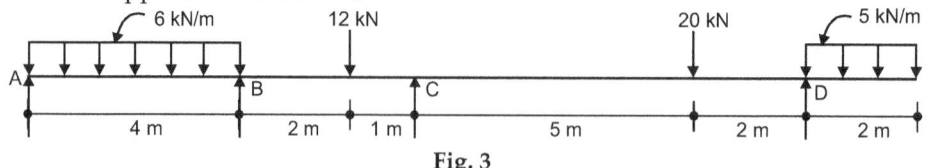

Fig. 3

(1) 16.32 kN-m   (2) 11.32 kN-m   (3) 7.32 kN-m   (4) 25.32 kN-m

17. To generate the jth column of the flexibility matrix

(1) a unit force is applied at co-ordinate j and the displacements are calculated at all co-ordinates.

(2) a unit displacement is applied at co-ordinate j and the forces are calculated at all co-ordinates.

(3) a unit force is applied at co-ordinate j and the forces are calculated at all co-ordinates.

(4) a unit displacement is applied at co-ordinate j and the displacements are calculated at all co-ordinates.

18. For stable structures, one of the important properties of flexibility and stiffness matrices is that the elements on the main diagonal
    (i)   of a stiffness matrix must be positive.
    (ii) of a stiffness matrix must be negative.
    (iii) of a flexibility matrix must be positive.
    (iv) of a flexibility matrix must be negative.
    The correct answer is
    (1) (i) and (iii)   (2) (ii) and (iii)
    (3) (i) and (iv)   (4) (ii) and (iv)

19. Which of the following methods of structural analysis is a force method ?
    (1) Slope deflection method   (2) Column analogy method
    (3) Moment distribution method   (4) none of the above

20. In the displacement method of structural analysis, the basic unknowns are
    (1) displacements   (2) force
    (3) displacements and forces   (4) none of the above

21. The width of the analogous column in the method of column analogy is
    (1) 2/EI   (2) 1/EI
    (3) 1/2EI   (4) 1/4EI

22. A beam is shown in Fig. 4. Reaction at C is

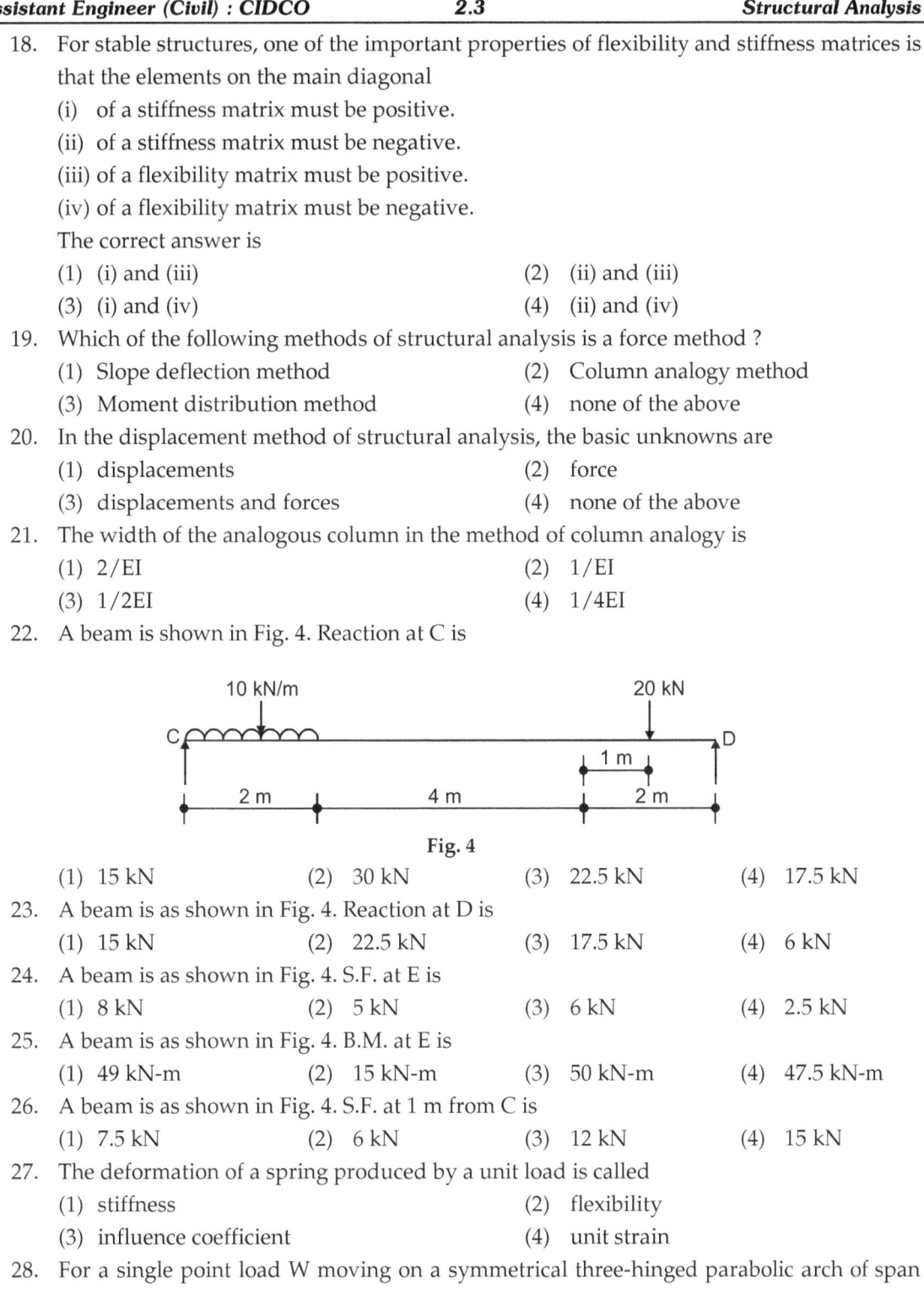

Fig. 4

    (1) 15 kN   (2) 30 kN   (3) 22.5 kN   (4) 17.5 kN

23. A beam is as shown in Fig. 4. Reaction at D is
    (1) 15 kN   (2) 22.5 kN   (3) 17.5 kN   (4) 6 kN

24. A beam is as shown in Fig. 4. S.F. at E is
    (1) 8 kN   (2) 5 kN   (3) 6 kN   (4) 2.5 kN

25. A beam is as shown in Fig. 4. B.M. at E is
    (1) 49 kN-m   (2) 15 kN-m   (3) 50 kN-m   (4) 47.5 kN-m

26. A beam is as shown in Fig. 4. S.F. at 1 m from C is
    (1) 7.5 kN   (2) 6 kN   (3) 12 kN   (4) 15 kN

27. The deformation of a spring produced by a unit load is called
    (1) stiffness   (2) flexibility
    (3) influence coefficient   (4) unit strain

28. For a single point load W moving on a symmetrical three-hinged parabolic arch of span L, the maximum sagging moment occurs at a distance x from ends. The value of x is
    (1) 0.211 L   (2) 0.25 L   (3) 0.234 L   (4) 0.5 L

29. A load 'W is moving from left to right support on a simply supported beam of span T. The maximum bending moment at 0.4 l from the left support is
    (1) 0.16 Wl (2) 0.20 Wl (3) 0.24 Wl (4) 0.25 Wl

30. A continuous beam ABCDE is as shown in Fig. 5. The support moment at B is

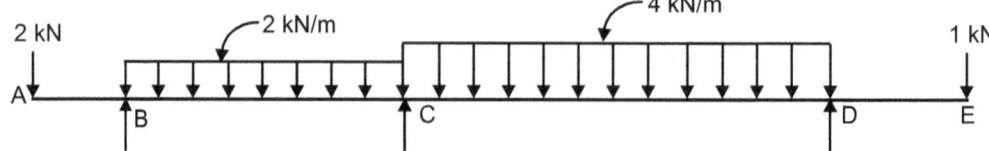

Fig. 5

    (1) 11.4 kN-m   (2) 21.3 kN-m   (3) 18.91 kN-m   (4) 26.67 kN-m

31. A continuous beam ABC is as shown in Fig. 6. The support moment at B is

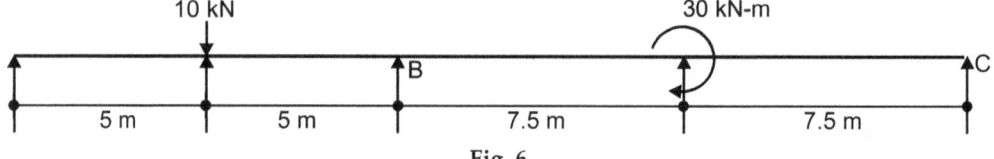

Fig. 6

    (1) 10.4 kN-m   (2) 14.3 kN-m
    (3) 5.25 kN-m   (4) 19.21 kN-m

32. A beam is as shown in Fig. 7. The reaction at A is

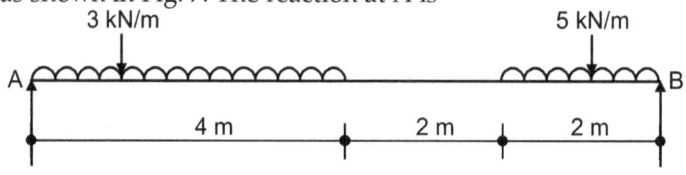

Fig. 7

    (1) 11.45 kN   (2) 12.13 kN   (3) 10.25 kN   (4) 21.55 kN

33. A beam is as shown in Fig. 7. The reaction at B is
    (1) 11.75 kN   (2) 11.45 kN   (3) 12.13 kN   (4) 10.89 kN

34. Determine the shear force at the centre of beam shown in Fig. 7.
    (1) 2.25 kN   (2) 17.5 kN   (3) 1.75 kN   (4) 2.5 kN

35. A Warren truss is as shown in Fig. 8. Maximum tensile force in member L_1L_2, due to dead load of 11 kN/m covering the entire span and a moving live load of 18 kN/m longer than the span, is

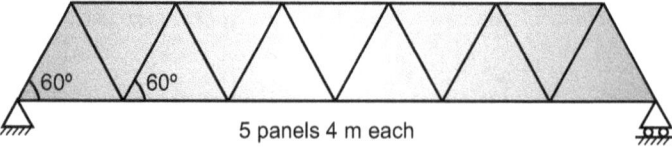

5 panels 4 m each

Fig. 8

    (1) 311 kN   (2) 335 kN   (3) 264 kN   (4) 218 kN

36. A Warren truss is as shown in Fig. 8. Maximum compressive force in member U_2U_3, due to dead load of 11 kN/m covering the entire span and a moving live load of 18 kN/m longer than the span, is
    (1) 415 kN   (2) 385 kN   (3) 300 kN   (4) 400 kN

37. A Warren truss is as shown in Fig. 8. Maximum tensile force in member U_2L_2, due to dead load of 11 kN/m covering the entire span and a moving live load of 18 kN/m longer than the span, is

    (1) 159 kN   (2) 138 kN   (3) 143 kN   (4) 184 kN

38. A Warren truss is as shown in Fig. 8. Minimum tensile force in member U_2L_2, due to dead load of 11 kN/m covering the entire span and a moving live load of 18 kN/m longer than the span, is

    (1) 40 kN   (2) 56 kN   (3) 24 kN   (4) 67 kN

39. A Warren truss is as shown in Fig. 8. Maximum compressive force in member U_2L_2, due to dead load of 11 kN/m covering the entire span and a moving live load of 18 kN/m longer than the span, is

    (1) 159 kN   (2) 138 kN   (3) 143 kN   (4) 184 kN

40. A Warren truss is as shown in Fig. 8. Minimum compressive force in member U_2L_2, due to dead load of 11 kN/m covering the entire span and a moving live load of 18 kN/m longer than the span, is

    (1) 40 kN   (2) 56 kN   (3) 24 kN   (4) 67 kN

41. A continuous beam ABC is as shown in Fig. 9. The support moment at B is

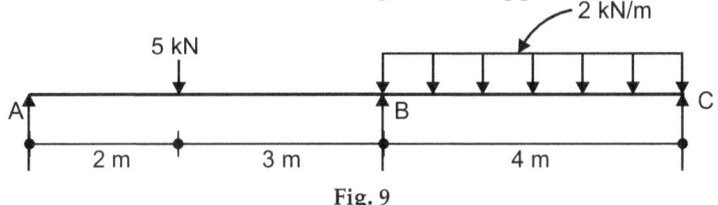

Fig. 9

    (1) 4.1 kN-m   (2) 2.5 kN-m   (3) 5.4 kN-m   (4) 8 kN-m

42. A cantilever beam CD has a span 6 m. A uniformly distributed load of intensity 24 kN/m is acting throughout the span. Deflection at 2 m from left end is

    (1) 188/EI   (2) 988/EI   (3) 288/EI   (4) 688/EI

43. A cantilever beam CD has a span 5 m. A uniformly distributed load of intensity 35 kN/m is acting throughout the span. Slope at 3 m from left end is

    (1) 682.5/EI   (2) 512.6/EI   (3) 570.2/EI   (4) 316.6/EI

44. A cantilever beam AB has a span 4 m. A uniformly distributed load of intensity 25 kN/m is acting on 2 m from left end. Slope at 3 m from left end is

    (1) 33.33/EI   (2) 51.63/EI   (3) 47.21/EI   (4) 36.6/EI

45. A beam is as shown in Fig. 10. The reaction at A is

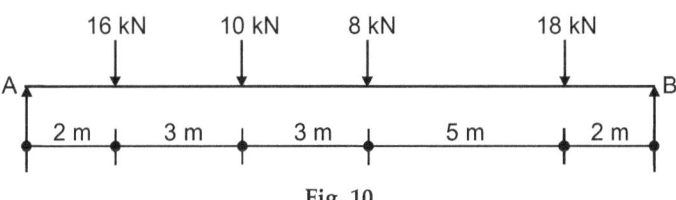

Fig. 10

    (1) 26.67 kN   (2) 27.77 kN   (3) 25.5 kN   (4) 23.33 kN

46. A beam is as shown in Fig. 10. The reaction at B is
    (1) 24.99 kN   (2) 25.33 kN   (3) 52.33 kN   (4) 26.67 kN
47. Determine the shear force at a section 7 m from left hand side of the beam as shown in Fig. 10.
    (1) 6.7 kN   (2) 0.67 kN   (3) 1.67 kN   (4) 5.67 kN
48. Find the bending moment at a distance 6 m from L.H.S., A of the beam given in Fig. 10
    (1) 43 kN-m   (2) 81 kN-m   (3) 86 kN-m   (4) 64 kN-m
49. A beam is as shown in Fig. 11. Ordinate of I.L.D. for reaction B at A is

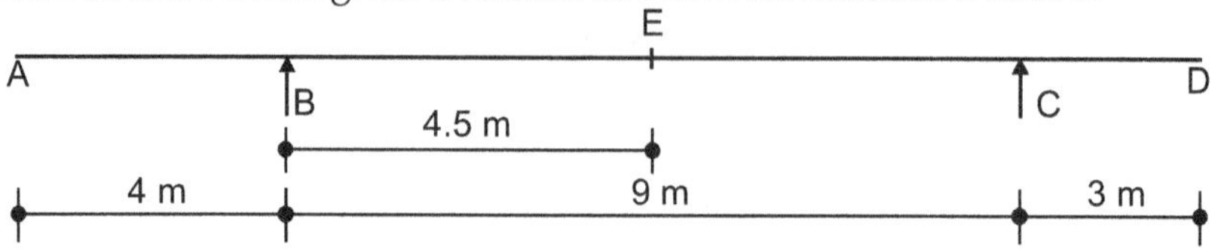

Fig. 11

    (1) zero   (2) 1   (3) 1.44   (4) 1.33
50. A beam is as shown in Fig. 11. Ordinate of I.L.D. for reaction B at D is
    (1) zero   (2) 1.33   (3) 1   (4) 0.33
51. A beam is as shown in Fig. 11. Ordinate of I.L.D. for reaction B at E is
    (1) 1.5   (2) 0.5   (3) 1   (4) zero
52. A beam is as shown in Fig. 11. Ordinate of I.L.D. for reaction C at B is
    (1) 1.44   (2) 1.33   (3) zero   (4) 1
53. A beam is as shown in Fig. 11. Ordinate of I.L.D. for reaction at C is
    (1) 1.44   (2) 1.33   (3) zero   (4) 1
54. When a uniformly distributed load, longer than the span of the girder, moves from left to right, then the maximum bending moment at mid-section of span occurs when the uniformly distributed load occupies
    (1) less than the left half span.   (2) whole of left half span.
    (3) more than the left half span.   (4) whole span.
55. When a uniformly distributed load, shorter than the span of the girder, moves from left to right, then the conditions for maximum bending moment at a section is that
    (1) the head of the load reaches the section.
    (2) the tail of the load reaches the section.
    (3) the load position should be such that the section divides it equally on both sides.
    (4) the load position should be such that the section divides the load in the same ratio as it divides the span.
56. A two -hinged arch is
    (1) statically indeterminate of 1 degree   (2) statically indeterminate of 3 degree
    (3) statically indeterminate of 2 degree   (4) statically determinate
57. Shape of I.L.D. for horizontal thrust in symmetric three hinge arch is
    (1) triangular   (2) parabolic
    (3) square   (4) rectangular

58. A symmetric three-hinged parabolic arch has span L and rise H. The area of I.L.D. for the bending moment at the left quarter point is..
    (1) $L^2/2H$ 　　　　　　　　　　　　　　(2) $L^2/3H$
    (3) increase or decrease 　　　　　　　　(4) none of above

59. A two hinged parabolic arch is subjected to temperature rise of t° then the horizontal thrust at the support will
    (1) decrease 　　　　　　　　　　　　　(2) increase or decrease
    (3) increase 　　　　　　　　　　　　　(4) remain constant

60. If the area of cross-section of tie of a tied arch is increased then the tension in the tie will
    (1) increase or decrease 　　　　　　　　(2) decrease
    (3) constant 　　　　　　　　　　　　　(4) increase

61. The line of thrust in parabolic arch is
    (1) funicular polygon 　　　　　　　　　(2) parabolic
    (3) square 　　　　　　　　　　　　　　(4) rectangular

62. The simply supported B.M. at the central hinge of three-hinged arch is 36　kN.m. The span and rise at the hinge are 12 m and 3 m respectively. The horizontal thrust in the arch is
    (1) 11 kN 　　　　(2) 12 kN 　　　　(3) 10 kN 　　　　(4) 9 kN

63. The arch resists the external load by
    (1) B.M. and thrust 　　　　　　　　　　(2) B.M. and radial shear
    (3) B.M., thrust and radial shear 　　　　(4) only B.M.

64. A symmetrical three-hinged parabolic arch has span of 24 m and central rise 6 m. It carries concentrated load of 60 kN at left quarter point. What is horizontal thrust in left support ?
    (1) 300 kN 　　　　(2) 30 kN 　　　　(3) 135 kN 　　　　(4) 45 kN

65. A symmetrical three-hinged parabolic arch has span of 24 m and central rise 6 m. It carries concentrated load of 60 kN at left quarter point. What is horizontal thrust in right support ?
    (1) 300 kN 　　　　(2) 30 kN 　　　　(3) 135 kN 　　　　(4) 45 kN

66. A symmetrical three-hinged parabolic arch has span of 24 m and central rise 6 m. It carries concentrated load of 60 kN at left quarter point. What is maximum bending moment ?
    (1) 30 kNm 　　　　(2) −30 kNm 　　　　(3) 45 kNm 　　　　(4) −45 kNm

67. A three-hinged symmetrical circular arch has span 20 m with central rise of 5 m. What is the maximum horizontal thrust due to 8 m long udl of 20 kN/m ?
    (1) 300 kN 　　　　(2) 150 kN 　　　　(3) 128 kN 　　　　(4) 138 kN

68. A three-hinged symmetrical parabolic arch has span 16 m with central rise of 4 m. What is the maximum horizontal thrust due to udl of 12 kN/m larger than the span ?
    (1) 100 kN 　　　　(2) 90 kN 　　　　(3) 96 kN 　　　　(4) 196 kN

69. A three-hinged symmetrical parabolic arch has span 16 m with central rise of 4 m. What is the maximum B.M. due to udl of 12 kN/m larger than the span ?
    (1) 58 kNm 　　　　(2) 90 kNm 　　　　(3) 60 kN 　　　　(4) 55 kNm

70. A three-hinged symmetrical parabolic arch has span 40 m with central rise of 5 m is subjected to rolling loads. What is the maximum positive moment at section 10 m from the left support due to concentrated load of 40 kN rolling from left to right of the span ?
    (1) 100 kNm   (2) 200 kNm   (3) 150 kNm   (4) 50 kNm

71. A three-hinged symmetrical parabolic arch has span 40 m with central rise of 5 m is subjected to rolling loads. What is the maximum negative moment at section 10 m from the left support due to concentrated load of 40 kN rolling from left to right of the span ?
    (1) 100 kNm   (2) 200 kNm   (3) 150 kNm   (4) 50 kNm

72. A three-hinged symmetrical parabolic arch has span 40 m with central rise of 5 m is subjected to rolling loads. What is the maximum negative moment at section 10 m from the left support due to udl of 20 kN/m longer than span rolling from left to right ?
    (1) 600 kNm   (2) 300 kNm   (3) 150 kNm   (4) 500 kNm

73. A cable of span 80 m and dip 6 m is subjected to rise in temperature of 20°C. If coefficient of thermal expansion of the cable material is 12×10^{-5} /°C, what is dip of the cable ?
    (1) 0.048 m   (2) 0.050 m   (3) 1.50 m   (4) 1.00 m

74. A cable of span 80 m and dip 6 m is subjected to rise in temperature of 20°C. If coefficient of thermal expansion of the cable material is 12×10^{-5} /°C when cable carries load of 15 kN/m, then what is the reaction in cable ?
    (1) 500 kN   (2) 300 kN   (3) 600 kN   (4) 1000 kN

75. A cable of span 80 m and dip 6 m is subjected to rise in temperature of 20°C. If coefficient of thermal expansion of the cable material is 12×10^{-5}/°C when cable carries load of 15 kN/m, then what is thrust in the cable ?
    (1) 1500 kN   (2) 1300 kN   (3) 1600 kN   (4) 2000 kN

76. A cable of span 80 m and dip 6 m is subjected to rise in temperature of 20°C. If coefficient of thermal expansion of the cable material is 12×10^{-5} /°C when cable carries load of 15 kN/m, then what is maximum tension in the cable ?
    (1) 2088 kN   (2) 1088 kN   (3) 1912 kN   (4) 2000 kN

77. A suspension cable of span 160 m and central dip of 16 m. It carries load of 5 kN/m of horizontal length. Then what is the maximum tension in cable ?
    (1) 1077 kN   (2) 1088 kN   (3) 1177 kN   (4) 1000 kN

78. A suspension cable of span 160 m and central dip of 16 m. It carries load of 5 kN/m of horizontal length. Then what is minimum tension in cable ?
    (1) 1077 kN   (2) 1088 kN   (3) 1177 kN   (4) 1000 kN

79. A suspension cable of span 160 m and central dip of 16 m. It carries load of 5 kN/m of horizontal length. When cable is passing over frictionless roller on the top of the pier, then what is thrust in the cable ?
    (1) 55 kN   (2) 65 kN   (3) 68 kN   (4) 60 kN

80. A suspension cable of span 160 m and central dip of 16 m. It carries load of 5 kN/m of horizontal length. When cable is passing over frictionless roller on the top of the pier, then what is reaction in the cable ?
    (1) 550 kN   (2) 940 kN   (3) 640 kN   (4) 900 kN

81. A cable resists the external loads by
    - (1) shear
    - (2) bending
    - (3) tension
    - (4) compression
82. A cable suspended between two points is subjected to temperature rise of $t°C$, then the horizontal component of tension in the cable
    - (1) decreases
    - (2) increases or decreases
    - (3) increases
    - (4) is constant
83. When the sag of the cable suspended between two points decreases then the horizontal component of tension will
    - (1) decrease
    - (2) increase or decrease
    - (3) increase
    - (4) remain constant
84. The shape of the cable suspended between two points is
    - (1) funicular polygon
    - (2) parabolic
    - (3) circular
    - (4) dependent upon the loads
85. The shape of the cable under horizontal udl is
    - (1) funicular polygon
    - (2) parabolic
    - (3) circular
    - (4) polygon
86. A suspension bridge with two hinged stiffening girders is
    - (1) statically indeterminate of 1 degree
    - (2) statically indeterminate of 3 degree
    - (3) statically indeterminate of 2 degree
    - (4) statically determinate
87. A cable of span L and central dip d is subjected to udl w per unit horizontal length. The horizontal component of tension in the cable is
    - (1) $wL^2/8d$
    - (2) $wL^2/16d$
    - (3) $wL^2/2d$
    - (4) $wL^2/4d$
88. The length of parabolic cable of span L and maximum dip D is
    - (1) $L + D^2/3L$
    - (2) $L + 8D^2/3L$
    - (3) $L + 8D^2/6L$
    - (4) $L + 8D^2/3L$
89. The area of I.L.D. for the reaction at the hinged end of uniform propped cantilever beam of span L is
    - (1) $L^2/12$
    - (2) $3L/8$
    - (3) $L^2/4$
    - (4) $3L/4$
90. The Muller-Breslau principle for influence line is applicable for
    - (1) continuous beam
    - (2) simple beam
    - (3) truss
    - (4) all of above
91. The influence lines for any stress function are used for obtaining the maximum value due to
    - (1) only single point load
    - (2) udl
    - (3) several point loads
    - (4) all of above
92. A live load of 45 kN/m and 5 m long moves on simply supported beam of 12 m span. What is the maximum B.M. at a section 4 m from the left support ?
    - (1) 100 kN
    - (2) 900 kN
    - (3) 475 kN
    - (4) 275 kN
93. A live load of 25 kN/m and 8 m long moves on simply supported beam of 24 m span. What is the maximum B.M. at a section 9 m from the left support ?
    - (1) 100 kN
    - (2) 900 kN
    - (3) 935 kN
    - (4) 275 kN

94. Four wheel loads spaced at 1 m intervals which are 30, 150, 100 and 60 kN with 30 kN load leading, cross a girder of 20 m span. What is the maximum B.M. at a section 8 m from the left support ?
    (1) 1515 kNm   (2) 1500 kNm   (3) 1000 kNm   (4) 2750 kNm

95. Four wheel loads spaced at 1 m intervals which are 30, 150, 100 and 60 kN with 30 kN load leading, cross a girder of 20 m span. What is the maximum positive S.F. at a section 8 m from the left support ?
    (1) 210 kN   (2) 110 kN   (3) 175 kN   (4) 275 kN

96. Four wheel loads spaced at 1 m intervals which are 30, 150, 100 and 60 kN with 30 kN load leading, cross a girder of 20 m span. What is the maximum negative S.F. at a section 8m from the left support ?
    (1) 210 kN   (2) 180 kN   (3) 175 kN   (4) 275 kN

97. Four wheel loads spaced at 1 m intervals which are 80, 160, 160 and 120 kN with 120 kN load leading, cross a girder of 25 m span. What is the maximum B.M. at a section 10 m from the left support ?
    (1) 2910 kNm   (2) 1500 kNm   (3) 2500 kNm   (4) 2750 kNm

98. Four wheel loads spaced at 1 m intervals which are 80, 160, 160 and 120 kN with 120 kN load leading, cross a girder of 25 m span. What is the absolute maximum S.F. in the beam ?
    (1) 290 kN   (2) 490 kN   (3) 175 kN   (4) 275 kN

99. Four wheel loads spaced at 1 m intervals which are 80, 160, 160 and 120 kN with 120 kN load leading, cross a girder of 25 m span. What is the absolute maximum B.M. in the beam ?
    (1) 3030 kNm   (2) 1500 kNm   (3) 2020 kNm   (4) 2750 kNm

100. Uniformly distributed load of intensity 30 kN/m crosses a simply supported beam of span 60 m from left to right. The length of udl is 15 m. What is the maximum B.M. at a section 20 m from the left support ?
    (1) 5250 kNm   (2) 5000 kNm   (3) 2500 kNm   (4) 2250 kNm

101. Uniformly distributed load of intensity 30 kN/m crosses a simply supported beam of span 60 m from left to right. The length of udl is 15 m. What is the absolute value of maximum B.M. ?
    (1) 5000 kNm   (2) 5900 kNm   (3) 2500 kNm   (4) 5550 kNm

102. Uniformly distributed load of intensity 30 kN/m crosses a simply supported beam of span 60 m from left to right. The length of udl is 15 m. What is the absolute value of maximum S.F. ?
    (1) 500 kN   (2) 390 kN   (3) 250 kN   (4) 490 kN

103. A symmetrical two-hinged parabolic arch when subjected to uniformly distributed load on the entire horizontal span, is subjected to ....
    (1) radial shear alone
    (2) normal thrust alone
    (3) normal thrust and bending moment
    (4) normal thrust, radial shear and bending moment

104. A three-hinged symmetric parabolic arch is hinged at the springing and at the crown. The span and rise are 40 m and 10 m respectively. The left half of the arch is loaded with U.D.L. of 3 t/m. The horizontal thrust at the springings will be ....
    (1) 15 t   (2) 20 t   (3) 30 t   (4) 40 t

105. The flexibility coefficient for shaft length L and torsional rigidity GJ under torsion at mid point is
    (1) 4L/GJ   (2) L/2GJ   (3) 2L/GJ   (4) L/4GJ

106. The number of unknowns to be determined in the stiffness method is equal to
    (1) kinematic indeterminacy   (2) dynamic indeterminacy
    (3) both (1) and (2)   (4) none of above

107. A uniform propped cantilever has a span L and flexural rigidity EI. The stiffness coefficient corresponding to rotation of propped end is
    (1) EI/4L   (2) 2EI/L   (3) 4EI/L   (4) EI/2L

108. A uniform cross-section beam of length 2L and flexural rigidity EI is fixed at the ends. The moment required for unit rotation at the centre of span is
    (1) EI/4L   (2) 8EI/L   (3) 4EI/L   (4) EI/2L

109. The force required to produce an unit translation displacement without rotation of one-third of fixed beam of span L and of uniform flexural rigidity EI is
    (1) $729EI/4L^3$ (2) $729EI/2L^3$ (3) $729EI/2L^2$ (4) $729EI/4L^2$

110. A simply supported beam of span L and flexural rigidity EI is subjected to moment M at one support. The strain energy due to bending is
    (1) $M^2L/4EI$ (2) $M^2L/6EI$ (3) $M^2L/2EI$ (4) M^2L/EI

111. Two uniform steel rods A and B of same length having diameter d and 2d are subjected to tensile forces P and 2P respectively.
    Which of the following statement is correct ?
    (1) Strain energy is same in both rods.
    (2) Elongation of rod A is twice that of B.
    (3) Axial strain in rod A is twice that of B.
    (4) All of the above.

112. The design of wind pressure depends upon
    (1) temperature   (2) wind velocity
    (3) altitude   (4) all of above

113. The percentage reduction in the floor imposed load per 50 m² transferable to the beam is
    (1) 15%   (2) 10%   (3) 5%   (4) 2.5%

114. The percentage reduction in the transferable live load in the building on a wall from the three floors above the wall is
    (1) 15%   (2) 10%   (3) 5%   (4) 20%

115. The percentage reduction in the transferable live load in the building on a column from the 8th floor above the column is
    (1) 15%   (2) 10%   (3) 40%   (4) 20%

116. The percentage reduction in the transferable live load from the roof of residential building over a column is
    (1) 0%   (2) 10%   (3) 40%   (4) 20%

117. The design concentrated live load in kN for living room is
    (1) 6   (2) 3   (3) 2   (4) 4

118. A cable of negligible weight is suspended between two points spaced 300 m apart horizontally, with the right support being 12 m higher than the left support. Four vertical loads of magnitudes 400, 200, 400 and 1200 kN are applied at points A, B, C and D which are 60, 120, 180 and 240 m horizontally respectively from the left support. The largest sag of the cable will be at
    (1) A   (2) B   (3) C   (4) D

119. In considering Plastic Analysis, which of the following is a valid comprehensive statement?
    (1) Shape factor is the ratio of plastic section modulus to the elastic section modulus.
    (2) Shape factor is the ratio of elastic section modulus to the plastic section modulus.
    (3) Shape factor is the ratio of plastic section modulus to the elastic section modulus and its value is always greater than 1.0.
    (4) Shape factor is the ratio of elastic section modulus to the plastic section modulus and its value is always less than 1.0.

120. Which one of the following statements is true with regard to the flexibility method of analysis ?
    (1) The method is used to analyse determinate structures.
    (2) The method is used only for manual analysis of indeterminate structures.
    (3) The method is used for analysis of flexible structures.
    (4) The method is used for analysis of indeterminate structures with lesser degree of static indeterminacy.

121. A single rolling load of 8 kN rolls along a girder of 15 m span. The absolute maximum bending moment will be
    (1) 30 kNm   (2) 15 kNm   (3) 20 kNm   (4) 25 kNm

122. Select the correct statement :
    (1) Flexibility matrix is a square symmetrical matrix.
    (2) Stiffness matrix is a square symmetrical matrix.
    (3) both (1) and (2)
    (4) none of the above

123. When a uniformly distributed load, longer than the span of the girder, moves from left to right, then the maximum bending moment at mid section of span occurs when the uniformly distributed load occupies
    (1) less than the left half span   (2) whole of left half span
    (3) whole span   (4) none of above

124. The maximum bending moment due to a train of wheel loads on a simply supported girder
    (1) always occurs at centre of span
    (2) always occurs under a wheel load
    (3) never occurs under a wheel load
    (4) none of the above

125. For a two-hinged arch, if one of the supports settles down vertically, then the horizontal thrust
    (1) increases
    (2) decreases
    (3) remains unchanged
    (4) becomes zero

126. Which of the following methods of structural analysis is a force method ?
    (1) Slope deflection method
    (2) Column analogy method
    (3) Moment distribution method
    (4) None of the above

127. Which of the following is not the displacement method ?
    (1) Equilibrium method
    (2) Column analogy method
    (3) Moment distribution method
    (4) Kani's method

128. When a series of wheel loads crosses a simply supported girder, the maximum bending moment under any given wheel load occurs when
    (1) the centre of span is midway between the centre of gravity of the load system and the wheel load under consideration.
    (2) the centre of gravity of the load system is midway between the centre of span and wheel load under consideration.
    (3) both of above
    (4) none of above

129. The deformation of a spring produced by a unit load is called
    (1) influence coefficient
    (2) flexibility
    (3) unit strain
    (4) none of above

130. Select the correct statement about two hinged arches.
    (1) statically indeterminate to first degree
    (2) structurally more efficient
    (3) both are correct
    (4) both are incorrect

131. Select the correct statement about three-hinged arches.
    (1) Statically indeterminate.
    (2) Increase in temperature causes increase in central rise, so no stresses.
    (3) Both are correct.
    (4) Both are incorrect.

132. A beam is as shown in Fig. 12. The reaction at A is

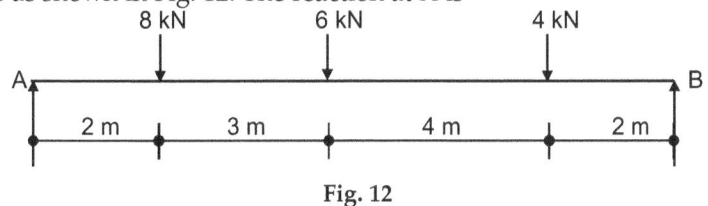

Fig. 12

    (1) 10 kN
    (2) 10.45 kN
    (3) 11.45 kN
    (4) 1.045 kN

133. A beam is as shown in Fig. 12. The reaction at B is
   (1) 13.45 kN   (2) 7.45 kN   (3) 9.5 kN   (4) 11.5 kN

134. A beam is as shown in Fig. 13. The reaction at A is

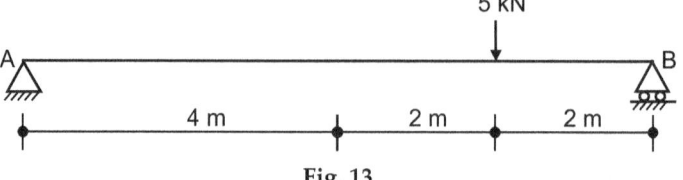

Fig. 13

   (1) 1.25 kN   (2) 3.75 kN   (3) 2.25 kN   (4) 5.25 kN

135. A beam is as shown in Fig. 13. The reaction at B is
   (1) 1.25 kN   (2) 3.75 kN   (3) 2.25 kN   (4) 5.25 kN

136. A beam is as shown in Fig. 14. The reaction at A is

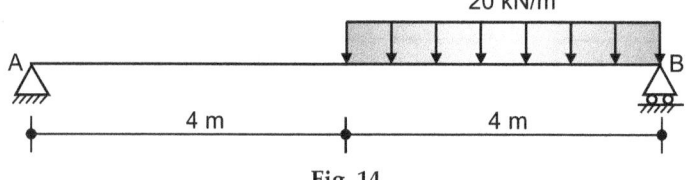

Fig. 14

   (1) 25 kN   (2) 37.5 kN   (3) 35 kN   (4) 20 kN

137. A beam is as shown in Fig. 15. Reaction at A is

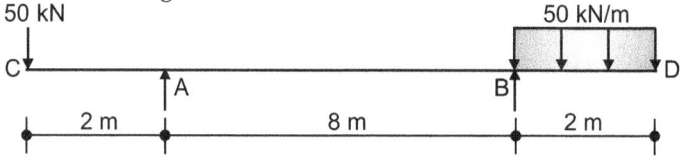

Fig. 15

   (1) 5.46 kN   (2) 9.12 kN   (3) 1.90 kN   (4) 3.55 kN

138. A beam is as shown in Fig. 15. Reaction at B is
   (1) 7.56 kN   (2) 5.88 kN   (3) 2.79 kN   (4) 4.04 kN

139. A beam is as shown in Fig. 16. Ordinate at C for I.L.D. of B.M. at D is

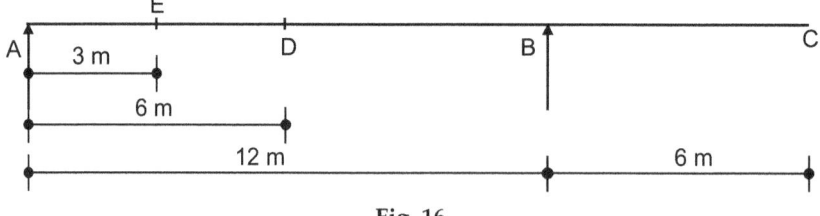

Fig. 16

   (1) 2   (2) 3   (3) 1   (4) zero

140. A beam is as shown in Fig 16. Ordinate at C for reaction at B is
   (1) 0.5   (2) 1   (3) 1.5   (4) zero

141. A beam is as shown in Fig. 16. Ordinate at C for reaction at A is
   (1) 0.5   (2) 1   (3) 0.75   (4) zero

142. A beam is as shown in Fig. 16. Ordinate at A for reaction at B is
   (1) 0.75   (2) zero   (3) 1.0   (4) 0.25

143. A truss is as shown in Fig. 17. Force in member U_4L_4, due to dead load of 10.5 kN/m covering the entire span and a moving live load of 21.5 kN/m longer than the span is

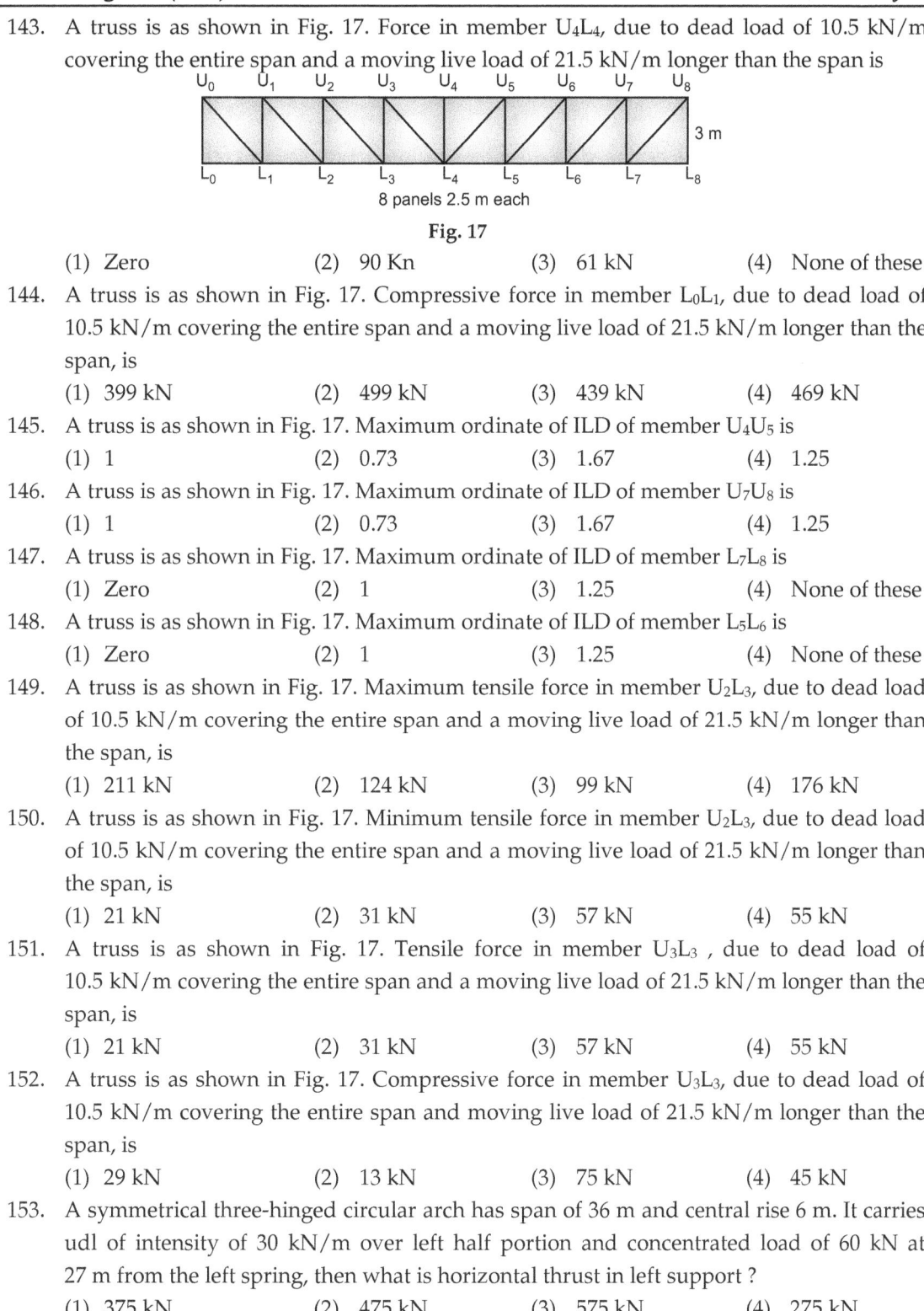

Fig. 17

(1) Zero   (2) 90 Kn   (3) 61 kN   (4) None of these

144. A truss is as shown in Fig. 17. Compressive force in member L_0L_1, due to dead load of 10.5 kN/m covering the entire span and a moving live load of 21.5 kN/m longer than the span, is

(1) 399 kN   (2) 499 kN   (3) 439 kN   (4) 469 kN

145. A truss is as shown in Fig. 17. Maximum ordinate of ILD of member U_4U_5 is

(1) 1   (2) 0.73   (3) 1.67   (4) 1.25

146. A truss is as shown in Fig. 17. Maximum ordinate of ILD of member U_7U_8 is

(1) 1   (2) 0.73   (3) 1.67   (4) 1.25

147. A truss is as shown in Fig. 17. Maximum ordinate of ILD of member L_7L_8 is

(1) Zero   (2) 1   (3) 1.25   (4) None of these

148. A truss is as shown in Fig. 17. Maximum ordinate of ILD of member L_5L_6 is

(1) Zero   (2) 1   (3) 1.25   (4) None of these

149. A truss is as shown in Fig. 17. Maximum tensile force in member U_2L_3, due to dead load of 10.5 kN/m covering the entire span and a moving live load of 21.5 kN/m longer than the span, is

(1) 211 kN   (2) 124 kN   (3) 99 kN   (4) 176 kN

150. A truss is as shown in Fig. 17. Minimum tensile force in member U_2L_3, due to dead load of 10.5 kN/m covering the entire span and a moving live load of 21.5 kN/m longer than the span, is

(1) 21 kN   (2) 31 kN   (3) 57 kN   (4) 55 kN

151. A truss is as shown in Fig. 17. Tensile force in member U_3L_3 , due to dead load of 10.5 kN/m covering the entire span and a moving live load of 21.5 kN/m longer than the span, is

(1) 21 kN   (2) 31 kN   (3) 57 kN   (4) 55 kN

152. A truss is as shown in Fig. 17. Compressive force in member U_3L_3, due to dead load of 10.5 kN/m covering the entire span and moving live load of 21.5 kN/m longer than the span, is

(1) 29 kN   (2) 13 kN   (3) 75 kN   (4) 45 kN

153. A symmetrical three-hinged circular arch has span of 36 m and central rise 6 m. It carries udl of intensity of 30 kN/m over left half portion and concentrated load of 60 kN at 27 m from the left spring, then what is horizontal thrust in left support ?

(1) 375 kN   (2) 475 kN   (3) 575 kN   (4) 275 kN

154. A symmetrical three-hinged circular arch has span of 36 m and central rise 6 m. It carries udl intensity of 30 kN/m over left half portion and concentrated load of 60 kN at 27 m from the left spring, then what is radial shear ?
 (1) 20 kN   (2) 30 kN   (3) 15 kN   (4) 45 kN

155. A symmetrical three-hinged circular arch has span of 36 m and central rise 6 m. It carries udl intensity of 30 kN/m over left half portion and concentrated load of 60 kN at 27 m from the left spring, then what is bending moment ?
 (1) 300 kNm   (2) 430 kNm   (3) 405 kNm   (4) 440 kNm

156. A symmetrical three-hinged parabolic arch has span of 36 m and central rise 6 m. It carries udl intensity of 30 kN/m over left half portion and concentrated load of 60 kN at 27 m from the left spring, then what is horizontal thrust in left support ?
 (1) 375 kN   (2) 475 kN   (3) 575 kN   (4) 275 kN

157. A symmetrical three-hinged parabolic arch has span of 36m and central rise 6 m. It carries udl intensity of 30 kN/m over left half portion and concentrated load of 60 kN at 27 m from the left spring, then what is radial shear ?
 (1) 20 kN   (2) 30 kN   (3) 0 kN   (4) 5 kN

158. A symmetrical three-hinged parabolic arch has span of 36 m and central rise 6 m. It carries udl intensity of 30 kN/m over left half portion and concentrated load of 60 kN at 27 m from the left spring, then what is bending moment ?
 (1) 300 kNm   (2) 430 kNm   (3) 440 kNm   (4) 540 kNm

159. The influence line for shear at section X (F_x) at a distance of 4 m from the left support of a simply supported girder AB is shown in figure. The shear force at section X due to a uniformly distributed dead load of intensity 2t/m covering the entire span will be .....

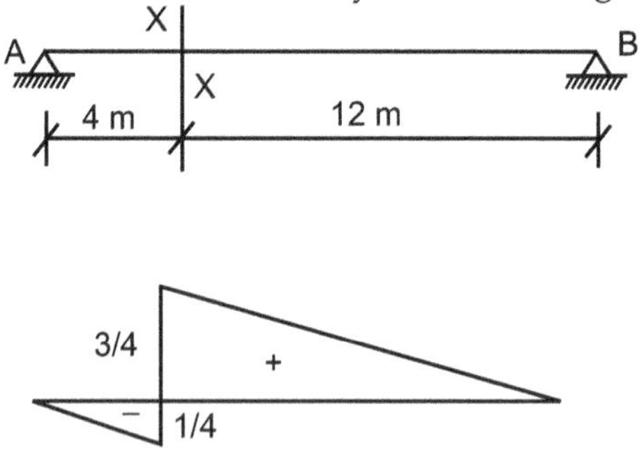

Fig. 18

 (1) 8 t   (2) 4 t   (3) 2 t   (4) 1 t

160. The moment area theorems in the structural analysis fall in the category of ....
 (1) force method   (2) displacement method
 (3) stiffness method   (4) iterative method

161. The analysis of statically indeterminate structures by the unit load method is based on ....
 (1) force method concept   (2) stiffness method
 (3) both (1) and (2)   (4) none of these

162. The analysis of statically indeterminate structures by the unit load method is based on ....
     (1) consistent deformation   (2) stiffness method
     (3) consistent force   (4) none of these

163. The force method in structural analysis always ensures ....
     (1) equilibrium   (2) kinematically admissible forces
     (3) equilibrium of forces   (4) none of the above

164. Unequal settlements in the supports of a statically indeterminate structure develop ....
     (1) member forces   (2) reactions from supports
     (3) no reactions   (4) strains in some members only

165. The method of virtual work in the analysis of structures results in ....
     (1) compitable deformations   (2) equilibrium of forces
     (3) stress-strain relations   (4) none of the above

166. Maxwell's reciprocal theorem in structural analysis can be applied in ....
     (1) all elastic structures   (2) plastic structures
     (3) symmetrical structures only   (4) prismatic element structures only

167. Castigliano's first theorem is applicable ....
     (1) for elastic structures   (2) for all statically determine structures
     (3) only when principle of superposition is valid
     (4) none of the above

168. The Muller-Breslau principle in structural analysis is used for ....
     (1) drawing influence line diagram for any force function.
     (2) superimposition of load effects.
     (3) writing virtual work equation.
     (4) none of the above.

169. What is the ordinate of influence line at B for reaction R_D in figure below ?

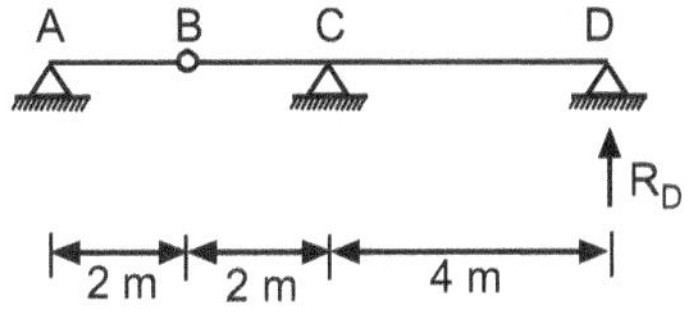

Fig. 19

     (1) 0.5   (2) 0.4   (3) 0.2   (4) Zero

170. When a load is applied to a structure with rigid joints ....
     (1) there is no rotation or displacement of joint.
     (2) there is no rotation of joint.
     (3) there is no displacement of joint.
     (4) there can be rotation and displacement of joint, but the angle between the members connected to the joint remains same even after application of the load.

171. A determinate structure ....
     (1) cannot be analyzed without the correct knowledge of modulus of elasticity.
     (2) must necessarily have roller support at one of its ends.
     (3) requires only statical equilibrium equations for its analysis
     (4) will have zero deflection at its ends.

172. Which one of the following methods is an approximate quick solution possible for frames subjected to transverse loads ?
   (1) By cantilever or portal method
   (2) By strain energy method
   (3) By moment distribution method
   (4) By matrix method

173. A statically indeterminate structure is the one which ....
   (1) cannot be analyzed at all
   (2) can be analyzed using equations of static only
   (3) can be analyzed using equations of statics and compatibility equations.
   (4) can be analyzed using equations of compatibility

174. The three moment equation in structural analysis is basically a ....
   (1) stiffness method
   (2) displacement method
   (3) energy method
   (4) flexibility method

175. In moment distribution method the sum of distribution factors of all the members meeting at any joint is always ....
   (1) zero
   (2) < 1
   (3) > 1
   (4) = 1

176. The influence line for force in member BC is

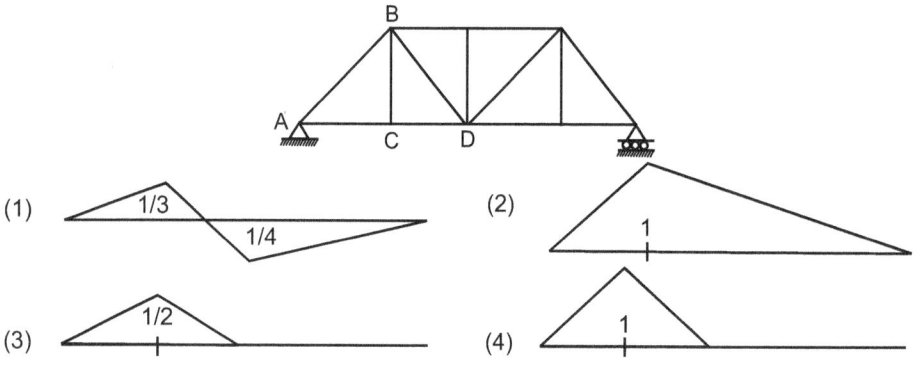

Fig. 20

177. For prismatic members, stiffness factor is ....
   (1) $\dfrac{I}{l}$
   (2) $\dfrac{l}{E}$
   (3) EI
   (4) $\dfrac{AEl}{I}$

   Where, I = Moment of inertia
   　　　l = Length of member
   　　　E = Young's modulus
   　　　A = Area of cross-sections

178. The carry over factor for prismatic member with far end fixed is ....
   (1) $-\dfrac{1}{2}$
   (2) $\dfrac{1}{2}$
   (3) $\dfrac{1}{4}$
   (4) $-\dfrac{1}{4}$

179. The absolute stiffness of a prismatic member with one end fixed is ....
   (1) $\dfrac{2EI}{L}$
   (2) $\dfrac{4EI}{L}$
   (3) $\dfrac{3EI}{L}$
   (4) none of these

180. The absolute stiffness of a prismatic member with one end hinged is ....
   (1) $\dfrac{2EI}{L}$
   (2) $\dfrac{4EI}{L}$
   (3) $\dfrac{3EI}{L}$
   (4) None of these

181. In the figure shown the degree of external indeterminacy is ......

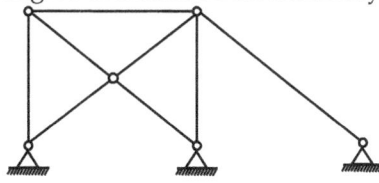

Fig. 21

(1) 1   (2) 2   (3) 3   (4) 4

182. A suspension bridge with a two-hinged stiffening girder is ....
   (1) statistically determinate   (2) indeterminate to one degree
   (3) indeterminate to two degrees   (4) a mechanism

183. What is the variation of influence line for stress function in a statically determinate structure ?
   (1) Parabolic   (2) Bilinear
   (3) Linear   (4) Uniformly rectangular

184. The influence line for force in member DC of the truss shown below will be ....

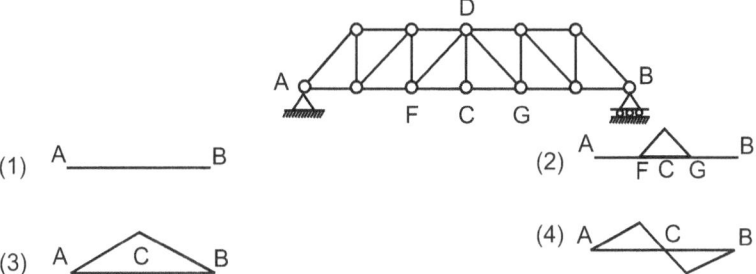

Fig. 22

185. The moment required to rotate the near end of a prismatic beam through unit angle without translation, when the far end is fixed.
   (1) $\dfrac{EI}{L}$ (2) $\dfrac{2EI}{L}$
   (3) $\dfrac{3EI}{L}$ (4) $\dfrac{4EI}{L}$

186. What is the area of influence line diagram for the reaction at the hinged end of a uniform propped cantilever beam of span L ?
   (1) $\dfrac{L}{B}$ (2) $\dfrac{L}{2}$
   (3) $\dfrac{L}{4}$ (4) $\dfrac{3L}{8}$

187. The expression given by Castigliano's first theorem to determine the deflection component of any point on structure is ....
   (1) $\int \dfrac{M}{EI} \dfrac{\rho M}{\rho P}$ (2) $\int \dfrac{\rho M}{\rho P} \dfrac{dx}{EI}$
   (3) $\int M \left(\dfrac{\rho M}{\rho P}\right) \dfrac{dx}{EI}$ (4) none of these

188. The influence line diagram for the support moment A of the fixed beam AB of constant EI is ......

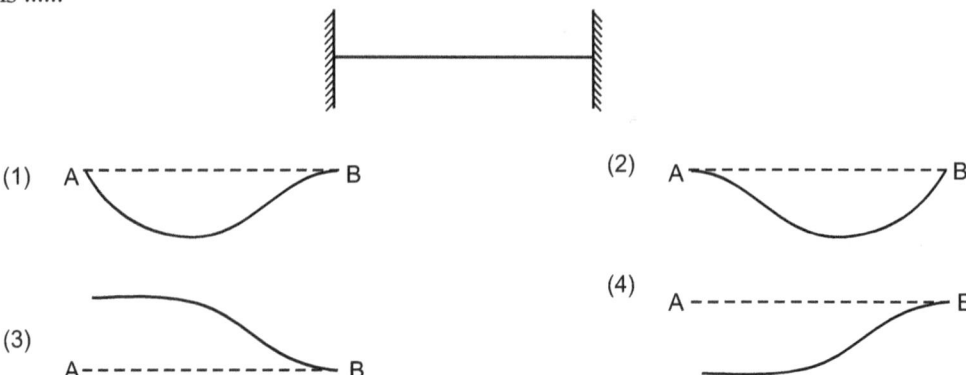

Fig. 23

189. In the moment-area method, the difference in slopes between any two sections of a loaded flexural member is equal to the .....

(1) Area of the $\dfrac{M}{EI}$ diagram between these two sections

(2) Moment of the $\dfrac{M}{EI}$ diagram between these two sections

(3) $\dfrac{1}{2}$ × area of the $\dfrac{M}{EI}$ diagram between these two sections

(4) $\dfrac{1}{2}$ × moment of the $\dfrac{M}{EI}$ diagram between these two sections

190. In the moment-area method, the deflection of a point A from a tangent at B is equal to the ....

(1) Area of $\dfrac{M}{EI}$ diagram between A and B

(2) Moment of $\dfrac{M}{EI}$ diagram between A and B about A

(3) Moment of $\dfrac{M}{EI}$ diagram between A and B about B

(4) $\dfrac{1}{2}$ × area of the $\dfrac{M}{EI}$ diagram between A and B

191. The conjugate beam method falls in the category of ....
    (1) force method　　　　　　　　　(2) stiffness method
    (3) displacement method　　　　　(4) none of these

192. Bending moment at any section in a conjugate beam gives in the actual beam ....
    (1) slope　　　　　　　　　　　　(2) curvature
    (3) deflection　　　　　　　　　　(4) none of the above

193. The kinematic indeterminacy of the plane frame shown in above figure is .... (disregrading the axial deformation of the members)
    (1) 7　　　　　　　　　　　　　　(2) 5
    (3) 6　　　　　　　　　　　　　　(4) 4

194. The three moments equation is applicable only when ....
    (1) the beam is prismatic
    (2) there is no discontinuity such as hinges within the span
    (3) the span are equal
    (4) there are atleast 2 spans.

195. Which one of the following is true example of statically determinate beam ?
    (1) One end is fixed and the other end is simply supported.
    (2) Both the ends are fixed.
    (3) The beam overhangs over two supports.
    (4) The beam is supported on three supports.

196. The influence line for vertical reaction at A of the beam ......

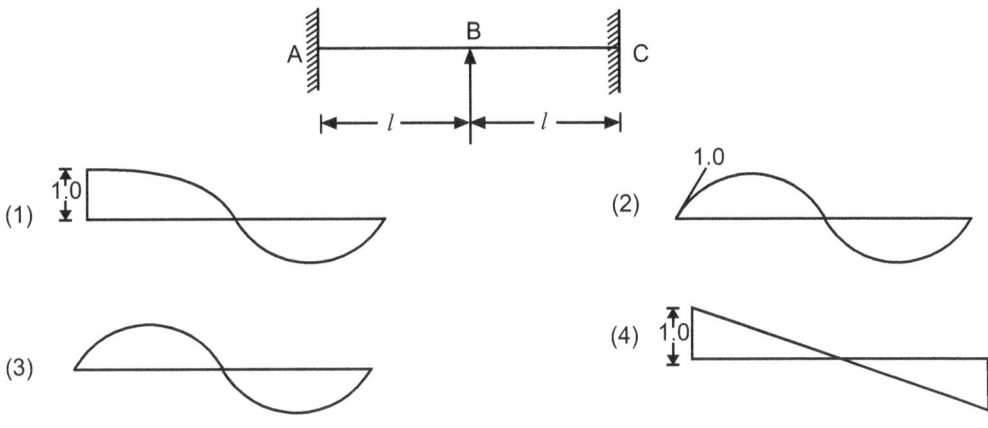

Fig. 24

197. If M is the external moment which rotates the near end of a prismatic beam without translation, the far end being fixed, then the moment induced at the far end is
    (1) zero   (2) $\dfrac{M}{2}$ in the same direction as M
    (3) $\dfrac{M}{2}$ in the opposite direction as M   (4) none of these

198. The method of moment distribution in structural analysis is ....
    (1) an iterative method   (2) an exact method
    (3) an approximate method   (4) none of these

199. The unit of flexural stiffness is ....
    (1) radians per unit rotation   (2) moment per unit rotation
    (3) force per unit deflection and rotation (4) extension per unit force

200. The torsional stiffness of a member can be defined as ....
    (1) torque for unit moment   (2) torque for unit twist
    (3) moment for unit twist   (4) torsion for unit twist

201. The stiffness method in structural analysis is also known as ....
    (1) unit load method   (2) consistent deformation method
    (3) force method   (4) displacement method

202. The flexibility of an element can be defined as ....
    (1) flexural moment per unit rotation   (2) rotation for unit moment
    (3) flexibility for unit translation   (4) none of these

203. The elements of flexibility matrix of a structure ....
    (1) are independent of the choice of co-ordinates
    (2) are dependent on the choice of co-ordinates
    (3) are always dimensionally homogeneous
    (4) both (1) and (2)

204. An increase in temperature on the top fibre of a simply supported beam will cause ....
    (1) downward deflection   (2) upward deflection
    (3) no deflection   (4) angular rotation about neutral axis

205. A fixed beam with central point load undergoes a slight settlement at one end. Select suitable answer from the following.
    (1) Moment induced at both ends will be same.
    (2) Moment induced at the end that has undergoes settlement will be maximum.
    (3) Moment induced will be maximum at the end having no settlement.
    (4) Zero moment at the end that has settled.

206. For a linear elastic material, ... where, U = strain energy, C = complementary energy
    (1) $U > C$ (2) $U = C$
    (3) $U < C$ (4) None of these

207. A uniformly distributed load (w) of length shorter than the span crosses a grider. The bending moment at a section in girder will be maximum when ....
    (1) head of the load is at the section
    (2) tail of the load is at the section
    (3) section divides the load in the same ratio as it divides the span
    (4) section divides the load in two equal lengths.

208. Consider the following settlements relating to structural analysis :
    (a) Flexibility matrix and its transpose are equal.
    (b) Elements of main diagonal of stiffness matrix are always positive.
    (c) For unstable structures, coefficients in leading diagonal matrix can be negative.
    Which of these statements is/are correct?
    (1) (a), (b) and (c)   (2) (a) and (b) only
    (3) (b) and (c) only   (4) (c) only

209. Flexibility matrix for a beam element is $[F] = \dfrac{1}{EI} \begin{bmatrix} 36 & 9 \\ 9 & 4 \end{bmatrix}$

    What is the corresponding stiffness matrix [S]?

    (1) $[S] = \dfrac{EI}{63} \begin{bmatrix} 36 & -9 \\ -9 & 4 \end{bmatrix}$ (2) $[S] = \dfrac{EI}{63} \begin{bmatrix} 36 & 9 \\ 9 & 4 \end{bmatrix}$

    (3) $[S] = \dfrac{EI}{63} \begin{bmatrix} 4 & -9 \\ -9 & 36 \end{bmatrix}$ (4) $[S] = \dfrac{EI}{63} \begin{bmatrix} 4 & 9 \\ 9 & 36 \end{bmatrix}$

210. Which one of the following statements is correct ?
    (1) In slope-deflection method, the forces are taken as unknowns.
    (2) In slope deflection method, the joint rotations are taken as unknowns.
    (3) Slope-deflection method is not applicable for beams and frames having settlements at the supports.
    (4) Slope deflection method is also known as force method.

211. What is the area of influence line diagram for the reaction at the hinged end of a uniform propped cantilever beam of span L ?
    (1) $\dfrac{L}{8}$
    (2) $\dfrac{L}{2}$
    (3) $\dfrac{L}{4}$
    (4) $\dfrac{3L}{8}$

212. A three-hinged symmetrical arch is loaded as shown in figure below. Which one of the following is the magnitude of the correct horizontal thrust ?

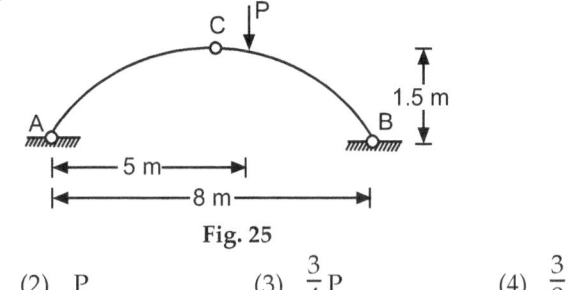

Fig. 25

    (1) $\dfrac{4}{3}P$
    (2) P
    (3) $\dfrac{3}{4}P$
    (4) $\dfrac{3}{8}$ P

213. For the elastic system under the action of loads the elastic strain and complementary strain energies are represented by U and U* respectively. Select the correct expression for displacement in the direction of load P ?
    (1) $\dfrac{\partial U}{\partial P}$
    (2) $\dfrac{\partial U^*}{\partial P}$
    (3) $\dfrac{\partial}{\partial P}(U + U^*)$
    (4) $\dfrac{1}{2}\dfrac{\partial}{\partial P}(U + U^*)$

214. The principle of superposition is made use of in structural computations when :
    (1) the geometry of the structure changes by finite amount during the application of the loads.
    (2) the changes in the geometry of the structure during the application of the loads is too small and the strains in the structure are directly proportional to the corresponding stress.
    (3) the strains in the structure are not directly proportional to the corresponding stresses, even though the effect of changes in geometry can be neglected.
    (4) none of the these conditions are met.

215. Consider the following statements :
    (I) In a two-hinged semi-circular, the reaction locus is a straight line.
    (II) The distance of reaction locus from abutment is $\pi R/2$.
    (1) Both I and II are true
    (2) I is true and II is false
    (3) I is false and II is true
    (4) Both I and II are false

216. A parabolic two-hinged arch carrying a load 'W' at center. Find the height from supports at which reactions at two ends intersect with load W. The central rise of arch is h ....

(1) $\dfrac{8\,h}{5}$ (2) $\dfrac{32h}{25}$ (3) h   (4) h

217. A plane frame ABCDEFGH shown in figure has a clamp support at A, hinge supports at G and H, axial force release (horizontal sleeve) at C and moment release (hinge) at E. The static (α_s) and kinematic (α_k) indeterminacies are ......

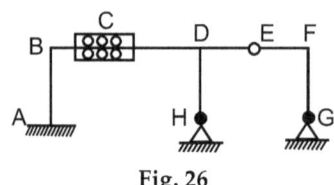

Fig. 26

	α_s	α_k
(1)	4	9
(2)	3	11
(3)	2	13
(4)	1	14

218. The plane frame shown in figure is .....
(1) stable and statically determinate
(2) unstable and statically determinate
(3) stable and statically indeterminate
(4) unstable and statically indeterminate

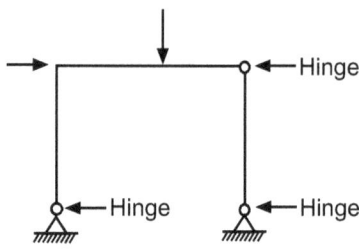

Fig. 27

219. The influence line diagram for the force in member of the truss shown below is given by

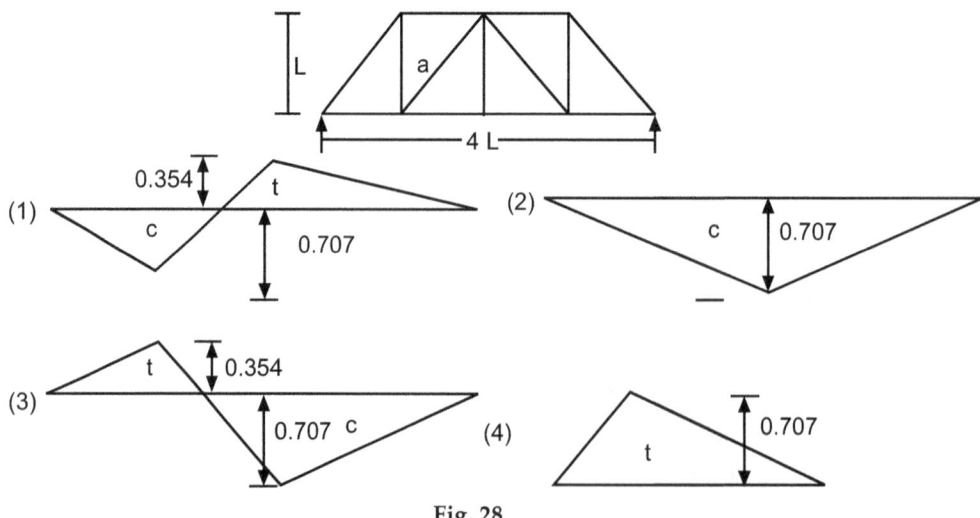

Fig. 28

220. A one-storey rigid portal frame, ABCD, carries loads P and Q as shown in the given figure. It is hinged at the two supports A and D. The structure is statically

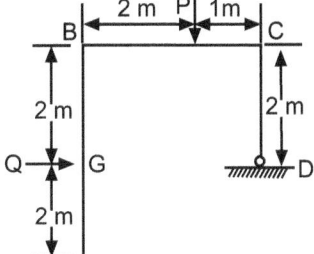

Fig. 29

(1) determinate
(2) indeterminate to the first degree
(3) indeterminate to the second degree
(4) indeterminate to the third degree

ANSWER KEY

1.	(2)	2.	(4)	3.	(3)	4.	(4)	5.	(2)	6.	(4)	7.	(1)	8.	(3)
9.	(2)	10.	(3)	11.	(4)	12.	(2)	13.	(2)	14.	(4)	15.	(3)	16.	(3)
17.	(1)	18.	(1)	19.	(2)	20.	(1)	21.	(2)	22.	(4)	23.	(2)	24.	(4)
25.	(4)	26.	(1)	27.	(2)	28.	(1)	29.	(3)	30.	(1)	31.	(3)	32.	(3)
33.	(1)	34.	(3)	35.	(2)	36.	(4)	37.	(3)	38.	(1)	39.	(3)	40.	(1)
41.	(1)	42.	(4)	43.	(1)	44.	(1)	45.	(1)	46.	(2)	47.	(2)	48.	(3)
49.	(4)	50.	(4)	51.	(2)	52.	(3)	53.	(4)	54.	(3)	55.	(4)	56.	(1)
57.	(1)	58.	(3)	59.	(3)	60.	(4)	61.	(1)	62.	(2)	63.	(3)	64.	(2)
65.	(3)	66.	(4)	67.	(3)	68.	(3)	69.	(1)	70.	(3)	71.	(1)	72.	(1)
73.	(1)	74.	(3)	75.	(4)	76.	(1)	77.	(1)	78.	(4)	79.	(3)	80.	(2)
81.	(3)	82.	(1)	83.	(3)	84.	(4)	85.	(2)	86.	(1)	87.	(1)	88.	(2)
89.	(2)	90.	(4)	91.	(4)	92.	(3)	93.	(3)	94.	(1)	95.	(2)	96.	(2)
97.	(1)	98.	(2)	99.	(1)	100.	(1)	101.	(2)	102.	(2)	103.	(2)	104.	(3)
105.	(2)	106.	(1)	107.	(3)	108.	(2)	109.	(2)	110.	(2)	111.	(4)	112.	(4)
113.	(3)	114.	(4)	115.	(3)	116.	(1)	117.	(3)	118.	(3)	119.	(3)	120.	(4)
121.	(1)	122.	(3)	123.	(3)	124.	(2)	125.	(3)	126.	(2)	127.	(2)	128.	(1)

129.	(2)	130.	(3)	131.	(4)	132.	(2)	133.	(2)	134.	(1)	135.	(2)	136.	(4)
137.	(1)	138.	(4)	139.	(2)	140.	(3)	141.	(1)	142.	(2)	143.	(1)	144.	(2)
145.	(3)	146.	(2)	147.	(1)	148.	(3)	149.	(4)	150.	(2)	151.	(1)	152.	(3)
153.	(2)	154.	(3)	155.	(4)	156.	(2)	157.	(3)	158.	(4)	159.	(1)	160.	(1)
161.	(1)	162.	(1)	163.	(3)	164.	(2)	165.	(2)	166.	(1)	167.	(3)	168.	(1)
169.	(2)	170.	(4)	171.	(3)	172.	(1)	173.	(3)	174.	(4)	175.	(3)	176.	(4)
177.	(1)	178.	(2)	179.	(2)	180.	(3)	181.	(2)	182.	(2)	183.	(3)	184.	(2)
185.	(4)	186.	(3)	187.	(3)	188.	(1)	189.	(1)	190.	(2)	191.	(1)	192.	(3)
193.	(4)	194.	(2)	195.	(3)	196.	(1)	197.	(2)	198.	(1)	199.	(2)	200.	(2)
201.	(4)	202.	(2)	203.	(2)	204.	(2)	205.	(3)	206.	(2)	207.	(3)	208.	(2)
209.	(3)	210.	(2)	211.	(3)	212.	(2)	213.	(2)	214.	(3)	215.	(1)	216.	(2)
217.	(3)	218.	(1)	219.	(1)	220.	(2)								

1. If the nominal shear stress (τ_v) at a section does not exceed the permissible shear stress (τ_c),
   (1) minimum shear reinforcement is still provided.
   (2) shear reinforcement is provided to resist the nominal shear stress.
   (3) no shear reinforcement is provided.
   (4) shear reinforcement is provided for the difference of the two.

2. Consider the following statements concerning both the working stress design and ultimate strength design of reinforced concrete.
   (i) Plane section before bending remains plane after bending
   (ii) The tensile strength of concrete is ignored.
   Which of these statements is/are correct ?
   (1) (i) alone   (2) (ii) alone
   (3) Both (i) and (ii)   (4) Neither (i) nor (ii)

3. In limit state design, permissible bond stress in the case of deformed bars is more than that in plain bars by :
   (1) 60%   (2) 50%   (3) 40%   (4) 25%

4. If f_{cu} and f_y are cube compressive strength of concrete and yield stress of steel respectively and E_s is the modulus of elasticity of steel for all grades of concrete, the ultimate flexural strain in concrete can be taken as
   (1) 0.002   (2) $\dfrac{f_{cu}}{1000}$ (3) 0.0035   (4) $\dfrac{f_y}{1.15E_s} + 0.002$

5. Limit state of serviceability for deflection including the effects due to creep, shrinkage and temperature occurring after erection of partitions and application of finishes as applicable to floors and roofs is restricted to :
   (1) $\dfrac{Span}{150}$ (2) $\dfrac{Span}{200}$ (3) $\dfrac{Span}{250}$ (4) $\dfrac{Span}{350}$

6. Shrinkage deflection in case of rectangular beams and slabs can be eliminated by putting
   (1) compression steel equal to tensile steel
   (2) compression steel more than tensile steel
   (3) compression steel less than tensile steel
   (4) compression steel 25% greater than tensile steel

7. What is the modular ratio to be used in the analysis of RC beams using working stress method if the grade of concrete is M20 ?
   (1) 18.6   (2) 13.3   (3) 9.9   (4) 6.5

8. Considering modular ratio as 13, grade of concrete as M20 and grade of steel as 415, what is the ratio of balanced depth of neutral axis as per limit state method ?
   (1) $\dfrac{12}{7}$ (2) $\dfrac{11}{3}$ (3) $\dfrac{7}{12}$ (4) $\dfrac{3}{11}$

(3.1)

9. What is the anchorage value of a standard hook of a reinforcement bar of diameter D ?

    (1) 4D   (2) 8D   (3) 12D   (4) 16D

10. How is the base-level bending moment of a cantilever retaining wall expressed as a function of its height H ?

    (1) H   (2) H^2 (3) H^3 (4) H^4

11. Match List-I with List-II and select the correct answer by using the codes given below the lists :

	List – I		List – II
A.	At end support for imposed load (not fixed)	1.	0.5
B.	At inside support, next inner to end support, for imposed load (fixed)	2.	0.55
C.	At end support, for dead load and (fixed) imposed load.	3.	0.60
D.	At all other interior supports (other than at 'B') for imposed load (fixed)	4.	0.45
		5.	0.4

    Codes :

	A	B	C	D
(1)	5	3	2	4
(2)	4	2	5	1
(3)	1	2	3	4
(4)	5	3	2	1

12. Match List-I with List-II and select the correct answer by using the codes given below the lists :

	List – I		List – II
A.	Moment and shear coefficients	1.	Durability
B.	Fire resistance	2.	Stability
C.	Sliding	3.	Analysis of structure
D.	Span to depth ratio of beam	4.	Deflection limits

    Codes :

	A	B	C	D
(1)	4	2	1	3
(2)	3	2	1	4
(3)	4	1	2	3
(4)	3	1	2	4

13. If a simply supported concrete beam, prestressed with a force of 2500 kN, is designed by load balancing concept for an effective span of 10 m and to carry a total load of 40 kN/m, the central dip of the cable profile should be :

    (1) 100 mm   (2) 200 mm   (3) 300 mm   (4) 400 mm

14. For a composite steel-beam and RCC-slab floor construction
    (1) the grade of concrete has to be M20 for the composite action to be satisfactory.
    (2) the longitudinal reinforcement of the slab has to be welded to the beam to develop monolithicity.
    (3) a notch is made in the slab to house the upper flange of the beam.
    (4) shear connectors are provided to develop the composite action.

15. In an underground warehouse, the external walls :
    (1) are designed as curtain walls.
    (2) are designed as retaining walls with or without surcharge.
    (3) are designed only for vertical loads imposed by the upper floors.
    (4) do not share any dynamic loads caused by the movement of trucks and fork-lift vehicles.

16. A six-storey 4-bay RC frame subjected to lateral loads would structurally behave :
    (1) more as a cantilever than as a portal frame.
    (2) more as a portal frame than as a cantilever.
    (3) neither as a cantilever nor as a portal frame.
    (4) as a cantilever or as a portal frame depending upon the load intensity.

17. IRC prescribes Coulomb's theory of earth pressure for the design of abutments and wing walls. The ratio of height of center of pressure above the bottom to the height of the wall is equal to :
    (1) 0.33   (2) 0.36   (3) 0.39   (4) 0.42

18. In an RCC beam of breadth 'b' and overall depth D exceeding 750 mm, side face reinforcement required and the allowable area of maximum tension reinforcement shall be respectively :
    (1) 0.2% and 0.2bD   (2) 0.3% and 0.03bD
    (3) 0.1% and 0.04 bD   (4) 0.4% and 0.01bD

19. For masonry built in 1 : 1 : 6 cement-lime-sand mix mortar or equivalent, the horizontal shear stress permissible on the area of a mortar bed joint is :
    (1) 0.15 MPa   (2) 0.125 MPa   (3) 0.1 MPa   (4) 0.075 MPa

20. Given that 'ϕ' is the angle of internal friction, 'p' is the safe bearing capacity and 'γ' is the unit weight of soil, the minimum depth of foundation of a masonry footing is given by :
    (1) $\dfrac{p}{\gamma}\left(\dfrac{1+\sin\phi}{1-\sin\phi}\right)$ (2) $\dfrac{p}{\gamma}\left(\dfrac{1-\sin\phi}{1+\sin\phi}\right)$
    (3) $\dfrac{p}{\gamma}\left(\dfrac{1+\sin\phi}{1-\sin\phi}\right)^2$ (4) $\dfrac{p}{\gamma}\left(\dfrac{1-\sin\phi}{1+\sin\phi}\right)^2$

21. The effective width 'b_t' of flange of a continuous T-beam in a floor system is given by :
    $$b_t = \dfrac{L_0}{6} + b_w + 6D_t,$$ where L_0 represents the
    (1) distance between points of contraflexure in a span
    (2) effective span of beams
    (3) clear span of beams
    (4) spacing between beams

22. Consider the following statements :

    (i) At a point or inflection, the embedment length need not exceed the development length L_d.

    (ii) The condition that $L_d \leq \left(\dfrac{M_1}{V} + L_0\right)$ need not be checked for negative reinforcement.

    (iii) At least one-third of the total negative reinforcement provided must extend beyond the point of inflection for a distance not less than 'd' or 12ϕ or clear span whichever is larger.

    Which of these statements are correct ?

    (1) (i), (ii) and (iii)   (2) (i) and (ii)   (3) (i) and (iii)   (4) (ii) and (iii)

23. In case of 2-way slab, the limiting deflection of the slab is

    (1) primarily a function of the long span.

    (2) primarily a function of the short span.

    (3) independent of long or short spans.

    (4) dependent on both long and short spans.

24. From limiting deflection point of view, use of high strength steel in RC beam results in :

    (1) reduction in depth   (2) no change in depth

    (3) increase in depth   (4) increase in width

25. In case of a composite construction, the effect of creep and shrinkage :

    (1) can be ignored even at the limit state of serviceability.

    (2) can be ignored at the ultimate limit state due to large inelastic strains induced.

    (3) can be completely eliminated if the props are removed after 28 days.

    (4) in the in-situ concrete has no interaction on the stresses in the pre-cast component at any stage.

26. A slab-beam floor system may be supported on brick walls or framed into a system of RC columns. The floor thickness (slab + beam web) for the same span will be :

    (1) less when framed into a system of RC columns.

    (2) less when supported on brick walls.

    (3) the same in both the cases.

    (4) equal to the wall thickness or size of column.

27. For maximum sagging bending moment at support in a continuous RC beam, live load should be placed on :

    (1) spans adjacent to the support plus alternate spans.

    (2) all the spans except the spans adjacent to the support.

    (3) spans next to the adjacent spans of the support plus alternate spans.

    (4) spans adjacent to supports only.

28. In a spherical dome subjected to a uniformly distributed load the meridianal force induced is :

    (1) compressive throughout   (2) zero at the crown

    (3) tensile below the plane of rupture

    (4) compressive for heavier loads, while being tensile for lower loads

29. Design of one-way RC slabs for concentrated load is done by :
    (1) using Pigeauds moment coefficients.
    (2) taking slab strip of unit width containing the load.
    (3) taking slab strip of width effective in resisting the deflection.
    (4) taking orthogonal slab strips of unit width containing the load.

30. In Pigeaud's coefficient method for the analysis of an interior panel of a T-beam bridge
    (1) notation for coefficients as ax^4 and ax^4 includes suffix 4 since the panel is continuous on all the four edges
    (2) Poission's ratio of concrete has no contribution
    (3) the applicability is restricted to the case when the wheel load is centrally placed
    (4) dispersion of load as considered through the wearing coat only.

31. Negative moment in reinforced concrete beams at the location of supports is generally much higher than the positive span moment. This is primarily due to curvature at the supports being :
    (1) very high   (2) very low
    (3) zero   (4) of reversing nature

32. Consider the following measures :
    (i) Keeping cement content within the range of 330 kg/m³ to 530 kg/m³.
    (ii) Using well-graded aggregate with water-cement ratio less than 0.5.
    (iii) Controlling the permissible stress in steel by the strain and crack widths rather than the strengths.
    (iv) Providing minimum steel of any grade amounting to 0.3 percent.
    Which of these measures have been recommended by IS:3370-1970 for the design of leak-proof liquid containers of impervious concrete ?
    (1) (i), (ii), (iii) and (iv)   (2) (i), (ii) and (iii)
    (3) (ii), (iii) and (iv)   (4) (i) and (iv)

33. Which one of the following components of the bridge deck is analyzed by using Courbon's method ?
    (1) Slabs   (2) Diaphragms   (3) Cross-beams   (4) Girders

34. In chimneys, the allowable axial compression reduces with the ratio d/t. (diameter d and plate thickness t) and not with the ratio l/r as in columns. This is to recognize the :
    (1) hoop compressive strain produced by axial compression
    (2) temperature gradient caused by hot gases
    (3) shell buckling
    (4) axial strain produced by hoop tension

35. If modular ratio is 'm', effective depth is D and stress ratio is 'r' $\left(r = \dfrac{\sigma_{st}}{\sigma_{cbc}} \right)$, the depth of neutral axis of a balanced section is :
    (1) $\left(\dfrac{m}{m-r} \right) \times D$ (2) $\left(\dfrac{m}{m+r} \right) \times D$ (3) $\left(\dfrac{m+r}{m} \right) \times D$ (4) $\left(\dfrac{m}{r} \right) \times D$

36. Side face reinforcement is provided in a beam when the depth of web exceeds
    (1) 300 mm (2) 450 mm (3) 500 mm (4) 750 mm
37. Drops are provided in flat slabs to resist
    (1) bending moment (2) thrust (3) shear (4) torsion
38. Consider the following statements :
    Assertion (A) : The behaviour of an over-reinforced beam is more ductile than that of an under reinforced beam.
    Reason (R) : Over-reinforced beam contains more steel and steel is more ductile than concrete.
    Of these statements :
    (1) both A and R are true, and R is the correct explanation of A.
    (2) both A and R are true, but R is not a correct explanation of A.
    (3) A is true, but R is false.
    (4) A is false, but R is true.
39. Flexural collapse in over-reinforced beams is due to :
    (1) primary compression failure   (2) secondary compression failure
    (3) primary tension failure   (4) bond failure
40. A reinforced cantilever beam of span 4 m, has a cross-section of 150 mm × 500 mm. If checked for lateral stability and deflection, the beam will :
    (1) fail in deflection only
    (2) fail in lateral stability only
    (3) fail in both deflection and lateral stability
    (4) satisfy the requirements of deflection and lateral stability
41. In a composite construction :
    (1) interface slipping is prevented by using shear connectors.
    (2) differential shrinkage is overcome by using the same grade of concrete for both the components.
    (3) precast member is always designed to carry the weight of in-situ concrete without props.
    (4) the in-situ concrete cannot be prestressed.
42. In a deep grain container :
    (1) only the horizontal pressure on walls approaches a limit.
    (2) only the vertical pressure on the bottom approaches a limit.
    (3) both vertical and horizontal pressures approach the limits.
    (4) the vertical pressure increases continuously, while the horizontal pressure approaches a limit.
43. The load carrying capacity of a column designed by working stress method is 500 kN. The ultimate collapse load of the column is :
    (1) 500 kN (2) 662.5 kN (3) 750 kN (4) 1100 kN

44. If the load acting on a commonly conventional sized RC column increases continuously from zero to higher magnitudes, the magnitude of the uniaxial ultimate moment that can be allowed on the column :
    - (1) increases
    - (2) decreases
    - (3) increases and then decreases
    - (4) remains constant

45. In RCC beams, as the percentage areas of tensile steel increases :
    - (1) depth of neutral axis increases
    - (2) depth of neutral axis decreases
    - (3) depth of neutral axis does not change
    - (4) lever arm increases

46. In the limit state method, balanced design of a reinforced concrete beam gives :
    - (1) smallest concrete section and maximum area of reinforcement.
    - (2) largest concrete section and maximum area of reinforcement.
    - (3) smallest concrete section and minimum area of reinforcement.
    - (4) largest concrete section and minimum area of reinforcement.

47. The maximum percent of moment redistribution allowed in RCC beams is :
    - (1) 10%
    - (2) 20%
    - (3) 30%
    - (4) 40%

48. When assessing the strength of a structure as per the limit state of collapse, the value of partial safety factor for steel is taken as :
    - (1) 2.0
    - (2) 1.5
    - (3) 1.15
    - (4) 1.00

49. The bending moment coefficient for continuous RC slabs in IS : 456-1978 code is based on:
    - (1) Pigeaud's method
    - (2) Marcus's method
    - (3) Yield - line theory
    - (4) Westerguard's mathematical analysis

50. In the design of prestressed concrete structure, which of the following limit states will come under the limit states of serviceability ?
    - (i) Flexure
    - (ii) Shear
    - (iii) Deflector
    - (iv) Cracking

    Select the correct answer using the codes given below :
    - (1) (i) and (iv)
    - (2) (iii) and (iv)
    - (3) (ii), (iii) and (iv)
    - (4) (ii) and (iii)

51. In the limit state method of design, the failure criterion for reinforced concrete beams and columns is :
    - (1) maximum principal stress theory
    - (2) maximum principal strain theory
    - (3) maximum shear stress theory
    - (4) maximum strain energy theory

52. To ensure adequate ductility for preventing failures during earthquakes, the percentage tension reinforcement 'p' on any face at any section in beams and girders should NOT exceed which one of the following values, when M15 concrete and mild steel bars are used for the construction of beams or girders (P_c is the percentage compression reinforcement and f_{ck} and f_{sy} have their usual meanings)?
    - (1) $p \le P_c + 0.011 \dfrac{f_{ck}}{f_{sy}}$
    - (2) $p \le P_c + 0.19 \dfrac{f_{ck}}{f_{sy}}$
    - (3) $p \le P_c + 0.15 \dfrac{f_{ck}}{f_{sy}}$
    - (4) $p \le P_c + 0.11 \dfrac{f_{ck}}{f_{sy}}$

53. As per IS : 456-1978, the ratio of stress in concrete to its characteristic strength at collapse in flexure for design purposes is taken as :
    (1) 0.67   (2) 0.576   (3) 0.447   (4) 0.138

54. Beam sections of reinforced concrete designed in accordance with ultimate strength or limit state design approach, as compared to sections designed by working stress method for the same conditions of load and span, and the same width, usually have :
    (1) a larger depth and smaller amount of reinforcement
    (2) the same depth and same reinforcement
    (3) smaller depth and more reinforcement
    (4) same depth as that of a deep beam

55. A doubly reinforced beam is considered less economical than a singly reinforced beam because :
    (1) tensile steel required is more than that for a balanced section.
    (2) shear reinforcement is more.
    (3) concrete is not stressed to its full value.
    (4) compressive steel is under-stressed.

56. In limit state design of reinforced concrete, deflection is computed by using :
    (1) Initial tangent modulus
    (2) Secant modulus
    (3) Tangent modulus
    (4) short-and long-term values of Young's modulus

57. As per IS : 456 - 1978 the vertical deflection limit for beams may generally be assumed to be satisfied, provided that the ratio of span to effective depth of a continuous beam of span upto 10 m is not be greater than :
    (1) 36   (2) 26   (3) 20   (4) 18

58. In limit state design method, the moment of resistance for a balanced section using M20 grade concrete and HYSD steel of grade Fe415 is given by $M_{u,lim}$ = Kbd². What is the value of K ?
    (1) 2.98   (2) 2.76   (3) 1.19   (4) 0.89

59. How is the deflection in RC beams controlled as per IS : 456 ?
    (1) By using large aspect ratio   (2) By using small modular ratio
    (3) By controlling span/depth ratio   (4) By moderating water-cement ratio

60. At what stress does the first flexural crack appear in RCC beams made of M25 grade concrete ?
    (1) 3.0 MPa   (2) 3.5 MPa   (3) 4.0 MPa   (4) 4.5 MPa

61. What is the adoptable maximum spacing between vertical stirrups in an RCC beam of rectangular cross-section having an effective depth of 300 mm ?
    (1) 300 mm   (2) 275 mm   (3) 250 mm   (4) 225 mm

62. A simply supported RC beam having clear span 5 m and support width 300 mm has the cross-section as shown in figure below.

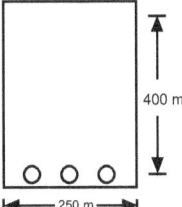

What is the effective span of the beam as per IS : 456 ?

(1) 5300 mm (2) 5400 mm (3) 5200 mm (4) 5150 mm

63. Consider the following statements dealing with flexural reinforcement to be terminated in the tension zone :

    (i) The shear at the cut-off point not to exceed two-third of the otherwise permitted value.

    (ii) Shear reinforcement is provided along each terminated bar overlapping three-fourth of the appropriate distance from the cut-off point.

    (iii) For 36 mm and smaller bars, the continuing bars shall provided double the area required for flexure at the cutoff and shear does not exceed three-fourth of the permitted value.

    Which of these statements is/are correct?

    (1) (i), (ii) and (iii) (2) (i) and (ii) only
    (3) (ii) and (iii) only (4) (iii) only

64. Match List-I with List-II and select the correct answer by using the codes given below the lists :

List – I		List – II	
A.	IS-875	1.	Earthquake resistant design
B.	IS-1343	2.	Loads
C.	IS-1893	3.	Liquid storage structure
D.	IS-3370	4.	Prestressed concrete

    Which of these statements on concrete ?

    Codes :

	A	B	C	D
(1)	3	1	4	2
(2)	2	1	4	3
(3)	3	4	1	2
(4)	2	4	1	3

65. Lateral ties in RC columns are provided to resist :

    (1) bending moment (2) shear
    (3) buckling of longitudinal steel bars (4) both bending moment and shear

66. For maximum sagging bending moment in a given span of a multiple span beam,
    (1) every span as well as alternate spans are loaded.
    (2) adjacent spans are loaded.
    (3) spans adjoining this span are loaded.
    (4) adjacent spans are unloaded and next spans are loaded.

67. What is the minimum width of roadway for a six-lane high-level bridge constructed for the use of road traffic only ?
    (1) 21.5 m   (2) 22.5 m   (3) 24.0 m   (4) 25.5 m

68. Partial safety factor for concrete and steel are 1.5 and 1.15 respectively, because
    (1) concrete is heterogeneous while steel is homogeneous.
    (2) the control on the quality of concrete is not as good as that of steel.
    (3) concrete is weak in tension.
    (4) voids in concrete are 0.5% while those in steel are 0.15%.

69. As compared to working stress method of design, limit state method takes concrete to
    (1) a higher stress level
    (2) a lower stress level
    (3) the same stress level
    (4) sometimes higher but generally lower stress level

70. While checking shear resistance of reinforced concrete beams for limit state of collapse as per IS : 456, which one of the following nominal shear stress recommendations is to be adhered to ? (V_u is shear force at vertical cross-section, 'b' and 'd' are overall breadth and effective depth of beam respectively)
    (1) $\dfrac{0.5V_u}{bd}$ (2) $\dfrac{2V_u}{5bd}$ (3) $\dfrac{V_u}{0.5\,bd}$ (4) $\dfrac{V_u}{bd}$

71. Consider the following statements :
    (i) In reinforced cement concrete, modular ratio is defined as the ratio of (modulus of elasticity of steel) and (Modulus of elasticity of concrete)
    (ii) Modulus of rupture of cement concrete is a function of its characteristic compressive strength.
    (iii) The characteristic compressive strength of M 20 grade cement concrete at 7 days is 20 N/mm².

    Which of these statements are correct ?
    (1) (i), (ii) and (ii)   (2) (i) and (ii) only
    (3) (ii) and (iii) only   (4) (i) and (iii) only

72. How can shear strength be ensured in a beam ?
    (1) By providing binding wire on main bars
    (2) By providing HYSD bars instead of mild steel bars
    (3) By providing rounded aggregate   (4) By providing stirrups

73. How is the depth of footing for an isolated column governed ?
    (i) By maximum bending moment   (ii) By shear force
    (iii) By punching shear
    Select the correct answer using the codes given below :
    (1) (ii) and (iii) only   (2) (i) and (ii) only
    (3) (i) and (iii) only   (4) (i), (ii) and (iii)

74. Usually stiffness of a simply supported beam is satisfied if the ratio of its span to depth does not exceed which one of the following ?
    (1) 7   (2) 10   (3) 20   (4) 26

75. When is an RCC roof slab designed as a two-way slab ?
    (1) If the slab is continuous over two opposite edges only.
    (2) If the slab is unsupported at one edge only.
    (3) If the ratio of spans in two directions is > 2.
    (4) If the ratio of spans in two directions is < 2.

76. When HYSD bars are used in place of mild steel bars in a beam, the bond strength :
    (1) does not change   (2) increases   (3) decreases   (4) becomes zero

77. In a singly reinforced beam, the tensile steel reaches its maximum allowable stress earlier than concrete. What is such a section known as ?
    (1) Under-reinforced section   (2) Over-reinforced section
    (3) Balanced section   (4) Economic section

78. Why is the design of a RC section as over-reinforced undesirable ?
    (1) It consumes more concrete.   (2) It undergoes high strains.
    (3) It fails suddenly.   (4) Its appearance is not good.

79. What is the moment capacity of an under-reinforced rectangular RCC beam ?
    (1) Rbd^2 (2) Rdb^2 (3) $A_{st}\, \sigma_{st}\, jd$ (4) $A_{st}\, jd$
    (Symbols have the usual meaning)

80. What is the bond stress acting parallel to the reinforcement on the interface between bar and concrete ?
    (1) Shear stress   (2) Local stress   (3) Flexural stress   (4) Bearing stress

81. In a singly reinforced concrete beam section, maximum compressive stress in concrete and tensile stress reach their permissible stresses simultaneously. What is such a section called ?
    (1) Under-reinforced section   (2) Economic section
    (3) Balanced section   (4) Over-reinforced section

82. What is the optimum mortar mix type of maximum masonry unit strength of $5\,N/mm^2$?
    (1) M_1 (2) M_2 (3) H_1 (4) H_2

83. Consider the following systems :
    (i) Trusses and purlins   (ii) Suspension system
    (iii) Flat grid roof   (iv) Shells

When these are used in single deck industrial structures, the correct sequence in increasing order of spans will be

(1) (iii), (i), (ii), (iv)   (2) (i), (iii), (ii), (iv)

(3) (iii), (i), (iv), (ii)   (4) (ii), (iv), (ii), (iii)

84. Design of foundation for a large generator is guided primarily by

    (1) frequency   (2) deformation   (3) strength   (4) stiffness

85. The 'effective width method' requires the :

    (1) wheel load to be dispersed through the wearing coat as well as deck slab in the transverse direction.

    (2) wheel load to be dispersed through the wearing coat as well as the deck slab in the longitudinal direction.

    (3) overlap to be considered in the transverse direction only.

    (4) impact factor to be considered for the dead load as well.

86. A concrete pedestal made of M20 mix is shown in the figure below. The tan α value in this case will be :

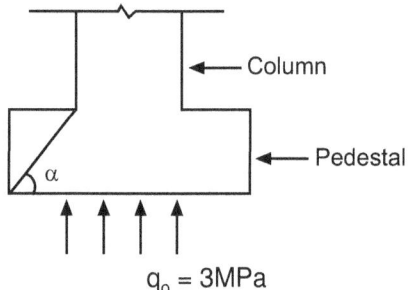

$q_o = 3MPa$

    (1) not less than 3.5   (2) less than or equal to 3.6

    (3) greater than 3.6   (4) greater than or equal to 3.6

87. A 200 mm thick wall made of modular bricks is 5 m long between cross walls and 8.8 m clear height between RCC slabs at top and bottom. The slenderness ratio of the wall is :

    (1) 15   (2) 19   (3) 20   (4) 25

88. A 200 mm thick brick masonry wall made of modular bricks carries an axial load of 30 kN/m from wall above and an eccentric load of 20 kN/m from RCC floor acting at a distance of 47.5 mm from the centre line of the wall. The resultant eccentricity ratio is :

    (1) 0.090   (2) 0.095   (3) 0.100   (4) 0.105

89. The reduction coefficient of a reinforced concrete column with an effective length of 4.8 m and size 250 mm × 300 mm is :

    (1) 0.80   (2) 0.85   (3) 0.90   (4) 0.95

90. Minimum percentage area of HYSD reinforcement in a 150 mm thick water tank wall is :

    (1) 0.16   (2) 0.20   (3) 0.23   (4) 0.24

91. In a load - balanced prestressed concrete beam under self load the cross section is subjected to :

    (1) axial stress   (2) bending stress

    (3) axial and shear stress   (4) axial and bending stress

92. A simply supported isotropically reinforced square slab of side 4 m is subjected to a service load of 6 kPa. The thickness of the slab is 120 mm. The moment of resistance required as per yield line theory is :
    (1) 9 kN-m   (2) 9 kN/m   (3) 13.2 kN-m   (4) 13.2 kNm/m

93. The load carrying capacity of a column designed by working stress method is 500 kN. The collapse load of the column is
    (1) 500.0 kN   (2) 662.5 kN   (3) 750.0 kN   (4) 1100.0 kN

94. Which one of the following statements is correct ?
    (1) Web shear cracks start due to high diagonal tension in case of beams with their webs and high prestressing force.
    (2) Shear design for a prestressed concrete beam is based on elastic theory.
    (3) In the zone where bending moment is dominant and shear is insignificant, cracks occur at 20° to 30°.
    (4) After diagonal cracking, the mechanism of shear transfer in a prestressed concrete member is very much different from that in reinforced concrete members.

95. The given figure shows the position of concentrated wheel loads on a bridge deck. For determining the bending moments in the girders by Courbon's theory, the reaction factors are respectively

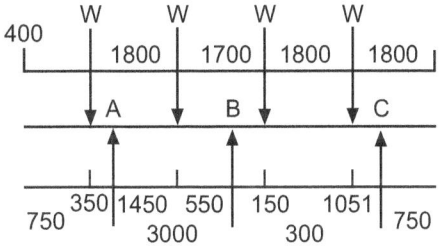

$$I_A = I_B = I_C$$

    (1) 1.80 W, 1.33 W and 0.87 W   (2) 1.73 W, 1.28 W and 0.99 W
    (3) 2.00 W, 1.50 W and 0.50 W   (4) 2.00 W, 1.25 W and 0.75 W

96. In chimneys, the allowable axial compression reduces with the ratio d/t (d being the diameter and t being the plate thickness) and NOT with the ratio l/r as in columns. This is to take into account the action of
    (1) hoop compressive strain produced by axial compression
    (2) temperature gradient due to hot gases
    (3) shell buckling
    (4) axial strain produced by hoop tension

97. High yield deformed bars have a :
    (1) definite yield value
    (2) chemical composition different from mild steel
    (3) percentage elongation less than that of mild steel
    (4) percentage elongation more than that of mild steel

98. The notching in a simply-supported timber beam of span L and depth 'd' should be restricted to the region :
    (1) L/6 from the support
    (2) L/6 from the mid-span
    (3) L/6 or 3d from the mid-span, whichever is less
    (4) L/6 or 3d from the supports, whichever is less

99. In brick masonry, arch action is possible only when the minimum height of wall above the top of lintel is X times the height of triangular distribution, where X is
    (1) 1.00   (2) 1.25   (3) 1.50   (4) 1.75

100. The basic stress in masonry unit having height to width ratio of 1.5 may be increased by a factor of :
    (1) 1.2   (2) 1.4   (3) 1.6   (4) 2.0

101. In an RCC beam, side face reinforcement is provided if its depth exceeds
    (1) 300 mm   (2) 500 mm   (3) 700 mm   (4) 750 mm

102. The limiting compressive strain in concrete is
    (1) 0.0035   (2) 0.0015   (3) 0.0025   (4) 0.015

103. The maximum spacing of vertical reinforcement in RCC wall should NOT exceed :
    (1) the thickness of wall
    (2) 1.5 times the thickness of wall
    (3) 2 times the thickness of wall
    (4) 3 times the thickness of wall

104. In a reinforced concrete retaining wall, a shear key is provided, if the :
    (1) shear stress in the vertical stem is excessive
    (2) shear force in the toe slab is more than that in the heel slab
    (3) retaining wall is not safe against sliding
    (4) retaining wall is not safe against overturning

105. In the case of a continuous RC beam, in order to obtain the maximum positive span moment, where should the live load be placed ?
    (1) On all the spans
    (2) On alternate spans starting from the left
    (3) On spans adjacent to the spans under consideration
    (4) On the span plus alternate spans

106. What is the allowable upward deflection in a prestress concrete member under serviceability limit state condition ?
    (1) Span/250   (2) Span/300   (3) Span/350   (4) Span/500

107. Which one of the following predicts the effective modulus of elasticity of concrete ?
    (1) $\dfrac{E_c}{1 + \theta}$ (2) $\dfrac{E_c}{1 + 2\theta}$ (3) $\dfrac{E_c}{1 + 3\theta}$ (4) $\dfrac{E_c}{1 + 5\theta}$

    where E_c is short-term elastic modulus and θ is the ultimate creep coefficient

108. What is the limiting principal tensile stress in prestress uncracked concrete member of M25 grade ?
    (1) 1 MPa   (2) 1.5 MPa   (3) 2 MPa   (4) 2.5 MPa

109. What is the minimum nominal percentage longitudinal reinforcement to be provided in a concrete pedestal as per relevant IS code ?
    (1) 0.4   (2) 0.2   (3) 0.15   (4) 0.1

110. Which is the minimum nominal percentage longitudinal reinforcement to be provided in a concrete pedestal as per relevant IS code ?
    (1) 0.4   (2) 0.2   (3) 0.15   (4) 0.1

111. Which one of the following is the correct expression to estimate the development length of deformed reinforcing bar as per IS code in limit state design ?
    (1) $\dfrac{\phi \sigma_s}{4.5 \tau_{bd}}$ (2) $\dfrac{\phi \sigma_s}{5 \tau_{bd}}$ (3) $\dfrac{\phi \sigma_s}{6.4 \tau_{bd}}$ (4) $\dfrac{\phi \sigma_s}{8 \tau_{bd}}$

    (where ϕ is diameter of reinforcing bar, σ_s is the stress in the bar at a section and τ_{bd} is bond stress.)

112. The cover of longitudinal reinforcing bar in a beam subjected to sea spray should not be less than which one of the following ?
    (1) 30 mm   (2) 70 mm   (3) 75 mm   (4) 80 mm

113. Which one of the following is correct in respect of the material efficiency of RCC flexural elements in rectangular beam, T-beam and two-way slab ?
    (1) All the three sections are equally efficient.
    (2) T-beam section is most uneconomical.
    (3) Two-way slab is most economical.
    (4) The efficiency of rectangular section lies between that of T-beam and two-way slab sections.

114. Working stress method of design for reinforced concrete is :
    (1) not a limit state design   (2) a serviceability limit state design
    (3) a limit state for crack width   (4) a collapse limit state

115. For a reinforced concrete beam section the shape of the shear stress diagram is :
    (1) parabolic over the whole section with maximum value at the neutral axis.
    (2) parabolic above the neutral axis and rectangular below the neutral axis.
    (3) linearly varying as the distance from the neutral axis.
    (4) dependent on the magnitude of shear reinforcement provided.

116. In a reinforced concrete T-beam (in which the flange is in compression). The position of neutral axis will :
    (1) be within the flange   (2) be within the web
    (3) depend on the thickness of flange in relation to total depth and percentage of reinforcement
    (4) at the junction of flange and web

117. Consider the following statements.
    The reinforcement in reinforced concrete shall have concrete cover, the thickness of such cover shall be not less than :
    (i) 25 mm   (ii) the diameter of bar
    (iii) the spacing between bars   (iv) 5 mm
    Which of these statements are correct ?
    (1) (iii) and (iv)   (2) (i) and (iv)   (3) (ii) and (iii)   (4) (i) and (ii)

118. In an axially loaded spirally reinforced short column, the concrete inside the core is subjected to :
    (1) bending and compression
    (2) biaxial compression
    (3) triaxial compression
    (4) uniaxial compression

119. The maximum permissible shear stress given in BIS : 456-1978 is based on :
    (1) diagonal tension failure
    (2) diagonal compression failure
    (3) flexural tension failure
    (4) flexural compression failure

120. The loading on a simply supported prestressed concrete beam is uniformly distributed, the centroid of tendons should be preferably :
    (1) a straight profile along the centroidal axis
    (2) a straight profile along with the lower kern
    (3) a parabolic profile with convexity downward.
    (4) a circular profile with convexity upward

121. In the design a masonry retaining wall, the :
    (1) vertical load should fall within the middle-third of base width
    (2) horizontal thrust should act at $\frac{h}{3}$ from base
    (3) resultant load should fall within distance of one-sixth of base width on either side of its midpoint
    (4) resultant load should fall within a distance of one-eighth of base width on either side of its midpoint.

122. The design for the limit state of collapse in flexure is based on the following assumptions.
    (i) Plane sections normal to the axis remain plane after bending.
    (ii) The maximum strain in concrete at the outermost tension fibre is 0.0035.
    (iii) The relationship between the compressive stress distribution in concrete and the strain in concrete may be assumed to be rectangular, trapezoidal, parabolic or any other shape which results in prediction of strength in substantial agreement with the results of tests.
    Select the correct answer using the codes given below :
    (1) (i) and (iii)   (2) (i), (ii) and (iii)   (3) (ii) and (iii)   (4) (i) and (ii)

123. Given that d = effective depth, b = width and D = overall depth, the maximum area of compression reinforcement in a beam is
    (1) 0.04 bd   (2) 0.04 bD   (3) 0.12 bd   (4) 0.12bD

124. The final deflection due to all loads including the effects of temperature, creep and shrinkage and measured from as cast level of supports of floors, roofs and all other horizontal member should NOT exceed
    (1) span/350   (2) span/300   (3) span/250   (4) span/200

125. A reinforced concrete slab is 75 mm thick. The maximum size of reinforcement bar that can be used is
    (1) 12 mm diameter
    (2) 10 mm diameter
    (3) 8 mm diameter
    (4) 6 mm diameter

126. Earthquake causes horizontal and vertical accelerations in the masonry structure. The magnitude of the forces induced in the structure depend on the :
    (1) age of the building
    (2) strength of mortar
    (3) type of roof
    (4) mass of the structure

127. In the design of two-way slab restrained at all edges torsional reinforcement required is :
    (1) 0.75 times the area of steel provided at midspan in the same direction.
    (2) 0.373 times the area of steel provided at midspan in the same direction.
    (3) 0.375 times the area of steel provided in the shorter span.
    (4) nil

128. At the time of initial tensioning, the maximum tensile stress in tendon immediately behind the anchorage shall NOT exceed
    (1) 50% of the ultimate tensile strength of the wire or bar or strand
    (2) 80% of the ultimate tensile strength of the wire or bar or strand
    (3) 40% of the ultimate tensile strength of the wire or bar or strand
    (4) 60% of the ultimate tensile strength of the wire or bar or stand

129. A square slab 4 m × 4 m is isotropically reinforced at the bottom. If it is subjected to a working load of 12 kPa (including self-weight), the moment capacity required as per yield line theory is
    (1) 6 kN/m/m
    (2) 8 kN/m/m
    (3) 10 kN/m/m
    (4) 12 kN/m/m

130. While designing multistorey in deep, trial structures, BIS code suggests the reduction in live loads because
    (1) all the floors may not be loaded simultaneously.
    (2) cross-section of the columns are different at different floors.
    (3) thickness of roof slab is smaller than the thickness of floor slabs.
    (4) of the cantilevering effect of the building.

131. Shear strength of concrete in a reinforced concrete beam is a function of which of the following :
    (i) Compressive strength of concrete
    (ii) Percentage of shear reinforcement
    (iii) Percentage of longitudinal reinforcement in tension in the section
    (iv) Percentage total longitudinal reinforcement in the section
    Selection the correct answer using the codes given below :
    (1) (i), (ii) and (iv)
    (2) (i), (ii) and (iii)
    (3) only (i) and (iii)
    (4) only (i) and (iv)

132. An axially loaded column is of 300 mm × 300 mm size. Effective length of column is 3 m. What is the minimum eccentricity of the axial load for the column ?
    (1) 0
    (2) 10 mm
    (3) 16 mm
    (4) 20 mm

133. In the case of isolated square concrete footing, match the locations at which the stress resultants are to be checked, where d is effective depth of footing and select the correct answer using the codes given below the lists :

	Stress Resultant		Location
A.	Bending moment	1.	At face of column
B.	One way shear	2.	At d/2 from face of column
C.	Punching shear	3.	At d from face of column

Codes :

	A	B	C
(1)	1	2	3
(2)	3	1	2
(3)	1	1	3
(4)	1	3	2

134. Which of the following deformations are important in case of deep beams when compared to flexure alone ?

(1) Shear   (2) Axial   (3) Torsional   (4) Bearing

135. The maximum depth of neutral axis for a beam with 'd' as the effective depth, in limit state method of design for Fe 415 steel is

(1) 0.46d   (2) 0.48d   (3) 0.50d   (4) 0.53d

136. Deck bridges have the main disadvantage that :

(1) their compression flanges have no lateral support

(2) the traffic is exposed to winds

(3) it is not possible to provide portal bracings

(4) the road level has to be very high

137. If σ_{cbc} is permissible compressive stress in flexural compression in N/mm² in service, the modular ratio is of the order of

(1) $\dfrac{280}{3\sigma_{cbc}}$ (2) $\dfrac{280}{4\sigma_{cbc}}$ (3) 19   (4) 13

138. In a Pedestal, the factor by which the effective length should not exceed the least lateral dimension is

(1) 2   (2) 3   (3) 4   (4) 5

139. The losses in prestress in pre-tensioning stem are due to :

(i) elastic deformation of concrete when wires are tensioned successively

(ii) friction   (iii) shrinkage and creep of concrete

Select the correct answer using the codes given below :

(1) (i), (ii) and (iii)   (2) (ii) and (iii)   (3) (i) alone   (4) (iii) alone

140. A simply supported rectangular beam of span 20.0 m is subjected to UDL. The minimum effective depth required to check deflection of this beam, when modification factor for tension and compression are 0.9 and 1.1 respectively will be :

(1) 2.0 m   (2) 1.8 m   (3) 1.3 m   (4) 1.0 m

141. Prestressing of indeterminate structures should take care of the following :
    (i) High strength concrete   (ii) High tensile steel
    (iii) Load balancing   (iv) Partial safety factors
    Select the correct answer using the codes given below :
    (1) (i) and (iii)   (2) (ii), (iii) and (iv)
    (3) (i), (ii) and (iv)   (4) (i), (ii), (iii) and (iv)

142. For a portal truss column fixed at the base, the point of contra flexure is assumed at :
    (1) a distance mid-way between the base and the foot of the knee brace
    (2) a distance mid-way between the base and top of the column
    (3) the foot of the knee brace
    (4) quarter distance between base and top of the column

143. As the span of a bridge increases, the impact factor :
    (1) decreases
    (2) increases
    (3) remains constant
    (4) increases upto a critical value of span and then decreases

144. A buttress in a wall is intended to provide :
    (1) lateral support to roof slab only   (2) lateral support to wall
    (3) to resist vertical loads only   (4) lateral support to roof beams only

145. Consider the following statements :
    In an under -reinforced concrete beam,
    (i)   actual depth of neutral axis is less than the critical depth of neutral axis.
    (ii) concrete reaches ultimate stress prior to steel reaching the ultimate stress.
    (iii) moment of resistance is less than that of balanced sections.
    (iv) lever arm of resisting couple is less than of balanced sections.
    Which of these statements is/are correct ?
    (1) (i) and (ii)   (2) (i) and (iii)
    (3) (ii), (iii) and (iv)   (4) (i) and (iv)

146. What is the effective height of a free standing masonry wall for the purpose of computing slenderness ratio ?
    (1) 0.5 L   (2) 1.0 L   (3) 2.0 L   (4) 2. 5 L

147. A square column section of size 350 mm × 350 mm is reinforced with four bars of 25 mm diameter and four bars of 16 mm diameter. Then the transverse steel should be
    (1) 5 mm dia @ 240 mm c/c   (2) 6 mm dia @ 250 mm c/c
    (3) 8 mm dia @ 250 mm c/c   (4) 8 mm dia @ 350 mm c/c

148. What shall be the maximum area of reinforcement (i) in compression and (ii) in tension to be provided in an RC beam, respectively, as per
    IS : 456 ?
    (1) 0.08 % and 2%   (2) 2% and 4%   (3) 4% and 2%   (4) 4% and 4%

149. Match List-I with List-II and select the correct answer using the codes given below the lists :

List- I		**List- II**	
A.	$\dfrac{V_0}{bd}$	1.	Modulus of rupture
B.	$0.7\sqrt{f_{ck}}$	2.	Development length
C.	$5000\sqrt{f_{ck}}$	3.	Nominal shear stress
D.	$\dfrac{\phi f_s}{4\tau_b}$	4.	Hook anchorage value
		5.	Modulus of concrete

Codes :

	A	B	C	D
(1)	3	1	5	2
(2)	2	1	4	3
(3)	3	5	1	4
(4)	2	4	1	3

150. Consider the following statements for minimum reinforcement to be provided in a wall as a ratio of vertical reinforcement to gross concrete area :
   (i) 0.0012 for deformed bars.
   (ii) 0.0015 for all other types of bars.
   (iii) 0.0012 for welded wire fabric with wires not larger than 16 mm in diameter.
   Which of these statements is/are correct ?
   (1) (i), (ii) and (iii)   (2) (i) only
   (3) (ii) and (iii) only   (4) (iii) only

151. A simply supported RC beam carries UDL and is referred to as beam A. A similar beam is prestressed and carries the same UDL as the beam A. This beam is referred to as beam B. The mid-span deflection of beam A will be :
   (1) more than that of beam B   (2) less than that of beam B
   (3) the same as that of beam B
   (4) generally less but sometimes more depending upon the magnitude of UDL

152. The critical section for two-way shear of footing is at the :
   (1) face of the column   (2) distance d from the column face
   (3) distance $\dfrac{d}{2}$ from the column face   (4) distance 2d from the column face
   (where d is the effective depth of the footing)

153. The limits of percentage 'p' of the longitudinal reinforcement in a column is :
   (1) 0.15% to 2%   (2) 0.8% to 4%   (3) 0.8% to 6%   (4) 0.8% to 8%

154. While designing combined footing, the resultant of the column loads passes through the centre of gravity of the footing slab such that the net soil pressure obtained is :
   (1) parabolic   (2) trapezoidal
   (3) uniform   (4) non-uniform

155. For shorter storey height, cheaper form work and better lighting facilities, what is the recommended slab floor ?
    (1) T beam and slab
    (2) Two way slab
    (3) Flat slab
    (4) Framed structure

156. What is the assumption in the steel beam theory of doubly reinforced beams ?
    (1) Only steel bars will resist tension
    (2) Only concrete will resist tension
    (3) Stress in tension steel equals the stress in compression steel
    (4) Both concrete and steel will resist compression

157. For ultimate load design of prestressed concrete girders used for bridges, combination of load factors is (where DL and LL are dead and live loads respectively)
    (1) 1.5 DL + 2.5 LL
    (2) 1.0 DL + 2.5 LL
    (3) 1.0 DL + 2.0 LL
    (4) 2.0DL + 2.0LL

158. The maximum strain in concrete at the outermost compression fiber in the limit state design of flexural member is (as per IS : 456-1978)
    (1) 0.0020
    (2) 0.0035
    (3) 0.0065
    (4) 0.0050

159. Deflection can be controlled by using the appropriate :
    (1) aspect ratio
    (2) modular ratio
    (3) span/depth ratio
    (4) water/cement ratio

160. In limit state approach, spacing of main reinforcement controls primarily :
    (1) collapse
    (2) cracking
    (3) deflection
    (4) durability

161. For the section of the beam shown in the given figure, span of the beam = 6.0 m, concrete = M 20, steel = Fe 415.

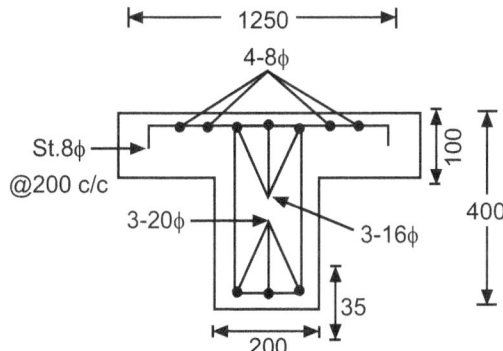

    If the section is checked for serviceability limit state of deflection, then it will be found that
    (1) the section is unsafe
    (2) the section needs revision
    (3) the section is safe
    (4) it cannot be judged from the given data

162. Unequal top and bottom reinforcement in a reinforced concrete section leads to :
    (1) creep deflection
    (2) shrinkage deflection
    (3) long-term deflection
    (4) large deflection

163. Temperature and shrinkage steel is provided in reinforced concrete slabs because :
   (1) it occupies larger area
   (2) its thickness is less
   (3) it is a main structural element
   (4) it is a flexural member

164. Match List-I (Reinforcement type) with List-II (Anchorage requirement) and select the correct answer by using the codes given below the lists :

List – I		List – II	
A.	Footing slab, tensile reinforcement	1.	$\frac{L_d}{3}$ into the support
B.	Cantilever beam, tensile reinforcement	2.	6ϕ for $135°$ bend
C.	Simply supported beam, tensile reinforcement	3.	L_d into the support
D.	Beam, shear stirrup	4.	L_d from the column face

   Codes :

	A	B	C	D
(1)	1	3	4	2
(2)	1	2	4	3
(3)	4	3	1	2
(4)	4	2	1	3

165. Minimum shear reinforcement in beams is provided in the form of stirrups :
   (1) to resist extra shear force due to live load
   (2) to resist the effect of shrinkage of concrete
   (3) to resist principal tension
   (4) to resist shear cracks at the bottom of beam

166. Diagonal tension reinforcement is provided in a beam as :
   (1) longitudinal bars
   (2) bent up bars
   (3) helical reinforcement
   (4) 90° bend at the bends of main bars

167. In a combined footing for two columns carrying unequal loads, the maximum hogging moment occurs at :
   (1) inside face of the heavier column
   (2) a section equidistant from both the columns
   (3) a section having maximum shear force
   (4) a section having zero shear force

168. The critical section for computing design shear force in an RC beam where the supports exert a compressive reaction is at :
   (1) the centre of support
   (2) the face of support
   (3) a distance of half of effective depth from the face support
   (4) a distance of effective depth from the face of support

169. Doubly reinforced beams are recommended when :
   (1) the depth of the beam is restricted
   (2) the breadth of the beam is restricted
   (3) both depth and breadth are restricted
   (4) the shear is high

170. In a reinforced concrete member, the best way to ensure adequate bond is
    (1) to provide minimum number of large diameter bars
    (2) to provide large number of smaller diameter bars
    (3) to increase the cover for reinforcement
    (4) to provide additional stirrups

171. Match List-I with List-II and select the correct answer by using the codes given below the lists :

	List – I		List – II
A.	Serviceability	1.	Sliding
B.	Shear key	2.	Deflection
C.	Shrinkage	3.	Cracking
D.	Concrete spalling	4.	Corrosion

Codes :

	A	B	C	D
(1)	1	3	4	2
(2)	2	1	3	4
(3)	1	3	2	4
(4)	2	1	4	3

172. The characteristic strength of concrete is :
    (1) higher than the average cube strength
    (2) lower than the average cube strength
    (3) the same as the average cube strength
    (4) higher than 90% of the average cube strength

173. What is the value of minimum reinforcement (in case of Fe 415) in a slab?
    (1) 0.1%   (2) 0.12%
    (3) 0.15%   (4) 0.2%

174. Match List-I (Condition of support) with List - II (Effective length of load bearing wall) and select the correct answer using the codes given below the lists (L = the length of wall between centers of piers, buttresses or cross walls)

	List- I		List- II
A.	Wall is continuous and supported by cross walls or buttresses and there is no opening within one eighth of the wall height	1.	2.0L
B.	Wall is supported by a buttress or cross wall at one end and continues with buttress or cross wall supported at other end.	2.	0.8L
C.	Wall is supported at each end by a buttress or a cross wall	3.	0.9L
D.	Wall is free at one end and supported by a buttress or cross wall at the other end	4.	1.0L

Codes :

	A	B	C	D
(1)	3	2	1	4
(2)	2	3	4	1
(3)	3	2	4	1
(4)	2	3	1	4

175. A brick masonry wall of nominal thickness 200 mm carries an axial load of 26 kN/m and another load of 19 kN/m acting at an eccentricity of 45 mm. The resultant eccentricity and eccentricity ratio are respectively :

    (1) 19 mm, 0.095   (2) 19 mm, 01   (3) 22 mm, 0.11   (4) 24 mm, 0.12

176. A T-beam roof section has the following particulars :

Thickness of slab	:	100 mm
Width of rib	:	300 mm
Depth of beam	:	500 mm
Centre to centre distance of beams	:	3.0 m
Effective span of beams	:	6.0 m
Distance between points of contraflexure	:	3.60 m

The effective width of flange of the beam is :

    (1) 3000 mm   (2) 1900 mm   (3) 1600 mm   (4) 1500 mm

177. Minimum tension steel in RC beam needs to be provided to :

    (1) prevent sudden failure   (2) arrest crack width

    (3) control excessive deflection   (4) prevent surface hair cracks

178. Consider the following statements :

    (i) The limit state of collapse is defined as the acceptable limit for the stresses in the materials.

    (ii) Limit state method is one that ensures adequate safety of structure against collapse.

    (iii) In the limit state design method, actual stresses developed at collapse differ considerably from the theoretical values

Which of these statements is/are correct ?

    (1) (i) and (ii)   (2) (i) and (iii)   (3) (ii) and (iii)   (4) None

179. From consideration of earthquake loading and lateral stability of tall building, which of the following measures are taken ?

    (i) Minimize gravity loads

    (ii) Add masses at floor levels

    (iii) Ensure ductility at the locations of maximum moments.

    (iv) Provide shear walls   (v) Provide stilt (ground) storey

Select the correct answer using the codes given below :

    (1) (i) and (v)   (2) (ii), (iii) and (v)

    (3) (i), (iii) and (iv)   (4) (ii), (iii) and (iv)

180. A reinforced concrete rectangular slab is built-in (fixed) on three edges and the other edge is free. The possible yield line patterns for the slab subjected to a uniformly distributed load and reinforced isotropically are shown below as (i), (ii), (iii) and (iv).

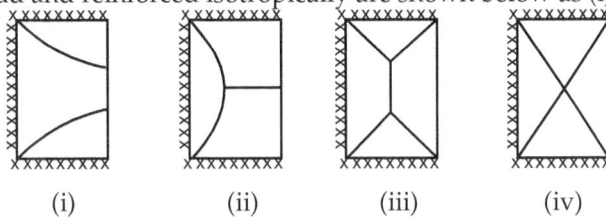

       (i)   (ii)   (iii)   (iv)

Which of these correctly exhibits the yield line pattern ?

(1) (i) or (iii)   (2) (ii) or (iii)   (3) (i) or (ii)   (4) (iii) or (iv)

181. A reinforced concrete beam is subjected to the following bending moments :

Dead load - 20 kN-m

Live load - 30 kN-m

Seismic load - 10 kN-m

The design bending moment for limit state of collapse is :

(1) 60 kN-m   (2) 75 kN-m   (3) 72 kN-m   (4) 80 kN-m

182. In the limit state design of prestressed concrete structures, the strain distribution is assumed to be

(1) linear   (2) non-linear

(3) parabolic   (4) parabolic and rectangular

183. Consider the following statements

Under -reinforced concrete flexural members

(i) are deeper   (ii) are stiffer   (iii) can undergo larger deflection

Which of these statements is/are correct ?

(1) (i), (ii) and (iii)   (2) (i) and (ii)   (3) (ii) only   (4) (i) and (iii)

184. Long term elastic modulus in terms of creep coefficient (θ) and 28-day characteristic strength (f_{ck}) is given by)

(1) $\dfrac{5000\sqrt{f_{ck}}}{1+\theta}$ MPa   (2) $\dfrac{50000\sqrt{f_{ck}}}{1+\theta}$ MPa

(3) $\dfrac{5000 f_{ck}}{1+\sqrt{\theta}}$ MPa   (4) $\dfrac{5000\sqrt{f_{ck}}}{\sqrt{1+\theta}}$ MPa

185. Minimum shear reinforcement is provided to :

(1) resist shear force at the support.

(2) resist shear on account of accidental torsion.

(3) arrest the longitudinal cracks on side faces due to shrinkage and temperature variation.

(4) resist shear in concrete developing on account of non-homogeneity of concrete.

186. In a cantilever beam carrying gravity load, main reinforcement is provided

(1) above the neutral axis   (2) as vertical stirrups

(3) as a helical reinforcement   (4) below the neutral axis

187. Match List-I (Beam variable) with List-II (Design provision) and select the correct answer by using the codes given below the lists :

	List – I		List – II
A.	Flexure	1.	Minimum depth of section
B.	Shear	2.	Longitudinal steel reinforcement
C.	Bond	3.	Stirrups
D.	Deflection	4.	Anchorage in support

Codes :

	A	B	C	D
(1)	3	2	1	1
(2)	2	3	1	4
(3)	3	2	4	1
(4)	2	3	4	1

188. Which one of the following sections performs better on the ductility criterion ?
(1) Balanced section
(2) Over-reinforced section
(3) Under-reinforced section
(4) Non-prismatic section

189. A beam of rectangular cross-section (b × d) is subjected to a torque T. What is the maximum torsional stress induced in the beam (b < d and α is a constant) ?

(1) $\dfrac{T}{\alpha b^2 d}$　　　　(2) $\dfrac{T}{\alpha b d^2}$　　　　(3) $\dfrac{T}{\alpha b d}$　　　　(4) $\dfrac{T}{bd}$

190. Match List-I (Codal Parameter) with List-II (Structural Member) and select the correct answer by using the codes given below the lists :

	List – I		List – II
A.	0.04 bD	1.	Column
B.	$250\,b^2/d$	2.	Cantilever
C.	$100\,b^2/d$	3.	Continuous beam
D.	$(k_x I_x)/D_x$	4.	Beam

Codes :

	A	B	C	D
(1)	4	1	2	3
(2)	2	3	4	1
(3)	4	3	2	1
(4)	2	1	4	3

191. For a bridge-deck the most economical section shall be :
(1) a double-tee section
(2) an I-section
(3) a box section
(4) a channel section

192. What is the value of flexural strength of M 25 concrete ?
(1) 4.0 MPa　　　　(2) 3.5 MPa　　　　(3) 3.0 MPa　　　　(4) 1.75 MPa

193. Consider the following statements with regard to crack formation and its control.
    (i) The surface width of the crack should not, in general, exceed 0.30 mm for structures not subjected to aggressive environment.
    (ii) When depth of web in a beam exceeds 750 mm, side face reinforcement @ 0.1 percent of web area should be provided on each face.
    (iii) The nominal spacing of main bars in a slab should not exceed three times the effective depth of a solid slab or 300 mm, whichever is smaller.
    Which of these statements is/are correct ?
    (1) (i) only   (2) (i) and (ii)   (3) (i) and (iii)   (4) (ii) and (iii)

194. Which of the following should be employed to provide lateral support to the beams ?
    (i) Bracing of compression flanges
    (ii) Shear connectors
    (iii) Bracing of tension flanges.
    (iv) Embedding compression flanges into RCC slab.
    Select the correct answer using the code given below :
    (1) (i) only   (2) (i) and (iv)
    (3) (ii) and (iii)   (4) (i), (ii) and (iv)

195. On which one of the following concepts is the basic principle of structural design based ?
    (1) Weak column and strong beam   (2) Strong column and weak beam
    (3) Equally strong column-beam   (4) Partial weak column-beam

196. What is the number of categories into which masonry buildings are divided on the basis of earthquake resistant features ?
    (1) Five   (2) Four   (3) Three   (4) Two

197. When is a masonry wall known as a shear wall ?
    (1) If the earthquake load is out of plane.   (2) If the earthquake load is in-plane.
    (3) If it is unreinforced.   (4) If it is placed as in fill to the frame.

198. Which of the following measures are resorted to for strengthening masonry wall ?
    (i) Provide cross walls   (ii) Prestressing
    (iii) Provide unit slab on the surface (s) of walls.
    (iv) Provide buttresses
    Select the correct answer using the codes given below :
    (1) (i), (iii) and (iv)   (2) (i) and (ii)
    (3) (ii) and (iii)   (4) (i), (ii), (iii) and (iv)

199. Drop panel is a structural component in
    (1) Grid floor   (2) Flat plate
    (3) Flat slab   (4) Slab beam system of floor

200. What is the minimum number of longitudinal bars provided in a reinforced concrete column of circular cross-section ?
    (1) 4   (2) 5   (3) 6   (4) 8

201. Consider the following statements :

The main reinforcement in the counterfort retaining wall of RCC is provided on the

(i)   inclined face in front counterfort   (ii)   bottom face in back counterfort

(iii) inclined face in back counterfort   (iv) bottom face in front counterfort

Select the correct answer using the codes given below

(1) (i) and (ii)   (2) (ii) and (iii)

(3) (iii) and (iv)   (4) (ii) and (iv)

202. A doubly reinforced concrete beam has effective cover d' to the centre of compression reinforcement, 'x_u' is the depth of neutral axis, and 'd' is the effective depth to the centre of tension reinforcement. What is the maximum strain in concrete at the level of compression reinforcement ?

(1) $0.0035 (1 - d'/d)$ (2) $0.0035 (1 - d'/x_u)$

(3) $0.002 (1 - d'/x_u)$ (4) $0.002 (1 - d'/d)$

203. A prestressed concrete beam of cross-sectional area A, moment of inertia 'I', distance of top extreme fibre from neutral axis 'y' and distance of bottom extreme fibre from neutral axis 'y_b' is subjected to a prestressing force such that stress at top fibre is zero. What is the value of eccentricity ('r' is radius of gyration)?

(1) A/y_b (2) r^2/y_b (3) r^2/y_t (4) ry_b/y_t

204. The net effect of vertical and lateral forces acting on a masonry wall can be expressed as vertical load 'p'/unit length acting at an effective eccentricity 'e'. If e $>$ (t/6), tension develops in the wall. Ignoring the part of thickness 't' in tension, what is the compressive stress in extreme fibre ?

(1) $p/\{(t/2) - e\}$ (2) $[2p/3\{(t/2) - e\}]$

(3) $[p/3\{(t/2) - e\}]$ (4) $[p/6\{(t/2) - e\}]$

205. Which one of the following is not a factor affecting strength of a brick masonry wall ?

(1) Size and location of door in a wall

(2) Positioning of cross walls

(3) Type of roof the wall bears and its connection.

(4) Type of plastering on the wall

206. As per IS 456-2000, which one of the following correctly expresses the modulus of elasticity of concrete ? (read with the relevant units)

(1) $E_c = 0.7\sqrt{f_{ck}}$ (2) $E_c = 500\sqrt{f_{ck}}$

(3) $E_c = 5000\sqrt{f_{ck}}$ (4) $E_c = 5700\sqrt{f_{ck}}$

207. Characteristic strength of M20 concrete is 20 MPa. What is the number of cubes having 28 days' compressive strength greater than 20 MPa out of 100 cubes made with this concrete?

(1) All   (2) 95   (3) 80   (4) 50

208. The distance between theoretical cut-off point and actual cut-off point in respect of the curtailment of reinforcement of reinforced concrete beams should not be less than :
   (1) Development length
   (2) 12 × diameter of bar or effective depth whichever is greater
   (3) 24 × diameter of bar or effective depth whichever is greater
   (4) 30 × diameter of bar or effective depth whichever is greater

209. The maximum strain in the tension reinforcement in the section at failure when designed for the limit state of collapse should be :
   (1) as a rectangular one throughout its span
   (2) as a tee-beam throughout its span
   (3) as a rectangular beam for span moments and tee-beam for support moments
   (4) as a tee-beam for span moments and as a rectangular beam for support moments

210. The reinforcement for tension, when required in members, shall consist of :
   (1) only longitudinal reinforcement in the tension face
   (2) only longitudinal reinforcement in the compression face
   (3) only two legged closed loops enclosing the corner reinforcement
   (4) both longitudinal and transverse reinforcement

211. The codal provisions recommend minimum shear reinforcement in the form of stirrups in the beams :
   (i) to cater for any torsion in the beam section
   (ii) to improve ductility of the cross section
   (iii) to improve dowel action of longitudinal tension bars
   Select the correct answer using the codes given below :
   (1) (i), (ii) and (iii)   (2) (ii) and (iii)   (3) Only (i)   (4) Only (ii)

212. A trapezoidal combined footing for two axially loaded columns is provided when :
   (i) Width of the footing near the heavier column is restricted.
   (ii) Length of the footing is restricted
   (iii) Projections of the footing beyond the heavier column are restricted.
   Select the correct answer using the codes given below :
   (1) (i) and (ii)   (2) (i) and (iii)
   (3) (ii) and (iii)   (4) (i), (ii) and (iii)

213. In case of two-way slab, the deflection of the slab is :
   (1) primarily a function of the long span
   (2) primarily a function of the short span
   (3) independent of the span, long or short
   (4) mostly long span but sometimes short span

214. A rectangular reinforced concrete footing is to be designed to support a column which transfers axial load and uniaxial moment to the footing as shown in the figure. The footing is to be designed to have uniform upward soil pressure. The dimensions L_1 and L_2 $(L = L_1 + L_2)$ of the footing would be :

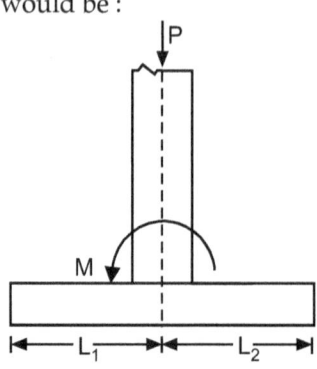

    (1) $L_1 = L_2$ (2) $L_1 > L_2$ (3) $L_1 < L_2$ (4) $L_1 = \dfrac{1}{2} L_2$

215. A reinforced concrete beam of 10 m effective span and 1 m effective depth is supported on 500 mm × 500 mm columns. If the total uniformly distributed load on the beam is MN/m, the design shear force for the beam is

    (1) 50 MN   (2) 47.5 MN

    (3) 37.5 MN   (4) 43 MN

216. A beam is designed for uniformly distributed loads causing compression in the supporting columns. Where is the critical section for shear ? (d is effective depth of beam and L_d is development length)

    (1) At distance $L_d/3$ from the face of the support.

    (2) At distance d from the face of the support.

    (3) At the centre of the support.

    (4) At the mid span of the beam.

217. As per codal provisions in two way slabs, the minimum mild steel reinforcement to be provided in the edge strip is :

    (1) On the basis of minimum bending moment.

    (2) Half of the area of steel provided in middle strip in the shorter span.

    (3) Half of the area of steel provided in middle strip in the longer span.

    (4) 0.15% of the cross-sectional area of concrete.

218. An RC structural member rectangular in cross section of width b and depth D is subjected to a combined action of bending moment M and torsional moment T. The longitudinal reinforcement shall be designed for a moment M_e given by :

    (1) $M_e = M + \dfrac{T(1 - D/b)}{1.7}$ (2) $M_e = M + \dfrac{T(1 - D/b)}{1.7}$

    (3) $M_e = M + \dfrac{T(1 + D/b)}{1.7}$ (4) $M_e = \dfrac{T(1 - b/D)}{1.7}$

219. A T-beam roof section has the following particulars :

    Thickness of slab   : 100 mm
    Width of rib   : 300 mm
    Depth of beam   : 500 mm
    Centre to centre distance of beams   : 3.0m
    Effective span of beams   : 6.0 m
    Distance between points of contraflexure   : 3.6 m

    What is the effective flange width of the T-beam ?
    (1) 3000 mm   (2) 1900 mm   (3) 1600 mm   (4) 1500 mm

220. A T-beam behaves as a rectangular beam of width equal to its flange if its neutral axis :
    (1) coincides with centroid of reinforcement
    (2) coincides with centroid of reinforcement.
    (3) remains within the flange
    (4) remains in the web

221. The profile of the centroid of the tendon is parabolic with a central dip h. Effective prestressing force is P and the span L. What is the equivalent upward acting uniform load ?

    (1) $\dfrac{8hL}{P}$ (2) $\dfrac{8hp}{L^2}$ (3) $\dfrac{8h^2L}{P}$ (4) $\dfrac{8h^2P}{L}$

222. What is the uplift at centre on release of wires from anchors due to pretensioning only for force P and eccentricity e for a pretensioned rectangular plank ?

    (1) $\dfrac{PeL^2}{6EI}$ (2) $\dfrac{Pe^2L}{6EI}$ (3) $\dfrac{PeL^2}{8EI}$ (4) $\dfrac{Pe^2L}{8EI}$

223. An ordinary mild steel bar has been prestressed to a working stress of 200 MPa. Young's modulus of steel is 200 GPa. Permanent negative strain due to shrinkage and creep is 0.0008. How much is the effective stress left in steel ?
    (1) 184 MPa   (2) 160 MPa   (3) 40 MPa   (4) 16 MPa

224. For the purpose of design as per IS:456, deflection of RC slab or beam is limited to :
    (1) 0.2% of span   (2) 0.25% of span   (3) 0.4% of span   (4) 0.45% of span

225. As per IS : 456, side face reinforcement, not less than 0.05% of web area, is provided on each side when the depth of web is not less than :
    (1) 300 mm   (2) 400 mm   (3) 500 mm   (4) 750 mm

226. Consider the following types of bridges :
    (i) Arch bridge   (ii) Double cantilever bridge
    (iii) Suspension bridge   (iv) Truss bridge

    What is the correct sequence in the ascending order of the span ranges, generally adopted for the bridges given above ?
    (1) (ii), (iv), (i), (iii)   (2) (i), (iii), (ii), (iv)
    (3) (ii), (iii), (i), (iv)   (4) (i), (iv), (ii), (iii)

ANSWER KEY

1. (1)	2. (3)	3. (1)	4. (4)	5. (4)	6. (1)	7. (2)	8. (3)
9. (4)	10. (3)	11. (2)	12. (4)	13. (2)	14. (4)	15. (2)	16. (1)
17. (4)	18. (3)	19. (3)	20. (4)	21. (1)	22. (2)	23. (2)	24. (3)
25. (2)	26. (1)	27. (3)	28. (1)	29. (1)	30. (3)	31. (4)	32. (2)
33. (4)	34. (1)	35. (2)	36. (4)	37. (3)	38. (4)	39. (2)	40. (3)
41. (1)	42. (4)	43. (3)	44. (3)	45. (1)	46. (3)	47. (3)	48. (3)
49. (2)	50. (2)	51. (2)	52. (3)	53. (3)	54. (3)	55. (4)	56. (4)
57. (2)	58. (2)	59. (3)	60. (2)	61. (4)	62. (1)	63. (1)	64. (4)
65. (3)	66. (1)	67. (1)	68. (2)	69. (1)	70. (4)	71. (2)	72. (4)
73. (4)	74. (3)	75. (4)	76. (2)	77. (1)	78. (3)	79. (3)	80. (1)
81. (3)	82. (1)	83. (3)	84. (1)	85. (1)	86. (4)	87. (2)	88. (2)
89. (2)	90. (3)	91. (1)	92. (2)	93. (3)	94. (2)	95. (1)	96. (1)
97. (3)	98. (4)	99. (2)	100. (1)	101. (4)	102. (1)	103. (4)	104. (3)
105. (4)	106. (2)	107. (1)	108. (1)	109. (3)	110. (3)	111. (3)	112. (2)
113. (4)	114. (1)	115. (2)	116. (3)	117. (4)	118. (3)	119. (2)	120. (3)
121. (3)	122. (1)	123. (2)	124. (3)	125. (3)	126. (4)	127. (1)	128. (2)
129. (4)	130. (1)	131. (3)	132. (4)	133. (4)	134. (1)	135. (2)	136. (4)
137. (1)	138. (2)	139. (4)	140. (1)	141. (3)	142. (1)	143. (1)	144. (2)
145. (2)	146. (3)	147. (3)	148. (4)	149. (1)	150. (1)	151. (1)	152. (3)
153. (3)	154. (3)	155. (3)	156. (3)	157. (4)	158. (2)	159. (3)	160. (2)
161. (4)	162. (2)	163. (1)	164. (3)	165. (3)	166. (2)	167. (4)	168. (4)
169. (1)	170. (2)	171. (2)	172. (2)	173. (2)	174. (2)	175. (1)	176. (4)
177. (1)	178. (3)	179. (3)	180. (3)	181. (2)	182. (1)	183. (1)	184. (1)
185. (3)	186. (1)	187. (4)	188. (3)	189. (1)	190. (3)	191. (3)	192. (2)
193. (3)	194. (4)	195. (2)	196. (1)	197. (2)	198. (1)	199. (3)	200. (3)
201. (3)	202. (2)	203. (3)	204. (2)	205. (4)	206. (3)	207. (2)	208. (2)
209. (3)	210. (4)	211. (2)	212. (3)	213. (2)	214. (2)	215. (3)	216. (2)
217. (4)	218. (1)	219. (4)	220. (3)	221. (2)	222. (3)	223. (3)	224. (3)
225. (4)	226. (4)						

1. Which one of the following sections is the most efficient for a simply supported gantry girder ?
   (1) I-section with equal flanges
   (2) I-section with a channel attached to the top flange
   (3) I- section with a wide bottom flange.
   (4) I- section with a heavy plate connected to the bottom flange.

2. Intermediate vertical stiffeners are provided in plate girders to .....
   (1) eliminate web buckling
   (2) eliminate local buckling
   (3) transfer concentrated loads
   (4) prevent excessive deflection

3. When the distance between centers of two adjacent rivets connecting the members subjected to either compression or tension exceeds the maximum pitch, then the additional rivets which are not subjected to the calculated stresses are known as .....
   (1) Packing rivets
   (2) Long-grip rivets
   (3) Tacking rivets
   (4) Auxiliary rivets

4. M is the moment due to a couple in a bearing plate whose width is b and allowable bending stress is P. The thickness (t) of the bending plate of the column splice is
   (1) $t = \sqrt{\dfrac{b \times P}{6M}}$
   (2) $t = \sqrt{\dfrac{6M}{b \times P}}$
   (3) $t = \dfrac{6M}{bP}$
   (4) $t = \sqrt{\dfrac{6M}{b \times P}}$

5. In a grillage column footing maximum bending moment M occurs at the centre of grillage beams. Its value is
   (1) $M = P (L - a)$
   (2) $M = \dfrac{P}{4} (L + a)$
   (3) $M = \dfrac{P}{8} (L - a)$
   (4) $M = \dfrac{P}{3} (L + a)$

6. In a tension member if one or more than one rivet holes are off the line, the failure of the member depends upon
   (1) pitch
   (2) gauge
   (3) diameter of the rivet hole
   (4) all the above

7. In a steel plate girder, the web plate is connected to the flange plates by fillet welding. The size of fillet welds is designed to safely resist
   (1) the bending stresses in the flanges
   (2) the vertical shear force at the section
   (3) the horizontal shear forces between the flanges and the web plate
   (4) the forces causing buckling in the web.

8. What is the distance away from midspan of a plastic hinge if developing in a simply supported beam of rectangular cross-section and span 6 m, subjected to a point load at the centre ?
   (1) zero
   (2) 1 m
   (3) 2 m
   (4) 3 m

9. When designing steel structures, one must ensure that local buckling in webs does not take place. This check may not be very critical when using rolled steel sections because
   (1) quality control at the time of manufacture of rolled sections is very good.
   (2) web depths available are small.
   (3) web stiffeners are in built in rolled sections.
   (4) depth to thickness ratio (of the web) is appropriately adjusted.

10. A cantilever arm is to be attached to a column. Which one among the following is the best connection ?
    (1) Framed connection
    (2) Stiffened connection
    (3) Seated connection
    (4) End plate connection

11. In a situation where torsion is dominant, which one of the following is the desirable section ?
    (1) Angle section
    (2) Channel section
    (3) I-section
    (4) Box type section

12. What is the maximum slenderness ratio permitted as per IS : 800-1984 for design of a tie member subjected to reversal of stress due to earthquake ?
    (1) 180
    (2) 250
    (3) 300
    (4) 350

13. The area A_P of cover plates in one flange of a built up beam, is given by
    (1) $A_P = \dfrac{Z_{reqd} + Z_{beam}}{h}$
    (2) $A_P = \dfrac{Z_{reqd} / Z_{beam}}{h}$
    (3) $A_P = \dfrac{Z_{reqd} \times Z_{beam}}{h}$
    (4) $A_P = \dfrac{Z_{reqd} - Z_{beam}}{h}$

14. Match List - I (Use) with List - II (Type of Weld) and select the correct answer using the codes given below the lists.

	List – I		List – II
A.	Structural member subjected to direct tension or compression	1.	Slot weld
B.	Joining two surfaces approximately at right angles to each other	2.	Seam weld
C.	A hole is made in one of the components and welding is done around the periphery of the hole	3.	Fillet weld
D.	Pressure is applied continuously	4.	Plug weld
		5.	Butt weld

    Codes :

	A	B	C	D
(1)	5	4	1	3
(2)	4	3	2	1
(3)	5	3	1	2
(4)	4	5	3	2

15. Match List - I (Type of stress) with List - II (Allowable value of stress) and select the correct answer using the codes given below the lists.

List – I		List – II	
A.	Axial tension	1.	$0.75 F_y$
B.	Bending tension	2.	$0.66 F_y$
C.	Maximum shear stress	3.	$0.60 F_y$
D.	Bearing stress	4.	$0.40 F_y$

(F = Minimum yield stress of steel)

Codes :

	A	B	C	D
(1)	2	3	1	4
(2)	3	2	4	1
(3)	2	3	4	1
(4)	3	2	1	4

16. A structural member subjected to tensile force in a direction parallel to its longitudinal axis is generally known is
    (1) a tie
    (2) a tie member
    (3) a tension member
    (4) all the above

17. When the length of a tension member is too long,
    (1) a wire robe is used
    (2) a rod is used
    (3) a bar is used
    (4) a single angle is used

18. For two plates of equal thickness, full strength of square-edged fillet weld can be ensured if its maximum size is limited to .....
    (1) 1.5 mm less than the plate thickness
    (2) 67% of the plate thickness
    (3) 80% of the plate thickness
    (4) thickness of the plate

19. For the welded joint shown in the figure, the direct vertical shear stress on the weld is 40 MPa and the bending stress is 120 MPa. For what strength should the weld be designed ?

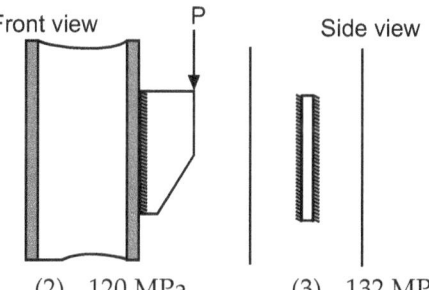

    (1) 80 MPa   (2) 120 MPa   (3) 132 MPa   (4) 160 MPa

20. An ISMB 500 is used as a beam in a multistorey construction. From the viewpoint of structural design, it can be considered to be 'laterally restrained' when
    (1) the tension flange is laterally restrained.
    (2) the compression flange is laterally restrained.
    (3) the web is adequately stiffened.
    (4) the conditions in both (1) and (3) are met.

21. Which of the following statements are correct in respect of welded connections ?
    (a) Strength of Butt weld is equal to the strength of components joined.
    (b) Fillet welds carry the loads computed based on the tensile strength characteristic of fusion material.
    (c) For effective transmission of load by fillet weld, the fusion faces shall subtend an angle between 60° and 120°.
    (1) (a), (b) and (c)   (2) (a) and (b) only
    (3) (b) and (c) only   (4) (a) and (c) only

22. At a certain location of a plate girder of web size 1000 mm × 10 mm, a pair of bearing stiffeners 100 mm × 5 mm is welded. The effective area of bearing stiffeners is .....
    (1) 1000 mm²   (2) 2000 mm²   (3) 3000 mm²   (4) 5000 mm²

23. For an I beam, the shape factor is 1.12. If the allowable stress (with factor of safety in bending as 1.5) is increased by 20% for wind and earthquake loads, the modified load factor is
    (1) 1.10   (2) 1.25   (3) 1.35   (4) 1.40

24. A group of rivets at a joint is subjected to in plane torsion moment M. The rivets have finished areas of cross-section A_i (i = 1, 2 ... n) and distances r_i (i = 1, 2 ..... n) from CG of the rivet group as shown in figure. The shear force developed in i^{th} rivet is proportional to
    (1) area of cross-section A only.
    (2) distance from CG of group, r_i only.
    (3) both A_i and r_i.
    (4) polar moment of inertia of group of area A_i.

25. Rivet value is defined as
    (1) lesser of the bearing strength of rivet and the shearing strength of the rivet.
    (2) lesser of the bearing strength of rivet and the tearing strength of thinner plate.
    (3) greater of the bearing strength of rivet and the shearing of the rivet.
    (4) lesser of the shearing strength of the rivet and the tearing strength of thinner plate.

26. A welded plate girder, consisting of two flange plates of 350 mm × 16 mm each and a web plate of 1000 mm × 6 mm, requires .....
    (1) no stiffeners   (2) horizontal stiffeners
    (3) intermediate vertical stiffeners   (4) vertical and horizontal stiffeners

27. **Assertion (A) :** In a plate girder of uniform cross-section, intermediate vertical stiffeners are provided at closer spacing in the middle rather than at supports.
    Reason (R) : Intermediate vertical stiffeners are provided to prevent the web from buckling under a complex and variable stress situation resulting from combined action of shear force and bending moment.
    (1) Both A and R are true and R is the correct explanation of A.
    (2) Both A and R are true, but R is not a correct explanation of A.
    (3) A is true, but R is false.   (4) A is false, but R is true.

28. A fillet-welded joint is shown in the figure. The size of the weld is 8 mm. Safe stress in the weld is 110 N/mm². What is the safe force (to the nearest magnitude) to which the weld can be subjected ?

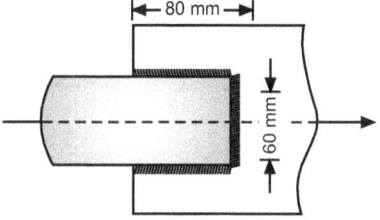

   (1) 125 kN   (2) 130 kN   (3) 140 kN   (4) 135 kN

29. The maximum longitudinal pitch allowed in bolted joints of tension members is .....
   (1) 16 times the diameter of the bolt   (2) 32 times the diameter of the bolt
   (3) 16 times the thickness of the plate   (4) 32 times the thickness of the plate

30. A tension member, if subjected to possible reversal of stress due to wind or earth quake, the slenderness ratio of the member should not exceed
   (1) 180   (2) 300   (3) 250   (4) 350

31. In case of single angles in tension connected by one leg only, the next effective area as per IS : 800 is ....
   (1) Gross area – Area of holes   (2) $a + \dfrac{b}{1 + 0.33\,(b/a)}$
   (3) $a + \dfrac{b}{1 + 0.2\,(b/a)}$ (4) $a + \dfrac{b}{1 + 0.35\,(b/a)}$

32. Efficiency of a riveted joint having the minimum pitch is
   (1) 40%   (2) 50%   (3) 60%   (4) 70%

33. As per IS : 800, the thickness of slab base is given by.........
   (1) $\dfrac{3W}{F_b}\left[A^2 - \dfrac{B^2}{4}\right]$ (2) $\sqrt{\dfrac{3W}{F_b}\left(A^2 - \dfrac{B^2}{4}\right)}$
   (3) $\sqrt{\dfrac{3W}{F_b}\left(A^2 - \dfrac{B^2}{2}\right)}$ (4) $\sqrt{\dfrac{W}{3F_b}\left(A^2 - \dfrac{B^2}{4}\right)}$

   where A and B are larger and smaller projections respectively of plate beyond column, W is the pressure on the under side of base and F_b is permissible bending stress in slab bases.

34. An equal angle of area A has been attached to the support by means of a lug angle. If allowable stress in tension is f, what is the load carrying capacity of the member ?
   (1) 0.5 fA   (2) 0.85 fA   (3) 0.9 fA   (4) 1.0 fA

35. The common assumption that 'All rivets share equally a non-eccentric load' is valid at a load
   (1) below the working load   (2) equal to the working load
   (3) above the working load   (4) equal to failure load

36. The shape factor for a solid circular section of diameter D is equal to
   (1) $\dfrac{D}{2\pi}$ (2) $\dfrac{15}{2\pi}$ (3) $\dfrac{16}{3\pi}$ (4) $\dfrac{\pi D}{8}$

37. The slenderness ratio in tension member as per BIS code where reversal of stress is due to loads other than wind or seismic shall not exceed
    (1) 350   (2) 180   (3) 100   (4) 60

38. A mild steel flat subjected to a tensile force of 840 kN is connected to a gusset plate using rivets. If the permissible forces required per pitch length (i) to shear a single rivet, (ii) to crush the rivet and (iii) to tear the plate are 50 kN, 80 kN and 60 kN respectively, then the number of rivets required is .....
    (1) 12   (2) 14   (3) 16   (4) 17

39. According to IS : 875 Part 3, design wind speed is obtained by multiplying the basic wind speed by factors k_1, k_2 and k_3, where k_3 is .....
    (1) terrain height factor   (2) structure size factor
    (3) topography factor   (4) risk coefficient

40. In the simple system shown in the figure, the load P is equal to 4 tones. What is the tension in the cable.
    (1) 4 t   (2) 5 t
    (3) 6 t   (4) 7 t

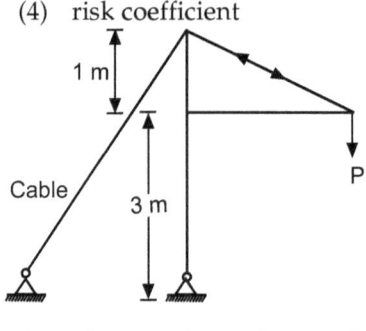

41. Match List - I with List - II and select the correct answer using the codes given below the lists.

	List – I		List – II
A.	Upper bound theorem	1.	Undeformed state
B.	Lower bound theorem	2.	Large rotation
C.	Equilibrium of forces	3.	Statical method
D.	Ductility of the material	4.	Mechanism method

    Codes :

	A	B	C	D
(1)	2	1	3	4
(2)	4	1	3	2
(3)	2	3	1	4
(4)	4	3	1	2

42. A propped cantilever beam shown in the figure has a plastic moment capacity of M_0.

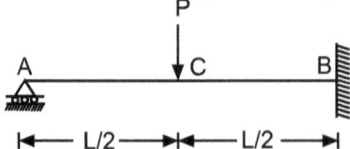

    The collapse load is
    (1) $\dfrac{4M_0}{L}$ (2) $\dfrac{6M_0}{L}$ (3) $\dfrac{8M_0}{L}$ (4) $\dfrac{12M_0}{L}$

43. Permissible bending tensile stress in high yield strength deformed bars of grade 415 in a beam is
    (1) 190 N/mm²   (2) 230 N/mm²   (3) 140 N/mm²   (4) None of these

44. A moment M of magnitude 50 kN-m is transmitted to a column flange through a bracket by using four 20 mm diameter rivets as shown in the figure.

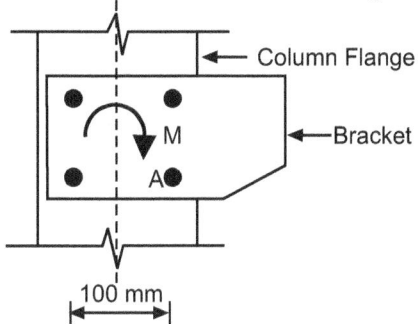

The shear force induced in the rivet A is
    (1) 250 kN   (2) 175.8 kN   (3) 125 kN   (4) 88.4 kN

45. Two plates of dimensions 150 mm × 16 mm and 150 mm × 12 mm at their welding edges are joined by butt welding as shown in the figure. What is the maximum tension that this single V-butt weld joint can transmit ? The permissible tensile stress in the plates is 150 MPa.

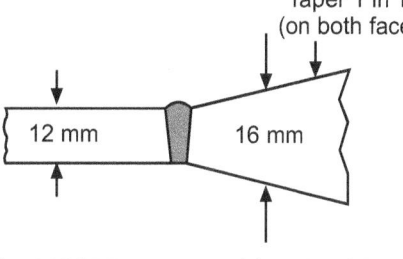

    (1) 168.75 kN   (2) 270 kN   (3) 218 kN   (4) 1350 kN

46. For heavy vibrating loads in industrial buildings, the roof trusses are provided with .....
    (1) diagonal bracing in the plane of lower chord members.
    (2) diagonal bracing in the plane of upper chord members.
    (3) knee bracing.
    (4) sway bracing.

47. If P is the allowable bending stress in a slab, whose greater and lesser projections from the column faces are A and B, the thickness (t) of the circular solid slab base is

(1) $t = \sqrt{\dfrac{3W}{P}\left(A^2 + \dfrac{B^2}{4}\right)}$ (2) $t = \sqrt{\dfrac{3}{P}\left(A^2 + \dfrac{B^2}{4}\right)}$

(3) $t = \sqrt{\dfrac{90W}{16P}\dfrac{B}{B-d_0}}$ (4) $t = \sqrt{\dfrac{P}{3}\left(A^2 - \dfrac{B^2}{4}\right)}$

48. Number of rivets required in a joint is
    (1) $\dfrac{\text{Load}}{\text{Shear strength of a rivet}}$ (2) $\dfrac{\text{Load}}{\text{Bearing strength of a rivet}}$
    (3) $\dfrac{\text{Load}}{\text{Tearing strength of a rivet}}$ (4) $\dfrac{\text{Load}}{\text{Rivet value}}$

49. A column splice is used to increase
    (1) length of column   (2) strength of column
    (3) cross-sectional area of the column   (4) none of these

50. As per IS : 800,the maximum deflection in a beam should not exceed ....
    (1) $\dfrac{L}{180}$ (2) $\dfrac{L}{250}$ (3) $\dfrac{L}{325}$ (4) $\dfrac{L}{360}$

51. Minimum pitch of the rivets shall not be less than...........
    (1) 1.5d   (2) 2.0d   (3) 2.5d   (4) 3.0d

52. The slenderness ratio of facing bars should not exceed
    (1) 100   (2) 120   (3) 145   (4) 180

53. A propped cantilever beam of span L and constant plastic moment capacity M_p carries a concentrated load at mid-span, then the load at collapse will be
    (1) M_p (2) $\dfrac{6\,M_p}{L}$ (3) $\dfrac{4\,M_p}{L}$ (4) $\dfrac{2\,M_p}{L}$

54. At the location of plastic hinge
    (1) radius of curvature is infinite   (2) curvature is infinite
    (3) moment is infinite   (4) flexural stress is infinite

55. A ductile structure is defined as one for which the plastic deformation before fracture
    (1) is smaller than the elastic deformation
    (2) vanishes
    (3) is equal to the elastic deformation
    (4) is much larger than the elastic deformation

56. What is the ratio of the yield stress in power driven shop rivets relative to the permissible bearing stress of mild steel ?
    (1) 1.0   (2) 0.8   (3) 0.6   (4) 0.4

57. What is the number of plastic hinges which will cause the overall total collapse of a structure ?
    (1) One more than the order of statical indeterminacy
    (2) Equal to order of statical indeterminacy
    (3) One less than the order of statical indeterminacy
    (4) Not determinable

58. The effective length of the fillet weld is
    (1) Total length – 2 × Throat size   (2) Total length – 2 × Weld size
    (3) 0.7 × Total length   (4) Total length – $\left(\text{Weld size}/\sqrt{2}\right)$

59. Lug angles
    (1) are necessarily unequal angles   (2) are always equal angles
    (3) increase the shear resistance of joint   (4) reduce the length of joint

60. For a standard 45° fillet, the ratio of size of fillet to throat thickness is
    (1) 1 : 2   (2) $1 : \sqrt{2}$ (3) $\sqrt{2} : 1$ (4) 2 : 1

61. Consider the following statements : Bearing stiffeners in a plate girders, are
    (a) provided at supports   (b) provided under concentrated loads
    (c) provided alternately on the web
    Which of these statement (s) is/are correct ?
    (1) (a) only   (2) (b) only
    (3) (a) and (b)   (4) (a), (b) and (c)

62. Tacking rivets in compression plates not exposed to the weather have a pitch not exceeding 300 mm or

    (1) 16 times the thickness of outside plate

    (2) 24 times the thickness of outside plate

    (3) 32 times the thickness of outside plate

    (4) 36 times the thickness of outside plate

63. Consider the following statements :

    (a) When analyzing by the Ultimate Load Method, the eccentrically loaded fastener group rotates about an instantaneous centre.

    (b) The rivet which is the farthest from the centre of gravity of the rivet group and may also be the nearest to the applied load line is the most 'critical' one.

    (c) The deformation at each rivet is not proportional to its distance from the centre of rotation.

    Which of the above statements are correct ?

    (1) (a) and (c) only   (2) (b) and (c) only

    (3) (a) and (b) only   (4) (a), (b) and (c)

64. Which one of the following four shapes for a compound, column of the same effective height formed with two equal angles has the largest axial compressive load carrying capacity ?

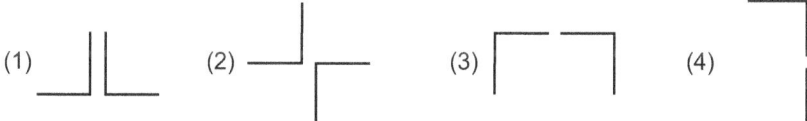

65. In a roof truss, if pitch is 1/2 and slope is 1, the angle of inclination with the horizontal would be .....

    (1) 30°   (2) 45°   (3) 60°   (4) 75°

66. The serviceability criterion for a plate girder design is based upon .....

    (1) width of flange   (2) depth of web

    (3) minimum thickness of web   (4) stiffness of web

67. The plastic moment at collapse is

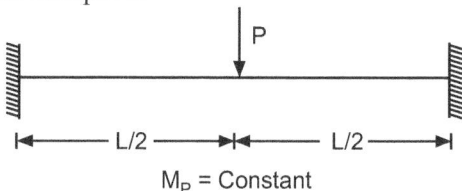

    (1) $\dfrac{PL}{6}$ (2) $\dfrac{PL}{8}$ (3) $\dfrac{PL}{12}$ (4) $\dfrac{PL}{16}$

68. A bracket connection is made with four bolts of 10 mm diameter and supports a load of 10 kN at an eccentricity of 100 mm. The maximum force to be resisted by any bolt will be

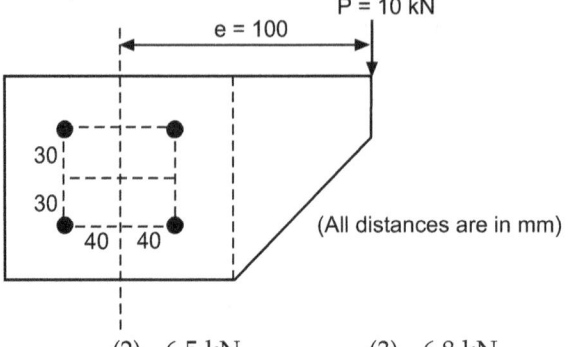

(1) 5 kN   (2) 6.5 kN   (3) 6.8 kN   (4) 7.16 kN

69. In a steel plate with bolted connection, the rupture of the net section is a mode of failure under

(1) tension   (2) compression   (3) flexure   (4) shear

70. The dimensions of a T-section are shown in the figure

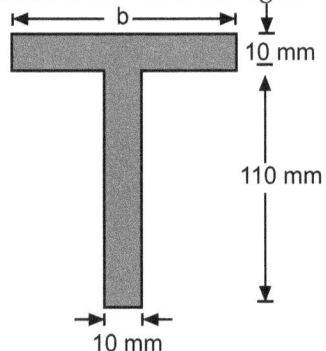

For the depth of plastic neutral axis from the top of the T-section to be 9.583 mm, the flange width b must be

(1) 100 mm   (2) 110 mm

(3) 120 mm   (4) 130 mm

71. Consider the following statements in respect of design of web and flange splices :

(a) Flange splice shall be designed for actual BM at the section.

(b) Flange splice shall be designed to resist the actual shear at the section.

(c) Web splice shall be designed to resist the actual shear at the section.

(d) Web splice shall be designed for actual BM.

Which of these statements are correct ?

(1) (a) and (c)   (2) (b) and (c)   (3) (c) and (d)   (4) (a) and (d)

72. The effective throat thickness of a fillet weld depends upon .....

(1) angle between fusion faces   (2) length of weld

(3) permissible shear stress   (4) type of weld

73. To transform an indeterminate frame with a degree of indeterminacy 'r' into a determinate one, the number of plastic hinges required is

(1) r + 2   (2) r + 1   (3) r   (4) r − 1

74. The maximum slenderness ratio of a compression member carrying both dead and superimposed load is
    (1) 180   (2) 200   (3) 250   (4) 350

75. The thickness of the web of a mild steel plate girder is less than d/200. If only one horizontal stiffeners is used, it is placed at
    (1) the neutral axis of the section
    (2) 2/3rd of the depth of the neutral axis from the compression flange
    (3) 2/5th of the depth of the neutral axis from the compression flange
    (4) 2/5th of the height of the neutral axis from tension flange

76. According to IS : 800, in the Merchant-Rankine formula, the value of imperfection index (n) is
    (1) 1.0   (2) 1.4   (3) 1.8   (4) 2.0

77. The angle of dispersion of a concentrated load on the flange to the web plate of a steel beam is
    (1) 90° with the horizontal   (2) 60° with the horizontal
    (3) 45° with the horizontal   (4) 30° with the horizontal

78. Load on connection is not eccentric for
    (1) lap Joint
    (2) single cover butt joint
    (3) double cover butt joint
    (4) all the joints mentioned in options (1), (2) and (3)

79. A continuous beam of constant M_p has three equal spans and carries total uniformly distributed load W on each span. The value of collapse load for the beam will be
    (1) $\dfrac{12\,M_P}{L}$ (2) $\dfrac{8.65\,M_p}{L}$ (3) $\dfrac{11.656\,M_p}{L}$ (4) $\dfrac{4\,M_p}{L}$

80. An angle ISA 50 × 50 × 6 is connected to a gusset plate 5 mm thick, with 16 mm bolts. What is the bearing strength of the bolt when the hole diameter is 16 mm and the allowable bearing stress is 250 MPa ?
    (1) 8 kN   (2) 20 kN
    (3) 22.5 kN   (4) 24 kN

81. ISMB 250 ($Ze = 410 \times 10^3$ mm³) has been chosen as a beam cross-section to resist a bending moment. Two plates 100 mm × 10 mm are welded to each flange to enhance the moment capacity. The enhanced moment capacity is .....
    (1) 71.5 kNm   (2) 79.5 kNm
    (3) 99.0 kNm   (4) 148.0 kNm

82. A mild steel tube of mean diameter 20 mm and thickness 2 mm is used as an axially loaded tension member. If f_y = 300 MPa, what is the maximum load that the member can carry ?
    (1) 11.25 kN   (2) 22.5 kN   (3) 30.0 kN   (4) 37.5 kN

83. An industrial building with 5 bays each 3 m wide has columns of height 4 m. The two end bays are braced by rods as shown in the figure. Each column carries an axial load of 120 kN. The design force for each brace is .....

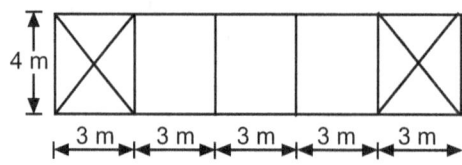

  (1) 6 kN   (2) 9 kN   (3) 15 kN   (4) 30 kN

84. Horizontal stiffener in a plate girder is provided to safeguard against web buckling due to .....
  (1) shear   (2) compressive force in bending
  (3) tensile force in bending   (4) heavy concentrated load

85. The length of beam over which the moment is greater than the yield moment is called as the plastic hinge length. What is the plastic hinge length for a simply supported beam of circular cross-section loaded at mid-span (shape factor for the section = 5/3) ?
  (1) 0.15 l (2) 0.33 l (3) 0.4 l (4) 0.5 l

86. The effective section of a fillet weld is represented by a triangle ABC with sides S_1, S_2 and S_3 such that $S_3 > S_2 > S_1$. If the allowable shear stress in weld material is τ, the resistance of weld per unit length is

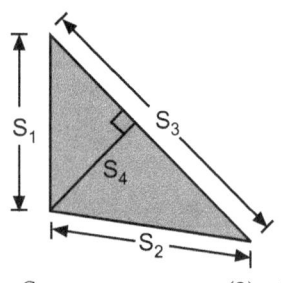

  (1) $S_1\tau$ (2) $S_2\tau$ (3) $S_3\tau$ (4) $S_4\tau$

87. A steel section is subjected to a combination of shear and bending actions. The applied shear force is V and the shear capacity of the section is V_s. For such a section, high shear force (as per IS 800 : 2007) is defined as
  (1) $V > 0.6\, V_s$ (2) $V > 0.7\, V_s$
  (3) $V > 0.8\, V_s$ (4) $V > 0.9\, V_s$

88. Prying forces are
  (1) shearing forces on the bolts because of the joints.
  (2) tensile forces due to the flexibility of connected parts.
  (3) bending forces on the bolts because of the joints.
  (4) forces due the friction between connected parts.

89. M60 structural steel tube has a radius of gyration 20 mm. The unbraced length upto which the tube can be used as a compression member is
  (1) 3.6 m   (2) 5.0 m   (3) 6.0 m   (4) 7.2 m

90. Racking force on a steel railway bridge is due to
    (1) tractive effect of the driving well
    (2) breaking effect
    (3) resistance offered by the bearing to the movement at the roller end
    (4) lateral movement of the train when moving on a straight track.

91. Which one of the following methods of design is not suitable for structures subjected to impact and fatigue ?
    (1) Simple design   (2) Semi-rigid design
    (3) Rigid design   (4) Plastic design

92. What is the maximum permissible longitudinal pitch in staggered riveted compression joint ?
    (1) 500 mm   (2) 400 mm   (3) 300 mm   (4) 100 mm

93. At the location of the plastic hinge of a deformed structure
    (1) curvature is infinite   (2) radius of curvature is infinite
    (3) moment is infinite   (4) flexural stress is infinite

94. The load factor to be used for plastic design of steel structures for dead load and imposed load is
    (1) 2.2   (2) 2.0   (3) 1.7   (4) 1.5

95. Which one of the following is the mode of failure in a fillet weld material ?
    (1) Tension   (2) Shear   (3) Bearing   (4) Crushing

96. In the design of steel bridges if wind or seismic forces are also considered, then the allowable stresses as per BIS may be increased by
    (1) 10 %   (2) $16\frac{2}{3}\%$ (3) 25 %   (4) $33\frac{1}{3}\%$

97. The working stress for structural steel in tension is of the order of
    (1) 15 N/mm²   (2) 75 N/mm²   (3) 150 N/mm²   (4) 750 N/mm²

98. An electric pole 5 m high is fixed into the foundation. It carries a wire at the top and is free to move sideways. The effective length of the pole is
    (1) 3.25 m   (2) 4.0 m   (3) 5.0 m   (4) 10.0 m

99. At the location of plastic hinge
    (1) radius of curvature is infinite   (2) curvature is infinite
    (3) moment is infinite   (4) flexural stress is infinite

100. According to IS : 800 – 1984, the minimum thickness of a vertically stiffened web plate shall not be less than
    (1) $\dfrac{d}{85}$ (2) $\dfrac{d}{200}$ (3) $\dfrac{d}{225}$ (4) $\dfrac{d}{250}$

101. Consider the following factors
    (a) Large number of loading cycles
    (b) Large variation in stress
    (c) large stress concentrations
    Those associated with fatigue failure would include
    (1) a and b   (2) a and c   (3) b and c   (4) a, b and c

102. For a pair of identical steel channel sections lack welded as a tension element, what is the net area of cross-section for design purposes ?
   (1) Net area of the webs only
   (2) Net area of the flanges only
   (3) Net area of the webs and flanges
   (4) Web area plus a portion of the area of the flanges

103. In a diamond riveting, for plate of width 'b' and rivet diameter 'd', the efficiency of the joint is given by
   (1) $\dfrac{b-d}{b}$
   (2) $(b-2d)$
   (3) $\dfrac{(b-d)}{d}$
   (4) $\dfrac{(b-2d)}{d}$

104. Match List-I (Type of connection) with list-II (Type of beams) and select the correct answer using the codes given below the lists.

List - I		List - II	
A.	Semi - rigid connection	1.	To permit large angles of rotation and to transmit negligible moment.
B.	Framed connection	2.	To allow small end rotation and transmit appreciable moment.
C.	Flexible connection	3.	When a beam is connected to a beam to stanchion by means of an angle at the bottom of the beam which is shop-riveted to the beam at an angle at the top of which is field riveted.
D.	Seated connection	4.	When a beam is connected to a beam or stanchion by means of two angles revited to them.

Codes

	A	B	C	D
(1)	2	4	3	1
(2)	4	2	1	3
(3)	2	4	1	3
(4)	4	2	3	1

105. The effective length of a fillet weld is taken as the actual length .....
   (1) plus twice the size of the weld
   (2) minus twice the size of the weld
   (3) plus the size of the weld
   (4) minus the size of the weld

106. A tie bar 100 mm × 16 mm thick is to be welded to another plate as shown in figure using 8 mm fillet welds. If the tensile stress in plates is 150 N/mm² and shear stress in weld is 110.0 N/mm², the minimum overlap required will be .....

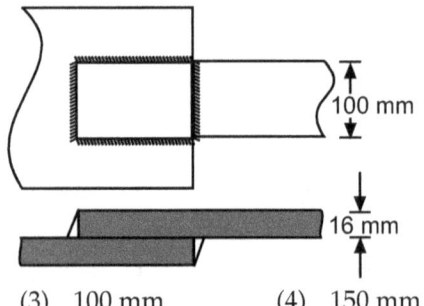

   (1) 50 mm
   (2) 75 mm
   (3) 100 mm
   (4) 150 mm

107. What is the maximum number of 20 mm diameter bolts that can be accommodated in a single row on a 140 mm wide flat strip used as one of the structural elements involved in the process ?
   (1) 4   (2) 3   (3) 2   (4) 5

108. Two angles of ISA 100 × 100 × 6 have been used as a tie member. The angles are welded on either side of a gusset and tag welded over its length. The maximum length of the member is ..... (For ISA 100 × 100 × 6, Area = 2334 mm² and Y_{xx} = 30 mm)
   (1) 5.4 m   (2) 6.0 m   (3) 12.0 m   (4) 24.0 m

109. The allowable shear stress in the web of mild steel beams decreases with .....
   (1) decrease in h/t ratio.   (2) increase in h/t ratio.
   (3) decrease in thickness.   (4) increase in height.

110. The height at which wind force acts on a moving vehicle on a bridge deck is
   (1) 1.2 m   (2) 1.5 m   (3) 1.7 m   (4) 2.0 m

111. Consider the following provisions to possibly improve the shear capacity of a steel girder :
   (a) Horizontal stiffeners   (b) Vertical stiffeners
   (c) Column splice   (d) Bearing stiffeners
   Which of these are correct ?
   (1) (a), (b), (c) and (d)   (2) (c) and (d) only
   (3) (a) and (b) only   (4) (b) and (c) only

112. In a plastic hinge, the actual distribution of strain across the section is essentially as

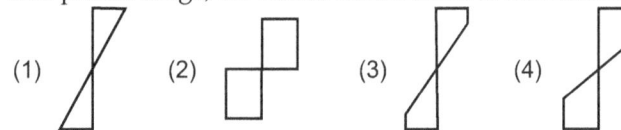

113. Consider the following statements :
   (a) The virtual work method is preferred to the equilibrium method for the determination of collapse load in a structure.
   (b) The number of plastic hinges required for the total collapse of a statically indeterminate structure is one less than the degree of indeterminacy of the structure.
   (c) In a large system the uniformly distributed load can be replaced by a number of concentrated loads to simplify the plastic analysis.
   Which of these statements are correct ?
   (1) (a), (b) and (c)   (2) (a) and b) only   (3) (a) and (c) only   (4) (b) and (c) only

114. Identify the most effective butt joint (with double cover plates) for a plate in tension from the patterns (plan view) shown below, each comprising 6 identical bolts with the same pitch and gauge.

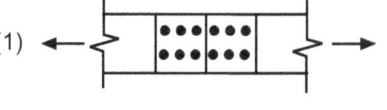 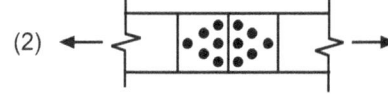

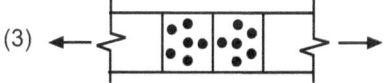 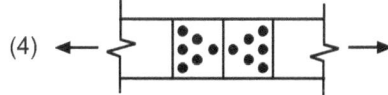

115. In the case of a tension member consisting of two angles back to back on the same side gusset plate, what is k equal to ? (Area of connected leg = A_1, Area of outstanding leg = A_2)

 (1) $\dfrac{3A_1}{3A_1 + A_2}$ (2) $\dfrac{3A_1}{A_1 + 3A_2}$ (3) $\dfrac{5A_1}{A_1 + 5A_2}$ (4) $\dfrac{5A_1}{5A_1 + A_2}$

116. The effective length of a structural steel compression member of length effectively held in position and restrained against rotation at one end, but neither held in position nor restrained against rotation at the other end, is

 (1) L (2) 1.2 L (3) 1.5 L (4) 2.0 L

117. A double cover butt riveted joint is used to connect two flat plates of 200 mm width and 14 mm thickness as shown in the figure. There are twelve power driven rivets of 20 mm diameter at a pitch of 50 mm in both directions on either side of the plate. Two cover plates of 10 mm thickness are used. The capacity of the joint in tension considering bearing and shear ONLY, with permissible bearing and shear stresses as 300 MPa and 100 MPa respectively is

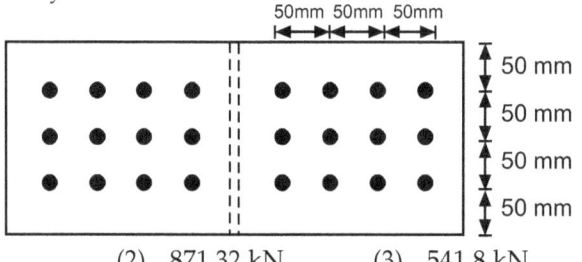

 (1) 1083.6 kN (2) 871.32 kN (3) 541.8 kN (4) 433.7 kN

118. As per IS 800 : 1984, the minimum pitch of rivets in a row is recommended as the diameter of the rivet times

 (1) 2.0 (2) 2.5 (3) 3.0 (4) 4.0

119. For portal frame shown in the figure, collapse load W has been calculated as per combined mechanism as $W = \dfrac{16M_p}{3l}$

What is the bending moment at B at collapse conditions ?

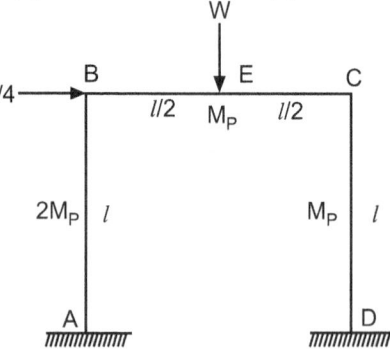

 (1) $\dfrac{Wl}{16}$ (2) $\dfrac{Wl}{8}$

 (3) $\dfrac{3Wl}{16}$ (4) $\dfrac{3Wl}{8}$

120. Which of the following statements is/are correct ?

 (a) A steel structure designer can guarantee the safety of the structure.

 (b) Working stress method of design of steel structures offers a safer and economical structure.

 (c) Strength and serviceability of a structure cannot be predicted on account of several unforeseen factors.

 (1) (a), (b) and (c) (2) (c) only (3) (b) only (4) (a) only

121. The thickness of web for unstiffened plate girder with clear distance 'd' between the flanges shall be not less than .....
    (1) $\dfrac{d}{200}$ (2) $\dfrac{d}{85}$ (3) $\dfrac{d}{100}$ (4) $\dfrac{d}{160}$

122. The best-suited rolled steel section for a tension member is .....
    (1) angle section   (2) T-section   (3) channel section   (4) flat section

123. When the load line coincides with the centroid of the rivet group, the rivets are subjected to .....
    (1) shear only   (2) tension only
    (3) bending only   (4) shear as well as tension

124. When the effect of wind or earthquake load is taken into account in the design of a riveted connection, the permissible stresses in rivets may be exceeded by .....
    (1) 16.66%   (2) 33.33%   (3) 25%   (4) 30%

125. The maximum longitudinal pitch in bolted joints, subjected to tensile forces, wherein t = thickness of the plate and D = diameter of bolt, is .....
    (1) 32 D   (2) 16 D   (3) 32 t   (4) 16 t

126. In the case of structural steel sections, the minimum ratio of thickness of elements in compression in terms of their outstanding length is specified to prevent
    (1) bending failure   (2) shear failure
    (3) local buckling   (4) tension failure

127. What is the maximum permissible slenderness ratio of major compression member which undergoes reversal of stress due to wind load ?
    (1) 180   (2) 250   (3) 300   (4) 120

128. Which one of the following is the correct maximum shear capacity of a prismatic beam under plastic design of steel structures ?
    (1) $0.5\,A_w\,F_y$ (2) $0.55\,A_w\,F_y$ (3) $0.75\,A_w\,F_y$ (4) $A_w\,F_y$

129. A steel beam supporting loads from the floor slab as well as from wall is termed as
    (1) stringer beam   (2) lintel beam
    (3) spandrel beam   (4) header beam

130. A simply supported beam of uniform cross-section has span L and is loaded by a point load P at it's mid-span. The length of elasto-plastic zone of the plastic hinge will be
    (1) $\dfrac{L}{3}$ (2) $\dfrac{2L}{5}$ (3) $\dfrac{L}{2}$ (4) $\dfrac{3L}{4}$

131. Upper yield point in the stress strain curve in structural steel can be avoided by
    (1) cold working   (2) hot working   (3) quenching   (4) galvanizing

132. The rolled steel section used in a cased beam has width B mm and diameter D mm. The minimum width of the finished cased beam in mm is given by
    (1) (B + 50)   (2) (B + 100)   (3) (B + D + 100)   (4) 2 (B + D)

133. The ratio of collapse load of a propped cantilever of span L carrying a UDL throughout the span to that of a simply supported beam carrying the same load is
    (1) 1.457   (2) 1.500   (3) 2.000   (4) 3.000

134. A circular shaft of diameter 120 mm is welded to a rigid plate by a fillet weld of size 6 mm. If a torque of 8 kNm is applied to the shaft, what is the maximum stress in the weld (to the nearest unit) ?

    (1) 84 N/mm²   (2) 87 N/mm²   (3) 90 N/mm²   (4) 95 N/mm²

135. A fillet welded joint of 6 mm size is shown in the figure. The welded surfaces meet at 60-90 degree and permissible stress in the fillet weld is 108 MPa. The safe load that can be transmitted by the joint is

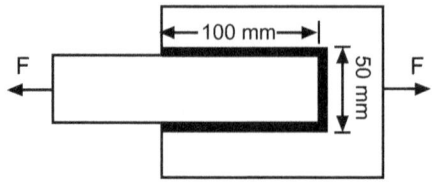

    (1) 162.7 kN   (2) 151.6 kN   (3) 113.4 kN   (4) 109.5 kN

136. If 'P' is the basic wind pressure, for buildings with large opening, design pressure on a wall is taken as

    (1) 0.5 P   (2) 0.7 P   (3) 1.0 P   (4) 1.2 P

137. In which of the following cases is the compression flange most susceptible to buckle laterally ?

    (1) An I-section supporting a roof slab with shear connection.
    (2) Purlin of a roof supporting dead and live loads.
    (3) Encased beam.
    (4) A steel I-section supporting a point load when acting as a cantilever.

138. Which of the following elements of a pitched roof industrial steel building primarily resists lateral load parallel to the ridge ?

    (1) Bracing   (2) Purlin   (3) Truss   (4) Column

139. In a plate girder, the web is primarily designed to resist .....

    (1) torsional moment   (2) shear force
    (3) bending moment   (4) diagonal buckling

140. A crane with two wheels per side has a capacity of 50 kN. Weight of the crane is 100 kN, weight of the trolley is 10 kN and the span is 12 m. The maximum static wheel load with hook clearance of 1.0 m from the wheel is .....

    (1) 50 kN   (2) 52.5 kN   (3) 55 kN   (4) 60 kN

141. A bracket plate connected to a column flange transmits a load of 100 kN as shown in the following figure. The maximum force for which the bolts should be designed is

    (1) 156.2 kN   (2) 100 kN
    (3) 200 kN   (4) 256.2 kN

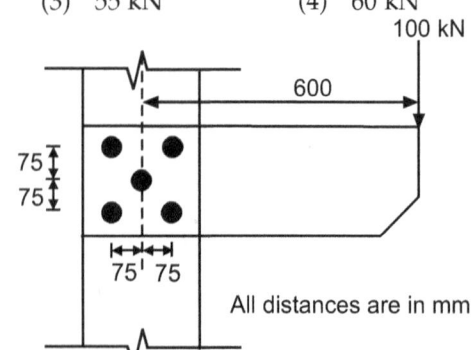

142. Generally, fatigue life of welded steel structure to fatigue life of riveted steel structure ratio is
   (1) smaller than 1   (2) equal to 1
   (3) greater than 1   (4) greater than 2.1

143. ISA 100 × 100 × 10 mm (cross-sectional area = 1908 mm²) serves as tensile member. This angle is welded to a gusset plate along A and B appropriately as shown in figure. Assuming the yield strength of the steel to be 260 N/mm², the tensile strength of this member can be taken to be approximately.

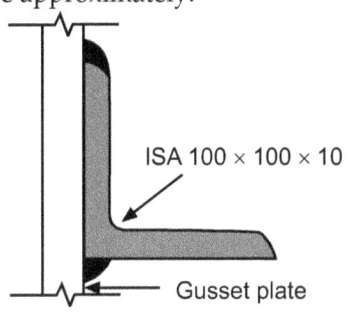

ISA 100 × 100 × 10

Gusset plate

   (1) 500 kN   (2) 300 kN   (3) 225 kN   (4) None

144. The allowable shear stress in stiffened webs of mid steel beams decreases with .....
   (1) decrease in the spacing of the stiffeners.
   (2) increase in the spacing of the stiffeners.
   (3) decrease in the effective depth.
   (4) increase in the effective depth.

145. The problems of lateral buckling can arise only in those steel beams which have .....
   (1) moment of inertia about the bending axis larger than the other.
   (2) moment of inertia about the bending axis smaller than the other.
   (3) fully supported compression flange.
   (4) none of the above.

146. Consider the following statements :
   Web crippling due to excessive bearing stress can be avoided by .....
   (a) increasing the web thickness.   (b) providing suitable stiffeners.
   (c) increasing the length of the bearing plates.
   Which of these statements are correct ?
   (1) (a) and (b) only   (2) (b) and (c) only   (3) (a) and (c) only   (4) (a), (b) and c)

147. Purlins are to be chosen for a roof truss of 20 m span, 4 m rise. Trusses are spaced at 4.5 m centre-to-centre. A most efficient design results from the use of .....
   (1) angle sections   (2) channel sections
   (3) circular hollow sections   (4) square hollow sections

148. The mechanism method and the statical method guide in estimating.
   (1) the lower and upper bounds respectively on the strength of structure.
   (2) the upper and lower bounds respectively on the strength of structure.
   (3) the lower bound on the strength of structure.
   (4) the upper bound on the strength of structure.

149. In a gabled industrial building in order to minimize the wind forces on the roof, the roof slope should be kept close to
   (1) 5°   (2) 15°   (3) 30°   (4) 45°

150. Purlins are provided in industrial buildings over roof trusses to carry dead loads, live loads and wind loads. As per IS code, what are they assumed to be ?
   (1) Simply supported   (2) Cantilever   (3) Continuous   (4) Fixed

151. Some steels do not show yield plateau and show continuous curve for such steel. How is the yield strength obtained ?
   (1) By drawing 0.2% offset of the strain   (2) By drawing 0.5% offset of the strain
   (3) By drawing initial tangent   (4) By drawing initial secant modulus

152. For a vertical stiffened web of a plate girder, the lesser clear dimension of the panel should not exceed .... ('t' is the thickness of the web)
   (1) 85 t   (2) 180 t   (3) 200 t   (4) 250 t

153. The economic spacing of a roof truss depends upon the
   (1) cost of purlins and cost of roof covering   (2) cost of roof covering and dead loads
   (3) dead loads and live loads   (4) live load and cost of purlins

154. In an industrial steel building, which of the following elements of a pitched roof primarily resist loads parallel to the ridge ?
   (1) Bracings   (2) Purlins   (3) Columns   (4) Trusses

155. For two plates of equal thickness, full strength of fillet weld can be ensured if it's maximum size, for square edge is limited to
   (1) 1.5 mm less than the thickness   (2) 75% of thickness
   (3) 80% of the thickness   (4) thickness of the plate

156. Consider the following statements :
   (a) The thickness of the gusset plate should not be more than the thickness of the structural members being connected.
   (b) A plate girder is essentially a beam and its moment of resistance depends upon its section modulus.
   (c) The function of the flanges in a plate girder is to resist the bending moment and hence their respective areas can be reduced near the supports of a simply supported beam.
   Which of the above statements are correct ?
   (1) (a) and (b) only   (2) (a) and (c) only
   (3) (b) and (c) only   (4) (a), (b) and (c)

157. If the shape factor of a section is 1.5 and the factor of safety to be adopted is 2, then the load factor will be
   (1) 3   (2) 4   (3) 1.5   (4) 2

158. Maximum size of fillet weld for a plate of square edge is
   (1) 1.5 mm less than the thickness of the plate.
   (2) one half of the thickness of the plate.
   (3) thickness of the plate itself.
   (4) 1.5 mm more than the thickness of the plate.

159. Consider the following statements : A grillage base is checked for
    (1) bending   (2) shear
    (3) web crippling   (4) All of these

160. Two plates, subjected to direct tension, each of 10 mm thickness and having widths of 100 mm and 175 mm, respectively are to be fillet welded with an overlap of 200 mm. Given that the permissible weld stress is 110 MPa and the permissible stress in steel is 150 MPa, the length of the weld required using the maximum permissible weld size as per IS 800 : 1984 is

    (1) 245.3 mm   (2) 229.2 mm
    (3) 205.5 mm   (4) 194.8 mm

161. In a fillet weld the weakest section is the
    (1) smaller side of the fillet   (2) throat of the fillet
    (3) side perpendicular to force   (4) side parallel to force

162. The permissible stresses in rivets under wind load conditions as per IS : 800 can be exceeded by about
    (1) 15%   (2) 25%   (3) 33%   (4) 50%

163. When the effect of wind or earthquake load is considered in the design of rivets and bolts for steel structures, by what percentage the permissible stresses may be exceeded ?
    (1) 15%   (2) 25%   (3) 33.33%   (4) 50%

164. What is the permissible tensile stress in bolts used for column bases ? (f_y is the yield stress of the steel)
    (1) 120 N/mm^2 (2) 150 N/mm^2 (3) $0.6 f_y$ (4) $0.4 f_y$

165. The moment of inertia of the pair of vertical stiffeners about the centre line of the web should not be less than
    (1) $1.5\, d^3 t^2/c$ (2) $1.5\, d^2 t^3/c$ (3) $1.5\, d^3 t^3/c^2$ (4) $1.5\, d^2 t^4/c^3$

166. If the 20 mm rivets are used in lacing bars, then the minimum width of lacing bar should be
    (1) 40 mm   (2) 60 mm   (3) 80 mm   (4) 10 mm

167. Angle of inclination of the lacing bar with the longitudinal axis of the column should preferably be between
    (1) 10° to 30°   (2) 30° to 40°   (3) 40° to 70°   (4) 70° to 90°

168. For steels structures proportioned using plastic design, the working load (dead load + imposed load) should be multiplied by which one of the following minimum load foctor ?
    (1) 1.3   (2) 1.5   (3) 1.7   (4) 2.0

169. A structural member carrying a pull of 700 kN is connected to a gusset plate using rivets of 20 mm diameter. If the pull required for shearing the rivets, to crush the rivets and to tear the plate per pitch length are 60 kN, 35 kN and 70 kN respectively, then the number of rivets required is .....

(1) 12   (2) 18   (3) 20   (4) 22

170. What is the nearest magnitude of strength of a 6 mm fillet weld of 100 mm length made between two flats each 10 mm thick ? The allowable shear stress on the weld is 110 MPa.

(1) 23 kN   (2) 33 kN   (3) 46 kN   (4) 66 kN

171. Gantry girders are designed to resist :

(a) lateral loads   (b) longitudinal loads

(c) vertical loads

(1) (a) and (b) only   (2) (a) and (c) only

(3) (b) and (c) only   (4) (a), (b) and (c)

172. A monorail crane runs on an I-section of span 6 m, which is simply supported. Estimate the deflection for crane capacity of 20 kN, crab weight of 4 kN, impact factor of 25% and $EI = 10 \times 10^{12}$ N-mm². Deflection due to self-weight is neglected.

(1) 6 mm   (2) 9 mm   (3) 12 mm   (4) 18 mm

173. The plastic modulus of a section is 4.8×10^{-4} m³. The shape factor is 1.2. The plastic moment capacity of the section is 120 kN-m. The yield stress of the material is

(1) 100 MPa   (2) 240 MPa   (3) 250 MPa   (4) 300 MPa

174. An ISMB 500 is used as a beam in a multi-storey construction. From the viewpoint of structural design, it can be considered to be 'laterally restrained' when

(1) the tension flange is laterally strained.

(2) the compression flange is laterally restrained.

(3) the web is adequately stiffened.

(4) the conditions in (1) and (3) are met.

175. For an I-beam, shape factor is 1.12. The factor of safety in bending is 1.5. If the allowable stress is increased by 20% for wind and earthquake loads, then the load factor is ......

(1) 1.10   (2) 1.25   (3) 1.35   (4) 1.40

176. For a fixed beam with a concentrated load W at $\frac{1}{4}$ of span from one end, the ultimate load is

(1) $\dfrac{16M_P}{3L}$ (2) $\dfrac{4 M_P}{L}$ (3) $\dfrac{32 M_P}{3L}$ (4) $\dfrac{6M_P}{L}$

177. Which one of the following is a compression member ?

(1) Purlin   (2) Boom   (3) Girt   (4) Tie

178. Factor of safety adopted by IS 800:1984 while arriving at the permissible stress in axial compression is

(1) 2.00   (2) 1.00   (3) 1.67   (4) 1.50

179. Diameter of a rivet hole is made larger than the diameter of the rivet by
    (1) 1.0 mm for rivet diameter upto 12 mm
    (2) 1.5 mm for rivet diameter exceeding 25 mm
    (3) 2.0 mm for rivet diameter over 25 mm
    (4) none of these

180. As per IS : 800, the rivets subjected to combined tensile and shear stresses are proportioned such that
    (1) $\left(\dfrac{F_s}{P_s}\right)^{1/2} + \left(\dfrac{F_t}{P_t}\right)^{1/2} \le 1.4$
    (2) $\left(\dfrac{F_s}{P_s}\right) + \left(\dfrac{F_t}{P_t}\right) \le 1.4$
    (3) $\left(\dfrac{F_s}{P_s}\right)^2 + \left(\dfrac{F_t}{P_t}\right)^2 \le 1.4$
    (4) $\left(\dfrac{F_s}{P_s}\right)^2 + \left(\dfrac{F_t}{P_t}\right)^2 \ge 1.4$

    where F_s and F_t are respectively actual shear and tensile stresses in a rivet, and P_s and P_t are respectively permissible shear and tensile stresses in the rivet.

181. The maximum slenderness ratio of steel column, the design of which is governed by wind or seismic forces, is
    (1) 150   (2) 180   (3) 250   (4) 350

182. Secant formula for direct stress in compression is applicable only for slenderness ratio upto
    (1) 120   (2) 160   (3) 140   (4) 150

183. If d is the distance between the flange angles, the vertical stiffeners in plate girders are spaced not greater than
    (1) d   (2) 1.25d   (3) 1.5d   (4) 1.75d

184. The greater gauge of long rivets should not exceed
    (1) 2d   (2) 4d   (3) 6d   (4) 8d

185. As per IS : 800, in the case of plate girder with vertical and   horizontal stiffeners the greater and lesser unsupported clear dimension of web panel in terms of web thickness 't' should not exceed respectively
    (1) 180 t_w and 8.5 t_w
    (2) 270 t_w and 200 t_w
    (3) 270 t_w and 180 t_w
    (4) 400 t_w and 250 t_w

186. Which one of the following is the load factor ?
    (1) $\dfrac{\text{Live load}}{\text{Dead load}}$
    (2) $\dfrac{\text{Failure load}}{\text{Working load}}$
    (3) $\dfrac{\text{Total load}}{\text{Dead load}}$
    (4) $\dfrac{\text{Dynamic load}}{\text{Static load}}$

187. Match List - I (Beam) with List-II (Collapse load) and select the correct answer using the codes given below the lists.

	List - I		List - II
A.	Fixed beam with a central point load	1.	$\dfrac{8 M_p}{L}$
B.	Fixed beam with a UDL of intensity 'w'	2.	$\dfrac{16 M_p}{L}$
C.	Propped cantilever with a central point load.	3.	$\left(\dfrac{6 M_p}{L}\right)$
D.	Simply supported beam with a central point load.	4.	$\dfrac{4 M_p}{L}$

Codes

	A	B	C	D
(1)	1	2	4	3
(2)	2	1	3	4
(3)	2	1	4	3
(4)	1	2	3	4

188. Which one of the following modes of failure is taken care of in plastic design of a steel beam ?
    (1) Plastic material deformation throughout the beam
    (2) Lateral buckling of the beam
    (3) Elastic buckling of the compression flange
    (4) Hinge formation in the beam due to yielding of steel

189. According to Indian Railway Board, in respect of steel girders of single track span for meter/board gauge, the impact factor for a span of 6 m is
    (1) 0.5   (2) 0.75   (3) 1   (4) 1.25

190. Which one of the following is NOT correct for steel sections as per IS 800 : 1984?
    (1) The maximum bending stress in tension or in compression in extreme fibre calculated on the effective section of a beam shall not exceed $0.66 f_y$.
    (2) The bearing stress in any part of a beam when calculated on the net area shall not exceed $0.75 f_y$.
    (3) The direct stress in compression on the gross sectional area of axially loaded compression member shall not exceed $0.6 f_y$.
    (4) None of the above

191. Two plates are connected by fillet welds of size 10 mm and subjected to tension, as shown in the sketch. The thickness of each plate is 12 mm. The yield stress and the ultimate tensile stress of steel are 250 MPa and 410 MPa respectively. The welding is done in the workshop (γ_{mm}= 1.25). As per the Limit State Method of IS 800 : 2007, the minimum length (rounded off to the nearest higher multiple of 5 mm) of each weld to transmit a force P equal to

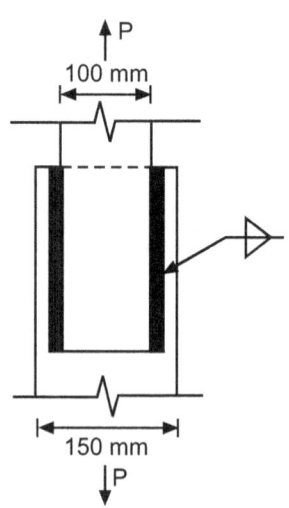

    (1) 100 mm   (2) 105 mm   (3) 110 mm   (4) 115 mm

192. The permissible stresses for main structural steel members under dynamic loads should be increased by
    (1) 20%   (2) 25%   (3) 30%   (4) 33.33%

193. The center to center maximum distance between bolts in tension member of thickness 10 mm is
    (1) 200 mm   (2) 160 mm   (3) 120 mm   (4) 100 mm

194. The type of stress induced in the foundation bolts fixing a columm to its footing is
    (1) pure compression   (2) bearing   (3) pure tension   (4) bending

195. Which of the following does not describe be a weld type ?
    (1) Butt   (2) Plug   (3) Zig - Zag   (4) Lap

196. A plate used for connecting two or more structural members intersecting each other is termed as ?
    (1) Template   (2) Base plate   (3) Gusset plate   (4) Shoe plate

197. Rivets and bolts subjected to both shear stress ($\tau_{vf, cal}$) and axial tensile stress ($\sigma_{tf, cas}$) shall be so proportioned that the stresses do not exceed the respective allowable stresses σ_{tf} and σ_{vf} and the value of $\left(\dfrac{\tau_{vf, cal}}{\tau_{vf}} + \dfrac{\sigma_{tf, cal}}{\sigma_{tf}} \right)$ does not exceed
    (1) 1.0   (2) 1.2   (3) 1.4   (4) 1.8

198. The tension and shear force (both in kN) in each bolt of the joint, as shown in the figure respectively are

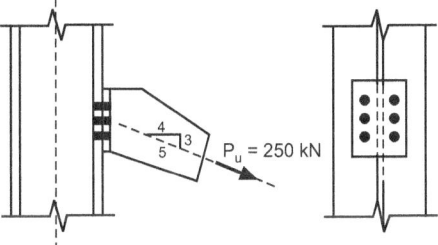

    (1) 30.33 and 20.00   (2) 30.33 and 25.00
    (3) 33.33 and 20.00   (4) 33.33 and 25.00

199. A 12 mm thick plate is connected to two 8 mm thick plates, on either side through a 16 mm diameter power driven field rivet as shown in the figure. Assuming permissible shear stress as 90 MPa and permissible bearing stress as 270 MPa in the rivet, the rivet value of the joint is

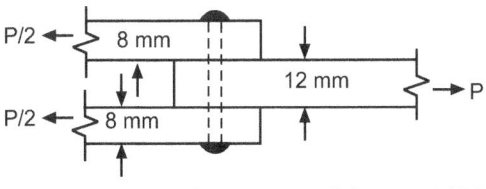

    (1) 56.70 kN   (2) 43.29 kN   (3) 36.19 kN   (4) 21.65 kN

200. The common assumption that all rivets share equally a non-eccentric load is valid at a load
    (1) below the working load   (2) equal to the working load
    (3) above the working load   (4) equal to the failure load

201. The rolled steel section used in a cased beam has width 'B' mm and diameter 'D' mm. The minimum width of the finished cased beam is given by
    (1) (B + 50) mm
    (2) (B + 100) mm
    (3) [(B/D) + 100] mm
    (4) 2(B + D) mm

202. For the fillet weld of size 's' shown in the figure, the effective throat thickness is

    (1) 0.61s
    (2) 0.65s
    (3) 0.70s
    (4) 0.75s

203. In the context of the ultimate load theory for steel, the stress-strain curve for steel is idealized as
    (1) a single straight line
    (2) bi-linear
    (3) a quadratic parabola
    (4) a circular arc

204. A structure has two degrees of indeterminacy. The number of plastic hinges that would be formed at complete collapse is
    (1) 0
    (2) 1
    (3) 2
    (4) 3

205. For a compression member having the same effective length about any cross-sectional axis, the most preferred section from the point of view of strength is
    (1) a box
    (2) an I- section
    (3) a circular tube
    (4) a single angle

206. In a riveted joint failure will occur due to which one of the following ?
    (1) Shear failure of rivet
    (2) Bearing failure of rivet
    (3) Teaning failure of plate
    (4) Minimum load value of shearing bearing of tearing failure

207. A_f is the area of flanges and A_w is the area of web. What is the effective flange area in the design of a plate girder ?
    (1) $A_f + \dfrac{A_w}{8}$
    (2) $A_f + \dfrac{A_w}{6}$
    (3) $A_f - \dfrac{A_w}{8}$
    (4) $A_f - \dfrac{A_w}{6}$

208. Horizontal stiffeners are needed in plate girders if the thickness of web is
    (1) < 6 mm
    (2) $< d/200$
    (3) $< L/500$
    (4) nearly equal to flange thickness
    (where d = distance between flanges and L = span)

209. At what value (nearly) is the maximum spacing of purlins for standard asbestos roofing sheets kept ?
    (1) 1.0 m
    (2) 1.4 m
    (3) 1.8 m
    (4) 2.0 m

210. A reduction in the allowable stress in steel chimney construction is necessary if the temperature exceeds
     (1) 75°C   (2) 100°C   (3) 200°C   (4) 300°C

211. What is the number of plastic hinges formed if an indeterminate beam with redundancy R is to become determinate ?
     (1) R – 1   (2) R   (3) R + 1   (4) R + 2

212. Which one of the following is correct ?
     Steel structures are ideally suitable for impact loads because they have high
     (1) toughness value   (2) elastic modulus
     (3) design stress   (4) plastic modulus

213. In a double- riveted double-covered butt joint, the strength of the joint per pitch length in shearing the rivets is 'n' times the shear strength of one rivet shear, where 'n' is equal to
     (1) 1   (2) 2   (3) 3   (4) 4

214. In a simply supported beam of span L each end is restrained against torsion, compression flange being unrestrained. According to IS : 800, the effective length of the compression flange will be equal to
     (1) L   (2) 0.85 L   (3) 0.75 L   (4) 0.70 L

ANSWER KEY

1.	(2)	2.	(1)	3.	(3)	4.	(2)	5.	(3)	6.	(4)	7.	(3)	8.	(1)
9.	(4)	10.	(4)	11.	(4)	12.	(4)	13.	(4)	14.	(3)	15.	(2)	16.	(4)
17.	(4)	18.	(1)	19.	(3)	20.	(2)	21.	(3)	22.	(4)	23.	(4)	24.	(4)
25.	(1)	26.	(3)	27.	(4)	28.	(4)	29.	(3)	30.	(4)	31.	(2)	32.	(3)
33.	(2)	34.	(4)	35.	(4)	36.	(3)	37.	(2)	38.	(4)	39.	(3)	40.	(1)
41.	(4)	42.	(2)	43.	(2)	44.	(2)	45.	(1)	46.	(3)	47.	(3)	48.	(4)
49.	(1)	50.	(3)	51.	(3)	52.	(3)	53.	(2)	54.	(2)	55.	(4)	56.	(2)
57.	(3)	58.	(2)	59.	(4)	60.	(3)	61.	(3)	62.	(3)	63.	(3)	64.	(2)
65.	(2)	66.	(4)	67.	(2)	68.	(4)	69.	(1)	70.	(3)	71.	(1)	72.	(1)
73.	(2)	74.	(1)	75.	(3)	76.	(2)	77.	(2)	78.	(3)	79.	(3)	80.	(2)
81.	(4)	82.	(2)	83.	(1)	84.	(2)	85.	(3)	86.	(4)	87.	(1)	88.	(2)
89.	(1)	90.	(4)	91.	(4)	92.	(3)	93.	(1)	94.	(3)	95.	(2)	96.	(4)
97.	(3)	98.	(2)	99.	(2)	100.	(2)	101.	(4)	102.	(3)	103.	(1)	104.	(3)
105.	(3)	106.	(3)	107.	(3)	108.	(3)	109.	(2)	110.	(2)	111.	(3)	112.	(1)
113.	(3)	114.	(2)	115.	(4)	116.	(4)	117.	(2)	118.	(2)	119.	(1)	120.	(3)

121.	(2)	122.	(2)	123.	(1)	124.	(3)	125.	(4)	126.	(3)	127.	(2)	128.	(2)
129.	(3)	130.	(1)	131.	(1)	132.	(2)	133.	(3)	134.	(1)	135.	(3)	136.	(2)
137.	(4)	138.	(2)	139.	(3)	140.	(2)	141.	(1)	142.	(1)	143.	(4)	144.	(2)
145.	(1)	146.	(1)	147.	(2)	148.	(2)	149.	(3)	150.	(3)	151.	(1)	152.	(2)
153.	(1)	154.	(1)	155.	(1)	156.	(3)	157.	(1)	158.	(1)	159.	(4)	160.	(2)
161.	(3)	162.	(2)	163.	(2)	164.	(1)	165.	(3)	166.	(2)	167.	(3)	168.	(3)
169.	(3)	170.	(3)	171.	(4)	172.	(3)	173.	(3)	174.	(2)	175.	(4)	176.	(3)
177.	(2)	178.	(3)	179.	(3)	180.	(2)	181.	(3)	182.	(2)	183.	(3)	184.	(4)
185.	(3)	186.	(2)	187.	(4)	188.	(4)	189.	(2)	190.	(4)	191.	(2)	192.	(4)
193.	(2)	194.	(3)	195.	(3)	196.	(3)	197.	(3)	198.	(4)	199.	(2)	200.	(4)
201.	(2)	202.	(2)	203.	(2)	204.	(3)	205.	(1)	206.	(4)	207.	(2)	208.	(2)
209.	(2)	210.	(2)	211.	(4)	212.	(1)	213.	(4)	214.	(1)				

1. The single grained, honey comb, flocculent, dispersed etc. are the ...., which are generally recognised.
   (1) classifications of soil
   (2) types of soil
   (3) soil structures
   (4) nature of soil

2. The flow index in soils indicates .....
   (1) shear strength variation with water content
   (2) variation of liquid limit
   (3) rate of flow of water through the soil
   (4) ratio of liquid limit to plastic limit

3. In which method of site exploration, soil and rock formations are broken by repeated blows of heavy chisel or bit suspended by a cable or drill rod ?
   (1) Rotary boring
   (2) Percussion boring
   (3) Wash boring
   (4) Auger boring

4. Which of the following methods is easiest method of determination of water content of a soil in the field ?
   (1) Oven drying method
   (2) Sand bath method
   (3) Alcohol method
   (4) Calcium carbide method

5. The ratio of plasticity index to flow index is called.....
   (1) activity ratio
   (2) liquidity index
   (3) toughness index
   (4) none of these

6. In an undrained triaxial test on a saturated clay, the Poisson's ratio is .....
   (1) $\dfrac{\sigma_3}{\sigma_1 + \sigma_3}$
   (2) $\dfrac{\sigma_3}{\sigma_1 - \sigma_3}$
   (3) $\dfrac{\sigma_1 - \sigma_3}{\sigma_3}$
   (4) $\dfrac{\sigma_1 + \sigma_3}{\sigma_3}$

7. The effective size of the soil is .....
   (1) D_{60}
   (2) D_{85}
   (3) D_{10}
   (4) D_{90}

8. Soil which contains the particles of different sizes in good proportion is called .....
   (1) uniform soil
   (2) well graded soil
   (3) consistent soil
   (4) none of these

9. Soil in which some of the intermediate size particles are missing is known as .....
   (1) poorly graded soil
   (2) non-uniform soil
   (3) ill proportional soil
   (4) skip graded soil or gap graded soil

10. D_{10} of the soil is the diameter in mm such that .....
    (1) 10% of the soil is coarser than this value
    (2) 10% of the soil is finer than this value
    (3) this value has no bearing on particle size distribution
    (4) none of the above

11. A steep grain size distribution curve presents .....
    (1) more uniform grain sizes   (2) non-uniform grain sizes
    (3) grains of all sizes   (4) none of these

12. A flat grain size distribution curve shows a .....
    (1) narrow range of grain sizes   (2) wide range of grain sizes
    (3) uniform grain sizes   (4) non-uniform grain sizes

13. Residual soil is a soil :
    (1) which stays at the place of its formation
    (2) which deposits at a place away from place of its origin
    (3) Both 1 and 2
    (4) Neither 1 nor 2

14. A direct shear test was conducted on a cohesionless soil (C = 0) specimen under a normal stress of 200 kN/m². The specimen failed at a shear stress of 100 kN/m². The angle of internal friction of the soil (degree) is .....
    (1) 26.6°   (2) 29.5°   (3) 30.0°   (4) 32.6°

15. The maximum water content, at which a reduction in water content does not cause a decrease in volume of soil mass, is known as .....
    (1) liquid limit   (2) plastic limit   (3) shrinkage limit   (4) ductile limit

16. The minimum water content at which the soil just begins to crumble when rolled into threads 3 mm in diameter is known as .....
    (1) shrinkage limit   (2) plastic limit   (3) liquid limit   (4) consistency limit

17. Theoretically, the void ratio in soils can have the following values :
    (1) less than one only   (2) more than one
    (3) can be less or more than one   (4) less than 0.5

18. The following data were obtained from a liquid limit test conducted on a soil sample

Number of blows	17	22	25	28	34
Water content (%)	63.8	63.1	61.9	60.6	60.5

The liquid limit of the soil is .....
    (1) 63.1%   (2) 62.8%   (3) 61.9%   (4) 60.6%

19. The equation of A-line is .....
    (1) $I_P = 0.73 (W_L - 10)$ (2) $I_P = 0.73 (W_L - 20)$
    (3) $I_P = 0.73 (W_L + 10)$ (4) $I_P = 0.73 (W_P - 20)$

20. In an undrained triaxial compression test, the sample failed at a deviator stress of 200 kN/m² when the cell pressure was 100 kN/m². The cohesion intercept is
    (1) 200 kN/m²   (2) 100 kN/m²   (3) 300 kN/m²   (4) 50 kN/m²

21. Over dried soil will have liquidity index of .....
    (1) negative value   (2) 0   (3) 1   (4) more than one

22. Which one of the following gives the correct decreasing order of the densities of a soil sample ?
    (1) Saturated, submerged, wet, dry   (2) Saturated, wet, submerged, dry
    (3) Saturated, wet, dry, submerged   (4) Wet, saturated, submerged, dry

23. By using sieve analysis, the particle size distribution curve has been plotted for a particular soil. The coefficient of curvature C_c is given by .....

(1) $\dfrac{D_{30}}{D_{60} \times D_{10}}$ (2) $\dfrac{\sqrt{D_{30}}}{D_{60} \times D_{10}}$ (3) $\dfrac{D_{30}}{\sqrt{D_{60} \times D_{10}}}$ (4) $\dfrac{(D_{30})^2}{D_{60} \times D_{10}}$

24. An undrained triaxial compression test is carried out on a saturated clay sample under a cell pressure of $100\ kN/m^2$. The sample failed at a deviator stress of $200\ kN/m^2$. The cohesion of the given sample of clay in kN/m^2 is .....

(1) 50   (2) 100   (3) 200   (4) 300

25. A dry sand specimen was tested in a triaxial machine with the cell pressure of 50 kPa. If the deviator stress at failure was 100 kPa, the angle of shearing resistance is

(1) 30°   (2) 15°   (3) 45°   (4) 60°

26. A fine grained soil has a liquid limit of 45% and lies above the A-line when plotted on a plasticity chart. The group symbol of the soil as per IS soil classification is .....

(1) CH   (2) CI   (3) CL   (4) MI

27. Sample procured in a sandy soil by split spoon sampler is :

(1) Disturbed sample   (2) Undisturbed sample

(3) Representative sample   (4) Wash sample

28. Plastic limit and liquid limit of a sample are 24%, 60% and flow index = 0.6. Toughness index will be .....

(1) 0.6   (2) 0.4   (3) 0.7   (4) 0.5

29. The laboratory test results of a soil sample are given below :

Percentage finer than 4.5 mm = 60

Percentage finer than 0.075 mm = 30

Liquid limit = 35%

Plastic limit = 27%

The soil classification is

(1) GM   (2) SM   (3) GC   (4) ML-MI

30. The liquid limit (LL), plastic limit (PL) and shrinkage limit (SL) of a cohesive soil satisfy the relation :

(1) LL > PL < SL   (2) LL > PL > SL   (3) LL < PL < SL   (4) LL < PL > SL

31. A fine grained soil has liquid limit of 60 and plastic limit of 20. As per the plasticity chart, according to IS soil classification, the soil is represented by the letter symbols :

(1) CL   (2) ML   (3) CH   (4) CL-ML

32. Sieve analysis on a dry soil sample of mass 1000 g showed that 980 g and 270 g of soil pass through 4.75 mm and 0.075 mm sieve, respectively. The liquid limit and plastic limits of the soil fraction passing through 425 µ sieves are 40% and 18% respectively. The soil may be classified as :

(1) SC   (2) MI   (3) CI   (4) SM

33. Match List-I with List-II and select the correct answer using codes given below the lists :

List – I		List-II	
(A)	Pycnometer	1.	Specific gravity
(B)	Core cutter	2.	Grain size analysis
(C)	Mechanical sieve	3.	Field density

    Codes :

	A	B	C
(1)	1	3	2
(2)	1	2	3
(3)	3	2	1
(4)	2	3	1

34. In a compaction test, G, w, S and e represent the specific gravity, water content, degree of saturation and void ratio of the soil sample, respectively. If γ_w represents the unit weight of water and γ_d represents the dry unit weight of the soil, the equation for zero air voids line is :

    (1) $\gamma_d = \dfrac{G\gamma_w}{1 + Se}$ (2) $\gamma_d = \dfrac{G\gamma_w}{1 + Gw}$ (3) $\gamma_d = \dfrac{Gw}{1 + \gamma_w S}$ (4) $\gamma_d = \dfrac{Gw}{1 + Se}$

35. The water content of a saturated soil and specific gravity of soil solids were found to be 30% and 2.70 respectively. The void ratio of the soil is .....

    (1) 0.71   (2) 0.30   (3) 0.45   (4) 0.45

36. A saturated soil mass has a total density 22 kN/m³ and a water content of 10%. The dry density of this soil is .....

    (1) 20 kN/m³   (2) 22 kN/m³   (3) 19.8 kN/m³   (4) 23.2 kN/m³

37. If correct value of cohesion of highly soft clay is to be determined, choose the correct type of test that should be carried :

    (1) Direct shear test   (2) Triaxial shear test

    (3) Field vane shear test   (4) Laboratory unconfined compression test

38. When porosity is 50%, the void ratio is :

    (1) > 1   (2) 0.50   (3) 1   (4) 1.5

39. For a soil in natural state, void ratio is 1, water content is 30% and G = 2.50, the degree of saturation is :

    (1) 0%   (2) 150%   (3) 75%   (4) 30%

40. A sample of dry soil weight is 120 gm and its volume is 80 ml. If the specific gravity is 2.70, the void ratio of the sample is :

    (1) 1.5   (2) 0.5   (3) 1.0   (4) 0.8

41. In a wet soil mass, air occupies one-sixth of its volume and water occupies one-third of its volume. The porosity of the soil is :

    (1) 0.25   (2) 0.5   (3) 1.00   (4) 1.50

42. In a soil mass if volume of voids is equal to volume of solids, then values of void ratio and porosity are :

    (1) 0.5, 1   (2) 1, 0.5   (3) 1.5, 0.5   (4) 0.5, 1.5

43. In liquid limit test by Casagrande apparatus, the water content for 10 and 100 blows are 40% and 10%. The flow index for the soil is :
    (1) 10   (2) 40   (3) 30   (4) 50

44. The void ratios of a solid in its densest and loosest state are 0.2 and 0.80. If void ratio in the natural state is 0.5, the relative density is :
    (1) 80%   (2) 66%   (3) 50%   (4) 20%

45. Match List - I with List - II and select the correct answer using codes given below :

List - I	List - II
(Field Test)	**(Parameters measured)**
(A) Plate Load Test	(i) Total and frictional resistance
(B) Standard Penetration Test	(ii) Load intensity and settlement values
(C) Static Cone Penetration Test	(iii) Ned values
(D) Dynamic Cone Penetration Test	(iv) SPT values

    Codes :

	(A)	(B)	(C)	(D)
(1)	(ii)	(iv)	(iii)	(i)
(2)	(iv)	(ii)	(iii)	(i)
(3)	(ii)	(iv)	(i)	(iii)
(4)	(iv)	(ii)	(i)	(iii)

46. A clay sample has void ratio of 0.70 in the dry condition. The grain specific gravity has been determined as 2.80. The shrinkage limit of this clay will be .....
    (1) 10%   (2) 15%   (3) 20%   (4) 25%

47. A soil has the liquid limit of 60% and plastic limit of 20%. Then the classification of soil as per IS soil classification system is.....
    (1) CL   (2) CI   (3) CH   (4) MH

48. Sieve analysis on a dry soil sample of mass 1000 g showed that 900 g and 300 g of soil pass through 4.75 mm and 0.075 mm respectively. The liquid limit and plastic limit of the soil passing 425 micron sieve are 40% and 20% respectively. The soil may be classified as .....
    (1) SC   (2) MI   (3) CI   (4) SM

49. Match the following

List I : Soil Property	List II : Range of Soil Property
(A) Void ratio	1. Always more than one.
(B) Uniformity coefficient	2. Can be more than one.
(C) Porosity	3. Always less than one.

    Codes :

	A	B	C
(1)	1	2	3
(2)	3	2	1
(3)	3	1	2
(4)	2	1	3

50. Match the following :

    List I : Phase of soil   List II : Consistency index (I_c)

    (A) In plastic stage   1. 0
    (B) At plastic limit   2. 0.5
    (C) At liquid limit   3. 1

    Codes :

	A	B	C
(1)	1	2	3
(2)	3	2	1
(3)	2	3	1
(4)	2	1	3

51. The coefficients of uniformity and curvature of a soil are 4 and 1 respectively. The ratio D_{30}/D_{10} will be :
    (1) 1   (2) 2
    (3) 3   (4) 4

52. A soil sample is having a specific gravity of 2.60 and a void ratio of 0.78. The water content in percentage required to fully saturate the soil at that void ratio would be :
    (1) 10   (2) 30
    (3) 50   (4) 70

53. Match List I with List II and select the correct answer using the codes given below the lists :

    List I (Property of soil)   List II (Laboratory equipment)
    (A) Field density   (1) Pycnometer
    (B) Specific gravity   (2) Permeameter
    (C) Coefficient of permeability   (3) Sand pouring cylinder

Codes :	A	B	C
(1)	3	1	2
(2)	1	3	2
(3)	2	1	3

54. Match List I with List II and select correct answer using codes given under the lists :

    List I (Soil)   List II (Grain size)
    (A) Clay   (1) 2.00 to 4.75 mm
    (B) Coarse sand   (2) 0.002 to 0.2 mm
    (C) Silt   (3) < 0.002 mm

Codes :	A	B	C
(1)	1	3	2
(2)	2	1	3
(3)	3	1	2

55. Match List I with List II and select the correct answer using the codes given below the lists :

List I [Field Test]

(A) Vane shear test

(B) Standard penetration test

(C) Static cone penetration test

List II [Useful for]

(a) End bearing and skin friction resistance

(b) Soft clay

(c) Sandy deposits

Codes :

	(A)	(B)	(C)
(1)	(c)	(b)	(a)
(2)	(b)	(c)	(a)
(3)	(a)	(c)	(b)
(4)	(c)	(a)	(b)

56. Match List I with List II and select correct answer using codes given below the lists :

List I

(A) Atterberg's experiments

(B) Clay

(C) Sand

List II

(1) Very plastic soil

(2) Least plastic soil

(3) Determination of plasticity of soils

Codes :

	A	B	C
(1)	3	1	2
(2)	1	2	3
(3)	2	1	3

57. Match List I with List II and select correct answer using codes given under the lists :

List I

(A) Shrinkage limit

(B) Liquid limit

(C) Plastic limit

List II

(1) The water content at which the soil looses its full plasticity.

(2) The boundary between liquid state and plastic state.

(3) The water content at which soil particles come as near to each other as physically feasible.

Codes :

	A	B	C
(1)	3	2	1
(2)	3	1	2
(3)	2	1	3

58. A soil has liquid limit of 60%, plastic limit of 35% and shrinkage limit of 20% and it has a natural moisture content of 50%. The liquidity index of soil is

(1) 1.5　　　(2) 1.25　　　(3) 0.6　　　(4) 0.4

59. A dry soil sample has equal amounts of solids and voids by volume. Its void ratio and porosity will be (Choose correct option given below).

	Void Ratio	Porosity (%)
(1)	1.0	100%
(2)	0.5	50%
(3)	0.5	100%
(4)	1.0	50%

60. Match List I with List II and select correct answer by using codes given below the lists.

    List I   **List II (Permeability)**

    (A) Gravels   (1) 10^{-7} cm/sec.

    (B) Clays   (2) 10^{-6} cm/sec.

    (C) Silt   (3) 10 cm/sec.

    Codes : A B C

      (1) 3 1 2

      (2) 1 2 3

      (3) 3 2 1

61. Match List I with List II. Select the correct answer using the codes given below the lists.

    List I   **List II**

    (Type of Soil)   **(Drainage Characteristics)**

    (A) Well graded gravels, or gravel sands or no fines.   (1) Poor

    (B) Silty gravels, gravel silt and sand mixture   (2) Practically impervious

    (C) Inorganic clays of high plasticity, fat clays   (3) Excellent

    Codes : A B C

      (1) 3 1 2

      (2) 1 2 3

      (3) 3 2 1

62. Lists I and II contain respectively terms and expressions related to soil classifications. Match the two lists and select the correct answer using the codes given below.

    List I   **List II**

    (A) Activity number   (1) $\dfrac{\text{Unconfined compressive strength of undisturbed soil sample}}{\text{Unconfined compressive strength of remoulded soil sample}}$

    (B) Liquidity index   (2) $\dfrac{\text{Plasticity index}}{\text{\% finer than 2 microns}}$

    (C) Sensitivity   (3) $\dfrac{\text{Natural moisture content} - \text{Plastic limit}}{\text{Plasticity index}}$

    Codes : A B C

      (1) 2 1 3

      (2) 1 2 3

      (3) 2 3 1

63. Match List I with List II and select the correct answer using codes given below the lists.

    List I   **List II**

    (Type of soil)   **(Mode of transportation and deposition)**

    (A) Lacurstrine soils   (1) Transportation by wind

    (B) Alluvial soil   (2) Transportation by gravitational force

    (C) Aeolian soils   (3) Deposited at the bottom of lakes

    (D) Colluvial soil   (4) Transportation by running water

Codes :   A   B   C   D
   (1)   1   2   3   4
   (2)   3   4   1   2
   (3)   2   3   1   4

64. Match List I with List II and select the correct answer using the codes given below the lists :

List I (Term)	List II (Formulae)
(A) Void ratio	(1) $\dfrac{V_v}{V}$
(B) Porosity	(2) $\dfrac{V_v}{V_s} \times 100$
(C) Degree of saturation	(3) $\dfrac{W_w}{V_v}$

Codes :   A   B   C
   (1)   3   2   1
   (2)   2   1   3
   (3)   1   2   3

65. Match List I with List II and select the correct answer using the codes given below the lists :

List I	List II
(A) Loess	(1) Deposited from suspension in running water
(B) Peat	(2) Deposits by wet land
(C) Alluvial-soil	(3) Deposits by wind

Codes :   A   B   C
   (1)   3   2   1
   (2)   2   3   1
   (3)   1   2   3

66. Match List I (Soils) with List II (Group symbols) and select the correct answer using the codes given below the lists :

List I	List II
(A) Clayey gravel	(1) SM
(B) Clayey sand	(2) SC
(C) Silty sand	(3) GC

Codes :   A   B   C
   (1)   1   2   3
   (2)   3   2   1
   (3)   3   1   2

67. Match List I (Densities) with List II (Expressions) and select the correct answer using the codes given below the lists :

(Symbols G, e, γ_w and S stand for specific gravity of soil grains, void ratio, unit weight of water and degree of saturation respectively).

List I (Densities)	List II (Expressions)
(A) Dry density	(1) $\left(\dfrac{G + Se}{1 + e}\right) \gamma_w$
(B) Moist density	(2) $\left(\dfrac{G}{1 + e}\right) \gamma_w$
(C) Submerged density	(3) $\left(\dfrac{G - 1}{1 + e}\right) \gamma_w$

Codes :	A	B	C
(1)	3	1	2
(2)	1	2	3
(3)	2	1	3

68. Match List I (Unit) with List II (Purpose) and select the correct answer using the code given below the lists :

List I (Unit)	List II (Purpose)
(A) Graded filter	(1) To reduce seepage of water through body of earth dam.
(B) Lime treatment	(2) To stabilize black cotton soils.
(C) Curtain grouting	(3) To drain water without losing fines from the soil.

Codes :	A	B	C
(1)	3	2	1
(2)	1	3	2
(3)	3	1	2

69. Match List I (Soil) with List II (Type) and select the correct answer using the codes given below the lists :

List I (Soil)	List II (Type)
(A) Fine sand	(1) Organic soil
(B) Silt	(2) Coarse grained soil
(C) Peat	(3) Fine grained soil

Codes :	A	B	C
(1)	3	1	2
(2)	2	3	1
(3)	2	1	3

70. Match List I (Soil classification symbol) with List II (Soil property) and select the correct answer using the codes given below the lists :

List I	List II
(A) GW	(1) Soil having uniformity coefficient > 6
(B) SW	(2) Soil having uniformity coefficient > 4
(C) ML	(3) Soil having low plasticity

Codes :   A   B   C
   (1)   1   2   3
   (2)   2   1   3
   (3)   1   3   2

71. Match List I with List II and select the correct answer using the codes given below the lists :

List I	List II
(A) ML	(1) Silty sand
(B) SM	(2) Inorganic silt with large compressibility
(C) MH	(3) Inorganic silt with small compressibility

Codes :   A   B   C
   (1)   2   3   1
   (2)   3   1   2
   (3)   2   1   3

72. A soil sample tested in a triaxial compression apparatus failed when the total maximum and minimum principal stresses were 100 kPa and 40 kPa, respectively. The pore pressure measured at failure was 10 kPa. The effective principal stress ratio at failure is .....

   (1)   2.5   (2)   2.0   (3)   2.75   (4)   3.0

73. A CD triaxial test was conducted on a granular soil. At failure, $\dfrac{\sigma_1}{\sigma_3}$, was 3.0. The effective minor principal stress of failure was 75 kPa. The principal stress difference at failure will be

   (1)   75 kPa   (2)   150 kPa   (3)   225 kPa   (4)   300 kPa

74. A cylinder of clayey soil fails under an axial vertical stress of 20 t/m^2 when it is laterally unconfined. The failure plane makes an angle of 45° with the horizontal. The cohesion of the soil sample will be ....

   (1)   10 t/m^2 (2)   20 t/m^2 (3)   14.14 t/m^2 (4)   28.28 t/m^2

75. The average friction angle (ϕ) for a homogenous sand deposit is 30. The ratio of the major and minor principal stresses at any point in the soil medium, at failure will be :

   (1)   2   (2)   3   (3)   4   (4)   1

76. A shear test was conducted on a sample. At failure the ratio of $\dfrac{\sigma_1 - \sigma_3}{2}$ to $\dfrac{\sigma_1 + \sigma_3}{2}$ is equal to unity. Which one of the following shear tests represents this condition ?

   (1)   Drained triaxial compression test   (2)   Undrained triaxial compression test
   (3)   Undrained triaxial compression test   (4)   Unconfined compression test

77. A dry sand specimen is put through a triaxial test. Cell pressure is 50 kPa and deviator stress is 100 kPa. The angle of internal friction for the sand specimen is .....

   (1)   15°   (2)   30°   (3)   37°   (4)   45°

78. A clayey sample when tested in unconfined compression, gave compressive strength of 100 kN/m². Specimen of same clay, with same initial condition is subjected to undrained, unconsolidated triaxial test under a cell pressure of 100 kN/m². Axial stress in kN/m² of failure would be .....

   (1) 150   (2) 220   (3) 250   (4) 300

79. A vane 20 cm long and 10 cm in diameter was pressed into a soft marine clay at the bottom of a bore hole. Torque was applied gradually and failure occurred at 1000 kg cm. The cohesion of the clay in kg/cm² is ......

   (1) $\dfrac{1}{\pi} \times \dfrac{6}{7}$ (2) $\dfrac{1}{\pi} \times \dfrac{5}{7}$ (3) $\dfrac{1}{\pi} \times \dfrac{4}{7}$ (4) $\dfrac{1}{\pi} \times \dfrac{3}{7}$

80. A soil fails under an axial vertical stress of 100 kN/m² in an unconfined compression test. The failure plane makes an angle of 50° with the horizontal. The shear parameters C and ϕ respectively will be ......

   (1) 41.9 kN/m², 0   (2) 50.0 kN/m², 0   (3) 41.9 kN/m², 10° (4) 50.0 kN/m², 10°

81. Stoke's law is used to determine .....

   (1) specific gravity of soil solids
   (2) density of soil suspension
   (3) grain size distribution of those soils whose grain size is finer than 0.075 mm
   (4) All of these

82. For a partially saturated soil, Δu the increase in pore water pressure, when no drainage is permitted, is expressed as (where A and B are Skempton's pore pressure parameters, $\Delta\sigma_1$ and $\Delta\sigma_3$ are major and minor principal stress increments)

   (1) $\Delta u = B (\Delta\sigma_3 + A (\Delta\sigma_1 - \Delta\sigma_3))$ (2) $\Delta u = A (\Delta\sigma_3 + B (\Delta\sigma_1 - \Delta\sigma_3))$
   (3) $\Delta u = \Delta\sigma_3 + A (\Delta\sigma_1 - \Delta\sigma_3)$ (4) $\Delta u = \Delta\sigma_3 + B (\Delta\sigma_1 - \Delta\sigma_3)$

83. For a sandy soil, the angle of internal friction is 30. If the major principle stress is 50 kN/m² at failure, then the corresponding minor principal stress (in kN/m²) will be ...

   (1) 12.2   (2) 16.66   (3) 20.8   (4) 27.2

84. Grain size of soil indicated that $D_{10} = 0.004$ mm, $D_{30} = 0.002$ mm and $D_{60} = 0.005$ mm. The uniformity coefficient of this soil is .....

   (1) 1.25   (2) 1.2   (3) 1.12   (4) none of these

85. Plastic limit and liquid limit of sample are 30%, 65% and flow index = 0.5. Toughness index will be .....

   (1) 0.6   (2) 0.4   (3) 0.7   (4) 0.3

86. A sample of soil having liquid limit 48%, plastic limit 20% and shrinkage limit 17% and percentage of water content is 40%. The consistency index is .....

   (1) 3.512   (2) 0.2580   (3) 0.2857   (4) 2.857

87. In a direct shear test, the shear stress and normal stress on a dry sand sample at failure are 0.6 kg/cm² and 1 kg/cm² respectively. The angle of internal friction of the sand will be nearly :

   (1) 25°   (2) 31°   (3) 37°   (4) 43°

88. Total sum of consistency index and liquidity index is always equal to .....
    (1) 0   (2) 1   (3) both   (4) none of these
89. When activity of soil is in between 0.75 to 1.25, then soil is considered to be .....
    (1) normal   (2) active   (3) inactive   (4) none of these
90. When activity of soil is greater than 1.25, then soil is considered to be .....
    (1) normal   (2) active   (3) inactive   (4) none of these
91. The area of cross-section A at failure or during any stage of Triaxial Compression Test and its initial length (L) and volume (V), are related by the equation
    (1) $A = \dfrac{V + \Delta V}{L - \Delta L}$ (2) $A = \dfrac{V - \Delta V}{V + \Delta L}$ (3) $A = \dfrac{V - \Delta V}{L - \Delta L}$ (4) $A = \dfrac{V + \Delta V}{L + \Delta L}$
92. Match List I (Field problems) with List II (Type of Laboratory shear test) and select the correct answer using the codes given below the lists :

List I	List II
(A) Stability of a clay foundation of an embankment, whose rate of construction is such that some consolidation occurs.	1. Undrained triaxial test.
(B) Initial stability of a footing on saturated clay.	2. Drained triaxial test.
(C) Long-term stability of a slope in stiff, fissured clay.	3. Consolidated undrained test.

    Codes :
    (1) A   B   C   (2) A   B   C
         1   3   4   1   3   2
    (3) A   B   C   (4) A   B   C
         3   1   2   3   1   4
93. Which of the following clay mineral gives maximum amount of swelling ?
    (1) Kalonite   (2) Montmerillonite
    (3) Illite   (4) All of these
94. When degree of saturation is 1, soil is considered to be .....
    (1) fully saturated   (2) dry soil
    (3) both   (4) none of these
95. The dry soil has a mass specific gravity of 1.55. If the specific gravity of solids is 2.7, then void ratio will be .....
    (1) 0.5   (2) 1.0   (3) 1.5   (4) 2.0
96. A triaxial shear test is prefered to direct shear test, because .....
    (1) it can be performed under all three drainage conditions with complete control.
    (2) precise measurement of pore pressure and change in volume during test, is not possible.
    (3) stress distribution on the failure plane, is non-uniform.
    (4) none of these

97. A saturated soil mass has total density 22 kN/m³ and water content of 10%. The dry density of soil is .....

 (1) 20 kN/m³   (2) 22 kN/m³   (3) 19.8 kN/m³   (4) 23.2 kN/m³

98. The neutral stress in a soil mass is .....

 (1) force per neutral area   (2) force per effective area

 (3) stress taken up by the pore water (4) stress taken up by solid particles

99. Which one of the following statements is true for Mohr-Coulomb envelope ?

 (1) Coulomb suggests that the relationship between shear strength and normal stress, is adequately represented by the straight line.

 (2) The generalised Mohr theory suggests that, though the shear stress depends on the normal stress, the relation is not linear.

 (3) Coulomb and Mohr suggest that a definite relationship exists among the principal stress and the angle of internal friction.

 (4) All the above.

100. On wetting, cohesive soils .....

 (1) loose permeability   (2) gain shear strength

 (3) loose elasticity   (4) decrease their shear strength

101. A soil has a bulk density of 1.75 gm/cm³ at a water content of 6%. If the void ratio remains constant, then its bulk density for a water content of 10% will be .....

 (1) 1.98 g/cm³   (2) 1.82 g/cm³   (3) 1.70 g/cm³   (4) 1.75 g/cm³

102. In a wet soil mass, air occupies one-sixth of its volume and water occupies one-third of its volume. The void ratio of the soil is .....

 (1) 0.25   (2) 0.5   (3) 1.00   (4) 1.50

103. The liquid limit and plastic limit of sample are 65% and 29% respectively. The percentage of the soil fraction with grain size finer than 0.002 mm is 24. The activity ratio of the soil sample is .....

 (1) 0.50   (2) 1.00   (3) 1.50   (4) 2.00

104. The dry density of a soil is 1.5 g/cc. If the saturation water content were 50% then its saturated density and submerged density would, respectively be.....

 (1) 1.5 g/cc and 1.0 g/cc   (2) 2.0 g/cc and 1.0 g/cc

 (3) 2.25 g/cc and 1.25 g/cc   (4) 2.50 g/cc and 1.50 g/cc

105. A fill having a volume of 1,50,000 cu.m is to be constructed at a void ratio of 0.8. The borrow pit soil has a void ratio of 1.4. The volume of soil required (in cubic metres) to be excavated from the borrow pit will be .....

 (1) 1,87,500   (2) 2,00,000   (3) 2,10,000   (4) 2,50,000

106. A truck can carry six cubic metres of loose earth at a void ratio of 1.4. This earth is to be excavated from a quarry where the void ratio e = 0.9. The volume of the earth in cubic metres which needs to be excavated would be :

 (1) $\dfrac{27}{7}$ (2) $\dfrac{19}{4}$ (3) $\dfrac{28}{3}$ (4) 6

107. The pressure that builds up in pore water due to load increment on the soil is termed as .....
     (1) excess pore pressure   (2) excess hydrostatic pressure
     (3) hydrodynamic pressure   (4) all of these

108. A sand deposit has a porosity of 0.375 and a specific gravity of 2.6, the critical hydraulic gradient for the sand deposit is .....
     (1) 2.975   (2) 2.225   (3) 1   (4) 0.75

109. If a soil sample of weight 0.18 kg having a volume of 10^{-4} m^3 and dry unit weight of 1600 kg/m^3 is mixed with 0.02 kg of water, then the water content in the sample will be .....
     (1) 30%   (2) 25%   (3) 20%   (4) 15%

110. The saturated and dry densities of a soil are respectively 2000 kg/m^3 and 1500 kg/m^3. The water content (in percentage) of the soil in the saturated state would be .....
     (1) 25   (2) 33.33   (3) 50   (4) 66.66

111. Through a point in a loaded soil mass, there exists n typical planes mutually orthogonal on which the stress is wholly normal and no shear stress acts, if n is .....
     (1) 1   (2) 2   (3) 3   (4) 4

112. A sample of saturated sand has a dry unit weight of 18 kN/m^3 and a specific gravity of 2.7. If γ_{water} is 10 kN/m^3, the void ratio of the soil sample will be .....
     (1) 0.5   (2) 0.6   (3) 0.4   (4) 0.9

113. The plasticity index and the percentage of grain size finer than 2 microns of a clay sample are 25 and 15 respectively. Its activity ratio is .....
     (1) 2.5   (2) 1.67   (3) 1.0   (4) 0.6

114. Based on grain distribution analysis, the D_{10}, D_{30} and D_{60} values of a given soil are 0.23 mm, 0.3 mm and 0.41 mm respectively. As per IS Code, the soil classification will be
     (1) SW   (2) SP   (3) SM   (4) SC

115. A soil sample having a void ratio of 1.3, water content of 50% and a specific gravity of 2.60, is in a state of .....
     (1) partial saturation   (2) full saturation
     (3) over saturation   (4) under saturation

116. A sample of sand above water table was found to have a natural moisture content of 15% and a unit weight of 18.84 kN/m^3. Laboratory tests on a dried sample indicated values of 0.5 and 0.85 for minimum and maximum void ratios respectively for densest and loosest states. Calculate the degree of saturation and the relative density. Assume G = 2.65.
     (1) 100% and 16.38 kN/m^3 (2) 67.7% and 16.38 kN/m^3
     (3) 50% and 19 kN/m^3 (4) 67.7% and 0.061 kN/m^3

117. The natural void ratio of a sand sample is 0.6 and its density index is 0.6. If its void ratio in the loosest state is 0.9, then the void ratio in the densest state will be .....
     (1) 0.2   (2) 0.3   (3) 0.4   (4) 0.5

118. The value of porosity of a soil sample in which the total volume of soil grains is equal to twice the total volume of voids, would be .....
    (1) 75%   (2) 66.66%   (3) 50%   (4) 33.33%

119. What are the factors influencing cost of soil investigation ?
    (a) Non uniformity of layers   (b) Undisturbed sampling
    (c) Depth of exploration   (d) Nature of project
    Answer options :
    (1) (a) and (b)   (2) (b) and (c)   (3) (c) and (d)   (4) All the above

120. Which one of the following represents relative density of saturated sand deposit having moisture content of 25%, if maximum and minimum void ratios of sand are 0.95 and 0.45 respectively and specific gravity of sand particles is 2.6 ?
    (1) 40%   (2) 50%   (3) 60%   (4) 70%

121. In a soil specimen, 80% of particles are passing through 4.75 mm I.S. sieve and 40% of particles are passing through 75 µ I.S. sieve. Its uniformity coefficient is 8 and coefficient of curvature is 2. As per I.S. classification, this soil is classified as :
    (1) SP   (2) GP   (3) SW   (4) GW

122. What are the respective values of void ratio, porosity ratio and saturated density (in kN/m^3) for a soil sample which has saturation moisture content of 20% and specific gravity of grains as 2.6 ? (Take density of water 10 kN/m^3)
    (1) 0.52, 1.08, 18.07   (2) 0.52, 0.34, 18.07
    (3) 0.77, 1.08, 16.64   (4) 0.52, 0.34, 20.14

123. Embankment fill is to be compacted at a density of 18 kN/m^3. The soil of the borrow area is at a density of 15 kN/m^3. What is the estimated number of trips of 6 cu. m capacity truck for hauling the soil required for compacting 100 m^3 fill of the embankment ? (Assume that the soil in the borrow area and that in the embankment are at the same moisture content.)
    (1) 14   (2) 18   (3) 20   (4) 23

124. A clay sample has a void ratio 0.54 in dry state. The specific gravity of soil solids is 2.7. What is the shrinkage limit of the soil ?
    (1) 8.5%   (2) 10.0%   (3) 17.0%   (4) 20.0%

125. The length/diameter ratio of cylindrical specimens used in triaxial test is generally .....
    (1) 1   (2) 1.5   (3) 2   (4) 2.5

126. A direct shear test possesses the following disadvantage.
    (1) A relatively thin thickness of sample permits quick drainage.
    (2) A relatively thin thickness of sample permits quick dissipation of pore pressure developed during the test.
    (3) As the test progresses, the area under shear gradually changes.
    (4) None of these.

127. In comparison to Atterberg limits of normal soils, the expansive soils have which of the following ?
     (a) More liquid limit
     (b) Less plastic limit
     (c) Less shrinkage limit
     (d) More volumetric shrinkage
     Select the correct answer using the codes given below :
     (1) (a), (b), (c) and (d)
     (2) (a), (c) and (d)
     (3) (b) and (c)
     (4) (a), (b) and (d)
         Except (3) all are valid.

128. Which one of the following represent relative density of saturated sand deposit with moisture content of 25% if maximum and minimum void ratio of sand are 0.95 and 0.45. Assume specific gravity of sand as 2.6.
     (1) 40%
     (2) 50%
     (3) 60%
     (4) 70%

129. The angle of internal friction is maximum for .....
     (1) angular-grained loose sand
     (2) angular-grained dense sand
     (3) round-grained dense sand
     (4) clays

130. Match the following
     (A) SM
     (B) MH
     (C) GP
     (D) CI
     (i) Clay with intermediate plasticity
     (ii) Poorly graded gravel
     (iii) Silty sand
     (iv) Silt of high compressibility
     Codes :

	(A)	(B)	(C)	(D)
(1)	(iv)	(iii)	(ii)	(i)
(2)	(iii)	(iv)	(i)	(ii)
(3)	(iv)	(ii)	(iii)	(i)
(4)	(iii)	(iv)	(ii)	(i)

131. The triaxial compression test is usually used for .....
     (1) unconsolidated-undrained test
     (2) consolidated-undrained test
     (3) drained test
     (4) all the tests

132. In a cohesionless soil, quick sand condition occurs when effective pressure is :
     (1) High
     (2) Zero
     (3) Less
     (4) None of the above

133. The seismic refraction methods cannot be used if the wave velocity is :
     (1) greater than the velocity in the upper layer
     (2) less than the velocity in the lower layer
     (3) more than four times
     (4) more than thrice

134. Submergence of foundation due to rise of water table causes :
     (1) increase in bearing capacity
     (2) decrease in bearing capacity
     (3) no change in bearing capacity
     (4) None of the above

135. The radius of friction circle is equal to :
   (1) $R \sin \phi$ (2) $R \cos \phi$ (3) $R \tan \phi$ (4) $R \phi$

136. To resist heavy lateral loads, which type of piles are used ?
   (1) Friction and bearing piles   (2) Displacement piles
   (3) Under reamed piles   (4) Batter piles

137. A shallow foundation is defined as foundation which has :
   (1) depth less than 0.6 m   (2) depth less than its width
   (3) depth less than 1 m   (4) None of the above

138. Allowable soil pressure for foundation in cohesive soils is generally controlled by :
   (1) settlements   (2) bearing capacity
   (3) Both 1 and 2   (4) Neither 1 nor 2

139. For testing a saturated clay for shear strength, the test recommended is .....
   (1) direct shear test   (2) triaxial compression test
   (3) unconfined compression test   (4) vane shear test

140. The shear strength of a soil .....
   (1) increases with an increase in the normal stress
   (2) is proportional to the cohesion of the soil
   (3) is proportional to the tangent of the angle of internal friction
   (4) all the above

141. In a falling head permeability test on a soil, the time taken for the head to fall from h_0 to h_1 is t. The test is repeated with the same initial head h_0, the final head h' is noted in time $t/2$. Which one of the following equations gives the relation between h', h_0 and h_1 ?
   (1) $h' = h_0/h_1$ (2) $h' = \sqrt{h_0/h_1}$
   (3) $h' = h_0 h_1$ (4) $h' = \sqrt{h_0 h_1}$

142. The upstream slope of an earth dam under steady seepage condition is
   (1) equipotential line   (2) phreatic line
   (3) flow-line   (4) seepage line

143. For a practically impervious type of soil, the coefficient of permeability is determined in labroatory using .....
   (1) variable head test   (2) constant head test
   (3) consolidation test   (4) pumping test

144. Consider the following factors pertaining to the flow through soil :
   (a) Hydraulic gradient   (b) Grain size
   (c) Void ratio   (d) Cross-sectional area of the sample
   Of these, the factors affecting permeability include
   (1) (a) and (d)   (2) (b) and (c)
   (3) (a), (b) and (c)   (4) (b), (c) and (d)

145. The shear strength in plastic undrained clay is due to .....
   (1) inter-granular friction   (2) internal friction
   (3) cohesion   (4) none of these

146. With the rise of temperature, the permeability .....
    (1) increases   (2) decreases
    (3) remains constant   (4) none

147. The soil is said to be impermeable when coefficient of permeability is .....
    (1) $< 10^{-7}$ cm/sec   (2) $< 10^{-10}$ cm/sec (3) $> 10^{-9}$ cm/sec   (4) $< 10^{-15}$ cm/sec

148. The soil is said to be highly permeable when coefficient of permeability is
    (1) $> 10^{-2}$ cm/sec   (2) $> 10^{-1}$ cm/sec   (3) $< 10^{-1}$ cm/sec   (4) $< 10^{-2}$ cm/sec

149. In a Darcian flow, flow velocity is .....
    (1) actual velocity   (2) seepage velocity
    (3) discharge velocity   (4) boundary velocity

150. In granular soil, K varies with the specific surface :
    (1) directly   (2) inversely   (3) logarithmically (4) not in order

151. A flow is taking place in a soil for which porosity is "n". If the discharge velocity is "v", then the seepage velocity will be :
    (1) $n \cdot v$ (2) n/v (3) v/n (4) v/n^2

152. The upward movement of a soil is called .....
    (1) heaving   (2) swelling   (3) creep   (4) none of these

153. Thixotropy is defined as .....
    (1) Ratio of the compressive strength of unconfined undisturbed soil to that of remoulded soil.
    (2) The rotation of soil particles into stable state while remoulding.
    (3) The water content at which a soil changes from the liquid state to solid state.
    (4) The water content at which a soil flows.

154. The angle of internal friction is least for .....
    (1) angular-grained loose sand   (2) angular-grained dense sand
    (3) clays   (4) round-grained loose sand

155. According to Darcy's law for flow through porous media, the velocity is proportional to ....
    (1) effective stress   (2) hydraulic gradient
    (3) cohesion   (4) stability number

156. Piping in soil occurs when ....
    (1) the soil is highly porous   (2) sudden change in permeability occurs
    (3) effective pressure becomes zero   (4) the soil is highly stratified

157. A flownet is drawn for a weir. The total head loss is 6 m, number of potential drops is 10 and the length of the flow path for the last square is 1 m. The exit gradient is ....
    (1) 0.6   (2) 0.7   (3) 1.0   (4) 1.6

158. An upward hydraulic gradient i of a certain magnitude will initiate the phenomenon of boiling in granular soils. The magnitude of this gradient is
    (1) $0 \le i \le 0.5$ (2) $0.5 \le i \le 1.0$ (3) $i = 1.0$ (4) $1 < i \le 2$

159. A deposit of fine sand has a porosity 'n' and specific gravity of soil solids is G. The hydraulic gradient of the deposit to develop boiling condition of sand is given by :

    (1) $i_c = (G - 1)(1 - n)$
    (2) $i_c = (G - 1)(1 + n)$

    (3) $i_c = \dfrac{G - 1}{1 - n}$
    (4) $i_c = \dfrac{G - 1}{1 + n}$

160. Consider the following statements about the properties of flownets :

    (a) Flow lines are perpendicular to equipotential lines.

    (b) No two flow lines or equipotential lines start from the same point.

    (c) No two flow lines cross each other.

    Of these statements

    (1) (a), (b) and (c) are correct
    (2) (b) and (c) are correct

    (3) (a) and (b) are correct
    (4) (a) and (c) are correct

161. A flow net is drawn to obtain :

    (1) seepage, coefficient of permeability and uplift pressure.

    (2) coefficient of permeability, uplift pressure and exit gradient.

    (3) exit gradient, uplift pressure and seepage quantity.

    (4) exit gradient, seepage and coefficient of permeability.

162. For an isotropic soil, permeabilities in x and y directions are k_x and k_y respectively in a two dimensional flow. The effective permeability k_{eq} for the soil is given by :

    (1) $k_x + k_y$
    (2) k_x / k_y
    (3) $(k_x^2 + k_y^2)^{1/2}$
    (4) $(k_x k_y)^{1/2}$

163. Consider the following statements regarding anisotropic soils

    (a) The coefficient of permeability has maximum value in the direction of stratification.

    (b) The coefficient of permeability has minimum value in the direction normal to the direction of stratification.

    (c) The coefficient of permeability has same value in both the directions.

    Of these statements,

    (1) (a) alone is correct
    (2) (a) and (b) are correct

    (3) (b) and (c) are correct
    (4) (a) and (c) are correct

164. From a flow net which of the following information can be obtained ?

    (a) Rate of flow
    (b) Pore water pressure

    (b) Exit gradient
    (d) Permeability

    Select the correct answer using the codes given below :

    (1) (a), (b), (c) and (d)
    (2) (a), (b) and (c) only

    (3) (b), (c) and (d) only
    (4) (a) only

165. The ratio of the undrained strength in the undrained state to the undrained strength, at the same water content, in the remoulded state, is called the sensitivity of the clay. Its value for quick clays is .....

    (1) 20
    (2) 8
    (3) 12
    (4) 16

166. For a practically impervious type of soil, the coefficient of permeability is determined using field test :
     - (1) variable head test
     - (2) constant head test
     - (3) consolidation test
     - (4) pumping test

167. Consider the following statements regarding confined aquifers :
     - (a) The aquifer is bound at the top and below by impervious strata.
     - (b) The pressure of water is greater than atmospheric pressure.
     - (c) A tubewell sunk in such an aquifer starts flowing always by itself.
     - (d) The aquifer is fully saturated.

     Of the above statements.
     - (1) (a), (b) and (c) are correct
     - (2) (b), (c) and (d) are correct
     - (3) (a), (b) and (d) are correct
     - (4) (a), (c) and (d) are correct

168. The quantity of seepage of water through soils is proportional to .....
     - (1) coefficient of permeability of soil
     - (2) total head loss through the soil
     - (3) neither (1) nor (2)
     - (4) both (1) and (2)

169. If N_f, N_d and H are total number flow channels, total number of potential drops and total hydraulic head differences respectively, then the discharge q through the complete flow is given by (where K is a constant)
     - (1) $q = \sqrt{H} \cdot \dfrac{N_f}{N_d}$
     - (2) $q = KH \cdot \dfrac{N_d}{N_f}$
     - (3) $q = KH \cdot \dfrac{N_f}{N_d}$
     - (4) $q = KH \cdot \sqrt{\dfrac{N_f}{N_d}}$

170. If the specific gravity and voids in soil sample are G and e respectively, the critical hydraulic gradient i is .....
     - (1) $\dfrac{G-1}{1+e}$
     - (2) $\dfrac{G+1}{1-e}$
     - (3) $\dfrac{1-G}{1+e}$
     - (4) $\dfrac{1+G}{1+e}$

171. The critical exit gradient of seepage water in soils, for G = 2.67, e = 0.67 is .....
     - (1) 1.0
     - (2) 1.5
     - (3) 2.0
     - (4) 0.8

172. For a homogeneous earth dam 50 m high having 2 m free broad, a flow net was constructed and the results were : Number of potential drops = 2.4, Number of flow channels = 0.4. If coefficient of permeability of the dam material is 3×10^{-3} m³/sec, the discharge per metre length of dam is .....
     - (1) 12×10^{-5} m³/sec.
     - (2) 24×10^{-3} m³/sec.
     - (3) 6×10^{-5} m³/sec.
     - (4) 24×10^{-5} m³/sec.

173. The soil moisture driven off by heat, is called .....
     - (1) free water
     - (2) hygroscopic water
     - (3) gravity water
     - (4) none of these

174. A phreatic line is defined as the line within a dam section below which there are :
     - (1) positive equipotential lines
     - (2) positive hydrostatic pressure
     - (3) negative hydrostatic pressure
     - (4) negative equipotential lines

175. Pick up the correct statement from the following :
    (1) The phenomenon of quick sand generally occurs in the cohesionless soil.
    (2) The quick sand occurs more in fine sand and silt than coarse material.
    (3) The critical gradient depends on the void ratio and the specific gravity.
    (4) All the above

176. The capillary rise of water .....
    (1) depends upon the force responsible
    (2) increases as the size of the soil particles increases
    (3) decreases as the size of the soil particles decreases
    (4) is less in wet soil than in dry soil

177. If the unit weight of sand particles is 2.696 g/cc and porosity in loose state is 44%, the critical hydraulic gradient for quick sand condition is .....
    (1) 0.91   (2) 0.95   (3) 0.93   (4) 0.94

178. Darcy's law is applicable to seepage if a soil is .....
    (1) homogeneous   (2) isotropic   (3) incompressible (4) all of these

179. When the seepage pressure becomes equal to the pressure due to submerged weight of a soil, the effective pressure is reduced to zero and the soil particles have a tendency to move up in the direction of flow. This phenomenon is generally known as .....
    (1) quick condition   (2) boiling condition
    (3) quick sand   (4) all of these

180. The phreatic line in an earth dam may be .....
    (1) circular   (2) elliptical   (3) parabolic   (4) a straight line

181. A critical hydraulic gradient may occur when .....
    (1) flow is in upward direction   (2) seepage pressure is in upward direction
    (3) effective pressure is zero   (4) all of these

182. The critical exit gradient of seepage water in soils, increases with .....
    (1) an increase in specific gravity   (2) a decrease in specific gravity
    (3) a decrease in void ratio   (4) both (1) and (3)

183. The property of a soil which permits water to percolate through it is called .....
    (1) moisture content   (2) permeability
    (3) capillarity   (4) none of these

184. A flow net may be utilised for the determination of .....
    (1) exit gradient   (2) seepage
    (3) seepage pressure   (4) all of these

185. During seepage through a soil, direction of seepage is always .....
    (1) parallel to equipotential lines   (2) perpendicular to stream lines
    (3) perpendicular to equipotential lines (4) none of these

186. The seepage exit gradient in a soil is the ratio of .....
    (1) total head to the length of seepage   (2) flow line to slope
    (3) head upstream to that at downstream
    (4) head loss to the length of the seepage

187. If there is no impervious boundary at the bottom of a hydraulic structure, stream lines tend to follow .....
    (1) a straight line
    (2) a parabola
    (3) a semi-ellipse
    (4) a semi-circle

188. When a cohesionless soil attains quick condition, it looses .....
    (1) shear strength
    (2) bearing capacity
    (3) both (1) and (2)
    (4) neither (1) nor (2)

189. In a flow net,
    (1) flow lines and equipotential lines cross each other at right angles
    (2) fields are rectangles whose length is twice the breadth
    (3) smaller the dimensions of the field, smaller will be the hydraulic gradient and velocity of flow through it
    (4) for homogeneous soil, the curves are smooth and circular

190. The following data were obtained when a sample of medium sand was tested in a constant head permeameter :
    Cross-sectional area of sample : 100 cm^2
    Hydraulic gradient : 10
    Discharge collected : 10 cc/s
    The coefficient of permeability of the sand is .....
    (1) 0.1 m/s
    (2) 0.01 m/s
    (3) 1×10^{-4} m/s
    (4) 1×10^{-8} m/s

191. Match List - I (Soil description) with List - II (Coefficient of permeability, mm/s) and select the correct answer using the codes given below the lists.

List - I	List - II
(Soil description)	**(Coefficient of permeability, mm/s)**
(A) Gravel	(1) > 1
(B) Clay slit admixtures	(2) < 10^{-6}
(C) Homogeneous clays	(3) 10^{-4} to 10^{-6}

    Codes :

	A	B	C
(1)	1	2	3
(2)	2	1	3
(3)	3	1	2
(4)	1	3	2

192. Consider the following statements :
    (a) Organic matter increases the permeability of a soil.
    (b) Entrapped air decreases the permeability of a soil.
    Which of these statements is/are correct ?
    (1) (a) only
    (2) (b) only
    (3) Both (a) and (b)
    (4) Neither (a) nor (b)

193. Consider the following statements regarding the factors affecting permeability of soils.
    (a) Permeability varies approximately as the square of the grain size.
    (b) Permeability is directly proportional to the unit coefficient of water and its viscosity.
    (c) Permeability is greatly influenced in fine grained soils.
    (d) Permeability is reduced in the presence of organic matter.
    Of these statements,
    (1) (a), (b) and (c) are correct   (2) (b), (c) and (d) are correct
    (3) (a), (c) and (d) are correct   (4) (a), (b), (c) and (d) are correct

194. Consider the following statements regarding the coefficient of permeability of soil.
    (a) For coarse-grained soils, the constant head permeability test is performed.
    (b) For fine grained soils, the falling head permeability test is performed.
    (c) For homogeneous coarse-grained soil strata, well pumping test is suitably employed.
    Of these statements,
    (1) (a) alone is correct   (2) (a), (b) and (c) are correct
    (3) (b) and (c) are correct   (4) (c) alone is correct

195. A soil mass under seepage has downward flow of water. Which of the following statements are correct with regard to stresses at any point in the soil mass ?
    (a) Effective stress is decreased by an amount equal to the seepage force.
    (b) Effective stress is increased by an amount equal to the seepage force.
    (c) Total stress will change.
    (d) Total stress will be unaltered.
    Select the correct answer using the codes given below :
    (1) (a) and (c)   (2) (b) and (c)   (3) (a) and (d)   (4) (b) and (d)

196. If drainage is permitted throughout the test, during the application of both normal, and shear stresses so that full consolidation occurs and no excess pore pressure is set up at any stage of the test, is known as .....
    (1) quick test   (2) drained test
    (3) consolidated undrained test   (4) none of these

197. A strata of 3.5 m thick fine sand has a void ratio of 0.7 and G of 2.7. For a quicksand condition to develop in this strata, the water flowing in upward direction would require a head of ....
    (1) 7 m   (2) 5.56 m   (3) 5 m   (4) 3.5 m

198. For a soil void ratio = 0.7 and specific gravity of solids 2.7, the head required to cause quicksand over a column of 5 m high sand will be ....
    (1) 3.5 m   (2) 4.5 m   (3) 5.0 m   (4) 9.0 m

199. If the critical hydraulic gradient of a soil is 1 and its specific gravity is 2.7, then the void ratio will be ....
    (1) 0.58   (2) 0.7   (3) 1.7   (4) 2.7

200. If the soil has a permeability of 2×10^{-6} m/s, determine the seepage loss per unit length of a sheet pile wall if the flow net gives the number of low paths, $N_f = 5$ and equipotential drops, $N_d = 10$. Effective head $= 10$.

    (1) 10^{-4} m³/sec   (2) 10^{-6} m³/sec   (3) 10^{-3} m³/sec   (4) 10^{-5} m³/sec

201. Due to rise in temperature, the viscosity and unit weight of percolating fluid are reduced to 70% and 90% respectively. Other things being constant, the change in coefficient of permeability will be :

    (1) 20.0%   (2) 28.6%   (3) 63.0%   (4) 77.8%

202. Consider the following statements regarding the flow nets in seepage flow in soils.

    (a) Every intersection of a flow line and an equipotential is made at right angles.

    (b) Difference in flows ($\Delta \psi$) between any two adjacent flow lines is the same.

    (c) Difference in potentials ($\Delta \phi$) between two adjacent equipotentials is the same.

    (d) The flow lines and equipotentials form curvilinear rhombuses.

    Of these statements,

    (1) (a) and (b) are correct   (2) (b) and (c) are correct

    (3) (a), (b) and (c) are correct   (4) (c) and (d)

203. Consider the following inequalities regarding the filters provided in a dam.

    (a) $\dfrac{[D_{15}]_f}{[D_{85}]_s} < 4.5$ (b) $\dfrac{[D_{15}]_f}{[D_{15}]_s} > 4.5$

    (c) $\dfrac{[D_{25}]_f}{[D_{75}]_s} < 20$ (d) $\dfrac{[D_{50}]_f}{[D_{550}]_s} < 25$

    Of these inequalities,

    (1) (a) alone is correct   (2) (b) and (c) are correct

    (3) (a), (b) and (d) are correct   (4) (c) and (d) are correct.

204. The shearing strength of a cohesionless soil depends upon

    (1) dry density   (2) rate of loading

    (3) confining pressure   (4) nature of loading

205. The property of the soil mass which permits the water through its body is termed as .....

    (1) capillarity   (2) permeability   (3) porosity   (4) none of these

206. While applying Darcy's law for soil we are assuming soil to be .....

    (1) incompressible   (2) homogenous and isotropic

    (3) flow conditions are laminar   (4) all of these

207. The permeability of soil is .....

    (1) directly proportional to the grain size

    (2) inversely proportional to the grain size

    (3) directly proportional to square of grain size

    (4) inversely proportional to square of grain size

208. The seepage pressure always acts .....

    (1) in the direction of flow   (2) in the opposite direction of flow

    (3) both of these   (4) none of these

209. Soil is generally having critical hydraulic gradient :
    (1) 0.5   (2) 1   (3) 1.5   (4) 2.5

210. The seepage force in soil is .....
    (1) proportional to head loss   (2) proportional to exit gradient
    (3) perpendicular to the equipotential lines
    (4) all of these

211. The flow net is used to determine .....
    (1) seepage flow   (2) seepage pressure
    (3) exit gradient   (4) all of these

212. If the flow net of a coffer dam foundation had six number of flow channels and sixteen number of equipotential drops, with head of the water lost during seepage being 6 m through the foundation having $k = 4 \times 10^{-5}$ m/min, the seepage loss (m³/day) per metre length at the dam will be :
    (1) 2.16×10^{-3} (2) 6.48×10^{-3} (3) 12.96×10^{-2} (4) 15.92×10^{-2}

213. Depending upon the properties of a material, the failure envelope may .....
    (1) be either straight or curved   (2) pass through the origin of stress
    (3) intersect the shear stress axis   (4) all of these

214. The shear resistance of a soil is constituted basically of the following component.
    (1) The frictional resistance to translocation between the individual soil particles at their contact point.
    (2) To the structural relation to displacement of the soil because of the interlocking of the particles.
    (3) Cohesion and adhesion between the surfaces of the soil particles.
    (4) All the above.

215. A soil mass has coefficients of horizontal and vertical permeability as 9×10^{-7} cm/sec and 4×10^{-7} cm/sec respectively. The transformed coefficient of permeability of an equivalent isotropic soil mass is .....
    (1) 9×10^{-7} cm/sec   (2) 4×10^{-7} cm/sec
    (3) 13×10^{-7} cm/sec   (4) 6×10^{-7} cm/sec

216. Through a point in a loaded soil, the principal stress is maximum on .....
    (1) minor principal plane   (2) intermediate principal plane
    (3) major principal plane   (4) none of these

217. The loose uniform sand with rounded grains has effective grain size of 0.05 cm. Coefficient of permeability of sand is .....
    (1) 0.25 cm/sec   (2) 0.50 cm/sec   (3) 1.00 gm/sec   (4) 1.25 cm/sec

218. A soil sample, 25 cm² in cross-sectional area and 12 cm long is tested for permeability in a variable head permeometer. The stand pipe of cross-sectional area 1.2 cm² and head drop from 32 cm to 12 cm in 8 minutes and 40 sec. The permeability of soil is .....
    (1) 1.08×10^{-3} cm/sec   (2) 2.16×10^{-3} cm/sec
    (3) 0.54×10^{-3} cm/sec   (4) none of these

219. The depth of water on the upstream side of a zoned earth dam is 20 cm. The coefficient of permeabilities of upstream and downstream zones are 1.5×10^{-7} m/sec and 6×10^{-7} m/sec respectively. Determine the quantity of seepage per unit length through the dam. ($N_f = 3.5$, $N_d = 8$).

(1) 13.1×10^{-7} m^3/sec   (2) 26.2×10^{-7} m^3/sec

(3) 6.85×10^{-7} m^3/sec   (4) none of these

220. The void ratio for sand deposit varies from 0.5 to 1. The specific gravity of sand is 2.75. What is the range of critical hydraulic gradient ?

(1) 1.16 to 0.94   (2) 3 to 0.9   (3) 1.19 to 0.90   (4) 0.9 to 1.16

221. When clay is dried below its shrinkage limit and suddenly immersed in water, it disintegrates in a soft wet mass. This process is known as .....

(1) bulking of sand (2) slaking of sand (3) soil suction   (4) none of these

222. The water in the soil mass above the water table has a negative pressure. This state of reduced pressure is known as .....

(1) soil suction   (2) bulking sand   (3) slaking of sand (4) none of these

223. Soil suction depends upon .....

(1) particle size   (2) temperature   (3) both of these   (4) none of these

224. The process of increase in volume of sand due to dampness is known as .....

(1) soil suction   (2) bulking of sand

(3) slaking of sand   (4) none of these

225. The field test to determine permeability of soil is .....

(1) pumping out method   (2) pumping in method

(3) both of these   (4) constant head permeability method

226. The flow net of earth dam gave the distance to the directrix from the focus as 5 m and coefficient of permeability of soil is 3×10^{-3} cm/s. What is the quantity of seepage per unit length of dam in m^3/s ?

(1) 1.5×10^{-5} (2) 15×10^{-5} (3) 15×10^{-3} (4) 15×10^{-4}

227. A circular pile of 30 cm diameter and 7 m length passes through a recently filled up material of 3.5 m depth. The unconfined compressive strength of the soil is 60 kN/m^2. The negative skin friction of the pile is :

(1) 110 kN   (2) 330 kN   (3) 99 kN   (4) 198 kN

228. Uniformity coefficient of a soil is :

(1) always less than 1   (2) always equal to 1

(3) ≤ 1 (4) ≥ 1

229. For conducting a Standard Proctor compaction test, the weight of hammer (P in kg), the fall of hammer (Q in mm), the number of blows per layer (R) and the number of layers (S) required are respectively.

Codes :	P	Q	R	S
(1)	5.89	550	50	3
(2)	4.89	450	25	3
(3)	3.60	310	35	4
(4)	2.60	310	25	3

230. In a compaction test if the compacting effort is increased, it will result in .....
    (1) increase in maximum dry density and OMC.
    (2) increase in maximum dry density, but OMC remains unchanged.
    (3) increase in maximum dry density and decrease in OMC.
    (4) No change in maximum dry density, but decrease in OMC.

231. The optimum moisture content of soil is obtained from a plot of .....
    (1) moulding water content versus compacted unit weight
    (2) dry unit weight versus water content
    (3) time versus compression
    (4) effective stress versus void ratio

232. Pick out the incorrect statement.
    (1) Swelling of compacted clay is greater for those compacted at optimum.
    (2) Cohesionless soils do not show a marked optimum content.
    (3) Moderately cohesive soils give best results when compacted in layers.
    (4) Sheep-foot rollers are most suitable for hill soils of low plasticity.

233. Soil is compacted at which one of the following when a higher compactive effort produces highest in dry density ?
    (1) Optimum water content.
    (2) Dry side of the optimum moisture content.
    (3) Wet side of the optimum moisture content.
    (4) Saturation moisture content.

234. Proctor needle is used to determine .....
    (1) Penetration value of bitumen used in road construction
    (2) Swelling index of black cotton soils
    (3) Plastic limit of the soil
    (4) Penetration resistance to control of field compaction

235. The number of blows required for compacting each layer of soil in compaction tests is .....
    (1) 36   (2) 56   (3) 25   (4) 45

236. Factors affecting the compaction is/are .....
    (1) soil type   (2) compactive energy
    (3) water content   (4) all of these

237. The following soil has the highest OMC.
    (1) Sand   (2) Gravel   (3) Slit   (4) Clay

238. Optimum moisture content is the moisture content at which .....
    (1) settlement is maximum   (2) permeability is more
    (3) dry density is maximum   (4) shear strength is less

239. Clay particles on the wet side of optimum moisture content exhibit .....
    (1) disperse structure   (2) single grained structure
    (3) honeycomb structure   (4) flocculent structure

240. Compaction of a soil is measured in terms of .....

    (1) specific gravity   (2) compressibility (3) permeability   (4) dry density

241. Sample of saturated cohesionless soil tested in a drained triaxial compression test showed an angle of internal friction of 30°. The deviatoric stress at failure for the sample at a confining pressure of 200 kPa is equal to .....

    (1) 200 kPa   (2) 400 kPa   (3) 600 kPa   (4) 800 kPa

242. The unit internal molecular attraction of a soil,

    (1) decreases as the moisture content increases

    (2) increases as the moisture content decreases

    (3) is more in well compacted clays

    (4) depends upon the external applied load

243. A compacted soil sample using 10% moisture content has a weight of 200 g and mass unit weight of 2.0 g/cm³. If the specific gravity of soil particles and water 2.7 and 1.0 respectively, then degree of saturation of the soil is .....

    (1) 11.1%   (2) 55.6%   (3) 69.6%   (4) none of these

244. W is the weight of soil having a moisture content w. If V is the volume of proctor's mould, the dry density of the soil is .....

    (1) $\dfrac{WV}{1+w}$ (2) $\dfrac{V}{w(1+w)}$ (3) $\dfrac{W}{V(1+w)}$ (4) $\dfrac{V(1+w)}{W}$

245. Pick up the incorrect statement from the following:

    (1) Compaction has no effect on the structure of a soil.

    (2) Permeability decreases with increase in the dry density of a compacted soil.

    (3) A wet side compacted soil is more compressible than a dry side compacted soil.

    (4) Dry side compaction soils swell more when given access to moisture.

246. Pick up the incorrect statement from the following :

    (1) OMC refers to the moisture corresponding to the maximum point on the moisture content dry density curve.

    (2) The line which shows moisture content dry density relation for soil containing a constant percentage of air voids, is known as air void line.

    (3) The weight of hammer used is 15 kg.

    (4) The free fall of hammer for compaction is 30.5 cm.

247. The factor which affects the compaction is .....

    (1) moisture content   (2) type of soil

    (3) method of compaction   (4) All of these

248. Compression of soil occurs rapidly if voids are filled with .....

    (1) air   (2) water

    (3) partly with air and partly with water (4) none of these

249. The density of soil can be increased .....

    (1) by reducing the space occupied by air

    (2) by elastic compression of soil grains

    (3) by expelling water from pores

    (4) All the above

250. Pick up the correct statement from the following
    (1) The dry density reduces by addition of water after attaining optimum moisture content
    (2) The line joining the peak of three moisture content graphs obtained by using three compactive energies is called line of optimum.
    (3) Well graded coarse grained soils can be compacted to a very high density as compared to fine grained soils.
    (4) All the above

251. The ratio of the energies imparted to a soil sample in Modified Procter's Compaction test and the Standard Proctor's Compaction test is about ......
    (1) 10.0   (2) 4.5   (3) 2.2   (4) 1.8

252. The vane shear test is used for the in-situ determination of the undrained strength of the intact fully saturated
    (1) sands   (2) clays   (3) gravels   (4) highly organic soils

253. Work out the theoretical maximum dry density for a soil sample having specific gravity of 2.7 and OMC = 16%.
    (1) 1.885 gm/cm³   (2) 0.530 gm/cm³   (3) 25.39 gm/cm³   (4) none of these

254. The following soils are compacted at the same compactive effort in the field. Which one of the following is the correct sequence in the increasing order of their maximum dry density ?
    (1) Silty clay - clay - sand - gravel sand - clay mixture.
    (2) Sand - gravel sand-clay mixture - silty clay - clay.
    (3) Clay - silty clay - sand - gravel sand-clay mixture.
    (4) Sand - gravel sand-clay mixture - clay - silty clay.

255. Which one of the following is correct ?
    In laboratory compaction tests, the optimum moisture content of soil decreases
    (1) with increase of compaction energy and with decrease of coarse grains in the soil.
    (2) with decrease of compaction energy and with increase of coarse grains in the soil.
    (3) with increase of both compaction energy and coarse grains in the soil.
    (4) with decrease of both compaction energy and coarse grains in the soil.

256. In a compaction test, with increase in compactive effort :
    (1) maximum dry density increases, but OMC decreases
    (2) the compaction curve is shifted to the right and higher
    (3) both the above
    (4) both maximum dry density and OMC increase

257. The unit weight of loose sand deposit is 18 kN/m³. Determine geostatics stresses at a depth of 3 m.
    (1) 44 kN/m²   (2) 50 kN/m²   (3) 60 kN/m²   (4) 54 kN/m²

258. The vertical stress at depth z directly below the point P is (k is a constant)
    (1) $k\dfrac{P}{z}$ (2) $k\dfrac{P}{z^3}$ (3) $k\dfrac{P}{z^2}$ (4) $k\dfrac{P^z}{\sqrt{z}}$

259. The intensity of vertical stress σ_z at a depth z due to point load Q acting on the surface of a semi-infinite elastic soil mass is .....
     (1) directly proportional to depth
     (2) inversely proportional to depth
     (3) directly proportional to the square of depth
     (4) inversely proportional to the square of depth

260. σ_z is the vertical stress at a depth equal to z in the soil mass due to a surface point load Q. The vertical stress at depth equal to $2z$ will
     (1) $0.25\,\sigma_z$ (2) $0.50\,\sigma_z$ (3) $1.0\,\sigma_z$ (4) $2.0\,\sigma_z$

261. The change in the vertical stress in the soil mass estimated by Boussinesq's equation when Poisson's ratio of soil changes from 0.3 to 0.5 will
     (1) reduce by 30%   (2) increase by 50%
     (3) reduce by 20%   (4) no change

262. Consider,
     (a) Modulus of elasticity   (b) Poisson's ratio
     (c) Homogeneity of soil
     Main difference between Boussinesq's and Westergaard theory is due to ....
     (1) (a) alone   (2) (b) alone   (3) (a) and (c)   (4) (b) and (c)

263. In the case of stratified soil layers, the best equation that can be adopted for computing the pressure distribution is ...... equation.
     (1) Prandtl's   (2) Skempton's   (3) Westerguaard's (4) Boussinesq's

264. Pick out the incorrect statements.
     (a) The vertical stress distribution on a horizontal plane is bell shaped.
     (b) The vertical stress first increases and then decreases with depth asymptotically.
     (1) (a) only   (2) (b) only   (3) (a) and (b)   (4) None of these

265. The intensity of vertical pressure at a depth z directly below the point load Q on its axis of loading is :
     (1) $\dfrac{0.4775\ Q}{z}$ (2) $\dfrac{0.4775\ Q}{z^2}$ (3) $\dfrac{0.4775\ Q}{z^3}$ (4) $\dfrac{0.4775\ Q}{\sqrt{z}}$

266. The Westergaard analysis is used for .....
     (1) sandy soils   (2) cohesive soils   (3) stratified soils   (4) clayey soils

267. For a triaxial shear test conducted on a sand specimen at a confining pressure of 100 kN/m² under drained conditions, resulted in a deviator stress $(\sigma_1 - \sigma_3)$ at failure of 100 kN/m². The angle of shearing resistance of the soil would be .....
     (1) 18.43°   (2) 19.47°   (3) 26.56°   (4) 30°

268. For a sample of dry, cohesionless soil with friction angle ϕ, the failure plane will be inclined to the major principal plane by an angle equal to .....
     (1) ϕ (2) 45°   (3) $45° - \phi/2$ (4) $45° + \phi/2$

269. A concentrated load of 50 kN acts vertically at a point on the soil surface. If Boussinesq's equation is applied for computation of stress, then the ratio of vertical stresses at depths of 3 m and 5 m respectively, vertically below the point of application of load will be .....
    (1) 0.36   (2) 0.60   (3) 1.66   (4) 2.77

270. A point load of 650 kN is applied on the surface of a thick layer of clay. Using Boussinesq's elastic analysis, what is the approximate value of the estimated vertical stress at a depth 2 m and a radial distance of 1.0 m from the point of application of load ?
    (1) 55 kN/m²   (2) 44 kN/m²   (3) 41 kN/m²   (4) 37 kN/m²

271. A concentrated load of 2000 kN is applied at the ground surface. Then the vertical stress at a point which is 7 m directly below the load is .....
    (1) 40.8 kN/m   (2) 140 kN/m   (3) 20 kN/m²   (4) 81.6 kN/m²

272. The vertical stresses calculated by the Boussinesq's theory and Westergaard's theory at a particular point will be identical when r/z ratio is equal to (r = radial distance and z = vertical depth of the point)
    (1) 1   (2) 0.817   (3) 1.5   (4) 205

273 Sensitivity is defined as follows :
    (1) The property of a soil that enables it to become stiff in a relatively short time on standing.
    (2) The ratio of shear strength in natural state to the remoulded shear strength under undrained conditions.
    (3) The difference between the undisturbed shear strength and remoulded shear strength.
    (4) The tendency of dense sand to expand on application of shearing load.

274. A footing 2 m × 1 m exerts uniform pressure of 150 kN/m² on the soil. Assuming a load dispersion of 2 vertical to 1 horizontal, the average vertical stress (kN/m²) at 1.0 m below the footing is .....
    (1) 50   (2) 75   (3) 80   (4) 100

275. The vertical stress at some depth below the corner of a 2 m × 3 m rectangular footing due to a certain load intensity is 100 kN/m². What will be the vertical stress in kN/m² below the centre of a 4 m × 6 m rectangular footing at the same depth and same load intensity ?
    (1) 25   (2) 100   (3) 200   (4) 400

276. A 25 kN point load acts on the surface of an infinite elastic medium. The vertical pressure intensity in kN/m² at a point 6.0 m below and 4.0 m away from the load will be :
    (1) 132   (2) 13.2   (3) 1.32   (4) 0.132

277. Westergaard's formula for vertical stress gives greater value of stress than that by the Boussinesq's formula, when r/z exceeds :
    (1) 1.5   (2) 2.5   (3) 3.5   (4) 4.0

278. Reduction in volume of soil due to expansion of air is called as .....
    (1) consolidation   (2) compaction
    (3) both of these   (4) none of these

279. Soil should be fully saturated in case of .....
    (1) consolidation   (2) compaction
    (3) both of these   (4) none of these

280. OMC means
    (1) optimum moisture content   (2) other moisture content
    (3) optimum meter content   (4) optimum moisture calorie

281. The angle between the directions of the failure and the major principal plane is equal to .....
    (1) 90° + effective angle of shearing resistance
    (2) 90° + half of the angle of shearing resistance
    (3) 45° – half of the angle of shearing resistance
    (4) 45° + half of the angle of shearing resistance

282. In heavy compaction, the compaction energy is ...... that in light compaction.
    (1) 4 times   (2) 5 times   (3) 6 times   (4) 4.25 times

283. What will be the dry density of soil sample, if water content is 15% and saturation is 90%? Assume G = 2.7.
    (1) 1.820   (2) 1.862   (3) 1.782   (4) 0.450

284. A soil sample is having optimum moisture content of 20% and bulk density of 1.86 gm/cc. Determine void ratio. Assume G = 2.7.
    (1) 0.59   (2) 0.74   (3) 0.78   (4) none of these

285. The equation $\tau = C + \sigma \tan \phi$ is given by .....
    (1) Rankine theory   (2) Coulomb theory
    (3) Culmann theory   (4) Mohr theory

286. The vertical stress at a point P at a depth of 4 m directly under the centre of the circular area of radius 3 m and subjected to load of 250 kN/m² is
    (1) 84   (2) 122   (3) 150   (4) none of these

287. Consolidation can be applied to :
    (1) cohesive soils only   (2) cohesive and cohesionless soil
    (3) both of (1) and (2)   (4) none of these

288. Factor which effects the compaction is .....
    (1) water content of soil   (2) type of soil
    (3) compaction effects   (4) all of these

289. The height from which the light compaction is done is .....
    (1) 310 mm   (2) 450 mm   (3) both of these   (4) none of these

290. In heavy compaction, number of blows per layer are .....
    (1) 25   (2) 10   (3) 5   (4) none of these

291. The mould in heavy compaction is filled with .... number of layers.
    (1) 6   (2) 10   (3) 5   (4) none of these

292. A line which connects all points below the ground surface at which the vertical pressure is the same is called as .....
    (1) isopoint   (2) isobar   (3) isostress   (4) none of these

293. Slip circle method is used for determination of :
    (1) stability of finite slope
    (2) stability of infinite slope
    (3) stability of finite and infinite slope
    (4) None of the above

294. The pre-compression method is useful for compacting :
    (1) silts
    (2) organic soils
    (3) clays
    (4) All the above

295. In situ vane shear test is used to measure shearing strength of :
    (1) very soft and sensitive clays
    (2) stiff and fissured clays
    (3) sandy soils
    (4) All of the above

296. A line or contour joining the points of equal vertical stress inside the soil mass is called as:
    (1) isobar
    (2) contour bar
    (3) vertical stress bar
    (4) None of the above

297. The zone witin which the stress have a significant effect on the settlement of structures is known as :
    (1) stress bulb
    (2) pressure bulb
    (3) strain bulb
    (4) None of the

298. Factors affecting permeability are .....
    (a) Grain size
    (b) Void ratio
    (c) Field condition
    (d) Impurities in the water
    Select the correct answer from below :
    (1) (a), (b) and (d) are correct
    (2) (a) and (c) are correct
    (3) only (c) is correct
    (4) all are correct

299. Properties of flow net are .....
    (1) Flow lines are perpendicular to equipotential lines.
    (2) No two flow lines or equpotential lines start from the same point.
    (3) No two flow lines cross each other.
    (4) All of these are correct

300. Flow net drawn for a weir, total head loss is 6 m, number of potential drops is 10 and length of the flow path for the last square is 1 m. The exit gradient is .....
    (1) 0.8
    (2) 1.6
    (3) 0.6
    (4) 1.8

301. Which one of the following is the appropriate triaxial test to assess the immediate stability of an unloading problem, such as an excavation of a clay slope ?
    (1) UU test
    (2) CU test
    (3) CD test
    (4) Unconsolidated drained tests

302. Consider the following statements :
    (a) A sand with its void ratio higher than its critical void ratio increases in volume when sheared.
    (b) A sand with its void ratio less than its critical void ratio increases in volume when sheared.
    (c) For a sand at critical void ratio, the volume change during shear is minimum.
    Which of these statements are correct ?
    (1) (a), (b) and (c)
    (2) Only (a) and (b)
    (3) Only (b) and (c)
    (4) Only (a) and (c)

303. In a shear test on cohesionless soils, if the initial void ratio is less than critical void ratio, the sample will .....
    (1) increase in volume.
    (2) initially increase in volume and then remain constant.
    (3) decreases in volume.
    (4) initially decrease and then increase in volume.

304. The ratio of unconfined compressive strength of an undisturbed sample of soil to that of a remoulded sample, at the same water content, is known as .....
    (1) activity   (2) damping   (3) plasticity   (4) sensitivity.

305. Undrained shear strength C_u of a saturated clay tested in an unconfined compression is given in terms of unconfined compressive strength q_u as .....
    (1) $C_u = 0.5\, q_u$ (2) $C_u = 0.66\, q_u$ (3) $C_u = q_u$ (4) $C_u = 2\, q_u$

306. In an unconfined compression test, sectional area at any instant of loading (A_0 = original area, ε = strain at that load) is .....
    (1) $\dfrac{A_o}{1+\varepsilon}$ (2) $\dfrac{A_o}{1-\varepsilon}$ (3) $A_o\,(1+\varepsilon)$ (4) $A_o\,(1-\varepsilon)$

307. Vane test is normally used for determining in situ shear strength of .....
    (1) soft clays   (2) sand   (3) stiff clays   (4) gravel.

308. Laboratory vane shear test can also be used to determine .....
    (1) shear parameters of silty sand   (2) shear parameters of sandy clay
    (3) liquid limit of silty clay   (4) plastic limit of clayey silt

309. Unconfined compression strength test is a
    (1) drained test   (2) undrained test
    (3) consolidated undrained test   (4) unconsolidated drained test

310. If a sample of dry sand is tested in direct shear test, it gives failure shear stress τ_f as 1 kg/cm^2 at a normal stress σ_f of 2 kg/cm^2, then the angle of internal friction of soil is given by .....
    (1) $\tan^{-1}(2)$ (2) $\tan^{-1}(1)$ (3) $\tan^{-1}\left(\dfrac{1}{2}\right)$ (4) $\tan^{-1}\left(\dfrac{1}{4}\right)$

311. Which one of the following planes is most likely to be the failure plane in sandy soils ?
    (1) Plane carrying maximum shear stress
    (2) Plane carrying maximum normal stress
    (3) Plane with the maximum angle of obliquity
    (4) Principal plane

312. Consider the following features of direct shear test
    (a) Failure takes place on the predetermined plane.
    (b) It is a quick test.
    (c) Drainage conditions cannot be changed.
    (d) Failure of the sample is progressive.
    Which of these are the disadvantages of direct shear test ?
    (1) (a), (b) and (c)   (2) (a), (c) and (d)   (3) (a), (b) and (d)   (4) (c) and (d)

313. If an unconfined compressive strength of 4 kg/cm^2 in the natural state of clay reduces by four times in the remoulded state, then its sensitivity will be :
    (1) 1   (2) 2   (3) 4   (4) 8

314. The undrained cohesion of a remoulded clay soil is 10 kN/m^2. If the sensitivity of the clay is 20, the corresponding remoulded compressive strength is .....
    (1) 5 kN/m^2 (2) 10 kN/m^2 (3) 20 kN/m^2 (4) 200 kN/m^2

315. What does the confining pressure used in triaxial compression tests on an undisturbed soil sample represent ?
    (1) The in-situ total normal stress.   (2) The in-situ total lateral stress.
    (3) The in-situ effective principal stress. (4) The in-situ shear stress.

316. Consider the following statements related to triaxial test .....
    (a) Failure occurs along pre-determined plane
    (b) Intermediate and minor principal stresses are equal
    (c) Volume changes can be measured
    (d) Field conditions can be simulated
    Of these statements,
    (1) (a), (b) and (c) are correct   (2) (a), (b) and (d) are correct
    (3) (a), (c) and (d) are correct   (4) (b), (c) and (d)are correct

317. For a fully saturated clay Skempton's pore pressure parameter B is
    (1) zero   (2) between zero and 1
    (3) 1   (4) more than 1

318. List I and List II contains respectively terms and expressions related to soil classification. Match the two lists and select the correct answer using the codes given below in the lists :

    List I   **List II**

    A. Activity number   1. $\dfrac{\text{Liquid limit} - \text{Water content}}{\text{Plasticity index}}$

    B. Liquidity index   2. $\dfrac{\text{Plasticity index}}{\text{Per cent finer than 2 microns}}$

    C. Sensitivity   3. $\dfrac{\text{Unconfined compressive strength of undistributed soil sample}}{\text{Unconfined compressive strength of remoulded soil sample}}$

    Codes :

	A	B	C
(1)	1	3	2
(2)	1	2	3
(3)	3	2	1
(4)	2	1	3

319. The direct shear test suffers from the following disadvantage.
    (1) Drain condition cannot be controlled.
    (2) Pore water pressure cannot be measured.
    (3) Shear stress on the failure plane is not uniform.
    (4) The area under the shear and vertical loads does not remain constant throughout the test.

320. The process by which a mass of saturated soil is caused by external forces to suddenly lose its shear strength and to behave as a fluid is called ....
    (1) piping   (2) slide   (3) quick condition (4) liquefaction

321. A vane shear test on a soil sample gives a moment of total resistance M. The shear stress at failure, 'S' being more or less uniform at the top bottom and surface of cylinder of soil is given by [where H = height of vane, D = Diameter of vane]

    (a) $S = \dfrac{2M}{\pi D^2 H}$ (b) $S = \dfrac{2M}{\pi D^2 [H + D]}$

    (c) $S = \dfrac{2M}{\pi D^2 \left(H + \dfrac{D}{3}\right)}$ (d) $S = \dfrac{2M}{\pi DH}$

    Of these statements :
    (1) (a) and (b) are correct   (2) (a) and (c) are correct
    (3) (b) and (c) correct   (4) (a), (b) and (c) are correct

322. For shear strength, triaxial shear test is suitable because :
    (1) it can be performed under all three drainage conditions
    (2) precise measurement of the pore pressure and volume change during the test is possible
    (3) state of stress within the specimen during any stage of the test as well as at failure, is completely determined
    (4) all the above

323. For a saturated soil, Skempton's B-parameter is .....
    (1) nearly zero   (2) nearly 0.5   (3) nearly 1.0   (4) very high

324. For a heavily over-consolidated clay, the pore pressure coefficient A_f is in the range of
    (1) 0.7 to 1.3   (2) 0.3 to 0.7   (3) – 0.5 to 0.0   (4) – 1.0 to 0.50

325. For saturated, normally consolidated soils, Skempton's pore pressure coefficients can be represented as
    (1) A < 1, B = 1   (2) A > 1, B > 1   (3) A > 1, B < 1   (4) A < 1, B > 1

326. The type of shear test (with regard to drainage conditions) in which no significant volume changes are expected and pore pressure develop throughout the test is
    (1) consolidated undrained test   (2) unconsolidated undrained test
    (3) consolidated drained test   (4) slow test

327. The maximum shear stress occurs on the filament which makes an angle with the horizontal plane equal to .....
    (1) 30°   (2) 45°   (3) 60°   (4) 90°

328. Pick up the correct statement from the following :
    (1) An unconfined compression test is a special case of triaxial compression test.
    (2) An unconfined compression test is a special case of direct shear test.
    (3) The confining pressure is maximum during an unconfined compression test.
    (4) The cylindrical specimen of a soil is subjected to major principal stress till it fails due to shearing along the plane of the failure.

329. If a pure cohesive soil specimen is subjected to a vertical compressive load only, the inclination of crack to the horizontal is .....
    (1) 30°   (2) 45°   (3) 90°   (4) 0°

330. The shear test that is more suitable in the field is .....
    (1) direct shear   (2) triaxial shear
    (3) unconfined compression   (4) vane shear

331. A sensitive clay has a shear strength of 45 kN/m² in natural state and 15 kN/m² in remoulded state. The sensitivity of the soil is .....
    (1) 1/3   (2) 30   (3) 3   (4) none

332. Which one of the following statements provides the best argument that direct shear tests are not suited for determining shear parameters of a clay soil.
    (1) Failure plane is not the weakest plane.
    (2) Pore pressures developed cannot be measured.
    (3) Satisfactory strain levels cannot be maintained.
    (4) Adequate consolidation cannot be ensured.

333. The phenomenon when the sand losses its shear strength due to oscillatory motion in saturated condition is known as.....
    (1) quick sand   (2) plastic sand   (3) liquefaction   (4) all of these

334. For a normally consolidated clay tested in a CD test, the cohesion of the clay will be .....
    (1) zero   (2) maximum   (3) minimum   (4) cannot be said

335. The strength envelope of a pure cohesive soil is .....
    (1) vertical   (2) inclined   (3) horizontal   (4) curvilinear

336. If the cohesion of a pure clay found in an unconfined compressive strength test is 1 kg/cm², the unconfined compressive strength in kg/cm² is .....
    (1) 0.5   (2) 1   (3) 2   (4) 4

337. For a highly fissured clay the best method to find the shear strength is .....
    (1) direct shear test   (2) triaxial test with $\sigma_3 = 0$
    (3) field vane shear test   (4) unconfined compression test

338. For the stability analysis of an earth dam for steady seepage case, the most appropriate test would be the .....
    (1) UU test   (2) CU test   (3) CD test   (4) UD test

339. The stress responsible for the mobilization of shearing strength of a soil is .....
    (1) effective normal stress   (2) neutral stress
    (3) total normal stress   (4) shear stress

340. The shear strength for a saturated clay from unconfined compression test is .....
    (1) twice the unconfined compression strength
    (2) half the unconfined compression strength
    (3) four times the unconfined compression strength
    (4) not related to the unconfined compression strength

341. When drainage is permitted under initially applied normal stress only and full primarily consolidation is allowed to take place, the test is known as .....
    (1) quick test
    (2) drained test
    (3) consolidated undrained test
    (4) none of these

ANSWER KEY

1.	(3)	2.	(1)	3.	(3)	4.	(4)	5.	(3)	6.	(1)	7.	(3)	8.	(2)
9.	(4)	10.	(2)	11.	(1)	12.	(2)	13.	(1)	14.	(1)	15.	(3)	16.	(2)
17.	(3)	18.	(3)	19.	(2)	20.	(2)	21.	(4)	22.	(3)	23.	(1)	24.	(2)
25.	(1)	26.	(2)	27.	(1)	28.	(1)	29.	(2)	30.	(2)	31.	(3)	32.	(1)
33.	(1)	34.	(1)	35.	(1)	36.	(1)	37.	(3)	38.	(3)	39.	(3)	40.	(4)
41.	(2)	42.	(2)	43.	(1)	44.	(3)	45.	(3)	46.	(4)	47.	(3)	48.	(1)
49.	(4)	50.	(3)	51.	(2)	52.	(2)	53.	(2)	54.	(3)	55.	(2)	56.	(1)
57.	(2)	58.	(3)	59.	(4)	60.	(1)	61.	(1)	62.	(3)	63.	(2)	64.	(2)
65.	(1)	66.	(2)	67.	(3)	68.	(1)	69.	(2)	70.	(2)	71.	(2)	72.	(4)
73.	(2)	74.	(1)	75.	(2)	76.	(4)	77.	(2)	78.	(2)	79.	(1)	80.	(3)
81.	(3)	82.	(1)	83.	(2)	84.	(1)	85.	(3)	86.	(3)	87.	(2)	88.	(2)
89.	(1)	90.	(2)	91.	(3)	92.	(3)	93.	(2)	94.	(1)	95.	(2)	96.	(1)
97.	(1)	98.	(3)	99.	(4)	100.	(4)	101.	(2)	102.	(2)	103.	(3)	104.	(3)
105.	(2)	106.	(2)	107.	(4)	108.	(3)	109.	(2)	110.	(2)	111.	(3)	112.	(1)
113.	(2)	114.	(2)	115.	(2)	116.	(2)	117.	(3)	118.	(4)	119.	(4)	120.	(3)
121.	(3)	122.	(4)	123.	(3)	124.	(4)	125.	(3)	126.	(3)	127.	(4)	128.	(3)
129.	(2)	130.	(4)	131.	(4)	132.	(2)	133.	(2)	134.	(2)	135.	(1)	136.	(4)
137.	(2)	138.	(1)	139.	(3)	140.	(4)	141.	(4)	142.	(1)	143.	(1)	144.	(2)
145.	(3)	146.	(1)	147.	(1)	148.	(b)	149.	(3)	150.	(2)	151.	(c)	152.	(1)
153.	(2)	154.	(3)	155.	(2)	156.	(3)	157.	(1)	158.	(3)	159.	(1)	160.	(1)
161.	(3)	162.	(4)	163.	(2)	164.	(2)	165.	(1)	166.	(4)	167.	(1)	168.	(4)
169.	(3)	170.	(1)	171.	(1)	172.	(4)	173.	(2)	174.	(2)	175.	(4)	176.	(1)
177.	(2)	178.	(4)	179.	(4)	180.	(3)	181.	(4)	182.	(4)	183.	(2)	184.	(4)

185.	(3)	186.	(4)	187.	(3)	188.	(3)	189.	(1)	190.	(2)	191.	(4)	192.	(2)
193.	(3)	194.	(2)	195.	(4)	196.	(2)	197.	(4)	198.	(3)	199.	(2)	200.	(4)
201.	(b)	202.	(2)	203.	(3)	204.	(3)	205.	(2)	206.	(4)	207.	(3)	208.	(1)
209.	(2)	210.	(4)	211.	(4)	212.	(3)	213.	(4)	214.	(4)	215.	(4)	216.	(3)
217.	(1)	218.	(1)	219.	(1)	220.	(1)	221.	(2)	222.	(1)	223.	(3)	224.	(2)
225.	(3)	226.	(2)	227.	(2)	228.	(4)	229.	(4)	230.	(3)	231.	(2)	232.	(4)
233.	(2)	234.	(4)	235.	(3)	236.	(4)	237.	(4)	238.	(3)	239.	(1)	240.	(4)
241.	(2)	242.	(3)	243.	(3)	244.	(3)	245.	(1)	246.	(3)	247.	(4)	248.	(1)
249.	(4)	250.	(4)	251.	(b)	252.	(2)	253.	(1)	254.	(3)	255.	(3)	256.	(3)
257.	(4)	258.	(3)	259.	(4)	260.	(1)	261.	(4)	262.	(2)	263.	(3)	264.	(4)
265.	(2)	266.	(3)	267.	(1)	268.	(4)	269.	(4)	270.	(2)	271.	(3)	272.	(4)
273.	(2)	274.	(1)	275.	(4)	276.	(4)	277.	(1)	278.	(2)	279.	(1)	280.	(1)
281.	(4)	282.	(4)	283.	(2)	284.	(2)	285.	(2)	286.	(2)	287.	(1)	288.	(4)
289.	(1)	290.	(1)	291.	(3)	292.	(2)	293.	(1)	294.	(4)	295.	(4)	296.	(1)
297.	(2)	298.	(1)	299.	(4)	300.	(3)	301.	(1)	302.	(3)	303.	(4)	304.	(4)
305.	(1)	306.	(2)	307.	(1)	308.	(2)	309.	(2)	310.	(3)	311.	(1)	312.	(2)
313.	(1)	314.	(3)	315.	(2)	316.	(4)	317.	(3)	318.	(4)	319.	(3)	320.	(3)
321.	(3)	322.	(4)	323.	(3)	324.	(3)	325.	(1)	326.	(2)	327.	(2)	328.	(1)
329.	(3)	330.	(4)	331.	(3)	332.	(2)	333.	(3)	334.	(1)	335.	(3)	336.	(3)
337.	(1)	338.	(2)	339.	(1)	340.	(2)	341.	(3)						

UNIT - 6 : FOUNDATION ENGINEERING

1. Taylor's stability number curves are used for the analysis of stability of slopes. The angle of shearing resistance used in the chart is called the ....
   - (1) effective angle
   - (2) apparent angle
   - (3) mobilized angle
   - (4) weighted angle

2. Taylor's stability number 'S_n' is ....
   - (1) $\dfrac{C}{F_c \gamma H}$
   - (2) $\dfrac{C}{\gamma H}$
   - (3) $\dfrac{CH}{F_c \gamma}$
   - (4) $\dfrac{C^2}{F_c \gamma H}$

3. The settlement of a footing in clays (S_F) is given by ....
   - (1) $\dfrac{S_P}{B_P} \times B_F$
   - (2) $\dfrac{S_P}{B_F} \times B_P$
   - (3) $\dfrac{S_P}{\left[\dfrac{B_P(B_F + 30.48)}{B_F(B_P + 30.48)}\right]^2}$
   - (4) $\dfrac{S_P(B_P + 30.48)^2}{(B_F + 30.48)^2}$

4. An infinite slope represents the inclined face of ....
   - (1) an earth dam
   - (2) an embankment
   - (3) an excavation
   - (4) a natural high hill slope

5. Pile foundation is one of the type of :
   - (1) Shallow foundation
   - (2) Raft foundation
   - (3) Deep foundation
   - (4) Machine foundation

6. The stability analysis of the upstream slope of earth dam has to be checked for the ....
   - (1) sudden draw down condition
   - (2) steady seepage condition
   - (3) steady seepage with sustained rainfall condition
   - (4) none of the above

7. In an earth dam the critical condition(s) for which the stability has to be checked during construction with or without partial pool is/are ....
   - (1) downstream slope
   - (2) upstream slope
   - (3) upstream and downstream slope
   - (4) none

8. The upstream and downstream slopes of an earth dam are critical for the ....
   - (1) reservoir partial pool condition
   - (2) sudden draw down condition
   - (3) steady seepage condition
   - (4) earthquake condition

9. The shape of a clay particle is ....
   - (1) rounded
   - (2) angular
   - (3) flaky
   - (4) any of (1), (2), (3)

10. Kerosene liquid doesn't cause plasticity to the clay because it is ....
    - (1) electrically neutral
    - (2) polar liquid
    - (3) non-polar
    - (4) not having montmorillonite

11. Allowable soil pressure for foundation in cohesive soil is generally controlled by :
    (1) settlement   (2) bearing capacity
    (3) Both 1 and 2   (4) Neither 1 nor 2

12. China clay is an example for ....
    (1) Kaolinite   (2) Illite
    (3) Montmorillonite   (4) Holloysite

13. The correct increasing order of specific surface i.e. surface area per mass of the given soil is ....
    (1) silt, sand, colloids, clay   (2) sand, silt, colloids, clay
    (3) sand, silt, clay, colloids   (4) clay, silt, sand, colloids

14. Black cotton soils exhibit large swelling and shrinkage due to presence of the following clay mineral :
    (1) Kaolinite   (2) Illite
    (3) Montmorillonite   (4) Holloysite

15. Flocculated structure is formed by attraction of particles and the particles have the ....
    (1) edge to face orientation   (2) edge to edge orientation
    (3) face to face orientation   (4) parallel orientation

16. In general element of flocculated soil has a ....
    (1) lower strength, lower compressibility and higher permeability
    (2) higher strength, higher compressibility and higher permeability
    (3) higher strength, lower compressibility and higher permeability
    (4) higher strength, lower compressibility and lower permeability

17. The soil sample used for liquid unit (W_L) and plastic limit (W_P) and for (W_S) tests should be finer than ....
    (1) 75 microns   (2) 150 microns
    (3) 200 microns   (4) 425 microns

18. Pick the incorrect pair

	Property of Soil		Scientist Concerned
(1)	Consistency	:	Alterberg
(2)	Liquid limit	:	Casagrande
(3)	Consolidation	:	Terzaghi
(4)	Sedimentation analysis	:	Darcy

19. In hydrometer analysis the principle used is ....
    (1) Newton's law   (2) Darcy's law   (3) Stoke's law   (4) Rehabann's law

20. A soil is said to be non-plastic when I_P ....
    (1) = 0%   (2) >7%   (3) = 1%   (4) is 7 to 17 %

21. For a well graded soil, the coefficient of curvature will be between ....
    (1) 1 and 10   (2) 2 and 8   (3) 3 and 7   (4) 1 and 3

22. The settlement of footing (S_F) in sandy soils is given by ....

    where S_P =   settlement of a plate in the bearing test

    B_P =   Width of the plate, and

    B_F =   Width of the footing

    (1) $\dfrac{S_P}{B_P} \times B_F$

    (2) $\dfrac{S_P}{B_F} \times B_P$

    (3) $\dfrac{S_P}{\left[\dfrac{B_P(B_F + 30.48)}{B_F(B_P + 30.48)}\right]^2}$

    (4) $\dfrac{S_P (B_P + 30.48)^2}{(B_F + 30.48)^2}$

23. The liquid limit exists for ....

    (1) sandy soils   (2) silty soils   (3) clayey soils   (4) gravelly soils

24. A shallow foundation is defined as foundation which has :

    (1) depth less than 0.6 m   (2) depth less than its width

    (3) depth less than 1 m   (4) None of the above

25. For proper field control, which of the following methods is best suited for quick determination of water content of a soil mass ?

    (1) Oven drying method   (2) Sand bath method

    (3) Alcohol method   (4) Calcium carbide method

26. Sand is said to be well graded when Cu is ....

    (1) 4 to 6   (2) > 6   (3) 2 to 4   (4) < 4

27. The ratio of plasticity index to flow index is called ....

    (1) activity ratio   (2) liquidity index

    (3) toughness index   (4) none

28. The minimum water content at which the soil just begins to crumble when rolled into threads 3 mm in diameter is known as ....

    (1) shrinkage limit (2) plastic limit   (3) liquid limit   (4) consistency limit

29. Plasticity index of a highly plastic soil is about ....

    (1) 10 - 20   (2) 20 - 40   (3) > 40   (4) > 10

30. Activity of montmorillonite clay mineral is ....

    (1) < 0.75   (2) 0.75 - 1.25   (3) 1.25 - 4   (4) > 4

31. For a dense sand, the relative density is ....

    (1) 35 - 65   (2) 65 - 85   (3) 85 - 100   (4) > 100

32. The coefficients of uniformity and curvature of a soil are 4 and 1 respectively. The ratio D_{30}/D_{10} will be ....

    (1) 1   (2) > 2   (3) 3   (4) 4

33. The consistency of a saturated cohesive soil is affected by ....

    (1) water content   (2) density index

    (3) particle size distribution   (4) coefficient of permeability

34. The void ratios of a soil in its closest and loosest state are 0.2 and 0.80. If void ratio in the natural state is 0.4, the relative density is ....
    (1) 80%   (2) 66%   (3) 40%   (4) 20%

35. To resist heavy lateral load which type of piles are used ?
    (1) Fraction and bearing piles   (2) Displacement piles
    (3) Under-reamed piles   (4) Batter piles

36. Pretreatment of soil to remove organic matter by oxidation is done with ....
    (1) sodium hexametaphosphate   (2) oxygen
    (3) hydrogen peroxide   (4) hydrochloric acid

37. When the plastic limit of a soil is greater than the liquid limit, then the plasticity index is reported as ....
    (1) negative   (2) zero   (3) non-plastic (NP) (4) 1

38. A flow is taking place in a soil for which porosity is 'n'. If the discharge velocity is 'v', then the seepage velocity will be ....
    (1) $n \cdot v$ (2) n/v (3) v/n (4) v/n^2

39. Flow can be assumed laminar in the following soils :
    (1) Clay only   (2) Clay, silt   (3) Clay, silt, sand   (4) All types

40. The soil is said to be impermeable when coefficient of permeability is ....
    (1) $< 10^{-7}$ cm/sec.   (2) $< 10^{-1}$ cm/sec.   (3) $> 10^{-9}$ cm/sec.   (4) $< 10^{-15}$ cm/sec.

41. The soil is said to be highly permeable when coefficient of permeability is ....
    (1) $> 10^{-2}$ cm/sec.   (2) $> 10^{-1}$ cm/sec.   (3) $< 10^{-1}$ cm/sec.   (4) $< 10^{-2}$ cm/sec.

42. Darcy's law is valid and flow will be laminar as long as Reynold's number is less than ....
    (1) 2000   (2) 100   (3) 10   (4) 1

43. Drop in head between adjacent equipotential lines is ....
    (1) dependent of up-stream head
    (2) dependent of down-stream head
    (3) dependent of number of equipotential lines
    (4) same

44. It has been mathematically shown that the basic shape of the top flow line in a dam is that of ....
    (1) an ellipse   (2) a parabola   (3) a circle   (4) a log-spiral

45. The shape factor of a flow net is given as ....
    (1) $\dfrac{N_d}{N_f}$ (2) $\dfrac{(N_d - 1)}{N_f}$ (3) $\dfrac{N_f}{N_d}$ (4) $\dfrac{(N_f - 1)}{N_d}$

46. The shape factor for a given flow domain ....
    (1) depends on number of flow lines   (2) depends on number of equipotential lines
    (3) depends on number of flow channels (4) is relatively unchanged

47. The pressure head at the intersection of the phreatic line and any equipotential line is ....
    (1) unity   (2) zero   (3) > 0 (4) < 0

48. The effective permeability used in a transformed section is ....
    (1) $\dfrac{K_h}{K_v}$ (2) $\left(\dfrac{K_h}{K_v}\right)^2$ (3) $\sqrt{K_h \cdot K_v}$ (4) $\sqrt{K_h/K_v}$

49. Consolidation of a soil is due to a load which is ....
    (1) static and short term   (2) dynamic and short term
    (3) dynamic and long term   (4) static and long term

50. 'Secondary Consolidation' is mainly due to expulsion of ....
    (1) highly viscous water   (2) plastic readjustment of solid particles
    (3) both (1) and (2)   (4) none of the above

51. Sample procured in a sandy soil by split spoon sampler is :
    (1) Disturbed sample   (2) Undisturbed sample
    (3) Representative sample   (4) Wash sample

52. Coefficient of consolidation depends upon ....
    (1) permeability   (2) coefficient of volume change
    (3) unit weight of water   (4) all the above

53. The unit of coefficient of consolidation is ....
    (1) cm/sec   (2) cm²/sec   (3) cm/sec²   (4) no units

54. The ratio of settlement at any time 't' to the final settlement is known as ....
    (1) coefficient of consolidation   (2) degree of consolidation
    (3) time factor   (4) consolidation of undisturbed soil

55. 'Isochrones' are the curves showing distribution of ....
    (1) Total settlement   (2) Total pressure
    (3) Excess hydrostatic pressure   (4) None

56. Time factor is ....
    (1) a non-dimensional parameter   (2) a function of degree of consolidation
    (3) directly proportional to permeability of soil
    (4) all the above are correct

57. Submergence of foundation due to rise of water table causes :
    (1) increase in bearing capacity   (2) decrease in bearing capacity
    (3) no change in bearing capacity   (4) none of the above

58. In the soil sample of a consolidometer test, pure water pressure is ....
    (1) minimum at the center   (2) maximum at the top
    (3) maximum at the bottom   (4) maximum at the center

59. Which of the following soils will generally have maximum compressibility ?
    (1) Gravels   (2) Sands   (3) Silts   (4) Clays

60. If coefficient of permeability is doubled and coefficient of volume compressibility is halved, the coefficient of consolidation ....
    (1) increases by 2 times   (2) decreases by 2 times
    (3) decreases by 4 times   (4) increases by 4 times

61. The time for 50% consolidation of a 'd' cm thick with double drainage is 't' hours. The time for 50% consolidation of another sample of similar soil with '3d' cm thickness and single drainage is ....
    (1) 6 t   (2) t/6   (3) 36 t   (4) 9 t

62. The ultimate consolidation settlement of a soil ....
    (1) is directly proportional to the compression index
    (2) decreases with the increase in the initial void ratio
    (3) both (1) and (2)
    (4) none

63. A saturated clay layer with single drainage face takes 4 years to attain 50% degree for consolidation. If the clay layer had double drainage face, then the time required to attain 50% is ....
    (1) 8 years   (2) 4 years   (3) 2 years   (4) 1 year

64. In consolidation testing, curve fitting method is used to determine ....
    (1) compression index   (2) swelling index
    (3) coefficient of consolidation   (4) time factor

65. Consolidation time of a soil sample ....
    (1) increases with an increase in permeability
    (2) increases with a decrease in compressibility
    (3) increases with decrease in unit weight of water
    (4) increases with decrease in permeability

66. The ultimate settlement of a soil deposit increases with ....
    (1) an increase in the compression index
    (2) an increase in the initial void ratio
    (3) a decrease in thickness of the stratum
    (4) an increase in time

67. A building constructed on a compressible layer settles 80 mm in 4 years. Assuming that the degree of consolidation at both the times is less than 60%, the settlement in 9 years is ....
    (1) 80 mm   (2) 100 mm   (3) 120 mm   (4) none of the above

68. In case of footing in sand, if the soil pressure distribution is triangular, the maximum soil pressure is .... the average soil pressure.
    (1) equal to   (2) double   (3) three times   (4) four times

69. An undrained triaxial compression test is carried out on a saturated clay sample under a cell pressure of 100 kN/m². The sample failed at a deviator stress of 200 kN/m². The cohesion of the given sample of clay in kN/m² is ....
    (1) 50   (2) 100   (3) 200   (4) 300

70. Which one of the following planes is most likely to be the failure plane is sandy soil ?
    (1) Plane carrying maximum stear stress.
    (2) Plane carrying maximum normal stress.
    (3) Plane with the maximum angle of obliquity.
    (4) A principle plane.

71. For a highly fissured clay the best method to find the shear strength is ....
    (1) Direct shear test
    (2) Triaxial test with $\sigma_3 = 0$
    (3) Field vane shear test
    (4) Unconfined compression test

72. A circular pile of 30 cm diameter and 7 m length passes through a recently filled up material of 3.5 m depth. The unconfined compressive strength of the soil is 60 kN/m². The negative skin friction of the pile is :
    (1) 110 kN
    (2) 330 kN
    (3) 99 kN
    (4) 198 kN

73. Match the pairs for safe bearing capacity :   ]
    (a) Moist clay which can be indented with strong thumb pressure
    (i) 245 kN/m²
    (b) Soft rock
    (ii) 150 kN/m²
    (c) Medium sand, compact and dry
    (iii) 100 kN/m²
    (d) Fine sand, loose and dry
    (iv) 440 kN/m²

	(a)	(b)	(c)	(d)
(1)	(iii)	(iv)	(ii)	(i)
(2)	(ii)	(iv)	(i)	(iii)
(3)	(ii)	(iv)	(iii)	(i)
(4)	(iii)	(i)	(iv)	(ii)

74. The shear test that is more suitable in the field is ....
    (1) Direct shear
    (2) Triaxial shear
    (3) Unconfined compression
    (4) Vane shear

75. The angle of inclination of the Coulomb's failure envelope with the horizontal is called ....
    (1) angle of repose
    (2) angle of friction
    (3) angle of internal friction
    (4) frictional resistance

76. A sensitive clay has a shear strength of 45 kN/m² in natural state, 15 kN/m² in remoulded state. The sensitivity of the soil is ....
    (1) 1/3
    (2) 30
    (3) 3
    (4) none

77. In a triaxial compression test on a soil, the relation between σ_1, σ_2 and σ_3 is ....
    (1) $\sigma_1 = \sigma_2 + \sigma_3$
    (2) $\sigma_2 = \sigma_1 - \sigma_3$
    (3) $\sigma_2 = \sigma_3$
    (4) none of the above

78. According to Terzaghi, the net ultimate bearing capacity of clay is given by ....
    (1) cN_q
    (2) cN_γ
    (3) cN_c
    (4) $1.3\, cN_c$

79. For saturated, normally consolidated soils, Skempton's pore pressure coefficients can be represented as ....
    (1) $A < 1, B = 1$
    (2) $A > 1, B > 1$
    (3) $A > 1, B < 1$
    (4) $A < 1, B > 1$

80. The settlement of a footing in sand depends upon the ....
    (1) stress deformation characteristics of sand
    (2) relative density of the sand
    (3) width of the footing
    (4) all of these

81. Match the following :

(a) Pneumatic tyre roller   (i) Static compression

(b) Sheep foot roller   (ii) Eccentric weight rotation

(c) Smooth wheel roller   (iii) Kneading action

(d) Vibratory roller   (iv) Tamping and kneading

	(a)	(b)	(c)	(d)
(1)	(iii)	(i)	(iv)	(ii)
(2)	(iv)	(iii)	(i)	(ii)
(3)	(iv)	(ii)	(i)	(iii)
(4)	(iii)	(iv)	(i)	(ii)

82. What are the factors influencing cost of soil investigation ?

(a) Non-uniformity of layers   (b) Undisturbed sampling

(c) Depth of exploration   (d) Nature of project

Answer options :

(1) (a) and (b)   (2) (b) and (c)   (3) (c) and (d)   (4) All the above

83. The lateral earth pressure coefficients K_a and K_p are based on ....

(1) total stress   (2) neutral stress

(3) effective stress   (4) elastic properties of soils

84. If 'μ' is Poisson's ratio of a soil, then the coefficient of earth pressure at rest is ....

(1) $\dfrac{\mu}{1-\mu}$ (2) $\dfrac{1-\mu}{\mu}$ (3) $\dfrac{\mu}{1+\mu}$ (4) $\dfrac{1+\mu}{\mu}$

85. The inclination of the failure plane behind a vertical wall in the passive pressure case is inclined to the horizontal at ....

(1) $45° - \phi/2$ (2) $45° - \phi$ (3) $45° + \phi/2$ (4) $45° + \phi$

86. The total active pressure after the development of tension cracks is equal to ....

(1) $1/2\, \gamma\, H^2\, K_a - 2c'\, H\sqrt{K_a}$ (2) $1/2\, \gamma\, H^2\, K_a + 2c'\, H\sqrt{K_a}$

(3) $1/2\, \gamma H^2\, K_a - 2c'\, H\dfrac{\sqrt{K_a} - 2\,(c')^2}{\gamma}$ (4) $\dfrac{\frac{1}{2}\gamma H^2 \sqrt{K_a} - 2(c')^2}{\gamma}$

87. The results (Curves A, B, C, D) of four compaction tests on different soils are shown in the graph.

Tests :

(a) Silty sand, modified test

(b) Silty sand, standard test

(c) Fat clay, modified test

(d) Fat clay, standard test

Curves A, B, C, D correspond respectively to tests

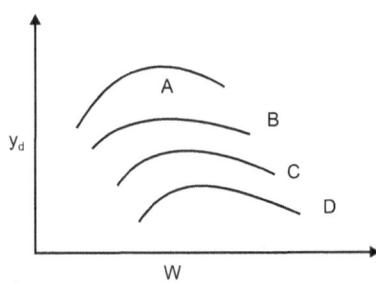

Fig.

(1) (a), (c), (b), (d)   (2) (a), (b), (c), (d)   (3) (c), (b), (a), (d)   (4) (b), (a), (c), (d)

88. Match List-I with List-II and select the correct answer using the codes given below the lists :

       List - I   **List - II**

  A.   Sheep foot roller   (a)   Hearting of earthen dam

  B.   Smooth heavy roller   (b)   Dry sand

  C.   Pneumatic roller   (c)   Casing of earthen dam

  D.   Vibrating roller   (d)   Gravel in WBM road

  Codes :

	A	B	C	D
(1)	(c)	(d)	(b)	(a)
(2)	(a)	(d)	(c)	(b)
(3)	(a)	(c)	(d)	(b)
(4)	(b)	(a)	(c)	(d)

89. In a compaction test, with increase in compactive effort ....
   (1) maximum dry density increases but OMC decreases
   (2) the compaction curve is shifted to the left and higher
   (3) both the above
   (4) both maximum dry density and OMC increase

90. The number of blows required for completing each layer of soil in case of compaction test, is ....
   (1) 25   (2) 36   (3) 56   (4) 45

91. While carrying out stability of slopes, by using the method of slices, it was noticed that for a 10 m high slope, the length of circular arc was 30 m. The sum of shearing forces 500 kN and unconfined compressive strength of soil was 30 kN/m². Assuming unit weight of soil as 20 kN/m³, what will be the factor of safety with respect to cohesion ?
   (1) 1.5   (2) 1.2   (3) 1.0   (4) 0.9

92. In which method of site exploration, soil and rock formations are broken by repeated blows of heavy chisel or bit suspended by a cable or drill rod ?
   (1) Rotary boring   (2) Percussion boring
   (3) Wash boring   (4) Auger boring

93. Optimum moisture content is the moisture content at which ....
   (1) settlement is maximum   (2) permeability is more
   (3) dry density is maximum   (4) shear strength is less

94. Vibrator rollers are useful for compacting ....
   (1) clayey soil   (2) cohesionless soil
   (3) gravel   (4) crusted rock

95. To avoid large selling pressure under pavements and floors, the soil is compacted ....
   (1) at OMC   (2) dry of optimum
   (3) wet of optimum   (4) none

96. The Poisson's ratio for a saturated clay will be ....

    (1) zero   (2) 0.25   (3) 0.5   (4) 0.15

97. Under a flexible footing, the contact pressure in the case of clayey soil is ....

(1)	(2)

(3)	(4)

98. Under rigid footing, the contact pressure in case of clayey soil is ....

    Options same as Q. No. 97

99. The vertical cross section of an isobar is ....

    (1) parabolic curve   (2) circle   (3) lemniscates   (4) none

100. Group index of soil ranges such that ....

    (1) $0 < GI < 20$ (2) $0 \leq GI \leq 20$ (3) $0 \leq GI \leq 25$ (4) $0 < GI < \infty$

101. Match List - I (giving method of estimation of pile capacity) with List - II (parameters to be estimated), and select correct answer using codes given below :

    List - I

    (a) Dynamic formulae

    (b) Static formulae

    (c) Pile load test

    (d) Cyclic pile load test

    List - II

    (i) Bearing capacity of cost in situ piles

    (ii) Separating end bearing and friction bearing capacity of pile

    (iii) Bearing capacity of timber pile

    (iv) Settlement of friction bearing pile

    Codes :

	(a)	(b)	(c)	(d)
(1)	(iii)	(i)	(iv)	(ii)
(2)	(iv)	(ii)	(iii)	(i)
(3)	(iii)	(ii)	(iv)	(i)
(4)	(iv)	(i)	(iii)	(ii)

102. Unified soil classification is based on 'Air field classification system' that was developed by ....

    (1) Casagrande   (2) Terzaghi   (3) Boussinesq   (4) Newmark

103. Match List - I (type of foundation) with List - II (use of the foundation) and select correct answer, using the codes given below :

      List - I   **List - II**
      (a) Floating piles   (i)   Closely spaced columns resting on compressible soil
      (b) Micro piles   (ii) Expansive soils
      (c) Combined footing   (iii) Deep soft clays
      (d) Under-reamed piles   (iv) Loose sands

      Codes :

	(a)	**(b)**	**(c)**	**(d)**
(1)	(ii)	(i)	(iv)	(iii)
(2)	(ii)	(iv)	(i)	(iii)
(3)	(iii)	(i)	(iv)	(ii)
(4)	(iv)	(iv)	(i)	(ii)

104. Match List - I with List - II and select the correct answer using codes given below :

      List - I   **List - II**
      (Field Test)   **(Parameters measured)**
      (a) Plate Load Test   (i)   Total and frictional resistance
      (b) Standard Penetration Test   (ii) Load intensity and settlement values
      (c) Static Cone Penetration Test   (iii) Ned values
      (d) Dynamic Cone Penetration Test   (iv) SPT values

      Codes :

	(a)	**(b)**	**(c)**	**(d)**
(1)	(ii)	(iv)	(iii)	(i)
(2)	(iv)	(ii)	(iii)	(i)
(3)	(ii)	(iv)	(i)	(iii)
(4)	(iv)	(ii)	(i)	(iii)

105. The ultimate unit bearing capacity for square footing is given by ....
      (1) $0.4\,cN_C + \gamma D_f N_q + 1.2\gamma BN_\gamma$ (2) $0.4\,cN_C + 1.2\gamma D_f N_q + \gamma BN_\gamma$
      (3) $1.3\,cN_C + \gamma DN_q + 0.4\gamma BN_\gamma$ (4) $0.5\,\gamma BN_\gamma + \gamma D_f N_q$

106. The net ultimate bearing capacity of a square footing in sand is given by ....
      (1) $0.3\,\gamma BN_\gamma + \gamma D_f\,(N_q - 1)$ (2) $0.3\,\gamma BN_\gamma + \gamma D_f\,(N_q + 1)$
      (3) $0.4\,\gamma BN_\gamma + \gamma D_f\,(N_q - 1)$ (4) $0.4\,\gamma BN_\gamma + \gamma D_f\,(N_q + 1)$

107. According to I.S. code, the total settlement for isolated footing for cohesive soil should be ....
      (1) 30 mm   (2) 40 mm   (3) 50 mm   (4) 65 mm

108. When the water table is close to the ground surface, the bearing capacity of a soil is reduced to ....
      (1) one-fourth $\left(\dfrac{1}{4}\right)$ (2) one-half $\left(\dfrac{1}{2}\right)$ (3) two-third $\left(\dfrac{2}{3}\right)$ (4) three fourth $\left(\dfrac{3}{4}\right)$

109. If the soil below the base of the footing is dry or moist, the confining pressure is approximately .... the confining pressure available when the water table is at the base of the footing.

    (1) equal to   (2) double   (3) three times   (4) four times

110. Foundation soil of the toe of a dam has a void ratio of 0.62, G = 2.62. Assuming a factor of safety of 5, the permissible exit gradient is ....

    (1) 0.2   (2) 0.5   (3) 1   (4) zero

111. The hydraulic head that would produce a quick condition in a sand stratum of thickness of 2 m, if G = 2.7 and e = 0.7, is ....

    (1) 0.5   (2) 1   (3) 2   (4) None

112. To satisfy the condition that the soil to be protected is not washed into the filter, the Terzaghi criteria is ....

    (1) (D_{15} of filter/D_{15} of soil) < 5
    (2) (D_{15} of filter/D_{85} of soil) < 5
    (3) (D_{15} of filter/D_{15} of soil) > 5
    (4) (D_{15} of filter/D_{85} of soil) > 5

113. Graded filter is one wherein ....

    (1) the finest layer is on the upstream side of the filter
    (2) the coarse layer is on the upstream side of the filter
    (3) the medium coarse layer is at the upstream side of the filter
    (4) any layer is at the upstream side of the filter.

114. Piping occurs when ....

    (1) effective stress is zero
    (2) flow is downwards
    (3) flow is upwards
    (4) flow is horizontal

115. Cohesionless soils are formed due to ....

    (1) oxidation of rocks
    (2) leaching action of water on rocks
    (3) blowing of hot and cold wind
    (4) physical disintegration of rocks

116. Peat is composed of ....

    (1) clay and sand
    (2) decayed vegetable matter
    (3) inorganic silt and silty clay
    (4) synthetic chemicals

117. The coefficient of passive earth pressure .... with the increase of angle of shearing resistance.

    (1) increases
    (2) decreases
    (3) does not change
    (4) none of these

118. The ultimate bearing capacity per unit area of a soil for general shear failure is ....

    where   C = Cohesion value   r = Radius of footing
          B = Width of footing D_f = Depth of foundation
          γ = Density of soil, and
       N_c, N_q and N_γ = Bearing capacity factors

    (1) $0.5\,\gamma\,BN_\gamma + \gamma D_f N_q$
    (2) $cN_c + 0.5\gamma\,BN_\gamma + \gamma\,D_f N_q$
    (3) $1.3\,cN_c + \gamma D_f N_q + 0.6\gamma \cdot \gamma N_\gamma$
    (4) $1.3\,cN_c + \gamma D_f N_q + 0.4\,BN_\gamma$

119. The unit bearing capacity of footing in sand ....
    (1) decreases with depth of footing
    (2) decreases with width of footing
    (3) increases with depth of footing
    (4) increases with width of footing

120. Loam means ....
    (1) sandy clay with a little slit
    (2) silty clay with a little sand
    (3) sand, slit and clay
    (4) sand, slit and gravel

121. Pick up the correct sequence of geological cycle for the formation of soil :
    (1) transportation - upheaval - deposition - weathering
    (2) transportation - deposition - weathering - upheaval
    (3) weathering - upheaval - deposition - transportation
    (4) weathering - transportation - deposition - upheaval

122. Match List-I (Soil deposit) with List-II (Soil name) and select the correct answer using the codes given below the lists :

	List - I		List - II
A.	Gravity	(a)	Stratified drift
B.	Lake	(b)	Talus
C.	Glacial	(c)	Loess
D.	Wind	(d)	Lacustrine

    Codes :

	A	B	C	D
(1)	(a)	(c)	(b)	(d)
(2)	(b)	(d)	(a)	(c)
(3)	(c)	(d)	(a)	(b)
(4)	(d)	(c)	(b)	(a)

123. For water table below ground surface, a rise in the water table causes ....
    (1) an increase in pore pressure and decrease in effective pressure
    (2) decrease in pore pressure and increase in effective pressure
    (3) no change in effective pressure
    (4) equal change in pore pressure and total pressure

124. The effect of capillary saturation will cause the effective stress ....
    (1) to increase
    (2) to decrease
    (3) either to increase or decrease
    (4) not to change

125. Neutral pressure (Pure pressure) is ....
    (1) always compressive
    (2) always tensile
    (3) compressive below water table and tensile above water table
    (4) compressive above water table and tensile below water table

126. The stress which controls the strength and deformation behaviour of soil is ....
    (1) Total pressure
    (2) Pore pressure
    (3) Effective pressure
    (4) None

127. The relation between total pressure σ effective pressure σ' and pore pressure μ is ....

   (1) $\sigma' = \sigma + \mu$ (2) $\sigma' = \sigma - \mu$ (3) $\sigma = \sigma' - \mu$ (4) none of the above

128. In the capillary saturated zone, pore pressure is ....

   (1) tensile   (2) compressive

   (3) either tensile or compressive   (4) zero

129. When ground water table is lowered ....

   (1) total stress decreases, neutral stress decreases, but effective stress increases.

   (2) total, neutral and effective stresses decrease

   (3) total stress remains constant, while the neutral and effective stress decrease

   (4) total stress and neutral stresses decrease, while effective stress remains constant

130. Increase in level of water table above ground level causes ....

   (1) increase in effective stress   (2) no change in effective stress

   (3) decrease in effective stress   (4) nothing can be said

131. Water table was found 1 m, below ground surface. Above the water table the soil was found saturated with capillary water. If saturated density is 20 kN/m³, the effective stress at the water table level in kN/m² is ....

   (1) 5   (2) 10   (3) 15   (4) 20

132. If the moisture content of a fully saturated soil is 100 %, then the void ratio is equal to ....

   (1) mass specific gravity   (2) true specific gravity

   (3) half of true specific gravity   (4) no relation with specific gravity

133. The soil that will have generally maximum void ratio is ....

   (1) gravel   (2) sand   (3) silt   (4) clay

134. The bulk density of coarse grained soils can be determined by ....

   (1) sand replacement method   (2) core cutter method

   (3) pycnometer method   (4) torsion balance method

135. Dry density of soil can be defined as the ratio of ....

   (1) mass of soil to the total volume

   (2) weight of the soil to the total volume of soil

   (3) unit weight the soil to the unit weight of water

   (4) none

136. The standard method of determining water content is ....

   (1) oven-drying method   (2) alcohol method

   (3) calcium carbide method   (4) pycnometer method

137. The bearing capacity of a soil depends upon ....

   (1) grain size of the soil   (2) size of the footing

   (3) shape of the footing   (4) all of these

138. The bearing capacity of a soil .... with the decrease in the area of the footing.

   (1) increases   (2) decreases

   (3) does not change   (4) none of these

139. If the void is 0.5, then the porosity is ....
    (1) 0.333   (2) 1   (3) 0.666   (4) 0.5

140. For a soil, $G = 2.5$ and the void ratio is 1. Then the value of $\gamma_{sat}/\gamma_{sub}$ is ....
    (1) 2.5   (2) 2   (3) 2.33   (4) none

141. In a wet soil mass, air occupies one-sixth of its volume and water occupies one-third of its volume. The void ratio of the soil is ....
    (1) 0.25   (2) 0.5   (3) 1.00   (4) 1.50

142. The lateral earth pressure is ....
    (1) directly proportional to the depth of soil
    (2) inversely proportional to the depth of soil
    (3) directly proportional to the square of the depth of soil
    (4) inversely proportional to the square of the depth of soil

143. The minimum depth for all foundations below the natural ground level is ....
    (1) 500 mm   (2) 1200 mm   (3) 250 mm   (4) 100 mm

144. Net allowable bearing pressure is ....
    (1) net safe bearing capacity   (2) net safe settlement pressure
    (3) smaller of (1) and (2)   (4) none of the above

145. Terzaghi's analysis is based on the assumptions ....
    (1) Base of footing is rough
    (2) Footing is shallow
    (3) The shear strength of soil is governed by Mohr - Coulomb equation
    (4) All of the above

146. The ultimate bearing capacity (q_u) and the net ultimate bearing capacity (q_{nu}) are connected by the relation ....
    (1) $q_{nu} = q_u + \gamma D$ (2) $q_u = q_{nu} + \gamma D$
    (3) $q_u = (q_{nu})/R + \gamma D$ (4) $q_u = (q_{nu} + \gamma D)/f$

147. Terzaghi's bearing capacity factor depends upon ....
    (1) angle of internal friction only   (2) cohesion also
    (3) cohesion only   (4) density of soil

148. For a square surface footing (rough), resting on clayey soil ultimate bearing capacity is given by (According to Terzaghi) ....
    (1) 5.14 C   (2) 5.7 C + γD (3) 5.7 C   (4) 7.4 C

149. The ultimate bearing capacity of a surface strip footing on clay, according to the Terzaghi's theory is ....
    (1) 5.7 C   (2) 5.14 C   (3) $q_u B$ (4) 9 C

150. General shear failure is characterized by ....
    (1) low strain before plastic failure
    (2) soil behaves like an ideally plastic material
    (3) occurs in stiff soils   (4) all of the above

151. The bearing capacity of a footing of pure clay soils is independent of ....
     (1) depth of footing   (2) width of footing
     (3) shape of footing   (4) water table
152. If water table rises to the ground level of a footing resting on cohesionless soils, the bearing capacity approximately ....
     (1) reduces to half   (2) reduced to one third
     (3) remains same   (4) none of the above
153. Which of the following factors affects the bearing capacity of a soil ?
     (1) Cohesion and angle of internal friction only
     (2) Width and depth of footing
     (3) Inclination factors also   (4) None of the above
154. As per IS code, maximum permissible differential settlement on clayey soil is ....
     (1) 25   (2) 40   (3) 65   (4) 100
155. Match List-I (Type of foundation and foundation soil) with List-II (Allowable settlement) and select the correct answer using the codes given below the lists :

     List - I   **List - II**
     A.   Isolated foundations on clay   (a)   40 mm
     B.   Isolated foundations on sand   (b)   65 mm
     C.   Raft foundation on clay   (c)   40 mm to 65 mm
     D.   Raft foundation of sand   (d)   65 mm to 100 mm

     Codes :

	A	B	C	D
(1)	(a)	(b)	(c)	(d)
(2)	(b)	(a)	(d)	(c)
(3)	(a)	(b)	(d)	(c)
(4)	(b)	(a)	(c)	(d)

156. The recommended size of a square bearing plate to be used in plate loads test for determining the ultimate bearing capacity of soil, should be 30 cm^2 to 75 cm^2 with a minimum thickness of ....
     (1) 10 mm   (2) 15 mm   (3) 20 mm   (4) 25 mm
157. The seating load for plate load test is ....
     (1) 1 kN/m^2 (2) 5 kN/m^2 (3) 7 kN/m^2 (4) 10 kN/m^2
158. The ultimate bearing capacity at ground surface for a purely cohesive soil and for a smooth base of a strip footing is ....
     (1) 5.7 C   (2) 5.14 C   (3) 2.85 C   (4) 7 C
159. In case of perfectly smooth base of a footing resting on surface of an ideal soil, the triangular wedge below the base of the footing is an ....
     (1) elastic equilibrium   (2) plastic equilibrium
     (3) Both (1) and (2)   (4) None

160. The permissible settlement is the maximum in the case of ....
    (1)   isolated footing on clay   (2)   raft on clay
    (3)   isolated footing on sand   (4)   raft of sand

161. If the gross bearing capacity of a strip footing 1.5 m wide located at a depth of 1 m clay is 400 kN/m², its net bearing capacity for γ = 20 kN/m² is ....
    (1)   370 kN/m²   (2)   380 kN/m²
    (3)   390 kN/m²   (4)   360 kN/m²

162. Identify the incorrect statement. Bearing capacity of a footing on sand depends on ....
    (1)   depth of footing   (2)   width of footing
    (3)   position of water table   (4)   undrained shear strength

163. In pure clay the safe bearing capacity of footing is approximately equal to ....
    (1)   unconfined compressive strength   (2)   undrained cohesion
    (3)   half of vane shear strength   (4)   none of the above

164. Plate load test results reflect only the characters of the soil located within a depth ...., the width of the bearing plate.
    (1)   of less than twice   (2)   equal to
    (3)   equal to 2.5 times   (4)   of more than twice

165. Negative skin friction can be developed from,
    (a)   a cohesive fill placed over a cohesion less soil deposit
    (b)   a cohesionless fill placed over a compressible cohesive deposit
    (c)   lowering of ground water table with resulting ground subsidence
    (d)   pile driving operation
    Select the correct option :
    (1)   (a), (b) and (c) are correct   (2)   (c), (b) and (d) are correct
    (3)   (a), (b) and (d) are correct   (4)   (a), (b), (c) and (d) are correct

166. When the number of bulbs is increased from one to two, the capacity of the pile increases by about ....
    (1)   100%   (2)   75%   (3)   50%   (4)   25%

167. Group efficiency of friction pile in clay is ....
    (1)   exactly 100%   (2)   > 100%   (3)   < 100%   (4)   almost 100%

168. Well foundation is commonly used as foundation for the following structure :
    (1)   Water tanks   (2)   Bridges
    (3)   Building   (4)   Reciprocating machines

169. The minimum number of piles needed in a group of piles to support a column is ....
    (1)   one   (2)   two   (3)   three   (4)   four

170. Underframed piles are usually ....
    (1)   precast piles   (2)   driven piles
    (3)   bored piles   (4)   bored or driven piles

171. For undistributed sampling, the area ratio for a thin-wall sampler should not normally exceed ....
   (1)   10%   (2)   25%   (3)   30%   (4)   35%

172. The range of N values for a very loose sand is ....
   (1)   0 to 4   (2)   4 to 10   (3)   10 to 30   (4)   30 to 50

173. Identify the incorrect statement : N values from SPT are corelated with ....
   (1)   unit weight   (2)   relative density
   (3)   angle of internal friction   (4)   sensitivity

174. For an undistributed sample, the area ratio of the samples should be ....
   (1)   zero   (2)   10% or less
   (3)   10% to 20%   (4)   more than 20%

175. In-situ vane shear test is used to measure shear strength of ....
   (1)   very soft and sensitive clays   (2)   stiff and fissured clays
   (3)   sandy soils   (4)   all the above

176. The coefficient of earth pressure at rest for loose sand is .... that of dense sand.
   (1)   more than   (2)   less than   (3)   same as   (4)   none of these

177. For cohesive soil, the height of the retaining wall for zero active earth pressure will be
   ....
   (1) $\dfrac{C}{\gamma} \tan\left[45° + \dfrac{\phi}{2}\right]$ (2) $\dfrac{2C}{\gamma} \tan\left[45° + \dfrac{\phi}{2}\right]$
   (3) $\dfrac{3C}{\gamma} \tan\left[45° + \dfrac{\phi}{2}\right]$ (4) $\dfrac{4C}{\gamma} \tan\left[45° + \dfrac{\phi}{2}\right]$

178. Mechanical weathering of soils is caused by ....
   (1)   periodical temperature changes   (2)   splitting action of flowing water
   (3)   splitting action of ice   (4)   all of these

179. Cohesionless soils are ....
   (1)   sands   (2)   clays   (3)   silts   (4)   silt and clays

180. The maximum size of grains of silts is about ....
   (1)   0.06 mm   (2)   0.2 mm   (3)   0.5 mm   (4)   1 mm

181. Black cotton soil ....
   (1)   is inorganic in nature   (2)   contains large percentage of clay mineral
   (3)   exhibits high compressibility   (4)   all of these

182. A fine grained soil ....
   (1)   has low permeability   (2)   has high compressibility
   (3)   may or may not be plastic   (4)   all of these

183. Consolidation and compressibility of soil ....
   (1)   is a measure of the ability of soil to allow the water to pass through its pores.
   (2)   is a measure of the ability of soil to bear stresses without failure
   (3)   deals with changes in volume of pores in a soil under load
   (4)   none of the above

184. The minimum size of grains of silts is about ....
     (1) 0.0002 mm   (2) 0.002 mm   (3) 0.02 mm   (4) 0.2 mm

185. The maximum size of the particles of clay is about ....
     (1) 0.0002 mm   (2) 0.002 mm   (3) 0.02 mm   (4) 0.2 mm

186. The unit weight of a soil at zero air voids depends upon ....
     (1) unit weight of water   (2) water content
     (3) specific gravity   (4) all of these

187. If W is the total weight of the soil mass and W_S is the weight of solids, then water content is equal to ....
     (1) $1 + \dfrac{W}{W_S}$ (2) $1 - \dfrac{W}{W_S}$ (3) $\dfrac{W}{W} - 1$ (4) $\dfrac{W_S}{W} + 1$

188. The earth pressure at rest is calculated by using ....
     (1) Euler's theory   (2) Rankine's theory
     (3) Bending theory   (4) Theory of elasticity

189. The contact pressure of flexible footing on non-cohesive soils is ....
     (1) more in the centre than at the edges   (2) less in the center than at the edges
     (3) uniform throughout   (4) none of these

190. The degree of saturation for fully saturated soil is ....
     (1) 0.25   (2) 0.50   (3) 0.75   (4) 1

191. The difference between maximum void ratio and minimum void ratio of a sand sample is 0.30. If the relative density of this sample is 66.6% at a void ratio of 0.40, then the void ratio of this sample at its loosest state will be ....
     (1) 0.40   (2) 0.60   (3) 0.70   (4) 0.75

192. A soil sample is having a specific gravity of 2.60 and a void ratio of 0.78. The water content in percentage required to fully saturate the soil at that void ratio will be ....
     (1) 10   (2) 30   (3) 50   (4) 70

193. The specific gravity of a soil is the ratio of unit weight of soil solids to that of water at a temperature of ....
     (1) 4°C   (2) 17°C   (3) 27°C   (4) 36°C

194. For a given soil mass, the void ratio is 0.60, water content is 18% and specific gravity of the soil particles is 2.6. The degree of saturation of the soil is ....
     (1) 30%   (2) 50%   (3) 78%   (4) 82.5%

195. The ratio of the difference between the void ratio in its loosest state and its natural void ratio to the difference between the voids ratio in the loosest and the densest state; is called ....
     (1) density index   (2) relative density
     (3) degree of density   (4) any one of these

196. The void ratio of soil is defined as the ratio of the ....
     (1) weight of water to the weight of solids
     (2) volume of water to the voids in the soil mass
     (3) total volume of voids to the volume of soil solids
     (4) total volume of voids to the total volume of soil

197. The degree of saturation for the moist soil is about ....
    (1) 0%   (2) 1 to 25%   (3) 25 to 50%   (4) 50 to 75%

198. Which of the following clay mineral has maximum swelling ....
    (1) Kalonite   (2) Montmorillonite
    (3) Illite   (4) All of these

199. Gravel and sand is a ....
    (1) cohesive coarse grained soil   (2) cohesive fine grained soil
    (3) non-cohesive coarse grained soil (4) non-cohesive fine grained soil

200. The specific gravity of sandy soils is ....
    (1) 1.2   (2) 1.8   (3) 2.2   (4) 2.7

201. The lateral earth pressure exerted by the soil when the retaining wall moves into the soil, is known as ....
    (1) earth pressure at rest   (2) active earth pressure
    (3) passive earth pressure   (4) total earth pressure

202. Bulk density of a soil is defined as the ratio of ....
    (1) total mass of soil to the total volume of soil.
    (2) weight of water to the weight of solids
    (3) unit weight of solids to the unit weight of water
    (4) weight of solid grains to the volume of solids

203. The contact pressure of rigid footing on cohesive soil is ....
    (1) more in the centre than at the edges (2) less in the center than at the edges
    (3) uniform throughout   (4) none of these

204. If W is the water content and γ is the unit weight of soil mass, then the unit weight of dry soil (γ_d) is equal to ....
    (1) $\dfrac{W}{\gamma} + 1$ (2) $\dfrac{\gamma}{W} + L$ (3) $\dfrac{\gamma}{1 + W}$ (4) $\dfrac{1 + W}{\gamma}$

205. The relation between dry unit weight (γ_d), specific gravity (G), void ratio (e) and porosity (n) is ....
    (1) $\gamma_d = \dfrac{G \cdot \gamma_w}{1 + e}$ (2) $\gamma_d = \dfrac{G \cdot \gamma_w}{1 + e}$
    (3) $\gamma_d = G \cdot \gamma_w (1 - n)$ (4) $\gamma_d = G \cdot \gamma_w (1 + n)$

206. The submerged unit weight for completely saturated soil is given by ....
    (1) $\dfrac{(G + e)\, \gamma_w}{1 + e}$ (2) $\dfrac{(1 + e)\, \gamma_w}{G + e}$ (3) $\dfrac{(G - 1)\, \gamma_w}{1 + e}$ (4) $\dfrac{(1 - e)\, \gamma_w}{G + e}$

207. The water content of soils can be accurately determined by ....
    (1) sand bath method   (2) calcium carbide method
    (3) oven drying method   (4) pycnometer method

208. The specific gravity of soil solids is determined by ....
    (1) pycnometer method   (2) hydrometer analysis
    (3) sieve analysis   (4) All of these

209. Stoke's law is used to determine the ....
    (1) specific gravity of soil solids   (2) density of soil suspension
    (3) grain size distribution of those soils whose grain size is finer than 0.075 mm
    (4) all of the above

210. The active earth pressure of a soil is defined as the lateral pressure exerted by soil ....
    (1) when it is at rest
    (2) when the retaining wall has no movement relative to the backfill
    (3) when the retaining wall tends to move away from the backfill
    (4) when the retaining wall moves into the soil

211. When the hydrometer analysis is performed, it requires correction for ....
    (1) temperature only   (2) meniscus only
    (3) dispersing agent only   (4) all of these

212. According to Stoke's law, the velocity at which grains settle out of suspension, all other factors being equal, depends upon ....
    (1) shape of the grain   (2) weight of the grain
    (3) size of the grain   (4) all of these

213. The smallest sieve size according to Indian Standards is ....
    (1) 0.0045 mm   (2) 0.045 mm   (3) 0.45 mm   (4) 0.154 mm

214. According to Indian Standards, in 92 mm sieve ....
    (1) there are two holes
    (2) each sieve is circular and its diameter is 2 mm
    (3) each hole is a square and its size is 2 mm
    (4) there are two holes per cm length of the mesh

215. The uniformity coefficient of soil is defined as the ratio of ....
    (1) D_{40} to D_{10} (2) D_{40} to D_{20} (3) D_{50} to D_{20} (4) D_{60} to D_{10}

216. The earth pressure at rest is defined as the lateral pressure exerted by soil ....
    (1) when it is at rest
    (2) when the retaining wall has no movement relative to the backfill
    (3) when the retaining wall tends to move away from the backfill
    (4) when the retaining wall tends to move towards the backfill

217. A soil having uniformity coefficient more than 10 is called ....
    (1) uniform soil   (2) poor soil
    (3) well graded soil   (4) coarse soil

218. Stoke's law is applicable to particles up to .... effective diameter.
    (1) 0.0002 mm   (2) 0.002 mm   (3) 0.02 mm   (4) 0.2 mm

219. The property of a soil which enables to regain its strength lost on remoulding in a short time, without change of moisture content, is called ....
    (1) unconfined compressive strength   (2) sensitivity
    (3) thixotropy   (4) relative density

220. The unconfined compressive strength of a hard clay is ....
    (1) 10 to 25 kN/m²   (2) 25 to 150 kN/m²
    (3) 150 to 400 kN/m²   (4) above 400 kN/m²
221. The sensitivity of a normal clay is about ....
    (1) 2 to 4   (2) 4 to 8   (3) 8 to 15   (4) 15 to 20
222. The maximum water content of a saturated soil at which a reduction in its moisture does not cause a decrease in volume of the soil, is called ....
    (1) liquid limit   (2) plastic limit
    (3) elastic limit   (4) shrinkage limit
223. The plastic limit of a soil is defined as the ....
    (1) limit of water that makes the soil to flow
    (2) amount of water content which makes the soil to go into the liquid state
    (3) amount of water content which makes the soil to go into the solid state from the liquid state
    (4) Minimum amount of water content which makes the soil to be rolled into 3 mm diameter threads
224. The consistency index is given by ....
    (1) $\dfrac{W_P - W}{I_p}$ (2) $\dfrac{W_L - W}{I_p}$ (3) $\dfrac{W_L - W_p}{I_p}$ (4) $\dfrac{W - W_p}{I_p}$
225. The liquidity index (in percentage) is given by ....
    (1) $\dfrac{W_P - W}{I_p}$ (2) $\dfrac{W_L - W}{I_p}$ (3) $\dfrac{W_L - W_p}{I_p}$ (4) $\dfrac{W - W_p}{I_p}$
226. When the consistency index is zero, then the soil is at its ....
    (1) elastic limit   (2) plastic limit   (3) liquid limit   (4) semi-solid state
227. A soil is in a semi-solid state, the consistency index is ....
    (1) zero   (2) one
    (3) more than unity   (4) none of these
228. Toughness index is the ratio of ....
    (1) flow index and plasticity index   (2) plasticity index and flow index
    (3) liquidity index and flow index   (4) flow index and liquidity index
229. A sample of soil has liquid limit 45%, plastic limit 25%, shrinkage limit 17% and natural moisture content 30%. The consistency index of the soil is ....
    (1) $\dfrac{15}{20}$ (2) $\dfrac{13}{20}$ (3) $\dfrac{8}{20}$ (4) $\dfrac{5}{20}$
230. The liquid limit exists in ....
    (1) sandy soils   (2) gravel soils   (3) silty soils   (4) clays
231. The plastic limit exists in ....
    (1) sandy soils   (2) gravel soils   (3) silty soils   (4) clays
232. The liquid limit minus plastic limit is termed as ....
    (1) flow index   (2) plasticity index
    (3) shrinkage index   (4) liquidity index

233. When the plastic limit is equal to or greater than the liquid limit, then the plasticity index is ....
    (1) negative   (2) zero   (3) one   (4) more than one

234. The shrinkage index is equal to ....
    (1) liquid limit + plastic limit
    (2) plastic limit – liquid limit
    (3) liquid limit – shrinkage limit
    (4) shrinkage limit – liquid limit

235. The flow index in soils indicates the ....
    (1) ratio of liquid limit to plastic limit
    (2) variation of liquid limit
    (3) variation of plastic limit
    (4) shear strength variation with water content

236. The moisture contents of a clayey soil is gradually decreased from a large value. The correct sequence of the occurrence of the limits will be ....
    (1) liquid limit, plastic limit and shrinkage limit
    (2) plastic limit, liquid limit and shrinkage limit
    (3) shrinkage limit, plastic limit and liquid limit
    (4) plastic limit, shrinkage limit and liquid limit

237. The activity of clay is defined as the ratio of ....
    (1) liquid limit to plastic limit
    (2) liquidity index to plasticity index
    (3) plasticity index to clay fraction
    (4) plasticity index to shrinkage index

238. When the particles of soil are oriented edge to edge or edge to face with respect to one another, the soil is said to have ....
    (1) single grained structure
    (2) double grained structure
    (3) honey-combed structure
    (4) flocculent structure

239. Which of the following is practically impermeable ?
    (1) Gravel   (2) Sand mixture   (3) Coarse sand   (4) Clay

240. A sample of clay and a sample of sand have the same specific gravity and void ratio. Their permeabilities will differ because ....
    (1) their porosities will be different
    (2) their densities will be different
    (3) their degrees of saturation will be different
    (4) the size range of their voids will be different

241. When applying Darcy's law to soils, it is assumed that the ....
    (1) soil is incompressible
    (2) soil is homogeneous and isotropic
    (3) flow conditions are laminar
    (4) all of these

242. Which of the following have an influence on the value of permeability ?
    (1) Grain size
    (2) Void ratio
    (3) Degree of saturation
    (4) All of these

243. The permeability of a given soil is ....
    (1) directly proportional to the average grain size
    (2) inversely proportional to the average grain size
    (3) directly proportional to the square of the average grain size
    (4) inversely proportional to the square to the average grain size

244. The coefficient of permeability of silt is .... that of clay.

    (1) same as   (2) less than   (3) more than   (4) None of the above

245. The quantity of seepage of water in a malicim is ....

    (1) directly proportional to the head of water at upsteam

    (2) inversely proportional to the head of water at upsteam

    (3) directly proportional to the coefficient of permeability

    (4) inversely proportional to the coefficient of permeability

246. The average velocity of flow that will take place through the total cross-sectional area of soil under unit hydraulic gradient is called ....

    (1) uniformity coefficient   (2) Darcy's coefficient

    (3) coefficient of permeability   (4) terminal velocity

247. The pressure exerted by water on the soil through which it percolates, is known as ....

    (1) hydrostatic pressure   (2) effective pressure

    (3) seepage pressure   (4) none of these

248. A flow line in seepage through a soil medium is defined as the ....

    (1) path of particles of water through a saturated soil mass

    (2) line connecting points of equal head of water

    (3) flow of movement of fine particle of soil

    (4) direction of the particle

249. The equipotential line in a seepage through an oil medium is defined as the ....

    (1) path of particles of water through saturated soil mass

    (2) line connecting points of equal head of water

    (3) flow of movement of fine particles of soil

    (4) direction of the flow particle

250. Quick sand is a ....

    (1) moist sand containing small particles

    (2) condition which occurs in coarse sand

    (3) condition in which a cohesionless soil loses all its strength because of upward flow of water

    (4) none of the above

251. Flow lines and equipotential lines are ....

    (1) perpendicular to each other   (2) parallel to each other

    (3) intersecting lines at 90° to each other (4) intersecting lines at 45° to each other

252. A flow net is used to determine the ....

    (1) seepage flow   (2) seepage pressure

    (3) exit gradient   (4) all of these

253. The exit gradient of the seepage of water through a soil medium is the ....

    (1) slope of the flow line   (2) slope of the equipotential line

    (3) ratio of total head loss to the length of seepage

    (4) ratio of the head loss to the length of seepage

254. The angle of internal friction ....
   (1) varies with the density of sand
   (2) depends upon the amount of interlocking
   (3) depends upon the particle shape and roughness
   (4) all of the above

255. A line showing the dry density as a function of water content for soil containing no air voids is called ....
   (1) saturation line   (2) zero air void line
   (3) liquid limit line   (4) none of these

256. The critical gradient of the seepage of water is ....
   (1) directly proportional to void ratio
   (2) increases with the decrease in void ratio
   (3) inversely proportional to specific gravity
   (4) increases with the decrease in specific gravity of soil

257. The critical gradient of the seepage of water .... with the increase in specific gravity of soil.
   (1) increases   (2) decreases
   (3) does not change   (4) none of these

258. The seepage force in soils is ....
   (1) proportional to head loss   (2) proportional to exit gradient
   (3) perpendicular to the equipotential lines
   (4) all of these

259. The critical gradient for all soils is normally ....
   (1) 0.5   (2) 1   (3) 1.5   (4) 2.5

260. The piping failure in a hydraulic structure can be prevented by ....
   (1) diverting the seepage water into filter wells
   (2) increasing the creep length of flow of water
   (3) increasing the stress due to weight of the structure
   (4) all of the above

261. The neutral stress on the soil is due to the ....
   (1) external load acting on the soil
   (2) weight of the soil particles
   (3) weight of water present in soil pores
   (4) both (1) and (2)

262. The natural stress is ....
   (1) transmitted through the points of contact of the interconnected particles of soil
   (2) transmitted to the soil base through the pore water
   (3) independent of the depth of water above the soil mass
   (4) due to weight of soil particles

263. The consolidation of a soil is defined as the ....
    (1) process of compression by gradual reduction of pore space under steady load
    (2) process which gives gradual decrease of water content at constant load
    (3) change in volume of soil due to expulsion of pure water under an applied load
    (4) Any one of the above

264. The coefficient of volume of compressibility is given by ....
    (1) $\dfrac{a_v}{1 + e_o}$ (2) $\dfrac{1 + e_o}{a_v}$ (3) $\dfrac{e_o}{a_v}$ (4) $\dfrac{e_o}{a_o}$

265. The decrease in void ratio per unit increase in pressure is called ....
    (1) coefficient of permeability   (2) coefficient of compressibility
    (3) coefficient of volume compressibility
    (4) coefficient of curvature

266. The coefficient of consolidation is measured in ....
    (1) cm^2/g (2) cm^2/s (3) $g/cm^2/s$ (4) $cm^2/g/s$

267. The coefficient of consolidation is used for evaluating ....
    (1) stress in the soil   (2) total settlement
    (3) over consolidation ratio   (4) time rate of settlement

268. The degree of consolidation is directly proportional ....
    (1) to time and inversely proportional to drainage path
    (2) to drainage path and inversely proportional to time
    (3) to time and inversely to the square of the drainage path
    (4) to square of drainage path and inversely proportional to time

269. The time factor for a clay layer is ....
    (1) a dimensionless parameter
    (2) directly proportional to permeability
    (3) directly proportional of drainage path
    (4) none of these

270. The relation between coefficient of consolidation (C_v), coefficient of volume change (M_v) and coefficient of permeability (k) is given by ....
    (1) $C_v = \dfrac{k}{M_v \cdot Y_w}$ (2) $C_v = \dfrac{k \cdot M_v}{Y_w}$ (3) $C_v = \dfrac{Y_w}{k \cdot M_v}$ (4) $C_v = \dfrac{M_v \cdot W}{k}$

271. The relation between coefficient of consolidation (C_v), time factor (T_v), drainage path (d) and time (t) is given by ....
    (1) $C_v = \dfrac{d^2 \cdot T_v}{t}$ (2) $C_v = \dfrac{d^2 \cdot t}{T_v}$ (3) $C_v = \dfrac{T_v \cdot t}{d^2}$ (4) $C_v = \dfrac{T_v}{d^2 t}$

272. The coefficient of volume compressibility is ....
    (1) directly proportional to the void ratio
    (2) inversely proportional to the void ratio
    (3) directly proportional to the coefficient of compressibility
    (4) inversely proportional to the coefficient of compressibility

273. The coefficient of volume compressibility .... with the increase in pressure.
    (1) increases
    (2) decreases
    (3) does not change
    (4) first increases and then decreases

274. The compression index of the soil ....
    (1) increases with the increase in liquid limit
    (2) decreases with the increase in liquid limit
    (3) increases with the decrease in plastic limit
    (4) decreases with the increase in plastic limit

275. The expansion of soil due to shear at a constant value of pressure is called ....
    (1) apparent cohesion
    (2) true cohesion
    (3) dilatacy
    (4) consistency

ANSWER KEY

1.	(3)	2.	(1)	3.	(1)	4.	(4)	5.	(3)	6.	(1)	7.	(3)	8.	(4)
9.	(3)	10.	(3)	11.	(2)	12.	(1)	13.	(3)	14.	(3)	15.	(1)	16.	(3)
17.	(4)	18.	(4)	19.	(3)	20.	(1)	21.	(4)	22.	(3)	23.	(3)	24.	(2)
25.	(4)	26.	(2)	27.	(3)	28.	(2)	29.	(2)	30.	(4)	31.	(2)	32.	(2)
33.	(1)	34.	(2)	35.	(4)	36.	(3)	37.	(2)	38.	(3)	39.	(3)	40.	(1)
41.	(2)	42.	(4)	43.	(4)	44.	(2)	45.	(3)	46.	(4)	47.	(2)	48.	(3)
49.	(4)	50.	(3)	51.	(1)	52.	(4)	53.	(2)	54.	(2)	55.	(3)	56.	(4)
57.	(2)	58.	(4)	59.	(4)	60.	(4)	61.	(3)	62.	(3)	63.	(4)	64.	(3)
65.	(4)	66.	(1)	67.	(3)	68.	(2)	69.	(2)	70.	(3)	71.	(1)	72.	(3)
73.	(2)	74.	(4)	75.	(3)	76.	(3)	77.	(3)	78.	(3)	79.	(1)	80.	(4)
81.	(4)	82.	(4)	83.	(3)	84.	(1)	85.	(1)	86.	(4)	87.	(2)	88.	(2)
89.	(3)	90.	(1)	91.	(4)	92.	(2)	93.	(3)	94.	(2)	95.	(3)	96.	(3)
97.	(2)	98.	(4)	99.	(2)	100.	(2)	101.	(1)	102.	(3)	103.	(1)	104.	(4)
105.	(3)	106.	(3)	107.	(4)	108.	(2)	109.	(2)	110.	(1)	111.	(3)	112.	(2)
113.	(1)	114.	(1)	115.	(4)	116.	(2)	117.	(1)	118.	(2)	119.	(3)	120.	(3)
121.	(4)	122.	(2)	123.	(1)	124.	(1)	125.	(3)	126.	(3)	127.	(2)	128.	(1)
129.	(1)	130.	(2)	131.	(4)	132.	(2)	133.	(4)	134.	(4)	135.	(1)	136.	(1)
137.	(4)	138.	(1)	139.	(1)	140.	(3)	141.	(2)	142.	(3)	143.	(1)	144.	(3)

145.	(4)	146.	(2)	147.	(1)	148.	(4)	149.	(1)	150.	(4)	151.	(2)	152.	(1)
153.	(3)	154.	(2)	155.	(2)	156.	(4)	157.	(3)	158.	(2)	159.	(2)	160.	(2)
161.	(2)	162.	(4)	163.	(1)	164.	(1)	165.	(4)	166.	(3)	167.	(3)	168.	(2)
169.	(3)	170.	(3)	171.	(1)	172.	(1)	173.	(4)	174.	(2)	175.	(1)	176.	(2)
177.	(4)	178.	(4)	179.	(1)	180.	(1)	181.	(4)	182.	(4)	183.	(3)	184.	(1)
185.	(2)	186.	(4)	187.	(3)	188.	(4)	189.	(1)	190.	(4)	191.	(2)	192.	(2)
193.	(3)	194.	(3)	195.	(4)	196.	(3)	197.	(4)	198.	(2)	199.	(3)	200.	(4)
201.	(3)	202.	(1)	203.	(3)	204.	(3)	205.	(1)	206.	(3)	207.	(3)	208.	(1)
209.	(3)	210.	(3)	211.	(4)	212.	(4)	213.	(2)	214.	(3)	215.	(4)	216.	(2)
217.	(3)	218.	(1)	219.	(3)	220.	(4)	221.	(1)	222.	(4)	223.	(4)	224.	(2)
225.	(4)	226.	(3)	227.	(3)	228.	(2)	229.	(1)	230.	(4)	231.	(4)	232.	(2)
233.	(2)	234.	(3)	235.	(4)	236.	(1)	237.	(3)	238.	(4)	239.	(4)	240.	(4)
241.	(4)	242.	(4)	243.	(3)	244.	(2)	245.	(3)	246.	(3)	247.	(3)	248.	(1)
249.	(2)	250.	(1)	251.	(3)	252.	(4)	253.	(4)	254.	(4)	255.	(1)	256.	(2)
257.	(1)	258.	(4)	259.	(2)	260.	(4)	261.	(3)	262.	(2)	263.	(4)	264.	(1)
265.	(2)	266.	(2)	267.	(4)	268.	(3)	269.	(2)	270.	(1)	271.	(1)	272.	(3)
273.	(2)	274.	(1)	275.	(3)											

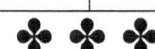

UNIT - 7 : FLUID MECHANICS AND HYDRAULICS

1. Fluid is defined as a substance which .....
   - (1) is essentially incompressible
   - (2) has a viscosity that always decrease with temperature
   - (3) cannot remain at rest when subjected to a shearing stress
   - (4) cannot be subjected to shear stress
2. An ideal fluid is defined as the fluid which .....
   - (1) has negligible surface tension
   - (2) obeys Newton's law of viscosity
   - (3) is incompressible and non-viscous
   - (4) satisfies the relation PV = RT
3. A practical fluid is the one .....
   - (1) which has weight
   - (2) which has viscosity and is compressible
   - (3 which has surface tension
   - (2) all of above
4. A prefect fluid is
   - (1) a real fluid
   - (2) the one which obeys perfect gas laws
   - (3) Compressive and gaseous
   - (4) incompressible and frictionless
5. _____ type of fluids do not exist in nature.
   - (1) Real
   - (2) Newtonian
   - (3) Ideal
   - (4) Thixotropic
6. In practice which of the following is generally treated as ideal fluid ?
   - (1) Air
   - (2) Kerosene
   - (3) Lubricating oil
   - (4) None of above
7. In a concept of fluid continuum .....
   - (1) fluid is non-homogeneous
   - (2) density of fluid is very low
   - (3) fluid particles are scattered in space
   - (4) fluid particles are very closely spaced
8. Mass density of fluid is .....
   - (1) $\dfrac{mass}{volume}$
   - (2) $\dfrac{volume}{mass}$
   - (3) $mass \times volume$
   - (4) none of these
9. Mass density is also called as .....
   - (1) specific weight
   - (2) specific gravity
   - (3) specific mass
   - (4) specific volume
10. Specific volume is .....
    - (1) $\dfrac{1}{\rho}$
    - (2) γ/g
    - (3) $\dfrac{W}{V}$
    - (4) $\dfrac{M}{V}$
11. Mass density of water on earth (g = 9.81 m/s²) is 1000 kg/m³. Its mass density on moon where the gravitational acceleration is $\dfrac{1}{6}^{th}$ that of earth, will be .....
    - (1) 166.67 kg/m³
    - (2) 1000 kg/m³
    - (3) 6000 kg/m³
    - (4) none of these
12. Specific weight of a liquid is .....
    - (1) $\dfrac{\text{weight of liquid}}{\text{volume of liquid}}$
    - (2) $\dfrac{\text{volume of liquid}}{\text{weight of liquid}}$
    - (3) weigh of liquid × volume of liquid
    - (4) none of these

13. The ratio of specific weight of liquid to specific weight of standard liquid (water at 4°C) is known as .....

    (1) weight density (2) specific volume (3) specific gravity (4) compressibility

14. If specific weight of fluid is 8210 N/m³ and its kinematic viscosity is 1.7 cm²/sec, its density is .....

    (1) 8210 kg/m³   (2) 4830 kg/m³   (3) 837 kg/m³   (4) 821 kg/m³

15. Two liquids of different specific gravity are mixed together. If the weight of mixture is 150 N and volume of mixture is 0.02 m³, the specific gravity of mixture is .....

    (1) 0.5   (2) 3   (3) 7.5   (4) 0.76

16. The net or effective head at the turbine is :

    (1) The sum of gross head plus the head loss in the penstock

    (2) Sum of gross head plus head loss in the penstock and velocity head at turbine exit

    (3) The difference between gross head minus head loss in penstock

    (4) The difference between gross head minus head loss in penstock and velocity head at turbine exit

17. Specific gravity of liquid is 0.9, its mass density is .....

    (1) 900 kg/m³   (2) 1111.11 kg/m³ (3) 9×10^{-4} kg/m³ (4) none of these

18. The weight of 8 litre of oil is 75 N. Its weight density is _____ N/m³.

    (1) 600   (2) 9196   (3) 7900   (4) 9375

19. If specific gravity of mercury is 13.6, its specific weight is .....

    (1) 1.386 kN/m³   (2) 133.416 kN/m³ (3) 98.10 kN/m³   (4) 1000 kN/m³

20. If a mercury has mass density of 13600 kg/m³, its specific weight is _____ (g = 9.81).

    (1) 1.386 kN/m³   (2) 133.416 kN/m³ (3) 98.10 kN/m³   (4) 1000 kN/m³

21. The property due to which fluid offers resistance to deformation under shear stress is .....

    (1) surface tension (2) viscosity   (3) compressibility (4) capillarity

22. As per Newton's law of viscosity, shear stress is directly proportional to .....

    (1) change of force w.r.t. distance   (2) change of displacement w.r.t. velocity

    (3) change of velocity w.r.t. distance   (4) change of viscosity w.r.t. distance

23. Newton's law of viscosity states that the shear stress is .....

    (1) proportional to angular deformation

    (2) proportional to rate of angular deformation

    (3) inversely proportional to angular deformation

    (4) inversely proportional to rate of angular deformation

24. Newton's law of viscosity is related to .....

    (1) shear stress and pressure   (2) shear stress and velocity gradient

    (3) pressure, velocity and viscosity   (4) stress and strain in a fluid

25. Newton's law of viscosity is given by .....

    (1) $\tau = \mu \cdot \dfrac{du}{dy}$ (2) $\tau = \mu^2 \cdot \dfrac{du}{dy}$ (3) $\tau = \mu \cdot \left(\dfrac{du}{dy}\right)^2$ (4) none of these

26. Boundary layer on a flat plate is called laminar boundary layer if :
    (1) Reynold number is less than 2000   (2) Reynold number is less than 4000
    (3) Reynold number is less than 5×10^5 (4) None of the above

27. In Netwon's law of viscosity, the term du/dy is called as .....
    (1) pressure gradient   (2) velocity gradient
    (3) temperature gradient   (4) none of the above

28. In Newton's law of viscosity, the unit of velocity gradient is .....
    (1) m   (2) s^{-1} (3) m/s   (4) m^{-1}

29. Poise is the unit of .....
    (1) viscosity   (2) surface tension
    (3) kinematic viscosity   (4) vapour pressure

30. One poise is .....
    (1) $\dfrac{Ns}{m^2}$ (2) kg/ms   (3) $\dfrac{dyne\text{-}sec}{cm^2}$ (4) $\dfrac{Ns}{m}$

31. The unit of viscosity is .....
    (1) $\dfrac{N\text{-}s}{m^2}$ (2) kg/ms   (3) poise   (4) all of these

32. An oil has viscosity of 9 poise, its conversion into Pa-s is .....
    (1) 90   (2) 0.9   (3) 9   (4) 900

33. Pascal-second is the unit of .....
    (1) Pressure   (2) Kinematic viscosity
    (3) Dynamic viscosity   (4) Surface tension

34. In case of liquids, viscosity .....
    (1) decreases with decrease in temperature
    (2) decreases with rise in temperature
    (3) does not change with temperature
    (4) does not change with pressure

35. In case of gases, viscosity .....
    (1) increases with increase in temperature
    (2) decreases with rise in temperature
    (3) does not change with temperature
    (4) does not change with pressure

36. If for a fluid, the relation between shear stress and velocity gradient is straight line, the fluid is classified as .....
    (1) Newtonian   (2) Non-newtonian
    (3) Dilatant   (4) Thixotropic

37. A real fluid in which shear stress is not proportional to the velocity gradient is called as ____ fluid.
    (1) Newtonian   (2) Thixotropic
    (3) Non-Newtonian   (4) Ideal plastic

38. A real fluid which satisfies Newton's law of viscosity is termed as ____ fluid.
    (1) thixotropic   (2) ideal   (3) Newtonian   (4) ideal plastic

39. If the relationships between the shear stress τ and the rate of shear strain $\dfrac{du}{dy}$ is given by

    $\tau = K\left(\dfrac{du}{dy}\right)^n$ the fluid with exponent $n < 1$ is known as .....

    (1) Dilatant fluid   (2) Bingham fluid
    (3) Pseudoplastic fluid   (4) Newtonian plastic fluid

40. For a turbulent flow in a circular pipe the mean velocity is 0.3 m/s. If the shear velocity is 0.015 m/s then the local velocity at a radial distance of '0.5 r' from the pipe axis is .....
    (1) 0.28 m/s   (2) 0.62 m/s   (3) 0.73 m/s   (4) 0.33 m/s

41. For a turbulent flow of water if the mean velocity is 0.25 m/s and friction factor is 0.02 then the shear stress at the pipe wall is ____ N/m².
    (1) 0.21   (2) 0.36   (3) 0.16   (4) 0.42

42. For the turbulent flow if the value of $\log_{10}\left(\dfrac{R}{k}\right) = 2$ then the friction factor is .....

    (1) 0.05   (2) 0.022   (3) 0.061   (4) 0.031

43. For a turbulent flow of water through a pipe of diameter 0.6 m the shear stress at the pipe wall is 45 N/m². The shear velocity is .....
    (1) 0.21 m/s   (2) 0.35 m/s   (3) 0.045 m/s   (4) none of the above

44. In a turbulent flow in a pipe, the shear stress is :
    (1) Maximum at the centre
    (2) Maximum at the boundary and decreases linearly to zero at the centre
    (3) Maximum at the boundary and decreases logarithmically towards the centre
    (4) Maximum at a finite distance from the boundary

45. The critical depth is the depth of flow at which :
    (1) Discharge is maximum   (2) Reynold number is unity
    (3) The specific energy is minimum   (4) Perimeter is minimum

46. The relation between the shear stress τ and the rate of angular deformation $\dfrac{du}{dy}$ is given by

    $\tau = \left(\dfrac{du}{dy}\right)^n$, the fluid with exponent $n > 1$ is known as

    (1) Dilatant fluid   (2) Bingham fluid
    (3) Pseudoplastic fluid   (4) Newtonian fluid

47. Printers ink is an example of .....
    (1) ideal fluid   (2) pseudoplastic fluid
    (3) ideal plastic fluid   (4) thixotropic fluid

48. Toothpaste is an example of .....
    (1) pseudoplastic fluid   (2) ideal plastic or bingham plastic fluid
    (4) ideal fluid   (4) elastic solid

49. Milk, paper pulp etc. are examples of ..... fluid.
    (1) dilatant   (2) thixotropic   (3) ideal plastic   (4) pseudoplastic

50. Water, kerosene, gasoline etc. are the examples of ____ fluid.
    (1) thixotropic   (2) ideal   (3) newtonian   (4) ideal plastic

51. Dynamic viscosity (μ) has the dimensions as .....
    (1) MLT^{-2} (2) $ML^{-1}T^{-1}$ (3) $ML^{-1}T^{-2}$ (4) $M^{-1}L^{-1}T^{-1}$

52. Dimensions of dynamic viscosity (in F, L, T, system) are .....
    (1) $FL^{-1}T^{-2}$ (2) $FL^{-1}T^{-1}$ (3) FLT^{-2} (4) FTL^{-2}

53. If velocity gradient is 250 m/s/m and viscosity of oil is 2 poise, shear stress is ____ N/mm².
    (1) 125×10^{-6} (2) 50×10^{-6} (3) 100×10^{-4} (4) 500×10^{-4}

54. The clearance between shaft and its sleeve is filled with Newtonian fluid when a force of 200 N is applied to sleeve parallel to shaft, the sleeve attains a speed of 1 cm/s. If a force of 1 kN is applied to the sleeve instead, the sleeve will move with a velocity of
    (1) 2 cm/s   (2) 3 cm/s   (3) 10 cm/s   (4) 5 cm/s

55. The power required to turn 100 mm diameter shaft is 25 W. If the tangential force on the shaft is 20 N, the speed of shaft is _____ rpm.
    (1) 239   (2) 393   (3) 452   (4) 297

56. The variation of velocity in a fluid flow is given as, $u = (3 + 3 \times 10^3 y^2)$ m/s, where y is in metres. If viscosity of oil is 0.1 N-s/m², the shear stress at y = 10 mm is
    (1) 12 N/m²   (2) 60 N/m²   (3) 6 N/m²   (4) 24 N/m²

57. Kinematic viscosity is the ratio of .....
    (1) dynamic viscosity and weight density of fluid
    (2) dynamic viscosity and mass density of fluid
    (3) dynamic viscosity and weight of fluid
    (4) dynamic viscosity and mass of fluid

58. For a turbulent flow in a circular pipe the mean velocity is 0.3 m/s. If the shear velocity is 0.015 m/s then the local velocity at a radial distance is '0.25 r' from the pipe axis is .....
    (1) 0.69 m/s   (2) 0.35 m/s   (3) 0.27 m/s   (4) 0.12 m/s

59. Stoke is the unit of .....
    (1) density   (2) kinematic viscosity
    (3) velocity gradient   (4) dynamic viscosity

60. The units of kinematic viscosity are .....
    (1) m²/s   (2) kg/m²s   (3) m/kg s   (4) Ns/m²

61. One stoke is equal to .....
    (1) 1 m²/s   (2) 1 cm²/s   (3) 1 mm²/s   (4) 10 mm²/s

62. To convert 1 stoke into m²/s, the multiplication factor is .....
    (1) 10^{-2} (2) 10^2 (3) 10^4 (4) 10^{-4}

63. A fluid has viscosity of 8 poise and density of 900 kg/m³. Its kinematic viscosity is _____ m²/sec.

    (1) 8.8×10^{-3} (2) 8.8×10^{-4} (3) 720   (4) 112.5

64. Mass of 6 m³ of water 20° C and 1 atm., pressure is 6000 kg and viscosity under similar condition is 1 centipoise, kinematic viscosity of water is .....

    (1) 10^{-3} m²/s   (2) 10^{-4} m²/s   (3) 10^{-5} m²/s   (4) 10^{-6} m²/s

65. Compressibility is .....

    (1) capillarity   (2) vapour pressure

    (3) reciprocal of bulk modulus   (4) bulk modulus of elasticity

66. The power required to pump 500 lps of water through a pipe of 0.5 m diameter over a length of 2 km is _____ kW. Take f = 0.0303.

    (1) 125.6   (2) 149.8   (3) 181.2   (4) 196.5

67. Bulk modulus of elasticity is .....

    (1) $\dfrac{dV}{(-dp/p)}$ (2) $\dfrac{dp}{(-dV/V)}$ (3) $\dfrac{-dp}{(-dV/V)}$ (4) $\dfrac{-dV}{(-dp/p)}$

68. Bulk modulus of water is _____ N/m².

    (1) 9.81×10^{6} (2) 1×10^{9} (3) 2.07×10^{9} (4) 101×10^{3}

69. Air is about _____ times more compressible than water.

    (1) 20   (2) 2000   (3) 10,000   (4) 20,000

70. Water is about _____ times more compressible than mild steel.

    (1) 10   (2) 100   (3) 1000   (3) 2000

71. 12 litre of a liquid (specific gravity 1.6) is mixed with 18 litre of another liquid (specific gravity 1.1). If the combination shrinks by 4% on mixing, the volume of mixture is .....

    (1) 0.028 m³   (2) 0.03 m³   (3) 0.012 m³   (4) 0.04 m³

72. Volume of sample of water is reduced by 1 per cent when pressure is increased by 22 MPa. The bulk modulus of elasticity of the sample in MPa is .....

    (1) 2.2   (2) 220   (3) 2200   (4) 0.22

73. Measure of the effect of compressibility in fluid flow is the magnitude of a dimensionless parameter known as .....

    (1) Froude number   (2) Weber number

    (3) Mach number   (4) Euler number

74. _____ is called as average height of roughness projections.

    (1) Total of all the irregularities   (2) Mean of all the irregularities

    (3) Both (1) and (2)   (4) None of the above

75. In turbulent flow $\dfrac{u}{u*} = 5.75 \log_{10}\left(\dfrac{u*y}{v}\right) + 5.55$ is called as _____ equation.

    (1) velocity deficiency   (2) Prandtl's universal velocity

    (3) Karman-Prandtl velocity   (4) none of the above

76. A pipe of 0.1 m diameter conveying water (turbulent flow) the velocities at the centre of pipe is 2.5 m/s and that of at 30 mm from the pipe centre is 2.2 m/s. The shear velocity is .....

    (1)   0.13 m/s   (2)   0.69 m/s   (3)   0.42 m/s   (4)   0.25 m/s

77. Value of bulk modulus of elasticity _____ with increase in pressure.

    (1)   increases   (2)   decreases   (3)   is unchanged   (4)   none of these

78. Vapour pressure of a liquid is due to .....

    (1)   pressure of flow   (2)   pressure of air above free surface

    (3)   molecules of liquid which hang over free surface

    (4)   free surface existence

79. Which of the following statements is true?

    (1)   Vapour pressure increases with increase in temperature.

    (2)   Vapour pressure decreases with increase in temperature.

    (3)   Vapour pressure does not change with temperature.

    (4)   None of these.

80. In fluid flow through a pipeline the mixing length '*l*' is assumed to be equal to .....

    (1)   ky²   (2)   ky   (3)   k log y   (4) $-\dfrac{k}{y}$

81. Shear stress in turbulent flow in a pipe .....

    (1)   is maximum at the centre and decreases logarithmically towards the wall

    (2)   is maximum at the centre and decreases linearly towards the wall

    (3)   is maximum at the pipe wall and decreases linearly to zero towards the centre

    (4)   none of the above

82. In case of turbulent flow over a smooth boundary, match the following:

    Flow zone   **Criterian**

    (1)   Purely laminar zone   (i) $\dfrac{u* \, y}{v} > 70$

    (2)   Turbulent zone   (ii) $\dfrac{u* \, y}{v} < 5$

    (3)   Transition zone   (iii) $5 < \dfrac{u* \, y}{v} > 70$

    (1)   A - ii, B - i, C - iii   (2)   A - i, B - iii, C - ii

    (3)   A - iii, B - ii, C - i   (4)   A - ii, B - iii, C - i

83. The boundary is treated as hydrodynamically smooth when .....

    (1)   the surface of the boundary is smooth

    (2)   average roughness projections are small in height

    (3)   average roughness projections are completely covered by laminar sub-layer

    (4)   the laminar sub-layer is thin as compared to average roughness projections

84. The kinematic viscosity of oil passing through a 20 cm diameter is 0.2 stokes. The critical velocity is .....

    (1)   0.4 m/s   (2)   0.2 m/s   (3)   0.5 m/s   (4)   0.8 m/s

85. In case of turbulent flow through a pipe of radius 'R', the average velocity occurs at a radial distance of .....
    (1) 0.707 R   (2) 0.5 R   (3) 0.2228 R   (4) 0.25 R

86. For turbulent flow through pipes, the pipe factor $\dfrac{u_{av}}{u_{max}}$ is given by .....
    (1) 0.267   (2) $\dfrac{1}{\left(1.43\sqrt{f}+1\right)}$ (3) $\dfrac{1}{(1.3\sqrt{f}+1)}$ (4) $1.43\sqrt{f}+1$

87. For the turbulent flow in a pipe the maximum velocity at the centre is 3.68 m/s. If friction factor is 0.025 the average velocity of flow in m/s is given by .....
    (1) 0.333   (2) 4.5   (3) 3   (4) 3.55

88. If Δp is the pressure drop in length L of horizontal pipe with radius R, the boundary shear is given by .....
    (1) $\dfrac{\Delta pR}{2L}$ (2) $\dfrac{\Delta pL}{2R}$ (3) $\dfrac{2\Delta p}{RL}$ (4) $\dfrac{2\Delta pR}{L}$

89. For turbulent flow in a pipe, the average velocity of flow is 3 m/s. If friction factor is 0.025, the maximum velocity is .....
    (1) 6.21 m/s   (2) 3.68 m/s   (3) 2.45 m/.s   (4) 4.5 m/s

90. For a pipe of 20 cm diameter carrying liquid at Reynold's number of 10^6, if friction factor is 0.02, the thickness of laminar sublayer δ' in mm is .....
    (1) 0.023   (2) 0.046   (3) 0.092   (4) 0.015

91. If for a pipe flow, the ratio of average height of roughness projections 'K' and the thickness of laminar sublayer δ' is 4, the flow can be classified as .....
    (1) fully rough turbulent   (2) fully smooth turbulent
    (3) transition from smooth turbulent to rough turbulent

92. If the wall shear stress is 300 Pa, the diameter of the pipe 80 mm and length of pipe 100 m, the total drag force in kN is .....
    (1) 7.54   (2) 0.151   (3) 30   (4) 3.77

93. Darcy-Weisbach friction factor 'f' for laminar flow is .....
    (1) $\dfrac{16}{R_e}$ (2) $16 \times R_e$ (3) $\dfrac{64}{R_e}$ (4) $64 \times R_e$

94. The boundary is treated as hydrodynamically rough
    (1) $\dfrac{K}{\delta'}<0.25$ (2) $\dfrac{K}{\delta}>6$ (3) $\dfrac{\delta'}{K}<0.25$ (4) $\dfrac{\delta'}{K}<6$

95. Blasius equation is used for .....
    (1) laminar flow
    (2) turbulent flow in rough pipes
    (3) turbulent flow in smooth pipes irrespective of value of R_e
    (4) turbulent flow in smooth pipes for $R_e < 10^5$

96. Relation between Reynold's number R_e and friction factor f in turbulent flow through smooth pipes is f =
    (1) $\dfrac{64}{R_e}$ (2) $\dfrac{0.316}{R_e}$ (3) $\dfrac{0.316}{R_e^{1/4}}$ (4) $\dfrac{64}{R_e^{1/4}}$

97. The plot of Nikurdase experiments on logarithmic scale is the relation between .....
    (1) friction factor, diameter and velocity
    (2) friction factor, Reynold's number and relative roughness of pipe
    (3) friction factor, velocity and relative roughness
    (4) friction factor, velocity and diameter of pipe

98. The friction factor for hydrodynamically smooth pipe .....
    (1) is function of relative roughness K/R only
    (2) is function of relative roughness, K/R and Reynold's number only
    (3) is function of Reynold's number only
    (4) is constant

99. From Stanton curves based on Nikradse's experiments it can be observed that the friction factor f, for fully rough pipes .....
    (1) becomes independent of Reynold's number and depends on relative roughness only
    (2) is mainly dependent on Reynold's number and is independent of relative roughness
    (3) is independent of both Reynold's number and relative roughness
    (4) is dependent on both Reynold's number and relative roughness

100. For turbulent flow shear velocity is .....
    (1) $\sqrt{\dfrac{\tau_o}{\gamma}}$ (2) $\sqrt{\dfrac{\tau_o}{\mu}}$ (3) $\sqrt{\dfrac{\tau_o}{\rho}}$ (4) none of the above

101. For turbulent flow unit of shear velocity is .....
    (1) $N\text{-}s/m^2$ (2) m^2/s (3) m/s^2 (4) m/s

102. The study of fluids at rest is called as fluid .....
    (1) dynamics   (2) kinematics   (3) statics   (4) all of the above

103. Fluid statics deals with .....
    (1) gravity and viscous forces   (2) gravity and pressure forces
    (3) viscous and surface tension forces   (4) gravity and surface tension forces

104. Prandtl mixing length is .....
    (1) dependent on viscosity of fluid   (2) constant for all fluids
    (3) independent of the distance from the fixed surface
    (4) zero at the pipe wall

105. If the force is uniformly distributed over the surface, then
    (1) $F = p \times A$ (2) $p = F \times A$
    (3) $F = p + A$ (4) none of the above

106. A pressure of 1 MPa = _____ N/m^2.
    (1) 10^6 (2) 10^2 (3) 1   (4) 10^4

107. For a fluid at rest
    (1) shear stress depends upon coefficient of velocity
    (2) shear stress is zero
    (3) shear stress is zero only on horizontal planes
    (4) shear stress is maximum on a plane inclined at 45° to horizontal

108. According to Pascal's law the pressure at a point is equal in all directions
     (1) in a liquid at rest   (2) in a fluid at rest
     (3) in a laminar flow   (4) in a turbulent flow

109. Pascal's law states that the hydrostatic pressure .....
     (1) is same at all points in horizontal plane
     (2) is same at all points in vertical plane
     (3) at a point is same irrespective of the direction
     (4) depends upon the specific gravity of liquid

110. For a lamina submerged in liquid making an angle of 45° with the free surface, the liquid pressure will act .....
     (1) parallel to the lamina   (2) making an angle of 45° to lamina
     (3) normal to the lamina   (4) none of these

111. According to Prandtl mixing theory, the turbulent shear stress is given by .....
     (1) $\rho l^2 \left(\dfrac{du}{dy}\right)^2$ (2) $\rho l \left(\dfrac{du}{dy}\right)$ (3) $\rho l \left(\dfrac{du}{dy}\right)^2$ (4) $\rho l^2 \left(\dfrac{du}{dy}\right)$

112. _____ equation represents hydrostatic law.
     (1) $P_x = P_y = P_z$ (2) $P = \gamma h$ (3) $\tau = \mu \dfrac{du}{dy}$ (4) $F = \gamma \times V$

113. Height of free liquid surface above a point is known as .....
     (1) static head   (2) piezometric head
     (3) intensity of pressure   (4) none of these

114. The piezometric head (p + γz) in a static liquid .....
     (1) remains constant at all points
     (2) remains constant only in horizontal direction
     (3) varies only in vertical direction
     (4) does not vary in vertical direction

115. For turbulent flow in a pipe .....
     (1) Reynold's number is < 2000
     (2) Reynold's number is between 2000 and 4000
     (3) Reynold's number is more than 4000
     (4) Reynold's number has no significance

116. For turbulent flow .....
     (1) the motion is streamline motion   (2) velocity variation is parabolic in nature
     (3) velocity is constant across the section
     (4) average velocity is superimposed by random fluctuating component velocity

117. The intensity of turbulence refers to
     (1) the average kinetic energy of turbulence per unit mass
     (2) correlation between the fluctuating velocity components, u' and v'
     (3) the Reynold's stresses
     (4) the root mean square value of turbulent velocity fluctuations

118. Eddy viscosity is also called as .....
    (1) turbulent mixing coefficient
    (2) apparent viscosity
    (3) virtual viscosity
    (4) all of the above

119. In case of turbulent flow the _____ stresses will exist .....
    (1) viscous shear
    (2) turbulent shear
    (3) both (1) and (2)
    (4) none of the above

120. Apparent viscosity is a .....
    (1) property of fluid
    (2) function of fluid property
    (3) function of flow characteristic
    (4) both (2) and (3)

121. Kinematic eddy viscosity is .....
    (1) μ/ρ
    (2) $\mu \times \rho$
    (3) η/ρ
    (4) $\eta \times \rho$

122. _____ is used to measure the fluid pressure.
    (1) U-tube manometer
    (2) Piezometer
    (3) Mechanical gauges
    (4) All of the above

123. Manometers are used to measure comparatively
    (1) high pressures
    (2) low pressures
    (3) very high pressures
    (4) both high and low pressures

124. Piezometers can be inserted .....
    (1) in the top of container
    (2) in the bottom of container
    (3) in the side of container
    (4) all of the above

125. In connection with Reynold's experiments, select correct statement related to turbulent flow .....
    (1) the filament remains straight and stable parallel to the side of the tube
    (2) loss of head is proportional to velocity of flow
    (3) the filament is more irregular and there is mixing of dye
    (4) Reynold's number is low

126. Mechanical gauges are used to measure .....
    (1) low pressures
    (2) high pressures
    (3) both high and low pressures
    (4) none of these

127. Sensitive manometer is used to measure _____ pressures accurately.
    (1) high
    (2) low
    (3) moderate
    (4) none of these

128. In _____ type of simple manometer a reservoir is connected to one of the limb.
    (1) piezometer
    (2) U-tube
    (3) single column
    (4) none of the above

129. Difference of pressure between two points is measured by .....
    (1) piezometer
    (2) barometer
    (3) differential manometer
    (4) none of these

130. _____ is used for the measurement of very small pressure differences.
    (1) U-tube differential manometer
    (2) Inverted U-tube manometer
    (3) Micromanometer
    (4) All of the above

131. _____ pressure is measured by using a barometer.
    (1) Gauge   (2) Atmospheric   (3) Absolute   (4) All of the above
132. Standard atmospheric pressure in terms of water column is .....
    (1) 7.5 m   (2) 8.33 m   (3) 9.80 m   (4) 10.33 m
133. If the pressure is below atmospheric pressure, it is called as _____ pressure.
    (1) vacuum   (2) negative gauge
    (3) suction   (4) all of the above
134. Bourdon gauge measures .....
    (1) gauge pressure   (2) absolute pressure
    (3) local atmospheric pressure   (4) standard atmospheric pressure
135. Equivalent column of water corresponding to 76 cm column of mercury is .....
    (1) 1033 cm   (2) 1020 cm   (3) 1060 cm   (4) 1000 cm
136. Mercury is used in barometers because .....
    (1) it has negligible capillarity effect   (2) it is easy to read
    (3) it has high density and low vapour pressure
    (4) it is not compressible
137. If standard atmospheric and local atmospheric pressures are 101.33 kPa and 90 kPa respectively, the gauge pressure of 20 kPa in terms of absolute pressure will be .....
    (1) 121.33 KPa   (2) 81.33 KPa   (3) 110 KPa   (4) 70 KPa
138. At some point the barometer reading is 750 mm of Hg and the pressure gauge reads 10 N/cm². The absolute pressure in KPa is
    (1) 100   (2) 200   (3) 250   (4) 350
139. The pressure due to a column of _____ m of water is 2.943 kPa.
    (1) 0.2   (2) 0.1   (3) 0.3   (4) 0.4
140. Differential manometers are used to measure .....
    (1) pressure difference between two points
    (2) pressure at a point in a pipe
    (3) both (1) and (2)   (4) none of the above
141. 1 m column of mercury is equivalent to .....
    (1) 1 m of water   (2) 1.36 m of water
    (3) 13.6 m of water   (4) 136 m of water
142. 32 m of column of water is equivalent to _____ of column of liquid of sp. gr. 1.6.
    (1) 48 m   (2) 4.8 m   (3) 20 m   (4) 2 m
143. The pressure due to a column of 0.5 m of oil having density 890 kg/m³ is .....
    (1) 4365 Pa   (2) 445 Pa   (3) 8730 Pa   (4) 4905 Pa
144. Pressure of 88.29 kN/m² will be equivalent to _____ of liquid of sp. gr. 0.9.
    (1) 98.1 m   (2) 79.46 m   (3) 10 m   (4) 9 m
145. Fluctuating velocity may be .....
    (1) positive   (2) negative   (3) zero   (4) all of the above

146. ____ velocity changes continuously w.r.t. time.
   (1) Time average   (2) Instantaneous
   (3) Fluctuating   (4) None of the above
147. Essential feature of turbulent flow is .....
   (1) high velocity
   (2) large discharge
   (3) irregular fluctuations of high frequency
   (4) none of the above
148. The magnitude of total pressure on a plane surface is independent of .....
   (1) area of surface   (2) type of fluid   (3) angle   (4) all of the above
149. When fluid is at rest, the total pressure acts ____ to the surface.
   (1) parallel   (2) inclined
   (3) perpendicular   (4) none of the above
150. The resultant hydrostatic force on a plain surface submerged in a liquid acts at .....
   (1) centre of buoyancy   (2) centre of gravity
   (3) centre of pressure   (4) none of these
151. Centre of pressure of a plain surface immersed in a liquid is .....
   (1) above centre of gravity of the surface
   (2) at centre of gravity of the surface
   (3) below centre of gravity of the surface
   (4) none of these
152. Match the following :

List - I	List - II
(1) Reynolds number	(i) Inertia force and elastic force
(2) Froude number	(ii) Inertia force and surface tension
(3) Weber number	(iii) Inertia force and gravity force
(4) Match number	(iv) Inertia force and viscous force

   Codes :

	(1)	(2)	(3)	(4)
(1)	(i)	(ii)	(iii)	(iv)
(2)	(iv)	(iii)	(ii)	(i)
(3)	(i)	(iii)	(ii)	(iv)
(4)	(iv)	(ii)	(iii)	(i)

153. In case of turbulent flow the velocity distribution is .....
   (1) uniform   (2) variable   (3) both (1) and (2) (4) none of the above
154. In case of a turbulent flow the velocity distribution is .....
   (1) logarithmic   (2) parabolic   (3) hyperbolic   (4) linear
155. In case of turbulent flow velocity fluctuation is due to .....
   (1) random nature of fluid motion   (2) irregular nature of fluid motion
   (3) haphazard nature of fluid motion   (4) all of the above

156. In turbulent flow the temporal mean velocity is also called as _____ velocity.
    (1) instantaneous
    (2) time average
    (3) fluctuating
    (4) none of the above

157. The position of CP of a lamina is independent of _____
    (1) angle
    (2) area of lamina
    (3) type of fluid
    (4) CG of lamina

158. For a rectangular lamina immersed vertically in water to a height of 3 m, the depth of centre of pressure is .....
    (1) $\frac{3}{4}$ m
    (2) 2 m
    (3) $\frac{9}{4}$ m
    (4) 1.5 m

159. A rectangular plate 1 m × 1 m is immersed vertically in water with its one edge horizontal. The force on one side of the plate was found to be 10 kN. If the plate is now turned in vertical plane through 45° without changing the depth of centre of gravity below water surface, the total force on the plate now will be .....
    (1) 5 kN
    (2) 15 kN
    (3) 10 kN
    (4) 20 kN

160. A square plate of diagonal 1.5 m is immersed in water with its diagonal vertical. Its upper corner is 0.4 m below the water surface. The total pressure on the plate is .....
    (1) 25.38 kN
    (2) 12.69 kN
    (3) 41.93 kN
    (4) 33.11 kN

161. The depth of centre of pressure for a rectangular lamina immersed vertically upto the height of 6 m is given by .....
    (1) 1.5 m
    (2) 4 m
    (3) 4.5 m
    (4) 3 m

162. A circular plate of 2 m diameter is completely immersed in water vertically. Its top edge is 0.8 m below the water surface. The total pressure on the plate is .....
    (1) 24.6 kN
    (2) 55.5 kN
    (3) 86.3 kN
    (4) 81.9 KN

163. A circular plate 2 m in diameter is submerged in water such that its least and greatest depths below water surface are 2 m and 3 m respectively. The total pressure on the plate is .....
    (1) 61.64 kN
    (2) 77.04 kN
    (3) 92.46 kN
    (4) 77.82 kN

164. An annular plate with 4 m external diameter and 2 m internal diameter is submerged in water. Its least depth below water surface is 1.5 m and greatest depth is 3 m. The pressure on one side of the plate is .....
    (1) 78.01 kN
    (2) 208.03 kN
    (3) 138.69 kN
    (4) 277.37 kN

165. The horizontal component of liquid pressure on a curved surface is equal to .....
    (1) weight of liquid retained by the curved surface
    (2) weight of liquid vertically above the curved surface
    (3) product of pressure at its centroid and area
    (4) force on projection of the curved surface on a vertical plane

166. The vertical component of pressure force on a submerged curved surface is equal to .....
    (1) product of pressure at its centroid and area
    (2) weight of liquid retained by the curved surface
    (3) force on vertical projection of the curved surface
    (4) weight of liquid vertically above the curved surface

167. An oil of viscosity 1 poise (specific gravity 0.9) flows between parallel fixed plates 25 mm apart. If u_{avg} = 1.8 m/s then the shear stress at the boundary (τ_{max}) = _____ Pa.
 (1) 36.1   (2) 23.5   (3) 49.7   (4) 43.2

168. In a laminar flow between fixed parallel plates of 50 mm apart a liquid with pressure gradient of 2500 N/m²/m flows. If velocity at 10 mm from the plate is 2.91 m/s then the coefficient of viscosity of a liquid is _____cP.
 (1) 123.4   (2) 239.6   (3) 187.5   (4) 171.8

169. An oil of viscosity 1 poise (specific gravity 0.9) flows between parallel fixed plates 25 mm part. If $\left(\dfrac{-\partial p}{\partial x}\right)$ = 3456 N/m²/m then the velocity at 5 mm from the plate is _____.
 (1) 95.1 m/min   (2) 103.8 m/min   (3) 112.2 m/min   (4) 119.4 m/min

170. A rectangular tank 4 m long, 2 m wide and 4 m deep is completely filled with liquid of sp. gr. 0.9. The ratio of hydrostatic forces on the bottom to that on any vertical side 4 m in length is .....
 (1) 4   (2) 2   (3) 1   (4) $\dfrac{1}{2}$

171. An oil of viscosity 1 poise (specific gravity 0.9) flows between parallel fixed plates 25 mm apart. If u_{avg} = 1.8 m/s then u_{max} = _____ m/min.
 (1) 125   (2) 189   (3) 162   (4) 153

172. Tendency of a submerged body to rise in a fluid against gravity due to upthrust produced by fluid is known as
 (1) buoyancy   (2) buoyant force   (3) adhesion   (4) capillarity

173. The principle related with the magnitude of buoyant force is .....
 (1) Newtons second law of motion   (2) Pascal's law
 (3) Archemede's principle   (4) Conservation of mass principle

174. The buoyant force on the body is equal to
 (1) the weight of the body itself
 (2) the weight of fluid displaced by the body
 (3) difference between the weight of the body and weight of fluid displaced by the body
 (4) none of the above

175. Following statement is false.
 (1) buoyant force is equal to the weight of fluid displaced by the body.
 (2) buoyant force acts only in vertical direction
 (3) buoyant force acts through the CG of displaced fluid
 (4) none of the above

176. If $\rho_{body} = \rho_{fluid}$, the body will .....
 (1) sink   (2) remain anywhere inside the liquid
 (3) start rising   (4) all of the above

177. The point of application of buoyant force is called .....
 (1) metacentre   (2) centre of gravity
 (3) centre of buoyancy   (4) instantaneous centre of rotation

178. For floating body, buoyant force passes through the .....
    (1) centre of gravity of the body
    (2) centre of gravity of the submerged part of the body
    (3) metacentre
    (4) centroid of the liquid displaced by the body

179. Buoyant force on a floating/submerged body is due to .....
    (1) gravity
    (2) force necessary to maintain equilibrium of a submerged body
    (3) submerged weight of the body
    (4) the resultant force on a body due to fluid surrounding it

180. When a ship enters sea from a river, its depth of submergence will
    (1) increase
    (2) decrease
    (3) remain at same level of draft
    (4) depend on the material of the ship

181. A block of ice floats on the surface of water contained in a vessel. When it melts the level of water in the container .....
    (1) rises
    (2) falls
    (3) remains the same
    (4) first falls and then rises

182. When a heavy body sinks deeper in liquid the buoyant force acting on the body .....
    (1) increases
    (2) decreases
    (3) remains same
    (4) none of these

183. An object weighing 60 N in air was found to weigh 45 N in water. The relative density of the object is .....
    (1) 4
    (2) 6
    (3) 4.5
    (4) 8

184. A pontoon has a displacement of 1000 metric tons whilst floating in a sea water. When a load of 20 metric tons is moved through a distance of 5 m across the deck, the pontoon heels over $\frac{1}{10}$. The metacentric height of pontoon is .....
    (1) 0.5 m
    (2) 1 m
    (3) 1.5 m
    (4) 2 m

185. The solid 'A' floats with its half volume submerged in water. The solid 'B' floats with 40% of its volume above water surface. The ratio of densities of 'A' and 'B' is .....
    (1) 1 : 4
    (2) 1 : 2
    (3) 5 : 6
    (4) 2 : 3

186. A metallic body floats at the interface of water and mercury (sp. gr. 13.6) in such a way that 50% of its volume is submerged in mercury and 50% in water. The specific gravity of metallic body is .....
    (1) 3.9
    (2) 7.3
    (3) 5.8
    (4) 9.75

187. Metacentre is .....
    (1) centroid of displaced volume of fluid
    (2) the mid point between centre of buoyancy and centre of gravity
    (3) the point of intersection of line of action of buoyant force and centre line of the body
    (4) the point of intersection of line of action of buoyant force and line of action of gravitational force

188. Metacentric height of a floating body is .....
    (1) distance between centre of buoyancy and centre of gravity
    (2) distance between centre of buoyancy and metacentre
    (3) distance between metacentre and centre of gravity
    (4) none of the above

189. In case of laminar flow through a circular pipe if shear stress at the pipe wall is 25 N/m² and pressure gradient is 1300 N/m²/m then the diameter of pipe is ___ m.
    (1) 0.02   (2) 0.04   (3) 0.06   (4) 0.08

190. An oil of viscosity 0.2 Pa-s and density 850 kg/m³ flows through a pipe of diameter 75 mm. If the flow rate of oil is 5 lps then the Reynold's number is _____.
    (1) 360.7   (2) 590.2   (3) 793.1   (4) 932.6

191. For laminar flow through a pipe Reynold's number is 1800. The kinematic viscosity of oil is 2.5×10^{-6} m²/s and mean velocity is 0.0225 m/s. The diameter of pipe is ____ cm.
    (1) 10   (2) 15   (3) 20   (4) 25

192. If the mass flow rate of oil (R.D. 1.2) through the circular pipe of radius 0.15 m is 35 kg/s, the average velocity of flow is .....
    (1) 0.31 m/s   (2) 0.29 m/s   (3) 0.68 m/s   (4) 0.41 m/s

193. If the body is given a slight angular displacement after which it comes back to its original position, then it is said to be _____ equilibrium.
    (1) unstable   (2) neutral   (3) stable   (4) none of the above

194. A submerged body will be in stable equilibrium if
    (1) the centre of buoyancy B is below the centre of gravity G
    (2) the centre of buoyancy B coincides with G
    (3) the centre of buoyancy B is above the metacentre M
    (4) the centre of buoyancy B is above G

195. For a submerged body if CG is below CB, it is in _____ equilibrium.
    (1) stable   (2) neutral   (3) unstable   (4) none of the above

196. If CG coincides with CB for the submerged body, then it is in _____ equilibrium
    (1) stable   (2) neutral   (3) unstable   (4) none of the above

197. When the metacentre of a floating body lies below the centre of gravity of the body, then the equilibrium is called as
    (1) stable   (2) unstable   (3) neutral   (4) none of these

198. When the metacentre of a floating body coincides with the centre of gravity of the body, the equilibrium is called as
    (1) stable   (2) unstable   (3) neutral   (4) none of these

199. If metacentric height GM is positive, then the body is in _____ equilibrium.
    (1) unstable   (2) neutral   (3) stable   (4) none of the above

200. The kinematic viscosity of oil flowing through the circular pipe of diameter 0.1 m is 4.5×10^{-2} cm²/s. If the maximum velocity of oil flow is 0.25 m/s then the flow is .....
    (1) transitional   (2) turbulent   (3) laminar   (4) none of the above

201. _____ deals with the motion of fluid particles without considering the forces causing the motion.
   (1) Fluid statics
   (2) Fluid dynamics
   (3) Fluid kinematics
   (4) All of the above

202. The motion of fluid particles can be studied by .....
   (1) Lagrangian method
   (2) Eulerian method
   (3) both Lagrangian and Eulerian method
   (4) Neither (1) nor (2)

203. The method in which a single fluid particle is selected and its motion is studied is known as .....
   (1) Lagrangian method
   (2) Eulerian method
   (3) Either of (1) and (2)
   (4) Neither of (1) and (2)

204. The method in which a point occupied by fluid is selected and study is made about the particles passing through the point, is known as .....
   (1) Lagrangian method
   (2) Eulerian method
   (3) Either (1) or (2)
   (4) Neither (1) nor (2)

205. A pathline represents .....
   (1) mean direction of number of particles at the same instant of time.
   (2) trace made by a single particle over a period of a time
   (3) instantaneous picture of positions of all particles in the flow which passed a fixed point
   (4) the line tangent to which at any point gives the velocity vector

206. A stream line is a line .....
   (1) which is normal to velocity vector at every point
   (2) tangent to which at any point gives the direction of velocity vector at that point
   (3) tangent to which at any point represents the velocity vector at that point
   (4) along which the velocity potential is constant

207. The velocity vector is always _____ to the stream line.
   (1) tangential
   (2) normal
   (3) both (1) and (2)
   (4) none of the above

208. An oil of viscosity 10 N-s/m² flows through a pipe of 200 mm diameter. If discharge through the pipe is 0.095 m³/sec, the maximum velocity of oil is .....
   (1) 7.83 m/s   (2) 5.29 m/s   (3) 6.04 m/s   (4) 11.72 m/s

209. An oil of viscosity 12 poise flows through a pipe of radius 125 mm. If the pressure drop over 200 m length of pipe is 2200 kPa, then the shear stress at 75 mm from the centre of pipe is .....
   (1) 325 Pa   (2) 380.5 Pa   (3) 412.5 Pa   (4) 480.2 Pa

210. A liquid flows through a pipe of 250 mm diameter in laminar regime. If maximum velocity of flow is 13 m/s then the velocity of 50 mm from the pipe wall is
    (1) 8.3 m/s   (2) 9.3 m/s   (3) 7.1 m/s   (4) 6.5 m/s

211. An oil viscosity 800 cP and density 1300 kg/m³ flows through a pipe of 0.1 m diameter. If pressure drop in 100 m length of pipe is 2000 kN/m², the velocity gradient at the pipe wall is .....
    (1) 520 s⁻¹   (2) 675 s⁻¹   (3) 625 s⁻¹   (4) 490 s⁻¹

212. A line traced by a series of fluid particles passing through a fixed point in the flowing fluid mass is known as .....
    (1) streak line   (2) stream line   (3) path line   (4) stream tube

213. The path traced by particles coming out of a chimney is an example of .....
    (1) path line   (2) stream line   (3) streak line   (4) stream tube

214. ____ is used in hydrodynamic theory of lubrication.
    (1) Flow through circular pipe   (2) Flow through fixed parallel plates
    (3) Couette flow   (4) None of the above

215. Match the following:
    List - I
    (1) Capillary tube viscometer
    (2) Falling sphere viscometer
    (3) Rotating cylinder viscometer
    Codes :

    List - II
    (i)   Stoke's law
    (ii) Newton's law of viscosity
    (iii) Hagen-Poiseuille equation

    (1) (1) - (iii), (2) - (i), (3) - (ii)   (2) (1) - (i), (2) - (ii), (3) - (iii)
    (3) (1) - (ii), (2) - (iii), (3) - (i)   (4) (1) - (ii), (2) - (i), (3) - (iii)

216. An oil of viscosity 10 N-s/m² flows through a pipe of 200 mm diameter. If discharge through the pipe is 0.095 m³/sec, the average velocity of oil is .....
    (1) 3.02 m/s   (2) 13.9 m/s   (3) 4.67 m/s   (4) 6.51 m/s

217. The steady flow is one in which .....
    (1) the velocity does not change with respect to distance
    (2) the velocity does not change at a point with respect to time
    (3) velocity changes at a point with respect to time
    (4) none of the above

218. If the flow characteristics like velocity, pressure etc. vary only in one of the three co-ordinate directions, the flow is .....
    (1) two-dimensional   (2) three-dimensional
    (3) one-dimensional   (4) all of the above

219. Uniform flow is the one in which .....
    (1) the velocity vector is identical at every point at any given instant
    (2) the velocity vector at a point does not change with time
    (3) the velocity at a point changes with respect to time
    (4) none of the above

220. When the velocity of fluid flow changes from point to point at the given instant of time, then the flow is .....
    (1) uniform   (2) steady   (3) non-uniform   (4) unsteady

221. The flow of liquid through a tapering pipe at varying rate is
    (1) steady uniform   (2) steady non-uniform
    (2) unsteady uniform   (4) unsteady non-uniform

222. Which of the following represents steady uniform flow?
    (1) Flow through a converging pipe at constant rate.
    (2) Flow through a converging duct at increasing rate.
    (3) Flow through a straight long pipe at constant rate.
    (4) Flow through a straight long-pipe with increasing rate.

223. The flow of liquid through a tapering pipe with constant discharge is
    (1) steady uniform   (2) steady non-uniform
    (3) unsteady uniform   (4) unsteady non-uniform

224. Reynold's number is
    (1) $\dfrac{\text{Inertia force}}{\text{Viscous force}}$ (2) $\dfrac{\rho VD}{\mu}$ (3) $\dfrac{VD}{v}$ (4) All of the above

225. The flow through a pipe is laminar if .....
    (1) Reynolds number is less than 2000
    (2) Reynolds number is between 2000 and 4000
    (3) Reynolds number is more than 4000
    (4) Reynolds number has any value

226. _____ is the example of laminar flow.
    (1) Flow of oil in bearings   (2) Flow of blood in veins
    (3) Flow of liquid in porous media   (4) All of the above

227. Which is the type of flow when pathlines, streamlines and streaklines coincide with each other?
    (1) uniform   (2) non-uniform   (3) steady   (4) unsteady

228. During the flow, if volume and hence density does not change, due to change in pressure and temperature, the flow is .....
    (1) irrotational   (2) rotational   (3) compressible   (4) incompressible

229. If the density of fluid changes from point to point during the flow, the flow is .....
    (1) unsteady flow   (2) non-uniform flow
    (3) compressible flow   (4) rotational flow

230. The friction factor 'f' for laminar flow through a pipe was found to be 0.064. The Reynold's number in the flow is .....
    (1) 400   (2) 800   (3) 1000   (4) 1600

231. The flow in which average values of flow parameters are used for flow analysis is .....
    (1) uniform flow   (2) steady flow
    (3) one dimensional flow   (4) incompressible flow

232. The flow in the river during period of heavy rainfall is .....
     (1) steady, non-uniform and three-dimensional
     (2) steady, uniform, two-dimensional
     (3) unsteady, uniform, three-dimensional
     (4) unsteady, non-uniform, three-dimensional

233. For one-dimensional flow, the velocity distribution is .....
     (1) parabolic   (2) logarithmic   (3) hyperbolic   (4) straight line

234. Flow over central part of long spillway is .....
     (1) one-dimensional   (2) two-dimensional
     (3) three-dimensional   (4) none of these

235. Flow in river, flow between parallel plates of large extent etc. are the examples of _____ flow.
     (1) two-dimensional   (2) one-dimensional
     (3) three-dimensional   (4) all of the above

236. Flow in open channel is an example of _____
     (1) two-dimensional   (2) one-dimensional
     (3) three-dimensional   (4) all of the above

237. A pipe 1 m in diameter carries water with a velocity of 1 m/s. The pipe bifurcates in 2 pipes of 0.5 m diameter each. The velocity of water in smaller pipes is .....
     (1) 0.5 m/s   (2) 1.5 m/s   (3) 2 m/s   (4) 4 m/s

238. In a steady flow velocities at A and B 1 m apart are 2 m/s and 6 m/s respectively. If velocity varies linearly between A and B the convective acceleration at B is .....
     (1) 12 m/s²   (2) 24 m/s²   (3) 6 m/s²   (4) 18 m/s²

239. In case of curved converging stream line pattern there is .....
     (1) convective tangential acceleration
     (2) convective normal acceleration
     (3) tangential as well as normal convective acceleration
     (4) no acceleration

240. In case of converging straight stream lines when the flow in steady, the flow .....
     (1) has uniform flow with local acceleration
     (2) has convective tangential acceleration
     (3) has convective normal acceleration
     (4) has convective normal as well as tangential acceleration

241. In case of steady flow with parallel curved stream lines, the flow .....
     (1) is uniform flow with local acceleration
     (2) has convective tangential acceleration
     (3) has convective normal as well as tangential acceleration
     (4) has convective normal acceleration

242. In case of steady flow with straight parallel stream lines, the flow .....
    (1) has convective tangential acceleration
    (2) has convective normal acceleration
    (3) has no acceleration
    (4) has tangential as well as normal convective acceleration

243. In case of laminar flow .....
    (1) fluid particles exhibit regular pattern of flow
    (2) fluid flows through a narrow passage
    (3) momentum transfer is on microscopic level
    (4) injection of a dye shows considerable dispersion

244. Which of the following is a possible case of turbulent flow?
    (1) flow of oil in measuring instruments (2) flow in sap in trees
    (3) flow of water through pipe   (4) flow of blood in arteries

245. Flow is rotational when .....
    (1) fluid element undergoes linear deformation
    (2) fluid element undergoes angular deformation
    (3) fluid particles rotate about their mass centres while moving along the flow
    (4) flow takes place in a circular path

246. Flow is an irrotational flow when .....
    (1) fluid element does not undergo angular deformation
    (2) fluid element does not undergo linear deformation
    (3) fluid particles do not rotate about their mass centres while moving along the flow
    (4) flow does not take place along a circular path

247. A steady irrotational flow is .....
    (1) uniform flow   (2) non-uniform flow
    (3) potential flow   (4) streamline flow

248. If $\dfrac{\partial u}{\partial y} = \dfrac{\partial v}{\partial x}$ in two dimensional flow, the fluid element will undergo .....
    (1) translation only   (2) translation and rotation
    (3) translation and deformation   (4) rotation and deformation

249. The friction factor 'f' in the formula $h_f = \dfrac{fL}{D} \times \dfrac{V^2}{2g}$ for laminar flow in a pipe is .....
    (1) $\dfrac{8}{R_e}$ (2) $\dfrac{16}{R_e}$ (3) $\dfrac{32}{R_e}$ (4) $\dfrac{64}{R_e}$

250. The continuity equation $\dfrac{\partial u}{\partial x} + \dfrac{\partial v}{\partial y} + \dfrac{\partial w}{\partial z} = 0$, is valid for .....
    (1) ideal fluid flow only
    (2) incompressible fluids, whether the flow is steady or unsteady
    (3) steady flow, whether compressible or incompressible
    (4) incompressible fluids and steady flow only

251. General form of continuity equation in Cartesian coordinates is given by .....

(1) $\dfrac{\partial u}{\partial x} + \dfrac{\partial v}{\partial y} + \dfrac{\partial w}{\partial z} = 0$

(2) $\dfrac{\partial \rho}{\partial t} + \dfrac{\partial u}{\partial x} + \dfrac{\partial v}{\partial y} + \dfrac{\partial w}{\partial z} = 0$

(3) $\dfrac{\partial(\rho u)}{\partial x} + \dfrac{\partial(\rho v)}{\partial y} + \dfrac{\partial(\rho w)}{\partial z} = 0$

(4) $\dfrac{\partial \rho}{\partial t} + \dfrac{\partial(\rho u)}{\partial x} + \dfrac{\partial(\rho v)}{\partial y} + \dfrac{\partial(\rho w)}{\partial z} = 0$

252. The velocity vector for a flow field is given by .....

$\overline{V} = a\,xy\,\overline{i} + \dfrac{a}{b}(x^2 - y^2)\,j$ The relevant equation of stream line is

(1) $\dfrac{dx}{x^2 - y^2} = \dfrac{dy}{b\,xy}$

(2) $\dfrac{dx}{b\,xy} = \dfrac{dy}{x^2 - y^2}$

(3) $\dfrac{dx}{a\,xy} = \dfrac{dy}{x^2 - y^2}$

(4) $\dfrac{dx}{x^2 - y^2} = \dfrac{dy}{xy}$

253. The continuity equation for steady, compressible flow in two dimensions is .....

(1) $u\dfrac{\partial \rho}{\partial x} + v\dfrac{\partial \rho}{\partial y} = 0$

(2) $\rho\dfrac{\partial u}{\partial x} + \rho\dfrac{\partial v}{\partial y} = 0$

(3) $\dfrac{1}{\rho}\dfrac{\partial u}{\partial x} + \dfrac{1}{\rho}\dfrac{\partial v}{\partial y} = 0$

(4) $\dfrac{\partial(\rho u)}{\partial x} + \dfrac{\partial(\rho v)}{\partial y} = 0$

254. The continuity equation in one dimension can take the form .....

(1) $\rho_1 A_1 = \rho_2 A_2$

(2) $A_1 V_1 = A_2 V_2$

(3) $\rho_1 A_1 V_1 = \rho_2 A_2 V_2$

(4) $\dfrac{A_1 V_1}{\rho_1} = \dfrac{A_2 V_2}{\rho_2}$

255. The shear stress in a circular pipe with laminar flow in it .....

(1)   is zero at the centre and varies linearly with pipe radius

(2)   remains constant over the section

(3)   is zero at the pipe wall and varies linearly towards centre

(4)   varies parabolically across the section

256. In case of laminar flow through a circular pipe the kinetic energy correction factor is .....

(1)   0.5   (2)   1.5   (3)   2.0   (4)   1.33

257. For a laminar flow through a circular pipe the ratio of maximum velocity to average velocity is .....

(1)   2   (2)   0.5   (3)   1.67   (4)   0.707

258. The momentum correction factor 'β' for laminar flow through circular pipe is .....

(1)   2   (2)   1.5   (3)   1.33   (4)   1.67

259. The distance 'r' from the centre of the pipe of radius 'R', at which the average velocity occurs in laminar flow is .....

(1) $r = 0.5\,R$ (2) $r = 0.77\,R$ (3) $r = 0.707\,R$ (4) $r = 0.35\,R$

260. The pressure drop for laminar flow in a circular pipe varies .....

(1)   directly with square of velocity   (2)   directly with diameter of pipe

(3)   directly as velocity of flow   (4)   inversely as viscosity of fluid

261. The shear stress at 5 cm from the axis of a pipe is 20 Pa. If the diameter of the pipe is 24 cm, the shear stress at pipe wall will be .....

(1)   50 Pa   (2)   48 Pa   (3)   96 Pa   (4)   6 Pa

262. For laminar flow with given discharge of a liquid through a circular pipe, the hydraulic gradient .....
    (1) varies directly as square root of diameter
    (2) varies directly as square of diameter
    (3) varies inversely as square of diameter
    (4) varies directly as fourth power of diameter
    (5) varies inversely as fourth power of diameter

263. The pressure drop in 8 cm diameter horizontal pipe is 60 kPa in a distance of 12 m. The shear stress at the pipe wall is .....
    (1) 0.2 kPa   (2) 0.1 kPa   (3) 5 kPa   (4) 10 kPa

264. If Reynold's number for a flow through a pipe is 960, 'f' the Darcy-Weisbach friction factor for this flow is .....
    (1) 0.017   (2) 0.067   (3) 0.096   (4) 0.064

265. The value of friction factor 'f' corresponding to the lower critical point in a laminar flow through a pipe is .....
    (1) 0.008   (2) 0.032   (3) 0.064   (4) 0.024

266. If the stream function exists and satisfies Laplace equation then .....
    (1) the flow is rotational
    (2) the flow is irrotational but does not necessarily satisfy continuity equation
    (3) the continuity is satisfied and the flow is irrotational
    (4) the continuity is satisfied but flow does not satisfy condition for irrotational flow

267. If potential function (ϕ) satisfies Laplace equation, it is possible case of fluid flow. This is called as ___ flow.
    (1) steady   (2) rotational   (3) potential   (4) uniform

268. ____ is a scalar function of space and time such that its derivative w.r.t. any direction gives velocity component at right angle to this direction.
    (1) circulation   (2) potential function
    (3) vorticity   (4) stream function

269. The relation between stream function and velocity potential is given by _____ equation.
    (1) Bernoulli's   (2) Cauchy-Rieman
    (3) Reynold's number   (4) Hagen-Poiseulle's

270. A streamline is a line :
    (1) Which is normal to the velocity vector at every point
    (2) Which represents lines of constant velocity potential
    (3) Which is normal to the lines of constant stream function
    (4) Which is tangental to the velocity vector everywhere at a given instant

271. ____ is the line along which the stream function is constant.
    (1) Stream line   (2) Streak line
    (3) Equipotential line   (4) Path line

272. The stream function in a two dimensional flow field is given by $\psi = x^2 - y^2$. The magnitude of the velocity at point (1, 1) is .....
    (1) 2   (2) $2\sqrt{2}$ (3) 4   (4) 8

273. The stream function for a two dimensional flow is given by $\psi = 2xy + $ constant, the flow between stream lines between (1, 1) and (3, 3) would be .....
    (1) 4 units   (2) 6 units   (3) 8 units   (4) 16 units

274. In laminar flow the shear stress is given by .....
    (1) Archimede's principle   (2) Netwon's law of motion
    (3) Pascal's law   (4) Netwon's law of viscosity

275. The lines of constant velocity potential ϕ .....
    (1) are parallel to streamlines   (2) are normal to streamlines
    (3) can intersect each other   (4) are parallel streamlines

276. The product of slopes of equipotential line and stream line is .....
    (1) 0   (2) 1   (3) – 2   (4) – 1

277. Existence of velocity potential in a fluid flow indicates that .....
    (1) velocity must not be zero
    (2) flow must be irrotational
    (3) flow is rotational and satisfies continuity equation
    (4) none of the above

278. The relation $\nabla^2 \phi = 0$ for an irrotational flow is .....
    (1) Reynold's equation   (2) Cauchy-Reimann equation
    (3) Laplace equation   (4) Euler equation

279. The velocity distribution across the section of a pipe for steady laminar flow is .....
    (1) exponential   (2) hyperbolic   (3) linear   (4) parabolic

280. ____ method is used for drawing flow net.
    (1) Analytical   (2) Graphical   (3) Relaxation   (4) All of the above

281. Indicate the incorrect statement in relation to flow net .....
    (1) it is applicable to irrotational flow
    (2) spacing between streamlines as well as that between equipotential lines is inversely proportional to local velocity
    (3) for a given boundary flow net will change with reversal of direction of flow
    (4) the streamlines and equipotential lines intersect each other at right angles

282. In case of flow net .....
    (1) streamlines and equipotential lines are parallel to each other
    (2) streamlines and equipotential lines intersect each other orthogonally
    (3) streamlines and equipotential lines intersect each other at a constant angle
    (4) none of the above

283. An oil of kinematic viscosity 0.25 stokes flows through a pipe of diameter 10 cm. The flow is critical at a velocity of .....
    (1) 5.0 m/s   (2) 0.5 m/s   (3) 1.5 m/s   (4) 2.0 m/s

284. In the analysis of flow of viscous fluid through horizontal circular pipe ____ force is considered.

    (1) pressure force   (2) shear force

    (3) both (1) and (2)   (4) none of the above

285. In a pipe if velocity at section A and B is 2 m/s and 6 m/s respectively, then $d_A / d_B =$

    (1) $\sqrt{3}$ (2) $\sqrt{5}$ (3) $\sqrt{6}$ (4) $\sqrt{2}$

286. The diameters of pipe at section A and B are 10 cm and 15 cm. If velocity of water through the pipe at A is 2.5 m/s, the velocity at section B is .....

    (1) 2.5 m/s   (2) 1.1 m/s   (3) 5.6 m/s   (4) 3.3 m/s

287. The pressure gradient in the direction of flow is equal to shear stress gradient in the direction .....

    (1) parallel to direction of flow   (2) normal to direction of flow

    (3) either of (1) and (2)   (4) none of (1) and (2)

288. A pipe of 20 cm diameter carries fluid of density 1250 kg/m³ at a velocity of 1.5 m/s. The mass flow rate of fluid is .....

    (1) 38.65 kg/s   (2) 58.9 kg/s   (3) 47.12 kg/s   (4) 26.59 kg/s

289. The mass flow rate of oil ($\gamma = 11.772$ kN/m³) flowing through the pipe is 75 kg/s. The diameter of pipe is 300 mm, the velocity of oil is ____ m/s.

    (1) 0.56   (2) 0.88   (3) 0.92   (4) 0.45

290. Reynold's experiments for studying the characteristics of flow in pipes involves .....

    (1) velocity measurement

    (2) measurement of flow only

    (3) observation of nature of dye filament with change in flow

    (4) none of the above

291. Reynold's observed that at low velocities the filament of dye

    (1) was stable straight line   (2) was wavy in nature

    (3) diffused completely   (4) none of these

292. Select the correct statement :

The laminar flow is characterised by

    (1) The Reynold's number is high for the flow

    (2) Movement of fluid particles is irregular

    (3) Existence of eddies

    (4) Reynold's number is less than its critical value

293. Laminar flow is also called as .....

    (1) irrotational flow   (2) uniform flow

    (3) viscous flow   (4) steady flow

294. Which of the following is an example of laminar flow?

    (1) flow of oil in measuring instruments (2) flow of fluid in capillary tubes

    (3) underground flow   (4) all of these

    (5) none of these

295. Rise of sap in trees is an example of .....
   (1) viscous flow (2) uniform flow
   (3) irrotational flow (4) steady flow

296. The criterian to decide whether the flow is laminar or turbulent is .....
   (1) Froude number (2) Mach number
   (3) Reynold's number (4) Euler's number
   (5) Weber's number

297. Reynold's number is related to the ratio of .....
   (1) inertia force to elastic force (2) inertia force to viscous force
   (3) inertia force to gravity force (4) inertia force to pressure force

298. In no slip condition .....
   (1) fluid has no velocity
   (2) fluid at the boundary has same velocity as that of boundary
   (3) both (1) and (2)
   (4) none of the above

299. The flow of fluid in a pipe is laminar only when .....
   (1) viscosity of fluid is high (2) velocity of flow is high
   (3) density of liquid is low (4) characteristics dimension is small
   (5) Reynold's number is less than 2000

300. The equations of motion for viscous flow are known as .....
   (1) Euler's equation (2) Reynold's equation
   (3) Navier-Stoke's equation (4) Hagen-Poiseuille's equation

301. In case of Navier-Stoke's equation the various forces which are taken into account are .....
   (1) gravity, pressure, turbulence (2) pressure, viscous, turbulence
   (3) gravity, pressure, viscous (4) pressure, gravity, viscous and turbulence

302. Boundary layer on a flat plate is called laminar boundary layer if :
   (1) Reynold number is less than 2000 (2) Reynold number is less than 4000
   (3) Reynold number is less than 5×10^5 (4) None of the above

303. Navier-Stoke's equations are useful in study of .....
   (1) turbulent flow (2) viscous flow
   (3) rotational flow (4) compressible flow

304. Navier-Stoke's equation are connected with .....
   (1) turbulence (2) viscosity
   (3) compressibility (4) surface tension

305. _____ equation of motion is used in the analysis of viscous flow.
   (1) Bernoulli's (2) Reynold's (3) Navier-Stoke's (4) Euler's

306. _____ equation is used in the analysis of steady, compressible and incompressible flow of non-viscous fluid.
   (1) Euler's (2) Navier-Stokes (3) Reynold's (4) All of the above

307. Euler's equation of motion is along a .....
   (1) streak line   (2) path line
   (3) stream line   (4) none of the above

308. In the analysis of Euler's equation of motion _____ force acting on the fluid element is considered.
   (1) pressure force in the direction of flow
   (2) pressure force in the opposite direction of flow
   (3) weight of the element
   (4) all of the above

309. Euler's equation of motion .....
   (1) is statement of energy balance
   (2) is moment of momentum equation
   (3) can be derived from Navier-Stoke's equation
   (4) is related to forces and the change in momentum

310. A tank containing water is provided with a sharp edge circular orifice. At a certain point the horizontal and vertical co-ordinates of jet from venacontracta are 12 cm and 8 cm. If $C_v = 0.69$, the head over the orifice is ___ cm.
   (1) 6.92   (2) 9.45   (3) 7.83

311. Euler's equation of motion .....
   $$gdz + \frac{dp}{\rho} + V \, dv = 0. \text{ Assume}$$
   (1) flow of non-viscous fluid only
   (2) steady flow of incompressible and non-viscous fluid
   (3) steady flow of non-viscous fluid
   (4) motion along a streamline, non-viscous and steady flow

312. Euler's equation of motion can be integrated only when .....
   (1) continuity is satisfied
   (2) fluid is compressible
   (3) flow is steady and irrotational
   (4) flow is non-viscous and when 'ρ' is either constant or is a function of pressure 'p' only

313. If power lost at orifice discharging water is 0.8 W, the loss of head is ____ . The discharge through orifice is 50 lit. in 5 min.
   (1) 0.31 m   (2) 0.62 m   (3) 0.49 m   (4) 0.22 m

314. Bernoulli's equation is obtained by integrating _____ equation.
   (1) Reynold's   (2) Euler's   (3) Navier-Stokes   (4) All of the above

315. If theoretical discharge of an orifice is 4278 lpm and actual discharge is 40 lps, the value of C_r is ____ . Take $C_c = 0.67$.
   (1) 0.28   (2) 0.51   (3) 0.61   (4) 0.43

316. Bernoulli's equation can be written as .....

(1) $Z + \dfrac{p}{\gamma} + \dfrac{V^2}{2g} = $ constant

(2) $Z + \dfrac{p}{\gamma^2} + \dfrac{V^2}{2g} = $ constant

(3) $Z + \dfrac{p}{\gamma} + \dfrac{V}{2g} = $ constant

(4) $Z^2 + \dfrac{p}{\gamma} + \dfrac{V^2}{2g} = $ constant

317. Datum head is given by .....

(1) Z (2) Z^2 (3) $\dfrac{1}{Z}$ (4) $\dfrac{1}{Z^2}$

318. Velocity head is given by .....

(1) $\dfrac{V^2}{g}$ (2) $\dfrac{V^2}{2g}$ (3) $\dfrac{V^2}{2g^2}$ (4) $\dfrac{V^2}{g^2}$

319. Pressure head is given by .....

(1) $\dfrac{\gamma}{p}$ (2) $\dfrac{p}{\gamma}$ (3) $\dfrac{\gamma^2}{p}$ (4) $\dfrac{p}{\gamma^2}$

320. Each term in Bernoulli's theorem $Z + \dfrac{p}{\gamma} + \dfrac{V^2}{2g} = $ constant, represents head that is .....

(1) energy per unit mass of fluid   (2) energy per unit volume of fluid
(3) energy per unit weight of fluid   (4) none of these

321. Each of the term of Bernoulli's equation stated in the form $Z + \dfrac{p}{\gamma} + \dfrac{V^2}{2g} = $ constant has unit of .....

(1) Nm/kg   (2) Nm/N   (3) Nm/s   (4) N

322. Conservation of energy principle as applied to fluid flow is .....
(1) Newton's law   (2) Pascal's law
(3) Bernoulli's equation   (4) Continuity equation

323. The total head of any particle in motion is .....
(1) datum head + pressure head + velocity head
(2) datum head – pressure head + velocity head
(3) datum head + pressure head – velocity head
(4) datum head – pressure head – velocity head

324. "In a steady flow of an ideal fluid, the total head of any particle is constant along a stream line". This statement is for .....
(1) Euler's equation   (2) Bernoulli's equation
(3) Reynold's equation   (4) Navier-Stokes equation

325. Identify the Bernoulli's equation in which each term represents the energy per unit volume

(1) $Z + \dfrac{p}{\gamma} + \dfrac{V^2}{2g} = $ constant

(2) $\gamma Z + p + \dfrac{\rho V^2}{2} = $ constant

(3) $gZ + \dfrac{p}{\rho} + \dfrac{V^2}{2} = $ constant

(4) none of these

326. ____ is the assumption made in the Bernoulli's equation.
(1) The flow is steady, continuous and irrigational
(2) The fluid is non-viscous and incompressible
(3) The gravity and pressure forces are only considered and velocity is uniform over the cross-section
(4) All of the above

327. Bernoulli's equation is applicable between any two points in .....
 (1) rotational flow of an incompressible fluid
 (2) steady irrotational flow of an incompressible fluid
 (3) steady rotational flow of an incompressible fluid
 (4) any type of rotational flow of fluid

328. In the Bernoulli's equation the term $\left(\dfrac{p}{\gamma} + Z\right)$ represents .....
 (1) datum head (2) velocity head
 (3) piezometric head (4) pressure head

329. _____ is the limitation of Bernoulli's equation.
 (1) Fluid is not ideal
 (2) Velocity across the section is not uniform
 (3) In addition to gravity and pressure forces, viscous force is also involved in the motion
 (4) All of the above

330. At a point 'A' in a pipe carrying water, the diameter is 1 m and the velocity is 1 m/s. The velocity at point where the diameter of the pipe is 0.5 m is .....
 (1) 0.5 m/s (2) 2 m/s (3) 4 m/s (4) 8 m/s

331. At a point 'A' in a pipe carrying water, the diameter is 1 m and velocity head is 1 m. The velocity head at point 'B' where the diameter of pipe is 0.5 m is .....
 (1) 0.5 m (2) 2 m (3) 4 m (4) 16 m

332. At a point in a pipe carrying liquid of sp. gr. 0.8, the pressure is 19.62 kN/m². The pressure head at a point is .....
 (1) 15.7 m (2) 1.6 m (3) 2 m (4) 2.5 m

333. A 30 cm diameter pipe is carrying water with the velocity of 7.5 m/s. If the pressure at a section is 125 kPa, the total head at the section is .....
 (1) 9.81 (2) 13.12 m (3) 15.61 m (4) 18.47 m

334. A 2 m diameter pipe carries water at the rate of 22 m³/s. The velocity head is .....
 (1) 0.714 m (2) 5 m (3) 2.5 m (4) 17.5 m

335. In an orifice if $C_d = 0.61$ and $C_c = 0.69$, the value of C_r is .....
 (1) 0.48 (2) 0.88 (3) 0.38 (4) 0.28

336. During the flow in an orifice if $C_c = 0.65$ and $C_v = 0.8$ then C_d =
 (1) 0.81 (2) 0.52 (3) 0.7 (4) 0.9

337. During the experiment a water jet is issued from the orifice under a head of 20 cm. At any point the horizontal co-ordinate of jet from vena-contracta is 10 cm. If $C_r = 0.2$, the vertical co-ordinate of jet is .....
 (1) 5 cm (2) 3.5 cm (3) 0.5 cm (4) 1.5 cm

338. The piezometeric head is defined as the sum of .....
 (1) datum head and velocity head (2) datum head plus pressure head
 (3) velocity head and pressure head
 (4) datum head plus velocity head plus pressure head

339. The value of kinetic energy correction factor '$\propto$' for laminar flow is .....
   (1) 1.01   (2) 1.15   (3) 2   (4) none of these

340. Hydraulic grade line indicates to some selected datum, the variation of
   (1) piezometric head in the direction of flow
   (2) velocity head in the direction of flow
   (3) the total energy in the direction of flow
   (4) pressure head in the direction of flow

341. A line joining all the liquids levels indicated by piezometers connected to the pipe line is called as .....
   (1) HGL   (2) TEL   (3) EGL   (4) stream line

342. Rise or fall of HGL in the direction of flow depends on the .....
   (1) change in velocity   (2) change in pressure
   (3) change in temperature   (4) all of the above

343. The total energy line indicates to some selected datum, the variation of .....
   (1) datum head plus pressure head
   (2) datum head plus velocity head
   (3) datum head plus pressure head plus velocity head
   (4) pressure head plus velocity head

344. In case of flow of real fluids .....
   (1) the energy line will be horizontal or sloping upwards in the direction of flow
   (2) the energy line can never be below centre line of pipe
   (3) the energy line can never be horizontal or sloping upwards in the direction of flow
   (4) the energy line can never be below hydraulic grade line

345. For real fluid TEL is .....
   (1) vertical   (2) horizontal
   (3) inclined   (4) curve

346. In a pipe line, the hydraulic grade line is above the centre of the pipe at section A and below the centre of the pipe at section B, this indicates
   (1) the positive pressure at B   (2) positive pressure at A
   (3) flow from A and B   (4) flow from B to A

347. The vertical distance between total energy line and hydraulic grade line represents
   (1) pressure head   (2) the elevation head
   (3) the velocity head   (4) the piezometric head

348. If H_A is the total head at point A, H_B is the total head at point B, H_L: the loss of head between A and B and H_P the head supplied by pump installed between A and B, the flow taking place from A to B, the equation for the heads can be written as
   (1) $H_A + H_P + H_L = H_B$ (2) $H_A + H_P - H_L = H_B$
   (3) $H_A - H_P - H_L = H_B$ (4) $H_A - H_P + H_L = H_B$

349. When the turbine is installed between section 1 and 2 of pipe then the Bernoulli's equation is

(1) $\dfrac{p_1}{\gamma} + \dfrac{V_1^2}{2g} + z_1 = \dfrac{p_2}{\gamma} + \dfrac{V_2^2}{2g} + z_2$ (2) $\dfrac{p_1}{\gamma} + \dfrac{V_1^2}{2g} + z_1 + h_T = \dfrac{p_2}{\gamma} + \dfrac{V_2^2}{2g} + z_2$

(3) $\dfrac{p_1}{\gamma} + \dfrac{V_1^2}{2g} + z_1 = \dfrac{p_2}{\gamma} + \dfrac{V_2^2}{2g} + z_2 + h_T$ (4) None of the above

350. When the pipes are connected in parallel, the total loss of head .....
    (1) is equal to the sum of the loss of head in each pipe
    (2) is same in each pipe
    (3) is equal to the reciprocal of the sum of loss of head in each pipe
    (4) none of the above

351. The pressure head at the summit of a syphon is 2 m (abs) and the atmospheric pressure is 10 m (abs). If the loss of head in the inlet leg of syphon is 3 m and the velocity head at the summit is 0.25 m, the elevation of the summit above the liquid level in the reservoir from which the flow is discharged out is .....
    (1) 4.75 m   (2) 8.75 m   (3) 5.75 m   (4) 10.75 m

352. A liquid jet issuing upwards out from a nozzle is inclined at an angle of $30°$ to horizontal. If the jet velocity is 20 m/s, the maximum height reached by the jet is .....
    (1) 15.29 m   (2) 5.1 m   (3) 10 m   (4) 15 m

353. A pump is installed on a uniform horizontal pipeline between point 'A" on the suction side and point 'B' on the delivery side. The pump develops a head of 20 m. The loss of head between A and B for the discharge is 5 m. If the pressure at B is 225.63 kPa, the pressure at point A is .....
    (1) 78.48 kPa   (2) 470.88 kPa   (3) − 19.62 kPa   (4) − 78.48 kPa

354. The suction head at the inlet to the pump is − 2m and the delivery head at the outlet of the pump is 8 m. The pump delivers at the rate of 100 L/s, the power of the pump is .....
    (1) 98.1 kW   (2) 5.89 kW   (3) 9.81 kW   (4) 0.981 kW

355. Total head at a section of pipe is 20 m. Datum head is 10 m and the pressure head is 6 m. The vertical distance between total energy line and hydraulic grade line is .....
    (1) 10 m   (2) 14 m   (3) 4 m   (4) 16 m

356. The stagnation pressure point is a point where .....
    (1) total energy is zero   (2) velocity of flow is zero
    (3) pressure is zero   (4) total energy is maximum

357. The stagnation pressure is .....
    (1) static pressure   (2) dynamic pressure
    (3) sum of static pressure plus dynamic pressure
    (4) sum of dynamic pressure plus vacuum pressure
    (5) none of the above

358. Pitot tube is an instrument for measuring .....
    (1) pressure of flow
    (2) velocity of flow
    (3) discharge of fluid
    (4) total head
    (5) none of these

359. Pitot static tube measures .....
    (1) static pressure
    (2) dynamic pressure
    (3) dynamic pressure plus static pressure
    (4) dynamic pressure minus static pressure

360. Pitot tube is dipped ____ in the flowing stream of liquid.
    (1) horizontally
    (2) inclined
    (3) vertically
    (4) all of the above

361. The alignment of the Pitot tube should be such that .....
    (1) its opening faces upstream and the horizontal leg is aligned perfectly with direction of flow
    (2) the horizontal leg is at right angles to direction of flow
    (3) its opening faces the downstream direction
    (4) the horizontal leg can make any angle with the direction of flow

362. Simple Pitot tube can be used to measure .....
    (1) velocity of liquids only
    (2) velocity of gas only
    (3) velocity of both liquid as well as gas
    (4) none of these

363. When the tube recording static pressure and stagnation pressure are combined into one instrument, it is called as .....
    (1) Pitot tube
    (2) Prandtl pitot tube
    (3) Pitot static tube
    (4) Both (2) and (3)

364. A pitot-static tube is used to measure velocity of oil of sp. gr. 0.8 flowing through a pipe. If oil-mercury differential manometer shows deflection of 0.2 m. Velocity of oil in the pipe is .....
    (1) 7.03 m/s
    (2) 8.16 m/s
    (3) 7.92 m/s
    (4) 5.78 m/s

365. A Pitot static tube used to measure velocity of an aeroplane indicates a differential head of 49 m of air. If coefficient of tube is 0.98 the velocity of air will be ____ m/s.
    (1) 6.86
    (2) 30.69
    (3) 30.38
    (4) 31.01

366. ____ is used to measure the discharge (flow rate) of fluid through the pipe.
    (1) Venturimeter
    (2) Orifice meter
    (3) both (1) and (2)
    (4) none of the above

367. The discharge through a pipeline can be measured with least loss of head by .....
    (1) Orifice meter
    (2) Venturimeter
    (3) Pitot tube
    (4) Notch

368. The venturimeter is used for measurement of .....
    (1) velocity head
    (2) pressure
    (3) flow rate
    (4) piezometric head

369. The coefficient of discharge of a venturimeter lies in the range of .....

    (1) 0.6 to 0.8   (2) 0.7 to 0.9   (3) 0.75 to 0.85   (4) 0.95 to 0.99

370. A convergent cone of venturimeter is .....

    (1) taper from pipe to the divergent cone

    (2) tapers from pipe to the throat

    (3) both (1) and (2)   (4) none of the above

371. For venturimeter the angle of converging cone is upto .....

    (1) 6°   (2) 10°   (3) 20°   (4) 15°

372. The height of a hydraulic jump in the stilling pool of 1.25 scale model was observed to be 10 cm. the corresponding prototype height of the jump is .....

    (1) Not determinable from the data given

    (2) 2.5 cm   (3) 0.5 m   (4) 0.1 m

373. For venturimeter the length of throat is _____ its diameter.

    (1) half of   (2) equal to   (3) twice of   (4) none of the above

374. In venturimeter the diameter of throat is generally _____ the diameter of the pipe.

    (1) half of   (2) equal to   (3) twice of   (4) none of the above

375. For venturimeter, flow always takes place from .....

    (1) diverging cone to converging cone   (2) converging cone to diverging cone

    (3) both (1) and (2)   (4) none of the above

376. Match the following in the case of a venturimeter .....

    (1) converging cone   (i) obtain accelerated flow

    (2) cylindrical portion - the throat   (ii) to convert kinetic energy into pressure energy

    (3) diverging cone   (iii) stabilize high velocity

    (1) (1) - (i), (2) - (iii), (3) - (ii)   (2) (1) - (ii), (2) - (i), (3) - (iii)

    (3) (1) - (iii), (2) - (ii), (3) - (i)   (4) (1) - (ii), (2) - (iii), (3) - (i)

377. The venturimeter is installed in a horizontal pipeline which carries a constant discharge. When the pipeline is inclined in the direction of flow the reading of the differential manometer installed between inlet and throat will .....

    (1) increase   (2) decrease   (3) remain same   (4) be unstable

378. An orifice of 0.1 m diameter discharges water under a head of 4.2 m. The diameter of jet at venacontracta is 82 mm. If the flow rate of orifice is 0.04 m³/s, the value of C_c is .....

    (1) 0.98   (2) 0.67   (3) 0.81   (4) 0.75

379. An orifice of 0.1 m diameter discharges water under a head of 4.2 m. The diameter of jet at venacontracta is 82 mm. If the flow rate of orifice is 0.04 m³/s, the value of C_d is .....

    (1) 0.56   (2) 0.95   (3) 0.81   (4) 0.72

380. Orifice is .....

    (1) opening in the side of the vessel   (2) opening in the base of the vessel

    (3) opening in side or base of the vessel

    (4) opening in side or base of the vessel where the liquid level is always above the top of the opening

381. The size of orifice can be .....
   (1) large   (2) small
   (3) both (1) and (2)   (4) none of the above

382. The condition of discharge of orifice is .....
   (1) free orifice   (2) fully submerged
   (3) partially submerged   (4) all of the above

383. The total energy at inlet section of venturimeter is 10 m and the loss of head between inlet and throat is 25% of the total energy at the throat. The total energy at the throat is .....
   (1) 8 m   (2) 12 m   (3) 15 m   (4) 7.5 m

384. An orifice meter with 0.15 m diameter is inserted in a pipe of 0.3 m diameter. The pressure difference measured by a mercury - oil differential manometer is 0.5 m of Hg. If specific gravity of oil is 0.9 and $C_d = 0.64$ the flow rate of oil is .....
   (1) 0.311 m³/s   (2) 0.092 m³/s   (3) 0.271 m³/s   (4) 0.137 m³/s

385. If area ratio of an orifice is 5 : 1 and C_d 0.65 then the flow rate of orifice is
   (1) $2.94\ a_0\sqrt{h}$ (2) $1.23\ a_0\sqrt{h}$ (3) $5.81\ a_0\sqrt{h}$ (4) $3.25\ a_0\sqrt{h}$

386. If discharge of an orifice is 2.26 lps and area ratio is 4, the pressure head of orifice is _____ . Take $C_d = 0.604$ and diameter of orifice is 1.5 cm.
   (1) 15.51 m   (2) 25.78 m   (3) 12.11 m   (4) 21.45 m

387. If the velocity of aeroplane measured by pitot tube is 141.2 km/hr and $C_v = 0.97$, the pressure head is .....
   (1) 91.6 m   (2) 83.3 m   (3) 86.7 m   (4) 72.5 m

388. Generally for a small sharp edged circular orifice the coefficient of discharge varies from .....
   (1) 0.62 – 0.65   (2) 0.7 – 0.85   (3) 0.95 – 0.99   (4) 0.5 – 0.6

389. In case of sharp-edged orifice coefficient of velocity C_v has average value of .....
   (1) 0.8   (2) 0.85   (3) 0.9   (4) 0.98

390. For an orifice, 10 cm in diameter, working under a head of 100 cm, the actual discharge is found to be 0.0216 m³/s. The C_d for the orifice is .....
   (1) 0.6   (2) 0.62   (3) 0.64   (4) 0.66

391. The orifice is treated as a large orifice when .....
   (1)   the head over the orifice is smaller than the vertical dimension of the orifice
   (2)   the vertical dimension of the orifice is large e.g. 2 m
   (3)   the head on the orifice is larger than the vertical dimension of the orifice
   (4)   the velocity across the vertical dimension of the orifice can be treated as constant

392. The discharge through a large rectangular orifice with usual notations is given by .....
   (1) $Q = \dfrac{2}{3} C_d \sqrt{2g}\ L\ \left(H_2^{3/2} - H_1^{3/2}\right)$ (2) $Q = \dfrac{2}{3} C_d \sqrt{2g}\ L\ \left(\sqrt{H_2} - \sqrt{H_1}\right)$

   (3) $Q = \dfrac{2}{3} C_d \sqrt{2g}\ L\ \left(\sqrt{H_1} - \sqrt{H_2}\right)$ (4) $Q = \dfrac{2}{3} C_d \sqrt{2g}\ L\ \left(H_1^{3/2} - H_2^{3/2}\right)$

   where, H_1 - Head upto top edge of orifice, H_2 = Head upto bottom edge of orifice

393. The coefficient of discharge C_d of an orifice is .....
 (1) equal to C_v (2) less than C_c
 (3) equal to C_c (4) greater than C_c

394. The area of an orifice is 314.16 cm² and the value of C_c for the orifice is 0.64. The diameter of the jet at venacontracta is .....
 (1) 12.8 cm   (2) 16 cm   (3) 14 cm   (4) 18 cm

395. If H is the head on the orifice, the loss of head H_L is
 (1) $H\left(1 - C_v^2\right)$ (2) $H\left(1 - C_v\right)$ (3) $H\left(C_v - 1\right)$ (4) $\sqrt{H}\left(1 - C_v^2\right)$

396. If 'H' is the head acting on an orifice and 'h' is the head indicated by a Pitot tube kept at the centre line at venacontracta, the coefficient of velocity for the orifice is
 (1) $\dfrac{h}{H}$ (2) $\sqrt{\dfrac{h}{H}}$ (3) $\sqrt{\dfrac{H}{h}}$ (4) $\dfrac{\sqrt{H}}{h}$

397. A vertical tank with constant area in plan was emptied with an orifice of a certain diameter. It took 100 seconds to lower the liquid level in the tank from 2 m to 1 m. If the diameter of orifice is halved, the time required for the above lowering of the liquid level is .....
 (1) 50 seconds   (2) 100 seconds   (3) 200 seconds   (4) 400 seconds

398. If whole of the outlet side of an orifice is submerged under liquid so that it discharges a jet of liquid into the liquid of same type then it is called as .....
 (1) small orifice   (2) large orifice   (3) free orifice   (4) drowned orifice

399. In case of submerged orifice if H_1 is the head on the upstream side and H_2 is the head on downstream side, the discharge is proportional to .....
 (1) $\sqrt{H_1}$ (2) $\sqrt{H_2}$ (3) $\sqrt{H_1 - H_2}$ (4) $\sqrt{H_1 H_2}$

400. The coefficient of discharge for drowned orifice as compared to that for free orifice working under similar condition is .....
 (1) $C_{d_{(drowned)}} = C_{d_{(free)}}$ (2) $C_{d_{(drowned)}} < C_{d_{(free)}}$
 (3) $C_{d_{(drowned)}} > C_{d_{(free)}}$ (4) depends upon the head

401. In case of an orifice plate, the coefficient of discharge C_d .....
 (1) independent of Reynold's number R_e
 (2) Increases with R_e
 (3) Decreases with R_e
 (4) First increases and then decreases with increase in R_e

402. Select the correct statement.
 (1) The value of C_d for orifice meter is greater than that of venturimeter.
 (2) Losses in the orifice meter are less than those in venturimeter.
 (3) As compared to venturimeter orifice meter can be conveniently used where the space is limited.
 (4) Orifice meter is more costly to install and replace as compared to venturimeter.

403. If 'd' is the diameter of orifice in the plate and 'D' is the diameter of the pipe, the value of C_d for the orifice .....
    (1) depends upon Reynold's number only
    (2) depends upon the ratio $\frac{d}{D}$ only
    (3) does not depend upon Reynold's number as well as $\frac{d}{D}$
    (4) depends upon both Reynold's number and $\frac{d}{D}$

404. Rotameter is used to measure .....
    (1) density of fluids   (2) viscosity of fluids
    (3) flow rate of fluids   (4) pressure of fluids

405. The pressure difference between the inlet and throat of inclined venturimeter measured by water-oil differential manometer is 40 cm. The density of oil flowing through the venturimeter is 1250 kg/m³. The pressure head is _____. Take $C_d = 0.98$.
    (1) 20 cm   (2) 5 cm   (3) 8 cm   (4) 15 cm

406. Water flows through a circular orifice under a head of 5 m. The co-ordinates of centerline of the jet are 2 m horizontally from venacontracta and 20.8 cm vertically below the centre of the orifice. The coefficient of velocity for the orifice is .....
    (1) 0.619   (2) 0.693   (3) 0.852   (4) 0.98

407. Diameter of the jet at venacontracta = 20 mm .....
    Diameter of the orifice = 25 mm
    The coefficient of contraction for the orifice is
    (1) 0.5   (2) 0.64   (3) 0.8   (4) 0.89

408. A jet of water from an orifice, 5 cm in diameter has a diameter of 4 cm at venacontracta. If the coefficient of velocity is 0.96, the coefficient of discharge of the orifice will be .....
    (1) 0.96 (0.8)²   (2) 0.96 (1.25)²   (3) (0.8)²/0.96   (4) (1.25)²/0.96

409. A tank containing water has two orifices of the same size situated at depths h_1 and h_2 below free water surface. The ratio of discharges $Q_1 : Q_2$ through the orifices is .....
    (1) $h_1 : h_2$ (2) $h_2 : h_1$ (3) $\sqrt{h_1} : \sqrt{h_2}$ (4) $h_1^2 : h_2^2$

410. Two identical orifices with diameters d_1 and d_2 and having same C_d are placed in vertical side of a tank. The heads on the orifices are h_1 and h_2 respectively. If the discharges through the orifices are to be same, the ratio of diameters $d_1 : d_2$ has to be .....
    (1) $h_1 : h_2$ (2) $h_2 : h_1$ (3) $\sqrt{h_2} : \sqrt{h_1}$ (4) $\sqrt[4]{h_2} : \sqrt[4]{h_1}$

411. A 10 cm diameter orifice discharges 30 liters per second of water under a head of 2.1 m. A jet exerts a force of 187.5 N on a flat plate held normal to the jet at venacontracta. The coefficient of velocity of the orifice is .....
    (1) 0.96   (2) 0.965   (3) 0.974   (4) 0.98

412. The coefficient of discharge of a mouthpiece is .....
    (1) less than that of the orifice   (2) equal to that of orifice
    (3) more than that of orifice
    (4) depends on way in which mouthpiece is running

413. For external cylindrical mouthpiece, the coefficient of discharge is more than that of an orifice .....
    (1) due to more length of the tube
    (2) due to negative pressure at venacontracta
    (3) due to less friction
    (4) none of these

414. There is a limit to maximum head under which a mouthpiece can work because of .....
    (1) large length of the mouthpiece required
    (2) large coefficient of discharge
    (3) likely cavitation at venacontracta
    (4) none of the above

415. The coefficient of discharge for an external cylindrical mouthpiece is .....
    (1) 0.5   (2) 0.707   (3) 0.853   (4) 0.62

416. Which of the following has maximum coefficient of discharge?
    (1) Circular orifice
    (2) Borda's mouthpiece
    (3) External mouthpiece
    (4) Convergent-divergent mouthpiece

417. Coefficient of discharge for internal mouthpiece running free is .....
    (1) 0.5   (2) 0.62   (3) 0.707   (4) 0.64

418. Discharge through circular orifice with $C_d = 0.62$ is 0.14 m³/s. The discharge through an external cylindrical mouthpiece of same diameter under similar conditions is .....
    (1) 0.193 m³/s   (2) 0.102 m³/s   (3) 0.119 m³/s   (4) 0.265 m³/s

419. A notch is an opening .....
    (1) in the side of a tank or vessel
    (2) at the base of a tank or vessel
    (3) in the side of a tank or vessel in which the liquid level is always above the top of the opening
    (4) in the side of a tank or vessel in which the liquid level is always below the top of the opening

420. The shape of the notch is .....
    (1) triangular   (2) rectangular   (3) trapezoidal   (4) all of the above

421. The bottom edge of the notch over which the liquid flows is called as .....
    (1) nappe
    (2) crest height
    (3) crest
    (4) head over the notch

422. The height of free liquid surface above the crest of notch is known as .....
    (1) nappe
    (2) crest height
    (3) crest
    (4) head over the notch

423. A notch is used to measure .....
    (1) velocity of flow in a channel
    (2) velocity of flow in a pipe
    (3) discharge in a pipe
    (4) discharge through a small channel

424. A device used for measuring discharge passing through a river is .....
    (1) notch   (2) weir   (3) orifice   (4) a large orifice

425. A venturimeter has an area ratio of 2 : 1. If $C_d = 0.98$ the flow rate of venturimeter is .....
    (1) $2.5\ a_1\sqrt{h}$ (2) $5\ a_2\sqrt{h}$
    (3) both (1) and (2)   (4) none of the above

426. A horizontal venturimeter of size 0.3×0.1 m is used to measure the flow rate of water. The pressure at inlet is 140 kPa and the vacuum pressure head at throat is 45 cm of Hg. The pressure head for venturimeter is .....
    (1) 14.71 cm   (2) 8.15 m   (3) 20.39 m   (4) none of the above

427. ____ notch is combination of rectangular notches only.
    (1) Stepped   (2) Trapezoidal
    (3) Both (1) and (2)   (4) None of the above

428. A triangular notch .....
    (1) must be right angled triangular notch
    (2) has no end contractions
    (3) is more accurate than rectangular notch
    (4) is more accurate than rectangular notch for measurement of low discharges

429. A rectangular notch is called suppressed notch when .....
    (1) there is only one end contraction   (2) there are two end contractions
    (3) there are many end contractions   (4) there is no end contraction at all

430. In case of rectangular weir, the length of the weir, due to one end contraction is .....
    (1) increased by 0.1 H   (2) decreased by 0.1 H
    (3) neither increased nor decreased   (4) increased by 0.2 H

431. The side slope of Cipolletti notch is .....
    (1) $1\ H : 2\ V$ (2) $2\ H : 1\ V$ (3) $1\ H : 4\ V$ (4) $4\ H : 1\ V$

432. An error of 1% in measuring head over a rectangular notch will produce _____ error in the discharge.
    (1) 1%   (2) 1.5%   (3) 2%   (4) 2.5%

433. An error of 1% in measuring head over a triangular notch will produce _____ error in the discharge.
    (1) 1%   (2) 1.5%   (3) 2%   (4) 2.5%

434. There is an error of 3% in measuring head over a rectangular notch. The error in the discharge will be .....
    (1) 3%   (2) 4.5%   (3) 6%   (4) 7.5%

435. The head over a triangular notch was measured as 50 cm as against the correct head of 51 cm. The error in the discharge is .....
    (1) 2%   (2) 3%   (3) 4%   (4) 5%

436. Aeration of nappe is required in case of .....
    (1) triangular weir   (2) a fully contracted rectangular weir
    (3) a fully suppressed weir   (4) none of these

437. The discharge over a 1 m long rectangular notch is given by $Q = 1.77\ H^{3/2}$, C_d for this notch is
    (1) 0.6   (2) 0.62   (3) 0.64   (4) 0.58

438. The discharge in meter units over a right angled triangular notch is given by $Q = 1.417\ H^{5/2}$. Value of C_d for the notch is
    (1) 0.62　　　　　　(2) 0.60　　　　　　(3) 0.848　　　　　　(4) 0.48

439. "The rate of change of momentum is proportional to the applied force and it takes place in the direction of the force". This is .....
    (1) Newton's law　　　　　　　　(2) Hydrostatics law
    (3) Pascal's law　　　　　　　　　(4) Archimede's principle

440. The flow rate through a circular pipe is measured by .....
    (1) Pilot-tube　　　　　　　　　(2) Venturimeter
    (3) Orifice meter　　　　　　　　(4) Both 1 and 3

441. Water is flowing from a tapered pipe having area 0.0962 m² and 0.0314 m² at section 1 and 2 respectively. If $Z_1 = 10$ m, $Z_2 = 5$ m and $p_1 = 0.5$ MPa and $p_2 = 0.55$ MPa then the flow rate through the pipe is _____ lpm.
    (1) 5000　　　　　　(2) 2000　　　　　　(3) 3000　　　　　　(4) 3500

442. A vertical pipe carrying oil of specific gravity 0.9 tapers uniformly from section 1 to section 2. If total energy at section 1 is 7.65 m and that of at section 2 is 9.72 m then the flow takes from .....
    (1) 1 to 2　　　　　　　　　　(2) 2 to 1
    (3) both (1) and (2)　　　　　　(4) none of the above

443. A horizontal venturimeter is used to measure the discharge of oil (ρ = 870 kg/m³). If the differential mercury manometer head is 50 cm then the pressure head for venturimeter is .....
    (1) 0.46 m　　　　　　(2) 7.32 m　　　　　　(3) 0.98 m　　　　　　(4) 5.41 m

444. A venturimeter of size 0.2 m × 0.1 m is used to measure the flow of oil (ρ = 850 kg/m³). If the mercury differential manometer head is 25 cm and C_d = 0.98, the discharge of venturimeter is .....
    (1) 0.055 m³/s　　(2) 0.093 m³/s　　(3) 0.081 m³/s　　(4) 0.068 m³/s

ANSWER KEY

1. (3)	2. (3)	3. (4)	4. (1)	5. (3)	6. (1)	7. (4)	8. (1)
9. (3)	10. (1)	11. (2)	12. (1)	13. (3)	14. (3)	15. (4)	16. (4)
17. (1)	18. (2)	19. (2)	20. (2)	21. (2)	22. (3)	23. (2)	24. (2)
25. (1)	26. (3)	27. (2)	28. (2)	29. (1)	30. (3)	31. (4)	32. (2)
33. (3)	34. (2)	35. (1)	36. (1)	37. (3)	38. (3)	39. (3)	40. (4)
41. (3)	42. (4)	43. (1)	44. (2)	45. (3)	46. (1)	47. (4)	48. (2)

49. (4)	50. (3)	51. (2)	52. (4)	53. (2)	54. (4)	55. (1)	56. (3)
57. (2)	58. (2)	59. (2)	60. (1)	61. (2)	62. (4)	63. (2)	64. (4)
65. (3)	66. (4)	67. (2)	68. (3)	69. (4)	70. (2)	71. (1)	72. (3)
73. (3)	74. (2)	75. (3)	76. (1)	77. (1)	78. (3)	79. (1)	80. (2)
81. (3)	82. (1)	83. (3)	84. (2)	85. (3)	86. (2)	87. (3)	88. (1)
89. (2)	90. (2)	91. (3)	92. (1)	93. (3)	94. (2)	95. (4)	96. (3)
97. (2)	98. (3)	99. (1)	100. (3)	101. (4)	102. (3)	103. (2)	104. (4)
105. (1)	106. (1)	107. (2)	108. (2)	109. (3)	110. (3)	111. (1)	112. (2)
113. (1)	114. (1)	115. (3)	116. (4)	117. (4)	118. (4)	119. (3)	120. (4)
121. (3)	122. (4)	123. (2)	124. (4)	125. (3)	126. (3)	127. (2)	128. (3)
129. (3)	130. (3)	131. (2)	132. (4)	133. (4)	134. (1)	135. (1)	136. (3)
137. (3)	138. (2)	139. (3)	140. (1)	141. (3)	142. (3)	143. (1)	144. (3)
145. (4)	146. (2)	147. (3)	148. (1)	149. (3)	150. (3)	151. (3)	152. (2)
153. (1)	154. (1)	155. (4)	156. (2)	157. (3)	158. (2)	159. (3)	160. (2)
161. (2)	162. (2)	163. (2)	164. (2)	165. (4)	166. (4)	167. (4)	168. (4)
169. (2)	170. (3)	171. (3)	172. (1)	173. (3)	174. (2)	175. (4)	176. (2)
177. (3)	178. (4)	179. (4)	180. (2)	181. (3)	182. (3)	183. (1)	184. (2)
185. (3)	186. (2)	187. (3)	188. (3)	189. (4)	190. (1)	191. (3)	192. (4)
193. (3)	194. (4)	195. (1)	196. (2)	197. (2)	198. (3)	199. (3)	200. (1)
201. (3)	202. (3)	203. (1)	204. (2)	205. (2)	206. (2)	207. (1)	208. (3)
209. (3)	210. (1)	211. (3)	212. (1)	213. (3)	214. (3)	215. (1)	216. (1)
217. (2)	218. (3)	219. (1)	220. (3)	221. (4)	222. (3)	223. (2)	224. (4)
225. (1)	226. (2)	227. (3)	228. (4)	229. (3)	230. (3)	231. (3)	232. (4)
233. (4)	234. (2)	235. (1)	236. (3)	237. (3)	238. (2)	239. (3)	240. (2)
241. (4)	242. (3)	243. (1)	244. (3)	245. (3)	246. (3)	247. (3)	248. (3)
249. (4)	250. (4)	251. (4)	252. (2)	253. (4)	254. (3)	255. (1)	256. (3)
257. (1)	258. (3)	259. (3)	260. (3)	261. (2)	262. (5)	263. (2)	264. (2)
265. (2)	266. (3)	267. (3)	268. (4)	269. (2)	270. (4)	271. (1)	272. (2)
273. (4)	274. (4)	275. (2)	276. (4)	277. (2)	278. (3)	279. (4)	280. (4)

281.	(3)	282.	(2)	283.	(2)	284.	(3)	285.	(1)	286.	(2)	287.	(2)	288.	(2)
289.	(3)	290.	(3)	291.	(1)	292.	(4)	293.	(3)	294.	(3)	295.	(1)	296.	(3)
297.	(2)	298.	2)	299.	(5)	300.	(3)	301.	(3)	302.	(3)	303.	(2)	304.	(2)
305.	(3)	306.	(1)	307.	(3)	308.	(4)	309.	(3)	310.	(2)	311.	(4)	312.	(4)
313.	(3)	314.	(2)	315.	(4)	316.	(1)	317.	(1)	318.	(2)	319.	(3)	320.	(3)
321.	(2)	322.	(3)	323.	(1)	324.	(2)	325.	(2)	326.	(4)	327.	(2)	328.	(3)
329.	(4)	330.	(3)	331.	(4)	332.	(4)	333.	(3)	334.	(3)	335.	(4)	336.	(2)
337.	(4)	338.	(2)	339.	(3)	340.	(1)	341.	(1)	342.	(2)	343.	(3)	344.	(3)
345.	(3)	346.	(2)	347.	(3)	348.	(2)	349.	(3)	350.	(3)	351.	(1)	352.	(2)
353.	(1)	354.	(3)	355.	(3)	356.	(2)	357.	(3)	358.	(2)	359.	(2)	360.	(3)
361.	(1)	362.	(1)	363.	(4)	364.	(3)	365.	(3)	366.	(3)	367.	(2)	368.	(3)
369.	(4)	370.	(2)	371.	(3)	372.	(2)	373.	(2)	374.	(1)	375.	(2)	376.	(1)
377.	(3)	378.	(2)	379.	(1)	380.	(4)	381.	(3)	382.	(4)	383.	(1)	384.	(4)
385.	(1)	386.	(1)	387.	(2)	388.	(1)	389.	(4)	400.	(2)	401.	(4)	402.	(3)
403.	(4)	404.	(3)	405.	(3)	406.	(4)	407.	(2)	408.	(1)	409.	(3)	410.	(4)
411.	(3)	412.	(3)	413.	(2)	414.	(3)	415.	(3)	416.	(4)	417.	(1)	418.	(1)
419.	(4)	420.	(4)	421.	(3)	422.	(4)	423.	(4)	424.	(2)	425.	(3)	426.	(3)
427.	(4)	428.	(4)	429.	(4)	430.	(2)	431.	(3)	432.	(2)	433.	(4)	434.	(2)
435.	(4)	436.	(3)	437.	(1)	438.	(2)	439.	(1)	440.	(4)	441.	(3)	442.	(2)
443.	(2)	444.	(1)												

1. The life of a reservoir is determined by its capacity (C), volume of annual inflow into the reservoir (I) and concentration of sediment in the incoming flow (C_s). Life will be more if
   (1) C, I and C_s are high
   (2) C and I are high but C_s is low
   (3) C is high but I and C_s are low
   (4) C, I and C_s are low

2. A catchment of area 200 ha has a run-off coefficient 0.5. A storm of duration larger than the time of concentration of the catchment and of intensity 3.6 cm/h causes a peak discharge of ....
   (1) 5 m³/s
   (2) 10 m³/s
   (3) 100 m³/s
   (4) 360 m³/s

3. The following four hydrological features have to be estimated or taken as inputs before one can compute the flood hydrograph at any catchment outlet:
   (a) Unit hydrograph
   (b) Rainfall hydrograph
   (c) Infiltration index
   (d) Base flow
   The correct order in which they have to be employed in the computation is ....
   (1) (a), (b), (c), (d) (2) (b), (a), (d), (c) (3) (b), (c), (a), (d) (4) (d), (a), (c), (b)

4. A watershed got transferred from rural to urban over a period of time. The effect of urbanization on storm run-off hydrograph from watershed is to ....
   (1) increase the time to peak discharge (2) decrease the volume of run-off
   (3) decrease the time base
   (4) decrease the peak discharge

5. Discharge per unit of drawdown of a well is called its ....
   (1) specific capacity
   (2) efficiency
   (3) well loss
   (4) yield

6. The rainfall hyetograph shows the variation of which one of the following ?
   (1) Cumulative depth of rainfall with time
   (2) Rainfall depth with area
   (3) Rainfall intensity with time
   (4) Rainfall intensity with cumulative depth of rainfall

7. Match List-I (Floods) with List-II (Parameters) and select the correct answer using the codes given below the lists :

List – I		List – II
A.	Standard Project Flood (SPF)	1. Includes catastrophic floods
B.	Maximum Probable Flood (MPF)	2. Includes floods of severe conditions
C.	Design Flood	3. Peak flow obtained from observed data
D.	Maximum Flood	4. Flood of desired recurrence interval

   Codes :

	A	B	C	D
(1)	2	1	4	3
(2)	1	2	3	4
(3)	2	1	3	4
(4)	1	2	4	3

8. Capacity-inflow ratio for a storage reservoir is defined as :

   (1) $\dfrac{\text{Reservoir capacity}}{\text{Average annual flood inflow}}$

   (2) $\dfrac{\text{Reservoir capacity}}{\text{Average annual sediment inflow}}$

   (3) $\dfrac{\text{Dead storage capacity of the reservoir}}{\text{Average annual sediment deposited}}$

   (4) none of these

9. Percentage of total sediment flow depositing in the reservoir, is called its ....
   (1) capacity-inflow ratio   (2) sediment coefficient
   (3) trap efficiency   (4) displacement efficiency

10. Specific capacity of a well
    (1) decreases with diameter
    (2) decreases with time from the start of pumping
    (3) increases with discharge rate
    (4) none of these

11. The percentage of the total sediment flow depositing in the reservoir is called its :
    (1) Capacity inflow ratio   (2) Sediment coefficient
    (3) Trap efficiency   (4) Displacement efficiency

12. Match the List-I with List-II and select the correct answer by using codes given below the lists.

	List – I		List – II
A.	Inglis formula	1.	North and central India
B.	Dicken's formula	2.	Maharashtra state
C.	Ryvis formula	3.	USA
D.	Greager's formula	4.	South India

    Codes :

	A	B	C	D
(1)	2	1	4	3
(2)	3	2	4	1
(3)	2	1	3	4
(4)	1	3	2	4

13. The theory of synthetic hydrograph based on flood routing techniques is based on the principle that rainfall impulse (net storm rain) is modified by the factors
    (a) The time of travel of the flow volume in channel and overland flow
    (b) Storage   (c) Both translation and storage
    (1) (a) and (b) only   (2) (a), (b) and (c)
    (3) (a) and (c) only   (4) (b) and (c) only

14. Water present in an artesian aquifer is usually
    (1) at sub-atmospheric pressure   (2) at atmospheric pressure
    (3) at 0.5 times of the atmospheric pressure
    (4) above atmospheric pressure

15. Borland and Miller's classification of reservoirs for distribution of sediments in the reservoir is based on a parameter m. The reservoir is classified as
    (1) Type I if m is in the range 2.5 to 3.5
    (2) Type II if m is in the range 1 to 1.5
    (3) Type III if m is in the range 1.5 to 2.5
    (4) Type IV if m is greater than 3.5

16. A new reservoir has a capacity of 12 Mm³ and its catchment area is 400 km². The annual sediment yield from the catchment is 0.1 ha.m/km² and the trap efficiency can be assumed to be constant at 0.90. The number of years it takes for the reservoir to loose 50% of its initial capacity is about
    (1) 167 years　　　(2) 30 years　　　(3) 17 years　　　(4) 16 years

17. A 3 hours unit hydrograph U_1 of catchment of area 235 km² is in the form of a triangle with peak discharge 30 m³/s. Another 3 hours unit hydrograph U_2 is also triangular in shape and has the same base width as U_1, but has a peak flow of 90 m³/s. What is the catchment area of U_2 ?
    (1) 117.5 km²　　　(2) 235 km²　　　(3) 470 km²　　　(4) 705 km²

18. Which one of the following characteristics describes a watershed system in system's parlance ?
    (1) Linear　　　　　　　　　　(2) Non-linear
    (3) Linear and time-invariant　　(4) Non-linear and time-variant

19. A unit hydrograph for a watershed is triangular in shape with base period of 20 hours. The area of the watershed is 500 ha. What is the peak discharge in m³/hour ?
    (1) 7000　　　(2) 6000　　　(3) 5000　　　(4) 4000

20. The rainfall on five successive days on a catchment was 3, 6, 9, 5 and 1 cm respectively. If the ϕ-index for the storm can be assumed to be 3 cm/day, the total direct run-off from the catchment due to this storm is ....
    (1) 11 cm　　　(2) 24 cm　　　(3) 9 cm　　　(4) 20 cm

21. Ombrometer (pluviometer) is used to measure ....
    (1) soil moisture stress of a plant　　(2) rainfall depth
    (3) leaf area　　　　　　　　　　　(4) root zone depth

22. Base-flow separation is performed
    (1) on a unit hydrograph to get the direct-runoff hydrograph
    (2) on a flood hydrograph to obtain the magnitude of effective rainfall
    (3) on flood hydrograph to obtain the rainfall hyetograph
    (4) on hydrographs of effluent streams only

23. Consider the following statements :
    (a) Time - Area histogram method aims at developing an IUH.
    (b) Isochrone is a line joining places with equal rainfall on a map.
    (c) Linear reservoir is a reservoir having straight boundaries.
    (d) Linear channel is a fictitious channel in which an inflow hydrograph passes through with only translation and no attenuation.

Which of these statements are correct ?

(1) (a), (b) and (c)
(2) (a) and (d)
(3) (b), (c) and (d)
(4) (a), (b), (c) and (d)

24. Match List-I with List-II and select the correct answer using the codes given below the lists :

	List – I		List – II
A.	Rising limb of a hydrograph	1.	Depends on intensity of rainfall
B.	Falling limb of a hydrograph	2.	Function of total channel length
C.	Peak rate of flow	3.	Function of catchment slope
D.	Drainage density	4.	Function of storage characteristics

Codes :

	A	B	C	D
(1)	3	4	1	2
(2)	1	4	3	2
(3)	3	2	1	4
(4)	1	2	3	4

25. The shape of the hydrograph of runoff is affected by
(1) the intensity of the storm
(2) the duration of the storm
(3) the real distribution of the storm
(4) All the above

26. Two observation wells penetrating into a confined aquifer are located 1.5 km apart in the direction of flow. Heads of 45 m and 20 m are indicated at these two observation wells. If the coefficient of permeability of the aquifer is 30 m/day and the porosity is 0.25, the time of travel of an inert tracer from one well to another is about
(1) 417 days
(2) 500 days
(3) 750 days
(4) 3000 days

27. In an aquifer extending 150 ha, the water table was 20 m below ground level. Over a period of time the water table dropped to 23 m below the ground level. If the porosity of the aquifer is 0.40 and the specific retention is 0. 15, what is the change in groundwater storage of the aquifer ?
(1) 67.5 ha.m
(2) 112.5 ha.m
(3) 180.0 ha.m
(4) 450 ha.m

28. In one-dimensional flow in a confined aquifer between two water bodies, the piezometric head line is
(1) a straight line
(2) a part of an ellipse
(3) a parabola arch
(4) an arc of a circle

29. The double mass curve technique is used for :
(a) determination of average annual rainfall
(b) determination of cumulative rainfall
(c) checking the inconsistency of a record of rainfall data
(d) measurement of effective rainfall

Which of the above given statements is/are correct ?

(1) (a) only
(2) (a) and (b) only
(3) (c) only
(4) (c) and (d) only

30. What is the probable maximum precipitation (PMP) ?
    (1) Projected precipitation for a 100 year return period.
    (2) Maximum precipitation for all past record storms.
    (3) Upper limit of rainfall, which is justified climatologically.
    (4) Effective precipitable water.

31. A tropical cyclone in the northern hemisphere is a ....
    (1) low-pressure zone with clockwise wind
    (2) low-pressure zone with anticlockwise wind
    (3) high-pressure zone with clockwise wind
    (4) high-pressure zone with anticlockwise wind

32. What is hydrological cycle?
    (1) Processes involved in the transfer of moisture from sea to land.
    (2) Processes involved in the transfer of moisture from sea back to sea again.
    (3) Processes involved in the transfer of water from snowmelt in mountains to sea.
    (4) Processes involved in the transfer of moisture from sea to land and back to sea again.

33. The following is not a direct stream flow measurement method.
    (1) Dilution method   (2) Ultrasonic method
    (3) Area - Velocity method   (4) Slope - Area method

34. Wading technique is used
    (1) to determine velocity of sea waves during Tsunami
    (2) to determine thickness of canal lining in alluvial soils
    (3) to measure the volume of dredging material in harbours
    (4) to determine velocity of flow in shallow streams

35. The Unit-Hydrograph theory is based on the assumption of ....
    (1) non-linear response and time invariance
    (2) linear response and non-linear time variance
    (3) time invariance and linear response
    (4) non-linear response and non-linear time variance

36. The land use of an area and the corresponding run-off coefficients are as follows:

Sr. No.	Land use	Area (ha)	Run-off coefficient
1.	Roads	10	0.70
2.	Lawn	20	0.10
3.	Residential area	50	0.30
4.	Industrial area	20	0.80

What is the equivalent run-off coefficient ?
(1) 0.15   (2) 0.36   (3) 0.40   (4) 0.51

37. The shape of the recession limb of a hydrograph depends on ....
    (1) basin as well as storm characteristics
    (2) storm characteristics only
    (3) basin characteristics only
    (4) base flow only

38. The following steps are involved in arriving at a unit hydrograph:
    (a) Estimating the surface run-off in depth.
    (b) Estimating the surface run-off in volume.
    (c) Separation of base flow.
    (d) Dividing surface run-off ordinates by depth of run-off.
    The correct sequence of these steps is ....
    (1) (c), (b), (a), (d)   (2) (b), (c), (d), (a)
    (3) (c), (a), (b), (d)   (4) (d), (c), (b), (a)

39. A watershed was transformed from rural to urban over a period of time. If two storm hydrographs, occurring under identical conditions, but belonging to before and after urbanisation phase are compared, the hydrograph of after urbanisation phase would show
    (a) a decrease in the volume of runoff (b) an increase in the volume of runoff
    (c) decrease in the time base   (d) decrease in the time to peak
    (e) Increase in the peak discharge
    The correct answers are
    (1) (b), (d) and (e)   (2) (a), (c) and (e)
    (3) (a) and (c) only   (4) (b) and (e) only

40. Match List - I (Well Hydraulics Parameter) with List – II (Definition) and select the correct answer by using the codes given below the lists.

	List – I		List – II
A.	Specific yield	1.	Discharge per unit drawdown
B.	Safe yield	2.	Same as specific retention.
C.	Specific capacity	3.	Measure of water that can be removed by pumping
D.	Field capacity	4.	Limit of withdrawal from a well without depletion of the aquifer
		5.	Water bearing capacity of aquifer

    Codes :

	A	B	C	D
(1)	4	3	2	5
(2)	3	4	1	2
(3)	3	4	2	5
(4)	4	3	2	1

41. The specific capacity of a well is the
    (1) volume of water that can be extracted by the force of gravity from unit volume of aquifer
    (2) discharge per unit drawdown at the well
    (3) drawdown per unit discharge of the well
    (4) rate of flow through a unit width and entire thickness of the aquifer

42. List - I contains parameters and List - II contains methods/instruments. Match the lists and select the correct answer using the codes given below the lists.

    List – I (Parameters)   **List – II (Methods/Instruments)**
    A. Stream flow velocity   1. Anemometer
    B. Evapotranspiration rate   2. Penman's method
    C. Infiltration rate   3. Harton's method
    D. Wind velocity   4. Current meter

    Codes :

	A	B	C	D
(1)	1	4	2	3
(2)	4	2	1	3
(3)	1	3	2	4
(4)	4	2	3	1

43. **Assertion (A) :** The available yield of a tubewell can be doubled by doubling the diameter of the well.
    Reason (R) : The yield of a tubewell varies inversely with the logarithm of the reciprocal of the diameter of the well.
    (1) both A and R are true and R is the correct explanation of A
    (2) both A and R are true, but R is not a correct explanation of A
    (3) A is true, but R is false
    (4) A is false, but R is true

44. Mean precipitation over an area is best obtained from gauged amounts by
    (1) arithmetic mean method   (2) Thiessen polygon method
    (3) linearly interpolated isohyetal method
    (4) orographically weighted isohyetal method

45. Double mass curve is used ……….
    (1) to check on the consistency of precipitation record
    (2) as basis for storm rainfall analysis
    (3) to determine average rainfall over an area
    (4) to indicate rainfall distribution

46. Shape of the recession limb of a hydrograph depends on ……….
    (1) basin as well as storm characteristics
    (2) storm characteristics only
    (3) basin characteristics
    (4) none of these

47. Match the following Lists :

    List – I   **List – II**
    (Measuring devices)   **(Soil parameter)**
    (a) Pycnometer   (i) Compressibility
    (b) Hydrometer   (ii) Permeability
    (c) Oedometer   (ii) Specific gravity
    (d) Perameter   (iv) Particle size analysis

Codes :

	(a)	(b)	(c)	(d)
(1)	(iv)	(ii)	(i)	(iii)
(2)	(iv)	(ii)	(iii)	(i)
(3)	(ii)	(iv)	(i)	(iii)
(4)	(iii)	(iv)	(i)	(ii)

48. Match the following lists :

List – I	List – II
(a) Anemometer	(i) Humidity
(b) Rain simulator	(ii) Evapotranspiration
(c) Lysimeter	(iii) Infiltration
(d) Hygrometer	(iv) Wind speed

Codes :

	(a)	(b)	(c)	(d)
(1)	(iv)	(iii)	(i)	(ii)
(2)	(iii)	(iv)	(i)	(ii)
(3)	(iv)	(iii)	(ii)	(i)
(4)	(ii)	(iv)	(iii)	(i)

49. An urban area is located in plains having "average climatic conditions". The impervious area thereof for which drainage must be provided is 3.6 ha and the design rainfall intensity is 2.0 cm/hr. The drains will be designed for a run-off of ....

(1) $0.05 \, m^3/s$ (2) $0.10 \, m^3/s$ (3) $0.20 \, m^3/s$ (4) $0.40 \, m^3/s$

50. Consider the following statements :

In case of flood rounting in a river by using Muskingum method, the coefficient x represents :

(a) a dimensionless constant indicating relative importance of inflow and outflow in determining storage.

(b) a storage constant having the dimension of time.

(c) a coefficient that has a value in the range 0.2 to 0.3 in natural channels.

(d) a coefficient that represents equal influence of inflow and outflow when its value is 0.5.

The correct statements are

(1) (a), (b), (c) and (d)   (2) (a), (c) and (d) only

(3) (a) and (c) only   (4) (b), (c) and (d) only

51. An accurate estimate of average rainfall in particular area can be obtained by ......

(1) arithmetic mean method   (2) isohyetal method

(3) normal ratio method   (4) Thiessen polygon method

52. A canal is 80 km long and has an average surface width of 15 m. If the evaporation measured in a class A pan is 0.5 cm/day, the volume of water evaporated in month of 30 days is .... (m^3)

(1) 12600   (2) 36000   (3) 360000   (4) 126000

53. The following figure shows a typical flood hydrograph. Match the labeled items using lists I and II given below.

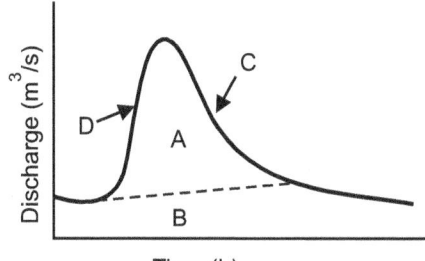

List – I (Items in Fig)		List – II (Labeled items are known as)	
A.	Item-A	1.	Recession limb
B.	Item-B	2.	Rising limb
C.	Item-C	3.	Direct runoff
D.	Item-D	4.	Base flow

Codes :

	A	B	C	D
(1)	3	4	2	1
(2)	3	4	1	2
(3)	4	3	1	2
(4)	4	3	2	1

54. The process by which plants dissipate water from the surface of their leaves, stalks and trunks is known as :

(1) evaporation   (2) transpiration (3) delta   (4) conjunctive use

55. What is the chemical symbol for ice as per UNESCO terminology ?

(1) H_8O_4 (2) H_2O (3) H_6O_5 (4) H_4O_2

56. The term annual flood denotes ……….

(1) mean flood in partial duration

(2) mean of annual flood flow series

(3) a flood with a recurrence interval of 2.33 years.

(4) None of these.

57. Consider the following zones in a soil profile

(a) Saturated zone   (b) Capillary zone

(c) Intermediate zone   (d) Soil-water zone

Which of these does not relate to the zone of aeration in the soil profile ?

(1) (a) and (d)   (2) (b) and (c)   (3) (c) only   (4) (a) only

58. The moving average of annual precipitation record is carried out to determine ……….

(1) trend   (2) annual mean

(3) extreme annual variation   (4) extreme seasonal variation

59. A catchment area of 90 hectares has a run-off coefficient of 0.4. A storm of duration larger than the time of concentration of the catchment and of intensity 4.5 cm/hr creates a peak discharge rate of ....
    (1) 11.3 m³/s   (2) 0.45 m³/s   (3) 450 m³/s   (4) 4.5 m³/s

60. By using Gumbel's method, the flood discharge with a return period of 500 years at a particular township neighbourhood was estimated as 18000 m³/s with a probable error of 2000 m³/s. What are the 95% confidence probability limits of the 500 year flood at the location ?
    (1) 16100 m³/s to 19900 m³/s   (2) 17050 m³/s to 18950 m³/s
    (3) 14080 m³/s to 21920 m³/s   (4) 13600 m³/s to 22400 m³/s

61. A culvert is designed for a flood magnitude of return period 100 years and has expected life of 20 years. The risk in this hydrologic design is ....
    (1) $1 - 0.99^{20}$ (2) $1 - 0.01^{20}$ (3) $1 - 0.09^{20}$ (4) None of these

62. The method of estimating high flood discharge is :
    (1) by empirical formulae developed for the region
    (2) by applying rational formulae
    (3) by flood frequency studies
    (4) All of the above

63. With the increase in its capacity-inflow ratio, trap efficiency of a reservoir ....
    (1) increases
    (2) remains unchanged
    (3) decreases
    (4) may increase or decrease depending on the reservoir characteristics.

64. The Standard Project Flood is ....
    (1) derived from the probable maximum precipitation in the region.
    (2) derived from the severe most meteorological conditions anywhere in the country.
    (3) the flood with return period of 1000 years.
    (4) the same as the probable maximum flood.

65. As a flood wave passes a given section of a river, the time of occurrence of the maximum stage and that of the maximum discharge will be such that ....
    (1) the maximum discharge passes down before the maximum stage is attained.
    (2) the maximum stage is attained before the maximum discharge passes down.
    (3) the two events occur simultaneously.
    (4) no specific sequence would be universally assignable.

66. Consider the following statements :
    (a) Over the oceans there is more evaporation than precipitation.
    (b) On land there is more precipitation than evapotranspiration.
    Which of these two statements are correct ?
    (1) Both (a) and (b)   (2) Neither (a) nor (b)
    (3) (a) only   (4) (b) only

67. If a tangent drawn parallel to the demand line from a ridge point of a mass curve does not intersect the mass curve again it can be inferred that the
    (1) frequency of the flood entering into the reservoir is less.
    (2) inflow into the reservoir cannot meet the demand.
    (3) reservoir is overflowing resulting in wastage.
    (4) reservoir can meet higher demand.

68. An unconfined aquifer of porosity 35%, permeability 35 m/day and specific yield of 0.15 has an area of 100 km². The water table falls by 0.20 m during a drought. The volume of water lost from storage in Mm³ is
    (1) 1.0   (2) 3.0   (3) 6.0   (4) 18.0

69. A DRH of a catchment of 216 km² area is shown in the following figure With respect to this DRH consider the following statements :

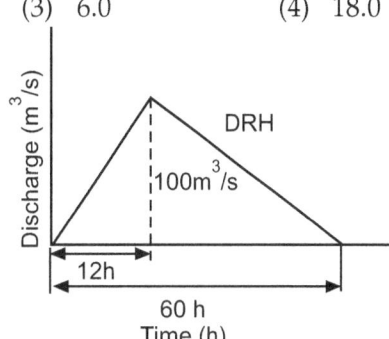

    (a) The effective rainfall producing the DRH is 5 cm.
    (b) The ordinate of a 6-h unit hydrograph of the catchment is 10 m³/s.
    (c) The peak of a DRH due to excess rainfall of 10 cm in 6 hours is 200 m³/s.
    (d) The base of a DRH of excess due to 10 cm of excess rainfall in 6 hours is 66 hours.
    Codes : The correct statements are
    (1) (a), (b) and (d)   (2) (c) and (d) only
    (3) (a) and (c) only   (4) (b),(c)and (d)

70. In a Flow - Mass curve the demand line drawn from a ridge in the curve did not intersect the mass curve again. This implies that :
    (1) The reservoir was not full at the beginning
    (2) The storage was not adequate
    (3) The demand cannot be met by the inflow as the reservoir will not refill
    (4) The reservoir is wasting water by spill

71. What does the Gumbel's distribution method require of the annual flood series to estimate the magnitude of a flood with a return period of T years ?
    (1) Mean value   (2) Length of record
    (3) Standard deviation   (4) All of the above

72. Appropriate value of the estimated average life of a dam reservoir is ……….
    (1) 10 years   (2) 25 years   (3) 75 years   (4) none of these

73. An aquifer is ……….
    (1) permeable geological stratum in which there is a storage of ground water.
    (2) geological stratum which does not have underground water upto 100 feet.
    (3) both (1) and (2)
    (4) none of these

74. Which one of the following statements is correct in respect of the two important aspects of flood forecast – (1) reliability of the forecast, and (2) the time available in between the forecast and the occurrence of flood ?
    (1) Meteorological forecast is least reliable and time available is also the least.
    (2) Hydrological forecast is most reliable, but the time available is the least.
    (3) River forecast is least reliable and the time available is the maximum.
    (4) River forecast is most reliable, but the time available is the least.

75. With reduction in the reservoir capacity over passage of time, trap efficiency ....
    (1) increases   (2) remains unaffected   (3)   decreases
    (4) may increase or decrease, depending upon reservoir characteristics

76. Match List - I (Equation) with List - II (Applicability/Principle of equation) and select the correct answer using the codes given below the lists.

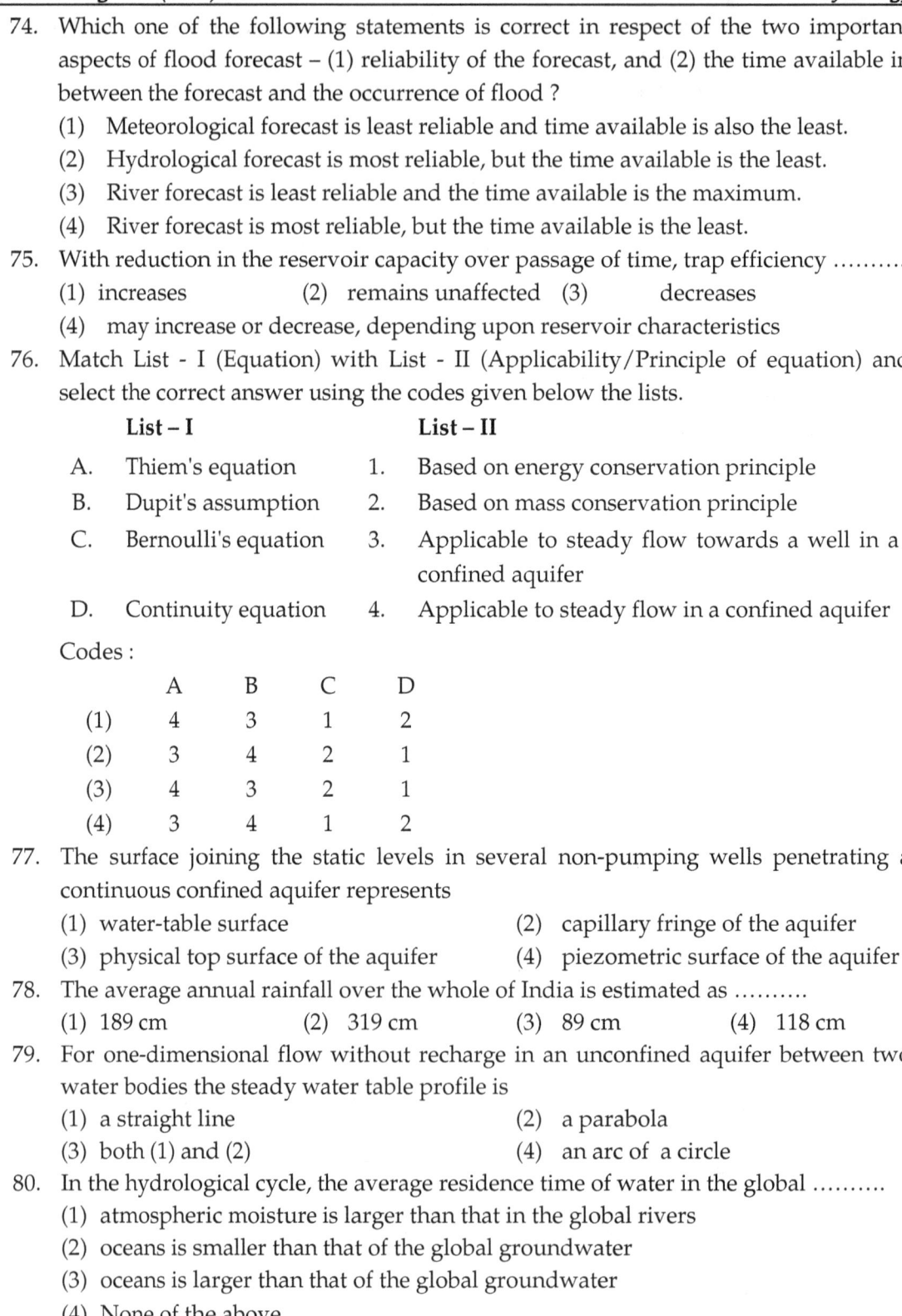

	List – I			List – II
A.	Thiem's equation		1.	Based on energy conservation principle
B.	Dupit's assumption		2.	Based on mass conservation principle
C.	Bernoulli's equation		3.	Applicable to steady flow towards a well in a confined aquifer
D.	Continuity equation		4.	Applicable to steady flow in a confined aquifer

Codes :

	A	B	C	D
(1)	4	3	1	2
(2)	3	4	2	1
(3)	4	3	2	1
(4)	3	4	1	2

77. The surface joining the static levels in several non-pumping wells penetrating a continuous confined aquifer represents
    (1) water-table surface   (2) capillary fringe of the aquifer
    (3) physical top surface of the aquifer   (4) piezometric surface of the aquifer

78. The average annual rainfall over the whole of India is estimated as ....
    (1) 189 cm   (2) 319 cm   (3) 89 cm   (4) 118 cm

79. For one-dimensional flow without recharge in an unconfined aquifer between two water bodies the steady water table profile is
    (1) a straight line   (2) a parabola
    (3) both (1) and (2)   (4) an arc of a circle

80. In the hydrological cycle, the average residence time of water in the global ....
    (1) atmospheric moisture is larger than that in the global rivers
    (2) oceans is smaller than that of the global groundwater
    (3) oceans is larger than that of the global groundwater
    (4) None of the above

81. The Flow - Mass curve is a graphical representation of :
    (1) cumulative discharge and time
    (2) discharge and percentage probability of flow being equalled or exceeded.
    (3) cumulative discharge, volume and time in chronological order.
    (4) discharge and time in chronological order.

82. When a ship enters sea from a river, one can expect it:
    (1) to rise a little
    (2) to sink a little
    (3) to remain at the same level of draft
    (4) to rise or fall depending on whether it is of wood or steel

83. The dimensions of the storage coefficient S are
    (1) L   (2) LT^{-1} (3) L^3/T (4) dimensionless

84. A stream that provides water to the water table is termed
    (1) affluent   (2) influent   (3) ephemeral   (4) effluent only

85. A soil has a coefficient of permeability of 0.51 cm/s. If the kinematic viscosity of water is 0.009 cm²/s, the intrinsic permeability in darcys is about
    (1) 5.3×10^4 (2) 474   (3) 4.7×10^4 (4) 4000

86. The discharge per unit drawn at the well is known as ....
    (1) specific yield   (2) specific storage
    (3) specific retention   (4) specific capacity

87. The salinity in water :
    (1) reduces the evaporation   (2) increases the evaporation
    (3) does not affect evaporation   (4) None of the above

88. Safe yield of an aquifer is the rate at which ground water can be withdrawn without causing ....
    (1) sand entering the well
    (2) overload of the pumping machine
    (3) long-term decline of the piezometric surface
    (4) all of these

89. The basic equation of flood routing through a reservoir can be modified for discrete successive intervals Δt by which one of the following ?

    (1) $\left[\dfrac{I_1 + I_2}{2}\right] \Delta t + \left[S_1 + \dfrac{O_1 \Delta t}{2}\right] = \left[S_2 + \dfrac{O_2 \Delta t}{2}\right]$

    (2) $\left[\dfrac{I_1 + I_2}{2}\right] \Delta t + \left[S_1 - \dfrac{O_1 \Delta t}{2}\right] = \left[S_2 + \dfrac{O_2 \Delta t}{2}\right]$

    (3) $\left[\dfrac{I_1 + I_2}{2}\right] \Delta t + \left[S_1 + \dfrac{O_1 \Delta t}{2}\right] = \left[S_2 - \dfrac{O_2 \Delta t}{2}\right]$

    (4) $\left[\dfrac{I_1 + I_2}{2}\right] \Delta t + \left[S_1 - \dfrac{O_1 \Delta t}{2}\right] = \left[S_2 - \dfrac{O_2 \Delta t}{2}\right]$

90. Dimensions of storage coefficient are ....
    (1) $M^0 L^0 T^0$ (2) $M^0 L^1 T^{-2}$ (3) $M^0 L^{-1} T^{-1}$ (4) $M^0 L^1 T^{-2}$

91. The surface joining the static water levels in several wells penetrating a confined aquifer represents
    (1) water-table surface　　　　　　　　(2) capillary fringe
    (3) piezometric surface of the aquifer　(4) cone of depression of the aquifer

92. What affects the shape of the hydrograph ?
    (1) Non-uniform a real distribution of rainfall
    (2) Varying rainfall intensity
    (3) Shape of the basin
    (4) All the above factors

93. For unconfined aquifers, storage coefficient is same as ....
    (1) porosity　　　　　　　　　　　　(2) specific retention
    (3) specific yield　　　　　　　　　(4) none of these

94. Match List-I (Technique/Principle) with List-II (Purpose) and select the correct answer using the codes given below the lists :

	List - I		List – II
A.	ϕ-index	1.	Dependable flow
B.	Slope – area method	2.	Reservoir regulation
C.	Flow duration curve	3.	Steady stream discharge determination
D.	Dilution technique	4.	Run-off volume
		5.	Unsteady stream discharge determination

    Codes :

	A	B	C	D
(1)	3	5	1	4
(2)	4	1	2	3
(3)	3	1	2	4
(4)	4	5	1	3

95. In constructing a 4 hour synthetic unit hydrograph for a basin, the lag time is estimated to be 40 hours. When will be peak discharge in the Synthetic Unit Hydrograph occur from the start of the storm ?
    (1) 36 hours　　　　(2) 40 hours　　　　(3) 42 hours　　　　(4) 44 hours

96. Match List-I with List-II and select the correct answer using the codes given below the lists :

	List – I		List – II
A.	Unit hydrograph	1.	Design flood
B.	Synthetic unit hydrograph	2.	Permeability
C.	Darcy's law	3.	Ungauged basin
D.	Rational method	4.	1 cm run-off

    Codes :

	A	B	C	D
(1)	2	3	4	1
(2)	2	1	4	3
(3)	4	3	2	1
(4)	4	1	2	3

97. Match List-I with List-II and select the correct answer using the codes given below the lists :

	List – I		List – II
A.	φ-index	1.	Used for measurement of evapotranspiration for given vegetation
B.	Lysimeter	2.	Used for flow measurement
C.	Dilution technique	3.	Average rainfall above which the rainfall volume is equal to the run-off volume
D.	Snyder's equation	4.	Relates the basin lag to the basin characteristics

Codes :

	A	B	C	D
(1)	3	1	2	4
(2)	4	2	1	3
(3)	3	2	1	4
(4)	4	1	2	3

98. Consider the following statements:

(a) An ephemeral stream is one which has a base-flow contribution.

(b) Flow characteristics of a stream depend upon rainfall and catchment characteristic and also the climatic factors which influence evapo-transpiration.

(c) Sequent Peak Algorithm is used for estimating run-off from rainfall.

Which of these statements is/ are correct ?

(1) (a), (b) and (c)   (2) (a) and (c)

(3) (b) and (c)   (4) (b) alone

99. Flowing artesian wells are expected in areas where

(1) the water table is very close to the land surface.

(2) the aquifer is confined.

(3) the elevation of the piezometric head line is above the elevation of the ground surface.

(4) the rainfall is intense.

100. The percentage standard error of precipitation averages is often expressed functionally or graphically in terms of (i) precipitating gauge network density expressed as area per gauge, and (ii) total area of catchment. The percentage standard error

(1) increases with area per gauge as well as with total area.

(2) decreases with area per gauge as well as with total area.

(3) increases with area per gauge, but decreases with total area.

(4) decreases with area per gauge, but increases with total sea.

101. In a reservoir, the sediment deposit is found to be made up of only sand and this deposit is always found to be submerged. The unit weight of this sediment deposit at any time T years after the commencement of operation of the reservoir is about
    (1) $1500 \, kgf/m^3$
    (2) $1500 + B \, Ln \, T \, kgf/m^3$, where B is a positive non-zero coefficient
    (3) $750 \, kgf/m^3$
    (4) $750 + BLn \, T \, kgf/m^3$, where B is a positive non-zero coefficient

102. In a Flow - Mass curve study, the demand line drawn from a ridge does not intersect the mass curve again. This implies that
    (1) the reservoir is not full at the beginning
    (2) the storage is not adequate
    (3) the demand cannot be met by the inflow as the reservoir will not refill
    (4) the reservoir is wasting water by spill

103. Match List - I with List - II and select the correct answer using codes given below :

List - I	List - II
(a) Convective	(i) Atmospheric disturbance
(b) Cyclonic	(ii) Mountain barrier
(c) Frontal	(iii) Pressure difference
(d) Orographic	(iv) Temperature difference
	(v) Warm and cold air masses

    Codes :

	(a)	(b)	(c)	(d)
(1)	(i)	(iv)	(v)	(ii)
(2)	(iv)	(iii)	(v)	(ii)
(3)	(i)	(iv)	(ii)	(v)
(4)	(iv)	(iii)	(ii)	(v)

104. A mean annual run-off of $1 \, m^3/s$ from a catchment area $31.54 \, km^2$ represents an effective rainfall of ....
    (1) 100 cm   (2) 1.0 cm   (3) 100 mm   (4) 31.54 cm

105. The theory of infiltration capacity was given by ....
    (1) Merrill & Bernard   (2) W.W. Horner
    (3) LeRoy K. Shermen   (4) Robert E. Horton.

106. The Slope-Area method is extensively used in ....
    (1) development of rating curve
    (2) estimation of flood discharge based on high-water marks
    (3) cases where shifting control exists
    (4) cases where back-water effect is present

107. The hydraulic risk of a 100 – year flood occurring during the 2 year service life of a project is ....
    (1) 9.8%   (2) 9.9%   (3) 19.9%   (4) 99%

108. A deep well ....
    (1) is always deeper than a shallow well
    (2) is weaker structurally than a shallow well
    (3) has more discharge than a shallow well
    (4) all of these

109. Specific capacity of a well is the
    (1) volume of water that can be extracted by the force of gravity from a unit volume of aquifer.
    (2) discharge per unit drawdown of the well.
    (3) drawdown per unit discharge of the well.
    (4) rate of flow through a unit width and entire thickness of aquifer.

110. A sand sample was found to have a porosity of 40%. For an aquifer of this material, the specific yield is
    (1) $= 40\%$ (2) $> 40\%$
    (3) $< 40\%$ (4) dependent on the clay fraction

111. Design yield (outflow demand) of a proposed storage reservoir is usually equal to ....
    (1) safe yield of its constant.
    (2) safe yield of its catchment minus the reservoir losses.
    (3) dependable yield of its catchment.
    (4) dependable yield of its catchment minus the reservoir losses.

112. "Economical height of a dam" is that height, for which ....
    (1) cost per unit of storage is minimum
    (2) benefit cost ratio is maximum
    (3) net benefits are maximum
    (4) none of these

113. Consider the following statements:
    (a) A 100 year flood discharge is greater than a 50 year flood discharge.
    (b) 90% dependable flow is greater than 50% dependable flow.
    (c) Evaporation from salt-water surface is less than that from fresh-water surface.
    Which of these statements are correct ?
    (1) (a) and (b)   (2) (b) and (c)   (3) (a) and (c)   (4) (a), (b) and (c)

114. Which of the pairs of terms used in groundwater hydrology are not synonymous?
    (1) Permeability and hydraulic conductivity
    (2) Storage coefficient and storativity
    (3) Actual velocity of flow and discharge velocity
    (4) Water table aquifer and unconfined aquifer

115. The sediment delivery ratio (SDR) of a watershed is related to watershed area (A), relief (R) and watershed length (L) as
    (1) $SDR = KA^m (R/L)^n$ (2) $SDR = KA^{-m} (R/L)^{-n}$
    (3) $SDR = KA^{-m} (R/L)^n$ (4) $SDR = KA^m (R/L)^{-n}$
    where K, m and n are positive coefficients.

116. The yield of a well depends upon
    (1) permeability of soil
    (2) area of aquifer opening into the wells
    (3) actual flow velocity
    (4) all of the above

117. Depth - Area - Duration curves of precipitation are drawn as ....
    (1) minimizing envelopes through the appropriate data points.
    (2) maximizing envelopes through the appropriate data points.
    (3) best fit mean curves through the appropriate data points.
    (4) best fit mean straight lines through the appropriate data points.

118. The Penman's evapotranspiration equation is based on ....
    (1) water budget method
    (2) energy budget method
    (3) mass transfer method
    (4) energy balance and mass transfer approach

119. Which one of the following flood routing method involves the concepts of wedge and prism storages ?
    (1) Coefficient method   (2) Muskingum method
    (3) Pull's method   (4) Lag method

120. Calibration of a current meter for use, in channel flow measurement is done in a ....
    (1) wind tunnel   (2) water tunnel
    (3) towing tank   (4) flume

121. Consider the following statements:
    (a) Only the surface flow constitutes the flood hydrograph due to an isolated storm.
    (b) For a given storm, the flood peak is dependent on the drainage density.
    (c) Fan shaped catchments give narrow hydrograph with low peak.
    Which of these statements is/are correct ?
    (1) (a), (b) and (c)   (2) (a) and (c)   (3) (b) only   (4) (c) only

122. The excess run-off hydrograph from a catchment area of 10 km^2 due to a storm of 6 hours duration has been observed to be triangular in shape. The peak flow is observed to be 10 m^3/s and the base length is 20 hours. The rainfall excess in the catchment is ....
    (1) 5.1 cm   (2) 3.6 cm   (3) 4.5 cm   (4) 2.5 cm

123. The word unit in hydrograph refers to the ....
    (1) unit depth of run-off   (2) unit duration of the storm
    (3) unit base period of the hydrograph   (4) unit area of the basin

124. A culvert is designed for a peak flow Q_p on the basis of rational formula. If a storm of the same intensity as used in the design and twice the duration occurs, then the resulting peak discharge will be ....
    (1) Q_p (2) $Q_p/2$ (3) $\sqrt{2}\,Q_p$ (4) $2Q_p$

125. In Snyder's method of synthetic unit hydrograph development, basin lag is taken as ………
    (1) the time interval between centroid of the rainfall excess and surface run-off.
    (2) the time interval from mid point of the unit rainfall excess to the peak of the unit hydrograph.
    (3) independent of rainfall duration.
    (4) independent of catchment characteristics.

126. Clark's method aims at which one of the following ?
    (1) Developing an IUH due to an instantaneous rainfall excess over catchment.
    (2) Developing stage-discharge relationship.
    (3) Measurement of infiltration.
    (4) Flood routing through channels.

127. Darcy's law is valid in a porous media flow if the Reynold's number is less than unity. This Reynold's number is defined as
    (1) (Discharge velocity $\times$ Maximum grain size)/μh
    (2) (Actual velocity $\times$ Average grain size)/vh
    (3) (Discharge velocity $\times$ Average grain size)/v
    (4) (Discharge velocity $\times$ Pore size)/v

128. When there is an increase in the atmospheric pressure, the water level in a well penetrating a confined aquifer
    (1) decreases
    (2) increases with pressure
    (3) does not undergo any change
    (4) decreases or increases depending on the elevation of the ground.

129. The current CWC practice in design of reservoirs adopts minimum drawdown level (MDDL) based on the bed elevation that will be reached in the reservoir after N years of sedimentation, where N is equal to
    (1) 25 years   (2) 50 years
    (3) 100 years   (4) 200 years

130. A tropical cyclone is a ……….
    (1) low-pressure zone that occurs in the northern hemisphere only
    (2) high-pressure zone with high winds
    (3) zone of low pressure with anticlockwise winds in the northern hemisphere
    (4) None of the above

131. A unit hydrograph is a hydrograph of a rain storm of a specified duration resulting from a run-off of ……….
    (1) 15 mm   (2) 20 mm   (3) 30 mm   (4) none of these

132. The Muskingham method of flood routing is a ……….
    (1) form of hydraulic routing of a flood
    (2) form of reservoir routing
    (3) complete numerical solution of St. Venant equation
    (4) hydrological channel routing method.

133. An acquifer, confined at the bottom, but open at top, is called ....
    (1) acquiclude   (2) unconfined acquifer
    (3) semiconfined acquifer   (4) acquifer

134. Energy is necessarily required in the utilisation of ....
    (1) ground water   (2) lake water   (3) reservoir water   (4) sea water

135. The relation between suspended sediment transport Q_s and stream flow Q is often represented by an equation of the form $Q_s = KQ^n$
    where the exponent n usually lies in the range
    (1) 0.1 to 0.3   (2) 0.4 to 0.6   (3) 0.6 and 1.0   (4) 1.0 and 3.0

136. The following rainfall data refers to station A and B which are equidistant from station X

	Station 'A'	Station 'X'	Station 'B'
Long-term normal annual rainfall in mm	200	250	300
Annual rainfall in mm for the year 1940	140	P	270

The value of P will be
    (1) 225   (2) 220   (3) 205   (4) 200

137. The volume of water that can be extracted by force of gravity from a unit volume of aquifer material is called
    (1) specific retention   (2) specific surface tension
    (3) specific storage   (4) specific capacity

138. For a given storm, other factors remaining same.
    (1) basins with large drainage densities give smaller flood peaks.
    (2) low drainage density basins give shorter time bases of hydrographs.
    (3) the flood peak is independent of the drainage density.
    (4) basins having low drainage density give smaller peaks in flood hydrographs.

139. Trap efficiency of a storage reservoir indicates sediment volume ....
    (1) trapped in the reservoir
    (2) let out from the reservoir
    (3) trapped in relation to the sediment volume entering the reservoir
    (4) none of these

140. If erosion in a watershed is estimated as 30 tonnes/ha/year, this watershed is in erosion class designated as
    (1) zero   (2) very high   (3) high   (4) moderate

141. Match List - I with List - II and select the correct answer using codes given below :

List - I

(a) Specific yield

(b) Specific capacity

(c) Specific retention

(d) Specific storage

List - II

(i) Volume of water retained per unit volume of aquifer

(ii) Volume of water drained by gravity per unit volume of aquifer

(iii) Difference of porosity and specific storage

(iv) Well yield per unit drawdown

(v) Volume of water released from unit volume of aquifer for unit decline in piezometric head

Codes :

	(a)	(b)	(c)	(d)
(1)	(ii)	(iv)	(i)	(v)
(2)	(iv)	(ii)	(iii)	(v)
(3)	(ii)	(iv)	(i)	(iii)
(4)	(iv)	(ii)	(i)	(iii)

142. The quantitative statement of the balance between water basin and losses in a certain basin during a specified period of time is known as which one of the following ?
    (a) Water budget (b) Hydrologic budget (c) Groundwater budget
    Select the correct answer using the codes given below:
    (1) (a) only   (2) (b) only   (3) (c) only   (4) all of these

143. A rectangular plot having direction of overland flow parallel to its larger side, has time of concentration of 25 minutes. Following four rainfall patterns are considered for purpose of design of drainage.
    A = 35 mm/h for 15 minutes   B = 45 mm/h for 10 minutes
    C = 10 mm/h for 60 minutes   D = 15 mm/h for 25 minutes
    The greatest peak rate of runoff is expected in the storm :
    (1) A   (2) B   (3) C   (4) D

144. Match List - I with List - II and select the correct answer using the codes given below the lists.

	List I		List II
(a)	Evapotranspiration	(1)	Penman method
(b)	Infiltration	(2)	Snyder's method
(c)	Synthetic unit hydrograph	(3)	Muskingum method
(d)	Channel routing	(4)	Hortoris method

    Codes

	(a)	(b)	(c)	(d)
(1)	1	3	4	2
(2)	1	4	2	3
(3)	3	4	1	2
(4)	4	2	1	3

145. The Mass - Flow curve is an integral curve of ....
    (1) the hydrograph   (2) the hyetograph
    (3) both of the above   (4) none of the above

146. A 4 hours storm had 4 cm of rainfall and the resulting direct run-off was 2.0 cm. If the ϕ-index remains at the same value, the run-off due to 10 cm of rainfall in 8 hours in the catchment is ....
    (1) 6.0 cm   (2) 7.5 cm   (3) 2.3 cm   (4) 2.8 cm

147. A stilling well is required when the stage measurement is made by employing ....
    (1) bubble gauge   (2) inclined staff gauge
    (3) vertical staff gauge   (4) float gauge recorder

148. For a return period of 1000 years the Gumbel's reduced variate Y_t is ....
    (1) 6.907   (2) 4.001   (3) 5.386   (4) 6.936

149. The time of concentration at the outlet in urban area catchment of 1.5 km² area with a run-off coefficient of 0.42 is 28 minutes. The maximum depth of rainfall with a 50 years return period for this time of concentration is 48 mm. What is the peak flow rate at the outlet for this return period ?
    (1) 12 m³/s   (2) 14 m³/s   (3) 16 m³/s   (4) 18 m³/s

150. A reservoir had an original capacity of 720 ha-m. The drainage area of the reservoir is 100 sq.km and has a sediment delivery rate of 0.10 ha-m/sq.km. If the reservoir has a trap efficiency of 80% , the annual percentage loss of original capacity is
    (1) 1.39%   (2) 1.11%   (3) 1.74%   (4) 0.28%

151. A groundwater basin consists of 10 km² area of plains. The maximum groundwater table fluctuation has been observed to be 1.5 m. Consider the specific yield of the basin as 10% and specific retention as 20%. What is the available groundwater storage in million cubic metres?
    (1) 1.0   (2) 1.5   (3) 0.5   (4) 0.3

152. In one-dimensional flow in an unconfined aquifer between two water bodies, when there is a recharge, the water table profile is
    (1) a parabola curve   (2) part of an ellipse
    (3) a straight line   (4) an arc of a circle

153. If 'p' is the precipitation 'a' is the area represented by a rain gauge, and 'n' is the number of rain gauges in a catchment area, then the weighted mean rainfall is
    (1) $\dfrac{\Sigma \, ap^3}{\Sigma \, a^2}$ (2) $\dfrac{\Sigma \, ap}{n}$ (3) $\dfrac{\Sigma \, ap}{\Sigma \, a}$ (4) $\dfrac{\Sigma \, ap^5}{\Sigma \, a^3}$

154. Trap efficiency of a storage reservoir is defined as :
    (1) $\dfrac{\text{Total annual sediment inflow}}{\text{Reservoir capacity}}$

    (2) $\dfrac{\text{Total sediment deposited in a given period}}{\text{Total sediment inflow in that period}}$

    (3) $\dfrac{\text{Total annual sediment deposited in the reservoir}}{\text{Dead storage capacity of the reservoir}}$

    (4) None of these

155. For open wells, ratio of the safe depression head to critical depression head is equal to ....
    (1) 1/3   (2) 1   (3) 2/3   (4) 0

156. An aquifer confined at top and bottom by impermeable layers is stratified into three layers as follows :

Layer	Thickness (m)	Permeability (m/day)
Top layer	4	30
Middle layer	2	10
Bottom layer	6	20

The transmissivity (m²/day) of the aquifer is
    (1) 260   (2) 227   (3) 800   (4) 230

157. Which one of the following is not a major type of storm precipitation ?
    (1) frontal storm   (2) air mass storm
    (3) orographic storm   (4) continental storm

158. If the base period of a 6-hour hydrograph of a basin is 84 hours, then a 12 hours unit hydrograph derived from this 6 hour unit hydrograph will have a base period of
    (1) 72 hours   (2) 73 hours   (3) 84 hours   (4) 90 hours

159. A catchment consists of 30% area with run-off coefficient 0.40 with the remaining 70% area with run-off coefficient 0.60. The equivalent run-off coefficient will be
    ....
    (1) 0.48   (2) 0.54   (3) 0.63   (4) 0.76

160. The trap efficiency of a reservoir is a function of ....
    (1) inflow into the reservoir
    (2) ratio of inflow to the storage capacity
    (3) ratio of reservoir to inflow
    (4) reservoir capacity

161. A catchment has an area of 150 hectares and a run-off/rainfall ratio of 0.40. If due to 10 cm rainfall over the catchment, a stream flow at the catchment outlet lasts for 10 hours, what is the average stream flow in the period ?
    (1) 60,000 m³/hr   (2) 100 m³/minute
    (3) 3.5 m³/s   (4) 1.33 m³/s

162. Match List-I with List-II and select the correct answer using the codes given below the lists :

	List – I		List – II
A.	Conservation reservoirs	1.	Uncontrolled outlets
B.	Retarding basins	2.	Flood fighting
C.	Flood plains	3.	Temporary storage of flood water
D.	Flood walls	4.	Controlled outlets

    Codes :

	A	B	C	D
(1)	1	4	3	2
(2)	1	4	2	3
(3)	4	1	3	2
(4)	4	1	2	3

163. The use of the unit hydrograph for estimating floods is limited to catchments of size less than:
    (1) 5000 km²   (2) 500 km²
    (3) 104 km²   (4) no upper limit

164. A two-hour storm hydrograph has 5 units of direct run-off. The two-hour unit hydrograph for this storm can be obtained by dividing the ordinates of the storm hydrograph by ....
    (1) 2   (2) 2/5   (3) 5   (4) 5/2

165. A mean annual run-off of 2 m³/s from a catchment of area 10 km² represents an effective rainfall of nearly:
    (1) 530 cm　　　　　(2) 590 cm　　　　　(3) 630 cm　　　　　(4) 658 cm

166. A 252 km² catchment area has 6 hours UH which is a triangle with time base of 35 hours. What is the peak discharge of the DRH due to 5 cm effective rainfall in 6 hours from that catchment ?
    (1) 45 cumecs　　　　(2) 115 cumecs　　　(3) 200 cumecs　　　(4) 256 cumecs

167. The dimensions of the coefficient of transmissibility T are
    (1) L^2/T　　　　　(2) L^3T^2　　　　　(3) L/T^2　　　　　(4) dimensionless

168. The specific capacity of a well in confined aquifer under equilibrium conditions and within the working limits of drawdown
    (1) can be taken as constant
    (2) decreases as the drawdown increases
    (3) increases as the drawdown increases
    (4) None of above.

169. The present CWC practice in design of reservoirs adopts area - capacity - elevation curves expected after M years of sedimentation for working table studies and checking for the performance of the project. In this M is equal to
    (1) 25 years　　　　　　　　　　(2) 50 years
    (3) 100 years　　　　　　　　　　(4) None of above

170. Depth-Area-Duration curves would seem to resemble
    (1) arcs of circle concave upwards with duration increasing outward
    (2) first quadrant limbs of hyperbolae with duration increasing outward
    (3) third quadrant limbs of hyperbolae with duration decreasing outward
    (4) first quadrant limbs of hyperbolae with duration decreasing outward

171. The standard Symons's type raingauge has a collecting area of diameter ....
    (1) 12.7 cm　　　　　　　　　　(2) 10 cm
    (3) 5.08 cm　　　　　　　　　　(4) 25.4 cm

172. Indicate the incorrect statement out of following four statements in which PET stands for Potential Evapo Transpiration :
    (1) PET depends essentially on climatic factors and is not critically dependent on soil and plant factor.
    (2) PET is same as the consumptive use of an irrigated crop.
    (3) Decrease in PET of an area on the basis of mean annual value reflects an increased runoff.
    (4) The ratio of PET to take evaporation is always greater than unity.

173. Which of the following instruments is not concerned with stream flow measurement ?
    (1) Sound hydrometer　　　　　　(2) Echo-depth recorder
    (3) Electromagnetic flow meter　　(4) Sounding weight

174. A stilling well is required when the stage measurement is made by employing ....

    (1) bubble gauge   (2) inclined staff gauge
    (3) vertical staff gauge   (4) float gauge recorder

175. Which of the following principles relate to a Unit Hydrograph ?
    (a) The hydrographs of direct runoff due to effective rainfall of equal duration have the same time base.
    (b) Effective rainfall is not uniformly distributed within its duration.
    (c) Effective rainfall is uniformly distributed throughout the whole area of drainage basin.
    (d) Hydrograph of direct run off from a basin due to a given period of effective rainfall reflects the combination of all the physical characteristics of the basin.
    Select the correct answer using the codes given below :
    (1) (a), (b) and (c)   (2) (a), (b) and (d)
    (3) (b), (c) and (d)   (4) (a), (c) and (d)

176. Match List-I (Hydrological terms) with List-II (Relationship/Nature of curve) and select the correct answer using the codes given below the lists :

	List – I		List – II
A.	Theissen Polygon	1.	Average depth of rainfall over an area
B.	Mass curve	2.	Relationship of rainfall intensity and time
C.	Hyetograph	3.	Relationship of accumulated rainfall and time
D.	DAD curve	4.	Relationship of river run-off and time
		5.	Always a falling curve

Codes :

	A	B	C	D
(1)	1	3	2	5
(2)	1	5	3	2
(3)	4	3	2	5
(4)	4	5	3	2

177. A direct run-off hydrograph due to isolated storm was triangular is shape with a base of 80 h and peak of 200 m^3/s. If the catchment area is 1440 km^2, the effective rainfall of the storm is ....

    (1) 20 cm   (2) 10 cm   (3) 5 cm   (4) 2 cm

178. A well of 20 cm diameter fully penetrates a confined aquifer. After a long period of pumping at a constant rate of 2720 litres/minute, the observation of drawdown taken, at 10 and 100 m distances from the centre of the well are found to be 3 m and 0.5 m respectively. The transmissivity of the aquifer is

    (1) 675 m^2/day   (2) 575 m^2/day   (3) 525 m^2/day   (4) 250 m^2/day

179. An isohyet is a line joining points of ....

    (1) equal temperature   (2) equal humidity
    (3) equal rainfall depth   (4) equal evaporation

180. According to Robert E. Horton, the equation of infiltration capacity curve, is ....
   (1) $f_t = f_c (f_o - f_c) e^{kt}$
   (2) $f_t = f_c - (f_o - f_c) e^{-kt}$
   (3) $f_t = f_c + (f_o - f_c) e^{-kt}$
   (4) $f_t = f_c + (f_o - f_c) e^{kt}$

181. The specific storage is
   (1) storage coefficient/aquifer depth
   (2) specific yield per unit area
   (3) specific capacity per unit depth of aquifer
   (4) porosity- specific detention

182. Evaporation losses from surface of a reservoir can be reduced by sprinkling ....
   (1) DDT
   (2) acetylalcohol
   (3) potassium permanganate
   (4) none of these

183. Dead storage zone in a reservoir is provided for the storage of ....
   (1) water for firm power
   (2) sand and silt
   (3) water for water supplies
   (4) all of the above

184. The unit of intrinsic permeability is
   (1) cm/day
   (2) m/day
   (3) darcy/day
   (4) cm^2

185. The percentage of total quantity of fresh water in the world available in the liquid from is about
   (1) 30 %
   (2) 70 %
   (3) 11 %
   (4) 51 %

186. Evapotranspiration is confined ....
   (1) to daylight hours
   (2) night-time only
   (3) land surface only
   (4) none of these

187. Specific yield of an aquifer is ....
   (1) proportional to soil porosity
   (2) volume of the water which drains freely
   (3) depends on soil conditions
   (4) none of these

188. The amount of water stored in river channel without any artificial storage is called ....
   (1) bank storage
   (2) river storage
   (3) valley storage
   (4) dead storage

189. Probability of a 10 year flood to occur at least once in the next 4 years is ....
   (1) 25%
   (2) 35%
   (3) 50%
   (4) 65%

190. An effective storage of a flood control reservoir is ....
   (1) the amount of water which can be supplied from it in a particular interval of time.
   (2) the storage between the minimum and maximum reservoir levels under ordinary operating conditions.
   (3) the useful storage plus the surcharge storage less the valley storage.
   (4) the storage volume of flood water above maximum reservoir level.

191. The total observed run-off volume during a 4 hour storm with a uniform intensity of 2.8 cm/hr is 25.2×10^6 m^3 from a basin of 280 km^2 area. What is the average infiltration rate for the basin ?
   (1) 3.6 mm/hr
   (2) 4.8 mm/hr
   (3) 5.2 mm/hr
   (4) 5.5 mm/hr

192. A 6 hour storm has 6 cm of rainfall and the resulting run-off was 3 cm. If φ-index remains at the same value, which one of the following is the run-off due to 12 cm of rainfall in 9 hours in the catchment ?
   (1) 4.5 cm   (2) 6.0 cm   (3) 7.5 cm   (4) 9.0 cm

193. In an underground profile, zone of aeration does not include ....
   (1) soil water   (2) capillary water
   (3) ground water   (4) lake water

194. An S-curve hydrograph has been obtained for catchments of 270 km² from a 3 hour unit hydrograph. The equilibrium discharge for the S-curve is ....
   (1) 750 m³/s   (2) 277.8 m³/s   (3) 250 m³/s   (4) 187 m³/s

195. A 1 hour of 10 cm has return period 50 years. The 1 hour of rainfall 10 cm or more will occur in each of two successive years is ....
   (1) 0.04   (2) 0.2   (3) 0.02   (4) 0.004

196. What would be the volume stored in a saturated column of aquifer with a porosity of 0.35, cross-sectional area of I square metre and of 3.0 metres depth ?
   (1) 3.0 m³   (2) 2.0 m³   (3) 1.05 m³   (4) 0.105 m³

197. The suspended sediment concentration C_s in ppm is determined from a sample of suspended sediment mixture as
   (1) $C_s = \dfrac{[\text{Weight of sediment in sample}]}{[\text{Weight of water in sample}]} \times 10^6$

   (2) $C_s = \dfrac{[\text{Weight of sediment in sample}]}{[\text{Weight of (sediment + water) in sample}]} \times 10^6$

   (3) $C_s = \dfrac{[\text{Volume of sediment in sample}]}{[\text{Volume of (sediment + water) in sample}]} \times 10^6$

   (4) $C_s = \dfrac{[\text{Weight of (sediment + water) in sample}]}{[\text{Volume of (sediment + water) in sample}]} \times 10^6$

198. Hyetograph is a plot of ....
   (1) cumulative rainfall *vs* time   (2) distribution of rainfall *vs* time
   (3) rainfall depth *vs* time   (4) none of these

199. A catchment was found to have a q index of 0.6 cm/h in winter season. If a rainfall of 3 cm occurs in that season at a uniform rate in a 6h in storm, the resulting direct runoff is :
   (1) 0.6 cm   (2) – 0.6 cm   (3) 0 cm   (4) 6.6 cm

200. For a free flowing well, piezometric surface is ....
   (1) above the G.L.   (2) below the G.L.
   (3) at the G.L.   (4) all of the above

201. A bridge has an expected life of 50 years and is designed for a flood magnitude of return period 100 years. What is the risk associated with this hydrologic design ?
   (1) $1 - (0.99)^{50}$ (2) $(0.5)^{50}$ (3) $(0.99)^{50}$ (4) $(0.99)^{100}$

202. Hydrograph is a graphical representation of ....
   (1) surface run off   (2) ground water flow
   (3) rain fall   (4) discharge flowing in the river

203. If the maximum depth of a 50 year – 15th rainfall depth at Bhubaneshwar is 260 mm, the 50 years-3h-maximum rainfall depth at the same place is :

    (1) < 260 mm   (2) > 260 mm   (3) = 260 mm   (4) None of the above

204. In a reservoir the capacity is 20 MCM and the annual inflow is estimated as 25 MCM.

    The trap efficiency of this reservoir under normal operating condition is about

    (1) 100%   (2) 45%   (3) 75%   (4) 95%

205. Match List-I (Names of scientists) with List-II (Contribution to field of hydrology) and select the correct answer using the codes given below the lists :

List – I		**List – II**	
A.	Dalton	1.	Unit Hydrograph
B.	Snyder	2.	Evaporation
C.	Blaney-Criddle	3.	Empirical flood formula
D.	Sherman	4.	Synthetic Unit Hydrograph
		5.	Consumptive use equation

    Codes :

	A	B	C	D
(1)	2	3	5	1
(2)	1	4	3	2
(3)	2	4	5	1
(4)	1	3	4	5

206. Interception losses ....

    (1) include evaporation, through flow and stem flow

    (2) consists of only evaporation loss

    (3) includes evaporation and precipitation loss

    (4) all of above

207. A geological formation which can absorb water but cannot transmit significant amount is called ....

    (1) acquifer   (2) acquiclude   (3) sand hole   (4) all of the above

208. The probability that a 100 year flood is equaled or exceeded, at least once in 100 years is ....

    (1) 99%   (2) 64%   (3) 36%   (4) 1%

209. Geological formation which may contain water, but does yield any, is ....

    (1) aquifer   (2) aquifuse   (3) aquiclude   (4) aquitard

210. A 4-hour unit hydrograph of a basin can be approximated as a triangle with a base period of 48 hours and peak ordinate of 300 m³/s. What is the area of the catchment basin ?

    (1) 7776 km²   (2) 5184 km²   (3) 2592 km²   (4) 1294 km²

211. A DRH due to a storm over a basin has a time base of 90 hours with straight line portions of the hydrograph with flow rates of 0, 10, 70, 90, 40 and 0 m³/s at elapsed durations of 0, 10, 20, 30, 50 and 90 hours as indicated in the following diagram, respectively. The catchment area is 300 km². What is the rainfall excess in the storm ?

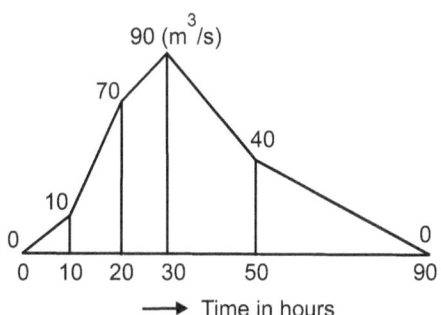

(1) 2.83 cm   (2) 3.46 cm   (3) 3.87 cm   (4) 4.02 cm

212. If a 4-hour unit hydrograph of a certain basin has peak ordinate of 80 m³/s, the peak ordinate of a 2 hour unit hydrograph for the same basin will be ....
     (1) equal to 80 m³/s   (2) greater than 80 m³/s
     (3) less than 80 m³/s   (4) between 40 m³/s to 80 m³/s

213. In wells, specific capacity ....
     (1) increases with time from the start of pumping
     (2) decreases with time from the start of pumping
     (3) is always constant
     (4) cannot be defined

214. Match the following lists :

List – I (Plot of)	**List II (Name)**
(a) Accumulated precipitation vs Time in chronological order	(i) Hydrograph
(b) Rainfall intensity vs time	(ii) Hyetograph
(c) Stream flow vs time in chronological order	(iii) Flow duration curve
(d) Steam discharge vs percent time. The flow is equaled or exceeded	(iv) Mass curve of rainfall

     Codes :

	(a)	(b)	(c)	(d)
(1)	(iv)	(ii)	(i)	(iii)
(2)	(iv)	(ii)	(iii)	(i)
(3)	(ii)	(iv)	(i)	(iii)
(4)	(ii)	(iv)	(iii)	(i)

215. A 3-hour storm on a small drainage basin produced rainfall intensities of 3.5 cm/hr, 4.2 cm/hr and 2.9 cm/hr in successive hours. If the surface runoff due to the storm is 3 cm, then the value of ϕ-index will be
     (1) 2.212 cm/hr   (2) 2.331 cm/hr   (3) 2.412 cm/hr   (4) 2.533 cm/hr

216. In a linear reservoir, the
  (1) volume varies linearly with elevation.
  (2) outflow rate varies linearly with storage.
  (3) storage varies linearly with time.
  (4) storage varies linearly with inflow rate.

217. Match List-I (Parameter) with List-II (Relatable term) and select the correct answer using the codes given below the lists :

	List - I		List – II
A.	Rainfall intensity	1.	Isohyets
B.	Rainfall excess	2.	Cumulative rainfall
C.	Rainfall averaging	3.	Hyetograph
D.	Mass curve	4.	Direct run-off hydrograph

  Codes :

	A	B	C	D
(1)	1	3	2	4
(2)	3	4	1	2
(3)	1	3	4	2
(4)	3	4	2	1

218. Steep rise in the Flow - Mass curve during a certain period indicates:
  (1) very high evaporation losses during that period
  (2) flash floods during that period
  (3) sudden spurt in irrigation demand during that period
  (4) sudden rise in demand for water to meet hydropower generation

219. The Water Year in India starts from the first day of ....
  (1) January   (2) April   (3) June   (4) September

220. A catchment area of 60 ha has a run-off coefficient of 0.40. If a storm of intensity 3 cm/h and duration longer than the time of concentration occurs in the catchment, then what is the peak discharge ?
  (1) $2.0 \, m^3/s$ (2) $3.5 \, m^3/s$ (3) $4.5 \, m^3/s$ (4) $2.5 \, m^3/s$

221. Base-flow separation is performed
  (1) on a unit hydrograph to get the direct-runoff hydrograph
  (2) on a flood hydrograph to obtain the magnitude of effective rainfall
  (3) on flood hydrograph to obtain the rainfall hyetograph
  (4) on hydrographs of effluent streams only

222. A stratified unconfined aquifer has three horizontal layers as below:

Layer	Coefficient of permeability (m/day)	Depth (m)
1	6	2
2	16	4
3	24	3

The effective vertical coefficient of permeability of this aquifer, in m/day, is about
  (1) 13   (2) 15   (3) 24   (4) 16

223. An IUH is a direct run-off hydrograph ....
     (1) of one cm magnitude due to rainfall excess of 1 hour duration.
     (2) that occurs instantaneously due to a rainfall excess of 1 hour duration.
     (3) of unit rainfall excess precipitating instantaneously over 1 hour duration.
     (4) None of the above

224. Recorded annual maximum 24-hour rainfall magnitudes at stations 'X' are as under:

Year	Rainfall (cm)
1960	12.0
1961	6.0
1962	4.8
1963	7.9
1964	12.0
1965	14.2
1966	13.6
1967	6.0
1968	3.7
1969	2.9

     What is the return period in years, for a 6.0 cm annual rainfall according to (i) Hazen formula and (ii) Weibull formula, respectively ?
     (1) $\dfrac{10}{7}, \dfrac{11}{7}$ (2) $\dfrac{20}{13}, \dfrac{22}{13}$ (3) $\dfrac{5}{3}, \dfrac{11}{7}$ (4) $\dfrac{20}{11}, \dfrac{11}{6}$

225. A triangular direct run-off hydrograph due to a storm has a time base of 60 hours and a peak flow of 30 m³/s occurring at 20 hours from the start. If the catchment area is 300 km², what is the rainfall excess in the storm ?
     (1) 50 mm   (2) 20 mm   (3) 10.8 mm   (4) 8.3 mm

226. Kirpich equation is used to determine which one of the following ?
     (1) Run-off from a given rainfall
     (2) Base time of a unit hydrograph
     (3) Time of concentration in run-off hydrograph
     (4) None of the above

227. A unit hydrograph has one unit of ....
     (1) peak discharge   (2) rainfall duration
     (3) direct run-off   (4) None of the above

ANSWER KEY

1. (4)	2. (2)	3. (3)	4. (3)	5. (1)	6. (3)	7. (1)	8. (1)
9. (3)	10. (2)	11. (3)	12. (1)	13. (2)	14. (4)	15. (3)	16. (3)
17. (4)	18. (3)	19. (3)	20. (1)	21. (2)	22. (2)	23. (4)	24. (1)
25. (4)	26. (3)	27. (2)	28. (1)	29. (3)	30. (3)	31. (2)	32. (4)
33. (4)	34. (4)	35. (3)	36. (1)	37. (3)	38. (1)	39. (1)	40. (1)
41. (3)	42. (4)	43. (4)	44. (4)	45. (1)	46. (1)	47. (4)	48. (3)

49. (3)	50. (1)	51. (2)	52. (4)	53. (2)	54. (2)	55. (2)	56. (3)
57. (4)	58. (1)	59. (4)	60. (3)	61. (1)	62. (4)	63. (1)	64. (2)
65. (1)	66. (1)	67. (2)	68. (2)	69. (3)	70. (3)	71. (4)	72. (3)
73. (1)	74. (4)	75. (3)	76. (4)	77. (4)	78. (4)	79. (2)	80. (3)
81. (3)	82. (1)	83. (4)	84. (2)	85. (2)	86. (4)	87. (1)	88. (3)
89. (2)	90. (1)	91. (3)	92. (4)	93. (3)	94. (4)	95. (3)	96. (3)
97. (1)	98. (3)	99. (3)	100. (1)	101. (1)	102. (3)	103. (2)	104. (1)
105. (4)	106. (2)	107. (4)	108. (3)	109. (2)	110. (2)	111. (4)	112. (1)
113. (3)	114. (3)	115. (3)	116. (4)	117. (2)	118. (4)	119. (2)	120. (3)
121. (3)	122. (2)	123. (2)	124. (1)	125. (2)	126. (1)	127. (3)	128. (1)
129. (3)	130. (3)	131. (2)	132. (4)	133. (2)	134. (1)	135. (4)	136. (4)
137. (1)	138. (4)	139. (3)	140. (2)	141. (1)	142. (1)	143. (1)	144. (2)
145. (1)	146. (1)	147. (4)	148. (1)	149. (4)	150. (2)	151. (2)	152. (2)
153. (3)	154. (2)	155. (1)	156. (1)	157. (4)	158. (4)	159. (2)	160. (3)
161. (2)	162. (3)	163. (1)	164. (3)	165. (3)	166. (3)	167. (1)	168. (2)
169. (2)	170. (3)	171. (1)	172. (4)	173. (1)	174. (4)	175. (4)	176. (1)
177. (2)	178. (4)	179. (3)	180. (3)	181. (4)	182. (2)	183. (2)	184. (4)
185. (3)	186. (4)	187. (4)	188. (3)	189. (2)	190. (3)	191. (4)	192. (3)
193. (1)	194. (3)	195. (4)	196. (3)	197. (2)	198. (2)	199. (3)	200. (3)
201. (1)	202. (4)	203. (1)	204. (4)	205. (3)	206. (2)	207. (2)	208. (2)
209. (2)	210. (3)	211. (4)	212. (2)	213. (2)	214. (1)	215. (4)	216. (2)
217. (2)	218. (4)	219. (3)	220. (1)	221. (2)	222. (1)	223. (3)	224. (4)
225. (3)	226. (3)	227. (3)					

UNIT - 9 : WATER REQUIREMENTS

1. The water supply system means .....
   (1) Construction of reservoirs
   (2) Construction of canals
   (3) The complete layout from the source of supply to the distribution .....
   (4) All of the above

2. Which of the following causes a decrease in per capita consumption ?
   (1) Modern living
   (2) Good quality of water
   (3) Metering system
   (4) Hotter climate

3. The hourly variation factor is usually taken of .....
   (1) 1.3
   (2) 1.5
   (3) 1.8
   (4) 2.7

4. The variation factor, applied to obtain peak hourly demand, in relation to the average daily demand is .....
   (1) 1.5
   (2) 1.8
   (3) 2.5
   (4) 2.7

5. Coincident draft in relation to water demand, is based on .....
   (1) Maximum daily demand
   (2) Fire demand
   (3) Maximum daily + fire demand
   (4) Peak hourly demand

6. The distribution mains are designed for .....
   (1) Maximum daily demand
   (2) Maximum hourly demand
   (3) Average daily demand
   (4) Maximum hourly demand on maximum day

7. In India, as per Indian Standards, water consumption per capita per day for domestic purpose is .....
   (1) 135 lit.
   (2) 100 lit.
   (3) 150 lit.
   (4) 153 lit.

8. Which of the following formula is used for computing the quantity of water for fire demand ?
   (1) Freeman's Formula
   (2) Kuichling Formula
   (3) Buston's Formula
   (4) All above

9. According to Kuichling Formula, the fire demand (α) in litre per minute is given by .....
   (1) $\phi = 1135 \left(\dfrac{P}{5} + 10 \right)$
   (2) $\phi = 3182 \sqrt{p}$
   (3) $\phi = 3821 \sqrt{p}$
   (4) $\phi = 5663 \sqrt{p}$

10. The design period for water supply scheme is taken as .....
    (1) 20-30 yrs
    (2) 35-45 yrs
    (3) 25-45 yrs
    (4) 20-50 yrs

11. The water mains should be designed for .... of average daily water requirement.
    (1) 200%
    (2) 225%
    (3) 250%
    (4) 275%

12. Filter and other units of treatment plant are designed for .....
    (1) two times the annual average daily demand of water
    (2) two times the maximum daily demand of water
    (3) maximum daily demand of water
    (4) all of the above

(9.1)

13. Water distribution systems are sized to meet the .....
    (1) maximum hourly demand   (2) average hourly demand
    (3) maximum daily demand and fire demand
    (4) average daily demand and fire demand

14. The suitable method for forecasting population for a young and rapidly developing city is .....
    (1) Arithmetic mean method   (2) Geometric mean method
    (3) Comparative graphical method   (4) None of these

15. The growth of population can be represented by a .....
    (1) Logistic curve   (2) Logarithmic curve
    (3) Semi-log curve   (4) Straight line curve

16. As compared to geometrical increase method of forecasting population, arithmetical increase method gives .....
    (1) lesser value   (2) higher value   (3) same value   (4) None of the above

17. Find the population at the end of 2011 by Arithmatical increase method ?

Year	Population
1951	1,00,000
1961	1,09,000
1971	1,16,000
1981	1,28,000

    (1) 1,26,000   (2) 1,36,000   (3) 1,46,000   (4) 1,56,000

18. The sub-surface water obtained under pressure is known as .....
    (1) Tube well   (2) Infiltration well
    (3) Artesian well   (4) Open well

19. A pipe sunk into the ground to tap the underground water is called .....
    (1) Open well   (2) Tube well   (3) Artesian well   (4) All of the above

20. Shallow horizontal tunnels constructed along the river on its bank to intercept are called .....
    (1) Infiltration galleries   (2) Canals
    (3) Spring   (4) None of the above

21. As compared to shallow wells, deep wells have .....
    (1) more depth   (2) less depth
    (3) more discharge   (4) less discharge

22. The maximum discharge of tube well is about .....
    (1) 5 lit./sec   (2) 10 lit./sec   (3) 50 lit./sec   (4) 75 lit./sec.

23. The quantity of water available from an infiltration gallery depends upon the .....
    (1) size of gallery   (2) nature of soil
    (3) yield of source   (4) All of the above

24. The layers such as sand and gravel which allow the water to pass through them are known as .....
    (1) Pervious layers   (2) Aquifers
    (3) Water bearing strata   (4) All of the above

25. The water bearing strata i.e. layers of sand, gravel etc. is called .....
    (1) An aquifer   (2) An aquiclude
    (3) An aquifuge   (4) Zone of saturation

26. The position of soil through which lateral movement of water takes place is called .....
    (1) Zone of saturation   (2) Water table
    (3) An aquiclude   (4) None of the above

27. The water of river has an important property called .....
    (1) Turbidity   (2) Self purification
    (3) Permeability   (4) Infiltration capacity

28. The specific retention is least in .....
    (1) Coarse gravel   (2) Sand
    (3) Clay   (4) Silt

29. Which of the following gives underground water?
    (1) Spring   (2) River   (3) Lake   (4) Reservoir

30. To determine the velocity of flow of ground water, the most commonly used non-empirical formula is .....
    (1) Darcy's formula   (2) Lacy's formula
    (3) Hazen formula   (4) All of the above

31. The suitable method for boring in hard rock, hard soil and boulder region is .....
    (1) Percussion method   (2) Rotatary method
    (3) Core drilling   (4) All of the above

32. The most important source of water for public water supply is .....
    (1) Lake   (2) Pond   (3) River   (4) Sea

33. The yield of a surface stream may be obtained by .....
    (1) c/s velocity method   (2) Stream guaging
    (3) Chemical method   (4) All of the above

34. The yield of well depends upon the .....
    (1) Permeability of soil   (2) Position of water table
    (3) Depth of well in impervious layer   (4) All of the above

35. Which one of the following tests employs Ethylene Diamine Tetra Acetic Acid as a titrating agent ?
    (1) Chlorides   (2) Dissolved oxygen
    (3) Hardness   (4) Residual chlorine

36. Run-off is the water which flows .....
    (1) In rivers   (2) In canals
    (3) In sewerpipes   (4) All of the above

37. According to Vermule's formula, the annual run-off (f) in cm is given by .....
    (1) $F = R - (0.279 + 0.116\ R)\ (0.063\ T + 0.47)$
    (2) $F = R + (0.279 - 0.116\ R)\ (0.063\ T + 0.47)$
    (3) $F = R - (0.279 - 0.116\ R)\ (0.063T - 0.47)$
    (4) None of the above

38. The type of valve, which is provided on the suction pipe in a tube well is .....
    (1) Air relief valve   (2) Reflux valve
    (3) Pressure relief valve   (4) Sluice valve

39. The device which are installed for drawing water from sources are called .....
    (1) Filters   (2) Intakes   (3) Aquifer   (4) None of the above

40. Select the correct relationship between porosity (N) specific yield (n) and specific retention (R) .....
    (1) N = V + R   (2) V = N + R   (3) R = N + V   (4) R 7 (N + V)

41. Strainer type tube wells are considered unsuitable for .....
    (1) Coarse gravel   (2) Fine sand strata
    (3) Clean gravel   (4) All of the above

42. 'Shrouding' is provided in case of .....
    (1) Slotted type wells   (2) Strainer wells
    (3) Cavity wells   (4) All of the above

43. The polluted water is one which .....
    (1) contains pathogenic bacteria
    (2) contains undesirable substances rendering it unfit for drinking and domestic use.
    (3) is contaminated   (4) All of the above

44. The amount of light absorbed or scattered by suspended material present in water is a measure of .....
    (1) Turbidity   (2) Diffraction   (3) Opacity   (4) None of the above

45. The turbidity which can be seen by naked eye is of the order of .....
    (1) 5 JTU   (2) 15 JTU   (3) 25 JTU   (4) 35 JTU

46. Hellige turbidimeter can measure turbidity in the range of .....
    (1) 0 to 50 ppm   (2) 10 to 60 ppm   (3) 50 to 100 ppm   (4) All of the above

47. Turbidity is measured on .....
    (1) Standard silica scale   (2) Standard platinum scale
    (3) Standard cobalt scale   (4) All of the above

48. The most common cause of acidity in water is .....
    (1) Carbon dioxide   (2) Oxygen
    (3) Hydrogen   (4) Nitrogen

49. The phenolic compound in public water supply should not be more than .....
    (1) 0.1 ppm   (2) 0.001 ppm   (3) 0.0001 ppm   (4) 1 ppm

50. Alkalinity in water is expressed as milli-gram per litre in terms of equivalent .....
    (1) Calcium carbonate   (2) Magnesium carbonate
    (3) Sodium carbonate   (4) Calcium hydroxide

51. The product of H^+ ions and OH^- ions in a stronger alkali is .....
    (1) 0   (2) 1   (3) 10^{-1} (4) 10^{-14}

52. Temporary hardness in water is caused by .....
    (1) bicarbonates of Ca and Mg   (2) Sulphates of Ca and Mg
    (3) chlorides of Ca and Mg   (4) Nitrates of Ca and Mg

53. One British degree of hardness is equal to .....
    (1) 1 ppm
    (2) 10 ppm
    (3) 14.25 ppm
    (4) 17.15 ppm

54. If the total hardness of water is greater than its total alkalinity, the carbonate hardness will be equal to .....
    (1) Total hardness
    (2) Total alkalinity
    (3) Carbonate hardness
    (4) All of the above

55. The taste of hard water is better than that of soft water due to presence of .....
    (1) Carbonates
    (2) Bicarbonates
    (3) Calcium
    (4) Sodium

56. Orthotolidine test is used for determination of .....
    (1) Residual chlorine
    (2) Dose of coagulant
    (3) Carbonate hardness
    (4) All of the above

57. Standard EDTA solution is used to determine the .....
    (1) turbidity of water
    (2) hardness of water
    (3) dissolved oxygen
    (4) None of above

58. The colour of water for domestic supplies, on standard platinum cobalt scale, should not exceed .....
    (1) 5-10 ppm
    (2) 10-20 ppm
    (3) 20-30 ppm
    (4) 35-45 ppm

59. An approximate estimation of total dissolved solids of a given water sample is often made by measuring ....
    (1) Electrical conductivity of the water sample
    (2) Electro-magnetic conductivity of the water sample
    (3) Sound conductivity of the water sample
    (4) Thermal conductivity of the water sample

60. One degree of hardness is equivalent to .....
    (1) 1.425 mg/lit.
    (2) 14.25 mmg/lit
    (3) 1.425 gm/m^3
    (4) 14.25 gm/m^3

61. The concentration of OH$^-$ ions in a water sample is measured as 17 mg/L at 25°C. What is the pH of water sample ?
    (1) 10
    (2) 11
    (3) 15
    (4) 21

62. The permissible pH value for public supply water is between .....
    (1) 6.5 to 8.5
    (2) 4 to 5
    (3) 7 to 10
    (4) 10 to 12

63. Permanent hardness can be removed by .....
    (1) Lime soda process
    (2) Base-exchange process.
    (3) De-mineralisation process
    (4) All of the above

64. Chlorides impart .....
    (1) Salty taste to water
    (2) Sweet taste to water
    (3) Irritating taste to water
    (4) None of the above

65. Mottling of teeth is associated with the presence of .....
    (1) Chlorides in water
    (2) Fluorides in water
    (3) Calcium in water
    (4) Sulphur in water

66. Water is considered as 'hard' if its hardness is of order .....
    (1) over 200 ppm   (2) over 100 ppm
    (3) over 50 ppm   (4) over 10 ppm

67. Which one of the following tests employs ferroin indication ?
    (1) Chemical oxygen demand   (2) Ammonia nitrogen
    (3) Nitrate nitrogen   (4) Fluoride

68. When fluoride concentration in water exceeds 1.5 mg/L or so, the disease that may be caused is .....
    (1) Dental problem   (2) Flurosis
    (3) Cholera   (4) All of the above

69. pH value of fresh sewage is usually .....
    (1) between 7 to 14   (2) between 1 to 7
    (3) Zero   (4) All of the above

70. The range of Baylis turbidimeter is .....
    (1) 0-2 ppm   (2) 0-10 ppm   (3) 10-20 ppm   (4) 0-50 ppm

71. When was the Water (Prevention and Control of Pollution) Act enacted by the Indian Parliament ?
    (1) 1970   (2) 1974   (3) 1980   (4) 1985

72. Match List-I (Industry and Unit of Production) with List-II (Water need in kL/Unit/Day) and select the correct answer using the codes given below the lists :

	List - I		List - II
A.	Automobile (per vehicle)	1.	1 to 2
B.	Leather (per 100 kg)	2.	4
C.	Paper (per tonne)	3.	40
D.	Crude petroleum refinery (per tonne)	4.	50-100
		5.	200-400

    Codes :

	A	B	C	D
(1)	3	2	5	1
(2)	1	3	5	4
(3)	3	2	4	5
(4)	1	4	2	1

73. Which one of the following Acts/Rules has a provision for "No right to appeal" ?
    (1) Environment (Protection) Act, 1986
    (2) The Hazardous Waste (Management and Handling) Rules, 1989
    (3) Manufacture, Storage and Import of Hazardous Chemicals Rules, 1989
    (4) Environment (Protection) Rules, 1992

74. Which among the following brings about the Hazardous Waste Management and Handling Rules in India ?
    (1) Central Pollution Control Board   (2) Ministry of Environment and Forests
    (3) Ministry of Urban Development   (4) Ministry of Rural Development

75. For water supply to a medium town, what is the daily variation factor ?
    (1) 1.5   (2) 2.5   (3) 3   (4) 3.5

76. Which one of the following factors has the maximum effect on figure of per capita demand of water supply of a given town ?
    (1) Method of charging of the consumption
    (2) Quality of water
    (3) System of supply - intermittent or continuous
    (4) Industrial demand

77. Match List-I with List-II and select the correct answer using the codes given below the lists :

	List - I		List - II
A.	Soil pipe	1.	Ventilating pipe
B.	Intercepting trap	2.	Wash basin
C.	P-trap	3.	Water closet waste
D.	Cowl	4.	House drainage

    Codes :

	A	B	C	D
(1)	3	4	1	2
(2)	3	4	2	1
(3)	4	3	2	1
(4)	4	3	1	2

78. Which one of the following pairs is not correctly matched ?
    (1) Check valve   : To check water flow in all directions
    (2) Sluice valve   : To control flow of water through pipelines
    (3) Air valve   : To release the accumulated air
    (4) Scour valve   : To remove silt in a pipeline

79. The trap used for a water closet is called ....
    (1) gully trap   (2) P-trap   (3) intercepting trap   (4) anti-siphon trap

80. Match List-I (Unit) with List-II (Purpose) and select the correct answer using the codes given below the lists :

	List - I		List - II
A.	Leaping weir	1.	To prevent grit, sand, debris etc. from entering the storm sewer.
B.	Gutter inlet	2.	To carry the sewer below a stream or railway line
C.	Inverted syphon	3.	To drain rain water from roads to the storm sewer
D.	Catch basin	4.	To separate storm water and the sanitary sewage

    Codes :

	A	B	C	D
(1)	4	3	1	2
(2)	4	3	2	1
(3)	3	4	2	1
(4)	3	4	1	2

81. In sanitary plumbing of buildings, a two pipe system signifies ....
    - (1) separate soil pipes and waste pipe without vent pipes
    - (2) a soil-cum-waste pipe and a ventilating pipe
    - (3) separate soil and waste pipe and a common ventilating pipe
    - (4) separate soil pipe and waste pipe, each with its own vent pipe

82. The least expensive and most suitable excreta disposal unit for rural areas would be the ....
    - (1) soak pit
    - (2) pit privy
    - (3) leaching cesspool
    - (4) septic tank

83. Match List-I (Valves) with List-II (Uses) and select the correct answer using the codes given below the lists :

	List - I		List - II
A.	Sluice valve	1.	Used where gravity flow is required through pipe line
B.	Check valve	2.	Used to maintain constant level of water
C.	Air inlet valve	3.	Used for reversal of flow
D.	Ball valve	4.	Used for isolating

    Codes :

	A	B	C	D
(1)	1	3	4	2
(2)	4	2	1	3
(3)	1	2	4	3
(4)	4	3	1	2

84. Consider the following valves in a water distribution system :
    1. Check valve   2. Pressure-reducing valve
    3. Air relief valve   4. Scour valve   5. Sluice valve
    Which of these work automatically ?
    - (1) 1, 3 and 4
    - (2) 2, 4 and 5
    - (3) 3, 4 and 5
    - (4) 1, 2 and 3

85. Match List-I (Fixture) with List-II (Purpose) and select the correct answer using the codes given below the lists :

	List - I		List - II
A.	Surge arrester	1.	Prevention of reversal of flow in a pipeline
B.	Butterfly valve	2.	Regulating or stopping the flow especially in large size conduits
C.	Scour valve	3.	Control of water hammer
D.	Check valve	4.	Draining or emptying the pipeline section

    Codes :

	A	B	C	D
(1)	1	2	4	3
(2)	3	2	4	1
(3)	1	4	2	3
(4)	3	4	2	1

86. Match List-I (Type of Pipe) with List-II (Purpose) and select the correct answer using the codes given below the lists :

	List - I		List - II
A.	Steel pipe	1.	House plumbing
B.	Cast iron pipe	2.	Hot water carrying
C.	GI Pipe	3.	Distribution main
D.	PVC pipe	4.	Pumping main

Codes :

	A	B	C	D
(1)	4	1	2	3
(2)	4	3	2	1
(3)	2	1	4	3
(4)	2	3	4	1

87. Match List-I (Equation/Method) with List-II (Application) and select the correct answer using the codes given below the lists :

	List - I		List - II
A.	Manning's Equation	1.	Frictional head loss estimation in pipe flow
B.	Darcy-Weisbach	2.	Sanitary sewer design
C.	Hardy Cross Method	3.	Storm sewer design
D.	Rational Method	4.	Water distribution system design

Codes :

	A	B	C	D
(1)	2	1	4	3
(2)	1	4	3	2
(3)	2	1	3	4
(4)	1	4	2	3

88. What is the depth of water seal in the traps ?
    (1) < 2.5 cm   (2) 2.5 - 7.5 cm   (3) 7.5 - 12.5 cm   (4) Not less than 15 cm

89. A commonly used hand pump is the ....
    (1) centrifugal pump   (2) reciprocating pump
    (3) rotary pump   (4) axial flow pump

90. Match List-I (Pump) with List-II (Requirement) and select the correct answer using the codes given below the lists :

	List - I		List - II
A.	Multistage centrifugal pump of moderate sized impellers	1.	High head and low discharge
B.	Archimedean screw type pump	2.	Low head and large discharge
C.	Simple reciprocating pump	3.	High head and moderate discharge
D.	Axial flow propeller pump	4.	Low head and low discharge

Codes :

	A	B	C	D
(1)	4	3	1	2
(2)	3	4	1	2
(3)	4	3	2	1
(4)	3	4	2	1

91. If the total hardness and alkalinity of a sample of water 300 mg/L and 100 mg/L ($CaCO_3$ scale) respectively, then its carbonate and non-carbonate hardness (in units of mg/L) will be respectively ....
    (1) 100 and 200   (2) 400 and 300   (3) 100 and 400   (4) 400 and zero

92. Electrical conductivity (EC) of water and total dissolved solids (TDS) are interrelated. The value of EC will ....
    (1) decrease with increase in TDS
    (2) increase with increase in TDS
    (3) decrease initially and then increase with increase in TDS
    (4) increase initially and then decrease with increase in TDS

93. Which one of the following would contain water with the maximum amount of turbidity ?
    (1) Lakes   (2) Oceans   (3) Rivers   (4) Wells

94. Eutrophication of water bodies is caused by the ....
    (1) discharge of toxic substances
    (2) excessive discharge of nutrients
    (3) excessive discharge of suspended solids
    (4) excessive discharge of chlorides

95. Zero hardness of water is achieved by ....
    (1) using lime soda process   (2) excess lime treatment
    (3) ion exchange method   (4) using excess alum dosage

96. Match List-I with List-II and select the correct answer using the codes given below the lists :

	List - I		List - II
A.	Absence of fluorides	1.	Methaemoglobinemia
B.	Excess of lead	2.	Goitre
C.	Presence of excess nitrates	3.	Dental caries
D.	Absence of iodide	4.	Anaemia

Codes :

	A	B	C	D
(1)	3	4	2	1
(2)	2	3	4	1
(3)	3	4	1	2
(4)	1	2	4	3

97. Which of the following determinations are NOT necessary for raw water from a lake for use as source of supply of water for boiler feed ?
    (i)   Turbidity   (ii) Bacterial count
    (iii) Iron   (iv) Hardness
    Select the correct answer using the codes given below
    (1) (i), (ii) and (iii)   (2) (i), (ii) and (iv)
    (3) (i), (iii) and (iv)   (4) (ii), (iii) and (iv)

98. If the methyl orange alkalinity of water equals or exceeds total hardness, all of the hardness is ....
    (1) non-carbonate hardness   (2) carbonate hardness
    (3) pseudo hardness   (4) negative non-carbonate hardness

99. The usual size of residential ferrule bore varies from ....
    (1) 1 mm to 5 mm   (2) 10 mm to 50 mm
    (3) 100 mm to 500 mm   (4) 1000 mm to 5000 mm

100. Match List-I with List-II and select the correct answer using the codes given below the lists :

	List - I		List - II
A.	Protozoa	1.	Mathaemoglobinemia
B.	Bacteria	2.	Poliomyelitis
C.	Presence of nitrate > 45 mg/L	3.	Dysentery
D.	Virus	4.	Typhoid fever

Codes :

	A	B	C	D
(1)	3	2	1	4
(2)	1	4	3	2
(3)	3	4	1	2
(4)	1	2	3	4

101. Match List-I (Type of impurity) with List-II (Effect) and select the correct answer using the codes given below the lists :

	List - I		List - II
A.	Carbonates and bicarbonates of calcium and magnesium	1.	Permanent hardness
B.	Carbonates and bicarbonates of sodium	2.	Temporary hardness
C.	Sulphates and chlorides of calcium and magnesium	3.	Alkalinity and softness
D.	Oxides of iron and manganese	4.	Colour and taste

Codes :

	A	B	C	D
(1)	1	3	2	4
(2)	2	4	1	3
(3)	1	4	2	3
(4)	2	3	1	4

102. Match List-I (Equipment) with List-II (Parameter) and select the correct answer using the codes given below the lists :

	List - I		List - II
A.	Tintometer	1.	Temperature
B.	Nephelometer	2.	Colour
C.	Imhoff cone	3.	Turbidity
D.	Muffle furnace	4.	Settleable solids
		5.	Volatile solids

Codes :

	A	B	C	D
(1)	4	3	1	5
(2)	2	5	4	3
(3)	4	5	1	3
(4)	2	3	4	5

103. After which of the following treatment units, the turbidity is maximum ?

(1) Chlorination
(2) Primary sedimentation
(3) Flocculation basin
(4) Secondary sedimentation

104. Match List-I with List-II and select the correct answer using the codes given below the lists :

	List - I		List - II
A.	Viruses in water	1.	Parasite-based disease
B.	Depletion of oxygen	2.	Fish extinction
C.	Excess nitrates in water	3.	Methemeglobinemia
D.	Excess fluorides in water	4.	Mottling of teeth

Codes :

	A	B	C	D
(1)	1	2	3	4
(2)	4	2	3	1
(3)	1	3	2	4
(4)	4	3	2	1

105. Match List-I (Process/Bacteria) with List-II (Energy/Material) and select the correct answer using the codes given below the lists :

	List - I		List - II
A.	Anabolism	1.	Providing energy for the synthesis of new cells and maintenance of other cell functions.
B.	Autotrophs	2.	Obtaining energy and material for growth from organic sources
C.	Catabolism	3.	Providing the material necessary for cell growth
D.	Heterotrophs	4.	Obtaining energy and material for growth from inorganic source

Codes :

	A	B	C	D
(1)	1	4	3	2
(2)	3	2	1	4
(3)	1	2	3	4
(4)	3	4	1	2

106. Match List-I (Pathogen) with List-II (Epidemic) and select the correct answer using the codes given below the lists :

	List - I		List - II
A.	Bacteria	1.	Gastroenteritis
B.	Virus	2.	Cholera
C.	Protozoa	3.	Worms
D.	Helminth	4.	Polio

Codes :

	A	B	C	D
(1)	2	4	1	3
(2)	3	1	4	2
(3)	2	1	4	3
(4)	3	4	1	2

107. Match List-I (Type of impurity) with List-II (Harm caused) and select the correct answer using the codes given below the lists :

	List - I		List - II
A.	Excess of nitrates	1.	Brackish water
B.	Excess of fluorides	2.	Goiter
C.	Lack of iodides	3.	Fragile bones
D.	Excess of chlorides	4.	Blue babies

Codes :

	A	B	C	D
(1)	4	2	3	1
(2)	1	2	3	4
(3)	4	3	2	1
(4)	1	3	2	4

108. Match List-I (Parameters) with List-II (Units) and select the correct answer using the codes given below the lists :

	List - I		List - II
A.	Turbidity	1.	TON
B.	Pathogen	2.	TCU
C.	Odour	3.	JTU
D.	Colour	4.	MPN

Codes :

	A	B	C	D
(1)	2	1	4	3
(2)	3	1	4	2
(3)	2	4	1	3
(4)	3	4	1	2

109. The maximum safe permissible limit of sulphates in domestic water supply is ....
    (1) 100 mg/L   (2) 200 mg/L   (3) 500 mg/L   (4) 600 mg/L

110. The following residual chlorine compounds are formed during chlorination of water:
    (a) NH_2Cl (b) $NHCl_2$ (c) HOCl   (d) OCl^-
    The correct sequence of formation of these residual chlorine compounds is
    (1) (b), (a), (c), (d)   (2) (a), (b), (d), (c)
    (3) (a), (b), (c), (d)   (4) (b), (a), (d), (c)

111. Match List-I (Type of Water Source) with List-II (Treatment to be given) and select the correct answer using the codes given below the lists :

List - I		List - II
A.	Surface water (river or canal)	1. Aeration, coagulation, sedimentation and disinfection
B.	Water from infiltration gallery	2. Disinfection
C.	Lake/pond water	3. $CuSO_4$ treatment, coagulation, sedimentation, filtration and disinfection
D.	Tube well water	4. Coagulation, flocculation, sedimentation, filtration and disinfection

    Codes :

	A	B	C	D
(1)	4	1	3	2
(2)	1	4	3	2
(3)	1	4	2	3
(4)	4	1	2	3

112. The cleaning of slow sand filter is done by ....
    (1) reversing the direction of flow of water
    (2) passing air through the filter
    (3) passing a solution of alum and lime through the filter
    (4) scraping off top layers of sand and admitting water

113. Match List-I (Name of impurity in water) with List-II (Removed by) and select the correct answer using the codes given below the lists :

List - I		List - II
A.	Fluorides	1. Activated carbon
B.	Manganese	2. Activated alumina
C.	Taste and odour	3. Manganese zeolite

    Codes :

	A	B	C
(1)	1	2	3
(2)	2	3	1
(3)	2	1	3
(4)	3	2	1

114. Match List-I with List-II and select the correct answer using the codes given below the lists :

List - I		List - II	
A.	Dead-end system	1.	Equal pressures and multiple flow paths
B.	Grid-iron system	2.	Both economy and reasonably equal pressures
C.	Ring system	3.	Economy and simplicity
D.	Radial system	4.	Zonal distribution

   Codes :

	A	B	C	D
(1)	3	2	1	4
(2)	2	4	1	3
(3)	3	1	2	4
(4)	2	1	4	3

115. Air-binding in rapid sand filters is encountered when ....
   - (1) there is excessive negative head
   - (2) the water is subjected to prolonged aeration
   - (3) the raw water contains dissolved gases
   - (4) the filter bed comprises largely of coarse sand

116. In a water treatment plant, dissolved iron and manganese can be removed from the water by ....
   - (1) aeration
   - (2) aeration and coagulation
   - (3) aeration and flocculation
   - (4) aeration and sedimentation

117. The effective size (ES) of sand and its uniformity coefficient (UC) are the usually specified parameters for sand filters. In slow sand filters, as compared to rapid sand filters ....
   - (1) ES is less but UC is more
   - (2) ES is more but UC is less
   - (3) both ES and UC are more
   - (4) both ES and UC are less

118. For proper slow mixing in the flocculator of a water treatment plant, the temporal mean velocity gradient G needs to be of the order of ....
   - (1) 5 to 10 s^{-1}
   - (2) 20 to 80 s^{-1}
   - (3) 100 to 200 s^{-1}
   - (4) 250 to 350 s^{-1}

119. Match List-I (Water treatment units) with List-II (Detention time) and select the correct answer using the codes given below the lists :

List - I		List - II	
A.	Rapid mixing unit	1.	1.5 hours
B.	Flocculator	2.	10 seconds
C.	Propeller mixing unit	3.	30 seconds
D.	Sedimentation tank	4.	30 minutes

   Codes :

	A	B	C	D
(1)	3	4	2	1
(2)	4	3	1	2
(3)	4	3	2	1
(4)	3	4	1	2

120. Match List-I (Nature of the solids) with List-II (Unit operation or process connected with its removal) and select the correct answer using the codes given below the lists:

	List - I		List - II
A.	Dissolved solids	1.	Sedimentation
B.	Colloidal solids	2.	Reverse osmosis
C.	Volatile solids	3.	Coagulation
D.	Settleable solids	4.	Digestion

Codes :

	A	B	C	D
(1)	2	3	4	1
(2)	3	2	4	1
(3)	2	3	1	4
(4)	3	2	1	4

121. The correct sequence of processes in a water treatment plant for rural water supply is ....
   (1) chlorination, aeration, sedimentation, rapid sand filter
   (2) coagulation, sedimentation, slow sand filter, chlorination
   (3) coagulation, flocculation, clarification, pressure filter
   (4) aeration, plain sedimentation, slow sand filter, chlorination

122. A rural water supply scheme serves a population of 10,000 at the rate of 50 litres per capita per day. For the chlorine dose of 2 ppm, the required amount of bleaching powder with 20% available chlorine will be ....
   (1) 0.5 kg   (2) 5 kg   (3) 10 kg   (4) 15 kg

123. Which one of the following filters will produce water of higher bacteriological quality ?
   (1) Slow sand filter   (2) Rapid sand filter
   (3) Pressure filter   (4) Dual media filter

124. Match List-I (Unit in water treatment plant) with List-II (Impurities removed) and select the correct answer using the codes given below the lists :

	List - I		List - II
A.	Aerator	1.	Excess CO_2 and H_2S
B.	Rapid sand filter	2.	Settleable and colloidal matter
C.	Slow sand filter	3.	Suspended matter
D.	Sedimentation tank (after coagulation and flocculation)	4.	Suspended, colloidal and bacteriological matter

Codes :

	A	B	C	D
(1)	1	3	2	4
(2)	3	1	2	4
(3)	3	1	4	2
(4)	1	3	4	2

125. Which of the following are the common problems associated with the operation of rapid sand-filter ?
     1. Air binding
     2. Cracking of sand beds
     3. Bumping of filter beds
     4. Mud balls
     Select the correct answer using the codes given below :
     (1) 1 and 2   (2) 2 and 3   (3) 2, 3 and 4   (4) 1, 2, 3 and 4

126. Match List-I (Impurities) with List-II (Effects) and select the correct answer using the codes given below the lists :

     List - I
     A. Dissolved sulphates and chlorides of Ca and Mg
     B. Dissolved bicarbonates of Ca and Mg
     C. Dissolved fluorides of Na
     D. Dissolved organic matter

     List - II
     1. Hardness and corrosion
     2. Bacterial infection
     3. Alkalinity and softness
     4. Impairment of dental health

     Codes :

	A	B	C	D
(1)	2	3	4	1
(2)	1	4	3	2
(3)	2	4	3	1
(4)	1	3	4	2

127. Match List-I (Water quality) with List-II (Method of determination) and select the correct answer using the codes given below the lists :

     List - I
     A. Hardness
     B. Chlorine
     C. DO
     D. Chloride

     List - II
     1. Winkler's method
     2. EDTA method
     3. Orthotolidine test
     4. Mohr method

     Codes :

	A	B	C	D
(1)	2	3	1	4
(2)	2	4	1	3
(3)	1	3	2	4
(4)	1	4	2	3

128. Match List-I (Different forms of nitrogen in water) with List-II (Inferences) and select the correct answer using the codes given below the lists :

     List - I
     A. Nitrate nitrogen
     B. Total nitrogen
     C. Nitrite nitrogen
     D. Ammonia nitrogen

     List - II
     1. Unsatisfactory microbial activity
     2. Satisfactory microbial activity
     3. Eutrophication may result
     4. Recent organic pollution

     Codes :

	A	B	C	D
(1)	3	2	1	4
(2)	1	4	3	2
(3)	3	4	1	2
(4)	1	2	3	4

129. 'Air binding' may occur in ....
    (1) Sewers   (2) Artesian well   (3) Aerator   (4) Filter

130. The purpose of re-carbonation after lime soda process of water softening is the ....
    (1) removal of excess soda from water
    (2) removal of non-carbonate hardness
    (3) recovery of lime
    (4) conversion of precipitates to soluble form

131. Which of the following treatment processes are necessary for removing suspended solids from water ?
    1. Coagulation   2. Flocculation   3. Sedimentation   4. Disinfection
    Select the correct answer using the codes given below :
    (1) 1 and 2   (2) 1, 2 and 3   (3) 2 and 4   (4) 1 and 4

132. Match List-I (Filter operating problems) with List-II (Effects) and select the correct answer using the codes given below the lists :

List - I	List - II
A. Air binding	1. Changes effective size of sand
B. Mud deposition	2. Mud penetrates deeper inside the bed
C. Cracking of bed	3. Mounds and balls of mud are formed in the bed
D. Sand incrustation	4. Air and gases get locked in the bed

    Codes :

	A	B	C	D
(1)	4	3	2	1
(2)	3	4	1	2
(3)	4	3	1	2
(4)	3	4	2	1

133. Which one of the following units is employed for the removal of particulate matter above 50 μm in size ?
    (1) Gravity settling chamber   (2) Cyclone
    (3) Fabric filter   (4) Electrostatic precipitator

134. Which one of the following is not a specific criterion for calculating surface overflow rates in sedimentation tank design ?
    (1) Total quantity of water to be treated (2) Total surface area available in the tank
    (3) Total length of the tank   (4) Total depth of the tank

135. Match List-I (Water/Waste water parameter) with List-II (Test) and select the correct answer using the codes given below the lists :

List - I	List - II
A. Potability of water	1. Mohr's method
B. Chloride	2. Orthotolidine test
C. Residual chlorine	3. EDTA method
D. Hardness of water	4. MF technique

Codes :

	A	B	C	D
(1)	4	3	2	1
(2)	2	1	4	3
(3)	2	3	4	1
(4)	4	1	2	3

136. Match List-I (Equation/Law) with List-II (Related Application) and select the correct answer using the codes given below the lists :

	List - I		**List - II**
A.	Chick's law	1.	Discrete particle settling
B.	Darcy-Weisbach equation	2.	Head loss in a pipe
C.	Stoke's equation	3.	Head loss in filters
D.	Carmen-kozeny equation	4.	Rate of bacterial kill

Codes :

	A	B	C	D
(1)	4	2	1	3
(2)	3	1	2	4
(3)	4	1	2	3
(4)	3	2	1	4

137. Which one of the following types of settling phenomenon can be analyzed by the classic sedimentation laws of Newton and Stokes ?
    (1) Discrete settling
    (2) Flocculent settling
    (3) Hindered settling
    (4) Compression settling

138. Match List-I (Treatment process) with List-II (Removed matter) and select the correct answer using the codes given below the lists :

	List - I		**List - II**
A.	Plain sedimentation	1.	Dissolved gases
B.	Chemical precipitation	2.	Dissolved solids
C.	Slow Sand Filtration	3.	Suspended solids with specific gravity more than 1.0
D.	Aeration	4.	Floating solids
		5.	Bacterial cells

Codes :

	A	B	C	D
(1)	5	1	4	2
(2)	3	2	5	1
(3)	5	2	4	1
(4)	3	1	5	2

139. Among the following, which is/are not pre-treatment unit(s) ?
    (1) Bar-screen and grit chamber
    (2) Flow equalization and proportioning tank
    (3) Neutralization of pH adjustment tank
    (4) Nutrient removal tank

140. Chlorides from water are removed by ....
    (1) Lime soda process
    (2) Reverse osmosis
    (3) Cation exchange process
    (4) Chemical coagulation

141. In which treatment unit is Schmutzdecke formed ?
    (1) Sedimentation tank
    (2) Rapid sand filter
    (3) Coagulation tank
    (4) Slow sand filter

142. Which one of the following chemicals is employed for dechlorination of water ?
    (1) Sodium sulphite
    (2) Sodium bicarbonate
    (3) Calcium carbonate
    (4) Hydrogen peroxide

143. Which one of the following is the correct sequence of slow sand filter (SSF), rapid sand filter (RSF), dual media filter (DMF) and mixed media filter (MMF) in the decreasing order of their filtration rates ?
    (1) MMF ≈ DMF > RSF > SSF
    (2) DMF > RSF > SSF > MMF
    (3) RSF > SSF > MMF ≈ DMF
    (4) SSF > MMF ≈ DMF > RSF

144. Match List-I (Parameter) with List-II (Impact) and select the correct answer using the codes given below the lists :

	List - I		List - II
A.	Excess sulphates	1.	Greater soap consumption
B.	Lack of iodide	2.	Laxative effect
C.	Excess hardness	3.	Goitre
D.	Excess dissolved oxygen	4.	Corrosion of pipes

    Codes :

	A	B	C	D
(1)	2	1	3	4
(2)	4	3	1	2
(3)	2	3	1	4
(4)	4	1	3	2

145. The concentration of hardness producing cations may be estimated using which one of the following ?
    (1) Conductivity meter
    (2) pH meter
    (3) Spectrophotometer
    (4) Flame photometer

146. Which one of the following treatments is economically effective in the control of guinea worm disease ?
    (1) Chlorination　　(2) Filtration　　(3) Ozonation　　(4) Sedimentation

147. Match List-I (Disinfectant) with List-II (Property) and select the correct answer using the codes given below the lists :

	List - I		List - II
A.	Chlorine	1.	No carcinogenic results
B.	Ozone	2.	Ineffective in the presence of suspended solids
C.	Iodine	3.	Not affected by the Ammonium ion
D.	Ultra-violet rays	4.	Feasible residual oxygen

Codes :

	A	B	C	D
(1)	4	3	1	2
(2)	1	2	4	3
(3)	4	2	1	3
(4)	1	3	4	2

148. What is the predominating coagulation mechanism for raw water having high turbidity and high alkalinity ?
(1) Ionic layer compression
(2) Adsorption and charge neutralization
(3) Sweep coagulation
(4) Inter particle bridging

149. Match List-I (Predominance of compounds) with List-II (pH range) and select the correct answer using the codes given below the lists :

List - I		List - II	
A.	Monochloramine	1.	Below pH 4.4
B.	Dichloramine	2.	Over pH 7.5
C.	Nitrogen trichloride	3.	Between pH 5 to 6.5

Codes :

	A	B	C
(1)	1	2	3
(2)	2	3	1
(3)	3	1	2
(4)	3	2	1

150. Which one of the following can fix atmospheric nitrogen ?
(1) Green algae
(2) Blue green algae
(3) Red algae
(4) Brown algae

151. What is the most important design parameter used in designing a continuous flow rectangular sedimentation tank for removal of discrete particles ?
(1) Length of the tank
(2) Surface overflow rate
(3) Depth of the tank
(4) Temperature of the water to be treated

152. Which combination of surface water quality parameters will indicate sweep coagulation as the preferred mechanism of coagulation ?
(1) High turbidity - low alkalinity
(2) High turbidity - high alkalinity
(3) Low turbidity - high alkalinity
(4) Low turbidity - low alkalinity

153. Which one of the following processes of water softening requires recarbonation ?
(1) Lime-soda ash process
(2) Hydrogen-cation exchanger process
(3) Sodium-cation exchanger process
(4) Demineralization

154. Consider the following treatment process units in a water treatment plant :
1. Coagulation   2. Disinfection   3. Sedimentation   4. Filtration
Which is the correct sequence of the process units in the water treatment plant ?
(1) 2–4–3–1
(2) 1–4–3–2
(3) 2–3–4–1
(4) 1–3–4–2

155. Which one of the following tests of water/wastewater employs Erichrome Black T as an indicator ?
    (1) Hardness   (2) COD
    (3) Residual chlorine   (4) DO

156. If organic sources of carcinogenic compounds in water persist even after chlorination, then what is the correct sequence among treatment processes listed below if all these are considered compulsory ?
    1. Coagulation   2. Sedimentation
    3. Filtration in general   4. Activated carbon bed filtration
    5. Flocculation   6. Chlorination
    (1) 4, 5, 3, 2, 6 and 1   (2) 1, 2, 3, 4, 5 and 6
    (3) 4, 2, 3, 1, 5 and 6   (4) 1, 5, 2, 3, 4 and 6

ANSWER KEY

1.	(3)	2.	(3)	3.	(2)	4.	(4)	5.	(3)	6.	(4)	7.	(1)	8.	(4)
9.	(2)	10.	(1)	11.	(2)	12.	(1)	13.	(3)	14.	(2)	15.	(1)	16.	(1)
17.	(4)	18.	(3)	19.	(2)	20.	(1)	21.	(3)	22.	(3)	23.	(4)	24.	(4)
25.	(1)	26.	(1)	27.	(2)	28.	(1)	29.	(1)	30.	(1)	31.	(1)	32.	(4)
33.	(4)	34.	(4)	35.	(3)	36.	(1)	37.	(1)	38.	(2)	39.	(2)	40.	(1)
41.	(2)	42.	(1)	43.	(2)	44.	(1)	45.	(1)	46.	(1)	47.	(1)	48.	(1)
49.	(2)	50.	(1)	51.	(4)	52.	(1)	53.	(3)	54.	(2)	55.	(2)	56.	(1)
57.	(2)	58.	(2)	59.	(1)	60.	(2)	61.	(2)	62.	(1)	63.	(4)	64.	(1)
65.	(2)	66.	(1)	67.	(1)	68.	(2)	69.	(1)	70.	(1)	71.	(2)	72.	(1)
73.	(1)	74.	(2)	75.	(1)	76.	(4)	77.	(2)	78.	(1)	79.	(2)	80.	(2)
81.	(4)	82.	(4)	83.	(4)	84.	(4)	85.	(2)	86.	(2)	87.	(1)	88.	(2)
89.	(2)	90.	(2)	91.	(1)	92.	(2)	93.	(3)	94.	(2)	95.	(3)	96.	(3)
97.	(1)	98.	(2)	99.	(2)	100.	(3)	101.	(4)	102.	(4)	103.	(3)	104.	(1)
105.	(4)	106.	(1)	107.	(3)	108.	(4)	109.	(2)	110.	(3)	111.	(1)	112.	(4)
113.	(2)	114.	(4)	115.	(1)	116.	(4)	117.	(1)	118.	(2)	119.	(1)	120.	(1)
121.	(4)	122.	(2)	123.	(1)	124.	(4)	125.	(4)	126.	(4)	127.	(1)	128.	(1)
129.	(4)	130.	(4)	131.	(2)	132.	(1)	133.	(1)	134.	(4)	135.	(4)	136.	(1)
137.	(1)	138.	(2)	139.	(4)	140.	(2)	141.	(4)	142.	(1)	143.	(1)	144.	(2)
145.	(3)	146.	(2)	147.	(1)	148.	(3)	149.	(2)	150.	(2)	151.	(2)	152.	(2)
153.	(1)	154.	(4)	155.	(1)	156.	(4)										

❖ ❖ ❖

UNIT - 10 : AIR POLLUTION AND NOISE POLLUTION

1. Air pollution from a variety of sources and contaminants which causes adverse social, economical and health effects, is classified under
   (1) Personnel air pollution   (2) Occupational air pollution
   (3) Community air pollution   (4) all of above
2. A small discrete mass of solid or liquid matter is called
   (1) particle   (2) dust   (3) fune   (4) droplet
3. Two primary air pollutants are
   (1) sulphur oxide and ozone   (2) nitrogen oxide and peroxy acetyl nitrate
   (3) sulphur oxide and peroxyacetylnitrate
   (4) ozone and peroxyacetylnitrate
4. Match the following :
   (A) Dust particles   (i) Death by asphyxiation
   (B) Hydrogen Fluoride   (ii) Asthama
   (C) CO   (iii) Mottling of teeth
   (D) Pollens   (iv) Silicosis
   Codes :

	(A)	(B)	(C)	(D)
(1)	(i)	(ii)	(iv)	(iii)
(2)	(iv)	(iii)	(i)	(ii)
(3)	(iv)	(iii)	(ii)	(i)
(4)	(ii)	(iv)	(i)	(iii)

5. Aerosol is a :
   (1) dispersion of small solids in liquid media
   (2) dispersion of small solids or liquid particles in gaseous media
   (3) finely divided particles of smoke
   (4) dispersion of liquid particles
6. Match the following :
   (A) Gravitational settler   (i) 50-90% removal efficiency of P.M. (particulate matter)
   (B) Electrostatic precipitator (ii) > 99% removal efficiency of P.M.
   (C) Fabric filtration   (iii) < 50% removal efficiency of P.M.
   (D) Centrifugal collector   (iv) 95-99% removal efficiency of P.M.
   Codes :

	(A)	(B)	(C)	(D)
(1)	(i)	(ii)	(iv)	(iii)
(2)	(iii)	(iv)	(i)	(ii)
(3)	(i)	(iv)	(ii)	(iii)
(4)	(iii)	(iv)	(ii)	(i)

7. The major source of 'carbon monoxide' in the urban atmosphere is due to,
   (1) decomposition of organics
   (2) chemical reaction between VOC and NO_x
   (3) incomplete combustion of fuel
   (4) incomplete combustion in the presence of sunlight

8. Consider the following statements :
   (a) Sound is a form of mechanical energy from a vibrating substance, transmitted by a cyclic series of compressions and rarefactions of the molecules of the material through which it passes.
   (b) In a pure tone, the wave pattern of the alternating positive and negative sound pressure is of ideal sinusoidal form with fixed wave length, frequency and amplitude.
   (c) The speed of transmission of sound is a function of the transmitting medium and its temperature.
   (d) The audible range of 200 to 25000 Hz is considered normal for young adults.
       Which of these statements are correct in respect of sound transmission ?
   (1) (a), (b), (c) and (d)   (2) (a), (b) and (d) only
   (3) (a), (b) and (c) only   (4) (b), (c) and (d) only

9. Consider the following statements :
   (a) Noise pollution can be reduced using double-glass window panes.
   (b) Glass absorbs the noise.
   (c) The air trapped in the double-glass system acts as an insulator and reduces the noise.
   (d) The noise totally reflects back due to the two layers of glass.
       Which of these statements are correct ?
   (1) (a), (b), (c) and (d)   (2) (a), (b) and (c) only
   (3) (a) and (c) only   (4) (b) and (d) only

10. Consider the following statements in regard to an electrostatic precipitator :
    (a) Power requirement is small compared to other devices.
    (b) Immune to variable particulate loadings and flow rates.
    (c) 99 % efficiency is obtainable. Very small particles can be collected wet or dry.
    (d) Can handle both gases and mists at high volume of flow.
        Which of these statements are correct ?
    (1) (a), (b), (c) and (d)   (2) (a), (c) and (d) only
    (3) (a), (b) and (c) only   (4) (b), (c) and (d) only

11. Environmental impact assessment includes :
    (1) Environmental statement   (2) Environmental management plan
    (3) Risk and hazard assessment and mitigation
    (4) All of the above

12. For noise measurement, formula for sound pressure level (SPL) is $20 \log \dfrac{P}{P_{ref}}$. What will be the resultant noise in dB if P is 0.0002 μbar ?
    (1) 0   (2) 60   (3) 90   (4) 100

13. Which of the following factors contribute to formation of photochemical smog ?
    (a) Stable atmospheres   (b) NO_x
    (c) Solar insolation   (d) CO
        Which options are correct ?
    (1) (a), (b), (c) and (d)   (2) (b), (c) and (d) only
    (3) (a) and (d) only   (4) (a), (b) and (c) only

14. Which of the following are responsible for the information of photochemical smog ?
    (a) Light intensity   (b) Ratio of hydrocarbons to nitric oxide
    (c) CO_2 (d) Hydrocarbon reactivity
    (e) SO_2
    Answer options :
    (1) (a), (b), (c), (d) and (e)   (2) (a), (b) and (d) only
    (3) (b), (c) and (d) only   (4) (b), (c) and (e) only
15. Particulate matter (fly ash) carried in effluent gases from the furnaces burning fossil fuels are better removed by
    (1) cotton bag house filter   (2) electrostatic precipitator (ESP)
    (3) cyclone   (4) wet scrubber
16. Consider the following statements relating zones of atmosphere to altitude :
    (a) Temperature decreases with altitude in troposphere.
    (b) Speed of sound decreases with altitude in troposphere.
    (c) Temperature increases with altitude in stratosphere.
    (d) Ozone is present in stratosphere which protects people from harmful effects of solar radiation.
    Which of the above statements are correct?
    (1) (a), (b), and (c) only   (2) (a), (b), and (d) only
    (3) (c) and (d) only   (4) (a), (b), (c), and (d)
17. The principle involved in collection and sampling of particulate matter in which the particles are drawn through a device by deflecting them from their original paths is called
    (1) filtration   (2) electronic precipitation
    (3) impaction   (4) gravitational settling
18. Consider the following statements related to noise pollution :
    (a) Silence zone is 100 m distance from institutions, hospitals etc.
    (b) Sound beyond 80 B harms human hearing system.
    (c) Noise from automobiles is measured at 2 m free field distance.
    Which of the above statements are correct
    (1) (a) and (b)   (2) (b) and (c)
    (3) (a) and (c)   (4) (a), (b) and (c)
19. Acid rain is caused by increase in the atmospheric concentration of :
    (1) Ozone and dust
    (2) Sulphur dioxide (SO_2) and nitrogen dioxide (NO_2)
    (3) Sulphur trioxide (SO_3) and carbon monoxide (CO)
    (4) Carbon dioxide (CO_2) and oxygen (O_2)
20. Efficiency of conventional cyclones as air pollution control device for particle size range 5 – 20 % lies between :
    (1) 50 to 80%   (2) Less than 50%
    (3) 80 to 95%   (4) 95 to 99%

21. The ambient air quality standards of noise in industrial area during day time and night time are respectively :
    (1) 75 and 70 dB (A) Leq.   (2) 70 to 75 dB (A) Leq.
    (3) 35 to 55 dB (A) Leq.   (4) 55 to 65 dB (A) Leq.

22. The term 'biological magnification' indicates which one of the following ?
    (1) Likelihood of increasing size of animals during evolution
    (2) Magnification pertaining to microscopy
    (3) Accumulation of pollutants in soil
    (4) Accumulation of pollutants in successive consumers

23. A heterotroph is an organism that obtains
    (1) its cell carbon from an inorganic source
    (2) its energy from the oxidation of simple inorganic compounds
    (3) its cell carbon as well as its energy from organic matter
    (4) its energy from a natural ecosystem

24. A machine in a steel plate fabricating industry is found to be producing a sound level of 50 dB. In the expansion plans one more such machine needs to be added. What will be the combined noise level ?
    (1) 80 - 100 dB (2) 101 - 150 dB (3) 51 - 70 dB (4) 40 - 50 dB

25. Which type of plume may occur during winter nights ?
    (1) Looping   (2) Inversion   (3) Coning   (4) Lofting

26. Match List-I (Air pollutant) with List-II (Impact on human health) and select the correct answer using the codes given below the lists :

        List - I   **List - II**
    (A) Particulates   (1) Impairs transport of O_2 in bloodstream
    (B) Carbon monoxide   (2) Irritation of mucous membranes of respiratory
    (C) Sulphur oxides   tract
    (D) Photochemical oxidants (3) Causes coughing, shortness of breath, headache,
                  etc.
                  (4) Causes respiratory illness

    Codes :

	A	B	C	D
(1)	2	3	4	1
(2)	4	1	2	3
(3)	2	1	4	3
(4)	4	3	2	1

27. Which one of the following pairs is not correctly matched ?
    (1) Coriolis effect : The effect of earth's rotation on wind direction and velocity
    (2) PAN :   Found during photochemical smog
    (3) Cyclone :   Employed for particulate matter removal
    (4) Wind rose :   Employed in forecast of pollutant dispersion in ambient air

28. Which one of the following is the range of ozonosphere in atmosphere ?
    (1) Troposphere to Stratosphere (2) Tropopause to Stratosphere
    (3) Tropopause to Mesophere   (4) Stratosphere to Mesophere

29. The reference pressure used in the determination of sound/pressure Level (SPL) is
     (1) 20 μpa   (2) 20 dB   (3) 10 μPa   (4) 40 dB

30. Which is the major pollutant present in photochemical smog ?
     (1) PAN   (2) SO_2 (3) HC   (4) NO_2

31. An air parcel having 40°C temperature move from ground level to 500 m elevation in dry
     air following the 'adiabatic lapse rate'. The resulting temperature of air parcel at 500 m
     elevation will be
     (1) 35°C   (2) 38°C   (3) 41°C   (4) 44°C

32. The presence of hardness in excess of permissible limit causes
     (1) cardio-vascular problems   (2) skin discolouration
     (3) calcium deficiency   (4)increased laundry expenses

33. According to the Noise pollution (Regulation and Control) Rules, 2000 of the Ministry of
     Environment and Ferots, India, the day time and night time noise level limits in ambient
     air for residential area expressed in dB (A) Leq are
     (1) 50 and 40   (2) 55 and 45   (3) 65 and 55   (4) 75 and 70

34. Consider four common air pollutants found in urban environments, NO, SO_2, Soot and
     O_3. Among these which one is secondary air pollutant.
     (1) O_3 (2) NO   (3) SO_2 (4) Soot

35. What is the Decibel (dB) value of sound during normal conversation?
     (1) 0 dB   (2) 20 dB   (3) 80 dB   (4) 60 dB

36. The cumulative noise power distribution curve at a certain location is given below.

The value of L_{40} is equal to
     (1) 90 dBA   (2) 80 dBA   (3) 70 dBA   (4) 60 dBA

37. Total Kjeldahl nitrogen is a measure of
     (1) total organic nitrogen   (2) total organic and ammonia nitrogen
     (3) total ammonia nitrogen   (4) total inorganic and ammonia nitrogen

38. Pneumoconiosis is caused due to inhalation of which one of the following ?
     (1) Silica   (2) NO_x (3) Lead   (4) Cadmium

39. Which one of the following conditions of automobile gives maximum unburned
     hydrocarbons ?
     (1) Idling   (2) Cruise   (3) Acceleration   (4) Deceleration

40. Electrostatic precipitator is most useful for which one of the following industries ?
     (1) Tannery   (2) Hydroelectric power generation
     (3) Thermal power generation   (4) Textile factory

41. What will be the resultant decibel level when two sources make noise of equal decibels ?
    (1) Decibel level will be the same.   (2) Decibel level will increase by 3 decibels.
    (3) Decibel level will decrease by 3 decibels.
    (4) Decibel level will be equal to the sum of decibels of the two sources.

42. Match List-I (Air pollutants) with List-II (Effects) and select the correct answer using the codes given below the lists :

	List - I		List - II
A.	CO	1.	Acid rain
B.	CO_2	2.	Acute toxicity
C.	SO_2	3.	Ozone liberation
D.	NO_x	4.	Green house effect

    Codes :

	A	B	C	D
(1)	4	3	1	2
(2)	4	3	2	1
(3)	2	4	1	3
(4)	3	4	1	1

43. Among the following which equipment cannot be used for measurement of noise?
    (1) Sound Level Meter   (2) Octave Band Analyser
    (3) Tintometer   (4) Cassette recorder

44. Which one of the following toxic gases has physiological action as asphyxiant ?
    (1) SO_2 (2) NO_2 (3) Cl_2 (4) CO

45. Assuming annual travel for each vehicle to be 20000 km, what is the quantity of NO_x produced from 50000 vehicles with emission rate of 2.0 g/km/vehicle ?
    (1) 1800 tonnes   (2) 1900 tonnes   (3) 2000 tonnes   (4) 2100 tonnes

46. What are the air pollutants responsible for acid rain within and downwind areas of major industrial emission ?
    (1) Hydrogen sulphide and oxides of nitrogen
    (2) Sulphur dioxide and oxides of nitrogen
    (3) Carbon dioxide and hydrogen sulphide
    (4) Methane and hydrogen sulphide

47. Consider the following air pollutants :
    (a) NO_x (b) PAN   (c) CO_2 (d) CO
    Which of the above air pollutants is/are present in an auto exhaust gas ?
    (1) (a) only   (2) (a) and (b)   (3) (b) and (c)   (4) (a), (c) and (d)

48. Noise pollution in a road-side building can be reduced by
    (1) providing a ditch around the building and filling it with water
    (2) providing a steel mesh around the building
    (3) providing a thick bush around the building
    (4) planting tall trees around the building and fencing them with barbed wires

49. In aerobic environment nitrosomonas convert
    (1) NH_3 to NO_2 (2) NO_2^- to NO_3^- (3) NH_3 to N_2O (4) NO_2^- to HNO_3

50. Which gas out of following is found highest by volume in air?
    (1) Nitrogen   (2) Ozone   (3) Oxygen   (4) Methane
51. Incomplete burning of petrol or diesel in vehicles creates .... gas which is very poisonous.
    (1) Carbon dioxide   (2) Carbon monoxide
    (3) Methane   (4) Ozone
52. Combustion of coal in power plant produces mainly .... which is a major pollutant of air.
    (1) Sulphur dioxide   (2) Nitrogen dioxide
    (3) Methane   (4) Chlorofluorocarbons
53. Taj Mahal is said to be suffering from "Marble Cancer " . What is Marble Cancer?
    (1) Acidic Rain which corrodes marble.
    (2) Large number of Fungus in Taj Mahal marbles.
    (3) Yellowing of the marble on account of soot particles.
    (4) Smokes filling the Taj Mahal from adjoining industries.
54. Which gas is responsible for depletion of ozone layer around earth which protects us from harmful ultraviolet rays ?
    (1) Chlorofluoro carbons   (2) Nitrogen
    (3) Oxygen   (4) Nitrogen oxide
55. Which gas is primarily responsible for Green House Effect i.e global warming. ?
    (1) Hydrogen dioxide   (2) Carbon dioxide
    (3) CFC   (4) Sulpher dioxide
56. What is Kyoto Protocol ?
    (1) It is an agreement among countries to take steps for reducing global warming.
    (2) It is an agreement among countries to take steps for reducing acid rain .
    (3) It is an agreement among countries to take steps for planting trees to control pollution.
    (4) It is an agreement among countries to start using nuclear energy.
57. Match List - I with List - II and select the correct answer using the codes given below the lists :

List-I		List-II	
(A)	Test with sound waves in the audible frequency range	(1)	To determine the ability of a distribution system to transmit water with adequate residual pressure
		(2)	Location and isolation of leaks
(B)	Fire flow tests	(3)	To determine the efficiency and adequacy of a distribution system during days of high demand
(C)	Hydraulic gradient tests		
		(4)	To determine the internal condition of pipeline with respect to friction loss
(D)	Coefficient tests		

Codes :

	A	B	C	D
(1)	2	1	3	4
(2)	2	3	1	4
(3)	4	1	3	2
(4)	4	3	1	2

58. Which one of the following procedures is used for sampling of the flue gas in a chimney for SPM ?
    (1) Isothermal sampling
    (2) Isokinetic sampling
    (3) Adiabatic condition
    (4) Variable rate of sampling

59. Acoustics of an auditorium is considered to be excellent when its reverberation time is between
    (1) 0.50 and 1.50 s
    (2) 1.50 and 2.00 s
    (3) 2.00 and 3.00 s
    (4) 3.00 and 5.00 s

60. Which type of light energy is effectively absorbed by CO_2 in the lower boundary of the troposphere ?
    (1) X-rays
    (2) UV-rays
    (3) Visible light
    (4) Infra-red rays

61. Which one of the following is the correct sound intensity expression with usual notations ?
    (1) $dB = 10 \log_{10}(I/I_0)^2$
    (2) $dB = 10 \log_{10}(I/I_0)$
    (3) $dB = 10 \log_{10}(I - I_0)^2$
    (4) $dB = 10 \log_{10}(I - I_0)$

62. What type of noise can be abated by providing lining on walls and ceiling with sound absorbing materials ?
    (1) Source noise
    (2) Reflection noise
    (3) Structural noise
    (4) Direct air-borne noise

63. Which one of the following pairs is not correctly matched ?
    Plume Behaviour   **Atmospheric Condition**
    (1) Looping :   Stable
    (2) Fumigation :   Inversion above and lapse below the stack
    (3) Fanning :   Inversion
    (4) Trapping :   Inversion above and below the stack with lapse in between

64. India celebrates Van Mahotsav every year in the month of .... in which lakhs of trees are planted across the country.
    (1) June
    (2) July
    (3) August
    (4) September

65. Match List-I (Equipment) with List-II (Pollutants removed) and select the correct answer using the codes given below the lists :

	List - I		List - II
A.	Electrostatic precipitators	1.	Coarse particles
B.	Cyclones	2.	Fine dust
C.	Wet scrubbers	3.	Gas
D.	Adsorbers	4.	Sulphur dioxide

    Codes :

	A	B	C	D
(1)	1	2	3	4
(2)	2	1	3	4
(3)	2	1	4	3
(4)	1	2	4	3

66. Two sources generate noise levels of 90 dB and 94 dB respectively. The cumulative effect of these two noise levels on the human ear is
    (1)   184 dB   (2)   95.5 dB   (3)   94 dB   (4)   92 dB

67. Match List-I (Pollutants) with List-II (Sources) and select the correct answer using the codes given below the lists :

	List - I		List - II
A.	Acid water	1.	Volcanoes
B.	SO_2	2,	Automobiles
C.	CO	3.	Thermal power station
D.	Fly ash	4.	Mining

Codes :

	A	B	C	D
(1)	4	1	2	3
(2)	4	1	3	2
(3)	1	4	3	2
(4)	1	4	2	3

68. In sampling of stack gases for measurement of concentration of Suspended Particulate Matter (SPM), the flue gases are sucked in the instrument at
    (1) any rate of flow from mid diameter of chimney.
    (2) any point of chimney cross-section and at any rate of flow.
    (3) a constant rate of flow but an hour equidistant points along the diameter.
    (4) controlled positions and controlled velocities along the chimney diameter to get isokinetic conditions.

69. Match List - I (Air pollutants) with List-II (Harmful effects) and select the correct answer using the codes given below the lists :

	List - I		List-II
A.	SPM	1.	Blood heamoglobin
B.	NO	2.	Vegetation
C.	CO	3.	Respiratory system
D.	SO_2	4.	Building materials

Codes :

	A	B	C	D
(1)	3	4	1	2
(2)	1	2	3	4
(3)	3	2	1	4
(4)	1	4	3	2

70. Match List-I (Air pollutants) with List-II (Emitted mainly by) and select the correct answer using the codes given below the lists :

	List - I		List - II
A.	Hydrocarbons	1.	Coal burning
B.	Particulates and gases	2.	Gasoline fuel
C.	Sulphur dioxide	3.	Tyres
D.	Carbon monoxide	4.	Carburettor

Codes :

	A	B	C	D
(1)	3	4	2	1
(2)	4	3	2	1
(3)	3	4	1	2
(4)	4	3	1	2

71. Which one of the following statements explains the term pyrolysis ?
    (1) Solid waste is heated in closed containers in oxygen-free atmosphere.
    (2) Solid waste is incinerated in presence of oxygen.
    (3) Wastewater is treated with oxygen.
    (4) Dissolved solids from water are removed by glass distillation.

72. In urban air pollution, the most poisonous gas is supposed to be carbon monoxide. It is hazardous because it
    (1) affects our sense of smell   (2) is carcinogenic in nature
    (3) combines with hemoglobin   (4) causes blindness

73. The graph shows the relationship of ambient lapse rates to the dry adiabatic lapse rate under different conditions of stability. Match stability situations A, B, C and D (as given in the graph) with the classes of stability as follows :
    (1) Super adiabatic   (2) Dry adiabatic
    (3) Sub adiabatic   (4) Inversion

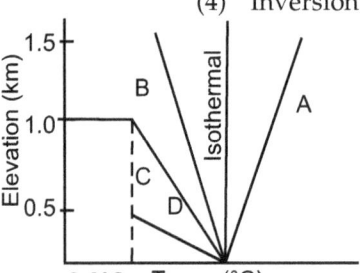

Select the correct answer using the codes given below :

Codes :

	A	B	C	D
(1)	3	4	1	2
(2)	4	3	2	1
(3)	3	4	2	1
(4)	4	3	1	2

74. Ozone layer in the stratosphere is being destroyed by :
    (1) Sulphur dioxide   (2) Carbon dioxide
    (3) Photochemical oxidants   (4) Chlorofluorocarbon

75. Which of the following is an air pollutant?
    (1) Nitrogen   (2) Carbon dioxide
    (3) Carbon monoxide   (4) Oxygen

76. Which of the following is a secondary air pollutant?
    (1) Ozone   (2) Carbon dioxide
    (3) Carbon monoxide   (4) Sulphur dioxide

77. The environmental lapse rate is found to be :
    (1) – 6.5°C/km   (2) 8.6°C/km   (3) 6.5°C/km   (4) 5.6°C/km

78. Among the following, the only secondary pollutant is:
    (1) Sulphur tetraoxide   (2) Sulphur dioxide
    (3) Ozone   (4) Sulphur tetraoxide

79. Which of the following groups of plants can be used as indicators of SO pollution of air?
    (1) Epiphytic lichens   (2) Ferns
    (3) Liver worts   (4) Horn worts

80. Which of the following on inhalation dissolved in the blood hemoglobin more rapidly than oxygen?
    (1) Sulphur dioxide   (2) Carbon mono-oxide
    (3) Ozone   (4) Nitrous oxide

81. Smog is :
    (1) a natural phenomenon   (2) a combination of smoke and fog
    (3) is colourless   (4) all of the above

82. Which of the following air pollutants are responsible for the green house effect ?
    (a) Methane   (b) Carbon dioxide
    (c) Chlorofluorocarbons   (d) Nitrogen oxides
    Select the correct answer using the codes given below :
    (1) (b) and (c)   (2) (a) and (b)
    (3) (a), (c) and (d)   (4) (a), (b), (c) and (d)

83. Which of the following pairs are correctly matched ?
    (a) Ringelmann chart   :   To grade density of smoke
    (b) Pneumoconiosis   :   Disease caused due to coaldust
    (c) PAN   :   Secondary air pollutant
    Select the correct answer using the codes given below :
    (1) (b) and (c)   (2) (a) and (b)   (3) (a) and (c)   (4) (a), (b) and (c)

84. Which of the following pairs are correctly matched ?
    (a) Reverberation time   :   Time required to reduce noise by 60 dB
    (b) NIPTS   :   Responsible for permanent hearing loss
    (c) Sound foci   :   Formed when sound waves are reflected from convex surface
    (d) TTS   :   Responsible for temporary hearing loss
    Select the correct answer using the codes given below :
    (1) (b), (c) and (d)   (2) (a), (c) and (d)   (3) (a), (b) and (d)   (4) (a), (b) and (c)

85. Which of the following air pollutants is/are responsible for photochemical smog ?
    (a) Oxides of nitrogen   (b) Ozone
    (c) Unburnt hydrocarbons   (d) Carbon monoxide
    Select the correct answer using the codes given below :
    (1) (a) alone   (2) (b), (c) and (d)   (3) (a), (c) and (d)   (4) (a) and (c)

86. The major photochemical oxidant is:
    (1) Ozone   (2) Hydrogen peroxide
    (3) Nitrogen oxides   (4) Peroxyl Acetyl Nitrate (PAN)

87. Which of the following are likely to be present in photochemical smog?
    (1) Sulphur dioxide   (2) Photochemical oxidants
    (3) Chlorofluorocarbon   (4) Smog
88. Which of the following devices is suitable for removal of gaseous pollutants?
    (1) Cyclone separator   (2) Electrostatic precipitator
    (3) Fabric filter   (4) Wet scrubber
89. Which of the following air pollution control devices is suitable for removing the finest dust from the air?
    (1) Cyclone separator   (2) Electrostatic precipitator
    (3) Fabric filter   (4) Wet scrubber
90. Air pollution from automobiles can be controlled by fitting:
    (1) Cyclone separator   (2) Electrostatic precipitator
    (3) Catalytic converter   (4) Wet scrubber
91. Taj Mahal at Agra may be damaged by :
    (1) Sulphur dioxide   (2) Chlorine
    (3) Hydrogen   (4) Oxygen
92. Gas leaked in Bhopal tragedy is :
    (1) Methyl isocyanate   (2) Potassium isothiocyanate
    (3) Ethyl isocyanate   (4) Sodium isothiocyanate
93. To atmosphere extends upto a height of 10,000 km. It is divided into the following four thermal layers :
    (a) Mesosphere   (b) Stratosphere   (c) Thermosphere (d) Troposphere
    The correct sequence of these starting from the surface of the earth upwards is
    (1) (b), (d), (a), (c)   (2) (d), (b), (a), (c)   (3) (d), (b), (c), (a)   (4) (b), (d), (c), (a)
94. Match List - I (Air pollutant) with List - II (Environmental effect) and select the-correct answer using the codes given below the lists :

List – I		List – II	
(A)	Carbon monoxide	(1)	Respiratory distress for living beings
(B)	Particulate matter	(2)	Chemical reaction with haemoglobin in blood
(C)	Nitrogen oxides	(3)	Reduction in visibility and aeroallergens
(D)	Sulphur dioxide	(4)	Photochemical smog in atmosphere

    Codes :

	A	B	C	D
(1)	2	3	1	4
(2)	3	2	4	1
(3)	2	3	4	1
(4)	3	2	1	4

95. If carbon monoxide is released at the rate of 0.03 m³/min from a gasoline engine and 50 ppm is the threshold limit for an 8 hour exposure, the quantity of air which dilutes the contaminant to a safe level will be
    (1) 60 m³/min   (2) 600 m³/min   (3) 60 m³/s   (4) 600 m³/s

96. The sound pressure level for a jet plane on the ground with sound pressure of 2000 μbar should be
   (1) 60 decibel   (2) 100 decibel   (3) 140 decibel   (4) 180 decibel

97. Which one of the following plume behaviours occurs when atmospheric inversion begins from the ground level and continues ?
   (1) Looping   (2) Fumigation   (3) Coning   (4) Fanning

98. Which one of the following pollutants or pairs of pollutants is formed due to photochemical reactions ?
   (1) CO alone   (2) O_3 and PAN   (3) PAN and NH_3 (4) NH_3 and CO

99. In the context of basic concept of an ecological system, the most appropriate definition of ecology is that it is a study of the
   (1) inter-relationship between organisms and the environment
   (2) relationship of human species with the industry
   (3) relationship of human species with natural resources
   (4) relationship of human species with air

100. Organisms that mineralize organic matter in an ecosystem are called
   (1) producers   (2) consumers   (3) decomposers   (4) carnivorous

101. Which of the following statements related to C/N (Carbon/Nitrogen) ratio is not correct ?
   (1) Lower initial C/N ratio leads to loss of nitrogen and slows down the rate of decomposition.
   (2) Higher initial C/N ratio leads to cell destruction to obtain nutrition.
   (3) Higher initial C/N ratio leads to lower conservation of nitrogen in the finished compost.
   (4) An initial C/N ratio of 30 to 50 is optimal for composting.

102. Fluoride pollution mainly affects:
   (1) Kidney   (2) Brain   (3) Heart   (4) Teeth

103. Which of the following is not a marine pollutant?
   (1) Oil   (2) Plastics
   (3) Dissolved oxygen   (4) All of the above

104. Noise pollution is :
   (1) Loud sound   (2) Sound of high frequency
   (3) Unwanted sound   (4) Constant sound

105. Sound becomes hazardous noise pollution at decibels:
   (1) Above 80   (2) Above 30   (3) Above 100   (4) Above 120

106. Which of the following is a major source of thermal pollution in water bodies?
   (1) Sewage treatment plant   (2) Solid waste disposal sites
   (3) Thermal power plant   (4) All of the above

107. The important gaseous pollutants contributing to acid rain are :
   (1) SO_2 and NO_x (2) NO_x and O_3
   (3) CO_2 and H_2S (4) None of these

108. Match List-I with List-II and select the correct answer using the codes given below the lists :

	List - I		List - II
A.	CO	1.	Green house effect
B.	CO_2	2.	Acid rains
C.	SO_2	3.	Acute toxicity
D.	NO_x	4.	Ozone liberation at ground level

Codes :

	A	B	C	D
(1)	3	2	1	4
(2)	2	3	4	1
(3)	3	1	2	4
(4)	4	1	2	3

ANSWER KEY

1. (3)	2. (1)	3. (3)	4. (2)	5. (2)	6. (4)	7. (3)	8. (1)
9. (3)	10. (2)	11. (4)	12. (1)	13. (4)	14. (2)	15. (2)	16. (4)
17. (3)	18. (1)	19. (2)	20. (1)	21. (1)	22. (4)	23. (3)	24. (3)
25. (4)	26. (2)	27. (4)	28. (4)	29. (1)	30. (3)	31. (1)	32. (4)
33. (2)	34. (1)	35. (4)	36. (3)	37. (2)	38. (1)	39. (1)	40. (3)
41. (2)	42. (3)	43. (3)	44. (4)	45. (3)	46. (2)	47. (4)	48. (3)
49. (1)	50. (1)	51. (2)	52. (2)	53. (1)	54. (1)	55. (4)	56. (1)
57. (1)	58. (2)	59. (1)	60. (4)	61. (2)	62. (2)	63. (1)	64. (2)
65. (2)	66. (4)	67. (1)	68. (4)	69. (3)	70. (4)	71. (1)	72. (3)
73. (2)	74. (3)	75. (3)	76. (1)	77. (1)	78. (4)	79. (1)	80. (2)
81. (2)	82. (4)	83. (4)	84. (2)	85. (4)	86. (4)	87. (3)	88. (4)
89. (2)	90. (3)	91. (1)	92. (1)	93. (2)	94. (2)	95. (2)	96. (3)
97. (4)	98. (2)	99. (1)	100. (3)	101. (3)	102. (4)	103. (3)	104. (3)
105. (1)	106. (3)	107. (1)	108. (3)				

UNIT - 11 : MUNICIPAL SOLID WASTES

1. A settling tank in a water treatment plant is designed for a surface overflow rate of $30 \text{ m}^3/\text{day}/\text{m}^2$. Assume specific gravity of sediment particles = 2.65, density of water (ρ) = 1000 kg/m³, dynamic viscosity of water (μ) = 0.001 N.s/m² and Stoke's law is valid. The approximate minimum size of particles that would be completely removed is
   (1) 0.01 mm   (2) 0.02 mm   (3) 0.03 mm   (4) 0.04 mm

2. A student began experiment for determination of 5-day, 20°C BOD on Monday. Since the 5th day fell on edurado, the Final DO reading was taken on Monday. On calculation, BOD (i.e. 7 day 20°C) was found to be 150 mg/L. What would be the 5-day 20°C BOD (in mg/L). Assume value of BOD rate constant (K) at standard temperature of 20°C as 0.23/days (base e)
   (1) 127.0345 mg/L   (2) 125.0679 mg/L (3) 128.0979 mg/L (4) 126.0539 mg/L

3. A sample of domestic sewage is digested with silver sulphate, sulphuric acid, potassium dichromate and mercuric sulphate in COD test. The digested sample is then titrated with standard Ferrous Ammonium Sulphate (FAS) to determine the unreacted amount of
   (1) mercuric sulphate   (2) potassium dichromate
   (3) silver sulphate   (4) sulphuric acid

4. The group of micro-organisms involved in production of methane from acetic acid (or acetate) in anaerobic waste water treatment processes is :
   (1) Methanothrix and Methanobacterium
   (2) Methanobacterium and Methanosarcina
   (3) Methanosarcina and Methanospirillum
   (4) Methanothrix and Mathanosarcina

5. Consider the following unit processes commonly used in water treatment; Rapid mixing (RM), Flocculation (F), Primary Sedimentation (PS), Secondary Sedimentation (SS), Chlorination (C) and Rapid Sand Filtration (RSF). The order of these unit processes (First to last) in a conventional water treatment plant is ....
   (1) PS → RSF → F → RM → SS → c   (2) PS → F → RM → RSF → SS → c
   (3) PS → F → SS → RSF → RM → c   (4) PS → RM → F → SS → RSF → c

6. During sewage treatment, effluent from which one of the following treatment units has minimum wt/vol amount of suspended solids ?
   (1) Detritus channel   (2) Primary sedimentation tank
   (3) Secondary sedimentation tank   (4) Activated sludge process aeration tank

7. A coastal city produces Municipal Solid Waste (MSW) with high moisture content, high organic materials, low calorific value and low inorganic materials. The most effective and sustainable option for MSW management in that city is ....
   (1) composting   (2) dumping in sea (3) incineration   (4) landfill

8. Secondary clarifier of an activated sludge process must be designed for effluent clarification and solids thickening, both of which are related directly to the ....
   (1) surface area
   (2) transport velocity due to sludge withdrawal
   (3) gravity settling of solids relative to the water
   (4) underflow solids concentration

9. Two biodegradable components of municipal solid wastes are
   (1) plastics and word   (2) cardboard and glass
   (3) leather and tin cans   (4) food waste and garden trimming

10. Which one of the following parameters is not included in the routine characterization of solid water for its physical composition ?
   (1) Moisture content   (2) Density
   (3) Particle size analysis   (4) Energy value

11. In an aerobic attached-culture system, the biomass at the biofilm-medium surface interface experiences ....
   (1) aerobic and endogenous metabolism (2) anaerobic and endogenous metabolism
   (3) anaerobic and exogenous metabolism
   (4) aerobic and exogenous metabolism

12. The alkalinity and the hardness of a water sample are 250 mg/L and 350 mg/L as $CaCO_3$ respectively. The water has
   (1) 350 mg/L carbonate hardness and zero non-carbonate hardness
   (2) 250 mg/L carbonate hardness and zero non-carbonate hardness
   (3) 250 mg/L carbonate hardness and 350 mg/L non-carbonate hardness
   (4) 250 mg/L carbonate hardness and 100 mg/L non-carbonate hardness

13. A synthetic sample of water is prepared by adding 100 mg Kaolinite (a clay mineral), 200 mg glucose, 168 mg NaCl, 120 $MgSO_4$, and 111 mg $CaCl_2$ to 1 L of pure water. The concentration of Tot al Solids (TS) and Fixed Dissolved Solids (FDS) respectively in the solution in mg/L are equal to ....
   (1) 699 and 599   (2) 599 and 399   (3) 699 and 199   (4) 699 and 399

14. To determine the BOD_5 of a waste water sample, 5, 10 and 50 mL aliquots of the waste water were diluted to 300 mL and incubated at 20°C in BOD bottles for 5 days. The results were as follows :

Sr. No.	Waste water volume (mL)	Initial DO (mg/L)	DO after 5 days (mg/L)
1.	5	9.2	6.9
2.	10	9.1	4.4
3.	50	8.4	0.0

Based on the data, the average BOD_5 of the waste water is equal to ....
   (1) 139.5 mg/L   (2) 126.5 mg/L   (3) 109.8 mg/L   (4) 72.2 mg/L

15.　1 TCU is equivalent to the colour produced by ....
　　(1)　1 mg/L of chloroplatinate ion　　(2)　1 mg/L of platinum ion
　　(3)　1 mg/L platinum is form of chloroplatinate ion
　　(4)　1 mg/L of organo-chloroplatinate ion

16.　In aerobic environment nitrosamines convert ....
　　(1)　NH_3 to NO_2　　(2)　NO_2^- to NO_3^-　　(3)　NH_3 to N_2O　　(4)　NO_2^- to HNO_3

17.　Bulking sludge refers to have ....
　　(1)　F/M < 0.3/d　　　　　　　　(2)　0.3/d < F/M < 0.6/d
　　(3)　F/M = zero　　　　　　　　(4)　F/M > 0.6/d

18.　Most of the turbidity meters work on the scattering principle. The turbidity value, so obtained is expressed in ....
　　(1)　CFU　　　　(2)　FTU　　　　(3)　JTU　　　　(4)　NTU

19.　Hardness of water is directly measured by titration with Ethylene Diamine Tetra-acetic Acid (EDTA) using ....
　　(1)　eriochrome black T indicator　　(2)　ferroin indicator
　　(3)　methyl orange indicator　　　　(4)　phenolphthalein indicator

20.　The organism, which exhibits very nearly the characteristics of an ideal pathogenic indicator is ....
　　(1)　Entamoeba histolytica　　　　(2)　Escherichia coli
　　(3)　Salmonella typhi　　　　　　(4)　Vibrio Cholera

21.　The results of analysis of a raw water sample are given below.
　　Turbidity　:　5 mg/L　　　　　pH　　　　　　　:　7.4
　　Fluorides　:　2.5 mg/L　　　　　Total hardness　:　300 mg/L
　　Iron　　　:　3.0 mg/L　　　　　MPN　　　　　:　50 per 100 mL
　　From the data given above, it can be inferred that water needs removal of ....
　　(1)　turbidity followed by disinfection　　(2)　fluorides and hardness
　　(3)　iron, followed by disinfection
　　(4)　fluorides, hardness and iron followed by disinfection

22.　Zero hardness of water is achieved by ....
　　(1)　lime soda process　　　　　　(2)　excess lime treatment
　　(3)　iron exchange treatment　　　　(4)　excess alum and lime treatment

23.　Which of the following sewage treatment methods has inherent problems of odour, ponding and fly nuisance ?
　　(1)　UASB system　　　　　　　(2)　Activated sludge process
　　(3)　Trickling filters　　　　　　　(4)　Stabilization ponds

24.　From amongst the following sewage treatment options, largest land requirements for a given discharge will be needed for ....
　　(1)　trickling filter　　　　　　　(2)　anaerobic pond
　　(3)　oxidation ditch　　　　　　　(4)　oxidation pond

25. The temporary hardness of water is caused by ....
    (1) dissolved carbon dioxide
    (2) bicarbonates and carbonates of calcium and magnesium
    (3) bicarbonates of sodium and potassium
    (4) carbonates of calcium and magnesium

26. Breakpoint chlorination of water involves addition of chlorine in an amount sufficient to
    (1) react with any ammonia and readily oxidisable organic matter
    (2) kill Giardia cysts
    (3) react with inorganic matter
    (4) reduce bacterial growth in filters

27. If tomato juice is having a pH of 4.1, the hydrogen ion concentration will be ....
    (1) 10.94×10^{-5} mol/L   (2) 9.94×10^{-5} mol/L
    (3) 8.94×10^{-5} mol/L   (4) 7.94×10^{-5} mol/L

28. List - I contains some properties of water/waste water and List - II contains some tests on water/waste water. Match List - I with List - II and select the correct answer using the codes given below the lists.

	List – I		List – II
A.	Suspended solids concentration	1.	BOD
B.	Metabolism of biodegradable organics	2.	MPN
C.	Bacterial concentration	3.	Jar test
D.	Coagulant dose	4.	Turbidity

    Codes

	A	B	C	D
(1)	2	1	4	3
(2)	4	1	2	3
(3)	2	4	1	3
(4)	4	2	1	3

29. Match List - I with List - II and select the correct answer using the codes given below the lists.

	List – I		List – II
A.	Thickening of sludge	1.	Decrease in volume of sludge by chemical oxidation
B.	Stabilization of sludge	2.	Separation of water by heat or chemical treatment
C.	Conditioning of sludge	3.	Digestion of sludge
D.	Reduction of sludge	4.	Separation of water by flotation or gravity

    Codes

	A	B	C	D
(1)	4	3	1	2
(2)	3	2	4	1
(3)	4	3	2	1
(4)	2	1	3	4

30. A circular primary clarifier processes an average flow of 5005 m^3/d of municipal waste water. The overflow rate is 35 $m^3/m^2/d$. The diameter of clarifier shall be

    (1) 10.5 m   (2) 11.5 m   (3) 12.5 m   (4) 13.5 m

31. Match List - I with List - II and select the correct answer using the codes given below the lists.

	List - I		List - II
A.	Release valve	1.	Reduce high inlet pressure to lower outlet pressure
B.	Check valve	2.	Limit the flow of water to single direction
C.	Gate valve	3.	Remove air from the pipeline
D.	Pilot valve	4.	Stopping the flow of water in the pipeline

    Codes

	A	B	C	D
(1)	3	2	4	1
(2)	4	2	1	3
(3)	3	4	2	1
(4)	1	2	4	3

32. Results of a water sample analysis are as follows.

Cation	Concentration (mg/L)	Equivalent weight
Na^+	40	23
Mg^{+2}	10	12.2
Ca^{+2}	55	20
K^+	2	39

    (Milliequivalent weight of $CaCO_3$ = 50 mg/meq).
    Hardness of the water sample in mg/L as $CaCO_3$ is ……….

    (1) 44.8   (2) 89.5   (3) 179   (4) 358

33. An ideal horizontal flow settling basin is 3 m deep having surface area 900 m^2. Water flows at the rate of 8000 m^3/d, at water temperature 20°C (μ = 10^{-3} kg/m–s and ρ = 1000 kg/m^3). Assuming Stoke's law to be valid, the proportion (percentage) of spherical sand particles (0.01 mm in diameter with specific gravity 2.65), that will be removed, is ……….

    (1) 32.5   (2) 67   (3) 87.5   (4) 95.5

34. Match List – I (Type of water impurity) with List – II (Method of treatment) and select the correct answer using the codes given below the lists.

	List - I		List - II
A.	Hardness	1.	Reverse osmosis
B.	Brackish water from sea	2.	Chlorination
C.	Residual MPN from filters	3.	Zeolite treatment
D.	Turbidity	4.	Coagulation and flocculation
		5.	Coagulation, flocculation and filtration

Codes

	A	B	C	D
(1)	1	2	4	5
(2)	3	2	2	4
(3)	2	1	3	5
(4)	3	1	2	5

35. Settling test on a sample drawn from aeration tank liquor of ASP (MLSS = 2800 mg/L) was carried out with 1L sample. The test yielded a settled volume of 200 mL. The value of sludge volume index shall be
   (1) 14.0   (2) 34.2   (3) 71.4   (4) 271

36. The manufacturer of aeration devices reports the oxygen transfer rate of the device obtained through laboratory tests carried under standard conditions. Such standard conditions are ....
   (1) Waste water at zero DO, 25°C and 760 mm Hg
   (2) Tap water at zero DO, 0°C and 700 mm Hg
   (3) Tap water at zero DO, 20°C and 760 mm Hg
   (4) Waste water at zero DO, 0°C and 700 mm Hg

37. Biochemical oxygen demand (BOD) of waste water is a measure of :
   (1) total concentration of biochemicals
   (2) total concentration of organic matter
   (3) concentration of biodegradable organic matter
   (4) concentration of chemically oxidisable matter

38. A trickling filter is primarily a ....
   (1) straining process to remove suspended solids from sewage
   (2) biological oxidation process to remove BOD from sewage
   (3) straining process to remove turbidity from water
   (4) straining process to remove bacteria from water

39. A septic tank is ....
   (1) an aerobic method of on-site sewage treatment
   (2) an anaerobic method of on sift treatment
   (3) a physical method of water treatment
   (4) a physicochemical method of water

40. At highway stretches, where overtaking sight distance cannot be provided, it is necessary to incorporate ....
   (1) atleast twice the stopping sight distance
   (2) half the, required overtaking sight distance
   (3) one-third the required overtaking sight distance
   (4) three times the stopping sight distance

41. The ideal form of curve for the summit curve is ....
   (1) spiral   (2) parabola   (3) circle   (4) lemniscate

42. In highway pavements emulsions are mainly used in ....
    (1) surface dressing
    (2) patching and maintenance operations
    (3) bitumen macadam
    (4) asphaltic concrete

43. In using the data from a plate bearing test for determining the modulus of subgrade reaction, the value of settlement to be used is ....
    (1) 1.25 mm
    (2) 2.50 mm
    (3) 3.75 mm
    (4) 1.75 mm

44. The function of ballast in railway tracks is to ....
    (1) facilitate drainage
    (2) serve as an elastic support for the track structure
    (3) provide the necessary resilience against the dynamic effect of the loads
    (4) all the above

45. The most important water quality parameter for domestic use of water is ....
    (1) carbonate hardness
    (2) non-carbonate hardness
    (3) coliform group of organisms
    (4) chlorides

46. Presence of fluoride in water greater than permissible level of 1.5 mg/L causes ....
    (1) cardiovascular disease
    (2) methemoglobinemia
    (3) hepatitis
    (4) dental fluorosis

47. Chemical Oxygen Demand (COD) of a sample is always greater than Biochemical Oxygen Demand (BOD) since it represents :
    (1) biodegradable organic matter only
    (2) biodegradable and non–biodegradable organic matter
    (3) non–biodegradable organic matter
    (4) inorganic matter

48. A waste water sample diluted to 100 times with aeration water had an initial dissolved oxygen (DO) of 7.0 mg/L and after 5 days of incubation at $20°$ C, the DO was zero. The BOD of waste water is ....
    (1) 700 mg/L
    (2) 100 mg/L
    (3) cannot be determined
    (4) 7 mg/L

49. The treatment that should be given to the water from a deep tube well is ....
    (1) pre–settling only
    (2) coagulation and flocculation only
    (3) filtration only
    (4) disinfection only

50. The drop manholes are provided in a sewerage system when there is ....
    (1) change in alignment of sewer line
    (2) change in size of sows
    (3) change in the elevation of ground level
    (4) change from gravity system to pressure system

51. The removal of dissolved organic matter occurs in ....
    (1) slow sand filters
    (2) trickling filters
    (3) rapid sand filters
    (4) dual media filters

52. The main constituents of gas generated during the anaerobic digestion of sewage sludge are ……….

    (1) carbon dioxide and methane   (2) methane and ethane

    (3) carbon dioxide and carbon monoxide (4) carbon monoxide and nitrogen

53. A single rapid test to determine the pollutional status of river water is ……….

    (1) biochemical oxygen demand   (2) chemical oxygen demand

    (3) total organic solids   (4) dissolved oxygen

54. Presence of excess nitrates in river water indicates :

    (1) Recent pollution of water with sewage

    (2) Past pollution of water with sewage

    (3) Immediate pollution of water with sewage

    (4) No pollution of water with sewage

55. Pathogens are usually removed by ……….

    (1) chemical precipitation   (2) sedimentation

    (3) activated sludge process   (4) chlorination

56. The 'sag' in the dissolved oxygen curve results because ……….

    (1) it is a function of the rate of addition of oxygen to the stream

    (2) it is a function of the rate of depletion of oxygen from the stream

    (3) a function of both addition and depletion of oxygen from the stream

    (4) the rate of addition is linear, but the rate of depletion is non-linear

57. Design parameters for mixing units are ……….

    (1) velocity gradient and the volume of mixing basin

    (2) viscosity and velocity gradient

    (3) viscosity, velocity gradient and the volume of the mixing basin

    (4) detention time and viscosity of water

58. The adsorbent most commonly used in water and waste water treatment is ……….

    (1) sand of grain size from 0.1 to 2 mm   (2) ordinary wood shavings of fine size

    (3) activated carbon granules of size 0.1 to 2 mm

    (4) coal tar

59. Among the following disinfectants of waste water, the one that is most commonly used is ……….

    (1) chlorine dioxide (2) chlorine   (3) ozone   (4) UV radiation

60. Alkalinity of water can be defined correctly in one of the following ways :

    (1) It is the measure of ability of water to neutralize oxygen.

    (2) It is the measure of ability of water to neutralize carbonates.

    (3) It is the presence of ions in water that will neutralize hydrogen ions.

    (4) It is the measure of ability of water to neutralize hydroxides.

61. A typical biological process in treating waste water using aerated lagoon can be described by one of the following schematic diagrams given below.

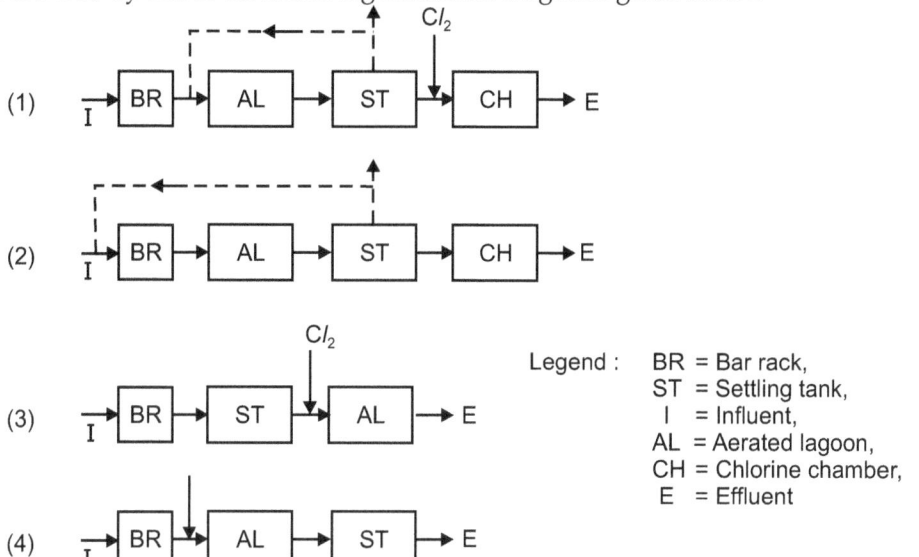

Legend : BR = Bar rack,
ST = Settling tank,
I = Influent,
AL = Aerated lagoon,
CH = Chlorine chamber,
E = Effluent

62. The BOD_5 of a surface water sample is 200 mg/litre at 20°C. The value of reaction constant is k = 0.2 day^{-1} with base 'e'. The ultimate BOD of the sample is
    (1) 126 mg/ litre   (2) 544 mg/litre   (3) 146 mg/litre   (4) 316 mg/litre

63. The Bowery ratio is defined as :
    (1) Ratio of heat and vapour diffusivities.
    (2) Proportionality constant between vapour heat flux and sensible heat flux.
    (3) Ratio of actual evapotranspiration and potential evapotranspiration.
    (4) Proportionality constant between heat energy used up in evaporation and the bulk radiation from a water body.

64. The microbial quality of treated piped water supplies is monitored by ....
    (1) microscopic examination   (2) plate count of heterotrophic bacteria
    (3) coliform MPN test   (4) identification of all pathokens

65. Excessive fluoride in drinking water causes ....
    (1) Alzheimer's disease
    (2) Mottling of teeth and embrittlement of bones
    (3) Methemoglobinemia   (4) Skin cancer

66. Coagulation-flocculation with alum is performed ....
    (1) immediately before chlorination   (2) immediately after chlorination
    (3) after rapid sand filtration   (4) before rapid sand filtration

67. Sewage treatment in all oxidation ponds is accomplished primarily by
    (1) alga-bacterial symbiosis   (2) algal photosynthesis only,
    (3) bacterial oxidation only   (4) chemical oxidation only

68. An inverted siphon is a ....
    (1) device for distributing septic tank effluent to a soil absorption system
    (2) device for preventing overflow from elevated water storage.
    (3) device for preventing crown corrosion of sewer
    (4) sewer which is dropped below the hydraulic grade line in order to avoid an obstacle

69. Water distribution systems are sized to meet the ....
    (1) maximum hourly demand   (2) average hourly demand
    (3) maximum daily demand and fire demand
    (4) average daily demand and fire demand

70. At highway stretches where the required overtaking sight distance cannot be provided, it is necessary to incorporate in such sections the following ....
    (1) at least twice the stopping sight distance
    (2) half of the required overtaking sight distance
    (3) one third of the required overtaking sight distance
    (4) half of the stopping sight distance

71. Symbiosis, the beneficial association between algae and bacteria is used for treatment of waste water in the following unit :
    (1) Activated sludge   (2) Rotating biological disc
    (3) Anaerobic digestor   (4) Oxidation pond

72. The ultimate BOD of the waste water whose 5 day BOD $(BOD)_5$ and rate constant (base e) are respectively 150 mg/L and 0.23/day is
    (1) 80 mg/L   (2) 150 mg/L   (3) 180 mg/L   (4) 220 mg/L

73. A small filter of 0.05 m depth removes 90 % of particles present in water. If the particle removal required is 99%, what should be the depth of filter ?
    (1) 0.10 m   (2) 0.50 m   (3) 0.75 m   (4) 1.00 m

74. Methemoglobinemia the 'blue baby' syndrome is caused by consuming water containing excess of ....
    (1) fluoride   (2) phosphate   (3) nitrate   (4) nitrite

75. Hardness of water is caused by the presence of the following in water ....
    (1) chlorides and sulphates   (2) calcium and magnesium
    (3) nitrites and nitrates   (4) sodium and potassium

76. The clariflocculator is the unit in which the following things will occur ....
    (1) Floc formation and its subsequent removal by filtration
    (2) Floc formation and its subsequent removal by sedimentation
    (3) Floc formation and its subsequent removal by decantation
    (4) Removal of bacteria by filtration and chlorination

77. A rapid test to indicate the intensity of pollution in river water is
    (1) Biochemical Oxygen Demand   (2) Dissolved Oxygen
    (3) MPN   (4) Total Dissolved Solids

78. Trickling filters are used to remove ....
    (1) suspended solids   (2) colloidal solids
    (3) organic matter   (4) pathogenic bacteria
79. When sufficient energy through mechanical mixing is supplied to keep the entire contents, including the sewage solids, mixed and aerated, the reactor is termed as ....
    (1) an aerobic lagoon   (2) an aerobic pond
    (3) a facultative lagoon   (4) a facultative pond
80. In transition of sewers from smaller diameter sewers to larger diameter sewers, the continuity of sewers is maintained at the ....
    (1) bottom of the concrete bed of sewers (2) inverts of the sewers
    (3) crowns of the sewers   (4) hydraulic gradients of the sewers
81. The slope of a 1.0 m diameter concrete sewer laid at a slope of 1 in 1000, develops a velocity of 1 m/s when flowing full. When it is flowing half-full, the velocity of flow through the sewer will be ....
    (1) 0.5 m/s   (2) 1.0 m/s   (3) 2 m/s   (4) 2.0 m/s
82. Self-cleansing velocity is ....
    (1) the minimum velocity of flow required to maintain a certain amount of solids in the flow.
    (2) the maximum velocity of flow required to maintain a certain amount of solids in the flow.
    (3) such flow velocity as would be sufficient to flush out any deposited solids in the sewer.
    (4) such flow velocity as would be sufficient to ensure that sewage does not remain in the sewer.
83. In the design of storm sewers, "time of concentration" is relevant to determine the ....
    (1) rainfall intensity   (2) velocity in the sewer
    (3) time of travel   (4) area served by the sewer
84. The maximum flow occurs in an egg shaped sewer when the ratio of flow to vertical diameter is ....
    (1) 0.33   (2) 0.50   (3) 0.95   (4) 1.00
85. A circular sewer of diameter 1 m carries storm water to a depth of 0.75 m. The hydraulic radius is approximately ....
    (1) 0.3 m   (2) 0.4 m   (3) 0.5 m   (4) 0.6 m
86. For the design of a storm sewer in a drainage area, if the time of concentration is 20 minutes, then the duration of rainfall will be taken as ....
    (1) 10 min   (2) 20 min   (3) 30 min   (4) 40 min
87. A sewer is commonly designed to attain self-cleansing velocity at ....
    (1) peak hourly rate of flow   (2) average hourly rate of flow
    (3) minimum hourly rate of flow (4) sewer running half full

88. Consider the following statements regarding building manholes :

    (a) They must be provided at every change of alignment, gradient or diameter.
    (b) They must be provided at the head of all sewers.
    (c) They must be provided at every junction of two or more sewers.
    (d) They must be provided at every 100 m, along straight runs of sewers.

    Which of these statements are correct ?

    (1) (a), (b), (c) and (d)   (2) (a), (c) and (d)
    (3) (a), (b) and (c)   (4) (b) and (d)

89. Which of the following statements is correct ?

    A combined sewer is one which transports domestic sewage and ....

    (1) storm water   (2) industrial waste
    (3) overhead flow   (4) industrial wastes and storm water

90. In the design consideration of sewerage system, the sewers must have which one of the following ?

    (1) Maximum velocity of flow
    (2) Only 50 % of maximum velocity of flow
    (3) Minimum velocity of not less than cleansing velocity of flow
    (4) High pressure at all times

91. At the same mean velocity of flow, the ratio of head loss per unit length for a sewer pipe running full to that for the same pipe flowing half-full is ....

    (1) 2.0   (2) 1.67   (3) 1.0   (4) 0.67

92. The self-cleansing velocity in a sewer depends on :

    (a) BOD (soluble)
    (b) Slope of the sewer
    (c) Ratio of depth of flow sewage to sewer diameter ratio
    (1) (a), (b) and (c)   (2) (a) and (b) only (3) (b) and (c) only (4) (a) and (c) only

93. If the slope of sewer A is 1/100 and that of sewer B is 1/400, the velocity of flow in the two sewers will be a ratio of (size of both the sewers being same) ....

    (1) $\dfrac{1}{2}$ (2) 1   (3) $2^{2/3}$ (4) 2

94. Non-disposal of solid waste may cause the spread of ....

    (1) malaria   (2) rodents related plague
    (3) typhoid   (4) dysentery

95. The following data pertains to a sewage sample :

    Initial DO = 10 mg/L

    Final DO = 2 mg/L

    Dilution ratio = 1%

    The BOD_5 of the given sewage sample is ....

    (1) 8 mg/L   (2) 10 mg/L   (3) 100 mg/L   (4) 800 mg/L

96. Sewage sickness occurs when ....
    (1) sewage contains pathogenic organisms
    (2) sewage enters the water supply system
    (3) sewers get clogged due to accumulation of solids
    (4) voids of soil clogged due to continuous application of sewage on a piece of land

97. The typical density in kg/m³ (in situ) of well-compacted municipal solid waste in landfill is in the range of ....
    (1) 100 to 300   (2) 310 to 500   (3) 550 to 850   (4) 900 to 1100

98. Consider the following statements :
    Ventilation of sewer lines is necessary to
    (a) avoid building up of sewer gases
    (b) ensure atmospheric pressure in the waste water surface
    (c) ensure the safety of sewer maintenance people
    (d) provide oxidation facility of sewage
    Which of these statements are correct ?
    (1) (a), (b) and (d)   (2) (a), (c) and (d)   (3) (b), (c) and (d)   (4) (a), (b) and (c)

99. For a colony of 10,000 persons having sewage flow rate of 200 L/capital/day, BOD of applied sewage of 300 mg/L and organic loading of 300 kg/day/hectare, the area of an oxidation pond required for treating the sewage of the colony is ....
    (1) 0.2 hectares   (2) 1 hectare   (3) 2 hectares   (4) 6 hectares

100. The second stage BOD as shown in the figure is due to ....

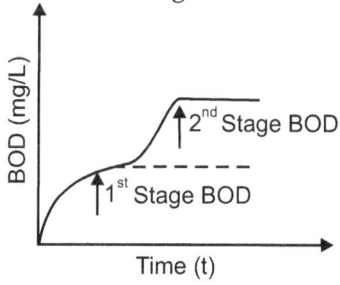

    (1) experimental error   (2) increased activity of bacteria
    (3) nitrification demand   (4) interference by certain chemical reactions

101. Sewage sickness is a term used for ....
    (1) persons who become sick after drinking polluted water
    (2) a treatment plant which does not function properly
    (3) a stream where the flora and fauna die due to sewage inflow
    (4) the condition of land where sewage is applied continuously for a long period

102. A 2 % solution of a sewage sample is kept at an incubation temperature of 20°C. If initial DO (Dissolved Oxygen) and final DO values after 5 days' incubation period are 8.5 mg/L and 5.5 mg/L respectively, then the BOD will be ....
    (1) 50 mg/L   (2) 150 mg/L   (3) 250 mg/L   (4) 350 mg/L

103. For a waste, the 5-day BOD at 20°C is found to be 200 mg/L. For the same waste, 5-day BOD at 30°C will be ....
    (1) less than 200 mg/L
    (2) more than 200 mg/L
    (3) 200 mg/L
    (4) zero, as the bacteria cannot withstand such a high temperature

104. The ultimate BOD value of a waste ....
    (1) increases with temperature
    (2) decreases with temperature
    (3) remains the same at all temperatures
    (4) doubles with every 10°C rise in temperature

105. The correct statement of comparison of ultimate BOD, COD, Theoretical Oxygen Demand (ThOD) on 5-day BOD (BOD_5) is ....
    (1) $BOD_u > COD > ThOD > BOD_5$ (2) $COD > ThOD > BOD_u > BOD_5$
    (3) $ThOD > COD > BOD_u > BOD_5$ (4) $COD > BOD_u > BOD_5 > ThOD$

106. Match List-I (Standards of sewage effluents for the discharge in surface water sources) with List-II (Tolerance limits in mg/L) and select the correct answer using the codes given below the lists :

	List - I		List - II
A.	BOD_5	1.	250
B.	COD	2.	30
C.	Oil and grease	3.	20
D.	Total suspended solids	4.	10

    Codes :

	A	B	C	D
(1)	3	4	1	2
(2)	2	4	1	3
(3)	3	1	4	2
(4)	2	1	4	3

107. A waste water sample of 2 mL is made upto 300 mL in BOD bottle with distilled water. Initial DO of the sample is 8 mg/L and after 5 days it is 2 mg/L. What is its BOD ?
    (1) 894 mg/L   (2) 900 mg/L   (3) 300 mg/L   (4) 1200 mg/L

108. A municipal sewage has BOD_5 of 200 mg/L. It is proposed to treat it and dispose off into a marine environment. For what minimum efficiency should the sewage treatment plant be designed ?
    (1) 85 %   (2) 60 %   (3) 50 %   (4) 33.67 %

109. What is 5-day 20°C BOD equal to ?
    (1) 3-day 27°C BOD   (2) 4-day 30°C BOD
    (3) 6-day 32°C BOD   (4) 7-day 35°C BOD

110. Match List-I (Parameter) with List-II (General standard for discharge into the inland surface water in mg/L (max)) and select the correct answer using the codes given below the lists :

	List - I			List - II
A.	BOD (5-day 20°C)		1.	250
B.	COD		2.	100
C.	Oil and grease		3.	20
D.	Suspended solids		4.	10
			5.	30

    Codes :

	A	B	C	D
(1)	2	1	4	5
(2)	5	4	3	2
(3)	2	4	3	5
(4)	5	1	4	2

111. In context of water polluted with sewage, what does BOD signify ?
    (1) Biological Oxygen Demand   (2) Bacteriological Oxygen Demand
    (3) Biochemical Oxygen Demand   (4) Biology Of Degradation

112. The daily cover of MSW landfills consists of which one of the following ?
    (1) Compacted soil   (2) Geomembrane
    (3) Geotextile   (4) Geocomposite

113. A sample of sewage is estimated to have a 5-day 20°C BOD of 250 mg/L. If the test temperature is 30°C, in how many days will the same value of BOD be obtained ?
    (1) 1.5 days   (2) 2.5 days
    (3) 3.3 days   (4) 7.5 days

114. Which one of the following solid waste disposal methods is ecologically most acceptable ?
    (1) Sanitary landfill   (2) Incineration
    (3) Composting   (4) Pyrolysis

115. A polluted stream undergoes self-purification in four distinct zones :
    (a) Zone of clear water   (b) Zone of active decomposition
    (c) Zone of degradation   (d) Zone of recovery
    The correct sequence of these zones is ....
    (1) (c), (d), (b), (a)   (2) (b), (c), (d), (a)
    (3) (b), (d), (c), (a)   (4) (c), (b), (d), (a)

116. The formation for BOD assimilation in a stream should include ....
    (1) BOD rate constant
    (2) sedimentation of organic matter
    (3) BOD rate constant and sedimentation of organic matter
    (4) pathogenic bacterial decay coefficient

117. Match List-I with List-II and select the correct answer using the codes given below the lists :

	List - I			List - II
A.	Sludge disposal		1.	Seeding
B.	Sludge digestion		2.	Biofilters
C.	Aerobic action		3.	Lagooning
D.	Recirculation		4.	Contact bed

Codes :

	A	B	C	D
(1)	3	1	4	2
(2)	3	1	2	4
(3)	1	3	2	4
(4)	1	3	4	2

118. Which one of the following would help to prevent the escape of foul sewer gases from a water closet ?

(1) Air gap   (2) Vent pipe   (3) Gully trap   (4) None of these

119. Self purification of running streams may be due to ....

(1) sedimentation, oxidation and coagulation

(2) dilution, sedimentation and oxidation

(3) dilution, sedimentation and coagulation

(4) dilution, oxidation and coagulation

120. The following zones are formed in a polluted river :

(a) Zone of clear water   (b) Zone of active decomposition

(c) Zone of recovery   (d) Zone of pollution

The correct sequence in which these zones occur progressively downstream in a polluted river is ....

(1) (d), (b), (a), (c)   (2) (d), (b), (c), (a)   (3) (b), (d), (c), (a)   (4) (b), (d), (a), (c)

121. Which one of the following methods can be employed for plastic and rubber waste disposal ?

(1) Composting   (2) Incineration   (3) Sanitary landfill (4) Pyrolysis

122. When a sewage is disposed off in a river, the rate of depletion of dissolved oxygen of the river mainly depends on ....

(1) biochemical oxygen demand of the sewage

(2) chemical oxygen demand of the sewage

(3) total organic carbon present in the sewage

(4) dissolved oxygen present in the sewage

123. From ecological considerations, the minimum level of Dissolved Oxygen (DO) necessary in the rivers and streams is ....

(1) 1 mg/L   (2) 2 mg/L   (3) 4 mg/L   (4) 8 mg/L

124. Which one of the following sets of processes is a part of self-purification of streams ?
     (1) Settling, bio-degradation and desalination
     (2) Settling, bio-degradation and aeration
     (3) Floatation, ion exchange and desalination
     (4) Desalination, ion exchange and reverse osmosis

125. When sewage enters a flowing river, the rapid depletion of dissolved oxygen is due to ....
     (1) change in temperature in river water
     (2) the suspended particles in river and waste
     (3) respiratory activity of aquatic plants in the river
     (4) microbial activity

126. Which one of the following methods would be the best suited for disposal of plastic and rubber waste ?
     (1) Composting   (2) Incineration   (3) Pyrolysis   (4) Sanitary landfill

127. Which one of the following comprehensive classifications is used for different types of solid wastes ?
     (1) Residential, commercial and treatment plant wastes
     (2) Food, demolition and construction wastes
     (3) Municipal, industrial and hazardous wastes
     (4) Rubbish, special wastes and wastes from open areas

128. The term 'Refuse' generally does not include ....
     (1) putrescible solid waste   (2) excreta
     (3) non-putrescible solid waste   (4) ashes

129. In dissolved oxygen sag curve, the sag curve results because ....
     (1) it is a function of rate of addition of oxygen to the stream.
     (2) it is a function of rate of addition of oxygen from the stream.
     (3) it is a function of both addition and depletion of oxygen from the stream.
     (4) the rate of addition of oxygen is linear, but the rate of depletion is non-linear.

130. In which type of lakes, does a perfect ecological equilibrium among the producers, decomposers and consumer groups of organisms exist ?
     (1) Senescent lakes   (2) Mesotrophic lakes
     (3) Oligotrophic lakes   (4) Eutrophic lakes

131. What is eutrophication of lakes primarily due to ?
     (1) Multiplication of bacteria   (2) Excessive inflow of nutrients
     (3) Increase in benthic organisms   (4) Thermal and density currents

132. What does the presence of excess nitrates in river water indicate ?
     (1) Recent pollution of water with sewage
     (2) Past pollution of water with sewage
     (3) Intermittent pollution of water with sewage
     (4) No pollution of water with sewage

133. Shallow ponds in which dissolved oxygen is present at all depths are called ....
    (1) aerobic lagoons   (2) aerobic ponds
    (3) facultative lagoons   (4) facultative ponds

134. Deep ponds, in which oxygen is absent except, perhaps, across a relatively thin surface layer, are called ....
    (1) aerobic ponds   (2) anaerobic ponds
    (3) facultative ponds   (4) polishing ponds

135. Match List-I (Process) with List-II (Biological agent) and select the correct answer using the codes given below the lists :

	List - I		List - II
A.	Oxidation ditch	1.	Facultative bacteria
B.	Waste stabilization pond	2.	Anaerobic bacteria
C.	Imhoff tank	3.	Aerobic bacteria (suspended culture)
D.	Rotating Biological Contractor (RBC)	4.	Aerobic bacteria (attached culture)

    Codes :

	A	B	C	D
(1)	4	1	2	3
(2)	3	1	2	4
(3)	1	2	3	4
(4)	3	4	1	2

136. One litre of sewage, when allowed to settle for 30 minutes gives a sludge volume of 27 cm³. If the dry weight of this sludge is 3.0 grams, then its sludge volume index will be ....
    (1) 9   (2) 24   (3) 30   (4) 81

137. The waste stabilization ponds can be ....
    (1) aerobic   (2) anaerobic   (3) facultative   (4) any of the above

138. Match List-I (Impurities to be removed from sewage) with List-II (Treatment unit used) and select the correct answer using the codes given below the lists :

	List - I		List - II
A.	Large floating matter	1.	Trickling filter
B.	Suspended inorganic matter	2.	Primary clarifier
C.	Suspended organic matter	3.	Grit chamber
D.	Dissolved organic matter	4.	Screens

    Codes :

	A	B	C	D
(1)	3	4	2	1
(2)	3	4	1	2
(3)	4	3	2	1
(4)	4	3	1	2

139. The following three stages are known to occur in the biological action involved in the process of sludge digestion :

(a) Acid fermentation   (b) Alkaline fermentation

(c) Acid regression

The correct sequence of these stages is ....

(1) (a), (b), (c)   (2) (b), (c), (a)   (3) (c), (a), (b)   (4) (a), (c), (b)

140. Fresh sludge has moisture content of 99 % and after thickening, its moisture content is reduced to 96 %. The reduction in volume of sludge is ....

(1) 3 %   (2) 5 %   (3) 75 %   (4) 97 %

141. In the oxidation ditch, the excess sludge is taken to ....

(1) anaerobic digester   (2) aerobic digester

(3) drying beds   (4) incinerator

142. The flow sheet of the liquid stream of a sewage treatment scheme consists of ....

(a) Trickling filter   (b) Primary settling tank

(c) Grit chamber   (d) Screen chamber

(e) Secondary settling tank

The correct sequence of these units in the sewage treatment scheme of a liquid stream is

(1) (c), (d), (a), (b), (e)   (2) (c), (d), (b), (a), (e)

(3) (d), (c), (a), (b), (e)   (4) (d), (c), (b), (a), (c)

143. The two main gases liberated from an anaerobic sludge digestion tank would include ....

(1) ammonia and carbon dioxide   (2) carbon dioxide and methane

(3) methane and hydrogen sulphide   (4) ammonia and methane

144. Which one of the following sewage treatment units has a partial flume ?

(1) Trickling filter   (2) Oxidation ditch

(3) Grit chamber   (4) Aerated lagoon

145. Which one of the following principal types of reactors is related to trickling filter ?

(1) Plug flow   (2) Complete-mix

(3) Packed-bed   (4) Fluidized-bed

146. Sludge bulking can be controlled by ....

(1) chlorination   (2) coagulation   (3) aeration   (4) denitrification

147. The correct sequence of the sludge digestion steps is ....

(1) acid formation, hydrolysis, methane formation

(2) methane formation, acid formation, hydrolysis

(3) hydrolysis, methane formation, acid formation

(4) hydrolysis, acid formation, methane formation

148. In which one of the following tests is the organic matter in the waste water is used as food by micro-organisms ?

(1) BOD   (2) Most probable number

(3) COD   (4) Chlorine demand

149. Aerobic method of composting practiced in India is called ....
    (1) Bangalore method   (2) Nagpur method
    (3) Delhi method   (4) Indore method

150. Match List-I (Treatment units) with List-II (Type of processes) and select the correct answer using the codes given below the lists :

	List - I		List - II
A.	Trickling filter	1.	Symbiotic
B.	Activated sludge process	2.	Extended aeration
C.	Oxidation ditch	3.	Suspended growth
D.	Oxidation pond	4.	Attached growth

    Codes :

	A	B	C	D
(1)	3	4	2	1
(2)	4	3	1	2
(3)	3	4	1	2
(4)	4	3	2	1

151. If the moisture content of a sludge is reduced from 98 % to 96 %, the volume of sludge will decrease by ....
    (1) 2 %   (2) 20 %   (3) 25 %   (4) 50 %

152. In a high rate trickling filter, the problem of ponding can be solved by ....
    (1) flooding and raking   (2) chlorination and supply of air
    (3) raking and chlorination   (4) flooding and supply of air

153. Which one of the following terms, correctly describes 'Biomagnification' ?
    (1) Reproduction of micro-organisms
    (2) Observation of micro-organisms under a microscope
    (3) Ability of micro-organisms to from zoological film
    (4) Concentration of toxic materials in the food chain

154. Bangalore method and Indore method of disposing solid wastes are ....
    (1) identical
    (2) different as Bangalore method is an anaerobic method
    (3) different as Bangalore method does not contain human excreta
    (4) different as Indore method is incineration method

155. Amongst the various sewage treatment methods, for the same discharge, the largest area is needed for ....
    (1) trickling filter   (2) anaerobic pond
    (3) oxidation ditch   (4) oxidation pond

156. In an activated sludge process, the sludge volume index can be controlled by ....
    (1) aeration   (2) adding chlorine
    (3) reducing recycling ratio   (4) increasing the depth of aeration tank

157. A primary sedimentation tank is not required for ....
   (1) activated sludge system
   (2) extended aeration system
   (3) trickling filtration system
   (4) tapered activated sludge process using pure oxygen for aeration

158. Match List-I (Parameter) with List-II (Treatment unit or process) and select the correct answer using the codes given below the lists :

List - I		List - II	
A.	F/M ratio	1.	Anaerobic digester
B.	Solar energy	2.	Detritus tank
C.	Effluent recirculation	3.	Waste stabilization pond
D.	Volatile fatty acids	4.	Trickling filter
		5.	Activated sludge process

   Codes :

	A	B	C	D
(1)	2	3	5	4
(2)	5	3	4	1
(3)	5	1	4	3
(4)	4	1	2	3

159. In aerobic conditions, the microbial decomposition of organics results in the formation of which one of the following ?
   (1) Stable and objectionable end products
   (2) Unstable and objectionable end products
   (3) Unstable and acceptable end products
   (4) Stable and unobjectionable end products

160. Which one of the following reactors can create a problem of short circuiting due to density currents ?
   (1) Batch   (2) Complete mix   (3) Plug flow   (4) Fluidized bed

161. Match List-I (Treatment process) with List-II (Related Terms) and select the correct answer using the codes given below the lists :

List - I		List - II	
A.	Lagoons	1.	Attached growth system
B.	Trickling filter	2.	Algae-bacteria symbiotic relationship
C.	Oxidation ponds	3.	Extended aeration
D.	Activated sludge process	4.	Low cost treatment method

   Codes :

	A	B	C	D
(1)	4	3	2	1
(2)	2	1	4	3
(3)	4	1	2	3
(4)	2	3	4	1

162. When the recirculation ratio in a high rate trickling filter is unity, then what is the value of the recirculation factor ?

    (1) 1   (2) > 1   (3) < 1   (4) Zero

163. Presence of nitrogen in a waste water sample is due to the decomposition of ....

    (1) carbohydrates   (2) proteins   (3) fats   (4) vitamins

164. Match List-I (Physical properties of filtering material for trickling filters) with List-II (Limiting value) and select the correct answer using the codes given below the lists :

	List - I		List - II
A.	Crushing strength N/mm^2	1.	12.0
B.	Hardness	2.	100.0
C.	Percent wear	3.	4.0
D.	Specific gravity	4.	2.6

Codes :

	A	B	C	D
(1)	3	1	2	4
(2)	2	4	3	1
(3)	3	4	2	1
(4)	2	1	3	4

165. Match List-I with List-II and select the correct answer using the codes given below the lists :

	List - I		List - II
A.	Suspended solids	1.	May cause eutrophication
B.	Nutrients	2.	Toxic, may interfere with effluent reuse
C.	Heavy metals	3.	May interfere with effluent reuse
D.	Dissolved inorganic solids	4.	Cause sludge deposits

Codes :

	A	B	C	D
(1)	4	1	2	3
(2)	2	3	4	1
(3)	4	3	2	1
(4)	2	1	4	3

166. Which one of the following methods of solid waste management conserves energy most efficiently in the form of gas or oil ?

    (1) Incineration with heat recovery   (2) Combusting

    (3) Fluidized-bed incineration   (4) Pyrolysis

167. Which one of the following is considered as the thermophilic range of sludge digestion ?

    (1) 60°C to 70°C   (2) 50°C to 57°C   (3) 29°C to 40°C   (4) 20°C to 30°C

168. In a well operating activated sludge process unit, what is the value of sludge volume index ?

    (1) < 50   (2) 100 – 150   (3) 200 – 300   (4) > 300

169. Bangalore and Indore processes of composting are ....
     (1) both anaerobic processes
     (2) both aerobic processes
     (3) anaerobic process and aerobic process, respectively
     (4) aerobic process and anaerobic process, respectively

170. Which of the following pollutants are generally not removed in a sewage treatment plant ?
     (1) Inorganic suspended solids   (2) Dissolved organic solids
     (3) Oil and grease   (4) Dissolved inorganic solids

171. Match List-I (Water/Wastewater treatment) with List-II (Operating Problem) and select the correct answer using the codes given below the lists :

	List - I		List - II
A.	Trickling filter	1.	Negative head
B.	Activated sludge process	2.	Fly-breeding
C.	Rapid gravity filter	3.	Sludge bulking
D.	Anaerobic sludge digester	4.	pH reduction

Codes :

	A	B	C	D
(1)	4	3	1	2
(2)	2	3	1	4
(3)	4	1	3	2
(4)	2	1	3	4

172. Which one of the following types of samples is relevantly employed for the design of wastewater treatment plant ?
     (1) Grab sample   (2) Composite sample
     (3) Integrated sample   (4) Any sample

ANSWER KEY

1.	(2)	2.	(3)	3.	(2)	4.	(4)	5.	(4)	6.	(4)	7.	(1)	8.	(1)
9.	(4)	10.	(4)	11.	(2)	12.	(2)	13.	(1)	14.	(3)	15.	(3)	16.	(1)
17.	(1)	18.	(3)	19.	(1)	20.	(2)	21.	(4)	22.	(3)	23.	(3)	24.	(4)
25.	(2)	26.	(1)	27.	(4)	28.	(2)	29.	(4)	30.	(4)	31.	(1)	32.	(3)
33.	(3)	34.	(4)	35.	(3)	36.	(3)	37.	(3)	38.	(2)	39.	(2)	40.	(1)
41.	(2)	42.	(4)	43.	(1)	44.	(4)	45.	(2)	46.	(4)	47.	(2)	48.	(1)

49.	(4)	50.	(3)	51.	(1)	52.	(1)	53.	(1)	54.	(2)	55.	(4)	56.	(3)
57.	(3)	58.	(3)	59.	(2)	60.	(1)	61.	(3)	62.	(4)	63.	(4)	64.	(3)
65.	(2)	66.	(4)	67.	(2)	68.	(4)	69.	(3)	70.	(1)	71.	(4)	72.	(3)
73.	(1)	74.	(3)	75.	(2)	76.	(2)	77.	(4)	78.	(3)	79.	(1)	80.	(4)
81.	(2)	82.	(3)	83.	(1)	84.	(3)	85.	(1)	86.	(2)	87.	(3)	88.	(1)
89.	(4)	90.	(3)	91.	(3)	92.	(3)	93.	(4)	94.	(3)	95.	(4)	96.	(4)
97.	(4)	98.	(4)	99.	(3)	100.	(3)	101.	(4)	102.	(2)	103.	(2)	104.	(3)
105.	(2)	106.	(3)	107.	(2)	108.	(3)	109.	(1)	110.	(4)	111.	(3)	112.	(1)
113.	(3)	114.	(3)	115.	(4)	116.	(1)	117.	(1)	118.	(4)	119.	(2)	120.	(2)
121.	(4)	122.	(1)	123.	(3)	124.	(2)	125.	(4)	126.	(3)	127.	(3)	128.	(2)
129.	(3)	130.	(3)	131.	(2)	132.	(2)	133.	(2)	134.	(2)	135.	(2)	136.	(1)
137.	(4)	138.	(3)	139.	(4)	140.	(3)	141.	(3)	142.	(4)	143.	(2)	144.	(3)
145.	(3)	146.	(1)	147.	(4)	148.	(1)	149.	(4)	150.	(4)	151.	(4)	152.	(3)
153.	(4)	154.	(2)	155.	(4)	156.	(3)	157.	(2)	158.	(2)	159.	(4)	160.	(3)
161.	(3)	162.	(2)	163.	(2)	164.	(4)	165.	(1)	166.	(4)	167.	(2)	168.	(2)
169.	(3)	170.	(4)	171.	(2)	172.	(1)								

UNIT - 12 : HIGHWAY PLANNING

1. What is traffic density ?
   (1) Number of vehicles moving in specific direction per hour.
   (2) Number of vehicles moving in specific direction per lane per day.
   (3) Number of vehicles per unit length.
   (4) Number of vehicles passing a given point in one hour.
2. Tentative Equivalency factor suggested by the I.R.C for bus, truck and agricultural tractor-trailer unit is _____.
   (1) 1.5   (2) 2.0   (3) 2.5   (4) 3.0
3. A pavement designer has arrived at a design traffic of 100 million standard axles for a newly developing national highway as per IRC : 37 guidelines using the following data :
   Design life = 15 years, commercial vehicle count before pavement
   Construction = 4500 vehicles / day, annual traffic growth rate = 8%
   The vehicle damage factor used in the calculations was
   (1) 1.53   (2) 2.24   (3) 3.66   (4) 4.14
4. In an urban area, it is proposed to provide 90° angle parking. The available length of kerb is 1000 meter. How many parking spaces will there be available ?
   (1) 410   (2) 400   (3) 415   (4) 425
5. How many number of crossing conflict points are there on a right angled road intersection with two-way traffic ?
   (1) 04   (2) 08   (3) 16   (4) 24
6. Consider the following statements in the context of geometric design of roads :
   (I) A simple parabolic curve is an acceptable shape for summit curves.
   (II) Comfort to passengers is an important consideration in the design of summit curves.
   The correct option evaluating the above statements and their relationship is
   (1) I is true, II is false.
   (2) I is true, II is true, and II is correct reason for I.
   (3) I is true, II is true, and II is not the correct reason for I.
   (4) I is false, II is true
7. The design speed for a two-lane road is 80 kmph. When a design vehicle with a wheelbase of 6.6 m is negotiating a horizontal curve on that road, the off-tracking is measured as 0.096 m. The required widening of carriage way of two-lane road on the curve applied is
   (1) 0.55 m.   (2) 0.65 m.   (3) 0.75 m.   (4) 0.85 m.
8. Consider the following statements in the context of cement concrete pavements.
   I. Warping stresses in the cement concrete pavements are caused by the seasonal variation in temperature.
   II. Tie bars are generally provided across transverse joints of cement concrete pavement.
   The correct option is
   (1) I is true, II is false   (2) I is false, II is true
   (3) I is true, II is true   (4) I is false, II is false

9. A crest vertical curve joins two gradients of +3% and −2% for a design speed of 80 km/hr and the corresponding SSD of 120 m. The heights of driver's eye and the object above the road surface are 1.2 m and 0.15 m respectively. The curve length (which is < SSD) to be provided is
   - (1) 120 m
   - (2) 152 m
   - (3) 163 m
   - (4) 240 m

10. The extra widening required for a two-lane national highway at a horizontal curve of 300 m radius, considering a wheel base of 8m and a design speed of 100 kmph is
    - (1) 0.42 m
    - (2) 0.62 m
    - (3) 0.82 m
    - (4) 0.92 m

11. While designing a hill road with a ruling gradient of 6%, if a sharp horizontal curve of 50 m radius is encountered, the compensated gradient at the curve as per the Indian Road Congress specification should be
    - (1) 4.4 %
    - (2) 4.75 %
    - (3) 5 %
    - (4) 5.5 %

12. The design speed on a road is 60 kmph. Assuming the driver reaction time of 2.5 sec. and coefficient of friction of pavement surface as 0.35, the required stopping distance for two-way traffic on a single lane road is
    - (1) 82.1 m
    - (2) 102.4 m
    - (3) 164.2 m
    - (4) 186.4 m

13. A subgrade soil sample was tested using standard CBR apparatus and observations are given below.

Load (kg)	Penetration (mm)
60.5	2.5
80.5	5.0

    Assuming that the load penetration curve is convex thoroughout, the CBR value (%) of sample is
    - (1) 6.5
    - (2) 5.5
    - (3) 4.4
    - (4) 3.9

14. The following observations were made of an axle load survey on a road.

Axle load (km)	Repetitions per day
35 - 45	800
75 - 85	400

    The standard axle load is 80 kN. Equivalent daily number of repetitions for the standard axle load are
    - (1) 450
    - (2) 480
    - (3) 800
    - (4) 1200

15. A road having a horizontal curve of 400 m radius on which a super- elevation of 0.07 is provided. The coefficient of lateral friction mobilized on the curve when a vehicle is travelling at 100 kmph is
    - (1) 0.07
    - (2) 0.13
    - (3) 0.15
    - (4) 0.4

16. For a road with camber of 3% and the design speed of 80 km, the minimum radius of the curve, beyond which no super-elevation needed is
    - (1) 1680 m
    - (2) 946 m
    - (3) 406 m
    - (4) 280 m

17. The coefficient of friction in the longitudinal direction of highway is estimated as 0.396. The breaking distance for a car moving at a speed of 65 km/hr is
    - (1) 87 m
    - (2) 45 m
    - (3) 42 m
    - (4) 40 m

18. The data given below for flexible pavement,

    Initial Traffic = 1213 cvpd,   Traffic growth rate = 8% per annum,

    Design life = 12 yrs,   Vehicle damage factor = 2.5,

    Distribution Factor = 1.0,

    The design traffic in terms of million standard axles to be catered would be

    (1) 0.06 msa   (2) 8.40 msa   (3) 21.00 msa   (4) 32.26 msa

19. The design speed for a NH is 108 kmph. If maximum permissible super-elevation is 0.10 and coefficient of lateral friction is 0.15, the ruling minimum radius of horizontal curve on the highway should be

    (1) 260 m   (2) 315 m   (3) 380 m   (4) 410 m

20. A traffic stream in a particular distance of two-lane road is moving with a constant speed of 50 kmph with an average headway of 2.52 sec. The longitudinal distance between two consecutive vehicles is

    (1) 30 m   (2) 35 m   (3) 38 m   (4) 42 m

21. A car is moving at a speed of 72 km/hr on a road having 2% upward gradient. The driver applies breaks when he sees an obstruction. If his reaction time is 1.5 sec, assuming that the coefficient of friction between the pavement and tyre as 0.15, calculate the distance traversed before the car finally stops.

    (1) 24 m   (2) 150 m   (3) 1056 m   (4) 324 m

22. The average daily traffic on a stretch of road is 300 m commercial vehicles per lane per day. Design traffic repetition for 10 years, when vehicle damage factor is 2.5 and traffic growth rate is 7 %, is

    (1) 3.8 msa   (2) 23.5 msa   (3) 45.4 msa   (4) 16 msa

23. A valley curve has a descending gradient of 1 in 40 followed by an ascending gradient of 1 in 50. The length of the valley curve required for a design speed of 80 km/hour for comfort condition is

    (1) 199 m   (2) 116 m   (3) 58 m   (4) 37 m

24. Width of carriage way for a single lane is recommended to be

    (1) 7.5 m   (2) 7.0 m   (3) 3.75 m   (4) 3.5 m

25. Stopping sight distance is the minimum distance available on a highway which is the

    (1) distance of sufficient length to stop the vehicle without collision.

    (2) distance visible to a driver during night driving.

    (3) height of the object above the road surface.

    (4) distance equal to the height of driver's eye above the road surface.

26. Bituminous materials are commonly used in highway construction because of their good

    (1) tensile and compression properties   (2) binding and water proofing properties

    (3) shear strength and tensile properties   (4) bond and tensile properties

27. The Indian Road Congress came into existence in :

    (1) 1927   (2) 1934   (3) 1943   (4) 1947

28. The road connecting two towns is called a
    (1) Country road   (2) Urban road   (3) Highway   (4) None
29. Carriage way is protected by shoulder having width :
    (1) 0.5 to 1.25 m   (2) 1.25 to 2 m   (3) 2 to 4 m   (4) 4 to 6 m
30. The G.T. road was constructed during :
    (1) 1540 to 1545 A.D.   (2) 2000 to 2500 B.C.
    (3) 2500 to 3000 B.C.   (4) 1950 to 1960 A.D.
31. The road connecting capital cities of states is called
    (1) National highway   (2) Express way
    (3) State highway   (4) Capital highway
32. The Central Road Research Institute (CRRI) was started in Delhi in :
    (1) 1951   (2) 1955   (3) 1964   (4) 1965
33. The head quarter of Indian Road Congress is at :
    (1) Kolkata   (2) Mumbai   (3) Chennai   (4) New Delhi
34. Nagpur road plan formulae were prepared by assuming
    (1) rectangular or block road pattern   (2) radial or star and block road pattern
    (3) radial or star and circular road pattern
    (4) radial or star and grid road pattern
35. The road length per hundred square km in India is :
    (1) 10-15 km   (2) 35-50 km   (3) 90-100 km   (4) 100-120 km
36. In Nagpur conference, the minimum width of village roads was recommended as :
    (1) 2 m   (2) 2.25 m   (3) 2.45 m   (4) 3.1 m
37. The Indian Roads and Transport Development Association (I.R.T.D.A.) was set up in :
    (1) 1934   (2) 1927   (3) 1947   (4) 1951
38. National Highway Act, 1956 came into force from :
    (1) 15th April, 1957 (2) 15th April, 1960 (3) 15th April, 1965 (4) 15th April, 1967
39. According to Indian Roads Congress, the maximum width of a road vehicle is :
    (1) 1.85 m   (2) 2.25 m   (3) 2.45 m   (4) 3.2 m
40. The Motor Vehicle Act was enacted in :
    (1) 1930   (2) 1932   (3) 1939   (4) 1942
41. Match the pairs :

	List - I		List - II
(A)	A Central Road Fund	(1)	1939
(B)	IRC	(2)	1943
(C)	Motor Vehicles Act	(3)	1934
(D)	Nagpur Road conference	(4)	1st March 1929

Codes :

	(A)	(B)	(C)	(D)
(1)	4	3	1	2
(2)	1	4	2	3
(3)	2	3	4	1
(4)	1	2	3	4

42. Match the Pairs

    List - I   List - II
    (Type of road)   (Width of Carriage Way)
    (A) Single Lane   (1) 7.0 m
    (B) Two-Lane road without kerbs   (2) 7.5 m
    (C) Two-Lane road with raised kerbs   (3) 3.75 m
    (D) Multi lane pavements   (4) 3.5 m

              (A)   (B)   (C)   (D)
        (1)   3   1   2   4
        (2)   1   2   3   4
        (3)   3   4   2   1
        (4)   1   3   4   2

43. For WBM road, the recommended camber is
    (1) 1 in 24 to 1 in 30   (2) 1 in 30 to 1 in 48
    (3) 1 in 60 to 1 in 80   (4) 1 in 80 to 1 in 120

44. The camber, for the drainage of surface water, was first introduced by :
    (1) Telford   (2) Tresaguet   (3) Sully   (4) Macadam

45. As per IRC the camber on cement concrete road should be :
    (1) 1 in 60 to 72   (2) 1 in 45 to 60   (3) 1 in 20 to 24   (4) 1 in 12 to 16

46. The recommended safe coefficient of friction is :
    (1) 1.5   (2) 0.15   (3) 1/15   (4) 15

47. Camber on road is provided for :
    (1) effective drainage   (2) counteracting the centrifugal force
    (3) having proper sight distance   (4) All of these

48. The rate of rise or fall along road alignment is known as
    (1) Gradient   (2) Camber   (3) Side slope   (4) Super-elevation

49. In WBM roads
    (1) small broken stones are laid in two layers
    (2) void between the stones are filled by stone dust
    (3) camber for drainage is given at the formation level itself
    (4) All of above

50. The top of ground on which the foundation of road rests, is called :
    (1) Sub-grade   (2) Soling   (3) Base   (4) Wearing layer

51. The super structure of road is called :
    (1) Wearing course (2) Wearing layer (3) Road surface   (4) All of above

52. The thickness of base in no case, should be more than :
    (1) 10 cm   (2) 12 cm   (3) 15 cm   (4) 30 cm

53. The highest point on road surface is called :
    (1) Crown   (2) Camber   (3) Gradient   (4) Bern

54. Road metal thickness of the layer to be compacted should exceed :
    (1) 5 cm   (2) 10 cm   (3) 15 cm   (4) 30 cm

55. The maximum side slope to be provided in cutting on a road can be :
    (1) 1 : 2   (2) 2 : 1   (3) 1 : 4   (4) Vertical

56. In case of WBM roads with traffic up to 1000 tonnes per day life may be expected as :
    (1) 1-2 yrs.   (2) 5-6 yrs.   (3) 8-10 yrs.   (4) 10-15 yrs.

57. On WBM road the roller used for rolling purposes is of weight :
    (1) 3 to 5 tonnes   (2) 5 to 8 tonnes   (3) 8 to 10 tonnes   (4) 15 to 20 tonnes

58. Generally life of an earthen road varies in between :
    (1) 12 to 30 yrs.   (2) 5 to 10 yrs.   (3) 2 to 4 yrs.   (4) Less than 1 year

59. The camber of road should be approximately equal to ....the longitudinal gradient.
    (1) 1/2   (2) 2 times   (3) 3 times   (4) 4 times

60. The main advantage of providing super-elevation is :
    (1) to decrease the intensity of stresses on foundation
    (2) to achieve higher speed of vehicles
    (3) to increase the stability of the fast moving vehicles, when they negotiate horizontal curve
    (4) All of above

61. In absence of super-elevation, pot holes occur at :
    (1) centre   (2) outer edge   (3) inner edge   (4) None of above

62. The equilibrium super-elevation is given by
    (1) V^2/R (2) V^2/gR (3) $V^2/127 R$ (4) None of above

63. The maximum super-elevation on hill roads should not exceed :
    (1) 7 %   (2) 8 %   (3) 9 %   (4) 10 %

64. As per IRC recommendations the maximum limits of super-elevations for mixed traffic in plain terrain is :
    (1) 1 in 15   (2) 1 in 12.5   (3) 1 in 10   (4) equal to camber

65. The attainment of super-elevation by rotation of pavement about the inner edge of the pavement :
    (1) is preferable in steep terrain   (2) results in balancing the earthwork
    (3) avoids the drainage problem in flat terrain
    (4) All of above

66. For a constant value of coefficient of lateral friction, the value of required super-elevation increases with :
    (1) increase in both speed and radius of curve
    (2) decrease in both speed and radius of curve
    (3) increase in speed and with the decrease in radius of curve
    (4) None of the above

67. According to IRC, super-elevation balances the centrifugal forces corresponding to
    (1) full design speed   (2) $\frac{1}{2}$ of design speed
    (3) $\frac{3}{4}$ of design speed   (4) None of above

68. The super–elevation is
    (1) directly proportional to the velocity of vehicles
    (2) inversely proportional to the velocity of vehicles
    (3) directly proportional to the width of pavement
    (4) inversely proportional to the width of pavement

69. Which one of following geometric features requires the magnitudes of weaving angle and weaving distance for its design ?
    (1) Rotary design   (2) Right-angle intersection
    (3) Round about   (4) Grade-separated junction

70. Super-elevation should not be ....than the camber.
    (1) less   (2) more   (3) more or less   (4) None of these

71. To prevent overturning of bullock cart on curves, the maximum value of super-elevation given by IRC is :
    (1) 1 in 15   (2) 1 in 17   (3) 1 in 10   (4) 1 in 22

72. The main advantage of providing super-elevation is :
    (1) to decrease the intensity of stresses on the foundation
    (2) to increase the stability of fast moving vehicles, when they negotiate a horizontal curve
    (3) to achieve higher speed   (4) All of above

73. As per IRC, in hilly roads, the ruling gradient should not be more than :
    (1) 3.33%   (2) 5%   (3) 6%   (4) 6.66%

74. In hilly roads, as per IRC, the limiting gradient should not be more than :
    (1) 1 in 10   (2) 1 in 15   (3) 1 in 12   (4) 1 in 30

75. The steepest gradient which is to be permitted on the road is called :
    (1) maximum gradient   (2) limiting gradient
    (3) Both (a) and (b)   (4) None of these

76. An essential gradient, provided for purpose of drainage, is called :
    (1) minimum gradient   (2) maximum gradient
    (3) exceptional gradient   (4) floating gradient

77. Exceptional gradient should not be provided in a length more than :
    (1) 10 m   (2) 15 m   (3) 40 m   (4) 100 m

78. The value of ruling gradient in plains as per IRC recommendation is :
    (1) 1 in 12   (2) 1 in 15   (3) 1 in 20   (4) 1 in 30

79. The maximum rate of super-elevation is given by :
    (1) $e = V^2/225\,R$ (2) $e = V^2/424\,R$ (3) $e = V^2/540\,R$ (4) $e = V^2/1000\,R$

80. As per IRC, the slope of earth in cutting should be :
    (1) 1 : 1   (2) 1 : 2   (3) 1 : 3   (4) 1 : 4

81. The SSD of a vehicle for Indian highway is given by :
    (1) $S = 0.28\,V.t + \dfrac{0.01\,V^2}{n}$ (2) $S = 0.28\,V.t + \dfrac{0.01\,n}{V^2}$

    (3) $S = 0.01\,V.t + \dfrac{0.28\,V^2}{n}$ (4) $S = 0.01\,V.t + \dfrac{0.28\,n}{V^2}$

82. The stopping sight distance depends upon :
    (1) speed   (2) braking time   (3) reaction time   (4) All of above

83. According to IRC, the absolute minimum radius of curve for safe operation for a design speed of 100 kmph is :
    (1) 100 m   (2) 200 m   (3) 300 m   (4) 400 m

84. The mechanical extra widening required for 10.5 m wide pavement on a horizontal curve of radius R m is given by
    (1) $l^2/2R$ (2) $2l^2/3R$ (3) l^2/R (4) $3l^2/2R$

85. If an ascending gradient of 1 in 50 meets a descending gradient of 1 in 50, the length of summit curve for a stopping sight distance of 80 m will be :
    (1) zero   (2) 60 m   (3) 64 m   (4) 80 m

86. The transition curve used in the horizontal alignment of highway as per IRC recommendation is :
    (1) spiral   (2) lemniscate   (3) cubic parabola   (4) Any of the above

87. The shift (S) of a transition curve is given by :
    (1) $S = L^2/6\,R$ (2) $S = L^2/12\,R$ (3) $S = L^2/24\,R$ (4) $S = L^2/40\,R$

88. The length of transition curve in m is :
    (1) $L = v^3/CR$ (2) $L = v^3/16\,CR$ (3) $L = v^3/24\,CR$ (4) $L = v^3/48\,CR$

89. In case of a cubic spiral, the polar deflection angle may be assumed to be equal to :
    (1) $\phi/2$ (2) $\phi/3$ (3) $\phi/4$ (4) $\phi/5$
    where ϕ = deviation angle of curve

90. The length of tangent of a simple curve having angle of deflection radius of curvature R is equal to :
    (1) $R \tan \phi/2$ (2) $R \cot \phi/2$ (3) $R \cos \phi/2$ (4) $R \sin \phi/2$

91. The intrinsic equation of an ideal transition curve representing a clothoid is given by :
    (1) $\phi = l^2/2RL$ (2) $\phi = l^2/4RL$ (3) $\phi = l^2/8RL$ (4) $\phi = l^2/16RL$

92. As per IRC, the maximum width of a vehicle should be :
    (1) 2 m   (2) 2.44 m   (3) 3.8 m   (4) 1.58 m

93. The width of shoulders provided on a road side varies in between 1.2 m and
    (1) 2.5 m   (2) 1.8 m   (3) 8 m   (4) 0.6 m

94. The factor which influences the design of curves is :
    (1) Speed of vehicle   (2) Maximum permissible super-elevation
    (3) Permissible centrifugal ratio   (4) All of the above

95. In India, a curve is expressed in terms of angle in degress subtended to the centre by an arc of .....radius.
    (1) 25 m   (2) 30 m   (3) 45 m   (4) 60 m

96. If L is the length of wheel base of vehicle and R is the mean radius of a curve, then the amount of extra width (b) to be provided on roads is given by :
    (1) $b = nL/R$ (2) $b = nL^2/R$ (3) $b = nL/2R$ (4) $b = nL^2/2R$

97. As per IRC, the minimum length of transition curve for a mountainous terrain road with radius of curvature 100 m and design speed of vehicle 100 kmph is

(1)   270 m   (2)   200 m   (3)   100 m   (4)   170 m

98. The maximum super-elevation to be provided on a road curve is 1 in 15. If the rate of change of super-elevation is specified as 1 in 120 and road width is 10 m, then the minimum length of transition curve on either end will be :

(1)   180 m   (2)   125 m   (3)   80 m   (4)   30 m

99. The radius of a horizontal curve is 100 m. The design speed is 50 kmph and the design coefficient of lateral friction is 0.15. What would be the rate of super-elevation if full lateral friction is considered :

(1)   1 in 2.12   (2)   1 in 15.8   (3)   1 in 25   (4)   1 in 32.6

100. Psychological widening on road curves is given by :

(1) $\dfrac{nL^2}{2R}$ (2) $\dfrac{0.1\ V}{\sqrt{R}}$ (3) $\dfrac{0.1\ nV}{\sqrt{R}}$ (4) $\dfrac{0.1\ V}{\sqrt{R}} + \dfrac{nl^2}{R}$

101. A road camber is given in following figure.

For designing this camber the equation to be used is :

(1) $y = x^2/60$ (2) $y = x^2/120$ (3) $y = x^2/210$ (4) $y = x^2/225$

102. While alignment of a hilly road with a ruling gradient of 1 in 20, a horizontal curve of radius 80 m is encountered. The compensated gradient on the curve will be :

(1)   1 in 15   (2)   1 in 17   (3)   1 in 25   (4)   1 in 27

103. Summit curves are required to be introduced at situations where :

(1)   +ve grade meets – ve grade   (2)   +ve grade meets another milder +ve grade

(3)   – ve grade meets steeper – ve grade (4)   All of the above

104. Alignment of a road is finally decided on the basis of :

(1)   selection of route   (2)   field survey

(3)   Trace cut   (4)   None of these

105. While deriving formula for length of valley curve, it is assumed that the head light is ..... above the road.

(1)   0.25 m   (2)   0.75 m   (3)   0.9 m   (4)   1.2 m

106. In detailed survey of hilly road, the interval for plotting the contours at sharp curves is generally :

(1)   1 m   (2)   2 m   (3)   4 m   (4)   6 m

107. A terrain with cross slope less than 10 % is called :

(1)   level terrain   (2)   steep terrain

(3)   mountainous terrain   (4)   rolling terrain

108. According to IRC, the length of valley curve, when length of curve exceeds the required sight distance (S), is given by :

   (1) $L = \dfrac{GS^2}{1.5 + 0.035\,S}$

   (2) $L = \dfrac{1.5 + 0.035\,S}{G^2}$

   (3) $L = 2S - \dfrac{1.5 + 0.035\,S}{G}$

   (4) $L = 2S - \dfrac{G}{1.5 + 0.035\,S}$

109. If S is the passing sight distance, then the length of summit curve (L), when S is less than L, is given by :

   (1) $L = \dfrac{GS^2}{4}$
       (2) $L = \dfrac{GS^2}{9.6}$
       (3) $L = 2S - \dfrac{9.6}{G}$
       (4) $L = 2S - \dfrac{4}{G}$

110. The minimum length of valley curve should be such that the head light beam sight distance is equal to the :

   (1) braking distance   (2) passing sight distance

   (3) stopping sight distance   (4) All of the above

111. In hilly roads, minimum sight distance required is :

   (1) SSD   (2) braking distance

   (3) passing sight distance   (4) All above

112. If R is the radius of curvature of a hilly road, the maximum grade compensation (%) is equal to :

   (1) 75 / R   (2) 100 / R   (3) 65 / R   (4) 85 / R

113. The minimum design speed for hair pin bends in hilly roads is taken as :

   (1) 20 kmph   (2) 30 kmph   (3) 40 kmph   (4) 50 kmph

114. Rolling terrain is a terrain with cross-slope of :

   (1) upto 10%   (2) 10 to 25 %   (3) 25 to 60 %   (4) greater than 60%

115. According to IRC : 52 – 1973, for a single lane national highway in a hilly area

   (1) the total width of the road-way must be 6.25 m.

   (2) the width of the carriage way must be 3.75 m.

   (3) the shoulder on either side must be 1.25 m.

   (4) All of the above

116. The IRC has recommended the following equation for finding the value of centrifugal acceleration 'C' for the design speed V kmph.

   (1) $C = \dfrac{80}{(75 + V)}$
     (2) $C = \dfrac{75}{(80 + V)}$
     (3) $C = \dfrac{(75 + V)}{80}$
     (4) $C = \dfrac{(80 + V)}{75}$

117. If the pavement is rotated about the inner edge, the length of transition curve is given by :

   (1) $L_s = eN\,(W + W_e)$
       (2) $L_s = \dfrac{eN}{2}\,(W + W_e)$

   (3) $L_s = eN\,(W - W_e)$
       (4) $L_s = \dfrac{eN}{2}\,(W - W_e)$

118. Grade compensation is given by formula :

   (1) $\dfrac{30 + R}{R}$
       (2) $\dfrac{R}{30 + R}$
       (3) $\dfrac{30 - R}{R}$
       (4) $\dfrac{R}{30 - R}$

119. According to IRC, grade compensation is not necessary for gradients flatter than :
   (1)   1 %   (2)   3 %   (3)   4 %   (4)   10 %

120. While aligning a hill road with ruling gradient of 6%, a horizontal curve of radius 60 m is encountered. Find the compensated gradient at the curve.
   (1)   1.75 %   (2)   4.75 %   (3)   3.5 %   (4)   None of above

121. According to IRC, the minimum length of summit or valley curve should not be less than .... the design speed in kmph.
   (1)   1/2   (2)   1/4th   (3)   2/3rd   (4)   3/4th

122. Summit curves in vertical curves are with convexity :
   (1)   upward   (2)   downward
   (3)   Both (a) and (b)   (4)   None

123. While designing summit curve we consider
   (1)   SSD   (2)   OSD
   (3)   Both SSD and OSD   (4)   None of the above

124. While designing summit curve if length of curve (L) is greater than SSD, then equation for length L of parabolic curve is given by :
   (1) $L = \dfrac{NS^2}{(\sqrt{2H} + \sqrt{2h})^2}$ (2) $L = \dfrac{N^2S}{(\sqrt{2H} + \sqrt{2h})^2}$
   (3) $L = \dfrac{NS}{(\sqrt{2H} + \sqrt{2h})^2}$ (4) $L = \dfrac{NS}{(\sqrt{2H} + \sqrt{2h})}$

125. While designing summit curve, if L > OSD, then the length of parabolic summit curve is given by :
   (1) $L = \dfrac{NS^2}{9.6}$ (2) $L = \dfrac{9.6}{NS^2}$ (3) $L = \dfrac{N^2S}{9.6}$ (4) $L = \dfrac{NS}{9.6}$

126. In a district where the rainfall is heavy, major district road of WBM pavement 3.8 m wide is constructed. What should be height of crown with respect to edge ?
   (1)   0.058 m   (2)   0.038 m   (3)   0.01 m   (4)   0.035 m

127. The width of carriage way as per IRC for single lane road is :
   (1)   3.75 m   (2)   7 m   (3)   5.5 m   (4)   3.5 m

128. The minimum width of shoulder recommended by IRC is :
   (1)   2.5 m   (2)   1.5 m   (3)   3.5 m   (4)   7.5 m

129. Longitudinal coefficient of friction F_1 for speed 100 kmph is given as :
   (1)   0.35   (2)   0.36   (3)   0.38   (4)   0.4

130. While calculating OSD, the minimum spacing between vehicles which depends on their speed is given by empirical formula :
   (1) $(0.7\,V_b + 6)$ m   (2) $(0.7 + V_b)\,6$ m   (3) $(0.7\,V_b - 6)$ m   (4) $(0.7\,V_b + 7)$ m

131. A water bound macadam road is an example of :
   (1)   rigid pavement   (2)   semi-rigid pavement
   (3)   flexible pavement   (4)   None of these

132. Los Angles testing machine is used to conduct :
   (1)   Abrasion test   (2)   Impact test
   (3)   Attrition test   (4)   Crushing strength test

133. Which of the following test measures the toughness of road aggregates ?
    (1) Crushing strength test   (2) Abrasion test
    (3) Impact test   (4) Shape test

134. If aggregate impact value is 20 to 30 %, then it is classified as :
    (1) Satisfactory for road surfacing (2) Strong
    (3) Unsuitable for road surfacing   (4) Exceptionally strong

135. Percentage of free carbon in bitumen is :
    (1) more than that in tar   (2) less than that in tar
    (3) equal to that in tar   (4) none of these.

136. The ductility value of bitumen for suitability in road construction should not be less than :
    (1) 30 cm   (2) 40 cm   (3) 50 cm   (4) 55 cm

137. Which of the following represents hardest grade of bitumen ?
    (1) 30/40   (2) 60/70   (3) 90/100   (4) 100/120

138. The maximum limit of water absorption for aggregate suitable for road construction is :
    (1) 0.4 %   (2) 0.6 %   (3) 0.8 %   (4) 1.0 %

139. Bitumen of grade 80/100 means :
    (1) Its penetration value is 8 mm   (2) Its penetration value is 10 mm
    (3) Its penetration value is 8 to 10 mm (4) Its penetration value is 8 cm

140. Penetration test on bitumen is used for determining its :
    (1) grade   (2) viscosity
    (3) ductility   (4) temperature susceptibility

141. RC-2, MC-2 and SC-2 correspond to :
    (1) same viscosity
    (2) viscosity in increasing order from RC- 2 to SC - 2
    (3) viscosity in decreasing order from RC – 2 to SC – 2
    (4) None of false

142. The recommended grade of tar for grouting purpose is ....
    (1) RT - 1   (2) RT - 2   (3) RT - 3   (4) RT - 5

143. Softening point of bitumen to be used for road construction, at a place where maximum temperature is 40° C, should be :
    (1) less than 40° C   (2) greater than 40° C
    (3) equal to 40° C   (4) None of these

144. For rapid curing cutbacks, the oil used in :
    (1) gasoline   (2) kerosene
    (3) light diesel   (4) heavy diesel

145. If in a Dorry abrasion test, the loss in weight is 21 gm, then the coefficient of hardness is :
    (1) 9.5   (2) 13   (3) 17   (4) 21

146. Bituminous materials are used in highway construction primarily because of their :
    (1) cementing and water proofing properties
    (2) load bearing capacity
    (3) high specific gravity
    (4) black colour which facilitates road marking

147. California Bearing Ratio (CBR) :
    (1) is a measure of soil strength
    (2) is a procedure for designing flexible pavements
    (3) is a method of soil identification
    (4) none of these

148. Match the pairs

List - I	List - II
(A) Penetration test	1. Design of bituminous concrete mix
(B) Marshall test	2. Overlap design
(C) Ring and ball test	3. Gradation of asphalt cement
(D) Bankelman beam test	4. Determination of softening point

    Options :

	(A)	(B)	(C)	(D)
(1)	3	2	4	1
(2)	3	1	4	2
(3)	2	3	1	4
(4)	4	2	3	1

149. Match the pairs

List - I	List - II
(Type of road surface)	(% of camber in areas of heavy fall)
(A) Cement concrete	1. 4 %
(B) Thin bituminous surface	2. 3 %
(C) Water-bound macadam	3. 2 %
(D) Earth	4. 2.5 %

    Options :

	(A)	(B)	(C)	(D)
(1)	4	3	2	1
(2)	3	2	1	4
(3)	4	3	1	2
(4)	3	4	2	1

150. Match the pairs :

List - I	List - II
(Type of curve)	(Suitable shape)
(A) Valley curve	1. Spiral
(B) Summit curve	2. Cubic parabola
(C) Horizontal highway transition curve	3. Simple parabola

Options :

	(A)	(B)	(C)
(1)	3	2	1
(2)	1	3	2
(3)	2	3	1
(4)	1	2	3

151. Match the pairs

List - I	List - II
(Test of Aggregates)	(Property)
(A) Abrasion test	1. Parability
(B) Crushing strength test	2. Toughness
(C) Impact test	3. Hardness
(D) Soundness Test	4. Compressive strength

Options :

	(A)	(B)	(C)	(D)
(1)	3	4	2	1
(2)	4	3	2	1
(3)	3	2	4	1
(4)	4	2	3	1

152. Which one of the following methods is used in the design of rigid pavements.
    (1) CBR method
    (2) Group index method
    (3) Westerguards method
    (4) Mc Leods method

153. In CBR test, the value of CBR is calculated at :
    (1) 2.5 mm penetration only
    (2) 5 mm penetration only
    (3) both 2.5 and 5 mm penetration
    (4) None of these

154. The group index method of designing flexible pavement is :
    (1) an empirical method based on the physical properties of the sub-grade soil
    (2) an empirical method based on the strength characteristics of the sub-grade soil
    (3) a semi-empirical method
    (4) None of these

155. Flexible pavement distributes the wheel load :
    (1) directly to sub-grade
    (2) through structural action
    (3) through a set of layers to the subgrade
    (4) None of these

156. Hot bitumen is sprayed over freshly constructed bituminous surface followed by spreading of 6.3 mm coarse aggregates and rolled. Which one of the following is indicated by this type of construction ?
    (1) Surface dressing
    (2) Gravel-bitumen mix
    (3) Liquid seal coat
    (4) Seal coat

157. Flexible pavement derive stability primarily from :
    (1) aggregate interlock, particle friction and cohesion
    (2) cohesion on alone
    (3) the binding power of bituminous materials
    (4) the flexural strength of surface course

158. The value of group index of a soil varies from
    (1) 0 to 20   (2) 0 to 22   (3) 0 to 25   (4) 0 to 36

159. The minimum thickness of the base of a flexible pavement is kept as :
    (1) 5 cm   (2) 10 cm   (3) 12 cm   (4) 15 cm

160. Group Index method of design of flexible pavement is :
    (1) a theoretical method
    (2) an empirical method based on physical properties of sub-grade soil
    (3) an empirical method based on strength characteristics of sub-grade soil
    (4) a semi-empirical method

161. If the group index value of sub-grade is between 5 and 9, then the sub-grade is treated as :
    (1) good   (2) fair   (3) poor   (4) very poor

162. The group index for a soil, whose liquid limit is 40 %, plasticity index is 10 % and % passing 75 µ IS sieve is 35, is :
    (1) 0   (2) 3   (3) 5   (4) 7

163. Main drawback of CBR method is that it :
    (1) does not consider the strength characteristics of sub-grade soil.
    (2) gives the total thickness which remains the same irrespective of the quality of materials used in the component layers.
    (3) does not give the thickness of individual layers.
    (4) is a complex method.

164. Rigidity factor for a tyre pressure greater than 7 kg/cm² is :
    (1) equal to 1   (2) less than 1   (3) greater than 1   (4) zero

165. Radius of relative stiffness in 1 m is given by :
    (1) $\left[\dfrac{Eh^3}{12(1 - \mu) k}\right]^{1/4}$ (2) $\left[\dfrac{Eh^3}{12(1 - \mu^2) k}\right]^{1/4}$

    (3) $\left[\dfrac{Eh^3}{12 (1 - \mu^2)}\right]^{1/2}$ (4) $\left[\dfrac{Eh^2}{12 (1 - \mu^2)}\right]^{1/3}$

166. If 'W' is the wheel load and 'σ' is the unit stress in tension, then the thickness of concrete pavement (t) is given by :
    (1) $t = \sqrt{\dfrac{W}{\sigma}}$ (2) $t = \sqrt{\dfrac{2W}{\sigma}}$ (3) $t = \sqrt{\dfrac{3W}{\sigma}}$ (4) $t = \sqrt{\dfrac{4W}{\sigma}}$

167. Critical load position in a rigid pavement design is taken as
    (1) interior loading   (2) edge loading
    (3) corner loading   (4) interior edge and corner loading

168. Rapid curing cutback bitumen is produced by blending bitumen with :
    (1)   kerosene   (2)   benzene   (3)   diesel   (4)   petrol

169. As per latest IRC guidelines for designing flexible pavement by CBR method, the load parameter required is :
    (1)   number of commercial vehicles per day
    (2)   cumulative standard axles in msa
    (3)   equivalent single axle load
    (4)   number of vehicles during design life

170. For carrying out bituminous patch work during rainy season, the most suitable binder is :
    (1)   Road tar   (2)   Hot bitumen
    (3)   Cutback bitumen   (4)   Bituminous emulsion

171. The difference in level between triangular disc and rectangular plate in cautionary sign should be :
    (1)   50 cm   (2)   10 cm   (3)   25 cm   (4)   15 cm

172. Which of the following tests measures the toughness of road aggregate?
    (1)   Abrasion test   (2)   Crushing strength test
    (3)   Impact test   (4)   Shape test

173. Mandatory signs are displaced on a disc having a diameter of :
    (1)   30 cm   (2)   60 cm   (3)   50 cm   (4)   100 cm

174. Tie bars in cement concrete pavements are at
    (1)   expansion joint   (2)   longitudinal joint
    (3)   contraction joint   (4)   None of these

175. The maximum spacing of contraction joints in rigid pavements is :
    (1)   10 mm   (2)   25 mm   (3)   35 mm   (4)   50 mm

176. The function of expansion joint at rigid pavement is to :
    (1)   allow free expansion   (2)   allow contraction
    (3)   relieve warping stresses   (4)   None of these

177. The thickness of bituminous carpet varies from :
    (1)   20 to 25 mm   (2)   25 to 30 mm
    (3)   50 to 75 mm   (4)   75 to 100 mm

178. Expansion joints in cement concrete pavements are provided at an interval of :
    (1)   15 m   (2)   20 m   (3)   18 to 21 m   (4)   25 to 30 m

179. The drain which is provided parallel to roadway to intercept and divert the water from hill slopes is known as
    (1)   Catch water drain   (2)   Sloping drain
    (3)   Side drain   (4)   Cross drain

180. For sand soils the most common method of stabilization is :
    (1)   Soil bitumen stabilization   (2)   Mechanical stabilization
    (3)   Soil cement stabilization   (4)   All of above

181. In bituminous pavement, alligator cracking is mainly due to :
    (1) use of excessive bitumen
    (2) fatigue arising from repeated stress applications
    (3) inadequate wearing course
    (4) All of above

182. The main function of prime coat is to :
    (1) provide bond between existing base and surface of new construction
    (2) control dust nuisance
    (3) improve rigiding quality of pavement :
    (4) All of above

183. Reflection cracking is observed in :
    (1) flexible pavement
    (2) rigid pavement
    (3) bituminous overlay over cement concrete surface
    (4) rigid overlay over flexible pavement

184. In Los Angeles Abrasion Test on aggregate if the speed of drum is increased to 50 rpm then abrasion value will
    (1) increase   (2) decrease   (3) remain unchanged (4) unpredictable

185. Which one of following causes raveling in bituminous pavement ?
    (1) use of soft bitumen   (2) excessive bitumen content
    (3) low bitumen content   (4) use of open grated aggregate

186. It is generally satisfactory to design the highway facilities for the traffic volume corresponding to :
    (1) peak hour   (2) annual average daily traffic
    (3) 30th hour   (4) 29th hour

187. In which one of the following grade of a highway is an emergency escape ramp provided ?
    (1) 1 in 200   (2) Zero grade
    (3) Down grade   (4) None of these

188. Which one of following is the chronological sequence in regard to road construction / design pavement?
    (1) Telford, Tresaguet, CBR, Macadam (2) Tresaguet, Telford, Macadam, CBR
    (3) Macadam, CBR, Tresaguet, Telford (4) Tresaguet, Macadam, Telford, CBR

189. The general requirement in constructing a reinforced concrete road is to place a single layer of reinforcement
    (1) near the bottom of slab   (2) near the top of lab
    (3) at middle   (4) equally distributed at top and bottom

190. The amount of mechanical energy imposed on the aggregate during the aggregate impact test is of order :
    (1) 5320 kg-cm   (2) 6750 kg-cm   (3) 7980 kg-cm   (4) 11400 kg-cm

191. With the reference to Marshal mix design criteria for highway, which one of the following pairs is not correctly matched ?
    (1) Stability value   -   340 min
    (2) Flow value   -   8 - 16
    (3) VFB   -   50 - 75
    (4) % Air voids   -   3 - 5

192. Which one of the following binders is recommended for a wet and cold climate ?
    (1) 80 / 100 penetration asphalt   (2) Tar
    (3) Cutback   (4) Emulsion

193. A wall constructed to retain the earth from slippage on the hill side of the roadway is called :
    (1) Breast wall   (2) Retaining wall
    (3) Parapet wall   (4) None of these

194. The thickness of cement concrete slab generally adopted varies in between :
    (1) 1 cm to 5 cm   (2) 5 cm to 10 cm
    (3) 15 cm to 20 cm   (4) 25 cm to 30 cm

195. Bituminous grouted macadam roads may be expected to have a useful life of about :
    (1) 3 to 5 yrs.   (2) 7 to 10 yrs.   (3) 10 to 12 yrs.   (4) 15 to 20 yrs.

196. Compaction of concrete slab is done with help of :
    (1) light roller   (2) heavy roller   (3) vibrator   (4) mixer

197. As per IRC, the difference in temperature in between aggregate and binder should not be :
    (1) more than 14° C   (2) less than 14° C
    (3) less than 20° C   (4) more than 20° C

198. The width of bay on a concrete road is generally taken as :
    (1) > 4.5 m   (2) < 4.5 m   (3) 3 to 4.5 m   (4) 4.5 to 5 m

199. The circular isolated depressions formed on flexible road pavements are known as :
    (1) Pot holes   (2) Rut   (3) Pit   (4) Crack

200. Patching should be done just :
    (1) after rainy season   (2) after summer season
    (3) before winter season   (4) before rainy season

201. The traffic volume is equal to :
    (1) $\dfrac{\text{Traffic speed}}{\text{Traffic density}}$ (2) $\dfrac{\text{Traffic density}}{\text{Traffic speed}}$
    (3) traffic density × traffic speed   (4) None of these.

202. Which set of traffic studies is needed for functional design as well as for highway capacity design ?
    (1) Origin and destination studies   (2) Parking and accident studies
    (3) Speed and volume studies   (4) Axle load studies

203. Which one of following traffic survey schemes is most relevant while deciding on locating major routes in city ?
    (1) Traffic volume survey
    (2) Origin and destination survey
    (3) Speed survey
    (4) Traffic capacity survey

204. On a right angled road intersection with two-lane, two-way traffic, the total number of potential conflict points will be :
    (1) 22
    (2) 24
    (3) 16
    (4) 32

205. An Enoscope is used for measuring :
    (1) Running speed
    (2) Time mean speed
    (3) Spot speed
    (4) Overall speed

206. The design capacity is also known as :
    (1) Practical capacity
    (2) Theoretical capacity
    (3) Basic capacity
    (4) Possible capacity

207. The instantaneous speed of vehicle as it passes a point in a highway is known as :
    (1) Design speed
    (2) Running speed
    (3) Spot speed
    (4) Overall speed

208. The average speed maintained by a vehicle over a particular stretch of road, while the vehicle is in motion, is known as :
    (1) Running speed
    (2) Design speed
    (3) Spot speed
    (4) Overall speed

209. The number of vehicles passing any point in one hour per lane is given by :
    (1) $C = \dfrac{1000\ V}{S}$
    (2) $C = \dfrac{100\ V}{S}$
    (3) $C = \dfrac{1000\ V}{S^2}$
    (4) $C = \dfrac{1000\ V^2}{S}$

210. According to IRC, for a passenger car, the PCU is :
    (1) 2
    (2) 3
    (3) 1
    (4) 5

211. The practical capacity of a highway is .... that of possible capacity.
    (1) same as
    (2) less than
    (3) more than
    (4) None of these

212. High way density is defined as the total number of vehicles
    (1) that can be accommodated on a unit length of the road.
    (2) that can pass a given point in a unit period of time.
    (3) that can pass a given point in a specified period of time.
    (4) None of above

213. Highway capacity is defined as the total number of vehicles :
    (1) that can be accommodated on a unit length of the road.
    (2) that can pass a given point in a unit period of time.
    (3) that can pass a given point in a specified period of time.
    (4) None of above

214. As per IRC recommendations, traffic volume study is carried out for rural roads for .... days continuously during harvesting and lean season.
    (1) 7
    (2) 14
    (3) 21
    (4) 28

215. The average number of vehicles passing on a section of road during a particular year is called :
   (1) Peak hour traffic   (2) Average daily traffic
   (3) Design heavy traffic   (4) None of these

216. In model choice studies which one of the following factors influences the shape of diversion curves ?
   (1) Trip purpose   (2) Trip length
   (3) Income   (4) Residential density

217. Highway facilities are designed for :
   (1) Annual average hourly volume   (2) Annual average daily traffic
   (3) 30th highest hourly volume   (4) Peak hourly volume of the year

218. For highway geometric design purposes the speed used is :
   (1) 15th percentile   (2) 50th percentile
   (3) 85th percentile   (4) 98th percentile

219. The maximum width of a vehicle as recommended by IRC is :
   (1) 1.85 m   (2) 2.44 m   (3) 3.81 m   (4) 4.72 m

220. Desire lines are plotted in :
   (1) Origin and destination studies   (2) Accident studies
   (3) Speed studies   (4) Traffic volume studies

221. The traffic manocurve shown in figure represents :

   (1) weaving   (2) crossing   (3) diverging   (4) all of the above

222. The diagram which shows approximate path of vehicles and pedestrians involved in accidents is known as :
   (1) Spot maps   (2) Pie charts
   (3) Condition diagram   (4) Collision diagram

223. If the average centre to centre spacing of vehicles is 20 m, then the basic capacity of a traffic lane at a speed of 50 kmph is :
   (1) 2500 vehicles per day   (2) 2000 vehicles per hour
   (3) 2500 vehicles per hour   (4) 1000 vehicles per hour

224. On a right angled road intersection with two-way traffic, the total number of conflict points is :
   (1) 6   (2) 11   (3) 22   (4) 24

225. When the speed of traffic flow becomes zero, then :
   (1) traffic density attains maximum value whereas traffic volume becomes zero.
   (2) traffic density and traffic volume both attain maximum value.
   (3) traffic density and traffic volume both become zero.
   (4) None of the above

226. The traffic census is carried out to study :
   (1) speed and delay   (2) traffic volume
   (3) road parking   (4) origin and destination
227. The overall height of vehicle determines the :
   (1) width of the pavement needed for the highway.
   (2) width of the bridges on the highway.
   (3) lengths of the valley curves at the under passes in the city areas.
   (4) Height of the tunnel along the highways.
   (5) both (3) and (4)
228. Weight of vehicle affects :
   (1) passing sight distance   (2) extra widening
   (3) pavement thickness   (4) width of lanes
229. Length of vehicle affects :
   (1) width of traffic lanes.
   (2) extra width of pavement and minimum turning radius.
   (3) width of shoulders and parking facilities.
   (4) clearance to be provided under stretch such as over-bridges, under-bridges etc.
230. Moving car observer methods is a procedure :
   (1) to find the traffic flow of a traffic stream.
   (2) to carry out origin and destination studies.
   (3) to estimate the traffic capacity of a road section.
   (4) All of the above
231. The traffic conflicts that may occur in a rotary intersection are :
   (1) Merging and diverging   (2) Crossing and merging
   (3) Crossing and diverging   (4) All of the above
232. Gravity model is used in transportation planning process for :
   (1) Modal split   (2) Trip distribution
   (3) Trip generation   (4) Trip assignment
233. According to IRC recommendations, the gross load of any vehicle (in kg) shall not exceed :
   (1) $1525 (L + 73) - 14.7 L^2$ (2) $1525 (2L + 37) - 14.7 L$
   (3) $1525 (L - 73) + 14.7 L^2$ (4) None of the above
234. The background colour of the informatory sign board is :
   (1) red   (2) yellow   (3) green   (4) white
235. 'Dead slow' is a :
   (1) Regulatory sign   (2) Warning sign
   (3) Informatory sign   (4) None
236. A complete signal-time cycle constitutes
   (1) Red timing   (2) Yellow timing
   (3) Green timing   (4) All of the above

237. Traffic-actuated signals may be :
    (1) full traffic-actuated signals
    (2) speed control signals
    (3) semi-traffic-actuated signals
    (4) All of the above

238. The most efficient traffic signal system is :
    (1) Flexible progressive system
    (2) Alternate system
    (3) Simple progressive system
    (4) All of the above

239. The purpose of traffic signal is to :
    (1) provide an orderly movement of traffic.
    (2) reduce the frequency of accidents of some special nature.
    (3) control speed on the main highway.
    (4) All of the above

240. Which of the following is indicated by a warning sign ?
    (1) No parking
    (2) Level crossing
    (3) Overtaking prohibited
    (4) All of the above

241. Centre line markings are used :
    (1) to designate traffic lanes.
    (2) in roadways meant for two-way traffic.
    (3) to indicate that overtaking is not permitted.
    (4) All of the above

242. The particular places where pedestrians are to cross the pavement are properly marked by the pavement marking known as :
    (1) Stop lines
    (2) Turn markings
    (3) Crosswalk lines
    (4) Lane lines

243. End of speed limit is a :
    (1) Informatory sign
    (2) Regulatory sign
    (3) Warning sign
    (4) None of above

244. The colour of light used for visibility during fog is :
    (1) Red
    (2) Yellow
    (3) Green
    (4) White

245. The length of side of warning sign boards of roads is :
    (1) 30 cm
    (2) 45 cm
    (3) 60 cm
    (4) 75 cm

246. When two equally important roads cross roughly at right angles, the suitable shapes of central island is :
    (1) Circular
    (2) Elliptical
    (3) Tangent
    (4) Turbine

247. The maximum number of vehicles beyond which the rotary may not function efficiently is :
    (1) 500 vehicles per hour
    (2) 500 vehicles per day
    (3) 5000 vehicles per hour
    (4) 5000 vehicles per day

248. Maximum number of vehicles can be parked with :
    (1) Parallel parking
    (2) 30° angle parking
    (3) 45° angle parking
    (4) 90° angle parking

249. As per IRC, the average level of illumination on important roads parking carrying fast traffic is :

    (1)   10 lux   (2)   15 lux   (3)   20 lux   (4)   30 lux

250. The most economical lighting layout which is suitable for narrow roads is :

    (1)   Single side lighting   (2)   Staggered system

    (3)   Central lighting   (4)   None of the above

251. When width of kerb parking space and width of street are limited, generally preferred parking system is :

    (1)   Parallel parking   (2)   30° angle parking system

    (3)   45° angle parking   (4)   90° angle parking

252. Match the following :

List - I	List - II
(A) Traffic volume study	1. Work spot interview method
(B) Speed and delay study	2. Doppler radar
(C) Spot-speed study	3. Floating car method
(D) Multiple character studies	4. Automatic vehicle counter and classifier
	5. Electronic detector

    Option :

	(A)	(B)	(C)	(D)
(1)	5	3	2	4
(2)	1	3	2	5
(3)	5	2	3	4
(4)	1	2	3	4

253. A road sign indicates 'No parking' is :

    (1)   Warning sign   (2)   Prohibitory sign

    (3)   Mandatory sign   (4)   Informatory sign

254. A direct interchange ramp involves :

    (1)   diverging to right side and merging from left

    (2)   diverging to left side and merging from right

    (3)   diverging to right side and merging from right

    (4)   diverging to left side and merging from left

255. A traffic rotary is justified when :

    (1)   number of intersecting roads is between 4 and 7.

    (2)   space is limited and costly.

    (3)   traffic volume is less than 500 vehicles per hour.

    (4)   traffic volume is more than 5000 vehicles per hour.

ANSWER KEY

1.	(3)	2.	(4)	3.	(2)	4.	(2)	5.	(3)	6.	(1)	7.	(3)	8.	(4)
9.	(2)	10.	(3)	11.	(1)	12.	(3)	13.	(3)	14.	(1)	15.	(2)	16.	(4)
17.	(3)	18.	(3)	19.	(2)	20.	(2)	21.	(2)	22.	(1)	23.	(3)	24.	(3)
25.	(1)	26.	(?)	27.	(2)	28.	(1)	29.	(2)	30.	(1)	31.	(3)	32.	(1)
33.	(4)	34.	(4)	35.	(2)	36.	(3)	37.	(2)	38.	(1)	39.	(2)	40.	(3)
41.	(1)	42.	(1)	43.	(2)	44.	(2)	45.	(1)	46.	(2)	47.	(1)	48.	(1)
49.	(4)	50.	(1)	51.	(4)	52.	(4)	53.	(1)	54.	(3)	55.	(4)	56.	(1)
57.	(3)	58.	(3)	59.	(1)	60.	(4)	61.	(2)	62.	(3)	63.	(4)	64.	(1)
65.	(3)	66.	(3)	67.	(3)	68.	(1)	69.	(1)	70.	(1)	71.	(1)	72.	(4)
73.	(2)	74.	(2)	75.	(3)	76.	(1)	77.	(4)	78.	(4)	79.	(1)	80.	(1)
81.	(1)	82.	(4)	83.	(4)	84.	(4)	85.	(2)	86.	(1)	87.	(3)	88.	(4)
89.	(2)	90.	(1)	91.	(1)	92.	(2)	93.	(2)	94.	(4)	95.	(2)	96.	(4)
97.	(3)	98.	(3)	99.	(1)	100.	(2)	101.	(3)	102.	(1)	103.	(4)	104.	(2)
105.	(2)	106.	(2)	107.	(1)	108.	(1)	109.	(2)	110.	(3)	111.	(1)	112.	(1)
113.	(1)	114.	(2)	115.	(4)	116.	(1)	117.	(1)	118.	(1)	119.	(3)	120.	(2)
121.	(1)	122.	(1)	123.	(3)	124.	(1)	125.	(1)	126.	(1)	127.	(1)	128.	(1)
129.	(1)	130.	(1)	131.	(3)	132.	(1)	133.	(3)	134.	(1)	135.	(2)	136.	(3)
137.	(1)	138.	(2)	139.	(3)	140.	(1)	141.	(1)	142.	(4)	143.	(2)	144.	(1)
145.	(2)	146.	(1)	147.	(1)	148.	(2)	149.	(4)	150.	(3)	151.	(1)	152.	(3)
153.	(3)	154.	(1)	155.	(3)	156.	(1)	157.	(2)	158.	(1)	159.	(2)	160.	(2)
161.	(3)	162.	(1)	163.	(2)	164.	(2)	165.	(2)	166.	(3)	167.	(4)	168.	(4)
169.	(2)	170.	(4)	171.	(3)	172.	(3)	173.	(2)	174.	(2)	175.	(2)	176.	(1)
177.	(1)	178.	(3)	179.	(1)	180.	(1)	181.	(2)	182.	(1)	183.	(3)	184.	(1)
185.	(3)	186.	(3)	187.	(3)	188.	(2)	189.	(2)	190.	(3)	191.	(3)	192.	(4)
193.	(1)	194.	(3)	195.	(2)	196.	(3)	197.	(1)	198.	(2)	199.	(2)	200.	(1)
201.	(3)	202.	(3)	203.	(2)	204.	(2)	205.	(3)	206.	(1)	207.	(3)	208.	(1)
209.	(1)	210.	(3)	211.	(2)	212.	(1)	213.	(2)	214.	(1)	215.	(2)	216.	(1)
217.	(3)	218.	(4)	219.	(2)	220.	(1)	221.	(1)	222.	(4)	223.	(3)	224.	(4)
225.	(1)	226.	(3)	227.	(5)	228.	(3)	229.	(2)	230.	(1)	231.	(1)	232.	(2)
233.	(1)	234.	(2)	235.	(1)	236.	(4)	237.	(4)	238.	(1)	239.	(4)	240.	(2)
241.	(2)	242.	(3)	243.	(1)	244.	(2)	245.	(2)	246.	(1)	247.	(3)	248.	(4)
249.	(4)	250.	(1)	251.	(1)	252.	(1)	253.	(3)	254.	(3)	255.	(1)		

1. Horizontal cross-wires is/are provided in the stadia diaphragm of tacheometer, these may be .....
   (1) one   (2) two   (3) three   (4) four

2. The multiplying constant of a tacheometer is .....
   (1) f/I (2) $(f/d) + I$ (3) $(f/I) + d$ (4) $f + d$

3. The stadia method in tacheometry is used to determine .....
   (1) horizontal angles   (2) vertical angles
   (3) horizontal distance   (4) horizontal and vertical distance

4. The local attraction at a place may be due to .....
   (1) key bunches   (2) steel buttons
   (3) current carrying wires   (4) none of these

5. When L denotes the Latitudes and D denotes the Departures, then the closing error is given by .....
   (1) $\dfrac{\Sigma L + \Sigma D}{2N}$ (2) $\dfrac{\Sigma L}{N} + \dfrac{\Sigma D}{N}$ (3) $\sqrt{\Sigma L + \Sigma D}$ (4) $\sqrt{(\Sigma L)^2 + (\Sigma D)^2}$

6. The magnitude azimuth of one end of a runway is 80° measured clockwise from the magnetic north. The other end of runway will be numbered as .....
   (1) 16   (2) 24   (3) 26   (4) 8

7. If the magnetic bearing of a line is 54°30′ and magnetic declination is 5°30′ E, the true bearing of line will be .....
   (1) 61°   (2) 59°   (3) 49°   (4) 60°

8. The process of determining the difference of elevations of stations from vertical angles and known distances, is known as .....
   (1) trigonometrical levelling   (2) geodetic surveying
   (3) field astronomy   (4) topographic surveying

9. In theodolite traverse computations, Gale's table is useful for determination of .....
   (1) independent co-ordinates   (2) dependent co-ordinates
   (3) both (1) and (2)   (4) none of these

10. The representative fraction (R.F.) of scale 1 cm = 500 m is .....
    (1) 1 : 500   (2) 1 : 5000   (3) 1 : 50000   (4) 1 : 50

11. A road section of length 2 km scales 9 cm on a vertical photograph. The focal length of the camera is 180 mm. If the terrain is fairly level, then the flying height will be .....
    (1) 40 m   (2) 4000 m   (3) 40 km   (4) 400 km

12. The process of determining the location of the station (on the map) occupied by the plane table is .....
    (1) intersection   (2) two-point problem
    (3) resection   (4) traversing

13. Consider the following statements :

    In aerial photogrammetry the 'filter' is placed in front of the lens to .....

    (a) reduce the effect of atmospheric haze.

    (b) protect the lens from dust.

    (c) provide uniform light distribution over the format.

    Which of these statements is/are correct ?

    (1) (a) and (b) only   (2) (b) only

    (3) (a) and (c) only   (4) (a), (b) and (c)

14. In the change point procedure, change point is the point of .....

    (1) the initial position of dumpy level.

    (2) the portion of staff where instrument is shifted.

    (3) the final position of dumpy level.

    (4) none of these

15. At a given place of observation, the declination of a circumpolar star is .....

    (1) greater than the latitude   (2) equal to the latitude

    (3) less than the co-latitude   (4) greater than the co-latitude

16. The tension at which the effect of pull is neutralised by the effect of sag is known as .....

    (1) appropriate tension   (2) neutral tension

    (3) equal tension   (4) normal tension

17. The least count of levelling staff is .....

    (1) 1 mm   (2) 1 cm   (3) 5 mm   (4) 5 cm

18. Given that δ denotes declination, θ denotes the latitude of the place of observation and α denotes the altitude of a star at the prime vertical, then .....

    (1) $\sin \theta = \sin \delta \cos \alpha$ (2) $\sin \theta = \sin \delta \operatorname{cosec} \alpha$

    (3) $\cos \alpha = \cos \delta \sin \theta$ (4) $\sin \delta = \sin \alpha \cos \theta$

19. The descending order of precision among the following types of survey is .....

    (a) chain   (b) compass   (c) theodolite   (d) total station

    (1) (a), (b), (c), (d)   (2) (c), (d), (b), (a)

    (3) (d), (c), (b), (a)   (4) (d), (c), (a), (b)

20. A rectangular plot in plan is 10 cm × 30 cm drawn to scale of 1 cm = 100 m. If the same plot is redrawn on a topo sheet to a scale of 1 cm = 1 km, what would be the area on the topo sheet in cm² ?

    (1) 0.3   (2) 3.0   (3) 30   (4) 100

21. Height of instrument (H.I.) in leveling is the .....

    (1) height of telescope axis above the ground

    (2) elevation of line of sight with respect to a datum

    (3) elevation of line of sight with respect to M.S.L.

    (4) none of above

22. A fore sight is a sight taken on a point which is .....

    (1) last point only   (2) turning point only

    (3) first point only   (4) both tunning and last points

23. From the probability equation it is found that the most probable values of a series of errors arising out of observations of equal weightage are those for which the sum of their squares is .....
    (1) zero   (2) infinity   (3) minimum   (4) maximum

24. It is required to produce a small-scale map of an area in magnetic zone by directly plotting and checking the work in the field itself. Which one of the following surveys will be most appropriate for purpose ?
    (1) Chain   (2) Theodolite   (3) Plane table   (4) Compass

25. Altimetry may be depicted most accurately by .....
    (1) hachures   (2) relief shading
    (3) layer tinting   (4) contour lines

26. The following steps are necessary to obtain sufficient accuracy with the tape :
    (a) Keeping uniform tension on tape for each measurement.
    (b) "Breaking" tape on slopes are necessary to keep the tape level.
    (c) Keeping accurate count of the stations.
    (d) Keeping the tape on the line being measured.
    The correct sequence of these steps is .....
    (1) (d), (b), (a), (c)   (2) (b), (c), (d), (a)
    (3) (d), (a), (b), (c)   (4) (c), (b), (a), (d)

27. A theodolite was set up at P and the angle of elevation to the top of a mobile tower ST was 30°. The staff reading held at a station of RL 110 m was 2.555 m, the telescope being horizontal. The horizontal distance between the foot of the tower and the instrument station is 810 m. The RL of the top of the tower is .....
    (1) 578.25 m   (2) 579.50 m   (3) 580.25 m   (4) 582.40 m

28. Match List-I (Type of survey) with List-II (Purpose) and select the correct answer using the codes given below the lists :

	List - I		List - II
A.	Topographical survey	1.	To determine boundaries of fields, houses etc.
B.	Reconnaissance survey	2.	To find relics of antiquity
C.	Cadastral survey	3.	To determine natural features of a country
D.	Archaeological survey	4.	To determine possibility and rough cost of the surveying system to be adopted.

    Codes :

	A	B	C	D
(1)	3	4	1	2
(2)	3	1	4	2
(3)	2	4	1	3
(4)	2	1	4	3

29. Which of the following set of terms does not relate to operation of a theodolite ?
    (1) Transiting and inverting   (2) Face left and face right
    (3) Right swing and left swing   (4) Gauging and sounding

30. Which of the following figures are equal to one acre ?
    (a)   43560 sq.ft.   (b)   40 gunthas
    (c)   10 sq. Gunter's chain   (d)   4850 sq.yds.
    Select the correct answer using the codes given below :
    (1)   (a), (b) and (c)   (2)   (b), (c) and (d)
    (3)   (a), (b) and (d)   (4)   (a), (c) and (d)

31. Which one of the following statements is correct ?
    (1)   In a retrograde vernier, (n − 1) divisions on the primary scale are divided into n divisions on the vernier scale.
    (2)   A double vernier consists of two simple verniers placed end-to-end forming one scale with the zero in the centre.
    (3)   In an extended vernier, (2n + 1) primary divisions are divided into n divisions on the vernier.
    (4)   In a direct vernier, (n + 1) primary divisions are divided into n equal divisions on the vernier scale.

32. Which one of the following is carried out by two theodolite method ?
    (1)   Circular curve ranging   (2)   Tacheometric survey
    (3)   Geodetic survey   (4)   Astronomical survey

33. The whole circle bearings of lines OP and OQ are 18°15′ and 335°45′ respectively. What is the value of the included angle QOP ?
    (1)   307°30′   (2)   42°30′   (3)   345°00′   (4)   177°00′

34. The magnitude of sag correction during measurement of lengths by taping is proportional to the .....
    (1)   cube of the weight of the tape, in kg per m run
    (2)   cube root of the weight of the tape, in kg per m run
    (3)   square of the weight of the tape in kg per m run
    (4)   square root of the weight of the tape, in kg per m run

35. The length of a survey line when measured with a chain of 20 m nominal length was found to be 841.5 m. If the chain used is 0.1 m too long, the correct length of the measured line is .....
    (1)   845.7 m   (2)   837.39 m   (3)   843.6 m   (4)   839.4 m

36. Staff reading on the floor of a verandah of a school building is 1.815 m and staff reading when held with bottom of staff touching the ceiling over the verandah is 2.870 m. R.L. of the floor is 74.500 m. Height of the ceiling above floor is .....
    (1)   4.270 m   (2)   4.685 m   (3)   3.955 m   (4)   4.920 m

37. In geodetical observations, the correction for refraction is .....
    (1)   subtractive to both the angle of elevation and the angle of depression
    (2)   additive to both the angle of elevation and the angle of depression
    (3)   subtractive to the angle of elevation and additive to the angle of depression
    (4)   additive to the angle of elevation and subtractive to the angle of depression

38. A survey which consists of observations of the heavenly bodies such as Sun or any fixed star, is known as .....
    (1) Celestial survey
    (2) Astrological survey
    (3) Heaven survey
    (4) Astronomical survey

39. Map is a graphical representation of the features on small scale as projected on a .....
    (1) horizontal plane
    (2) horizontal line
    (3) plane parallel to feature
    (4) in any plane

40. The imaginary line joining the intersection of cross hairs of diaphragm to the optical centre of object glass and its continuation is called as .....
    (1) Axis of telescope
    (2) Line of sight
    (3) Axis of diaphragm
    (4) Line of telescope

41. To determine the length of bridge proposed to be built across a very wide river, the surveying method of choice would be .....
    (1) chain survey
    (2) hydrographic survey
    (3) topographic survey
    (4) geometric survey

42. The basic principal of "working from whole to part" .....
    (1) prevents accumulation of errors
    (2) makes plotting easier
    (3) localized minor errors
    (4) both (1) and (3)

43. Which of the following angles can be set out with the help of a French cross staff ?
    (1) any angle   (2) 45° only   (3) 90° only   (4) both 45° or 90°

44. A "Level Surface" is a .....
    (1) horizontal surface
    (2) inclined surface
    (3) curved surface
    (4) horizontal or curved surface

45. An example for level surface is .....
    (1) still water in a lake
    (2) sea level unaffected by tides
    (3) a plane ground
    (4) both (1) and (2)

46. Consider the following statements about theodolites :
    (a) Transit theodolite is a theodolite in which the telescope can be transited.
    (b) EDMI is a theodolite fitted with a micrometer for measurements.
    (c) A double reading theodolite is one in which diametrically opposite segments of the graduated circle are brought into view and the readings are averaged.
    Which of these statements are correct ?
    (1) (a), (b) and (c)
    (2) (a) and (c) only
    (3) (a) and (b) only
    (4) (b) and (c) only

47. Consider the following in the context of variations in magnetic declination :
    (a) Secular   (b) Diurnal   (c) Annual   (d) Regular
    Which of these are relevant ?
    (1) (a), (b) and (c)   (2) (a), (b) and (d)   (3) (b) and (c) only   (4) (c) and (d) only

48. The type of needle used in prismatic compass is .....
    (1) Edge bar type
    (2) Broad needle
    (3) Blunt needle
    (4) none of these

49. Least count of a theodolite is .....
    (1) 1 minute (2) 30 minutes (3) 1 degree (4) 20 seconds

50. If the whole circle bearing is 315°20′, its quadrantal bearing would be .....
    (1) S 36°30′ W (2) N 44°40′ W (3) N 57°24′ W (4) S 60°40′ W

51. The magnetic bearing of a line is 55°30′ and the magnetic declination is 4°30′ east. The true bearing of a line will be .....
    (1) 60° (2) 34°30′ (3) 49°30′ (4) 51°

52. In a transit theodolite, any incidental error due to eccentricity of verniers is primarily counteracted by .....
    (1) reading both the verniers (2) reading different parts of main scale
    (3) reading right and left faces (4) taking both right swing readings

53. To find the RL of a roof slab of building, staff readings were taken from a particular set-up of the levelling instrument. The readings were 1.050 m with staff on the Bench Mark and 2.300 m with staff below the roof slab and held inverted. Taking the RL of the Bench Mark as 135.15 m, the RL of the roof slab will be .....
    (1) 129.8 (2) 131.9 (3) 134.4 (4) 138.5

54. Match List-I (Phenomenon) with List-II (Method of survey) and select the correct answer using the codes given below the lists :

	List - I		List - II
A.	Crab and drift	1.	Triangulation
B.	Stadia inercept	2.	Astronomical survey
C.	Culmination and elongation	3.	Aerial photogrammetry
D.	Baseline measurement	4.	Tacheometric survey

    Codes :

	A	B	C	D
(1)	3	1	2	4
(2)	2	4	3	1
(3)	3	4	2	1
(4)	2	1	3	4

55. Which one of the following Remote Sensing Systems employees only one detector ?
    (1) Scanning (2) Framing
    (3) Electromagnetic spectrum (4) All of these

56. The suitable contout interval for a map is suitable 1 : 10000 is .....
    (1) 2 m (2) 5 m (3) 10 m (4) 20 m

57. The multiplying constant of tachometer is generally about .....
    (1) 200 (2) 100 (3) 50 (4) 1

58. Which of the following can be held it hand while taking observation .....
    (1) prismatic compass (2) surveyor's compass
    (3) both (1) and (2) (4) none of these

59. Which one of the following methods of levelling eliminates the error due to curvature and refraction ?
    (1) Fly levelling
    (2) Levelling by equalizing the distances of back sight and foresight
    (3) Check levelling
    (4) Precise levelling

60. Consider the following statements :
    Reciprocal levelling eliminates the effect of .....
    (a) errors due to earth's curvature
    (b) errors due to atmospheric refraction
    (c) mistakes in taking levelling staff readings
    (d) errors due to line of collimation
    Which of these statements are correct ?
    (1) (a), (b) and (c)　　　　　　　(2) (a), (c) and (d)
    (3) (b), (c) and (d)　　　　　　　(4) (a), (b) and (d)

61. How high should a helicopter pilot rise at a point a just to see the horizon at point B, if the distance AB is 40 km ?
    (1) 101.75 m　　　(2) 110.50 m　　　(3) 107.75 m　　　(4) 105.50 m

62. What is the angle of intersection of a contour and a ridge line ?
    (1) 30°　　　(2) 0°　　　(3) 180°　　　(4) 90°

63. Consider the following pre-conditions for correct use of a theodolite :
    (a) The vertical axis need not be perpendicular to the plane of the plate level bubble.
    (b) The line of sight must be perpendicular to the horizontal axis.
    (c) The axis of the level tube attached to the telescope need not be parallel to the line of sight.
    (d) The vertical axis, the horizontal axis and the line of sight should all pass through a point known as stadia centre.
    Which of these conditions is/are necessary ?
    (1) (a), (b), (c) and (d)　　　　　(2) (b) only
    (3) (c) only　　　　　　　　　　　(4) (a) and (d) only

64. For better accuracy in measuring and plotting the sides of a triangle by triangulation, the angles of the triangle .....
    (1) should not be more than 30°
    (2) should not be less than 30° or more than 120°
    (3) are not restricted in magnitude
    (4) should not be less than 120°

65. If an overlapping pair of vertical photographs taken with a 150 mm focal length camera has an air base of 2100 m and the elevation of the control point A on it is 900 m above MSL and the parallax of the point is 75 mm, then the flying height above MSL of the stereopair will be .....
    (1) 3000 m　　　(2) 3150 m　　　(3) 5100 m　　　(4) 5250 m

66. A road section of length 1 km scales 8 cm on a vertical photograph. The focal length of the camera is 160 mm. If the terrain is fairly level, then the flying height will be .....
    (1) 20 m   (2) 2000 m   (3) 20 km   (4) 200 km

67. Setting off the 'proper principal distance' in the projectors of projection stereoplotters is a procedure for which one of the following ?
    (1) Finding the focal length of the camera used
    (2) Evaluating the digital terrain model
    (3) Carrying out the interior orientation
    (4) Filling the quotation for the purchase of A_1 stereoplotters.

68. Refraction error is the least in case of .....
    (1) stadia techeometry   (2) tangential techeometry
    (3) subtense bar tacheometry   (4) omnimeters

69. An object on the top of a hill 100 m high is just visible above the horizon from a station at sea level. The distance between the station and the object is .....
    (1) 38.53 km   (2) 3.853 km   (3) 3853 km   (4) 385.3 km

70. Which one of the following statements is not correct ?
    (1) Parallax error is eliminated when there is no change in the staff reading when eye is moved up and down.
    (2) The objective lens is to be focused towards a white or bright background for clear visibility of cross-hairs.
    (3) Temporary adjustments of the dumpy level are to be performed at every set up.
    (4) The eyepiece need not be adjusted after the first set up when the same surveryor is taking readings.

71. R.L. of floor at a building is 74.4 m, staff reading on the floor is 1.625 and staff reading when it is held inverted with bottom touching the ceiling of a hall is 2.870; then the height of the ceiling above the floor is .....
    (1) 3.593 m   (2) 3.953 m   (3) 4.495 m   (4) 4.594 m

72. Match List-I (Instrument) with List-II (Use) and select the correct answer using the codes given below the lists :

List - I	List - II
A. Subtense bar	1. To determine difference in elevation between points
B. Sextant	2. To determine horizontal distance
C. Tangent clinometer	3. To measure angles
D. Range finder	4. To establish right angles

Codes :

	A	B	C	D
(1)	2	4	1	3
(2)	1	3	2	4
(3)	2	3	1	4
(4)	1	4	2	3

73. In a plane table survey, the process of determining the plotted position of a station occupied by the plane table by means of sights taken towards known points, the locations of which have already been plotted, is known as .....
    (1) Intersection   (2) Radiation   (3) Resection   (4) Traversing

74. The plotting of inaccessible points in a plane table survey can be done by the method of .....
    (1) Interpolation   (2) Radiation   (3) Intersection   (4) Traversing

75. Match List-I (Measurements) with List-II (Instruments) and select the correct answer using the codes given below the lists :

List - I		List - II	
A.	Displacement measurement from photograph	1.	Box sextant
B.	Electronic distance measurement	2.	Subtense bar
C.	Base line measurement	3.	Tellurometer
D.	Horizontal angle measurement	4.	Parallax bar

Codes :

	A	B	C	D
(1)	4	3	2	1
(2)	1	3	2	4
(3)	4	2	3	1
(4)	1	2	3	4

76. In levelling between two points A and B on the opposite sides of a river, the level was first set up neat A and the staff readings on A and B were 2.645 m and 2.30 m respectively. The level was then moved near B and set up; the respective staff readings then were 1.085 m and 1.665 m on A and B respectively. What is the true difference of level between A and B ?
    (1) A and B are at same level   (2) A is 0.5825 m below B
    (3) A is 0.4825 m below B   (4) B is 0.5825 m below A

77. In setting up the plane table at a station P, the corresponding point on the plan was not accurately centred above P. If the displacement of P was 50 cm in a direction perpendicular to the ray, how much on the plan would be the consequent displacement of a point from its true position if the scale was 1 cm = 10 m ?
    (1) 5 mm   (2) 1 mm   (3) 0.5 mm   (4) 0.05 mm

78. The levelling staff held at a distance of 200 m is read at 4.54 m with the bubble out of centre by two divisions towards the observer. If the sensitiveness of the bubble is 25 secs/division, and 1 division = 2 mm, then actual staff reading must have been .....
    (1) 4.5 m   (2) 4.492 m   (3) 4.54 m   (4) 4.62 m

79. What is the volume of a 6 m deep tank having rectangular shaped top 6 m × 4 m and bottom 4 m × 2 m (computed through the use of prismoidal formula) ?
    (1) 96 m³   (2) 94 m³   (3) 92 m³   (4) 90 m³

80. Which one of the following methods of computing area assumes that the short lengths of the boundary between the ordinates are parabolic arcs ?
    (1) Average ordinate rule   (2) Middle ordinate rule
    (3) Simpson's rule   (4) Trapezoidal rule

81. Match List-I with List-II and select the correct answer using the codes given below the lists :

List - I		List - II	
A.	Clinometer	1.	Area measuring instrument
B.	Pantagraph	2.	Gradient finding instrument
C.	Tellurometer	3.	Angle measuring instrument
D.	Ghat tracer	4.	Plan enlarging instrument
		5.	Microwave instrument

Codes :

	A	B	C	D
(1)	1	2	5	3
(2)	1	5	4	3
(3)	3	4	1	2
(4)	3	4	5	2

82. Which one of the following is measured by the area between the balancing line and the mass haul curve ?
    (1) Haul between the balancing points   (2) Earthwork accumulated up to that point
    (3) Excess of excavation   (4) Excess of filling

83. Which of the following pairs are correctly matched ?
    (a) Telemeter : Measurement of distance
    (b) Price meter : Measurement of difference in elevation between points.
    (c) Sounding sextant : Measurement of horizontal angles
    (d) Clinometer : Measurement of vertical angles
    Select the correct answer using the codes given below :
    (1) (b), (c) and (d)   (2) (a), (c) and (d)
    (3) (a), (b) and (d)   (4) (a), (b) and (c)

84. The standard measurement of the Geodimeter 510 is .....
    (1) ± 1 cm   (2) ± 5.1 mm   (3) $\sqrt{5.1}$ mm   (4) ± 1 mm

85. Which one of the following verniers is employed in Abney Level ?
    (1) Retrograde vernier   (2) Double vernier
    (3) Double folded vernier   (4) Extended vernier

86. For air borne application and materialization of GPS receiver and easy construction, which is the most frequently used antenna ?
    (1) Microstrip   (2) Micropole   (3) Spiral helix   (4) Choke ring

87. Which one of the following is not strictly a method of remote sensing ?
    (1) Thermal and multi-spectral scanning
    (2) Microwave sensing
    (3) Earth resource satellite
    (4) Stereoscopy

88. Match List-I with List-II and select the correct answer using the codes given below the lists :

List - I

A. Visual interpretation

B. Geographical information system

C. National remote sensing agency

D. Supervised image classification

List - II

1. Creation of data bank of multi-information for a project area

2. Visual identification of objects from image characteristics

3. Computer classification of digital image data

4. Supplier of aerial and satellite based remote sensing data products in India

Codes :

	A	B	C	D
(1)	2	1	3	4
(2)	2	1	4	3
(3)	1	3	2	4
(4)	1	4	2	3

89. For setting out right angles, the instrument used is .....
    (1) Optical square (2) Abney level (3) Alidade (4) Ceylon ghat tracer

90. The angle between the index glass and the horizon glass of a box sextant is 40°; the horizontal angle between the two points sighted by the instrument is .....
    (1) 20° (2) 60° (3) 40° (4) 80°

91. Which one of the following methods estimates best area of an irregular and curved boundary ?
    (1) Trapezoidal method (2) Simpson's method
    (3) Average ordinate method (4) Mid-ordinate method

92. A parabolic vertical curve is to be set out connecting two uniform grades of + 0.6% and + 1.0%. The rate of change of grade is to be 0.06% per 30 m. The length of the curve will be .....
    (1) $66\frac{2}{3}$ m (2) $133\frac{1}{3}$ m (3) 200 m (4) $266\frac{2}{3}$ m

93. A lemniscate curve between the tangents is transitional throughout, if the polar deflection angle of its apex is equal to .....
    (1) $\phi/2$ (2) $\phi/4$ (3) $\phi/6$ (4) ϕ

94. For a chord of 60 m, the mid-ordinate for a circular curve of 50 m radius will be .....
    (1) 10 m (2) 12.5 m (3) 15 m (4) 18.75 m

95. If 'g_1' and 'g_2' are the two gradients, 'r' is the rate of change of grade (%) per chain, the length of the vertical curve will be .....
    (1) $\left(\dfrac{g_1 - g_2}{r^2}\right)$ (2) $\left(\dfrac{g_1 - g_2}{\sqrt{r}}\right)$ (3) $\left(\dfrac{g_1 - g_2}{r}\right)$ (4) $\dfrac{\sqrt{g_1 + g_2}}{r^3}$

96. If two triangulation singals of 6.75 m height each, are to be just visible over ground mutually, what is the maximum distance between their locations on the ground surface ?
   (1) 10 km   (2) 20 km   (3) 30 km   (4) 40 km

97. What ratio do the versines of a circular curve when measured at the quarter point of a full chord and, when measured at the same point on half chord bear ?
   (1) 100 : 1   (2) 60 : 1   (3) 3 : 1   (4) 1 : 1

98. R. L. of a floor level is 200.490 m. Staff reading on the floor is 1.695 m. Reading on the staff held upside down against the bottom of the roof is 3.305 m. Height of the ceiling is ...
   (1) 3.5 m   (2) 4.0 m   (3) 5.0 m   (4) 6.0 m

99. Which one of the following linear methods of setting out a circular curve needs reference of the centre of the curve ?
   (1) Offset from chord produced   (2) Radial offset
   (3) Perpendicular offset   (4) Successive bisection of arcs

100. In accordance to 'Gauss rule', weights to be assigned are proportional to .....
   (1) 1/(Sum of the residual errors of observations.
   (2) 1/(Sum of the square of the residual errors of observations).
   (3) Sum of the square roots of the residual errors of observation.
   (4) Sum of the cube roots of the residual errors of observations.

101. The purpose of a 'satellite station' in triangulation can be served by .....
   (1) A 'Church spire' in order to secure a well-shaped triangle.
   (2) A 'Flag pole' in order to secure a well shaped triangle.
   (3) A 'Steeple' in order to secure a well-shaped triangle.
   (4) An 'Eccentric station' near the true station whereon the instrument cannot be setup.

102. The sum of the three interior angles of a triangle, the vertices of which lie on the surface of the earth, covering a vast area of several hundreds of sq. km is .....
   (1) less than 180°   (2) equal to 180°
   (3) more than 180° but not less than 270°
   (4) more than 180° but not more than 225°

103. Regarding plane table survey, which of the following statements does not hold ?
   (1) All the plotting work including contouring can be done in the field.
   (2) It is quite suitable for small scale surveys
   (3) Less number of control points are required
   (4) It can be done in all seasons

104. If the angle of deflection of a simple curve is θ and its radius is R, then the length of the chord is .....
   (1) $2R \sin \theta$ (2) $2R \sin \dfrac{\theta}{2}$ (3) $2R \cos \theta$ (4) $2R \tan \dfrac{\theta}{2}$

105. The standard time meridian in India is 82°30′ E. If the standard time at any instant is 20 hours 10 minutes, the local mean time for the place at a longitude of 20° E would be .....
   (1) 4 hrs. PM   (2) 4 hrs. 10 min. PM
   (3) 1 hr. 20 min PM   (4) 0 h. 20 min. PM

106. In a tilted aerial photograph, if the swing is 230°, then the rotation angle is equal to .....
     (1) 140° (2) 130° (3) 50° (4) 25°

107. The declination of a star is 21°15′ N at a latitude of 43°30′N. The zenith distance at the upper culmination is .....
     (1) 22°15′ (2) 21°15′ (3) 64°45′ (4) 43°30′

108. Which one of the following surveys is required in observations of stars ?
     (1) Astronomical survey (2) Cadastral survey
     (3) Aerial survey (4) Photogrammetric survey

109. Which one of the following is the angular distance between the observer's meridian and the vertical circle passing through a star measured along the celestial horizon ?
     (1) Right ascension (2) Azimuth (3) Declination (4) Hour angle

110. A vertical photograph of a chimney was taken from an elevation of 500 m above MSL. The elevation of the base of the chimney was 250 m. If the relief displacement of the top of chimney was 51.4 mm and the radial distance of the image of the top of the chimney was 110 mm, the height of the chimney is .....
     (1) 233.64 m (2) 133.2 m (3) 116.82 m (4) 58.41 m

111. Consider the following statements :
     IRS series satellites are .....
     (a) Low orbiting satellites (b) Geostationary satellites
     (c) Meteorological satellites (d) Resource survey satellites
     Which of these statements are correct ?
     (1) (a) and (d) (2) (b) and (c)
     (3) (a), (b) and (d) (4) (b), (c) and (d)

112. Consider the following :
     (a) Linear ranger (b) Reciprocal ranging
     (c) Random line method (d) Optical square
     Which of these are the correct methods of ranging employed to solve the problem of vision obstructed but with chaining free ?
     (1) (a), (b), (c) and (d) (2) (b) and (c) only
     (3) (b) and (d) only (4) (c) and (d) only

113. What is the actual ground area covered by a 20 cm × 20 cm size vertical aerial photograph, at an average scale of 1 cm = 200 m having 60% forward overlap and 30% side overlap ?
     (1) 1.92 km² (2) 4.48 km² (3) 6.72 km² (4) 2.88 km²

114. If the mean temperature of Sun's surface 6000 K and λ m of its radiation is 0.5 μm, what is the mean temperature of earth's surface for which λ m is 10.0 μm, according to Wien's Displacement law in Remote Sensing concept ?
     (1) 25°C (2) 28°C (3) 27°C (4) 30°C

115. A particular runway measures 6 cm on a vertical photograph, whereas the same runway measures 4 cm on a map plotted on a scale of 1/24000. The scale of the photograph at the runway elevation is .....
     (1) 1/36000 (2) 1/24000 (3) 1/3600 (4) 1/16000

116. Which one of the following conditions requires geodetic surveying ?
     (1) Horizontal curve ranging   (2) Vertical curve ranging
     (3) Survey of a country   (4) Reconnaissance survey
117. 'Iso-centre' is the point .....
     (1) in which the titled axis of the camera meets the vertical photograph.
     (2) in which the bisector of the angle of tilt meets the vertical photograph.
     (3) in air space, the location of the optical centre of the lens of the camera at the time of exposure.
     (4) where the perpendicular from the nodal point meets the photograph.
118. The declination of a celestial body is the arc of the declination circle intercepted between that body and the .....
     (1) prime vertical through that body   (2) azimuth of the body
     (3) equinoxes of the earth   (4) equator of the earth
119. When compared with the co-latitude of the place of observation, the declination of a circumpolar star is always. ......
     (1) lesser   (2) greater
     (3) equal   (4) either lesser or equal
120. When H is the flight height, R is the appropriate radial measure and d is the relief displacement, the vertical height of an object appearing on an aerial photograph is .....
     (1) $\dfrac{R}{dH}$ (2) $\dfrac{dH}{R}$ (3) $\dfrac{H}{dR}$ (4) $\dfrac{RH}{d}$
121. In plane table surveying, detailed plotting is generally done by .....
     (1) radiation   (2) traversing   (3) resection   (4) none of these
122. To orient a plane table by solving two point problem is adopted only when .....
     (1) intersection   (2) traversing
     (3) two point problem   (4) three point problem
123. The amount of correction due to local attraction at a place .....
     (1) varies with the bearing   (2) is a constant for all bearing
     (3) as time variant   (4) none of these
124. The first temporary adjustment of a prismatic compass is .....
     (1) leveling   (2) centering   (3) focusing   (4) parallax
125. The chainages of point of curvature and point of tangency of a simple circular curve are 1050.50 m and 1314.90 m respectively. The number of full chords for a peg interval of 30 m will be .....
     (1) 7   (2) 8   (3) 6   (4) 9
126. In plane table survey, the method used for locating points is .....
     (1) resection   (2) radiation
     (3) intersection   (4) either radiation or intersection
127. The method of tacheometric surveying in which stadia hairs are not used and the readings are taken against the horizontal cross hair with measurement of vertical angle twice for one single observation is known as .....
     (1) Substance method   (2) Tangential system
     (3) Fixed hair method   (4) None of these

128. Arithmatic check in levelling indicates .....
    (1) Accuracy of field work   (2) Correctness of computations
    (3) Instrumental error   (4) Error in staff readings

129. The magnetic bearing of sun at noon was 170°. Hence, magnetic declination is .....
    (1) 10° E   (2) 10° W   (3) 10° S   (4) 10° N

130. A back sight reading on B.M. = 200 m, was 2.250 m. The inverted staff reading to the bottom of a beam was 1.450 m. The R.L. of bottom of beam is .....
    (1) 200.800 m   (2) 201.450 m   (3) 201.000 m   (4) 203.700 m

131. The area of irregular plotted figure can be easily determined by using instrument named as .....
    (1) Pentagraph   (2) Planimeter   (3) Subtense bar   (4) Vernier

132. In case of a truly vertical photographic survey, which of the following points coincide ?
    (a) Principal point   (b) Isocentre   (c) Plumb point
    (1) (a) and (b) only   (2) (a) and (c) only
    (3) (b) and (c) only   (4) (a), (b) and (c)

133. The process of establishing number of intermediate points between two fixed end points on ground is known as .....
    (1) Ranging   (2) Offsets   (3) Station points   (4) Auxiliary points

134. The latitude of a line of closed traverse is its length multiplied by .....
    (1) tangent of reduced bearing   (2) sine of reduced bearing
    (3) cosine of reduced bearing   (4) secant of reduced bearing

135. A chain of nominal length 30 m is found to be 0.30 m too long. If the area of the field measured with this defective chain is 300 hectares, the correct area of the field is .....
    (1) 294.03 hectares   (2) 300.03 hectares   (3) 306.03 hectares   (4) 300 hectares

136. The R.L. of the ground level is 100 m. The levelling staff reading on the ground surface is 1.355 m. The staff reading 2.355 m is recorded when the levelling staff is held inverted touching its bottom to the base of chajja. The height of chajja from the ground will be .....
    (1) 103.071 m   (2) 1.0 m   (3) 101.00 m   (4) 3.71 m

137. The U fork blumb bomb is used for .....
    (1) masonry work   (2) levelling of plane table
    (3) centering of plane table   (4) orientation of plane table

138. The latitute of the line is given as .....
    (1) $l \cos \theta$ (2) $l \sin \theta$ (3) $l \tan \theta$ (4) None of these

139. Example of an obstacle to both chaining and ranging is .....
    (1) hill   (2) pond   (3) river   (4) tall building

140. The following equipments can be used to layout horizontal angles in filed .....
    (a) microtic theodolite   (b) chain and metallic tape
    (c) varnier theodolite   (d) prismatic compass
    (1) (b), (d), (c), (a)   (2) (b), (c), (d), (a)
    (3) (a), (c), (d), (b)   (4) (a), (b), (c), (d)

141. The balancing of sights generally means .....
    (1) B.S. distance = F.S. distance
    (2) B.S. distance = intermediate sight distance
    (3) F.S. distance = intermediate sight distance
    (4) none of above
142. The diaphragm of a stadia theodolite is normally fitted with two additional .....
    (1) Horizontal hair   (2) Vertical hair
    (3) Horizontal and two vertical   (4) None of these
143. A 30 m metric chain is found to be 0.1 m too short throughout the measurement. If the distance measured is recorded as 300 m, then the actual distance measured will be .....
    (1) 300.1 m   (2) 301.0 m   (3) 299.0 m   (4) 310.0 m
144. Offsets are .....
    (1) lateral measurements made with respect to main survey lines
    (2) prependiculars erected from chain lines
    (3) taken to avoid unnecessary walking between stations
    (4) measurements which are not made at right angles to the chain line
145. The true length of a line is known to be 200 m. When this is measured with a 20 m tape, the length is 200.80 m. The correct length of the 20 m tape is .....
    (1) 19.92 m   (2) 19.98 m   (3) 20.04 m   (4) 20.08 m
146. A line of true length 500 m when measured by a 20 m tape is reported to be 502 m long. The correct length of the tape is .....
    (1) 19.92 m   (2) 20.08 m   (3) 20.80 m   (4) 21 m
147. What is the slope correction for a length of 30.0 m along a gradient of 1 in 20 ?
    (1) 3.75 cm   (2) 0.375 m   (3) 37.5 m   (4) 0.0375 cm
148. In the case of which natural feature do the two contour lines intersect ?
    (1) hill   (2) valley   (3) saddle   (4) vertical clift
149. A scale of 1 inch = 50 ft. is mentioned on an old map. What is the corresponding equivalent scale ?
    (1) 1 cm = 5 m   (2) 1 cm = 6 m   (3) 1 cm = 10 m   (4) 1 cm = 12 m
150. An invar tape, 50 m in length, standardized at 20°C temperature and 10 kg pull, is used to measure a base line. The correction per tape length, if at the time of measurement the temperature was 30° and the coefficient of linear expansion of the tape was 1×10^{-6} per °C, will be .....
    (1) 0.0200 m   (2) 0.0050 m   (3) 0.0005 m   (4) 0.0001 m
151. In an instrument, the bubble tube with divisions of 1 mm and a radius of 0.9 m has the sensitivity of .....
    (1) $\dfrac{1}{2}$ (2) $\dfrac{1}{70}$ (3) $\dfrac{1}{90}$ (4) $\dfrac{1}{900}$
152. If L is the length of the chain, W is the weight of the chain and T is the tension, the sag correction for the chain line is .....
    (1) $\dfrac{W^2L^2}{24T^3}$ (2) $\dfrac{W^2L}{24T^2}$ (3) $\dfrac{W^2L^2}{24T^2}$ (4) $\dfrac{W^2L^3}{24T^3}$

153. Consider the following statements :

   (a) The component of the distance between two points measured in the north-south direction is called the latitude of the line, between the points.

   (b) The component of the distance between two points measured in the east-west direction is called the departure of the line, between the points.

   (c) The latitude is considered as positive when reckoned southward.

   (d) The departure is considered as negative when recknoed westward.

   Which of the above statements are correct ?

   (1) (a), (b) and (c) only   (2) (b), (c) and (d)

   (3) (a), (b) and (d) only   (4) (a), (b), (c) and (d)

154. In a closed traverse, the sum of south latitudes exceeds the sum of north latitudes and the sum of east departures exceeds the sum of west departures. The closing line will lie in the .....

   (1) N-W quadrant   (2) N-E quadrant   (3) S-E quadrant   (4) S-W quadrant

155. In a closed traverse with five sides, the error found from the fore bearing and back bearing of the last line is + 2°. The correction to the third line will be .....

   (1) 0°24'   (2) 0°48'   (3) 1°12'   (4) 1°36'

156. Error due to inclination of line of collimation in levelling across a river can be eliminated by .....

   (1) reversion   (2) reciprocal ranging

   (3) reciprocal levelling   (4) keeping level in middle

157. What is the minimum number of satellites required from which signals can be recorded to enable a global positioning system receiver to determine latitude, longitude and altitude ?

   (1) One   (2) Two   (3) Three   (4) Four

158. Which one of the following pairs is not correctly matched ?

   (1) Declination   :   Horizontal angle between magnetic meridian and true meridian

   (2) Bowditch's rule   :   Employed to adjust closing error of a closed traverse

   (3) Deflection angle   :   Measured in case of open traverse instead of measuring included angle

   (4) Reconnaissance survey   :   Employed for detailed and precise survey

159. Diurnal variation in greater .....

   (1) in winter than in summer

   (2) at smaller latitudes than at higher latitudes

   (3) at magnetic equator points

   (4) in summer than in winter

160. The whole circle bearings of lines AB and BC are 30°15' and 120°30'. What is the included angle ABC between the lines AB and BC ?

   (1) 229°45'   (2) 89°45'   (3) 269°45'   (4) 90°15'

161. In a transit theodolite, error due to eccentricity of verniers is eliminated by reading .....
     (1) both verniers   (2) both right swing and left swing
     (3) right and left faces   (4) different parts of main scale

162. Consider the following pairs in the context of a theodolite :

     (a) Plunging   : The process of turning the telescope over its supporting axis through 180° in a vertical plane.

     (b) Face left   : When the vertical circle of the theodolite is on the left of the observer while taking the reading

     (c) Telescope normal : It implies 'bubble up' and face of the vertical circle left

     (d) Swining the telescope : It implies turning the telescope in a vertical plane.

     Which of these pairs are correctly matched in case of theodolite ?
     (1) (a), (b) and (d)   (2) (a), (c) and (d)
     (3) (b), (c) and (d)   (4) (a), (b) and (c)

163. Working from the whole to the part is followed as the fundamental principle of surveying so as to .....
     (a) Distribute errors   (b) Improve ease of working
     (c) Prevent accumulation of errors   (d) Compensate errors in a way
     (e) Refer to a common datum, say MSL
     (1) (a), (b) and (d)   (2) (a), (c) and (e)
     (3) (c) and (d)   (4) (b) and (e)

164. Consider the following statements :
     Reciprocal levelling is a method of levelling adopted when .....
     (a) the difference of levels between two points at a considerable distance apart is to be determined with great precision.
     (b) it is not possible to set up the level midway between two points as in the case of a deep valley or a river
     (c) error due to improper centering of level is to be eliminated
     Which of these statements is/are correct ?
     (1) (a) only   (2) (a) and (b)   (3) (b) and (c)   (4) (a) and (c)

165. If the observed fore bearing of a line xy is 16°26′, the back bearing of this line is .....
     (1) 103°26′   (2) 118°36′   (3) 196°26′   (4) 206°26′

166. The needle of a magnetic compass is generally supported on a .....
     (1) bush bearing   (2) ball bearing   (3) needle bearing   (4) jewel bearing

167. The Whole Circle Bearing of line AB is 50° and of line BC is 120°. The deflection angle at AB to BC is .....
     (1) 50°   (2) 70°   (3) 110°   (4) 120°

168. Reading a Prismatic Compass, which one of the following statements is correct ?
     (1) The object is sighted first. The observer then moves to the side of the object vane to take the reading.
     (2) Sighting and reading are done simultaneously.
     (3) The readings are taken from the north end.
     (4) The compass has an edge bar needle.

169. The three-point problem is hydrographic surveying considers the data on the location of three shore signals A, B and C and the angles α and β subtended by AB and BC at the boat P and then proceeds to plot the position of P. The problem may become indeterminate in special cases when .....
    (1) B and P are an opposite sides of the line AC
    (2) both B and P are on the same side of the line AC
    (3) P is within the triangle ABC
    (4) P is very close to the extension of one of the edges of the triangle ABC.

170. The combined correction of curvature and refraction for a distance of 1400 m is .....
    (1) 0.153 m   (2) 0.132 m   (3) 0.094 m   (4) 0.021 m

171. The sensitiveness of a bubble tube in a level would decrease if .....
    (1) the radius of curvature of the internal surface of the tube is increased
    (2) the diameter of the tube is increased
    (3) the length of the vapour bubble is increased
    (4) the viscosity of the liquid is increased

172. Theory of errors and adjustments deals with minimizing the effects of .....
    (1) instrumental errors   (2) mistakes
    (3) systematic errors   (4) personal and accidental errors

173. Match List-I (Terms) with List-II (Description) and select the correct answer using the codes given below the lists :

List - I		List - II
A.	Contour	1. Line joining magnetic North and South
B.	Line of collimation	2. Line joining subsidiary station on the main line
C.	Tie line	3. Line joining points of same elevation
D.	Magnetic meridian	4. Line joining optical centre of the objective lens with point of intersection of cross-wires

    Codes :

	A	B	C	D
(1)	3	4	2	1
(2)	4	3	2	1
(3)	3	4	1	2
(4)	4	3	1	2

174. Which of the following sights will be applicabale for a change point ?
    (1) Back sight   (2) Intermediate sight and fore sight
    (3) Fore sight   (4) Back sight and fore sight

175. A level when set up 25 m from peg A and 50 m from peg B reads 2.847 m on staff held on A and 3.462 m on staff held on B, keeping bubble at its centre while reading. If the reduced levels of A and B are 283.665 m and 284.295 m respectively, what is the collimation error per 100.0 m ?
    (1) 0.015 m   (2) 0.30 m   (3) 0.045 m   (4) 0.060 m

176. There are ten instrument stations occupied in succession during a traverse survey. An observer makes equal error in each station, the magnitude of which is $\delta\theta$ in each instance at all the stations. What is the probable error of the final bearing at the end of the traverse ?

(1) $\pm 10 \, \delta\theta$ (2) $+ 100 \, (\delta\theta)^2$ (3) $\pm 10\sqrt{\delta\theta}$ (4) $+ 10\sqrt{\delta\theta}$

177. Which one of the following surveys employs alidade ?

     (1) Contour survey   (2) Archelogical survey

     (3) Plane table survey   (4) Reconnaissance survey

178. Consider the following statements :

In surveying operations, the word 'reciprocal' can be associated with .....

     (a) ranging   (b) levelling   (c) contouring

Which of these statements is/are correct ?

     (1) (a) only   (2) (a) and (b)   (3) (b) and (c)   (4) (a), (b) and (c)

179. Which one of the following errors in more servere in plane table surveying ?

     (1) Defective sighting

     (2) Defective orientation

     (3) Movement of board between sights

     (4) Non-horizontality of board when points sighted are at large differences of their elevation.

180. A light-house is visible just above the horizon at a certain station at the sea level. Distance between the station and the light-house is 60 km. The height of the light-house is .....

     (1) 243.5 m   (2) 4.0 m   (3) 287.5 m   (4) 5.4 m

181. In a solution of the three-point problem in plane table surveying, the converging of error is attained through .....

     (1) Concyclic concept   (2) Bessel's method

     (3) Triangle of error   (4) Tracing paper method

182. Which one of the following statements is correct ?

     (1) The axis of the plate level should be parallel to the vertical axis.

     (2) The axis of the striding level must be parallel to the horizontal axis.

     (3) The axis of the altitude level must be perpendicular to the line of collimation.

     (4) The line of collimation must be perpendicular to the plate level axis.

183. A contour may be defined as an imaginary the passing through .....

     (1) Points on the longitudinal section   (2) Points of equal elevation

     (3) Point of equal local ground slope   (4) Points of transverse section surveys

184. A closed contour line with two or more higher contours inside it will represent a .....

     (1) Depression   (2) Hill   (3) Cave   (4) Well

185. In case of levelling, backsight is .....

     (1) A fixed point of known elevation.

     (2) The last staff reading taken before shifting the instrument.

     (3) The first staff reading taken after setting the instrument.

     (4) Any staff reading taken on a point of unknown elevation.

186. A sailor, standing on the deck of a ship, just sees the light beam from a lighthouse on the shore. If the height of the sailor's eye and of the light beam at the lighthouse, above the sea level, are 9 m and 25 m respectively, what is the distance between the sailon and the lighthouse ?
    (1)   29.8 km   (2)   31.1 km   (3)   31.9 km   (4)   33.2 km

187. A plane, which is perpendicular to the plumb line through a point and is tangential to the level surface at that point is called a .....
    (1)   Tangential plane   (2)   Vertical plane
    (3)   Level plane   (4)   Horizontal plane

188. Staff reading on the floor of a verandah of a school building is 1.815 m and staff reading when held with bottom of staff touching the ceiling over the verandah is 2.870 m R.L. of the floor is 74.500 m. Height of the ceiling above floor is .....
    (1)   4.270 m   (2)   4.685 m   (3)   3.944 m   (4)   4.920 m

189. In a levelling survey, the summation of all backsights and the summation of all foresights are 7.475 m and 7.395 m, respectively. The reduction level of the initial benchmark is 1000.000 m. The reduced level of the point where the staff is held will be .....
    (1)   100.000 m   (2)   100.080 m   (3)   107.395 m   (4)   107.475 m

190. In a mass-haul diagaram, the distance (D) of the centre of mass of excavation or embankment from the line representing the volume to be hauled over is given by .....
    (1)   D = Area × Horizontal scale × Vertical scale/Volume ordinate
    (2)   D = Area × Volume ordinate/(Horizontal scale × Vertical scale)
    (3)   D = Area × Volume ordinate
    (4)   D = Area × Horizontal scale/Vertical scale

191. Following offsets were taken from a survey line to a hedge :

Distance (in m)	0	5	10	15	20	30	40
Offsets (in m)	3	4	5.5	5	6	4	4.5

    The area between survey line and the hedge is (by trapezoidal method) .....
    (1)   185.5 m²   (2)   187.5 m²   (3)   189.5 m²   (4)   289.5 m²

192. The measured radius of a circle is 80 m with a possible error of 0.05 m in its diameter. The error in the computed area will nearly be .....
    (1)   + 6.5 m²   (2)   − 0.65 m²   (3)   ± 12.6 m²   (4)   ± 8.2 m²

193. On which one of the following are the third generation electro-optical instruments based ?
    (1)   Microwave   (2)   Infra-red   (3)   UV light   (4)   He-Laser light

194. Which of the following instruments have both horizon glass and index glass ?
    (a)   Optical square   (b)   Line ranger   (c)   Box sextant   (d)   Pedometer
    Select the correct answer using the codes given below :
    (1)   (b), (c) and (d)   (2)   (a), (c) and (d)
    (3)   (a) and (c) only   (4)   (b) and (d) only

195. Match List-I with List-II and select the correct answer using the codes given below the lists :

	List - I		List - II
A.	Sextant	1.	Measurement of depth below the water surface
B.	Sounding	2.	The line on which soundings are taken
C.	Fathometer	3.	The lines which are usually used for depths above about 6 m
D.	Range	4.	Instrument used for measuring angles from a boat
		5.	Instrument used for measuring depth is ocean

Codes :

	A	B	C	D
(1)	5	1	4	2
(2)	4	2	5	3
(3)	5	3	4	1
(4)	4	1	5	2

196. Which one of the following instruments can be used as clinometer ?
(1) Prism square   (2) Line ranger   (3) Abney level   (4) Optical square

197. Electronic theodolites of various ranges in which measured angles are displayed originally on display board are based on which one of the following ?
(1) Special optical technology   (2) Introduction of microprocessor technology
(3) Electro-optical technology   (4) Special gearing

198. Consider the following equipments :
(a) Tacheometer   (b) Odometer   (c) Passometer   (d) Perambulator
Which of the above equipments can be employed for measurement of horizontal distance ?
(1) (a) and (b) only   (2) (a) and (c) only
(3) (b) and (c) only   (4) (a), (b), (c) and (d)

199. Which one of the following surveys is employed for collecting sufficient data in connection with sewage disposal and water supply works ?
(1) Topographic survey   (2) Cadastral survey
(3) Geodetic survey   (4) Cross-sectioning and profile levelling

200. The following readings were taken with a Dumpy level and a 4 m levelling staff on a continuously sloping ground at 30 m intervals; 0.680 m, 1.455 m, 1.855 m, 2.330 m, 2.885 m, 3.380 m, 1.055 m. The RL of the fourth point was calculated to be 79.100 m. The RL of the point that was read 0.680 m is .....
(1) 80.750 m   (2) 79.780 m   (3) 78.420 m   (4) 77.740 m

201. In an external focussing tacheometer, the fixed interval between stadia hairs is 5 mm, the focal length of the objective is 25 cm, and the distance of the vertical axis of the instrument from the optical centre of the objective is 15 cm. Which one of the following is the set of constant of the tacheometer ?
(1) 30, 0.15   (2) 30, 0.40   (3) 50, 0.25   (4) 50, 0.40

202. Triangulation station selected close to the main station for avoiding intervening obstruction is called .....
    (1) total station   (2) pivot station
    (3) satellite station   (4) tie station

203. Match List-I with List-II and select the correct answer using the codes given below the lists :

	List - I		List - II
A.	Adjustment of surveying instruments	1.	Bringing the various fixed parts of the instruments into proper relations with one another
B.	Bowditch rule	2.	Solution of three point problem
C.	Triangulation	3.	Measuring all the angles and base line
D.	Bessel's method	4.	Balancing the latitudes and departures

Codes :

	A	B	C	D
(1)	1	2	3	4
(2)	3	4	1	2
(3)	1	4	3	2
(4)	3	2	1	4

204. If the weight of an angle A (= 40°24'24" say) is 2, then the weight of the angle A/3 (13°28'08") will be .....
    (1) 4   (2) $\pm\sqrt{3}$ (3) 9   (4) 18

205. Match List-I with List-II and select the correct answer using the codes given below the lists :

	List - I		List - II
A.	Traverse surveying	1.	Weddel's sounding machine
B.	Geodetic surveying	2.	Alidade
C.	Plane table surveying	3.	Chain and compass
D.	Hydrographic surveying	4.	Theodolite

Codes :

	A	B	C	D
(1)	3	4	2	1
(2)	1	4	2	3
(3)	3	2	4	1
(4)	1	2	4	3

206. The subtense tacheometry method is adopted when the ground is .....
    (1) flat   (2) inclined   (3) undulating   (4) a water body

207. If the radius of a simple curve is R, then the length of the chord for calculating the offsets by the "method of chords produced" should not exceed .....
    (1) R/5   (2) R/10   (3) R/20   (4) R/25

208. With regard to Trigonometric Levelling, which one of the following statements is correct at its simplest application ?
   (1) Determination of the elevations of stations is based on the observed vertical angles and the horizontal distance.
   (2) Determination of the horizontal distance is based on the observed vertical angles.
   (3) Determination of the vertical angles is based on the observed horizontal distances.
   (4) Determination of the horizontal distance.

209. An image of the top of the hill is 96 mm from the principal point of the photograph. The elevation of the top of the hill is 500 m and the flying height is 4000 m above the datum. The relief displacement will be .....
   (1) 768 mm   (2) 88 mm   (3) 12 mm   (4) 8 mm

210. Which one of the following methods would give accurate results in determining the direction of the observer's meridian ?
   (1) Observation of circumpolar stars on the same vertical.
   (2) Observation of circumpolar stars at culmination.
   (3) Extra-meridian observation of a circumpolar star.
   (4) Observation of the Sun at equal altitudes.

211. If the equation of time is – 13'28.5", then the Greenwich Apparent Time corresponding to zero hour Greenwich Mean Time on a day is .....
   (1) 13' 28.5"   (2) 46' 31.5"
   (3) 23 hrs. 46' 31.5" of same day   (4) 23 hrs. 46' 31.5" of previous day

212. Vertical photograph was taken at an attitude of 1500 m above MSL. If the focal length of the camera is 20 m, the scale of photograph for a terrain lying at an elevation of 500 m is .....
   (1) 1 : 50   (2) 1 : 100   (3) 1 : 1000   (4) 1 : 25

213. **Assertion (A) :** At a given station, a celestial body can be fixed by its co-altitude and co-declination.
   Reason (R) : In the astronomical triangle. ZPS, ZP is constant for the given place and S is the intersection of the vertical circle and declination of circle.
   (1) Both A and R are true and R is the correct explanation of A.
   (2) Both A and R are true but R is not a correct explanation of A.
   (3) A is true but R is false.
   (4) A is false but R is true.

214. The relationship between the air-base B, photographic base 'b', flying height H and focal length 'f' of lens in a vertical photograph is given by .....
   (1) $B = \dfrac{bH}{f}$ (2) $B = \dfrac{f}{bH}$ (3) $B = \dfrac{b}{fH}$ (4) $B = \dfrac{b}{H - f}$

215. Which one of the following represents a circumpolar star ?
   (1) Upper culmination above horizon, lower culmination below horizon.
   (2) Both upper and lower culminations below horizon.
   (3) Both upper and lower culminations above horizon.
   (4) Altitude at upper culmination is minimum.

216. In an aerial photogrammetric survey, if the exposure interval is 20 seconds to cover ground distance of 1000 m between exposures, what would be the ground speed of the aircraft ?
    (1) 90 km/hour   (2) 120 km/hour   (3) 150 km/hour   (4) 180 km/hour

217. Which of the following can be used as a map substitute ?
    (1) Terrestrial photographs   (2) Vertical aerial photographs
    (3) Oblique aerial photographs   (4) Vertical aerial photo-mosaics

218. Flamsteed gave numbers to stars observed by him in each constellation according to their .....
    (1) Brilliance   (2) Altitudes
    (3) Co-declinations   (4) Right ascensions

219. Which of the following co-ordinate systems is the most convenient way to specify the position of the star on celestial sphere ?
    (1) Latitude and longitude   (2) Altitude and azimuth
    (3) Declination and right ascension (4) Declination and hour angle

220. How many sidereal days are there in a solar year ?
    (1) 365.2840   (2) 366.2422   (3) 360.2500   (4) 365.000

221. The difference between the apparent solar time and mean solar time is known as .....
    (1) real time   (2) average time
    (3) equation of time   (4) sidereal time

222. If a 'vertical aerial photograph', (20 cm × 20 cm) in size, on a R.F. 1 : 10,000 has 60% longitudinal overlap and 40% side overlap, the actual ground length covered by each photograph in the longitudinal direction of the flight will be .....
    (1) 4 km   (2) 6 km   (3) 0.8 km   (4) 0.4 km

223. The observations made over the same area on different dates to monitor ground features like crop growth is called .....
    (1) Temporal resolution   (2) Radiometric resolution
    (3) Spatial resolution   (4) Spectral resolution

224. To uniquely determine the position of the user using GPS, one needs to receive signals from at least .....
    (1) 1 satellite   (2) 2 satellites   (3) 3 satellites   (4) 4 satellites

225. The angle of intersection of a contour and a ridge line is .....
    (1) 30°   (2) 60°   (3) 90°   (4) 120°

226. Closed contours with lower value in words representation .....
    (1) hillock   (2) plain surface   (3) depression   (4) uniform slope

227. "Temporary adjustment" means those made .....
    (1) periodically   (2) at every setup
    (3) to restore fundamental relations between various parts
    (4) none of these

228. On the graduated range of the prismatic compass, 90° is marked at ..... end of needle.
    (1) North   (2) South   (3) East   (4) West

229. An observer standing on the deck of a ship just sees the top of a lighthouse which is 30 m above the sea level. If the height of the observer's eye is 10 m above the sea level, then the distance of the observer from the lighthouse will be nearly .....

(1) 22.5 km   (2) 24.3 km   (3) 33.3 km   (4) 59.7 km

230. Overturning of a vehicle on a curve can be avoided by using .....

(1) Transition curve   (2) Vertical curve

(3) Reverse curve   (4) Compound curve

231. In Global Positioning System (G.P.S.), there are more than 24 numbers of G.P.S. Satellites moving in circular orbits around the earth with the inclination of .....

(1) 65°   (2) 35°   (3) 45°   (4) 55°

232. A compound curve consists of .....

(1) Proportionate super elevation   (2) Curves with different radius

(3) Combined horizontal curves   (4) Two circular curves of different radii

233. A tower is situated on the far side of the river and is inaccessible. But it is visible. It can be located by .....

(1) radiation   (2) traversing   (3) instersection   (4) resection

234. The length of a survey line when measured with a chain of 20 m nominal length was found to be 841.5 m. If the chain used is 0.1 m too long, the correct length of the measured line is .....

(1) 845.7 m   (2) 837.39 m   (3) 843.6 m   (4) 839.4 m

235. Measurement of discharge of river usually forms a part of .....

(1) Topographic surveying   (2) Hydrographic surveying

(3) Geodetic surveying   (4) Route surveying

236. A total station is an instrument consisting of the combination of .....

(1) prismatic compass, theodolite and dumpy level

(2) auto level, tacheometer and compass

(3) electronic theodolite and electronic distance meter

(4) digital planimeter with auto level

237. When lines come close together in a contour map, it indicates .....

(1) hill   (2) reservoir   (3) steep slope   (4) flat slope

238. Which of the following shapes is preferred in valley curve ?

(1) Spiral   (2) Lemniscate

(3) Cubic parabola   (4) Simple parabola

239. If R is the radius of the circular cuve and ϕ is the deflection angle, then tangent length of the curve is given by .....

(1) $R \tan \phi/4$ (2) $R \tan \phi$ (3) $R \tan \phi/4$ (4) $R \tan \phi/8$

240. Precision represents repeatability of a measurement and is concerned with only .....

(1) natural errors   (2) instrumental errors

(3) personal errors   (4) random errors

241. Two tangents intersect at the chainage 1200 m, the deflection angle being 40°. The number of 30 m long normal chords for setting a circular curve of 300 m radius between these two tangents are .....

(1) 7   (2) 4   (3) 5   (4) 6

242. The representative fraction of a map scale 1 cm = 5 km is .....

    (1) 1/500000   (2) 1/500   (3) 1/5000   (4) 1/50000

243. "Offsets" are .....

    (1) short measurement from chain line

    (2) ties or check lines which are perpendicular to chain line

    (3) sets of minor instruments   (4) parallel to the survey line

244. A subsidy line is same as .....

    (1) range line   (2) tie line   (3) survey line   (4) none of these

245. The object of leveling is to determine .....

    (1) level differences only   (2) elevations of stations

    (3) level difference of elevations   (4) level differences and elevation

246. Leveling deals with distances in a .....

    (1) vertical plane only   (2) horizontal plane only

    (3) oblique planes   (4) none of these

247. For minor adjustments of horizontal angles measured using a theodolite, the tangential screw is adjusted after .....

    (1) both the plates are unclamped.

    (2) the lower plate in clamped and the upper plate is unclamped.

    (3) the upper plate is clamped and the lower plate is unclamped.

    (4) both the plates are clamped.

248. For locating an inaccessible point with the help of only a Plane table, one should use .....

    (1) traversing   (2) resection   (3) radiation   (4) intersection

249. The direction of the magnetic meridian is established at each traverse station and the direction of the line is determined with reference to the magnetic meridian. This method of traversing is called .....

    (1) fast needle method   (2) loose needle method

    (3) bearing method   (4) fixed needle method

250. The true bearing of a line is 34°20′40″ and the megnetic declination at the place of observation is 2°00′20″W on the date of observation. The magnetic bearing of the line is .....

    (1) 36°21′00″   (2) 34°20′20″   (3) 32°20′20″   (4) 32°00′20″

251. The magnetic needle in a prismatic compass is placed .....

    (1) at the bottom of the graduated aluminium ring

    (2) above the graduated aluminium ring

    (3) below the brass box

    (4) below the needle lifter, but above the bottom inside the compass

252. What is ∠ ABC if FB of line AB is 40° and BB of line BC is 280° ?

    (1) 90°   (2) 120°   (3) 240°   (4) 320°

253. The length of a line measured with a 30 m chain was found to be 734.6 m. It was afterwards found that the chain was 0.05 m too long. The true length of the line was .....

    (1) 630.82 m   (2) 680.82 m   (3) 735.82 m   (4) 780.92 m

254. The bearing of line AB is 150° and the angle ABC is 124°. Bearing of line BC is .....

    (1) 94°   (2) 98°   (3) 198°   (4) 90°

ANSWER KEY

1.	(3)	2.	(1)	3.	(4)	4.	(3)	5.	(4)	6.	(3)	7.	(4)	8.	(1)
9.	(3)	10.	(3)	11.	(2)	12.	(3)	13.	(4)	14.	(2)	15.	(4)	16.	(4)
17.	(3)	18.	(2)	19.	(3)	20.	(2)	21.	(2)	22.	(4)	23.	(3)	24.	(3)
25.	(4)	26.	(3)	27.	(3)	28.	(1)	29.	(4)	30.	(1)	31.	(2)	32.	(1)
33.	(2)	34.	(3)	35.	(1)	36.	(2)	37.	(3)	38.	(4)	39.	(1)	40.	(2)
41.	(2)	42.	(4)	43.	(4)	44.	(4)	45.	(4)	46.	(1)	47.	(1)	48.	(2)
49.	(4)	50.	(2)	51.	(1)	52.	(1)	53.	(4)	54.	(3)	55.	(1)	56.	(1)
57.	(2)	58.	(1)	59.	(2)	60.	(4)	61.	(3)	62.	(4)	63.	(4)	64.	(2)
65.	(3)	66.	(2)	67.	(2)	68.	(3)	69.	(1)	70.	(4)	71.	(3)	72.	(3)
73.	(3)	74.	(3)	75.	(1)	76.	(3)	77.	(3)	78.	(2)	79.	(3)	80.	(3)
81.	(4)	82.	(1)	83.	(2)	84.	(2)	85.	(4)	86.	(1)	87.	(3)	88.	(2)
89.	(1)	90.	(4)	91.	(2)	92.	(3)	93.	(3)	94.	(1)	95.	(3)	96.	(2)
97.	(3)	98.	(3)	99.	(2)	100.	(2)	101.	(4)	102.	(4)	103.	(4)	104.	(2)
105.	(1)	106.	(3)	107.	(1)	108.	(1)	109.	(2)	110.	(3)	111.	(1)	112.	(2)
113.	(2)	114.	(3)	115.	(4)	116.	(3)	117.	(2)	118.	(4)	119.	(3)	120.	(2)
121.	(1)	122.	(3)	123.	(2)	124.	(2)	125.	(1)	126.	(4)	127.	(2)	128.	(2)
129.	(1)	130.	(4)	131.	(2)	132.	(4)	133.	(1)	134.	(3)	135.	(3)	136.	(4)
137.	(3)	138.	(1)	139.	(1)	140.	(3)	141.	(2)	142.	(1)	143.	(3)	144.	(2)
145.	(1)	146.	(1)	147.	(1)	148.	(4)	149.	(2)	150.	(3)	151.	(4)	152.	(2)
153.	(3)	154.	(3)	155.	(3)	156.	(3)	157.	(3)	158.	(4)	159.	(4)	160.	(2)
161.	(1)	162.	(2)	163.	(3)	164.	(2)	165.	(3)	166.	(4)	167.	(2)	168.	(2)
169.	(2)	170.	(3)	171.	(4)	172.	(4)	173.	(1)	174.	(4)	175.	(4)	176.	(1)
177.	(3)	178.	(2)	179.	(2)	180.	(1)	181.	(3)	182.	(2)	183.	(2)	184.	(2)
185.	(3)	186.	(2)	187.	(3)	188.	(2)	189.	(2)	190.	(1)	191.	(2)	192.	(3)
193.	(2)	194.	(3)	195.	(4)	196.	(3)	197.	(3)	198.	(4)	199.	(4)	200.	(1)
201.	(4)	202.	(3)	203.	(3)	204.	(4)	205.	(1)	206.	(1)	207.	(3)	208.	(1)
209.	(3)	210.	(2)	211.	(4)	212.	(1)	213.	(4)	214.	(1)	215.	(3)	216.	(4)
217.	(4)	218.	(4)	219.	(2)	220.	(2)	221.	(3)	222.	(3)	223.	(1)	224.	(4)
225.	(3)	226.	(3)	227.	(2)	228.	(4)	229.	(3)	230.	(1)	231.	(4)	232.	(4)
233.	(3)	234.	(1)	235.	(2)	236.	(3)	237.	(3)	238.	(3)	239.	(1)	240.	(4)
241.	(4)	242.	(1)	243.	(2)	244.	(2)	245.	(4)	246.	(3)	247.	(4)	248.	(4)
249.	(2)	250.	(1)	251.	(1)	252.	(2)	253.	(3)	254.	(1)				

❧ ❧ ❧